GW01375020

MALAVITA

Wendy Newman

This book was written by local author, Wendy Maynard. She lives in Bugle + hopes you enjoy this.

Too close to the Sun, and The Shadow Side (set in Cornwall) are available to buy on Amazon.co.uk.

xxx

AuthorHouse™
1663 Liberty Drive, Suite 200
Bloomington, IN 47403
www.authorhouse.com
Phone: 1-800-839-8640

© 2008 Wendy Newman. All rights reserved.

No part of this book may be reproduced, stored in a retrieval system, or transmitted by any means without the written permission of the author.

First published by AuthorHouse 9/25/2008

ISBN: 978-1-4343-7555-1 (sc)
ISBN: 978-1-4343-7556-8 (hc)

Printed in the United States of America
Bloomington, Indiana

This book is printed on acid-free paper.

CHAPTER ONE

The rear door of the black Lincoln opened and the young English girl emerged from the air conditioned coolness of the interior. She took in the wild and isolated surroundings of the Florida Everglades while she waited.

It was hot, far too hot to be out in the open and away from shade or air conditioning. June in Florida was stiflingly hot and notoriously humid. Already, sweat beads began to form and she felt the hot sun begin to burn her bare arms and neck. She put on her new Prada sunglasses to stop her from squinting in the glare of the sun as she looked to the other side of the car.

A tall, confident Italian-American man appeared from the other passenger door and Sarah could not help but smile. Even after two years of a rocky marriage, he still had an effect on her that made her grin at how lucky she was to have married this man, with all his faults, and he had many. One of which was an infamous temper, which he showed now by slamming the car door behind him.

The heat did not seem to bother him, he had other more pressing things on his mind. He walked around to the same side of the vehicle where his wife waited, and roughly taking her hand, he walked along the dirt track that would take them deep into the Everglades, pulling her behind him. He turned to smile at her but the smile was not full of the warmth he would usually reserve for her, more the smile of a man possessed by Satan.

Sarah's smile had disappeared with the slam of the car door. She was confused- romantic walks were not usually Marco's favourite pastime. Neither was he dressed for a walk, his dark grey Armani suit and black Bruno Magli shoes were not conducive to these rustic pathways in the 'Glades.

Nonetheless, she followed him albeit reluctantly, along the stony path of the swampy interior of Florida. The heat was debilitating and the effort of keeping up with the fast pace of her husband made her pale pink silk blouse began to stick to her upper body.

She felt the trickle of sweat flow down her back before it was soaked up by the waistband of her white skirt. Her heels scraped against the stones on the path and her feet, hot and perspiring began to slip around in the shoes, making it almost painful to walk.

The eerie silence began to concern her slightly as they kept on walking, just the occasional call of a bird and a splash of some unknown amphibian in the water that ran alongside the track that passed for a footpath on which they were walking. Insects buzzed annoyingly around her face and she kept swatting them away as they walked along, with Sarah beginning to feel very uncomfortable and extremely agitated.

"Marco?" She tried to keep the whine out of her voice but Sarah had had enough. This was no romantic walk. She was hot and fed up and she wanted to go back to the coolness of the car. She had a can of cola in the car, which she would devour the instant she got back there, such was her thirst.

"I just want to talk to you away from any interruptions." He continued walking without looking back at her. His steps were sure and purposeful even on the uneven path. On they went, further and further from anyone, just 'gators and other feral creatures for company. Crickets chirping in the background. A snake slithered across their path causing Sarah to startle slightly. She had never got used to their presence. Marco did not bat an eyelid at it's intrusion but continued walking, pulling her along by the hand with a strength she hadn't realised he possessed.

Eventually, they came to the end of the path. The waterway alongside them joined another and then flowed even deeper into the heartland getting lost forever. Marco looked around and nodded, satisfied of the location and he sat. A tree had been felled, perhaps from the recent hurricane and the trunk provided somewhere for them both to sit and talk although little shade was afforded the couple.

Sarah sat obediently next to her husband, leaning backwards and turned her face up towards the sun. She relaxed slightly and stretched her legs out in front of her, kicking off her shoes. In the far off distance she heard an occasional shot ring out, probably an illegal hunter somewhere in the swamp. She was glad to be sitting as their walk had exhausted her. It must be nearly one hundred degrees today. Although it was hot and sticky, the wildness was beautiful. After the bustling of Miami and the closeness of Palm Beach, it was nice to have some space. She was also pleased to be spending time alone with Marco. He had just been released from Federal prison after charges of tax evasion and other alleged crimes had been dropped. It had been a huge relief to the whole family as he had been looking at spending the next twenty years in prison, missing out on both seeing their daughter grow up and the opportunity for more children. Sarah wasn't sure how it had happened although she had some ideas but she wasn't one to ask questions of Marco Delvecchio. But it had happened and he was back home with her. Now they had their whole lives ahead of them to get back to where they had been before this nasty business had arisen.

"It's lovely out here." Her English accent was still perfect and not showing any lilt of the American vernacular despite living in the Sunshine State for two years now. She reached for his hand but Marco abruptly pulled it away.

"What's the matter?" She asked, suddenly uneasy with his reticence.

He stood now and turned to look down on her, threatening and imposing. "While I was away, I have it on good authority that you slept with my brother!" His eyes were black with anger, accusing. Gone was the twinkle that usually resided in his beautiful brown eyes. His face was full of calm, a complete antithesis of the rage burning behind his eyes and it was this that made Sarah's spine tingle with fearful apprehension. She knew what he was capable of when in such a rage.

"You are my wife and were supposed to remain faithful to me. I was only away for a few weeks but you couldn't stop yourself. Christ,

Sarah, of all people, you had to screw my BROTHER?!"

She snickered. "What makes you say such a thing?" Sarah finally found her voice although her mouth was dry. Her heart was beating so fast that she thought she would have heart failure and she felt sick. She was glad she was seated as her legs had turned weak and her arms felt heavy. Unable to look him in the eyes, she looked down at the ground crawling with fire-ants.

"Vinnie told me. His loyalty was to me, in the end. You just couldn't help yourself, could you? How many times? Where did you do it, in my house? In my bed?" His voice was rising with ire. He leant down and was just inches away from her face as he said these next words. "My father was right all along, you know that? He said I should have married an Italian girl who would do exactly as she was told and respect her marriage vows. A nice, submissive woman. Our daughter deserves a better mother than you!" Spittle was leaking from his mouth in his rage. He grabbed her long dark hair and with Sarah screaming his name hysterically, he pulled her, stumbling, into the undergrowth. She lost a shoe in the process. "You are evil!" He spat at her and pushed her away from him unable to stand her being too close any longer. She fell towards the thorny brush and it scratched her arms as it tore through the costly material, droplets of blood piercing through the flimsy silk.

With horror, Sarah saw Marco reached behind him and take out his gun from the waistband of his trousers. He aimed it at her.

"Sweetheart, no! You don't have to do this. Whatever the problem is, we can deal with it! Think about Grace!" She pleaded with him but he was unreachable. She began to sob with fear and turned to run from him.

Marco didn't move but just looked at her trying to run away from him, and shaking his head very, very slightly, he pulled the trigger. He had the faintest trace of a smile of his lips as he did so. This was his business, what he enjoyed doing. He felt a buzz as he watched the bullet tear into his slut of a wife and suddenly felt free. He laughed out loud and turned to go back to the car.

Sweating as always when this recurring nightmare crept up on her, Sarah sat up in bed and pushed the damp hair away from her face. She gulped for air until she caught her breath and she felt her heartbeat steady and return to normal as she realised it was just another bad dream and she was safe in her bed.

Sarah's mouth was dry and she needed a drink so she stepped out of her warm bed and reached for her dressing gown and slippers. She looked across at her precious daughter sleeping in the bed next to Sarah's and was relieved to see Grace still asleep and unaware of her mothers anguish.

In the small kitchen of her apartment, Sarah ran the tap and poured a glass of water. She sat at the rickety kitchen table while she sipped her water and thought about her dream. She dreamt the same dream often and it always made her think of Marco. Despite his many failings, she often missed him. She wondered, not for the first time, where her life had gone wrong and which path she had taken that had lead her here, to this basement flat in the Castro district of San Francisco. Her landlords lived on the two floors above her, Ted and Henry and were just about her only friends left in the world. They did not know about Sarah's past – she was known as Amy Cooper now, a single mother whose husband had beaten her up before she had fled with her daughter. Sarah did not want any one to know about her real past, it would put too many people in danger, especially her. It was a far cry from the mansion in Palm Beach, Florida with a black American Express card and the luxurious lifestyle but Sarah was eking out a life for them both, a life free of crime and dirty money.

Sarah padded quietly back into the bedroom and crawled back into the warmth of her bed. She slept with a clear conscience now even if she was as lonely as hell and barely scratching a living.

A diner just off Market Street in downtown San Francisco provided a minuscule income for Sarah and she worked five days a week from seven until four. Henry or Ted, sometimes both, took Grace to school for her everyday she worked. Sarah knew she could not survive without either of them, they were like a pair of uncles to her and to Grace. They had been together since they were in their twenties and now, both in their fifties knew their own children were not going to be part of their plan. They idolised Grace. She was a beautiful child with deep brown eyes, chestnut brown shoulder length hair and the manipulation skills of her father. She loved them both and did not question why two men lived together.

This particular morning, Sarah was on the crowded F-Line heading for downtown that took her within two blocks of the diner she worked and hated. She had taken on her fictional name not long after being shot by her husband. Marco's usually sure-fire aim had not hit its intended target and the bullet hit her in the neck, just missing her jugular. She had been thrown back into the undergrowth and lay there unconscious and bleeding profusely. Marco, again unusually had not checked to see if Sarah was dead and his work was done but just walked away. Sarah's saving grace had been an illegal hunter who had been close by. He had hidden just yards away from the incident as he had heard a woman screaming and went closer to investigate. He watched the scene play out while hiding in the nearby brush, hoping not to be seen. After he had watched Marco Delvecchio walk away, he rushed to the fallen woman and tried to stem the blood flow while calling 911 on his cellphone. Once the airborne paramedics had arrived in their helicopter, the hunter had sneaked away, not wanting to get involved any more than he had been. He had recognised the local Mafia Don and did not want to have to be a witness against him. He knew the Everglades backwaters like the back of his hand and it was not difficult to creep away with the medics putting all of their attentions to a young bleeding woman.

"Amy! Table seven!" Hank, the manager of the diner yelled at her. It was only eight-thirty and Sarah was already at the end of her tether. She was tired. It had taken her so long to fall back asleep after her dream and she now just wanted to sleep all day. Trying to smile for she needed the meagre tips the diner produced, Sarah forced herself to walk over to the four twenty-something lads at table seven and asked politely if they were ready to order.

One of the lads seemed to be transfixed by Sarah as she took his buddies orders. He stared at her all the time while taking their breakfast orders. He was very good looking and had an easy smile, which he turned on Sarah as soon as she gave him her attention. He laughed and joked with her while ordering his pancakes and sausage. With a spring in her step, Sarah took the orders to Hank for cooking up and then went back with the coffee pot. Sarah felt dowdy and unattractive most days and even with losing about twenty pounds through near starvation since living in Palm Beach, she felt tired and drained but that small smile from a handsome young man a few years younger than she had buoyed her.

Still grinning to herself, Sarah went over to the corner table by the steamed up window. A single woman sat facing outside, her back to the occupants of the diner and seemed to Sarah that she was very expensively dressed and not the sort of clientele this hick diner would normally attract. However, a large tip was the forefront of Sarah's mind and she was all smiles as she approached the woman from behind.

As Sarah drew level and the stranger looked up on her approach, Sarah's smile and her usual greeting died in her throat as she recognised the woman immediately.

"Hello Sarah. I thought it was you." The English accent chilled Sarah to the core.

"Sarah? No, my name is Amy" Sarah's hand touched her name badge as if for support which she needed as her wobbly legs were about to fail her.

Liz placed her perfectly manicured fingertips under her chin and smiled in glorious victory. "No, you are definitely Sarah. I would recognise the woman who ruined my life absolutely anywhere. I take it you do remember my fiancé, Vinnie? Well after you seduced him, he refused to marry me and now I'm left with nothing." Liz's words cut straight through Sarah as she tried to compose herself.

"I'm sorry for your trouble ma'am, but my name is Amy. I'll go get your coffee" Sarah put on her best American accent she could muster in an effort to convince Liz that she was indeed Amy Cooper. She tried to keep her voice level but felt like she was going to faint.

She picked up a fresh coffee pot, one was always on the go, and headed back to the corner table. As the strong black liquid was poured into the chipped coffee mug, Liz put her hand on Sarah's wrist and dug her nails in hard.

"You know, I think I may be mistaken. This slut I know, she is nothing like you. She was overweight and had long, dark hair not short and blond like yours, although darling, you could do with a root touch up. And a holiday – you look pale and pasty. I do apologise." She took five dollars out of her purse, put it on the table and left the diner with regal grace.

Sarah bristled at Liz's words but felt herself become less agitated at the apparent let-off.

Sarah's shift was long, hard and busy. She did not get chance to sit all day and had to eat lunch on the go. On the plus side, she did earn eighty bucks in tips. At the end of her working day, Sarah put on her long coat brought from a second hand shop in the Castro and left the steamy diner and out into the cold late afternoon air. The air was damp and the fog would soon drift in across the bay and envelope the city. She hurried to the F-line stop for her journey home and to collect Grace.

Sarah suddenly became aware of footsteps behind her that seemed to get closer with every second. Panic gripped her but she was too scared to turn around or to scream. Liz's visit that morning had really unnerved her and she was terrified once again in case Marco had found her.

"Amy?" An unfamiliar voice called her from no more than three feet away. "Amy, it's me!"

With her heart hammering away in fear, a familiar feeling of late, Sarah slowly turned to face the man with the voice. As she pivoted her head, she saw a vaguely familiar face.

"I just want to talk to you." He insisted. He realised that she did not recognise him and went on to explain. "We met in the diner this morning. I was with three other guys?"

Realisation and relief grew evident on Sarah's face and she half-smiled. "I'm sorry. I see a lot of people during the day." She offered by way of explanation. "What did you want to talk to me about? If the coffee's bad, talk to Hank" She said lightly.

He laughed. "The coffee's fine. I wondered if you wanted to go with me and get a coffee somewhere else, just you and me?"

Sarah hesitated. She knew she mustn't trust him, how many times had she warned Grace not to talk to strangers?

"I'm kinda busy" She said eventually.

"Just a quick coffee?" He almost pleaded. "My name is Nathan, by the way." He held out his hand for Sarah to shake.

"I have to get my daughter." His outstretched hand was ignored.

"You have a child?"

Sarah nodded. "I'm already late. I really have to go."

Nathan nodded. "How about you and your daughter meet me later for a pizza? I can meet you at Dom Beni's in Union Square at six-thirty? No strings. I would just like to get to know you. That's if you are single…" He said slowly.

Sarah hesitated again. She was in no position to turn down a free meal and Grace would love to go out for pizza.

Nathan sensed her irresolution and shrugged. "I'll be there at six-thirty. If you are there, that will be great. If not, I won't pester you again."

Sarah relented. "Okay. We'll see you there. Thank you." She trusted her instincts with this man and after all, it was only a pizza.

Trying to put thoughts of Liz out of her mind, Sarah later collected Grace from school, although she was still nervously looking around all the time. After picking up her daughter, they wandered slowly back home. As Sarah safely shut the front door behind them, Sarah told her daughter that they were going out to eat that night with a new friend of hers.

"Great! Can I wear my new jeans?" The little girl asked. The jeans were new to Grace but not new per se, as they were bought in the same thrift shop that Sarah's coat had been bought. Grace had been looking for an occasion to wear them for several days now.

"Sure. You go and get dressed and I'm going upstairs to tell Ted and Henry." Sarah kissed the top of Grace's head and left her in their bedroom.

The internal stairway to the first floor of the building took Sarah to Ted and Henry's door. She knocked lightly, hearing classical music from inside and knowing they were in.

Ted answered almost immediately. "Hi!" His green eyes lit up as he saw his tenant at the door. "You want to come in? Henry has just opened up a bottle of his best red." He opened the door for Sarah to pass through.

Ted and Henry were serious wine buffs and barely a Saturday

night went by when the two men did not invite Sarah up for a glass or two. They often went up the coast to the many vineyards for weekend tasting sessions and a chance to buy some of the wonderful locally produced wine.

"Thanks, Ted but I can't. I have a sort of a date tonight."

His eyes lit up further. "A good man, I hope."

Sarah shrugged. "I only met him today. He has invited Grace and me out for a pizza so I was just letting you know that I'm meeting Nathan at six-thirty at Dom Beni's in Union Square. Just being safety conscious, and all that!"

"Thank you for telling me. We'll be up later tonight if you want to stop by and tell us all about him."

Sarah laughed. "I might just do that!" She stroked his arm affectionately and appreciatively that they cared enough and smiling to herself and feeling good for a change, went back down the stairs to see if Grace was ready.

Liz arrived at Miami International Airport just as Sarah, Grace and Nathan were enjoying their pizzas in Union Square. She stood in line for a cab with only her hand luggage – she had been in too much of a hurry to leave San Francisco that morning to pack. Liz had made the necessary calls home to say she would be away for another few days and then rushed to Oakland airport. She wanted to tell Marco the news straight away and face to face.

As the cab headed north to Palm Beach, she thought about what to say and how to use her recently acquired knowledge to her best advantage. She had heard rumours about how certain issues were dealt with in Marcos world and was looking forward to using her wily feminine skills to get her revenge.

Liz hated Sarah Delvecchio with a vengeance.

In her twisted mind, the Englishwoman blamed Sarah for everything that had gone wrong in her recent life. The slut had slept with her fiancé Vinnie and when her husband had found out, Vinnie practically dropped Liz from a great height and rushed off to be with her. Only by then, Sarah had disappeared.

Marco was by now living the single, almost monk-like life and Liz hoped she could reap double revenge on Sarah.

Liz thought she had spotted Sarah Delvecchio quite by accident in San Francisco a few days ago while she was in the city on one of her regular shopping trips. She'd followed Marco's wife to the awful diner and then wondered quite what to do next. Over a few drinks in the bar of her hotel that night, she decided that the best thing was direct contact and face her. So this morning Liz had gone into the dreadful little place for a coffee. Delighted by the fact that Sarah had waited on her with the poor excuse for coffee, she knew damn well that the waitress was not anyone called Amy, but was indeed Marco's strumpet wife. Her eyes showed too much fear that she had been discovered. Sarah had lost quite a few pounds since Liz had last seen her in England when Marco was in prison, and her hair was bottle blond and short but underneath the flimsy disguise was still the scared, weak person Liz always knew Sarah to be.

The taxi cab driver had long since stopped trying to engage Liz in conversation when he pulled to a halt in front of the gates outside the luxurious mansion in Palm Beach that belonged to the Delvecchio family. A short, muscular man came out of the gatehouse to talk to the driver and Liz noticed a CCTV camera readjust to train itself directly onto her. She stared into the lens defiantly.

The man from the gatehouse bent down to peer into the back of the cab at Liz and she stared just as defiantly back at him. He half grinned to her but not recognising her, he went into the little building to make a call. After a few minutes, he came back out and told her that the cab was not permitted into the grounds and she would have to walk the rest of the way.

Cursing under her breath but at the same time making her annoyance very clear, Liz paid the cab fare and got out of the vehicle, slamming the door behind her with a heavy hand. Scowling at the man who had refused her the luxury of a drive up to the house, Liz began the long walk. She cursed under her breath again at the indignity of having to walk up the gravel drive and in the heels she was wearing, which would surely be ruined on this surface.

Arriving at the beautiful house, she walked into the cool of the portico and tried to compose herself. The American flag flacketed about in the gentle breeze on it's flagpole to the left of the front of the house. The beds and borders were beautifully kept and several palm trees edged the driveway. It was so tropical and very unlike Liz' home town of Chicago at this time of year. No small wonder so many people came to Florida for the winter.

The front of the mansion had huge glass windows and the front door was made of heavy English oak which had a huge brass knocker for which to attract the attention of it's occupants. Liz lifted the heavy metal and banged it down hard and heavy three times, hearing the echo resound inside. Liz prepared her sweetest smile for when the door was opened.

Marco's only sister opened the door with a smile but her face fell when she saw who was clouding her doorstep. Rosa did not like anyone from this side of the family. "Rosa, darling!" Liz oozed fake sincerity. The feeling of dislike was mutual. "Is your gorgeous brother at home?"

"Which one?" Rosa replied petulantly.

"Why, Marco of course!" Liz was not interested in any other.

Without saying another word, Rosa slammed the door and went off in search of her eldest brother.

Left to wait on the doorstep in the heat, Liz felt her temper bubble again. She would bet with her life that if she were Vinnies wife, she would have at least been invited to wait inside. It was just one more reason to hate Marco's whore of a wife.

Liz took off her long and heavy fur coat, so welcome in the cold of Chicago and San Francisco at this time of year. Here in the warmth of Florida, it was too much. Her wool sweater and skirt was still too warm for the temperature but she had left in such a hurry. Maybe she would have cause to stay a few days and would go shopping for some cool summer clothes to holiday in.

After being kept waiting for a few more minutes, which was far too long in Liz's eyes, she banged on the door again.

She heard hurried footsteps from inside and this time it was yanked open almost immediately by a scowling Marco Delvecchio. Liz caught her breath at the very sight of him.

"What do you want?" He asked gruffly and barely able to hide his contempt.

Without bothering to reply, Liz barged her way passed Marco and into the cool of the large hallway. She looked around at the grandness and opulence of the interior and once again felt aggrieved. The hallway was floored with a light coloured marble and a central staircase swept up before splitting into two and going in opposite directions. Marble statues dotted the area and large plants blended in to add life to the large foyer. On the wall opposite the front door was a large painting, a Degas, Liz thought, most likely an original and it added to the richness of the house. She should have a show home like this, a grand palatial residence that comes with being the wife of a Mafia hoodlum living in Chicago. That she didn't was down to the wife of the man who stood in front of her now.

She looked at him with a cheeky, almost schoolgirl glint in her eyes. "Marco, I'm sad to say the rumours about you are true. You ARE like a bear with a very bad hangover." She handed Marco her coat.

He threw the coat to the floor. "You didn't come here to discuss rumours! Pick your coat up on your way out or get to the point."

Liz nodded. "A gin and tonic would be nice first. It's hot. I'm thirsty. Ice and a slice, please."

He stood with his hands on his hips for a second before realising that he would not get rid of her that easily unless force were used. He sighed and walked into the sitting room where a drinks trolley was set. He poured Liz a strong gin and tonic but refrained from one himself.

Liz took a long sip and said what she had come here to say.

"I've just come from San Francisco. I thought you might like to know that while I was there, I ran into your wife." She watched Marco's face for a reaction but saw none save a slight twitch by his left eye that could have been the start of a frown. It gave her a moment to study his handsome features; the chocolate brown eyes that could be both beguiling and malevolent, the short, always tidy dark brown almost black hair that had a slight wave to it if ever it was permitted to grown too much. Today, Marco was clean shaven but Liz had known him previously to have grown a goatee which didn't well suit him. Not that he was ever over weight, but Marco had certainly dropped a few pounds and he was lean and had the ever present Florida tan. It all added up to one intensely desirable man in Liz's view and that was not even mentioning the power and wealth that Marco had which Liz ached for.

Marco turned his back on the gloating woman, not wanting

her to see any reaction or emotion that he was trying to hide from her. He slowly walked away and over to the window that overlooked the grounds to the rear of the house. Empty grounds, not dissimilar to his life.

"Marco, I'm telling you it was definitely her. I'd know that bitch anywhere and she was scared stiff when she knew she'd been rumbled."

"And what, Liz? Say it is her – what do you want me to do? Go and drag her back home? It seems to me that she has a life of her own now, with or without your fiancé!" He added the last part to be cruel. They were point scoring against each other and were now level.

Unbeknown to Liz, Marco had known for some time where Sarah and Grace had settled. He had known the supposed kidnapping of his daughter was down to the FBI and not a family rival not long after it had taken place. Marco knew where Grace went to school and how she was doing, knew Sarah worked in a greasy diner and how much she earned. Not much got by Marco when he set his mind to something. But he had been warned to stay away from his wife as long as she kept herself to herself and did not harm anyone's interests. He had been refused permission to contact her in any way and she was unknowingly protected by the Commission.

Liz had sidled up to Marco and her face was just inches away from him, her breasts touching his lower arm. "I just thought you might want to take back that beautiful little girl of yours. She is very much a Delvecchio child you know. She should be here, with you." Liz could not help but push herself closer to him and Marco allowed her to run her hand down his forearm.

"We all know Grace is better off with her mother. Now if you don't mind," Marco grabbed her hand away from his arm and shoved her away. "Get the hell out of my house!" His patience, not something he was famous for, deserted him and he stormed out of the room and headed up the stairs.

Unperturbed by his reaction and eager for the challenge, Liz followed him up the stairs, passing pictures of Delvecchio family members, past and present up the central stairway. At the intersection of the stairs, Liz waited a moment, trying to decide which way to go until she heard a door slam to the west side of the house. She tiptoed along the highly polished marble hallway trying not to step too heavily and make a noise with her shoes until she came to the only door off this way. She opened the door and saw Marco having just taken his shirt off.

"My! My! What a pleasant sight." Liz smiled, almost drooling.

"Do you mind?" Marco fumed. He was beginning to think he would have to resort to force to rid himself of this woman.

"Not at all. You go right ahead. Are you taking a shower?" Feeling dizzy at the very thought of rivulets running down his naked body, she sidled up to him, smiling lasciviously. She ran her plum coloured nails through the sprinkling of dark hair on his chest, entwining it in her fingertips and looked into his eyes. "You know Marco, you are a very handsome man. It's not fair on you or any woman to keep this body to yourself, you know."

Marco snatched her hand away and squeezed it menacingly, making her wince. "That's how it is. I may not have been the perfect husband but I am still married. I also won't lower my standards." He left his meaning unmistakable.

Liz took the hint. "Well, I don't know why you are waiting around for that bitch. She has a string of boyfriends and lots of uncles for Grace. Never was very faithful, as I recall." With a point ahead, Liz left the cruel lie hanging in the air and waltzed out of Marco's bedroom.

Marco lashed out and kicked the post of his bed in anger. With a sore foot and cursing the pain, he limped into his bathroom and got under the shower. He was angry with himself at getting into this whole situation. He still had feelings for his wife and thought maybe he did still love her. The mere fact that he couldn't move on and be with anyone else was proof to him that there was still something there, at least for him. But he had blown his last chance with Sarah and with Grace with the squeeze of that trigger. If Grace ever found out about him, she would never forgive him for trying to kill her mother.

Marco was desperately sad at missing out on being a father to Grace but he would have to be content with the monthly reports from her head teacher about how well she was doing, how clever she was. He also received a yearly photo from the school with Grace in it, a small face among many but he knew how beautiful she was. Marco was aware he had done many wrong things in his life but fathering such an intelligent and beautiful child was something to be proud of, even if his daughter never knew about him. He was a very powerful Don in Florida but there was no way he could go to San Francisco without permission as long as Sarah and Grace were residing there.

When he had tried to kill Sarah four years ago, the powers that be throughout the country had been horrified by his actions. Many of them withdrew their support and did not allow Marco to be a part of any new joint business ventures. He was excluded from many things and lost a great deal of trust and as an end result, money. If Marco Delvecchio could kill his wife, they felt none of them would be safe from him. The Dons rallied around and decided that they would protect Sarah from Marco, at least for as long as she kept the FBI at bay and kept her mouth shut about what she may or may not know. She was untouchable to Marco.

Maybe it was time to seek permission to bring them both home.

CHAPTER TWO

It had been two days since Sarah had seen Nathan. They had been out on another 'safe' date with Grace to the movies and had also been out for a dinner date, just the two of them to a Japanese restaurant where Sarah had become addicted to sushi. He had called every day since they met, but now it had been two days since she had heard from him. Nathan had told Sarah that he had some business to attend to, but hadn't elaborated. He had been very cagey and Sarah did not want to put pressure on him or pry. She wasn't sure she really wanted to know anyway. In a strange kind of way getting close to Nathan made her feel more alone than ever before. It just made it harder to keep up the lie that her life seemed to be and she struggled to remember the lies she told him so as not to trip herself up further. Grace was already talking seemingly non-stop about Nathan and she didn't want her little girl becoming attached to him. Sarah would always be running scared from the Mafia and the FBI. She had enough to worry about with being responsible for hers and for Grace's life – she couldn't be responsible for Nathan too and neither could she tell him the truth.

Ten days after their first meeting, he showed up at the apartment with flowers for Sarah and some candy for Grace. He hoped they might sit in and watch a DVD and revel in the cosiness of the three of them. Nathan had taken a real shine to Sarah, her vulnerability attracted her to him. Her daughter was the cutest thing in history and he really wanted to make a go of things with Sarah. However, Sarah's words knocked him off balance.

"What do you mean we can't see each other any more? I thought we were getting along just fine?"

"We are Nathan, but it's complicated. I have my reasons."

"Amy, I just want us to be friends right now. We don't have to rush into anything that you're not ready for. Where's the harm in that?" He tried to hold Sarah's hand but she pulled away, not wanting any contact, nothing intimate.

"I just can't have any sort of friends. I should never have let this go any distance, it's not fair. I know you don't understand and I can't explain it, but believe me, it's best for everyone if we just call it a day."

Nathan put his hands on Sarah's shoulders and forced her to look him in the eye as he spoke to her.

"Then make me understand. Is it Grace's father? Is he back on the scene hassling you?"

Sarah shook her head and looked at his feet, unable to face him. "He was never really off the scene. I can't get close to anyone as I just don't know what the man is capable of."

"Has he threatened you? I can get you protection." Nathan led Sarah to the old sofa, sagging in the middle and they sat, knees barely touching. She looked away from him as he spoke, just hoping he would take the hint and go away. "Amy, my father knew some very influential people in this city, people I work for now. They will help you out."

Sarah just sighed. "It wouldn't be enough." She knew that if Marco was determined enough, nothing and nobody could stop him.

"Sweetheart, listen to me. Do you know Don Alessandro Miotto?"

Sarah groaned. She shook her head. She had a nasty sinking feeling in the pit of her stomach. She put her head in her hands in despair.

Nathan continued unaware of Sarahs reservations. "Don Miotto is a very important man in the city of San Francisco. I work for him and I know he would protect you and Grace if I asked him. He would talk to Grace's father and tell him to stay away from the two of you."

Sarah shook her head in defeat. It seemed as though for some reason, she was a Mafia magnet and would never be free of them. She wondered if this friend of Nathan's would protect her from Marco, himself a powerful Don in Florida. For all she knew, they were pals and business associates and Sarah could not put her trust in Nathan or his friends and began to think it was time to move on again. South this time, where it would be warmer.

For days after Liz's visit, Marco was still unable to think of anything else but his wife and daughter. He'd had several business meetings but had been unable to concentrate and in the end had called a halt to proceedings. Gabe had taken over some decisions as his near-second in command but nothing much had been accomplished. Gabriel was concerned for his boss - he'd never seen him so distracted before. When he had tried to talk to Marco, he had become a victim if his temper and received a verbal berating for having the audacity to offer Marco any advice.

Marco could not help remembering the good times he and Sarah had shared. He hadn't been the best of husbands to her and despite this, she had still loved him. She also stood up to him which he found a turn on, unlike most of the other subservient women he had encountered. Her temperamental behaviour was what made him fall in love with her way back in France. It was that very same behaviour that should have made him realise that she would never put up with him having a mistress but he was too stupid and too arrogant to think about the consequences of being found out.

He kept asking himself why hadn't he fought harder to keep her?

Joe, the younger Delvecchio brother thought Marco should bring her home.

"Marco, she knows too much. She may have been silent until now but for what reason, we don't know. What if she gets scared? What if the FBI get to her first? At least if she is here, you can keep a real close eye on her."

Marco shrugged. "She's just a woman. What can she possibly know? If she did know anything, she would have talked to them by now."

Joe shook his head. "You said yourself that you told her more that was necessary, careless pillow talk. What about the Carusos? We've only just made peace with them and if Sarah talks about them, all of your diplomatic reasoning will be for nothing and there will be a real war. You want that?" Joe's voice was rising gradually. Marco shook his head and scowled at his brother. Of course he didn't want that. The so-called cold war between the Delvecchios and the Carusos had taken the best part of a year to resolve, not to mention the bloodshed on both sides and Marco did not want that again. He was good at what he did but preferred to reign on peaceful times.

Marco looked across the car at his brother and could not believe the change in him. When Marco had first brought Sarah home as his bride, Joe had been young and carefree. He'd been involved in the family business in some small way but his priorities then had been having a good time, going to the clubs and looking for women. The typical rich playboy lifestyle.

Then he'd met Lydia.

She had been a very quiet young lady who had swept Joe off his feet in much the same way Sarah had Marco. Lydia also had not taken any nonsense off Joe and this was the big attraction for him. He was done with the simpering women he'd known until then. Lydia had become pregnant and Joe was going to marry her, despite her parents being against him, his whole family and what they stood for. Lydia had moved into the house and the young couple seemed very much in love and began their wedding plans. Before the plans became too advanced, Lydia had gone into labour early and died while giving birth to Joe's son, Sammy. The baby born at only 25 weeks had lived just hours and this had brought about a dramatic change in Joe, one that Marco didn't much care for. The only thing Joe appeared to care about anymore was his drug refineries in Southern Georgia and the vast profits to the family business that he contributed to.

Marco was perfidious when it came to the money. He was happy to see the columns of figures rack up and happier still to spend it, but didn't approve of where it came from. He publicly slammed drugs. Marco tended to concern himself with his many other businesses, some legal, some not quite so and tried to keep his nose at least a little clean so the authorities would stay away. For the most part it worked.

Marco's only real regret in life was how he had handled the situation with his wife. Maybe now was the time to put that right. He booked three first class tickets to San Francisco for the following day, preferring commercial to his private plane to play down his arrival.

Nathan called out to Amy as he let himself in through the front door to the basement apartment. Sarah had decided that at some stage she must start to trust people and had decided to stay in San Francisco, at least for the time being. She loved the city and her small clutchful of friends and did not want to give that up just yet. She had given Nathan his own key already and he was in the apartment most evenings, although their relationship had not yet become physical. Just chaste goodnight kisses and the odd furtive touch.

"I'm in the kitchen!" Sarah replied to him calling out.

Nathan closed the front door firmly behind him and he was glad to be out of the cold. It was mid-November and quite chilly with a stark breeze whipping in off the Pacific. He rubbed his hands together to get the circulation going as he headed for the kitchen but he wasn't so sure it was much warmer inside the apartment. He knew Amy had a severe lack of funds and was frugal with her heating bills but Nathan thought he just might have a solution to that.

The kitchen was warm as the oven had been on to cook Grace's dinner of Spaghetti Bolognese, her favourite dish and her eyes lit up when she saw Nathan. He walked over to her to mop her face of the tomato sauce that had somehow missed her mouth.

"Can we go to the park after dinner, Nathan?" The child was barely able to contain her excitement.

"It's real cold outside, Grace and it will be dark soon. We'll go another day?" He tried to let her down gently. In reality, he hated being in the Castro at all, thinking that all the homosexual men would be after him.

Nathan was just over six foot tall and with his daily runs in the park and games of squash whenever time allowed, he was in good shape. His light brown hair and hazel eyes all contributed to a very good-looking man and Nathan was convinced that not only did every female want to fall at his feet, but so did most men. He really did not want to be out in the Castro after dark.

He kissed Sarah chastely on the cheek in greeting and she stood from the table to make him a cup of coffee. She felt a little uncomfortable in showing her true feelings to him and she was beginning to think that maybe she liked Nathan more than she cared to admit. She liked his eyes mostly. They were innocent and sparkled when he laughed, which was often. She quite fancied him and thought she might even be able to go to bed with him, that really wouldn't be such a chore. The only slight hesitation Sarah had in really going for it was Nathan's gangster friends and whether they were linked to Marco. "I've been to see Don Alessandro today." He began a little tentatively.

"How pleasant." Sarah's words were laced in sarcasm.

He pressed on, impervious to the acerbic reply. "I had a talk with him and I hope you don't mind but we got to talking about your situation. He's more than willing to find you a job, and in actual fact, he could do with an office assistant…"

"Nathan, I'm not interested. I'm happy at the diner, the money isn't too bad…"

"Bullshit!" Nathan exploded, causing Grace to look up from her dinner in alarm and dropped her fork.

Sarah scowled at Nathan. She walked over to the table and took Grace's nearly empty plate away. "Sweetheart, why don't you go and wash your hands and face? It looks like you have really enjoyed your dinner. Most of it's on your face!" Sarah said gently to her daughter in an effort to calm her. Grace stole a worried look at Nathan before leaving the room.

As the five year old girl went into the small bathroom and out of earshot, her mother spoke forcefully to their guest.

"I would appreciate it if you would not discuss my private matters with strangers!" She raged.

"Amy, he could pay you so much more than what you could hope for at the diner. The hours will fit around Grace's school hours." Nathan tried to explain.

"Perhaps. But where would this money come from? Drugs? Protection racketeering?" Sarah's voice was getting higher, almost hysterical.

Nathan looked at her in disbelief. "Does it matter? You could provide so much more for Grace!"

"To me, yes, it does matter!"

"Why don't you at least go and see the Don? He has some free time at eleven tomorrow."

Sarah glared at him in anger before flouncing out of the room as his answer. She went into the bathroom to see to Grace and help her put her pyjamas on in an effort to try to calm herself down. While they were in the bathroom, the front door could be heard slamming as Nathan left the apartment, himself very angry.

He walked back out into the cold and tried to cool his temper. He didn't understand Amy's reticence to her potential new job and thought she should be pleased. He knew he should drive to Marin County straight away and deliver the bad news.

He made his way in the traffic though the Haight and onto Fulton before picking up the 101 that would take him over the Golden Gate Bridge. It was slow going this time of the evening with the city workers making their way back to Marin County, to their rich lives, leaving the closeness of the city behind them for the trees and open spaces. Once the twinkling lights of the Bay City were in the rear view mirror, Nathan put his foot down. The engine of his silver BMW roared and the cold air blasted in through the small open window and Nathan began to relax a little.

After twenty minutes or so, he came to the large estate that belonged to his employer. His car was, as usual, searched thoroughly for any life threatening devices that might be hidden before he was allowed into the grounds and then proceed up the driveway. The November rain had turned heavy and he rushed from his car to the large porch and banged on the door getting soaked in the process.

After a few moments, the heavy door was opened by the Dons young housekeeper, Sofia. She recognised him immediately and smiled shyly.

"Hello Nathan. I'm not sure Don Alessandro is expecting you." She allowed him to come in anyway. Sofia had long since had a huge crush on Nathan Dando but was far too shy and traditional to do anything about it. Besides, her old-fashioned father, who also worked for Don Miotto disliked Nathan for reasons that he kept to himself and this prohibited Sofia to act upon her feelings.

Nathan returned Sofia's smile with his ever ready friendly one. "No, I didn't call ahead." He confirmed. "Can I come in and wait?"

Sofia would never say no to Nathan so she showed him into the dining room to wait while she went off to inform her employer of his arrival.

Nathan had but a few flaws and one of them was his impatience. After just a few minutes of waiting for Don Alessandro, Nathan began to get antsy. He got up from the green leather wing back chair that adorned the outside circle of the dining room and wandered over to the huge array of family photographs on the window sill. He saw some of his late father with the Don on a ski-ing holiday in Zermatt and another with his mother and the Dons now dead wife in Bermuda. Nathan smiled fondly at the photographs, even though he felt a pang in his chest at losing his father in such a way. Scott Dando had been killed ten years ago whilst protecting Don Alessandro when a bullet aimed for him had hit Scott instead. He'd pushed the Don to the ground and taken the bullet in the back and it had lodged itself in his heart, killing him instantly. Nathan had become a very angry fifteen year old boy, no mother or father left and he blamed Don Alessandro for the death of his father. The Don felt very remorseful at the loss of both a friend and a bodyguard. He treated Nathan as one of his own sons from there on in, fulfilling a promise made to Scott. He put Nathan through college, wanting him to have a career away from the family business. Nathan, on finishing college had decided he wanted to follow in his fathers footsteps and insisted on a job from Alessandro. Against his better judgement, the Don had found him a job as his driver hoping Nathan would get bored and eventually go elsewhere for employment. Nathan, like his father before him had since proven to be a valuable asset in the Miotto family business.

Putting the sunny Bermuda photo down, he caught a glimpse of a photo towards the back of the others and picked it up. It was of a wedding, a few years old judging by the fashions being worn and Nathan frowned as he brought it in for a closer inspection. The bride looked nervous and the groom looked as if he had better places to be, but it was the bride that looked somehow familiar, a face from another life time.

The door to the dining room creaked open and Nathan turned to greet the Don. "Nathan my boy! Twice in one day, huh?" The old man greeted him.

"Just a courtesy visit, Don Alessandro."

The older man ambled over to Nathan. "Looking at my memories, are you?"

"Yes sir. There is something familiar about this one, but I'm not sure what." Nathan offered it to Don Alessandro.

The Don took the teak framed photo from the younger man and pulled it very close to his eyes. He smiled at Nathan as he took his spectacles out of his breast pocket. "Age." he muttered as he placed the glasses on his nose and once again looked at the picture. "Ah yes, I remember this being taken. I had a good friend who lived in Palm Beach, Florida. His name was Giorgio Delvecchio and this was taken at his eldest sons wedding. Marco had a bit of a holiday romance, by all accounts and came back from the South of France with a bride. This was at his wedding party after the event. Giorgio was not best pleased about the rush wedding but he grew to love his new daughter in law – I believe her name was Sarah. After Giorgio died about five years ago, Marco took over the family businesses and the power went to his head. He killed Sarah for having an affair with the hired help. Shame he did that, he lost a lot of respect killing the mother of his child." Giorgio put the photo back in its place. "But Nathan, you have not come here to discuss my photographs."

Nathan, still unsure why the faces in the photos looked familiar, came to say what he had to. "Don Alessandro, I have been speaking to my friend Amy and despite your very generous offer, she feels unable to accept."

Don Alessandro shrugged. "That's her decision. You needn't have made a special journey in this rain." The rain had intensified outside and was pounding against the window and falling down the panes in rivers. "Did she say why?"

Nathan shifted uncomfortably from one foot to the other and said nothing, not sure of the right thing to say.

"Ah. She's heard the rumours. Why don't you get her here and see if I can't persuade her that I'm not such a monster." The old man smiled.

Nathan assured him that he would at least try.

Mid afternoon the following day, Don Marco Delvecchio

arrived at the International airport of San Francisco and eased through to his waiting car. He didn't want to draw any attention to himself and his small party in case Sarah got a heads up and took flight. Now that he'd made his mind up, nothing was going to stop Marco from getting what he came here for.

Settling down in the back seat of the car, he told Peter, his driver he brought with him from home to go by the diner. Although he got regular reports of what Sarah and Grace were doing, he wanted to get a feel for his wife's new life before he went in with both feet and upset everything.

CHAPTER THREE

Liz had just flown in from Miami, cross, tired and more than just a little angry with herself that her plan had not gone as she had expected. She had decided she had wasted enough time with the wrong brother and during the flight back to Chicago, she tried to think how she could get Marco for herself. She had just poured herself her second gin and a little splash of tonic when the lock in the front door clicked open.
It was her one-time fiancé, Vinnie Bonnetti, illegitimate brother of her new object of desire letting himself in with his key. Liz had been on at him for months to hand it in to her. True, the apartment was in his name and he paid for the upkeep but that didn't give him the right to come and go as he pleased.

"What do you want?" Her words were slightly slurred already. She hadn't eaten since last night in San Francisco. She swallowed half of her drink down.

He looked at her with mild distaste. "I want to see my son. The Nanny said you were out of town." He said, more than a little irked at even having to see her.

"I was." She smiled and walked over to him, kicking off her heeled shoes as she walked. She wanted to be close to him when she told him her news – to see every muscle on his face. To see how worried he might be. "I've been to Palm Beach."

He froze for a split second. "Palm Beach?"

"Hmmm" The second half of the drink disappeared down Liz's

throat. "You'll never amount to a hill of beans so I went to see the man with the power." She turned her back on him and walked over to the kitchen counter to pour herself another drink.

"About?" Vinnie was getting bored with this conversation. He doubted Liz would have the courage to see Marco, she had always been wary of him.

"I had some business to attend to."

"Ah-huh. What sort of business would Marco have with you?"

Liz smiled secretly.

"I can always call and ask him." Vinnie pushed.

Liz just laughed. "Yes, and I'm sure he'd love to hear from you!" She responded with sarcasm. It was well known that since Sarah's disappearance, the two half-brothers had not spoken. "Since you ask, I'll tell you. I'm trying to get him into bed. A worthy catch, I hear. Shame of it is I think he's still in love with that slut he's married to." She took another gulp of gin and tonic. "Well, of course, when I realised that, I just had to tell him that I'd seen her alive and well only that day in San Francisco." Liz didn't miss the look of anguish that flashed across Vinnies face so she continued. "I reckon he's on a plane right now to California." A drunken, distorted smile spread across her face.

Vinnie snapped. He felt such a hatred course through his veins that he had never felt before. In an uncontrollable rage that he didn't see coming, he smashed Liz across her face with his clenched fist. The force of it sent her flying across the glass coffee table, breaking it and several expensive ornaments in the process. She landed on the broken table and shards of glass surrounding her with the remains of her gin and tonic spilled on the white carpet. She looked confused and dazed and her finger went to touch her bloody lip.

"You are an evil bitch! You aren't even fit to mention her name! I'm leaving now and taking my son with me – you will never see him again!" he practically spat the words at the drunken woman on the floor. She had landed on her side, her stockings torn and her white sweater had blood spattered on it from where her lip had split with the force from Vinnie's fist. She was sprawled with legs akimbo and drunk as skunk.

"You think I care about that little wretch?" She referred to her son. "I couldn't care less if I never saw him again – you are welcome to him. You still owe me, Bonnetti! I gave up my life to have your bastard son!"

He leant down toward her. Her cheek was already welling up and would be black and blue. His job sometimes required him to commit acts of violence but never against a woman, let alone the mother of his son. "I want you out of this apartment by the end of the week. I owe you nothing. I'm letting you out of here with your life so consider that your severance pay. If anything happens to Sarah or to Grace, that will be revoked and I will hunt you down and kill you." He looked down at her again. "You disgust me." He left the room and went into his sons room to collect the sleeping child from his bed.

Liz let him go. She had never wanted the baby after she had got pregnant but hoped it would enforce Vinnie to marry her. All she ever wanted was the lifestyle Vinnie could offer her, power and wealth. When he refused, she resented the child and never really showed him any kind of love. The baby, James got more love from his father and his Nanny than Liz would ever be capable of showing.

Vinnie left the apartment with Liz's hysterical drunken laughter ringing in this ears, his half sleeping child in his arms. The nanny carried a small bag with some of James's favourite toys. Vinnie would buy his son and the nanny a whole new wardrobe.

The party of three headed for Vinnies apartment across town. James had fallen back asleep in Wendy's arms. Vinnie knew he must go to San Francisco to try and find Sarah before her murderous husband did. He owed her that much at least.

As soon as James and Wendy were settled, Vinnie made some phone calls to the West Coast. A friend of his late fathers lived in San Francisco and he invited Vinnie to stay with him for a few days. Vinnie hadn't told him exactly why he was in the city, just that he was looking for an old friend.

The following day, after a four hour flight from O'Hare airport, the Boeing aircraft touched down in San Francisco after a bumpy descent across the water. Vinnie did not much like flying and was pleased when the wheels landed onto the tarmac. It was windy but sunny outside, not as cold as Chicago but chilly all the same.

Outside the terminal building, Vinnie's ride was waiting for him. The driver of the car recognised him immediately even though the two of them had never met, for he made a bee-line for Vinnie.

"Mr Bonnetti? Welcome to San Francisco." The dark-haired young man took Vinnies small bag from him and led him to the waiting car. "I'm Nathan. Don Miotto regrets that he was unable to meet you personally."

Vinnie sat in the back of the car while Nathan put his bag in the trunk. "How is my old friend?" Vinnie asked Nathan when the younger man had got behind the wheel. He was eager to see the Don – it had been a year or so since their last meeting.

Alessandro Miotto was one of just a few people who knew about Giorgio Delvecchio's love child. Giorgio had met Justine Bonnetti not long after his marriage to Graziella. Justine was a secretary at his lawyers office and they had struck up a friendship which developed into a full blown affair. It had lasted only a few months – Giorgio had ended it the day Marco was born. A month or so later, Justine had told Giorgio she was pregnant but promised Giorgio she wanted nothing from him. She moved back to Chicago and Giorgio had given her a monthly allowance in return for her silence. Despite his shortcomings, Giorgio loved his wife and did not want to hurt her with this explosive news. Justine was true to her word and never told a soul who her child's father was, not even Vincenzo. Giorgio had told only Alessandro, his closest friend and ally.

Until things became complicated, that is.

Fate conspired to a chance meeting with Vinnie and Rosa on the beaches of Miami when Rosa was there celebrating graduation with some girlfriends. She had taken a liking to Vinnie, going out on several dates with him during her break. She rang home excitedly one evening to say that she had met the love of her life and was going to marry him and could she bring Vinnie home to meet her family. Her father probed Rosa for more information about her new love and Rosa divulged much information to him in an effort to win her beloved Pops over. Giorgio listened with horror as Rosa told him his name, that he lived in Chicago, his mother was a legal secretary and his father was dead and unknown to him. Giorgio could not believe that Rosa and Vinnie had met and panicked that his daughter and his son were a couple. He called Justine in Chicago to tell her to call Vinnie and tell him he must end it. All Rosa knew was that Vinnie changed his mind about her and would not and could not see her again. She was left devastated and still unaware of the fact that Vinnie was her illegitimate brother.

Vinnie was suddenly aware that Nathan was chatting inanely , something about a girl called Amy. Assuming Amy was Nathan's girlfriend and disinterested in the conversation, he stared out of the window and watched the passing countryside.

At the entrance to the Miotto estate, the car was once again searched before they were permitted to enter the grounds. Nathan parked the car and the two men went inside the house and out of the cold. Sophia showed them into the sitting room to wait while she went to get them some coffee. She informed them that the Don should not be too long, that he was with his new secretary.

"That's the girl I was telling you about - Amy." Nathan became animated.

"Your boss's secretary?" Vinnie frowned. He had an image of a prissy school mistress type whereas he thought Nathan would be more interested in braggers, showgirls and good time girls perhaps, but not a secretary.

"She's amazing. She is such an enigma that I'm drawn to her and she drives me crazy. She's running from someone – she has become a bottle blond to try and hide and she's always looking over her shoulder. Grace's dad, I guess."

"Grace?" It was Vinnies turn to have his interest piqued.

"Her daughter. She's five and has me wrapped around her finger already. A beautiful child, but dark, not like her mother."

"Dark?" Vinnie repeated.

"Yes, and olive skinned too. I guess she takes after her father, who ever he is."

The door creaked open and Don Miotto shuffled in, disabling Vinnie from asking anymore questions for the time being.

"Talking about your girlfriend?" The silver-haired man asked. "She's ready to be taken home now, if you don't mind Nathan." He was very amused that someone like Nathan was so infatuated with Amy but that it was one-way traffic. He could have any woman he wanted, except Amy or so it seemed.

Nathan stood at Don Miotto's dismissive words and saying goodbye to both the men in the room, he left to go and find Amy.

She had just come out of the Don's office and was buttoning her coat up, ready for the intense weather outside. She smiled when she saw Nathan.

"Hey! You're back from the airport?" She stated.

"Sure. You ready to go home? Amy nodded. "Are you coming back tomorrow?" He asked.

"Sure! Like you said, the money is much better, not to mention the working conditions. I asked him about his businesses and although he's a bit of an old hound, he seems mostly legal. I'll give it a go."

Nathan took her hand and they went outside. Nathan was astounded that Amy had asked the Don about his businesses, no-one usually dared.

Dark, angry eyes watched them leave the house.

That night, Sarah dreamt of Marco again only this time he wasn't trying to kill her. She dreamt of the time when they had first met. Sarah had been on holiday in the South of France with her then best friend, Helen. Helen had gone off in search of cold drinks, leaving Sarah on the beach soaking up the sun. Marco had seen her earlier that morning and was sitting at a nearby beach bar waiting for an opportunity to approach her. When Helen left, Marco strode up to Sarah and sat next to her on the empty sun-bed. They began to talk and he asked her and Helen out to the casino that evening with Joe, who he as vacationing with. Sarah was very taken with the good looking young American and accepted his invitation. She was almost engaged to Steve at the time, at least, he had asked her to marry him before she left for France and was pondering his proposal. The fact that she had accepted Marco's invitation told her all she needed to know about that relationship.

Marco and Joe had taken Sarah and Helen to the casino that evening and Sarah became even more enamoured with Marco. He was full of charm and easy to talk to, full of compliments that flowed off his tongue in a true sense. The men were both natural gamblers and bet heavily but also won plenty. They asked the girls out for dinner the following night to spend their winnings. Marco felt Sarah was his lucky charm and just wanted an excuse to spend more time with her.

After dinner the following night, Marco and Sarah went for a drunken walk along the dark beach. He was arrogant enough to try and kiss her, feeling he had spent enough money on her and deserved something in return. Sarah took exception and after a good slap around his face, she left him on the deserted beach and stormed off back to her hotel. Marco, undeterred, went looking for her the next morning and found her having coffee in the cafe of her hotel. He apologised for his behaviour and despite the fact that Sarah was leaving for home the next day, he promised he would call her everyday.

Sarah went home, finished with Steve and waited eagerly for Marco's phone calls every night. He left Nice about five days later and stopped in London to see Sarah on his way home. It was then he proposed, he told her that he had never met anyone like her and he wanted her to come to Florida with him. Sarahs life at the time had consisted of a rented room in a friends house, a dreary job in a jewellery shop and a drunken mother that she didn't care for. What did she have to lose? She accepted Marcos proposal and they married three days later at Reading registrars office. Their wedding night was spent at the Renaissance at Heathrow and it was the first time they had slept together, full of passion but not much tenderness. The following day they headed off to their new life together. She arrived at the Delvecchio mansion full of awe and surprise. Sarah had thought that Marco and his family were not short of a penny of two, but this opulent palace surprised even her.

Sarah had known nothing of Marco's life at the time, his family or how this might affect her. That all came much later.

Sarah awoke at five am feeling sad. Remembering the nice Marco made her ache for him again and she could almost feel his strong arms around her, although it had been five years since she had had the pleasure. She wished whole-heartedly that things had been different and Vincenzo Bonnetti had never come into her life.

Sarah felt unable to concentrate at work the following day and was relieved when Sophia came in at eleven am with some coffee. The young girl set the tray down next to Sarah and poured her some of the syrupy black liquid, strong, just as Sarah needed it.

"I will be doing a light lunch at one o'clock today, Amy." Sophia informed her politely.

"That's nice, Sophia but Nathan is taking me to town for a quick bite to eat today. You know that little bistro by the waterfront?" Sarah smiled, not taking her eyes of the computer screen and so missed the look of jealousy on the younger girls face.

At a quarter to one, Don Alessandro came into Sarahs little office with a hand written letter. His face seemed calm and relaxed and Sarah knew he was meeting with an old friend, one which he was obviously pleased to be spending time with.

"Amy, before you go out to lunch, could you please type this so it is legible and fax it to the number at the bottom? It's a Chicago fax number. For my house guest."

"Sure." Sarah smiled and took the letter from him. As she looked at the letter, badly written in a scrawl, Sarah felt she recognised the almost unreadable writing and scanned through it quickly. She immediately recognised the signature at the bottom of the page and her head began to swim.

"He's here?" Sarah half whispered, unaware she had said anything out loud.

Don Miotto turned and saw Sarah go moderately pale and swaying on her chair.

"Who?" he asked puzzled.

Sarah found some strength. "What? Nothing. I have to go. I have to get my daughter and go. I can't work here anymore." Her eyes began to swim with tears and grabbing her bag she tried to walk passed Miotto and out of the room.

"Wait." He commanded, stopping Sarah in her tracks. "What's going on?" He took the letter still in Sarah's shaking hand and read it through. It had nothing offensive in it; it was just a fax from his house guest to his sons nanny. He frowned and looked at his secretary again. He felt an overwhelming compassion for the girl; she looked so frail and vulnerable. Knowing he must be going soft in his old age, Miotto took her hand and lead her back to her seat at the desk. He perched himself on the desk next to her.

"Talk to me Amy."

"I can't." She was struggling to hold back the tears of fear. She was more scared for her daughter than herself.

"Well I can't help you if you don't tell me the problem. Nathan told me that there is something in your past that you are scared of. Isn't now the time to tell me?"

Sarah sobbed and looked into the old mans eyes. "The problem, Don Alessandro, is your house guest." She plunged over the ravine and knew there was no going back.

"Vincenzo? How do you know him?" He seemed very confused.

"He is my husbands brother." She had nothing to lose anymore. He may as well know the whole story. Maybe he would give her a head start before he sent Vinnie and Marco after her. "Vinnie and I had a brief affair, Vinnie betrayed me and my husband tried to kill me for it. My name is Sarah Delvecchio." She looked him in the eye as she said these last words.

There was absolute stony silence in the room and Don Alessandro digested these words.

"Every one knows Sarah Delvecchio is in hiding in England. You look nothing like her."

Sarah stood, calmer now and walked a few steps away from her employer.

"Why would I lie?" She turned to face him again.

She had him. He had no answer to that question.

He shrugged.

"I wouldn't put my daughters life at risk by making things like that up. For all I know, Vinnie has already called Marco and he could be on his way here now to get me. He is always so thorough with matters like this and I don't know why he didn't actually kill me in the Everglades five years ago but I am sure that if he got a second chance, he wouldn't make such a mistake again."

"Amy – Sarah – whatever your name is, you are under my protection here and he will not harm you. Your husbands influence means nothing in my city. You are safe, please believe me."

"You mean to tell me that you are not going to hand me over to him?" She was incredulous and was expecting some sort of double crossing to take place.

He shook his head. "Why would you think such a thing?"

"Isn't that what your kind is all about? Protecting each other, whatever the cost?"

"No. I have a duty to protect an innocent employee. The only thing you seem guilty of is being unfaithful to your husband but in this country, that is not yet a capital offence or God help us, we'd all be in the fires of hell!" He said this lightly to try and relax Sarah.

She ventured a half smile but was still not entirely convinced.

"You say Vinnie betrayed your secret?"

She nodded.

"How can you be sure it was him?"

"Well, I sure as hell wasn't going to tell Marco. It was one night, a stupid mistake while we were in London when Marco was in jail awaiting trial."

Don Alessandro nodded. He had heard about Marco being caught and then let free for lack of evidence. Sarah's story began to add up.

"I was low and I thought Marco would be in prison for years. I didn't know what was going to become of me and Vinnie seemed to have the answers. Of course, I was naïve back then and didn't know how things were. I should have known that Marco would walk away a free man." She smiled wryly.

"I really have no idea what you mean!" The old man returned her droll smile.

Sarah sighed, once again remembering the severity of her situation. "I have to go and get Grace. I don't want to leave her unprotected and Ted and Henry are innocent in this. I don't want them caught up in anything." She picked up her hand bag. "Three hours ago, I was happy. I had a nice new friend and a good well paid job. Now I find myself back in Mafia city and my past is quickly catching up on me."

"You cannot run forever. Let me protect you."

Sarah shook her head.

"Let me at least talk to Vincenzo, find out what he knows and why he is really here. I'll have Nathan stay at your apartment with you and will put a couple of guys surreptitiously outside the house, across the road so you'll know you'll be safe."

She turned to look at him again. "You think Nathan needs an

excuse to stay in my apartment? If Marco found out, Nathan would end up dead also."

"I have told you. He cannot do anything in my city. He lost a lot of respect when he chose to dispose of you in that way. People thought that if he could do that to his wife and mother of his child, he would have no business scruples. He would have to go over my head to seek permission for retribution, permission that I know he would not get."

Sarah frowned. "Permission from whom?"

"From those who matter. Trust me, you will be safe." He put his hands on her shoulders.

"Don Miotto, I don't think I trust anyone right now, but I have very little else to believe in. I will take your offer of protection and I hope it will be enough."

He smiled. Don Alessandro Miotto liked to look after lost sheep.

Nathan drove Sarah back to the city straight away. He was confused but would never question his boss. He was even more confused when Sarah pulled Grace out of school early and took her home, locking the door twice over when she arrived at the apartment. Grace was now happily drawing a picture of the three of them at the kitchen table when Sarah opened a bottle of Californian red wine, despite the early hour – it was just passed three o'clock.

Nathan stood leaning against the refrigerator, arms crossed over his chest, wanting some kind of explanation.

"The Don said I have to look after you, to spend the night on that sofa."

Sarah drained her glass and refilled it. "Yep" She grabbed the now full wine glass with one hand and the remainder of the bottle with her other and headed for the front room.

"Why?" He called after her.

She didn't reply.

"Amy?" He prompted as he came into the front room. "What's going on?"

She sat at one end of the sofa, one leg folded underneath her and the other stretched out onto the coffee table opposite. "Sarah." The drink had emboldened her.

"What?" He was very confused.

"You want me to talk, I'll talk. You'll find out soon enough anyway, why not now? My real name is Sarah Delvecchio."

"Delvecchio?" Nathan subconsciously backed away from Sarah.

She nodded. "Yes, as in Marco Delvecchio." She sighed deeply. "He is my husband and may well be on his way to the city to kill me and claim his daughter. That's why you are here. Protection." She laughed over the last word as if the idea was ludicrous.

Nathan recovered his composure a little. "Why didn't you tell me?" He looked hurt. "Don't you think you being married to a boss has some bearing on our friendship?"

She looked at him. "I haven't told anyone at all. I don't know who I can trust and I don't want to trust anyone anyway. There is too much at stake. I didn't want to get too close to you and that's why I tried to end our relationship. I do not know what Marco is capable of and I don't want to be responsible for anyone getting hurt."

"So why tell Miotto? Why trust him?"

"Because I am sick of running scared and looking over my shoulder. He claims he will protect me and Grace and I have nothing else to believe in."

Nathan pondered Sarahs words for a while. "At least I know now why you won't sleep with me." He made a half attempt at humour.

Sarah laughed softly. "Marco once had someone killed that he thought I was sleeping with."

"You must never say that, you don't know who might be listening! Besides, I'd take my chances for you. You know that I want to spend the night with you and not on the sofa, Amy…" He murmured softly.

Sarah leant forward to get away from his advances and to refill her wine glass. "Amy no longer exists." She made her meaning quite clear.

To the north, in Marin County, Don Miotto was having dinner with his house guest. They were in the library having a pre dinner drink, served as ever by Sophia, while their sumptuous meal was being prepared. Vinnie sat relaxed in one of the leather wing back chairs that the Don favoured throughout his house and sipped his martini, unaware of the information that his host had on him.

"So, Vinnie, do you want to tell me why you are in my city?" The older man questioned.

Vinnie looked over his glass at the Don. "I thought I had. I'm looking up an old girlfriend."

The Don stared at him for a moment long enough to make Vinnie feel just a little nervous. "Really?" He said.

Vinnie just shrugged. "What would make you think otherwise?"

Don Alessandro stood and went to refill both their glasses. When he had done so, he turned and looked at his guest, still sat in the chair. "I think that you are on a contract for your brother."

Vinnie stared at him in disbelief. "Marco? But we haven't spoken in years. I don't owe him anything and I wouldn't do him any favours."

"Years?" The old man pushed.

Vinnie nodded. He hesitated a moment before continuing, wondering what relevance any of this had and why he was being interrogated, however gently, on it. "I did a bad thing to him but I thought everyone knew. I had a brief affair with his wife while he was in jail awaiting trail about four years ago. It was a stupid thing to do but I did care for Sarah and we all thought Marco would go down for a few years, the charges were that big. He got off and came after me."

"Does this have anything to do with why you are here, in San Francisco?"

Vinnie finally put his glass down on the table beside his chair. "I still care for Sarah. I did a terrible thing to her and to Marco and want to put that right. I have heard that she may be in the city and that Marco may be on his way here to find her. I just want to warn her and to protect her."

Don Alessandro nodded. "So why come to me?"

"You have many contacts, on street level. One of your people may know her."

"It's a big city…"

Vinnie nodded. "That's why I need your help."

"What will you do if you find her?"

"Take her back to Chicago. Marry her, if she'll have me."

"And what if she wants nothing to do with you? Why should she trust you – you told her husband about your affair after all."

Vinnie narrowed his eyes. Something the Don had just said didn't tally. "How do you know that?"

The old man smiled a half smile. "She told me."

Stunned, Vinnie could say nothing.

"Let's just say that I happened upon her and that she is in my protection right now."

"Don Alessandro, I need to talk to her and put things right."

"Vincenzo, you are the son of my eldest friend and he was an honourable man, but how do I know that your intentions are as honourable as your father was?"

Vinnies voice took on an almost pleading tone. "You have my word. I just need to talk to her, to explain things. I have no regrets about our affair, only that Marco found out. I care for her and for Grace."

Sophia knocked softly on the door and announced that dinner was about to be served in the dining room. The two men stood, Vinnies eyes still pleading with his host as they walked out into the hallway and across to the room opposite. The large table was laid for two places, at the far end of the eight-seater and as Sophia served the goats cheese wrapped in prosciutto, the Don spoke to Vinnie.

"Here's what we'll do. I will ask Sarah to come to the house to speak to you tomorrow. You will have one chance and one chance only. If you harm that girl or her daughter by action or omission, I'll kill you myself. If you allow her husband to harm her, I shall also kill you. Do you understand me?"

Vinnie nodded enthusiastically, his appetite suddenly failing him as adrenaline rushed through him at the thought of seeing Sarah again.

After spending an uncomfortable night on the sofa, Nathan took Sarah to work the following morning. He had some business to attend to at the Don's house anyway and he knew Sarah's nerves were jangled and could do without the long bus journey.

Sarah sat staring out of the window all the way north. Every car they passed, she feared held a car full of assassins. In her minds eye, she saw 1920's style gangsters dressed like Al Capone, waiting to jump out of a vehicle with old fashioned Tommy guns blazing. In reality, she knew it was more likely to be on a crowded street with a silenced revolver. Sarah knew that paranoia was setting in and for the sake of her sanity, she had to trust Don Miotto.

Outside the house, Nathan stopped the car to let her out. He leant over to kiss her cheek without turning the engine off.

"I have to be off. I have some stuff to do." He said by way of an explanation.

She nodded and got out of the car into the warm sunny late November day. The rain had finally stopped and a false late Autumn had set in. Sarah turned her head upwards to let the sun fall on her pale face. She had barely slept last night, jumping at every noise.

She got straight to work, Don Miotto was headed to New York for a couple of days for a meeting and she had his flights and accommodation to arrange. It served well to clear her mind of her worries as she negotiated hotel rates in some of New York's top hotels.

At just after eleven, the Don called Sarah on his internal line, inviting her into his office for coffee. She left her small office and went through the connecting doors into his, relieved to see he was alone.

She sat at his invitation and he poured them both a cup of coffee. "How are you feeling today?" He asked out of genuine concern.

"Fine, thank you. A little nervous, I guess but I'm okay all things considered."

"Well, you have no need to be nervous or insecure. I have spoken at length to Vincenzo and he assures me that he only wants to put things right between you both. To look after you."

Sarah snickered in disgust. "Look after me? If it wasn't for him and his tell-all bragging, I wouldn't need looking after. I wouldn't be in this position."

"That's not strictly true…" A sickeningly familiar voice said from the doorway to the right. Sarah stood quickly, her chair tumbled over backwards and she spun around to the source of the voice. Vinnie was leaning in the doorway to the office. His green eyes stared at her in what he hoped was not menacing but pleading for her to believe him. His fair hair was immaculate as always, although short, like a Marine's might be. He looked very smart in his dark grey suit and tie but his business like image did not stop the feeling of terror Sarah felt rising up inside her.

"I just want to explain…" He began.

Sarah would not let him finish. "Explain?" Hysteria had taken hold and her voice was high and loud. "Explain what? Why you slept with me and then bragged to my husband? Just tell me this, Vinnie. Who do you hate more? Me or Marco?"

"It wasn't…" he tried to talk

Sarah rounded on Don Alessandro in a way no other would dare but she felt she had nothing to lose. She was as good as dead anyway.

"And you! You told me to trust you, that I was safe. How the hell do you explain this?" Her face was scarlet with rage.

"I explain nothing. Sit down, calm down and listen to what the man has to say. You are safe, believe that if nothing else." He left the room and closed the door behind him.

Sarah sat in the chair and barely whispered. "I hate you so much. Do you have any idea of what you have done with your spiteful words? What was it? If you couldn't have me, then you'd make damn sure that Marco wouldn't want me? Is that it?" She couldn't look at him.

He shook his head and sat in the chair next to Sarahs. She was trembling as he tried to take her hand in his. She forcefully drew it away.

"I have a good idea of what I have done and I want to make it up to you. I swear I never told Marco what happened between us and I didn't know what he was capable of or I would have never let you go back to him."

"So who the hell told him then, because it sure as hell wasn't me!"

He shrugged. "Marco guessed."

Sarah laughed hysterically. "He may have his spies but he's not that good."

Vinnie sighed and sat back in the chair. "Marco asked me one evening what had happened in London. I told him about Grace being taken and you being upset. We talked about lots of things and out of the blue, he asked me if I knew if you had been faithful to him. The question knocked me off guard and for a moment, I didn't answer him. He went mad, completely crazy like I'd never seen him before and asked me if I knew who it was that you'd been with. I told him that he was acting crazy and that you had stayed faithful. Then he just got this scary, deranged look in his eye and he said he knew who it was, that it was me who slept with you." He looked away from Sarah. "I protested, told him he was an idiot for even thing that but he had already made his mind up and had me thrown out of the house. I'm so sorry." He looked back at her, searching her hazel eyes for forgiveness.

"Sorry? " Sarah was incredulous. "Sorry doesn't even begin to cover it. Do you know what you have done to me, to my daughter?" She thought for a moment. "Is Marco on his way here?"

He shrugged. "I don't know for sure, but I believe so. We haven't spoken since he threw me out of the house. Liz has been to see him so my guess is yes, he's on his way."

"Liz? But why would she do that?"

He sighed deeply. "She's as deranged as Marco. Perhaps they deserve each other. I just want to help you and take you back to Chicago with me."

She looked at him coldly. "I don't want to go to Chicago and certainly not with you."

"Please Sarah. What happened between us in London was real, at least for me. Now that I've found you again, we can try to work things out." He begged her with his eyes as he swivelled around to face her on the chair.

"All I know is I once had a life with a husband and the father of my child, not running from him, scared. He may have many faults but I did love him and then you came along and all of that disappeared."

Vinnie stood up. "Do you still love him?"

She shrugged. "I miss having him around, having someone to tell me I look good in this dress or bad in that one. I want someone to discuss my daughters schooling with. I miss having someone hold me when I wake up in the middle of the night screaming from a nightmare, and believe me, there are plenty of those. Do you know what I'm trying to say?" She looked up at him, his hands on his hips.

    Vinnie nodded. He knew exactly what she was trying to say, or at least, he thought he did. He would be the one to give her what she was missing out on and if he could convince her to come to Chicago with him, they would have a great future together.

Chapter Four

Marco and his small army arrived at the Dons mansion just as Sarah had arrived home early to start packing.

He wanted to do this by the book, to get Don Miotto's permission to conduct his business in the Bay City. He had thought about calling ahead but then decided against it. Don Alessandro was one of the men who had vetoed Marco from going after Sarah four years ago and he thought a face to face meeting might better convince Alessandro of his good intentions.

First, Marco had to get passed Sophia.

"No, I do not have an appointment." Marco growled at the young housekeeper prohibiting his entrance to the great house. She had answered the door and not knowing who he was, tried to get rid of him. Don Alessandro wanted no more visitors today.

"Then I'm sorry but Don Miotto cannot see you today." She was bold, despite the intimidating, glowering looks from the handsome man on the doorstep.

He was about to make a scene, already gruff from the indignation of having to suffer a body search when a door off the large hallway opened and an old grey framed face peered from within. It was Don Miotto, looking to see who was making a noise in his house. He recognised the young Don from Florida.

"Marco. What a surprise." He exuded false pleasantries and sent Sophia scurrying away.

This visit was anything but a surprise although Miotto was not expecting it quite so soon.

Marco was beckoned inside and smiled at his superior in age and in rank. He knew he had just one shot at getting this right and wanted to sound sincere yet convincing.

"I am sorry to have called by unexpectedly. I'm only in town for a few days and I wanted to pay my respects to my dear late father's friend." He tried to be deferential to the older man.

Miotto led him into the library, making small talk about the weather in San Francisco and irrelevant business talk as they walked. Once in the large wood panelled library, they both took a seat, Marco on the Chesterfield and Miotto on the wing back chair.

"So Marco, what is your business in my city?"

Marco decided honesty covered in flattery would be the best policy. "Don Miotto, our families have been friends and allies for several decades now and you were my fathers closest friend. He loved you like the brother he never had and I know I can be candid with you." He crossed his legs and began. "As you know, my wife and daughter went missing several years ago and I know they are in your city. My intentions were always honest, but doubted in the past and I have been up until now, refused permission to seek them out. I know you are held in high esteem with your peers and I am asking for your help in finding them."

Miotto looked away from Marco and crossed with his legs. He had never thought that Marco would be so up front and honest so, stalling for time, he asked how he could be of assistance.

"You have many employees in this city, many contacts. I know where Sarah and Grace live and I know where Grace goes to school and I…"

"Marco, I cannot give you permission." Miotto interrupted him. "I cannot have the deaths of two innocent people on my hands."

Marco was confused. "That's not…"

Miotto stood to intimidate his now unwelcome guest. "I want you to leave my house and my city and return to Florida. You are not to seek them out in any way or the ties between our two Families will be irrevocably broken. Do I make myself clear?"

Marco stood to try and regain control of the conversation.

"Don Miotto, please let me explain…"

"You may be Giorgio Delvecchio's eldest son but you are no testament to him. I know he would abhor the fact that you tried to kill your wife and the mother of your child. They are both best left alone and without you."

The library door opened and Miotto's eldest son Frankie appeared in the open doorway. He was a very mean character and although Marco thought he could take him on his own, he knew there would be many more men to come out of the woodwork and he would not stand a chance. Instead, the Florida Don was escorted off the premises and into his hired car where Pete and Gabe were waiting inside.

Sinking back into the leather seats of the hired Lincoln, Marco suddenly felt defeated. Miotto had him all wrong. He just wanted Sarah and Grace to go home with him.

Towards the end of the long drive, Peter slammed on the brakes of the car and a bang on the hood was heard in the back by Marco and Gabriel. Gabriel got out of the car and after a brief struggle and girlish protests, a young girl was forced into the back with Marco. Gabe got in beside her and blocked her exit.

Sophia looked fearfully at Marco and then back at Gabe. Marco returned the defiant stare of the girl who had earlier tried and to some extent succeeded in giving him a hard time, waiting patiently for her to talk.

Sophia wondered briefly if she was doing the right thing, but then realised she was trapped and it was too late to back out. This was for Nathan's sake.

"I'm sorry I was rude to you earlier. I didn't know who you are." She began.

"And now you do?" He raised an eyebrow.

She nodded. "Don Marco Delvecchio."

Marco smiled. "I'm impressed. What do you want? I'm busy" His brusqueness returned abruptly.

"I thought you might like to know that we've had a visitor for the last few days. I think you may know him – his name's Vincenzo Bonnetti, from Chicago."

Marco's interest picked up. He hadn't heard from his half-brother in four years since he'd confessed to having sex with his wife. Why was Vinnie in San Francisco?

"Continue." He instructed.

"Well, he left the house this morning with Don Alessandro's secretary, Amy to get her daughter, Grace from school. I may be wrong but I'm sure I heard on several occasions people calling the secretary Sarah Delvecchio and I just wondered if there was any connection?" She asked slyly, knowing full well that there would be.

Marco turned away from the young girl and looked out of the window. He should have known Vinnie would come for Sarah and try to steal his wife away again. Marco was determined that he would not get away with it this time.

He turned back to Sophia. "Do you know what their plans are?"

She smiled slowly. "Sure I do. What's in it for me?" Never before did she have such power over such a powerful man.

He leant close to her so he only had to speak low and with malice. "You tell me and I won't have to kill you."

Sophia told him everything she knew.

Back in his suite at the St Francis hotel in downtown San Francisco, Marco poured himself another Jack Daniels from the bar and swallowed it in one gulp. He looked down over Union Square at the late night shoppers. It was just getting dark and the Christmas lights were already lit up and brightly shining in an effort to make people part with their hard earned greens. A huge decorated Christmas tree was displayed in the centre of the square and a school band were hammering out Christmas carols that were just about in tune underneath its fan-like branches. Even from this height, Marco could see parents with their children, their small eager faces glowing with excitement even though Christmas was still four weeks away. It bought it home to him what he was missing out on and what he had lost. He wasn't sure if Sarah and Vinnie were picking up where they left off, but Marco was determined that he would make life difficult for them, especially Vinnie. His half-brother always seemed to get what he wanted. After the chance meeting with Rosa in Miami, Giorgio had taken Marco aside and being the eldest son, had told him all about his relationship with Justine Bonnetti. Giorgio had made out that Vincenzo was a poor little orphan boy who had missed out on what should have been his because of the wrong doings of his father. Giorgio had made Marco promise him that he would keep the secret but that he would give Vincenzo something for himself. Marco, true to his fathers word had given Vinnie a piece of the business to take back to Chicago. Vinnie had ingratiated himself, with Giorgio's help with a crew in Chicago to help him build up his business and become somebody important. Over the years, Giorgio's secret son had become less secret and more accepted by everyone who mattered. Despite this rise in fortune for Vinnie, it had not been enough. He wanted Marco's wife and maybe his position too, but Marco was determined that the ungrateful bastard would not get his own way this time.

Marco landed at Chicago's O'Hare airport at seven o'clock the next evening. He had sent Pete home but Gabe had joined Marco on this extended trip east. Marco was tired and very grouchy – even on the first class seat from Oakland Airport, he hadn't slept well and had had little or no sleep the night before. In fact, his sleep had been largely disrupted since his meeting with Liz a week before. Marco hated the cold and as the airport doors slid open, blowing in a blast of ice cold air, he turned up his collar and tried to make the best of it. He just wanted to get his business done and head home to the warmth of the Sunshine State.

He gave the taxi driver the address of his brothers apartment in Chicago and they joined the traffic headed away from the airport. It was slow going at this time of night and it gave Marco more time to think about what he was going to say as he confronted his wife and her lover. He would try and stay calm but his temper had a mind of it's own at times.

Marco paid the driver of the taxi a hundred dollars and asked him to wait. He didn't think he'd be that long and didn't want to have to wait in the freezing temperatures for another cab. He looked up at the tall building of which his brother owned the top two floors and with a deep breath, Marco went inside with Gabe following him. He pushed the heavy glass double doors open and headed to the back of the lobby where the elevators were positioned.

"Excuse me, Sir, but you need to sign the visitors book" A voice from their left called out.

Marco looked over and saw the concierge of the building behind a large light wood coloured desk. He had on the typical uniform of a apartment block concierge and was probably an ex-cop. Not wanting to make a fuss, Marco and Gabe went over to the desk to sign in. He scrawled his name in the book and had a quick look up to see if he could see any familiar names, but there were none, at least on this page.

After Gabe had signed in, the concierge looked at who they were visiting.

"I don't believe anyone is home in the Penthouse, Sir. Save the nanny anyway." He offered helpfully.

Marco managed a smile. "I'll go and check anyway, if that's okay?"

"Go right ahead." The reply was given with an equally forced smile.

Gabe called for the elevator and after just a few seconds, it arrived, spilling out a couple who looked as though they were heading out for a night on the town. Marco envied them as they left the building laughing and holding hands.

The ride to the top of the thirty floor building seemed to take an eternity. Marco and Gabe did not speak, Gabe sensing that his boss was not in the mood for conversation. At last, the elevator pinged to signal that they had arrived at the top and the doors slid open. Marco had only been here a handful of times and not for many years, yet he still remembered the way the Vinnies home.

They stood outside the door to apartment 301 and Marco hesitated. Did he really want to know what was going on between his wife and his brother? Would he not be better off if he just left them to it and got on with his own life?

"Marco?" Gabe prompted.

Gabe's words prompted him out of his reverie and with a confidence he did not feel, he banged heavily on the door.

After just a few moments, the door was opened by a young redhead, presumably the nanny. She had the security chain on and peered suspiciously out at the two men on the doorstep.

"Is Mr Bonnetti home, please?" Marco enquired as politely as he could.

"No, he is away on business." She replied timidly.

"Where?"

She hesitated a moment, unsure if she should tell strangers of her boss's whereabouts. However, she knew of Vinnies reputation and what he was into. She wanted rid of these two men and she had James's safety to consider.

"He's in San Francisco."

"Still? I thought he was headed home yesterday?" Marco was confused.

"He called to say that he would be required to stay on a few days longer. Can I have your name and I will let him know you called by. He usually phones home everyday." The nanny offered.

Marco didn't reply but instead turned and slowly walked towards the elevators. He'd had enough of chasing after them and it was obvious to him that Sarah didn't want to be found, by Marco at least. He went back downstairs to his waiting taxi. He knew now what he had to do, his last course of action.

Sarah poured the three of them another glass of white wine, Californian, the only type Henry would drink. Ted came in from their kitchen with a tray of pizza that had just been delivered and Grace immediately dived in for a slice of cheese and tomato, her favourite, giggling as she did so.

Sarah sat back in the large, comfy chair that she claimed for her own on the numerous occasions she was invited upstairs and sipped the wonderfully fruity wine. She smiled inwardly as she watched Grace watching the television, oblivious to the adult conversation that had been interrupted by the pizza delivery. Ted was eager to pick up from where they had left off.

"So this Vinnie then. He is Marco's brother?" He prompted Sarah for more details of her recently confessed life story.

"Half-brothers. They share the same father." Sarah explained. "I have no excuse, it was a terrible thing to do to Marco. What can I say? I thought Marco would be gone for years and I already felt very alone. I should have known how things worked and that it would just be a matter of time."

"So does he know where you are?" Henry enquired, quite excitable.

"I don't think so. San Francisco is a big city and there are plenty of places to hide. If he knew, he would have been here by now. Marco is not one to suffer in silence."

"And what about Vinnies marriage proposal?" Ted laughed. Ted and Henry had arrived home earlier today just as Vinnie was down on one knee proposing to Sarah.

Sarah had decided yesterday that she wasn't going to go to Chicago with Vinnie. She liked San Francisco and was settled as was Grace in her school. Vinnie hoped that by asking Sarah to divorce Marco and marry him, it would change her mind. Sarah had promised him she would think about it but had already made her decision.

"I don't believe Marco would grant me a divorce, especially to marry his brother. Besides, I've been a Don's wife, why would I lower myself and settle for the hired help?" They all laughed loudly and Sarah helped herself to a slice of meaty pizza.

After an uneventful and quiet day, Vinnie called Sarah the following evening from Don Alessandros house.

"Hi, I'm sorry I missed you today." He began. "I thought you might like to know that Marco has gone back to Palm Beach today. He went to Chicago yesterday, looking for you. I don't know what gave him the idea that you would have headed there."

"No." Sarah didn't really know what to say to him. The conversation became a little stilted.

"I would say Marco will leave you alone for good now. It might be the best time to ask him for a divorce."

Sarah stayed silent.

"Sarah?"

"I don't think Marco would allow that." She replied softly.

"Well, it's not about what he would allow. You two have been separated for four years now, he wouldn't contest it. I'll get my lawyer to start looking in to it." He promised.

"No, Vinnie, don't. Not just yet. I need more time to think."

Now it was time for Vinnie to stay silent. After a few minutes, he said, "I'm going back to Chicago tomorrow. I need to know if you still love him?"

More silence.

"Vinnie, there is someone at the door. I have to go."

Sarah put the phone down, her hands shaking. There was nobody at the door.

CHAPTER FIVE

In the run up to Christmas, Sarah began to relax. Her job at Miotto's was easy and the money was good. There were no more run ins with her past and Vinnie had returned to Chicago without a fiancé and hadn't called Sarah since. Nathan had agreed to stay friends with Sarah and decided that now he knew who she was married to, it was for the best. They went out once a week for dinner or to the movies, sometimes taking Grace. About a week before Christmas, Sarah took Grace downtown to look at the Christmas tree in Union Square. The band was still there but now more in tune and Grace sang along with the crowd to the carols she knew and hummed along to those she didn't. Sarah watched her little girls face glowing with the thrill of just being there and the cold that had turned her nose pink even under the black fleece hat she wore. Her eyes were bright and she giggled as Sarah got some of the words wrong.

Some of Grace's classmates were also by the tree with their parents and Grace stood next to a friend of hers called Corey, who was very shy and kept trying to hide behind his mother.

Corey's mother tried to engage Sarah in conversation as the first round of carols came to an end.

"I'm Susan, Corey's mother." She held out her hand to Sarah.

Sarah shook it, introducing herself still as Amy.

"My Corey has thing for your little girl. He comes home and it's Grace this and Grace that. Now that I've seen her, I can understand why. She is just adorable." Susan gushed. "She has Corey tongue tied, even at this early age."

"Yes, very much like her father." Sarah said quietly as a pang shot through her chest, a sense of loss she felt acutely when she thought of Grace's father.

"Is Mr Cooper here?" Susan looked around. All the mothers at school were more than a little intrigued with Grace's parentage. Nine times out of ten, one of the two gay men would collect Grace from school and the gossips at school thought Grace was the product of a very strange threesome.

"There is no Mr Cooper." Sarah replied honestly.

It became apparent that Sarah was not going to divulge anything else so Susan made her excuses, said her goodbyes and disappeared into the crowd.

Sarah grabbed hold of Graces hand. "Let's go and get something to eat. What would you like?"

"Anything?" The little girl asked.

"Sure. You've been really good today."

"Cherry pie and ice cream!" Grace giggled.

"Okay then."

They found a small cheap restaurant where Grace could have her cherry pie and ice cream and Sarah had the healthier option of a Caesar salad. Grace picked some of Sarahs croutons from the plate and dipped them into the cherry pie filling, making both girls laugh raucously at Grace's grossness but they had a good time.

Afterwards, they went window shopping around the square. Most of the stores had fantastic Christmas window displays, much like that of Oxford Street in London from Sarahs childhood – the happier times, before her mother had become an alcoholic.

Needless to say, Grace insisted they go into the Disney store and wander around. She picked up a huge, soft Pooh Bear, bigger than Grace almost and she hugged him fiercely.

"I would love for Santa to bring me this for Christmas. Do you think I have been good enough?" Grace asked innocently.

Sarah surreptitiously looked at the price tag. At two hundred and fifty dollars, Grace would have to be for all of next year too.

"Let's see what happens, darling." Grace gave the bear another hug before replacing him in the display.

Sarah felt all of her previously good spirits drain away from her. Her little girl had a millionaire father and by rights, she should be able to have whatever she wanted, not second hand clothes and good will toys. The evening had lost its sparkle for Sarah so they headed for the F-Line stop to take them home.

The day before Christmas Eve, Sarah was home alone wrapping some presents up. Ted and Henry had taken Grace round the local shops in the Castro do some shopping but mainly to give Sarah a little time to herself.

A fresh coffee pot was being made and she unwrapped her pecan pastry, feeling sinful, and put it on a plate. She was going to have a fine time!

The radio was playing dreadful Christmas songs, the ones that got wheeled out year after year and she settled down to start wrapping her meagre presents up.

The doorbell rang.

Sarah sighed at the interruption for she didn't know how long Ted and Henry would be able to entertain her rumbustious daughter. She put on her happy Christmas face and went to answer the door. A silhouette of a large man could be seen through the mainly frosted glass front door and with a knot in her stomach, Sarah unlatched the door. Before her stood a figure dressed in black leather biking gear from neck to toe. In his left hand, he held a black motorcycle helmet with a red flash down one side. In the other, which he held out to Sarah was a package.

"Federal Express delivery, ma'am." He handed the package to Sarah and then offered her the clipboard with the docket for signing. She signed her real name for some unknown reason, thanked the man and wished him the compliments of the season.

Frowning, Sarah closed the front door to keep the snow out that had just started to fall. She walked slowly back into the cosy front room and sat in front of the gas fire that was on full, her pecan pastry all but forgotten. She thought the parcel must be from Vinnie. It was only a small packet with something fairly heavy inside. She turned it over to get some clues before opening it.

Her blood ran cold.

Her heart appeared to stop for a few moments before it started up again and raced away with the spinning room.

The packet was from Palm Beach. The senders name was M. Delvecchio and there was no denying that he had found her.

She pondered for a few moments what she should do. Her initial hysteria began to dissipate as she turned the packet over and over in her hand. She set it down in front of her and watched it for a few seconds, half expecting it to blow up.

She laughed softly to herself. Marco wouldn't send her a letter bomb. He wouldn't know if Grace would be around when it was delivered and he would never hurt his daughter. Sarah wasn't so sure about his intentions towards her, but he obviously knew where she was now and if he wanted to harm her, it was his M O. to come personally.

The more she thought about it, the more Sarah realised the packet would be harmless. Still, with more care than usual, she slit the brown parcel tape around the packet and unwrapped the brown parcel paper. Underneath this was a black leatherette box about five inches wide by seven inches long. It was tied very neatly with a yellow ribbon which Sarah unravelled and opened the lid.

She gasped.

Inside the box were neat bundles of one hundred dollar bills. All used. She counted the money twice over and made it five thousand dollars both times. As she pulled the last note out of the box, she saw a note.

It was from Marco. It read:

'I have treated you both very badly and providing for you both is the least I can do, if you will allow it. What I did to you, Sarah, was unforgivable and that is why I will not come after you and will never contact you again after this. I have set up an account for you and Grace and will deposit money into it every month for you to use as you see fit. If it is not enough, you can contact Cliff who will increase it for you. I understand from Vinnie that you want a divorce and although I never wanted it to end up like this, I will not contest it, if that is what you truly want.'

He had signed it in his usual flowing way.

Sarah looked down at the pile of cash before her and then at the clock on the wall above the fire. It was two-thirty. She scribbled a note to Ted and Henry and then, still doing her coat up, ran outside to find a cab to town.

Sarah became aware that it was very dark and that Grace was shouting for her. "Mummy! Mummy! Come quickly! Look at this!" Her voice came from the front room.

Sarah opened one eye and looked at the clock by her bedside. It was five o'clock on Christmas Day morning. Grace's excitement had obviously overcome her and she had sneaked out of her bed to where the presents were in the front room.

Before Sarah could rouse herself sufficiently to get out of bed, a massive yellow bear wearing a red tee-shirt came into the room, held up from behind by Grace. The bear swamped Grace and she struggled to carry it.

"Santa must have read my letter!"

Sarah managed a smile and grabbed her dressing gown. She gave her daughter a Christmas Day kiss and helped her back into the front room with the giant bear.

"No-one deserves that bear more than you, my darling!" Sarah said as Grace threw her arms around her mother and gave her lots of sloppy kisses.

"Santa left lots of presents for us." The little girl could hardly contain herself.

After Sarah had received the package the day before yesterday, she had gone into town and spent an inordinate amount of money. She had forgotten how good it felt to be able to spend and not worry about it. She bought Grace the bear, some puzzles, books, dolls, clothes, shoes and everything Sarah felt she had missed out on the last four Christmases. She had splashed out on presents for Ted and Henry and they would come downstairs later to swap presents and have their Christmas goose later on in the day. Sarah had bought them an expensive bottle of brandy and they were going to have a fine time today.

Ted and Henry knocked on Sarahs front door at 12 noon with

armfuls of presents. They spilled into Sarah's front room and plonked themselves down onto the sofa. Grace would not hold back any longer and handed them their presents that she and Sarah had brought for them. A late gesture, Sarah had bought them each a bottle of cologne, one Hugo Boss and one Hilfiger, both of which Sarah knew they would share.

They helped with making the dinner which Sarah was happy to make for them, and they all got quite merry even before dinner.

After their dinner, Grace fell asleep and the men left to go to a party at a friends house around the corner.

Sarah sat back and relaxed with a cup of tea and listened to her new CD that Ted and Henry and bought her for Christmas. Her mind drifted off to the other side of the country – it was coming up for noon in the Panhandle and she wondered what they might be doing.

Without giving it a second thought, Sarah picked up the phone and dialled the number she knew she would never forget. After three long dragging rings, the phone was picked by a young girl laughing and sounding joyous.

"Rosa? Is that you?" Sarah asked quietly.

At the other end of the phone, thousands of miles away, the line went quiet. Rosa Delvecchio was lost for words.

"Sarah?" She barely whispered.

"Yes, it's me. Are you alone?"

"Marco and Joe aren't here, if that's what you mean. I'm here with Sal, my fiancé."

"Fiancé? How wonderful!"

"Sarah, I've got so much to tell you and I miss you terribly. When are you coming home?"

Rosa had guessed wrong. "Ro, I don't think I am. I'm not even sure why I called."

"Well, Marco will be thrilled to know you did. He's at church at the moment."

Sarah stifled a laugh. "Praying for redemption? You want to tell him that his soul is already damned."

Rosa spoke quietly. "I can see why you might think that. He's very different now to how you remember him."

"I'm sure." Sarah was unconvinced. "Will you thank him for

the money?"

"I'll have him call you." Rosa sounded childishly desperate to get the lines of communication open between her brother and her sister-in-law.

"No, don't do that." Sarah replied quickly. "Just thank him for me, will you?"

"Sure. Will you call again?

"I don't know. Merry Christmas Rosa, and congratulations on the engagement."

Sarah pressed the stop button on the phone and retracted the aerial. Her emotions were in turmoil and calling Rosa was probably the worst thing she could have done.

The phone trilled almost immediately, making Sarah jump.

"Hello?" She asked rather cautiously.

"Hey Sarah, it's Vinnie. Just wanted to wish you Happy Holidays"

"Vinnie, what a surprise. Happy Christmas to you too." She chose, as always the un-PC way to greet him.

"I thought I would give you plenty of space before I called. See if you'd changed your mind."

"Not about you and me, Vinnie, I'm sorry. Even if I loved you, life would be too complicated given the history and the relationship between you and Marco. I just want out of all of it."

"So are you gonna give me the 'we'll always stay friends' crap?" He asked, hostility showing in his voice.

"No, I wouldn't patronise you. We have no real reason to stay in touch at all."

"No, I guess not." He said with a quiet anger before cutting the line dead.

Sarah sighed. She hated being mean spirited but wanted to put an end to Vinnie's calls and attentions once and for all.

After two more days of torturing herself, Sarah could stand it no more. Wrapping Grace up firmly against the cold, they took a tram to the city centre and they called in at a travel agents. Half an hour later, they left with tickets for two seats from Oakland to Miami for the red-eye tomorrow morning, returning three days later. Sarah wasn't due back at work until the 2nd January so there was plenty of time for a few days sojourn to warmer climes.

They stopped at the department store to see what clothes they had on sale to take with them. Sarah picked up a white linen skirt with matching top and a couple of tee- shirts that would go well with her jeans. Grace wanted only a tee-shirt with a Disney Princess on it and then they went home with their purchases to pack.

Later in the evening, Sarah went upstairs to tell Ted and Henry that they would be out of town for a few days.

Ted raised an eyebrow questioningly.

"I just need some sun, Ted, that's all."

"But Florida? What's the attraction?"

"I need to know how I feel about Marco. I can't move on until I have more answers and suddenly, I'm not scared of him anymore." She shrugged. "I'll see you both back here on Sunday evening." She promised, kissing them both on the cheek.

CHAPTER SIX

The taxicab driver knocked gently on Sarah's door at four thirty the following morning. Grace had barely been able to dress herself, she was so tired. Sarah carried her out into the cold and the darkness to the taxi while the driver very kindly loaded her small suitcase into the trunk.

The journey to the airport at this time of the morning took just about half an hour and Grace slept the whole way.

Once they had checked in and relieved themselves of their suitcase, Sarah took Grace to a café for some orange juice and coffee for Sarah. Grace had a chocolate muffin as her breakfast but Sarahs knotted stomach would not permit her to eat.

The flight was called with incredible quickness and it seemed all too soon that Sarah was strapping her daughter into the window seat of the United Airlines flight to Miami. There really was no going back now.

Grace fell asleep just after take off and Sarah closed her eyes to rest, although sleep would not come for her. She kept asking herself what exactly was she doing, what did she hope to achieve? She wondered how Marco would react to her being there and how angry with her he would be. She had spoken to Rosa at length the day before and Rosa had assured her that Marco would be fine with her visit. Sarah tried to convince herself that it was for Grace's benefit so she could meet her father after so many years. Rosa would meet them at the airport and they would stay at the house. Apparently, Marco had an all day meeting in the Bahamas and his private plane would not touch down until later on in the day and he would gone again early the next morning, so Sarah wouldn't see much of him, Rosa had promised.

Half an hour before the flight was due to land, Sarah roused her daughter. "Come on, sweetheart, let's get you ready."

The little girl opened her eyes and sleepily looked around. "Are we there?" She yawned and rubbed her eyes with her balled up fists.

"Nearly, darling. Let's go and brush your hair and wash your face."

Sarah led the way down the aisle to a vacant washroom at the back of the plane before the lines got too long. They both squeezed in the tiny space and Sarah sat on the lid of the toilet while Grace washed her hands and face in the minute basin. Sarah did her best to decrease Grace's navy blue polka dot dress. The child looked doll like in her dress with her ankle socks with the lace edging and navy blue leather shoes. She had a portion of her hair tied in a blue ribbon that fell the length of her chestnut hair. Sarah knew she was going to be a heartbreaker one day.

Like her father.

Sarah felt a faint rush of pleasure course through her as she though of her brutish husband and was suddenly looking forward to seeing him. She borrowed Grace's hair brush and tried to sort out her own short locks.

They went back to their seats and buckled themselves back in as the PA system announced they were five minutes from landing. Sarah could feel the plane descending and both the nerves and excitement of everything made her heart beat fast and she took Graces hand to try and steady herself. As the wheels of the Boeing 737 hit the tarmac and the breaks were slammed on, Grace looked across at her mother and grinned. It was her first memory of a plane ride and she loved it. The plane taxied for what seemed like an eternity before the plane found its disembarking bay and the seatbelt signs were switched off. A loud clicking noise resounded around the cabin as people unbuckled and stood to empty the overhead lockers of their belongings.

Sarah picked her in-flight bag up and taking Grace's hand, they joined throngs of people eager to exit the plane and feel the first piece of Florida sun on their faces.

Just over forty minutes later, Sarah was pushing the luggage trolley with Grace sitting atop the case through the automatic double doors to the airport and out into the sunshine. She looked around for Rosa, suddenly worried in case she had forgotten and would be left stranded. Across the road, away from the main throng of people waiting for passengers was a young girl and a handsome man, leaning against the hood of a silver and burgundy Pontiac and Sarah knew it was Rosa. She called out to her.

Rosa looked up and grabbing the mans hand, walked over to where her sister was struggling with the trolley that had developed a mind of its own and wanted to go in the opposite direction.

"Oh my god, Rosa! Why didn't you tell me you are pregnant?" Sarah threw her arms around the younger woman who with her small bump, was just beginning to show in her fourth month.

"I hoped to be able to tell you in person!" She was weeping with joy at finally seeing Sarah again.

They eventually parted and Rosa introduced the handsome man who accompanied her. "This is Sal, my fiancé. We're getting married in February."

Sarah appraised Rosa's fiancé. He was very tall, easily six foot five and had thick dark hair. His face looked kind and sincere, almost innocent. Sarah wondered how long that would remain if he stayed as one of Marco's crew.

Sarah said hello and then turned to her daughter who was still sitting shyly on top of the luggage trolley, having gone surprisingly coy.

"Grace, this is your Aunt Rosa and Uncle Sal." Sarah announced as she lifted Grace down onto the pavement.

Grace shot them a winning smile and said hello to her new family. She just nodded and answered with one word replies when any question was asked of her. Sal put the case and the bags in the back of the car and after everyone had got into the car, he drove off and away from the airport.

"Are we staying with you?" Grace asked quietly of her aunt.

"Of course you are, sweetheart. Would you like that?"

Grace nodded her head enthusiastically. She turned her attention to the outside, watching the traffic and huge trucks go passed lost in her own world of adventure.

Rosa turned round in her front seat to talk to Sarah.

"Marco doesn't know of your visit. We've managed to keep it quiet. He flew out from West Palm Beach this morning to the Bahamas and is due to touch down around eight tonight. I believe he has an early meeting in Miami in the morning so you will only see as much of him as is needed to break the ice."

"Private plane, huh? Life must be good for him."

Rosa sighed lightly. "Not really. I think he misses you and misses being able to be a father to Grace. He has lots of regrets, you know."

Sarah turned to stare out of the window to see what was holding Grace's attention. "So how do you think he will react to us being here?"

Rosa shrugged. "I don't know. Stunned disbelief, maybe? He's given up hope now of ever seeing either of you again. He won't try anything, if that's what you mean." Rosa thought Sarah might be scared of how Marco may react.

Sal interjected. "He was nearly strung up four years ago after what he did to you. He won't try that again. It's taken him all this time to get his contacts and respect back. You are well protected, both of you."

"Is that enough?" She murmured, mainly to herself. She reached for Graces hand for comfort again.

Sal drove them away from Miami and North on Route One towards the rich town of Palm Beach. The sea glittered in the sun to the East of where they were travelling. Grace stayed silent, unsure of her surroundings and at the same time, content to watch the passing scenery. She'd heard that alligators lived down here and was looking out for some. All she saw were road kill armadillos on the road side.

After an hours journey, during which Grace opened up to her new-found aunt and uncle, they arrived in Palm Beach. Sal drove slowly down the once familiar roads to Sarah and then suddenly pulled up in front of a small white hut that guarded two huge iron gates. A small, squat man came out of the hut and on seeing Rosa inside the car he turned and went back inside. The iron gates slid open and disappeared into the shrubbery to the side. The car was waved through and Sal hit the gas to drive slowly up the drive. Oleander bushes grew to either side of the gravel drive and in the late afternoon sun, they gave off a beautiful aroma.

After a few moments, the mansion came into view and Sarah felt as though she had come home. Marco still showed his patriotism with the American flag in front of the house and it was in full show today in the gentle breezes. The car rounded the large decorative fountain with the cherubs blowing water out of trumpets and the soft tinkle of water could be heard as Sarah and Grace got out of the car.

Sarah stretched her stiffened muscles as Grace looked around in awe.

"Do you live in this house?" She asked of Rosa.

Rosa smiled at her niece and nodded. "Would you like to see the gardens at the back of the house? We have a swimming pool as well."

Grace looked at her mother for permission which she got with a smile.

"I'll go and put our cases away, if that's okay Rosa?" Sarah was no longer the woman of the house and was a guest in Rosa's home.

"Sure. I've put you both in the yellow room – you remember where that is, don't you? Grace and I will meet you once we've had a look around and then we can all get some lemonade?" Rosa suggested.

"Sounds great. I'll see you in the kitchen in about ten minutes."

Sal opened the huge double doors at the front of the house for Sarah and led her inside with the case. He offered to take it upstairs for her, but it was not very heavy and Sarah told him she could manage. She wanted to be here on her own. Sal smiled at her and disappeared through to the kitchen that would lead to the rear of the house where Rosa and Grace would surely be by now.

Sarah picked up the case and turned to the grand staircase that swept up from the marble floored hallway to the second floor of this Mediterranean style mansion. She walked up the stairs on the carpeted area to the centre so her footsteps would not make too much noise. She didn't want to disturb the memories and ghosts of the house. At the juncture of the stairs, old habits wanted her to turn left, to go towards Marco's bedroom at the end of the hallway. She smiled to herself as she remembered the shenanigans that went on in that room when she and

Marco were together and felt herself redden slightly. Returning her thoughts back to the here and now, she instead turned right under the huge picture window and walked towards the guest suite, also known as the Yellow Room. Opening the door to the Yellow Room, Sarah felt as though she had been transported back in time by five years. It had not been changed at all in the time she had been away. She closed the door behind her and put the suitcase on the huge king-sized bed that occupied the outside wall of the bedroom. There were yellow linen sheets and blankets on the bed, a yellow rug was either side of the bed on the dark wooden floor and the yellow drapes fluttered gently in the breeze through the open window, like a large butterfly.

Sarah unpacked the few clothes that she and Grace had brought with them, hung them in the antique wardrobe and then went into the bathroom. The suite was white and had yellow adornments – yellow bath mat and a yellow blind at the window. Large yellow fluffy towels hung on the towel rail next to the walk in shower.

The thought of a shower was on Sarahs mind before she had to meet Marco again and she walked back into the bedroom and began to take out some fresh clothes. She became distracted and walked onto the balcony. The sun was just starting to set across the sea and the sun threw long shadows across the extensive lawns at the back of the mansion. From this balcony, she could see the tennis court at the side of the house. Giorgio had taught her to play many years before and she had enjoyed their games together before he became sick. She wondered if Marco still played. She gazed around and saw that the security around the grounds was tight – a youngish man, probably early twenties was stationed at the rear entrance to the house. It was just a gate in the wall that led down a path and eventually to the water but Marco had never had it guarded before. She wondered who he had upset this time.

Sarah turned to go back inside for her much longed for shower and did a double take. Looking back towards the top of the drive, passed the Oleanders and Pine trees, she could just make out the gatehouse from this side-on position and she thought she saw the gates closing. She stayed where she was for just a moment and then saw dust from the drive being kicked up by a car being driven in a hurry, followed up by the roar of the engine.

A black Lexus being driven by a blond headed man screamed

to a halt behind Rosa's car in front of the fountain. The back door opened but due to the side on view and the portico blocking her view, Sarah couldn't make out who was in the car. She didn't need to see the occupants of the car, she knew it was Marco.

Her heart hammered as the car doors slammed and she heard footsteps on the tiled veranda that led to the front door. She stayed partially hidden in the doorway to the bedroom, the yellow drapes covering her. The sound of the front door being closed with a heavy hand reverberated around the house and Sarah knew he wasn't in a good mood. She also knew it would probably get a lot worse.

Sarahs legs began to give way and she sat down on one of the two yellow sun chairs that were on the balcony. She was concerned at what Marcos reaction to her and Grace being here might be and her earlier bravado had disappeared. She wished she could go downstairs and be with her daughter as she was introduced to her father but her courage failed her.

Instead, she sat on the chair and waited. She watched the sun setting, the shadows now gone but brilliant colours of purple, red and orange stretched across the sky as the blackness drew in from the east. A few clouds scudded across the twilight sky as the darkness drew in. It was still very warm for a December evening and she thought about how cold it would be back home in San Francisco.

Sarah was so engrossed in her thoughts that she did not hear the door to the Yellow Room open and then close shortly after. In fact, she was unaware that anyone was in the room at all until she heard faltering footsteps on the wooden floor of the bedroom. She braced herself for whatever was going to be flung at her, waiting for the crash.

"Sarah?" The deep masculine voice came from behind her.

Rosa had told Marco that Sarah was in the Yellow Room but this woman sat here on the balcony in the deepening gloom was not his wife. She was blond, short-haired and quite skinny, not how he liked his women at all. He stopped short on the steps from the room and looked at her.

As she turned to look at him, he knew that this was the woman he had married. Her looks had changed quite dramatically, but he knew. He knew from the look in her beautiful hazel eyes that were so longingly familiar. That look of adoration she could not hide but also a slight look of fear.

"Wow!" Was the involuntary reaction from Sarah. Marco too, had changed since she had last seen him. He had never been overweight but was still much leaner, more toned. His hair which could be unruly and wavy had been trimmed right back and with his ever present tan, he left her breathless.

"I hope you don't mind us being here." She murmured as she returned her gaze to the now dark estate. Garden lights and security lights were being switched on around the grounds making the garden seem almost enchanted.

Marco shook his head as he came down the last step and stood to absorb her with his eyes. "Of course not. It's good to see you, but why are you here?"

"I've been asking myself the same question since I booked our tickets. I still have no answers really." She played with her wedding ring, something which was always on a chain around her neck, usually hidden, but on full show today. "Maybe to thank you for the money."

Marco finally sat on the step next to Sarahs chair. He stretched his legs out in front of him and rested his arms on his knees. "That would have been eaten up by the airfares." He stared out at his lands in the same direction as Sarah was looking.

"Pretty much."

"Do you want more money? A bigger allowance?" He seemed eager to please.

"No." She still didn't look back at him. "Have you seen Grace yet?"

Marco melted inside at the mere mention of his beautiful daughter. Marco had walked into the kitchen and saw Rosa making up lemonade with a young girl and they were laughing. Rosa had introduced Grace to him a little warily, she had hoped Sarah was going to arrive and make the introductions. Grace stopped stirring the jug and looked up at her daddy who had frozen in shock at her sudden appearance in his life. As soon as Marco looked at her properly, he knew it was his baby girl. She had smiled shyly at him and said hello and he had wanted to cry with joy. They conversed for a few minutes before Marco realised that if Grace was here, then so too must her mother. Rosa directed him to their guest suite.

Marco grinned. "Yes. She is so beautiful for a five year old. She seemed a bit shy, a bit wary of me."

"Grace doesn't know you and besides, she is a good judge of character." Sarah shot at him, unable to resist the barb.

"That's not fair. I never wanted to be a stranger to my own daughter!"

"I know." Sarah replied calmly. "Grace you wanted, it was just me that you wanted rid of."

"That's not how it was!" Marco's famous temper began to rise. He was angry only at himself for allowing the situation to have ever happened.

Sarah's temper began to soar and match Marcos. She got up from the chair and stood in front of him, hands on hips while he still sat on the step, four years of frustration getting the better of her and finally reaching boiling point.

"So how was it then? Come on, after all this time, I really want to know why you found it so necessary to try and kill me. Was it because I slept with Vinnie?" She shouted down at him.

He looked straight at her, sorting his thoughts. "So it's true then?" He asked quietly.

She nodded once, abruptly, her face still like thunder.

"Why? You are my wife and you should have waited however long it took! Christ, I was only away for a few weeks, even you should have been able to hold out!"

"We are not discussing me! I want to know why you pointed a gun at me and pulled the bloody trigger!" She forced her arms to her side. She just wanted to punch him and kick him, to make him hurt physically as much as he had hurt her mentally. She wanted to make him bleed and bruised and beg for her to stop.

He just looked down between his knees at his Gucci loafers and brushed a fleck of mud away absently.

"Drugs. Cocaine." He muttered.

Sarah wasn't sure she had heard correctly. "I'm sorry?"

He looked up at her, still standing above him with the angry scowl on her face. "I wasn't addicted, but I thought I could handle it. Joe gave me some when I was in prison, just to help me get through a tough time. When I came out, I went to a sort of welcome home party and had some more. That's when I got my suspicions about you and HIM. His face was one of a guilty man. I have to say it, Sarah. That revelation turned my world upside down and I couldn't think straight. I didn't know who to turn to for advice or commiseration. I took one more line and decided to confront you about it. That's all it was ever meant to be but the coke had me wired and I took a shot at you."

"Took a shot at me? Why didn't you just ask for a divorce like any other pissed off husband? Do you realise that if it hadn't been for that illegal hunter, I would be dead now. Maybe that's what you really want."

He shook his head. "I never wanted that, I was just hurt and angry."

Sarah sat back down on her chair. She realised that some of the blame lay squarely on her shoulders for all of this. Had she been able to keep her knickers on, none of this would have happened. She suddenly felt an overwhelming compassion for the man sat next to her, he looked lost and alone. He was usually impeccably dressed, but his designer suit looked crumpled and after running his hands though his hair several times, his hair was awry. She turned her attention back to the darkness and heard several dogs yip and yowl in the distance.

"Were you addicted?" She asked quietly, dreading the answer.

Marco shook his head forcibly. "Definitely not! I don't really know what possessed me in the first place." He looked at her puzzled face as she tried to absorb all of the information she had just received. After a few minutes silence, he could no longer bear the silence. "What are you thinking?" He asked softly. He squatted in front of her, searching her face for some kind of reaction.

She shook her head. "I have no idea what to think. I didn't come here for explanations or money or for you." She looked into his eyes. "I just wanted Grace to meet you. She has been asking questions."

"Will you be going to Chicago?" Marco had to ask the question although he did not really want to know the answer.

"No. I don't love Vinnie, I never did and I'm not even sure that I was attracted to him. I was just drunk and felt alone."

"So what are you going to do? What do you want to do?" Marco stood up and stretched. He was too old to be squatting for too long and his knees were stiff.

"I want for the last four years to have been a bad dream. From you being arrested and imprisoned to me being shot and going on the run. I'm sick of running scared and looking over my shoulder, waiting for a gun to go off and doing a proper job this time. I'm plain worn out raising Grace alone and struggling for every cent."

Marco smiled. "Well, you never need worry about money again. That much at least, I can help out with."

Sarah thanked him with a smile, genuine.

"How long are you staying?" He asked.

"Just a day or so, if that's okay?"

"Sure. Listen, I really have to go. I only came back for some papers that I forgot to take this morning. I will be back late tonight and gone early in the morning." He paused. "Do you want to go out for dinner tomorrow? Just the two of us? We clearly have more to talk about."

Sarah blanched at his unexpected invitation. "What about Grace?" She fumbled for an excuse.

"I'm sure Rosa will love to look after her." He made a move towards the balcony door and back into the Yellow Room.

It was just dinner. Where was the harm? "Okay." She relented.

"Great. Ring Carlotti and tell him we're coming. Make sure he books our table." With a wink, Marco disappeared through the door.

Sarah breathed deeply and felt the adrenaline and excitement flow through her. She stayed where she was until she heard Marco's car start up and roar back down the driveway. It was only then that she found the strength to go and talk to Grace.

Sarah woke at seven-thirty the next morning and turned over to see if Grace was awake. Panic filled her as she realised the bed beside her was empty, her mind working overtime and thinking that perhaps Marco had taken her.

Trying to suppress her mounting fear, she slipped out of bed and pulled on her dressing gown and slippers. As she opened the bedroom door, she heard laughter from below filtering upstairs. At the top of the stairs, Sarah heard her daughter giggling with delight at something Sal had said, his voice too low for Sarah to make out his words. She hurried down the stairs, relief flooding though her and feeling ridiculous that she could have started to think that Marco would harm his daughter. She walked calmly into the kitchen with a smile on her face. Grace was sat at the breakfast bar on a high stool next to Sal, while Rosa was stood at the hob making pancakes for them both.

"Hey Sarah! You sleep okay?" She asked when she saw Sarah come through the door.

Sarah nodded and sat next to Grace at the breakfast bar.

Rosa handed Sarah a cup of coffee which Sarah took gratefully. She smiled at her daughter who was revelling in the attention from her new-found aunt and uncle. She didn't seem too concerned about her father and Sarah was thankful as she didn't want Grace to get attached to him, just to know who he is.

"We don't have any tea in." Rosa said apologetically. "If you're going to be around, I'll have Enza include it on her shopping list?" She was fishing.

"A few teabags would be a good idea." Sarah was noncommittal in her reply. She loved tea and before her arrival here six years before, there was never any English breakfast tea in the cupboards. Coffee didn't really do it for her first thing in the morning.

"Marco left you this." Rosa handed her an envelope.

Sarah took it and frowned. She looked at Rosa for clues but found none on her sister in laws face.

Sarah put her coffee cup down and opened the letter. Marco had wrote:

'Good morning, I hope you slept well. Pete is around today and will be at your beck and call. I have left some cash with Rosa in case you wanted to go shopping. Enjoy your day and I'll see you for dinner.'

It was signed with the usual 'M'.

She folded the letter and put it safely in the pocket of her dressing gown. Rosa handed her a plate with some freshly made pancakes and fruit that she dived into, feeling ravenously hungry all of a sudden.

"What are your plans for today?" Rosa asked as she sat down to eat.

"I thought we'd go along and see Andrea this afternoon. I have some things to take care of this morning."

"On a Thursday, Andrea is always at the Country Club, according to Cliff. Did you know that they finally got around to having kids? They had a boy who'd be about eighteen months old now. I think his name is David."

"That's great news! I'll go along there for lunch and surprise her. I feel as though I have so much to catch up on." Sarah and Rosa had caught up plenty last night after Grace had gone to bed, including how she had met Sal, details of her wedding in February and her plans for the future. Sarah had no reply when Rosa had asked her what her future plans were.

At just after twelve-thirty, Peter pulled up outside the Country Club in Marco's black Lexus. Marco had driven himself to Miami for his meeting in the Mercedes; he wanted Sarah to enjoy herself while she was here and have all of his means at her disposal. If that meant he himself was slightly inconvenienced, he figured it would be worth it.

Sarah got out of the car and thanked Peter for the ride while Grace scrambled out behind her. Peter would wait close by for as long as was required. Sarah looked at the front of the single storey building to which she had once been a member of and startled at how much it had changed. The change was more evident when she and Grace walked in through the glass sliding doors. The air conditioning blasted them both cooling them down from the warmth outside. Gone were the tacky turnstiles to count members in and out. In their place was a spacious lobby with a large desk for enquiries and dotted around were a few soft black leather sofas for people to relax on while they waited for friends. A large café and bistro had opened off to the side and the aroma of food being cooked got Sarahs juices flowing. It all befitted the most exclusive club in Palm Beach.

Sarah held Grace's hand as they walked past all of this and attempted to go Through the lobby back into the sunshine where the tennis courts, swimming pool and sun-beds were.

"Excuse me, ma'am but children are not allowed in this establishment." A strange male voice stopped Sarah in her tracks. "And it is for members only."

Sarah turned to the source of the voice and saw a strikingly handsome man. Despite his feminine sounding voice, he was well over six foot tall and Sarah figured he worked out a lot, considering his solid muscles evident even under his clothes. He wore knee length shorts and a white polo shirt. He had short hair, marine style, once probably black but now very grey which he quite suited. He had the resident tan of a Palm Beach inhabitant and a decidedly unfriendly smile.

"And you are?" She enquired of him.

"I'm Andy Knezevic. I am the manager here." He removed his sunglasses to reveal ice cold blue eyes.

"Okay. I used to know the owner, Mr Townsend?"

"That's nice." His tone indicated that he had conversed enough with the skinny blond time waster in his foyer.

"I just want to see a friend of mine who I haven't seen for a few years. Would you mind?" Sarah was beginning to get agitated herself.

"Take a seat and I'll find someone to get your friend. Who's your friend?"

"Andrea Hill"

"And who are you?"

"Sarah Delvecchio."

He looked up sharply at the mention of the name and studied Sarah intently. He was puzzled. He and the merry widow Townsend were bedfellows as well as business associates. He'd heard the rumours of Mrs Delvecchio and Mr Townsend. He'd also heard that the local Don had found out about his wife's affair and had had Brad Townsend beaten up until he could barely walk. When he could finally walk again after months of rehabilitation, he was mown down and killed by a mystery car and the perpetrators had never been caught. Nothing was ever proven that it was the Delvecchio's as they were very clever at covering their tracks. Violence was in their blood and Sarah had eventually been driven away by her drug crazed husband and lived in fear for her life.

So were the rumours around town.

"Mrs Hill. I'll go and find her personally."

Sarah smiled smugly at his change in attitude towards her and relished the benefits of being Marcos wife, however tenuous.

Sarah and Grace sat in the air conditioned foyer on one of the soft black leather sofas and waited patiently. They played eye spy and some counting games but Grace soon began to get bored and testy.

"Can we go soon, mummy?" She asked.

"Soon darling. Let's give Andrea another five minutes."

With delighted squeals of 'Oh my god!' Andrea arrived through the door. She had on her tennis gear and her game had obviously been interrupted. She rushed over to Sarah and hugged her. The two had been close friends in Sarahs previous life. Andrea had introduced her to life as a rich mans wife in Palm Beach and taken her to social gatherings and coffee mornings, none of which Sarah had enjoyed but felt she owed it to Marco to endure. Sarah had always been top of peoples list to invite as no-one would dare not to. Most of their husbands livelihoods depended on Marco and they could not consider insulting his wife. There was nothing forced between Sarah and Andrea, they had been genuine friends.

"Cliff thought he saw you at the airport yesterday. I was hoping it was you and you'd come and see me!" Andreas face was beaming.

"We only flew in yesterday for a few days. You remember Grace?"

"Shit yes, but only as a baby!" Andrea looked down at Grace and then smiled apologetically at her mother for her choice of words in front of the impressionable five year old.

Sarah waved the error away. "Any chance of a drink? We're both parched."

"No problem. Andy has a no child rule but I'm sure he'd waive that for the child of Palm Beach's most respected citizen!" She laughed and linking arms with Sarah, they went out by the pool for a cool drink.

Walking out to the pool, they passed Andy who said nothing about Grace being there. Andrea knew there was history between him and the Delvecchio's. Her husband, Cliff was a business associate of Marco's and worked closely with him so she got hear some of the stories.

"I hear you're a mum now?" Sarah asked as they sipped their cool drinks.

"Yes, I finally gave in and gave Cliff the son he always wanted. I do love David, but I'm not really the maternal type so we have a nanny. That way, everyone's happy." She took a sip of her spritzer. "What about you? I can't believe how much you've changed. And not just the physical changes, you have a certain hardness in your face"

Sarah rolled her eyes heavenward. "I know, skinny and blond. It's not really me but now I don't have to hide anymore, I can go back to being how I was. I'm not sure Marco approves of the way I look now anyway."

Andrea stared at her friend. "Does it matter what he thinks?" She asked softly, glancing at Grace.

Sarah shrugged. "I don't know. We're on delicate speaking terms at least. We're going out for dinner tonight."

Grace piped up. "I met my daddy yesterday. I didn't know I had a daddy and he's handsome and he has a big house that he shares with my auntie and my uncle. Mummy, can I be Auntie Rosa's flower girl at her wedding? She wants me to wear a pretty dress and throw petals on the floor so she can walk on them. Can I please? Can I?" She turned those huge brown eyes pleadingly towards Sarah in the innocent yet manipulative way just like her fathers.

"We'll see, darling."

"My dress will be so pretty and have roses on and I'll have to have my picture taken too. Please can I, mummy?"

Sarah laughed at her insistence. "If you really want to, then of course you can. We'll talk to Rosa about it when we get home."

Andrea looked at Sarah. "Home?"

Sarah shrugged as she took a sip of her drink.

"Rosa and Sal aren't getting married until February. Does that mean you'll be 'home' until then?" Andrea pushed.

"I have to see if my boss in San Francisco can give me leave until then."

She proceeded to tell Andrea of her life since leaving San Francisco.

She recounted the time when she woke up in her hospital bed, a little dazed and confused at the armed guard at her doorway. As soon as she had opened her eyes, a man in a black suit was at her bedside. He introduced himself as Agent Jack Robbins from the FBI. He'd heard that Sarah Delvecchio had been shot and none of the Family members had turned up at the hospital, which he found strange so he mounted his own bedside vigil.

Eventually, Agent Robbins had surmised that Marco Delvecchio had been responsible for the shooting of his wife and tried to pressure her into pressing charges. Sarah was unsure. She was frightened of what might happen to her or to Grace if she did that and wanted to give it considerable thought. After much thought while still in hospital, she told Robbins she wanted Grace and then when she was well away, she would tell him anything he needed to know. It was well known that the FBI had been after Marco since his miraculous escape from justice and was on a mission for further information that would get him back in jail, where Robbins felt he belonged.

So the FBI set a plan in motion to kidnap the then one year old Grace from her fathers clutches and make it look like it was a rival Family that had staged it. Grace was reunited with her mother after three months apart and they moved to Memphis for a while. Agent Robins and his cohorts drove to Memphis to see Sarah and to start to gather the evidence on her husband, only Sarah and Grace had disappeared. They had absconded with their few belongings and a small amount of cash Robbins had given Sarah in order to start her life over. She went on the run from the FBI and the Mafia and moved every few months for the first eighteen, until she found herself in the Castro district of San Francisco and decided to stop running for a while and settled down. Grace needed schooling and stability.

"So I have a job with someone who happens to be an old friend of Marco's father, Giorgio. What are the chances of that, huh?" Sarah grinned at her friend. She was pleased to be back and catching up.

After Sarah had promised Grace a day of doing whatever she wanted the following day, Grace was happy to spend the evening with Rosa and Salvatore. Rosa had made the little girl her favourite dinner of spaghetti Bolognese with a secret family twist, so Grace was happy really just wanted to see how far she could push her mother.

As Sarah came down the stairs that evening, Peter came out of Marcos office

"Sarah, Marco has been held up and will go straight to the restaurant. He has asked me to take you there." He smiled apologetically at her.

Sarah shrugged. "Fine. Are you ready to go now?"

Peter led her out to the front of the house where he had been instructed to get the stretch limo out – it only came out for show or special occasions.

Sarah laughed nervously. "It's not worth going in that! Carlotti's isn't far."

"The Boss wants all the stops pulled out. He's glad you are here and wants special treatment for you. "He opened the back door and with a glance in the chauffeurs direction, Sarah climbed in.

Inside, the C.D player was playing some soft jazz music and a bottle of red wine had been opened with a glass ready. Sarah poured herself half a glass for courage as Peter pulled away from the house. She felt very underdressed in her beige linen trousers and pale blue silk blouse – she felt as though she should have been wearing a ball gown for this occasion.

The drive to the restaurant was short and Sarah barely had time to finish her wine before Pete pulled up outside Carlottis restaurant over looking the sea. This place had always been a favourite of hers and Marcos when they were together and it was very romantic – worryingly so. She wondered what Marco had in mind for tonight.

Carlotti himself opened the door to the limo and she stepped out smiling.

"Mrs Delvecchio. How very nice to see you again.' He smiled back at her. "Mr Delvecchio is waiting for you. Please, follow me."

Carlotti led Sarah through the intimate restaurant and to the outside terrace. The patio heaters were on to take the evening chill off the terrace. The awning was open at the side but the roof was drawn. She saw Marco at a table on the far side by the railing overlooking the inky black sea. He looked towards her as he became aware that she and Carlotti were approaching. He stood to greet her.

"Hi. You okay?" He asked a little nervously.

"Good, thanks." She sat opposite him and settled herself in while Marco ordered a bottle of Dom Perignon.

"Something to celebrate?" She asked.

He shook his head. "I just like the taste." He leant back in his chair and began to relax. He looked more composed now than he had when the two had met last night and he had a sparkle in his deep brown eyes. He wore a dark navy suit with a pale blue collar shirt, open at the neck with no tie. Sarah tried hard to focus on his words.

"So how was your day?" He asked when the Carlotti had gone to fetch their champagne.

"Good, thanks. We went to see Andrea at the club."

"Yes. Cliff told me last night that he'd thought he'd seen you at the airport yesterday and called Andrea."

"I'm surprised he would have recognised me. Didn't he ring you?" Sarah was surprised.

He shook his head. "I was in a meeting all day and couldn't be disturbed. I knew nothing of your arrival until I got home last night." He put his hand on his heart to push home that he was telling the truth.

The champagne arrived and Carlotti poured them both a glass and after putting it in the ice bucket next to their table, he discreetly left.

"Cheers." The couple both toasted and took a sip. The bubbles felt good on Sarahs tongue and she felt it go all the way to her toes. "That would explain why Andrea wasn't surprised to see me." She returned to their conversation. "We had drink there and a bit of lunch. That place sure has changed."

"Yes. Run by Andy Knezevic now, I believe." Marco mused as he turned his attention to the menus, although he knew by heart what was on offer.

"You know him?"

"Just a little business deal really. I don't play tennis any more and have no reason to go there much, apart from the occasional meeting. It's a nice place when you want to impress people."

"Well, all that has nothing to do with me really." Sarah didn't want him to tell her too much about his business.

He looked up over the menu at her. "Doesn't it? Isn't that why we are here? To discuss what does concern us?" He leant forward slightly, putting his menu down.

"I think we just need to get to know each other again." She looked up at the approaching waiter who had come to see if they were ready to order.

Sarah ordered figs with goats cheese wrapped in prosciutto, followed by seafood linguine and Marco ordered a medium rare steak to follow his scallops. When the waiter left, Marco poured out some more champagne.

"So. Have you had many girlfriends while I was away?" Sarah resumed their conversation on a light hearted and somewhat cheeky level.

Marco raised one eyebrow in mock indignation and smiled. "No-one serious." He responded earnestly. "A few dates when I was invited to parties or functions, that kind of thing. I didn't see anyone more than twice and I never stayed over. They were just dalliances, conveniences. What about you?"

She shook her head. "A few dates only. I never wanted to get close and trust anyone."

"In case I sent them?"

She nodded. "I was scared." She shrugged as though it was no big deal but in reality, it had been a very big deal. She had spent the last four years looking over her shoulder and petrified for her and for Grace.

"Christ, I've been a real prick!" Marco slammed a fist on the table in anger at himself. "I know I treated you badly but I never really stopped to think how it really affected you or Grace." He reached over and stroked Sarahs hand gently. She did not pull away. "I'm glad you are back for whatever reason and for how ever long. I want to make it up to you both in any way I can. Will you let me?"

She shrugged. She enjoyed Marcos caressing of her hand. "How do you make up for four years of running scared?"

Their starters arrived and Marco thought about her question as he dug into his scallops. He had no answers but whatever Sarah wanted, he would get for her.

"And you and Vinnie are over?" He asked cautiously.

"Never really started. He was a mistake, much like your cocaine taking."

"Touché." He smiled over his glass of bubbly at her. "Listen, I need a date for a New Years eve party tomorrow night. Would you like to come or do you have plans?"

"Will I just be a dalliance?"

"No." He laughed. It felt good to be in her company again.

"Well, I would love to but I have nothing to wear that I can face Palm Beach's elite socialites in." Sarah was a little regretful.

"Well, I can fix the first." He handed over a credit card. "Go shopping tomorrow. No limits. Rosa and Sal have no plans, they will sit in with Grace again. As for the bitches, do you really think they will say anything? I own most of their husbands."

"Maybe."

"Please. I don't want to go on my own." He turned those eyes on her. The same look that their daughter had pleaded with her with earlier that afternoon.

Sarah laughed. "Okay but it will cost you dear. I'm not one of your cheap tarts that are happy just to be out with you." She teased.

"No limits." He said again as he finished his starter. "It will be worth every cent just to have you on my arm again."

Sarah looked closely for any duplicitous signs at these words but found none.

On the drive home, both were merry from the champagne and talking in soft low tones in the back of the limo even though the partition was closed and Pete would not have heard anything they said. They sat close, hips touching and arms brushing one another's as they spoke. They had got through two bottles of champagne and both felt heady and relaxed.

As they got out of the car, Marco reached for Sarahs hand and they went inside while Pete put the limo away for the next special occasion. They quietly opened the front door and headed for the sitting room. Sarah stopped.

Marco turned to her. "I was just going to get us a night-cap? It's still quite early."

"I have to call it a night. Grace gets up early and it will be a long night tomorrow." She offered her feeble explanation.

"Okay." He made it sound like it was no big deal but Marco did not want the night to end. They still had so much to talk about and they were getting on so well.

Sarah turned to go up the stairs and realised that he was following close behind.

At the junction of the stairs, Sarah turned right but Marco took hold of her hand and gently pulled her down the first step back towards him. The gentle pressure propelled her to him and he caught her in his arms, their faces close.

"Stay with me tonight." He murmured, his lips brushing hers in a titillating manner. "Come to bed with me." He kissed her passionately and although Sarah willed herself not to respond and to pull away, she was as ever powerless to resist him and followed him into his bedroom.

CHAPTER SEVEN

Consciousness rolled over Sarah late the next morning and dread and regret hit her like a sledgehammer. She couldn't deny that she'd had fun last night and being with Marco again had been wonderful and exciting but she wondered if she had done the right thing by spending the night with him. She looked up at the ceiling and closed her eyes again trying to shut out the reality of what she had done. Knowing the bed beside her was empty before she even looked in that direction, Sarah kicked off the sheet and got out of the king-sized bed. She padded naked across the room to Marco's bathroom and pushed the door open. It was, as it always had been, a mess. Wet towels were discarded on the floor, which was wet from footstep puddles. She tidied up briefly before getting into the double shower.

About half an hour later, she went downstairs to face Rosa. It would have been obvious to any idiot that she had had drunken sex with her husband last night and was embarrassed by her lack of self control.

Rosa was unperturbed by it and didn't say a word, not even a knowing smile. Instead, she just offered to go with Sarah to Worth Avenue to shop.

They returned several hours later having spent a huge amount of money on Marcos black American Express card. Grace had been brought a few new outfits as a sweetener for her mother abandoning her for the second night in a row as well as a pair of pink suede boots with a faux fur trim that would be needed once they went back home.

Sarah had been taken to a new boutique by Rosa and had fallen in love with a midnight blue satin and lace dress. It had off the shoulder lace caps, a boned bodice and was loose from the hips down. It fell to the ankles and Sarah had even been able to find a pair of three inch strappy shoes that were almost an exact match of colour to the dress. Her new blue bag was made of satin and had silver sequins and small blue feathers on the top sown into it.

Arriving back at the mansion at just after five, Rosa went to have a lie down while Sarah and Grace took their purchases to the Yellow Room.

"Will you be sleeping in here with me tonight, mummy?" Grace asked out of the blue as Sarah hung her new dress up.

Sarah had always had a policy of never lying to her child so with complete honesty, she turned to Grace and told her that she didn't know.

Grace's bottom lip quivered. "But I don't know where you are and the house is so big!" A tear escaped from her eye.

Sarah picked her up and cuddled her to comfort her. "Then let me show you where daddy sleeps. You know that mummies and daddies usually sleep in the same bed?"

Grace nodded and allowed herself to be carried down the hallway to where Marco slept. Sarah hoped the maid had been in to tidy up.

Once inside the room, Sarah let Grace walk around. She went over to the large bed and seemed to take it in before looking inside the walk in closets where Marcos many suits were hanging neatly next to his folded clothes on the shelves and countless pairs of designer shoes. She wandered over to the French doors that led onto the wrap around balcony outside and peered her head through the open doors.

"You see, Grace. This is where Daddy sleeps and it's not far from where your room is."

Grace came back to her Mothers side, seemingly content with what she had seen. "Can I show daddy my new clothes? I just saw his car coming."

Sarah nodded. "Why don't you go and try them on for him now?"

Grace cheered and ran out of the bedroom to change, almost bowling Marco over in the process as they passed in the hallway. She called out to him that she'd be back in a minute but didn't break her stride.

"Hi." He smiled at his wife as he walked into his bedroom and saw her standing there looking slightly awkward.

"I was just…" She couldn't look at him.

He walked over to her and took both her hands in his. "Are we okay after last night?"

She nodded but didn't say anything, overcome with embarrassment.

He bent his knees slightly to match her height with his so he could meet her eye.

"It's okay, we are married. I know it was a little fast but I have no regrets. Do you?"

Finally she looked at him. "I guess not. It just complicates things further."

"Things are only as complicated as you make them." He looked at her again, more thoroughly this time. "I love what you've done to your hair! It suits you better." He smiled and ran his fingers through her soft hair looking at it in wonder.

Sarah had taken herself to the hairdressers for extensions and a colour. Her hair was now almost back to the light brown that was her natural colour, but with golden highlights and shoulder length extensions.

Grace came charging back into the room, kitted out in one of her new outfits and furry boots. She was laughing as Marco picked her up and whirled her around in delight.

Sarah closed the door to the Yellow Room quietly behind her and walked nervously down the hallway towards the top of the stairs. She felt slightly nauseous as though she was on a first date. Her satin dress swished around her calves and her heels clipped on the marble flooring. At the top of the stairs, she took a deep breath, holding onto the banister with her left hand. She could hear Marcos booming voice giving orders to his right hand man, Gabe and to his young apprentice, Scott Wolfe. Sarah began the descent down the stairs trying to control her breathing and clutching her bag as though it were her safety net, still not letting go of the hand rail. She heard the door to Marco's office close loudly, followed by fast paced footsteps. Marco came into view wearing a tuxedo, standard dress for a Palm Beach New Years Eve party and he looked up the stairs at Sarah and did a double take.

"Wow!" He barely whispered under his breath. He stopped walking and just gazed up at her.

Sarah almost glided down the remainder of the stairs, buoyed by his reaction and kissed him chastely on the cheek.

"Will I do?" She asked resting a hand on his hip.

He shook his head in disbelief that she was here. He had seen her hair extensions earlier in the day and while they had a little family dinner but all dressed up like this, she looked fabulous.

Sarah looked into his eyes and thought maybe she had gone too far too soon with the credit card, but she had had so much fun. "Marco, you did say no limits…"

"No. No limits. You look fantastic. I can barely believe it. That dress…" He took a step back to further admire her in it. "I can't wait to show you off." He frowned a moment. "Something is not right."

"What?"

"Something is missing." He looked ponderous for a minute before realisation pretended to hit. "I know. I have just the thing." He winked as he reached into his inside jacket pocket and withdrew a red velvet box. Sarah gasped as he opened it to reveal a stunning Van Cleef platinum necklace embedded with six emerald-cut diamonds which dropped to a pear shaped diamond pendant.

"I didn't know what colour dress you'd be wearing and figured diamonds go with everything." Marco carefully took it out of the box and Sarah turned round and lifted her hair up so he could fasten it around her neck, his fingertips brushing across the nape of her neck. The pear-shaped pendant settled just above her cleavage and for a moment, Marco couldn't bare to look away.

"It's beautiful, Marco. Thank you." She kissed his lips passionately and he drew her into an embrace. Feeling the effect it was having on him, he reluctantly pulled away. He cleared his throat but his voice was husky as he announced that they should be heading out.

The limousine had been wheeled out again for tonight, cleaned inside and out and was waiting outside the front door for them. Sarah got in first, then Marco slid in next to her. An open bottle of champagne was on ice waiting for them and Marco grinned as he poured it into two flutes. He handed one to her, laughing with excitement.

Sarah sipped her champagne as the limo moved through the dark streets of Palm Beach and allowed the bubbles go to her head. The journey would take about ten minutes and she wanted to be drunk by the time she got there. She was dreading seeing most of the people again. Marco held her hand and her nerves were slightly calmer by the time they arrived at the marina. That Cliff and Andrea would be there was her saving grace and she hoped that they would already have arrived by the time she and Marco arrived. Marco held her hand as they walked the short distance from the car to the dockside at West Palm Beach marina. Sarah could hear the soft music punctuating the night air as they approached the moorings of the luxury yacht Aurora which belonged to Dominic and Shelley Russell.

Marco showed his invitation to the security men at the bottom of the gangway that lead onto the yacht while Sarah practically hid behind him. She hadn't yet had enough to drink to face this and really wanted to run back to the safety of the limo, finish the champagne off and go home to see the New Year in with a pizza, as she had for the last few years.

Marco stepped onto the gangway and encouraged Sarah to follow him by taking her arm in his and leading her onto the yacht. Dominic and Shelley were on the main deck to greet each and every one of their guests with a glass of champagne. Marco shook hands in a friendly manner with Dominic and then kissed Shelley on the cheek hello. Her girlish giggle did not escape Sarah and she wandered briefly if there was any history between Marco and Shelley. She didn't have time to dwell on the matter as Marco had moved away and Sarah was now in front of her hosts.

Dominic and Shelley said a pleasant, if distant hello to Sarah. It was obvious to her that they did not know who she was, which was fine by her. She wanted to remain anonymous for as long as possible. She knew the curious gossips would form little cliques to find out who Marco Delvecchio's companion for the evening was and she would soon be outed.

Marco saw Cliff and Andrea quaffing champagne almost immediately they got by Dominic and Shelley and went over to them standing by the rails of the yacht, pulling Sarah by her hand.

"My God! You look fantastic!" Cliff said as he kissed Sarah hello. "So different to the woman I saw at the airport the other day. Being separated from Marco obviously suits you." He joked.

"No, but his Amex card certainly does!" She jested back. She looked over at Marco, who was smiling seductively at her.

The four of the chatted amiably for a few minutes before business came up and Andrea and Sarah headed up to the sun deck.

The centre of the deck was laid stern to bow with tables covered in a wonderful array of food. There were lobsters, oysters and shrimp, sliced meats, salads and candied fruit. Only a few other people were on this deck so the two women were able to chat comfortably. They leant over the railings at the black water below as they headed out to sea. On the deck below, Sarah could hear Marco and Cliff and all their kiss-ass business associates with their plastic wives, cow-towing to anything Marco said.

"God! I hate all this crap. I'd rather be with just a bunch of friends with a few beers and some good food." Sarah turned to her friend who felt pretty much the same way.

"It's our duty as wives to successful men. Dress up nice, look pretty and nod and smile in the right places."

"Perhaps, but I'm only a part time wife. Nothing has been discussed yet." A waiter passed then with a tray of full champagne glasses. Sarah and Andrea swapped their empty ones.

"He'd be devastated if you left. Cliff says Marco thinks you're here to stay or at least to try again." Andrea confided to Sarah.

"I've only been here for a day, he'll get over it. I guess we'll talk but I'm due back in San Francisco on the second of January. Besides, he won't be lonely – there must be plenty of women wanting a shot at Marco."

"Too true!" Came an interrupting voice coming up the stairs. It was Shelley Russell in her skimpy black dress and cleavage desperate to break free. Her black hair, short and straight hung down beside her face like some kind of Martian spider. Her eyes were almost as black as her hair.

"Do you like Marco?" Sarah asked as she sneaked a wink at Andrea. "But aren't you married to Dominic?"

"Well sure, but who would turn down a chance with Marco Delvecchio?"

"But Shelley, Dominic has this lovely boat and he is very successful!" Sarah teased.

"Of course he is but Marco had so much more to offer a girl. Look at him. Those smouldering good looks, money to make Dom look like a pauper, those alleged connections. I mean, who wouldn't?" She clearly had no idea who Sarah was.

"You got me!" Sarah murmured and took another glug of champagne.

Shelley turned away from the obvious object of her lust and turned to Sarah. She looked her up and down and decided that she didn't like her. Sarah was naturally pretty and Shelley envied anyone who was attractive without having to try too much. Unlike herself, who spent several weeks a year in a clinic in Austin, Texas having various pieces of work done.

"So how well do you know him then?" Shelley asked.

"Oh, pretty well I'd say."

"Are you from the escort agency? I haven't seen you before." The question was cold and without any real interest.

Andrea stifled a snigger next to Sarah and Sarah smothered a smile.

"No, I'm not from any escort agency. I don't think even Marco Delvecchio would give a call girl, however high class, THIS" Sarah pointed to the diamonds around her neck.

Shelley looked slightly deflated. "I didn't know he had a girlfriend."

"No, he didn't mention it to me either." Sarah said mysteriously.

Andrea was unable to hold back the giggle.

"Will one of you children tell me the joke?" Shelley was getting annoyed.

Sarah didn't fancy the prospect of swimming back to shore in this dress so she decided not to play with Shelley any more and tell her.

"I'm Sarah, Marcos wife."

It completely floored Shelley.

"Wife? I had no idea! When did you two..?"

"About six years ago now. I've been away for a while, with our daughter."

Shelley nodded and tried to smile. "I'm very happy for you. Please excuse me." She hurried down the stairs to her stateroom to compose herself.

Sarah and Andrea burst into hysterical laughter.

"That was the best laugh I have had in quite some time. That bitch has been coming onto Marco for months, she had that coming." Andrea said, wiping away tears of laughter.

"How could she not know Marco is married? He's not exactly a shrinking violet."

"Dom and Shelley are what is referred to a new wealth. They have only been in our social circle for about two years now and I think they lived out of the area before that so it is entirely possible that stupid woman had no idea. Maybe now she will stop making a play for your husband."

"That's between the two of them, Andrea."

"Aren't you jealous?"

Sarah shook her head. "Not really. Come on, let's mingle."

Word soon got around that Marco's guest that evening was in fact his wife. Peoples attitudes towards her changed rather rapidly as they found out that she was not just another high class call girl. People went over to her to say hello, how nice it was that she was back, how fabulous she looked, some false, most sincere.

Marco stood to the side and watched these people, his people bedazzled by her. He was spellbound himself and was surprised at his strength of feelings for her.

Friday night arrived and Sarah was persuaded by all to stay a little longer. Grace was eager to stay so Sarah relented and they decided to stay for another week. Sarah had some phone calls to make first.

"You're staying a while longer?" Don Miotto repeated.

"Yes. Marco and I are getting on so well that I don't want to call a halt to it just yet. He has work he cannot put off for more than a few days so I will return by next weekend." She promised.

"Okay but if you need anything, anything at all, you call me." His point was unmistakable.

"I will." She assured him.

"And take Grace to the Magic Kingdom, she'll love it."

Sarah laughed for she and Marco had planned to do exactly that the following day.

Next, she called Ted and Henry.

"Don't worry guys, I'll make sure you get the next rent cheque on time." She assured Henry.

"You needn't worry honey. It's been taken care of for the next six months." Henry told her.

"What?"

"It came today. I guess your husband wants to provide for you."

"Well, he owes me." Sarah said cattily. "Well. We'll see you both next weekend."

"Bye, darling, you take care. Kisses for Grace." He blew kisses down the phone and hung up. Sarah almost longed to be back at their house sharing a chat and a bottle of wine. She would have plenty to tell them when she got home.

CHAPTER EIGHT

The trip to the Magic Kingdom was a huge success. Marco, Sarah and Grace set off early and arrived in Orlando at around ten-fifteen. They parked in the Goofy car park and hopped on the land train which took them to the boat landing. They raced onto the boat that would take them across the lake to the Magic Kingdom. Grace was so excitable on the boat ride that Marco could barely constrain her, and the first thing she saw when stepping off the boat was Piglet. She ran off to speak to him with Marco calling out to her to slow down. When Sarah had caught up with them, Grace was in an embrace with Piglet and Marco was taking her photograph. Once they had paid for their tickets, been searched for weapons - another sad post 9/11 sign of the times, they went through the barriers. A jazz band was playing in an open top truck that drove slowly though the throngs of people. Kids were everywhere, parents shouting for them to wait or come back. Marco lifted Grace onto his shoulders so she could not run off in her excitement and become a lost child statistic.

They walked all around the huge park and went on many of the rides – It's a Small World, the Peter Pan ride, the Mary Poppins carousel. They watched the parade At three o'clock while having a huge ice-cream that dripped down Graces tee-shirt as it melted. Grace was bought a princess outfit by her father which she insisted on changing into and wearing around the park for the rest of the day. They had photos taken with Mickey, Minnie, Baloo and Rafiki and Grace was beside herself with the excitement. Grace began to flag about five o'clock so they wandered down Main Street where they stopped for a coffee and a pastry and more gifts for Grace before getting back on the boat to take them back to the car park. As the boat drifted back across the lake, strains of a Caribbean steel band could be heard echoing across the water. Grace had to be carried to the car by Marco, she was exhausted. By the time they reached the car, she was asleep in his arms.

They got underway for the long drive home with Marco at the wheel and Grace asleep in the rear of the car, safely strapped in her newly acquired child seat. Sarah was weary – it had been a long day all round. They drove in comfortable silence for the first half an hour.

They had been on the Florida Turnpike for about twenty minutes when Marco broke the silence.

"So Sarah, tell me what you are going to do."

"About what?" She stared ahead at the black top being eaten up by the Lincoln.

"Well as I understand it, you have a job and a life in San Francisco. What about our daughters schooling?"

"Oh that." She shifted in her seat, angling away from Marco. "I guess we'll be going home next week. We'll be back for Rosa's wedding."

"You guess?"

Sarah shrugged.

"Don't you want to stay?"

She shrugged again.

Marco sniggered at her indecisiveness. "Okay, let me ask you an easier question. Do you love me?"

At this, she dared a glance to her left. Marco was still looking straight ahead. "That's supposed to be an easier question? You want an honest answer?" She sighed. "I don't know for sure, that's one of the reasons I came back. To find out."

"Well, do you at least trust me?"

"Not one hundred percent, no. Strange that." She ventured a half smile.

"If you go back, I don't want to lose contact with either of you. We've built up some kind of relationship over the last week or so."

"And what if we are to stay?"

Marco grinned. "That would be fantastic." He looked over at her hopefully.

They drove in silence for another few miles.

"What if I were to stay just a little bit longer?" Sarah said slowly. "Say another month or so and see how things pan out."

Marco nodded enthusiastically. It was a decent enough start. "Stay until after Rosa and Sal get married. Then you and I can sit and have a good long chat. Will you move into my bedroom?"

"No, I don't think that's a good idea just yet. I can still wonder in if the mood takes us though" She smiled across at him. There had never been any problem in that part of their relationship. "You have already fronted my rent so I'll just call Ted and Henry and let them know. I don't know how Don Alessandro will feel about me having another few weeks off. He's already been more than generous."

"I'll talk to him." Marco assured Sarah.

She shook her head. "That's not a good idea. I have to talk to him. If you call him and tell him I'm not coming back just yet, he'll think you've had me clipped." She giggled.

"Clipped? You've been watching too many movies!" He smiled and reached across for her hand.

A few days later Sarah was in the kitchen at the breakfast bar reading a magazine. Rosa, Sal and Grace had gone to the beach for a spell. The weather was glorious for January. Marco was attending one of his numerous meetings somewhere in the State.

"Oh, it's you. I wondered if you'd ever come back." The voice from the doorway was none too friendly.

Sarah looked back over her shoulder and looked aghast at her brother in law. Marco had warned her that he had changed but it did not fully prepare her for what she saw. The once well-kept, tidy and proud man Joe had been had turned into nothing less than a monster. He had lost perhaps twenty pounds and didn't look well on it. His hair was shoulder length, greasy and dull. His once handsome face was gaunt and dark circles lay beneath his bloodshot eyes. He looked seriously hung over, unshaven and was sweating profusely.

Sarah was appalled.

"Yes, I'm back for a time. She looked back at her magazine, not really knowing what to say to him. "How are you?" She asked out of politeness.

Joe didn't answer. He had nothing much to say to this woman, who he deemed a slut and one his pathetic brother should have been well rid of by now. Joe couldn't understand the hold she had over Marco and as far as he was concerned, Sarah had messed with Marco's head and turned him into a soft touch which was not good for their business.

He walked through the kitchen, passing Sarah and out into the hallway. "I hope you aren't staying too long. You should just crawl back to wherever my lamentable brother found you." He called out as he walked away.

Angry, Sarah got up and followed him. She saw him disappearing into Marco's empty office.

"What gives you the right to talk to me like that? What the hell happened to you?" She asked the question although she knew.

Joe was rummaging through Marco's drawers, obviously looking for something. "Just shut up, bitch! You've turned my brother into an asshole, sleeping around while he was in prison. Now he doesn't have what it takes to run this business – you've ripped out his backbone."

"He seems to be doing okay to me."

"That just shows how much you know. He's a laughing stock, has been since he picked you up on that beach in France." He slammed the drawer shut, annoyance showing on his face that he could not find what he was looking for. He walked menacingly towards Sarah who back away slightly.

"No wonder your own brother kicked you out of the family home. I wouldn't want you in my house." Sarahs words were stronger and braver than she was feeling. She was acutely aware that she was alone in the house. There were guards at the gatehouse at the bottom of the drive who knew Joe was here and Scott was at the back gate as usual but no-one in the vicinity to hear her shouts if things turned really nasty.

Joe's face was just inches from hers as he spoke and she recoiled at his foul smelling breath. "You have no house and you have no family. Isn't that why you came back, because you have no options left?"

A strong, familiar and welcome voice answered the question. "Yes, she does. She has both. I hope you aren't threatening my wife in her home?"

Sarahs eyes wandered to the doorway to where Marco was stood. She was relieved that he was here but didn't want to make the situation worse by his choosing Sarah over Joe. He would have heard at least some of the conversation.

Joe backed away from Sarah, his sense of power evaporating.

He smiled sardonically. "How are you brother dear?"

Marco stared at Joe. "I'd be much better if you were to leave. It might be better if you stayed away Joe, at least while your head is full of coke. When you are clean, you can come back into the Family." Marco's meaning was unmistakable. He was edging his brother out of the family business.

"You can't do that. This is my family home too and it was also my father who built up everything you see here. You have no right to exclude me." Joe's voice was threatening.

"I have every right. The buck stops with me now. That's what Pops wanted and that's how it is. I make the decisions. Your 'habits' are a liability to this family and I have other people and their livings to think about. Like I said, clear your head permanently and we'll talk."

"Talk, my ass! You are making a big mistake choosing her over me."

"It has nothing to do with Sarah. It's a business decision, firing the deadwood."

"You will regret it."

"Is that a threat?"

"I don't make threats. You should know that!" Joe barged past Marco, shoving him with his shoulder as he passed. He stormed to the front door and slammed it after he left.

Sarah looked at Marco, her heartbeat returning to normal after the unexpected confrontation. "Marco, I'm sorry. I don't want to come between you two."

He went to her and put his arms around her. "It's been a long time coming. He has a habit that he doesn't want to kick. He uses more than he sells and it's affecting our business. He'll make a good living selling that stuff but I don't want to be involved in it anymore.

Besides, you are my wife and deserve more respect that he was giving you." He kissed her softly. It was an enticement to make her stay.

Along with the black American Express card that arrived shortly after with Sarahs name on it. Marco told her that it was hers to keep whether she stayed or went, but knew it would be an enticement.

CHAPTER NINE

Much of the family's time and energy was spent on the run up to Rosa and Sal's wedding. Graces dress was put together skilfully and quickly by the same designer who had made Rosa's wedding dress and the material for the two were carefully matched.

Marco's thirty sixth birthday at the end of January went by barely noticed, just a small intimate dinner for close family and friends at Carlottis restaurant, which Marco now owned fifty one percent of. Joe was conspicuous only by his absence.

Two days before the wedding, Rosa invited all of her girlfriends to a private party at the country club for a wedding shower. She did not want a fuss being five months pregnant, just a tasteful get together with no blown up condoms, male strippers or tacky gifts.

Rosa was blooming in her pregnancy. She'd had a tough time of it for the last few weeks with morning sickness and dizzy spells but was now past that and looked radiant. She welcomed her guests with a glass of champagne and introduced them all to Sarah. Eighteen women in all sat around the table having a sumptuous lunch talking about how Rosa and Sal had got together just last year. Salvatore Ricci's brother is a business associate of Marcos and had been at the house one day when Rosa walked into Marcos office with coffee and he had been blown away with her beauty. There was no doubting that Rosa was a stunner — long black hair with the Delvecchio wave in it that framed her oval shaped face and delicate features. She had been quite taken with Sal but refused to trust her instincts and Sarah knew the reason for that. The last person she had really fallen for had turned out to be her half brother. Sarah didn't air this thought though, she didn't want to embarrass Rosa and neither did she even want to think about Vinnie.

The women laughed as they heard stories of how Sal had tried to win Rosa over and finally it was a broken glass that had melted her heart towards him.

When Sarah got Rosa alone later that day, Sarah quizzed Rosa about this.

"A broken glass?"

"He cut himself and I tended to his wound." She said simply.

"I didn't have you down as the Florence Nightingale sort."

"I'm not. I had his blood analysed."

"What?"

"I had to make sure that I wasn't about to make another mistake. I loved my father very much but he had a very shady past and I didn't want another brother popping up to seduce me. We have friends in various places and one of them is at the crime lab. He tested Sal's DNA and made sure we weren't even remotely related. Once I knew that, I let myself fall for him and I'm happy I did it."

"Unbelievable." Sarah said softly.

"By the way, Sal doesn't know about blood test or Vinnie and he doesn't need to know. The less people know, the better. It makes me feel ill." Rosa glanced at Sarah apologetically, suddenly remembering her past with Vinnie. "Sorry."

Sarah patted her arm. "Don't worry, Ro. I'm over it now. Besides, you didn't miss out on much. He was a very selfish lover and didn't do much for me!"

Rosa burst out laughing. "God! It's good to have you back!" She hugged her sister in law.

Rosa's wedding day finally dawned a beautiful sunny day. It was St Valentines day and Marco brought Sarah breakfast in bed and a dozen red roses. Sarah was embarrassed that she hadn't got him anything – she had been too caught up in the wedding to even think about it. When Grace was out of earshot, Sarah promised him sexual favours later.

It was difficult to know who was more excited – Rosa or Grace. In the six weeks since arriving from San Francisco, Grace had settled into life in Palm Beach very nicely indeed and had her father eating out of the palm of her hand. It would difficult to take her back to California now.

After lunch, everyone disappeared to get ready and Sarah helped Grace with her hair and to finally put her dress on. She had wanted to wear it as soon as she got up but despite her promises to keep it clean had not been allowed to. When finally it was time, she was a bag of excitement. Sarah made her sit on the edge of the bed and not move while she went down the hallway to Marcos room to see him. Downstairs, the party planners were just putting the last few wedding adornments along the stairway, pink and white roses sewn into silk brocades.

Sarah walked into Marcos bedroom without knocking. They had gone past such niceties.

"Hi." She smiled at him. He looked scrumptious in his tuxedo. He had not been very happy when told he must wear a pink silk cummerbund and matching bow-tie but he looked fabulous despite this slight on his masculinity. He was just finishing tying his bow-tie. Sarah could not help but put her arms around him and give him a passionate kiss. "It's a bit different to our wedding day, huh?" He asked when she finally freed his lips.

"Hmm. Grace is in our bedroom sitting very still and waiting for you." She said looking into his eyes. "Have we got time for a quickie? You look good enough to eat." She asked in all seriousness.

Marco burst out laughing. "No! Behave yourself woman. It's taken me half an hour to get this monkey suit on. You'll have to contain yourself until later." He found time to kiss her again though, a promise of what was to come later.

"I just thought I'd ask." She smiled as they left the room and headed back to the Yellow Room to fetch Grace.

At five o'clock, Sarah was sat in the garden with fifty other carefully selected guests, in the front row of chairs that had been set out for the occasion. In front of her, the family priest waited in the gazebo that was also adorned in the pink and white roses that showered the rest of the house. Sal was sat next to her waiting for the bridal party to arrive, nervously wringing his hands and behaving as to be expected of a groom. The orchestra was to the side of the gazebo playing gentle music waiting for their cue that Rosa was ready. With a split second silence, followed by the beginnings of the wedding march, everyone knew it was time. Sal stood first followed by Sarah, anxious for her daughter to put on a good show. She turned round and saw Grace beaming as she walked along the carpeted boardwalk, throwing fresh rose petals on the floor. She looked as cute as a button in her pink silk dress that fell to her shins and the skirt was overcoated in delicate white lace. Grace wore pink ballet shoes, each one had a fresh pink rose bud sewn into it. Her shoulder length dark had was crowned in a tiara with gypsophila wound into it. A few paces behind her was Rosa and if Graces' dress was fantastic, there were no words to describe Rosa's. It was a full length ivory Thai silk dress, with pink roses sewn into the skirt. The bodice was covered in sequins and ivory silk roses and it hid her pregnancy well. Her hair was bundled up and secured with clips with ivory silk roses also. She was radiant and beaming.

Giving her away was Marco who couldn't have looked prouder if he were giving away his own daughter. Sarah was so pleased and proud to be a part of this wonderful day. Her emotions threatened to run away as the party walked towards the priest.

Once Marco had given his sister to Salvatore, he sat down next to Sarah in Sal's now vacant seat.

"Beautiful." Sarah whispered as he sat and took her hand.

He turned to her and smiled in pure joy and began to relax a little.

As soon as the formal proceedings were done and Sal and Rosa were married, the French champagne began to flow and the sumptuous wedding feast was served not long after wards under the newly erected marquee. As darkness set in, the garden lights were put on which cast a romantic glow around the grounds. The candles in storm glasses flickered on the tables as the band struck up it's first song after the speeches were finally done and the dinner plates cleared away.

As Rosa and Sal started off the dancing, Marco saw Joe in the crowd trying to look inconspicuous but failing. Marco decided to let it drop, he did not want to cause a scene today, he was too happy and relaxed from the champagne. Joe was with a man Marco did not know but was not causing any problems. He'd let Gabe know Joe was here and ask him to get rid of Joe if anything kicked off.

Marco moved from his seat at the head table to where Sarah was sat talking to Andrea and Cliff. They were laughing at one of Cliffs infamous jokes or stories as Marco arrived with a half glass of champagne left. There was a bottle on the table and he refilled his and sat next to his wife. He was happy to be with Sarah but also concerned that their time together may be coming to an end. He had done all he could think of to make Sarah stay.

He looked out at the dance floor and saw his delightful daughter dancing with some little friends and edging out the only boy who wanted to dance. He laughed at her and hoped she would not want to have boys around her for many years to come. She was going to be beautiful when she was older and he knew he would have his hands full with her. That's when he knew he was getting old – he was starting to think like his father had. He looked back at Sarah and picked up the champagne bottle to refill her glass. She put her hand over her flute to decline.

"Why not?" Marco was curious.

"I'm just hot and thirsty that's all. I need a soft drink. It's no big deal." She assured him.

"Okay." He handed the bottle to Cliff to refill his and Andrea glasses. "As long as you are okay." He said to Sarah.

"I'm fine." She flashed a smile at him. That simple thing made his heart leap. He felt like a dumbstruck virgin teenager lately if she even so much as looked at him. Maybe it was the thought of losing her that cut him to the core.

"Marco, do you mind if I dance with your wife?" Cliff asked Marco as he stood to take Sarahs hand.

Marco acquiesced and Cliff lead Sarah to the dance floor where a jazzy number had just been struck up.

Marco watched the two laughing as they danced and realised for the first time in their history that he was not jealous of another man being close to his wife. But it was more than the fact that Cliff was one of his oldest friends from school. He thought of her one time tennis coach, Brad Townsend and how he been insanely jealous when rumours of them having an affair reached his ears. He laughed to himself as he remembered how he had dealt with that. He hoped maturity was finally setting in.

Sal cut in half way through the song and Cliff walked back to the table for a dance with Andrea and the two left Marco alone at the table and while they danced.

Sarah danced with Sal and felt happy and light headed. She looked into Sal's eyes and saw a man who was just as happy and also in love.

"It's been a great day Sal. I'm glad I've been here and a part of it."

"We have your husband to thank for that. He's done Rosa proud with this."

"Rosa is his only sister. He wants the best for her, to make her happy. That makes him happy too."

Sal shook his head. "The reason for Marcos happiness is you. He's been a changed man since you have been back."

"You think so?" Sarah was pleasantly surprised.

They were interrupted by Grace's wailing at their feet.

"I've spilt cherry-ade on my dress!" The little girl was sobbing hysterically and hiccuping. She held the dress up with the large pink stain for her mother to see. She was fisting her tired tearful eyes.

Sarah released herself from Sal's dancing embrace. "Sweetheart, lets go and tidy you up. We can get the dress cleaned and it will be as good as new." She promised her. Sarah apologised to Sal and with a slight groan, she picked Grace up. They walked through the crowd and back into the house through the open French doors that lead into the sitting room. A few people had come inside for a few minutes and Rosa was also inside. She came over to the still crying Grace to see what the fuss was about. Grace told her with a fresh wail that she had ruined her dress and was sorry.

"Don't worry about the dress, sweetie. We can fix that and make it as good as new." Rosa looked at Sarah and half smiled.

"Grace is just tired, Auntie Rosa. It's been a busy day for her. We are going upstairs to watch a DVD in bed and we will get the dress fixed tomorrow."

Grace sniffled as she was carried through the sitting room and into the hallway. Her bedroom was towards the front of the house so it would be nice and quiet and away from the celebrations. Sarah put on her daughters latest favourite DVD and settled the child into the large bed and sat with her for a while. Grace soon drifted off to sleep and while Sarah felt she could have joined her in her slumber, she quietly closed the bedroom door and went back outside to look for her husband.

Sarah mingled with the guests in the cooling night with a glass of iced tea, all the while her eyes darting around looking for Marco.

"Hey!" He caught up with Sarah as she passed, circling her waist and gently spinning her around to face him.

"I was searching for you." She spoke softly and kissed his cheek. "I was hoping to have a dance with you if you are not too busy."

"I'll always have time for you." He assured her as they headed towards the dance floor under the marquee.

They danced close to a slow romantic melody and Sarah breathed deeply and inhaled his cologne. He still looked and smelt wonderful.

"Are you happy?" He asked her.

Sarah pulled him even closer, enjoying the closeness they shared. "Yes, kind of." She replied mysteriously.

Marco pulled away slightly and still dancing, he frowned at her. "Kind of? What's the matter?"

Sarah shook her head slightly. "Nothing really. I have something to tell you and I'm a little concerned about what your reaction may be."

"What? Are you going back to San Francisco?" Marco look totally bewildered and stopped dancing in the middle of the floor and looked at her, hurt and angry. He thought they were getting on great and couldn't see a reason for Sarah not to stay.

Sarah grabbed his hand and pulled him back close. She kissed his lips. "I consider this to be my home and I want to stay with you. Especially now."

The relief was evident on his face as he began to sway to the music, their hips almost joined. "That's great." He buried his face in Sarahs soft hair humming gently to the tune. It took a minute for her words to sink in, the effect of too much champagne. "Why especially now?"

Sarah looked at his boyishly happy face. "Marco, I know it's not the best timing in the world and it wasn't done intentionally. I know what people will say…"

"About what?" He interrupted her ramblings.

"I need to know your initial reaction to what I'm going to tell you…"

"Sarah, just tell me."

"I'm pregnant."

Marco looked at her and frowned. A thousand thoughts went through his head and he could think of nothing to say.

"Marco?" Sarah prompted

"Don't react badly to this, but is it mine?"

"Of course it is! I told you I hadn't been with anyone else while we were apart and I swear on Grace's life that is the truth. That first night I was back in Palm Beach, you caught me unawares. I was a little drunk and too happy to care about the consequences and just hoped it would be okay. I thought that would be our only time together and just wanted to make the most of it. If you're not happy about it, Grace and I will leave, you don't need to have anything to do with it."

"Mrs Delvecchio, that is really great news!" He finally broke out into a huge grin and kissed her.

"Really? You're not cross with me?"

"Cross? How can I be cross with you, it was down to me also. What better way to celebrate us getting back together than with a new baby. I take it you do want us back together?"

"Of course I do. Are you sure it's okay?"

"It's great news. Now I know what you're needs are, we can start to plan accordingly. For now though, can we keep it between the two of us, at least until Sal and Rosa get back from honeymoon. I don't want this to over shadow their wedding." He kissed the top of her nose affectionately.

Sarah would insist on ground rules. He was not going to walk all over her again.

CHAPTER NINE

The next few days were a blur to both Sarah and Marco. Both felt like the carpet had been pulled from under their feet as they began to make plans for their future life together and yet another whirlwind romance. Arrangements were made to retrieve Sarah's and Grace's belongings from San Francisco and Marco wanted to have a meeting with Don Alessandro. The three of them flew to San Francisco in Marco's jet and landed around three o'clock one Wednesday afternoon in mid February. They took a taxi to their hotel, the Westin St Francis where Marco had booked his family into a two bedroomed suite for the duration.

Marco carried Grace through the lobby while the bellhop carried their luggage behind them. They did not have to check in, the concierge was already waiting for them and showed them straight up to the Suite on the top floor. It was very opulent. The master bedroom was decorated in gold and cream furnishings, complete with a king sized bed which had a crowned canopy in the middle of the room. It overlooked Union Square and the wonderful noise of the city drifted up from the street. The sitting / dining area was a deep red with dark wood furniture. This led onto the second bedroom, Grace's for the duration, which was powder blue and white, the large bed which would swallow the little girl who was to occupy it. Each bedroom had its own en-suite bathroom, the master suite even having a flat screen television set in the wall at the foot of the Jacuzzi bath. Sarah was as worn out as her daughter so the two of them decided to have a snooze while Marco went north to take care of business.

    Marco's business with Don Alessandro was peaceable. He wanted to clear the air between himself and his late fathers best friend. The old Don was Sarahs protector and Marco had to convince him that Sarah was back in his life on her own terms and her own volition. He had to assure the Don that Sarah would be safe, happy and would want for nothing. It would be the only way there would not be any bad blood between the two families.

    Marco was let into the house by the same timid housekeeper who had tried to blackmail him on his previous visit here. She kept her eyes to the floor as she let the Florida Don into the house. She lead him into the library which had a large roaring fire blazing away. A plethora of family photos were on top of the mantle piece above the fire and on the sideboard beside it. As Sophia left the room and closed the door behind her, Marco went over to the pictures. He immediately saw one of his and Sarahs wedding blessing a few years before. He laughed to himself. He looked miserable and Sarah looked petrified. They both had good reason for their feelings, neither really knowing the other or what lay ahead for them. This time, they were going in with their eyes wide open. They had love enough to see them through the good and the bad times, of that he was sure.

    Marco heard the door open and turned to see Don Miotto enter the room. The old mans eyes were full of distrust and he didn't say a word until he had sat in the chair next to the fire.

    "Do you want a drink?" He asked Marco gruffly.

    Marco declined the offer and sat down as Don Alessandro motioned for him to do so.

    "So you have your wife back then?" The old man felt a strange affinity towards Sarah and this was one of the reasons he didn't trust Marco for personal or for business reasons.

    "She came to me. I did not seek her out." Marco replied a little frostily.

    Alessandro nodded. "Where is she now?"

    "At the Westin with Grace. She has a few things to sort out and then we are all returning to Florida. I don't want for our Families to disagree on this. It is what Sarah wants."

    "I find it hard to believe that you did not encourage her feelings on this matter. She was so dead against you not too long ago and I would even go so far as to say she feared you. Feared for her life."

"Those feelings were unfounded. I would never hurt her or Grace. We have talked everything through over the past few weeks and we have agreed to give our marriage another go. We are having a baby." Marco fairly swelled with pride.

"That was clever work, Marco. That's one way to ensure she stayed with you." Marco began to get angry and struggled to keep his anger in check. It would do him no good to show any flashes of temper. "It wasn't planned but we are very happy about it. I gave her the option to return here if she wanted but for some strange reason, she loves me and wants to stay with me."

Miotto finally smiled in a semi-friendly way. "There is no accounting for taste. So, why are you here Marco?"

"I want you to be assured that Sarah will be safe. I will not let any harm come to her or to Grace. It has taken until now to realise what I so nearly lost and I will not allow that to happen again. My father often said that a man is nothing without a woman who loves him and a family to care for and I now realise how important and true his words are. I do not want any of this to affect our business dealings."

Don Miotto breathed deeply. "I appreciate you coming here and telling me all of this but words are just words, Marco. However, I will trust Sarahs judgement on this, she seems to know what she wants after all. She will continue to remain in my protection as will Grace. Do you understand that, Marco?"

Marco nodded, feeling patronised and more than just a little affronted. He knew he only had himself to blame for peoples perception of him and Don Miotto's words would be enough for him to build up a positive image of himself in the business fraternity. He would just have to be patient.

"I have also come to discuss my brother, Joe." Marco stated.

Alessandro had heard of the problems in Florida between Marco and Giusseppe Delvecchio. Whatever the problems were, he did not want his businesses affected by them. He was interested in what Marco had to say and leant back in his chair.

Sarah and Grace had ordered room service and were in bed

eating Club Sandwiches with curly French fries when Marco returned. It was late, past nine o'clock when he walked into the sitting room pleased that his meeting with the Don of San Francisco had gone better than expected. Marco had told him why they had fallen out, namely drugs, something not many people were taken into Marco's confidence about. He was not proud of it. Marco had told Miotto that he no longer wanted to be a part of that side of things and wanted out before it had a denigrating effect on his and indeed, some of Alessandros other businesses. Alessandro was pleased to hear of this and seemed impressed with Marcos new business plan.

Grace fell asleep soon after finishing most of her sandwich while Marco finished off her fries. He was famished, he hadn't eaten since breakfast and ordered some food for himself. While he was waiting for it to be delivered, he carefully picked his sleeping daughter from out of his bed and gently carried her into the second bedroom. He waited until she was sound asleep before returning to the master bedroom, leaving the doors ajar in case Grace awoke.

"How was Alessandro?" Sarah asked as she snuggled next to her husband entwining her legs in his as they lay on the bed.

"Dubious of my intentions." He said quietly and placed a hand on her flat belly thrilled at the thought of his child inside.

"Do you blame him?"

"Not really and it will be a slow process to get him and others to trust me fully again. But I am willing to go through that for all of our sakes." He began to kiss her neck.

"Everything will work out fine." She promised. "Marco, we can't. Grace is through there." His hands had begun to wander and Sarah could see that he was aroused. Grace was unsettled and could wander through at any moment.

He sighed knowing she was right but that didn't stop the blood rushing south. The doorbell to the suite rang to signify his food had arrived and at least one appetite was fed.

The following morning after breakfast, the family got into a cab and headed for the Castro district of San Francisco. Ted and Henry were eagerly expecting them, looking forward to finally meeting Sarahs husband.

As Sarah got out of the taxi, Ted and Henry came down the steps from the front door to meet her. They both hugged Sarah. She had been very much missed while she had been out of town. They hugged Grace also having missed her very much. They were introduced to Marco by Grace who delighted in telling everyone that he was her daddy. Ted and Henry were enthusiastic in their welcoming of Marco but he was as usual a little reserved. He smiled politely as they shook hands and then followed his wife and daughter into the basement apartment that they had called home.

They got to work packing the things that were to be shipped to Palm Beach. Most of it was personal items, toys, photos and school pictures. Most of their clothes would go to the charity shop. They weren't really Palm Beach outfits and besides, Sarah had Marcos credit card now to replenish their wardrobes.

Marco and Grace were in the bedroom sorting through her toys and DVDs.

"God Amy – I mean, Sarah! No wonder you wanted him back. He's so handsome." Ted said as Henry elbowed him in the ribs.

"Isn't he just?" Sarah said dreamily.

"Rich too, and connected, I hear." Henry added.

"He's not just connected, Henry. He is Mr Big in Florida. I sometimes wonder what he sees in me, there are so many better women who want him – why does he want me?"

Henry stroked Sarahs hand. "He's Italian. You are the mother of his child. That's a big thing. Apart from the fact that you are gorgeous and funny and no doubt you please him in the bedroom department!" He laughed.

Sarah joined in the laughter. "I guess you men are all the same, whatever your orientation!"

"Oh yes. Now, do you want this blouse?" Ted held it up against himself, trying it for size.

Marco came in to the room to see what the laughter was about. He saw Ted holding the blouse up against him and began to feel uncomfortable. He already felt claustrophobic being in the basement and these two men were doing nothing to make him feel any better. He told Sarah to hurry it up, that he would buy them both new stuff when they got back home.

Ted and Henry offered to sit with Grace that evening while Sarah and Marco went out for dinner. Grace wanted to stay the night and after much pleading with her doting father, he relented. He just wanted to get out of the house.

Marco and Sarah headed back to the hotel and they spent a couple of leisurely hours in bed. As Marco lay dozing in Sarahs arms, she thought about what Ted and Henry had said. When she was first married, she often wondered why Marco had married her after such a short courtship and the truth had come out just before she knew she was expecting Grace. Marco was due to be married to Lucia but had changed his mind. In his own crazy world, he thought the best way out was to marry a near stranger and when his father objected, he would have to get a divorce. Lucia would no longer want him and he could continue his life as he saw fit.

Only his father hadn't objected. Yes, he was a little unhappy at the rush marriage but he had fallen in love with his sons bride almost straight away. Little by little, Marco had got to know Sarah and fell in love with her also. This much Marco had told her when she had caught him sleeping with his ex-fiancée, in an effort to convince her that perhaps he didn't love her to begin with but now couldn't live without her.

Their first stab at their marriage had been a fiasco. If one wasn't having an affair, the other one was. There was much distrust and disharmony in their relationship and perhaps their time apart had done them both some good. Marco seemed to be very happy that she was back and Sarah was beginning to feel that she had made the right decision. Maybe now they were ready to commit to each other. She had some hold on him and perhaps what Ted and Henry said was right. It could be Grace. Whatever it was, Sarah was determined to hold on to it and to Marco.

Sarah took a taxi-cab to the Castro the next morning to collect Grace alone. The reason for this was two-fold – one, Marco had some business calls to make and wanted some privacy; two – Sarah wanted to say goodbye to Ted and Henry without Marco skulking around in the background.

When Sarah arrived, Grace was sat in her favourite beanbag – a black leatherette squishy one that Grace always commandeered whenever she was in the upstairs apartment. Sarah began to feel very emotional. Ted and Henry had been her only real friends since she had left Marco and she had no idea when she would get to see them again. She would soon be too pregnant to fly and Marco had an inherent distrust of strangers in his home.

She had one final cup of coffee with them and they chatted about how much fun they had had over the last few years and reliving some of the funny moments. At eleven thirty, Sarah stood up.

"Well, we really ought to be getting back to Daddy now, Grace."

Grace stood up and went to stand next to her mother.

"The last of your boxes were collected last night after you left. The guy said they would go on the plane without a problem." Ted informed her.

"Good."

The adults suddenly seemed at a loss for words.

Grace, with the temerity due of a child of her age had plenty to say.

"I'm going to live with my Daddy now. I liked living in your house but my Daddy has a much bigger house and it has a swimming pool." The adults all laughed.

"Palm Beach through and though after just a few weeks!" Sarah said as she fondly stroked her daughters hair.

"Well, my lovely girls. I hope you will both be very happy." Ted decided to start the difficult goodbyes.

"Yes, our front door will always be open to you, no matter what." Henry added.

He walked towards Sarah and hugged her fiercely. He loved Sarah as a sister and would be very sorry to see her leave.

"We will be happy." Sarah promised them both as she sniffled.

Ted had no compunction about that. Sarah was a feisty woman who knew how to survive. She had proven that by keeping up her deception with them for two years. He kissed her cheek and then bent down to hug Grace who had just been released from Henrys bear-like hug.

They finished their emotional goodbyes and went outside to where a taxi was waiting. Henry placed Graces overnight bag in the back seat of the car and blew them both a kiss as he closed the door. The cab pulled away from the curb and Grace clambered up onto the seat and kneeling, looked out of the rear window and waved to them. Sarah held onto her daughters waist to steady her and risked a look behind her. Ted and Henry were waving goodbye with their arms entwined. Sarah choked back a sob and looked to the front. She thought of all the wonderful things those two had done for her and she knew she wouldn't have made it through the last two years without them. She hoped one day to come back to visit.

She wiped away her tears and thought of her future, her new baby and her life with Grace and Marco. Her thoughts were now firmly in Florida.

Marco was sat in the lobby of the St Francis when they returned. He was reading the Chronicle and drinking coffee when Grace saw him and ran over to him. With a delighted shout of "Daddy!" she launched herself at him and through the newspaper. With a groan as the full force of Graces weight landed on his lap, Marco put the now ripped San Franciscan paper aside and smiled at the enthusiastic face of his daughter.

"I thought my girls could take me out for the afternoon and show me what this city has to offer." He suggested as he stood up with Grace in his arms.

"Sure. Why don't we get the cable down to the Wharf and mingle with the tourists?" Sarah suggested.

"Yeah! We can show Fred to Daddy!" Grace squealed with excitement. She grabbed her fathers hand and began to pull him towards the door to the amusement of the doorman.

Sarah ran over and put Graces bag with security to collect later and then hurried outside to find her husband and daughter. By the time she had caught up with them both, they were at the cross walk waiting for the lights to change with a crowd of people. They were headed three blocks down to the cable stop on Powell Street where a line was already forming, perhaps indicating that the next car would be along soon.

Sure enough, within just a few minutes of waiting, the clanging of the car could be heard as it came over the hill and began it's descent to the bottom. It slowed down to a stop to let the passengers off and be turned around.

Grace had always been fascinated with the way the cable car was turned. It took three men to pull and push the car onto the wooden roundabout and be rotated so that it faced the way it had just come from, back up the hill. Once it was in position, the riders all clambered on, jostling for the best seats. Tourists of various nationalities climbed on, a cacophony of Japanese, French, German and English all excitedly grabbing what they deemed to be the best seats. Marco was just as animated as the rest of the passengers and Sarah was pleasantly surprised by this. He was usually so reserved and reluctant to show his true emotions that it was nice to see this side of him. Now he was like a young boy as he paid the three fares and gleefully pulled Grace onto his lap. He cheered and shouted with the other passengers as the car made it ascent up the hill. He took hold of Sarahs hand sitting next to him and they sat on the seats that faced outwards and watched the city go by. They went by many city landmarks and saw the Coit Tower, Alcatraz in the distance and coming ever closer, the famous Golden Gate Bridge. Marco made some teasing comment to the elderly lady from Iowa sat next to him as inertia made their thighs touch as the car made its way down the steepest hill towards the Wharf. The whole car yelled in mock fear as the brakeman pretended (as he always did for the benefit of the tourists) that the brakes had failed, and hurrahed in relief when the same hero brakeman managed to stop the cable car before it plunged into the bay.

Grace was still laughing along with her father as all the passengers disembarked. They had to stop and watched to car being turned again, for Grace's benefit before they walked along to the aquatic park in Victoria Park.

They wandered along slowly enjoying the February sunshine and looked up at the Golden Gate Bridge, marvelling at what a fantastic feat of engineering it was. It was two miles long and was orange more than gold. The painting of the bridge was never ending for as soon as it was finished, they painters had to start again at the other end.

They walked along the Golden Gate promenade towards Jefferson Street , Grace in the middle holding each of her parents hands. They walked though the Cannery, now a trendy shopping arcade but which had once been a fruit canning factory. Grace found, in Sarahs opinion, a tacky pink tee-shirt with a huge yellow hibiscus embroidered on the front, which she said she just had to have. It would most likely shrink after one wash but Grace gave her father those 'poor me' eyes.

"Sarah, if she wants it, she can have it. It's only eight dollars." Marco said as he took out his Gucci wallet. He peeled off a twenty dollar bill and gave it to his daughter, who looked up at her mother for a split second before going to the cash register under the watchful eye of her parents to make her purchase.

"Marco, it's not the cost, it really isn't. She has been brought up so far, anyway, to not get everything she wants. Just because she is in with her rich daddy now, there's no reason for that to change. I don't want Grace to be spoiled." Sarah tried to be authoritative.

Marco just looked at her, amused but trying not to show it. Then he said, "Let me tell you a secret." He leant in close, looking around as he did so, so no-one close by would hear the big conspiracy. "I gave her mother a black American Express card." He kissed her cheek.

Sarah smiled wryly. "Point taken. But you know I won't turn out to be a Palm Beach bitch and I don't want our daughter to be either."

"Okay." He kissed her again as Grace returned with her tee shirt wrapped up in a parcel. She gave Marco the change.

Marco just looked at Sarah.

They meandered along the Embarcadero looking at the shops and listening to the street buskers. Once at Pier 39 Grace seemed to take control and pulled Marco along towards the edge of the pier and towards a raucous sound.

"It's Fred, Daddy. Come on and let me show you!"

Laughing, Marco picked Grace up and carried her on his shoulders all the while Grace giving out the directions.

They soon came to the cause of the noise - hundreds of Sea Lions basking in the warm February sun. They were vociferous and malodorous. 'Fred' turned out to be several of the larger male creatures, depending on which one Grace liked the best at the time.

They watched the beasts on the floating wooden decks, some would fight a little, others just lay there sunning themselves. After a while, the stench became too much for Sarah and, feeling quite nauseous, she left the area and walked away until she found a vacant bench to sit on. It was near the ice cream shop and there were street entertainers nearby so she settled in to wait until Marco came looking for her, pleased to give her aching feet a rest.

"Amy?" A familiar voice sounded from behind her.

Sarah looked around and saw the smiling face of Nathan. She smiled back.

"Nathan! What a nice surprise." She patted the bench beside her, a gesture for him to sit with her.

"What are you doing here? I thought you'd gone to Florida."

Sarah nodded. "We have. We're in town for a couple of days to tie up loose ends and fetch our belongings. Marco is with Grace at the Sea Lions."

"How is Grace?"

"Good. She loves having her daddy around."

"So no regrets then?"

Sarah shook her head. "Not a one. It's still early days and me and Marco are still really getting to know one another again. But so far, it's good. How about you?"

"I'm okay. I'm…"

"Sarah. There you are." Nathan had been interrupted by Marco returning with Grace. Marco looked at his wife's companion and thought he recognised him from somewhere.

"Marco, this is Nathan. He works for Don Alessandro." Sarah introduced them. Marco nodded curtly in acknowledgement, recognising Nathan now with Sarah's help but not wanting to make conversation with him.

Nathan suddenly felt very uncomfortable and sensed an atmospheric barrier between himself and Marco. He made his excuses and rose to leave. He felt only friendship towards Sarah now but did not want Marco Delvecchio to get the wrong idea – it would not be in Nathan's best interests. He said goodbye to the family and walked off in the direction of the café where he was meeting a colleague.

Once Nathan had gone, the Delvecchios meandered slowly to the front of the pier and hailed a cab, which took them to Caffe Macaroni in North Beach. They were all very hungry as it was well after lunch time. Sarah ordered a panini with mushrooms, mozzarella and tomatoes with French fries and salad. Marco was quite taken aback when Sarah finished her entire meal and had some of Graces left over chicken salad. He slyly offered her half of his sandwich, which she declined.

When Sarah had been pregnant with Grace, she had lived away from Marco in her own apartment in town. They had separated when Sarah was just two months pregnant as she had discovered her husband was seeing another woman, and not just any other woman, but Marcos ex-fiancée. Sarah being pregnant now was a whole new experience to him and he was quite surprised at how much she was eating. He found it quite a turn on to see her wolf down her food when she was usually so refined when it came to eating. He enjoyed watching her eat and laughed when it gave her indigestion.

In the taxi on the way back to the hotel, Sarah asked to be dropped off at Neimann-Marcus. She had some business to attend to.

Marco frowned questioningly at her.

"You take Grace to the hotel pool, I'll be there shortly. I have something I need to do." She said mysteriously.

He shrugged as Sarah got out of the taxi outside the exclusive department store.

Sarah walked into the building and walked over to the elevators. Seeing the department she wanted, she pushed the button to the floor and waited as the box rose through the building.

Getting out on the third floor with a well dressed lady, Sarah felt as though she had walked into another world. She had rarely been in this building previously, money being a factor. Now, with her husbands unlimited American Express card in her possession, she strode purposefully towards the handbags department and surreptitiously looked around. She could smell the money on the people in the building and although she would always claim she was not interested in Marco's money, she felt very powerful knowing she could buy anything in the store, maybe even the entire building. Seeing the person she wanted Sarah then looked through all the bags until she found the most expensive one there. Picking it up, she went over to the cash desk to pay.

"Oh, hello Amy. We haven't seen you in school for a while." Corey's mother Susan smiled politely at her.

"No, Grace and I have moved back to Palm Beach, Florida with my husband. We are just in town tying up some loose ends" Sarah explained as she handed Susan the two thousand dollar bag to purchase.

Awkwardly, Susan took it from her and glanced at the price tag. "You know, we do have some less expensive than this one." Her little crowd at the school all knew Sarah and Grace wore second hand clothes from the charity shops. This bag was worth more than Sarah earned in a month. Susan felt a little embarrassed for her.

Sarah just smiled as she handed over her American Express card. "I'm sure my husband can afford it."

Susan looked at the card with the different name emblazoned across the bottom. "Is this yours?" She asked, hesitantly.

Sarah nodded. "That's my real name. I was just posing as Amy Cooper to see how underprivileged people live and to see how much we were ostracised for having nothing. It was quite interesting." She spun her yarn.

Susan said nothing as she wrapped Sarahs purchase up but made a note of the name Delvecchio. She would investigate that later. Susan had to admit that Amy or Sarah, whatever her name was certainly looked richer with the clothes she wore and her hair and make up. She no longer looked dowdy. She would run the Delvecchio name through the internet later and see what came up. She couldn't wait to tell the other mums about this!

Sarah never did see Susan or her coven of witches again and so had no idea of the effect that her little stunt had on them. Sarah enjoyed putting the seed into Susan's mind and imagining the effect it would create. Those women had practically ignored her for all the time she was in San Francisco and her daughter never got any invitations to parties or after school teas. Sarah knew Susan would investigate her name and she thrilled in the idea of Susan finding out about her husbands family. It was enough for her to just know that.

Early the next morning, Marco's plane took them all back to West Palm Beach airport and the aircraft landed late in the afternoon local time. Sarah was glad to be back in the warm sunshine and she even felt her daughters spirits lift as they walked down the steps to the waiting car. Their belongings rescued from the Castro were unloaded into a truck to be sent on to the house.

Almost from the moment they arrived home, Marco was shut away in his office with Gabe. He'd been away for just a few days but had things to catch up on and Cliff arrived soon after. There were undercurrents of tension which Sarah assumed were caused by Joe. With Rosa still away on her honeymoon, the house felt empty. Sarah set about organising Graces room and thinking about redecoration. She wanted it more child friendly for her and not still looking like the guest room.

When Marco finally came to bed that night, it was late and Sarah had long since fallen asleep. He crawled into bed beside her failing in his efforts to not wake her.

"What time is it?" She asked sleepily without opening her eyes.

"Just after two." He whispered as he snuggled up beside her, putting his arms around her with his hands settling on her abdomen. He kissed her neck gently.

"Everything okay?"

"It will be." He closed his eyes and fell asleep almost instantly. It had been a long day.

Sarah didn't see much of Marco over the next few days. She kept herself busy by enrolling Grace in the local school to start next Monday. She commissioned a decorator for Graces room, a small firm based in Miami that was headed up by a guy called Jake Shaw. Rosa and Sal returned from their honeymoon with stories to tell of Paris and almost immediately, Rosa lost Salvatore to Marco as there was work to be done.

Both feeling like widows, they decided to go to Miami for a shopping trip. Most of their clothes had been left at a Castro charity shop. Grace needed some new clothes for school and Rosa was looking forward to buying some baby items. Sarahs pregnancy was still a secret so she would have to be careful with her selections.

On the Friday morning, Sarah, Rosa and Grace set off early for the designer shopping mall in Miami. Peter was originally going to drive them but at the last minute, he was needed by Marco. Marco was working in his marina side office all day with Rico, Cliff and Gabe. Sarah didn't ask why Peter suddenly couldn't take them, she just smiled nicely at Marco and drove off in her new Mercedes SUV.

After the hour long drive south to Miami, they decided to start off with refreshments. They headed for a street café and sat outside in the sun drinking coffee and juice for Grace. They mentally planned their route and what they wanted to buy while they were relaxing. Sarah decided she would concentrate on building up Graces wardrobe as until Sarah had had her first scan, she didn't want to tempt fate with maternity clothes. They paid for the drinks and strolled along in the warm sunshine chatting comfortably. The first store they came to was a children's store so they disappeared inside.

Grace immediately found the pink clothes and picked off several items from the racks. Rosa tried to turn her attention to anything other than pink, which because Auntie Rosa had picked them out, Grace naturally liked. Anything her mother liked, Grace turned her nose up at.

With armfuls of jeans, tee-shirts, skirts and sweaters for Grace, they then headed for the baby department. Sarah kept looking at things for her own baby but was pretending to be interested for Ross sake. Rosa bought unisex coloured clothes and a few toys and they all went to pay for them.

In the next store, Sarah bought herself a few bits of clothing to include black linen trousers and some baggy tops, all of which brought about a frown from Rosa.

"I thought you'd be buying some designer clothes for all the functions you have to attend with Marco."

"I need some practical clothing for when I'm sitting around the house on my own while my husband makes his millions." She jested although she was feeling a little bit neglected. She did not want to appear high maintenance but had hoped the honeymoon period would have lasted a little bit longer. She thought back to before she went away, when she and Marco were living together and it had been very different then. Before Giorgio died, Marco had played the part of the heir in waiting and had done just enough to let his father think he was worthy of the responsibility of the family business. Now, it was all on his shoulders and if he got anything wrong, it would be down to him and there would be no-one else to blame. She knew he had a heavy commitment to a lot of people.

After a visit to the lingerie department, they were all weighed down with a fair few shopping bags. Rosa pulled up short, puffing with the exertion.

"The car isn't parked far from here. Why don't we go back and drop these bags off and then we'll be able to carry more!" Rosa laughed. She was enjoying spending money with Sarah.

"Sure. Why don't you two wait here and…"

Sarah was interrupted by a voice behind her.

"Mrs Delvecchio?"

Sarah turned her head and was confronted by an FBI badge in her face. Her heart began to pound.

"Yes." She looked up at the owner of the badge and her heart plummeted.

"Agent Jack Robbins. I believe we have met."

"Yes. What do you want?" Sarah turned her body towards him to give him her full attention. She tried to stay calm but with the intimidating Robbins in front of her and another man in a black suit to her left she felt a little nervous. A car drew up to the curb next to the little crowd.

"We just want to talk to you, Mrs Delvecchio. I understand you are known by that name again?"

"That is my name, yes. What is this all about?"

"It might be better if you came with us, ma'am." Robbins put his hand on Sarahs elbow to lead her to the car at the curb-side.

"To where?" Panic began to grip Sarahs insides although she was still trying to appear outwardly calm. She tried to shrug off Robbins' hand.

"To the FBI office in North Miami." He forcefully pulled her towards the car.

"Mummy?" A timid voice full of tears whimpered.

Sarah forcefully shook off Robbins's hand from her and bent down to calm her daughter whose eyes were full of frightened tears.

"Sweetheart, I want you to go home with Auntie Rosa. I'm just going to have a chat with this man and then I'll be home." She kissed her daughters forehead and stood up. "Daddy will see to that." She said for Robbins benefit.

Sarah looked at Rosa. "Can you call Marco?" She gave her sister the keys to her car.

Rosa nodded, looking more annoyed that their shopping trip had been interrupted than concerned. She knew this was just a hiccup and it would be sorted soon enough.

Sarah went almost willingly to the waiting car so as not to alarm her daughter further and as they pulled away, she saw Rosa already on the phone, presumably to Marco.

"Marco, Sarah has been picked up by the FBI." She wasted no time with any pleasantries. "They have taken her to North Miami."

"Shit! Why now?" he said down the phone more to himself than his sister. "Rico and I are on our way. Who's got her?"

"Jack Robbins."

"Well, that figures." He knew all about Robbins and how he had tried to corner Sarah into trapping him. "What about Grace?"

"She is with me. I'll bring her home now. She is okay, just a little confused."

"As we all are. Thanks Ro, I'll speak to you soon."

Marco disconnected his cell phone as he and Rico practically ran out of the door of his office. He got in the first car he saw which happened to be Rico's and they raced to the FBI regional office in North Miami.

Sarah had arrived at the FBI building and was escorted by Robbins' little side kick to an office. She had been searched for weapons before trundling through miles of corridors in the FBI regional office but had not had her personal effects taken away from her. This surprised Sarah as she was expecting to be strip-searched and thrown into an interrogation room. She allowed herself a little smile. Marco was right - she DID watch too many movies!

She sat alone in the office in front of a desk which had Jack

Robbins name plate on it. The blinds were all closed allowing no view from the office to the outside corridor. The only view in or out of the office came through the pane of glass in the door. There were no family photos adorning the desk in front of Sarah and she was not surprised. Although Robbins was quite good looking, and to some, Sarah supposed, quite attractive, he came across as very anal and obviously more into his job than his private life. Sarahs perception of him was that he would have no time for a personal life. The office was very modern but also sparse, just a desk, two chairs and some filing cabinets against the walls. A large framed black and white photograph of the New York skyline before the collapse of the twin towers was the only decorative object. The room was very tidy, nothing out of place and the papers on Robbins's desk were stacked up neatly.

    Sarah was made to wait in an effort to intimidate her. She would have walked out only there was an armed uniformed officer guarding the door. She didn't think she was under arrest so figured she could just get up and walk out at any time. However, her knowledge of U.S law was very limited and didn't want to try and find out. Besides, she knew Marco and Rico would be here soon and they'd straighten all this out.

    After a half hour or so, Robbins walked into his office with a file under his arm and a Styrofoam cup of coffee, which he sipped from.

    He was perhaps in his mid forties. His jet black hair had streaks of grey at the temples which only added to his good looks. He was just short of six foot and carried a few extra pounds although he carried it well. With no family to go home to, he probably ate a lot of take-outs, Sarah assumed.

    Behind him, his side kick wandered in. He looked barely out of high school and went to lean against the far wall next to the filing cabinet. He glared at Sarah to try and intimidate her but it made her want to laugh. She'd seen scarier pelicans on the beach than this little upstart.

    "So, why am I here?" Sarah decided to kick-start the conversation. She felt she had been here long enough without any real explanation.

    "We have things to discuss." He said without looking at her. Robbins sat down in his comfortable looking chair opposite Sarah and placed his coffee on a mat on the desk. He opened up the file he had brought in with him and browsed through it, saying nothing.

"Aren't you going to offer a pregnant woman a drink?" She glared at him. "I could also do with a comfort break."

He looked up at her surprised but quickly recovered. "Later. I want to know why you are back in Florida."

Sarah looked surprised. "I decided to give my marriage another go. Is that a crime?"

"No, but three and a half years ago, you and I made a deal. Now I think I have lived up to my side of the bargain. We kept you alive, kept you safe and delivered your daughter safely back to you. We even gave you the cash advance you requested. You don't seem to have kept your agreement with us. That's the crime."

Sarah smiled icily at him. "So that's what this is all about. You want your money back?" Sarah asked facetiously, knowing full well that it had nothing to do with the five thousand dollars.

"I don't want the money, Sarah. I want the information you promised me." He closed the file and folded his arms across his chest.

"What information, Agent Robbins?"

"Information on your slime ball husband and his Family. His associates."

"That's not very complimentary. He is the father of my children."

"Yes, how about that? Are you happy sleeping with the man who tried to kill you and left you for dead?"

"That's very personal, Robbins. Besides, I don't know who it was but I do now know that it wasn't Marco who shot me." She lied.

"Really? That's not what you said three years ago."

"I was confused and wanted my daughter back. I was angry with my husband at the time."

"So why run from him?"

"That is between my husband and me. My marital affairs are nothing to do with the FBI. Now, I really need that comfort break." She smiled sweetly at him, although it was covered in acid.

He looked across the desk for a moment and then stood. "I'll see if I can find someone to take you then." He left the room with the Prom King following obediently behind.

As the door closed, Sarah breathed deeply. She had handled it well but her hands were shaking. She hoped Marco and Rico would be here soon. She knew she would have to keep stalling Robbins until the cavalry arrived and surely they couldn't be much longer? It was only lunchtime so the traffic on the I-95 shouldn't be an issue.

A few minutes later, Robbins came back into the office and he was alone. He looked pointedly at his reluctant witness.

"There are no women around to escort you at the moment. You'll have to wait." No preamble, no apology.

Sarah stared at him. "Robbins, are you married?"

He shook his head.

"So I'm guessing no kids then?"

He shook his head again. "Why?" He should be the one to the ask the questions.

"Well, that would explain why you are being such a numbnuts then. Even so, you must realise that pregnant woman need comfort breaks more often?"

He looked at her with mild distaste. She was a harder woman than she had been last time they had met. He wondered for a moment what had changed her from the scared, naïve but likeable woman she had once been. When she had woken up from the hospital bed after being left for dead in the Glades, she was like a scared rabbit and it was only the presence of his armed officers that had enabled her to sleep. He remembered her tears as she told him that she wanted Grace back safely and then she would tell him whatever he wanted. He had almost lost his heart to the terrified woman and did everything he could to help her, to the point of going against protocol while getting her out of a dangerous situation. Without the knowledge or approval of his superior, Robbins had hidden Sarah in Memphis with the five thousand dollars and arranged to get Grace to her with a staged kidnapping that was made to look like the work of the Delvecchios enemy at the time, the Caruso family. Robbins had nearly lost his job over the incident and had been severely reprimanded, a blot on his copybook that he now blamed Sarah for.

Robbins turned his attention back to the present. "Do you have proof that you are pregnant?"

"Sorry." Although her tone intimated that she was anything but. "Only eight weeks gone so no scans or anything yet. Do you want to give me an internal exam to prove it?"

He just shrugged.

Sarah leaned forwards towards Robbins. "Marco will rip your fucking heart out for this!" She hissed viciously, her face screwed up in anger

"The language is not necessary, Mrs Delvecchio and neither is the threat."

"We don't make threats, Robbins." She smiled, her facial features changing back to a sweet delicate lady.

They stared at each other for a few moments, neither wanting to back down. A knock at the door forced Robbins gaze away and Sarah smiled in victory. It was the Prom King beckoning for his superior to come outside.

Sarah sat back in the chair and wondered again how much longer Marco would be. She looked over her shoulder to see what Robbins was doing. He was having a conspiratorial close-up with the Prom King. They both kept glancing through the glass door at Sarah. Robbins suddenly shrugged and then came back into the room.

Robbins sat back in his chair and stared at Sarah for a moment sizing up the situation. "It would appear your legal counsel have arrived, Sarah. I understand that your murderous husband is waiting outside the building."

The door had opened during Robbins' last statement.

"That's slander, Robbins. You have no proof of any wrongdoing." Rico had arrived and stood behind Sarah with his hand on her shoulder as if to reassure her.

The FBI agent stared up at Rico and Sarah could almost see the look of defeat in his eyes. She gloated inwardly. She had suddenly grasped the same dislike of law enforcement as her husband had. She felt almost smug knowing that she would be out of here straight away now that Rico was here to guide her.

"Perhaps we would have proof if your 'client' started talking." He described Sarah with distaste.

"Mrs Delvecchio doesn't have any idea of what you might want."

"Three years ago she knew plenty. Are you telling me that she has forgotten all of that or is it just selective memory loss?"

"Robbins, I think you have forgotten my bathroom request." Sarah piped up. She was getting desperate now. She also wanted to see if he would refuse her again now that Rico was here.

"I already told you. There are no female officers to escort you." He attempted to make a stand against her.

"Is my client under arrest?" Rico enquired.

Robbins said nothing but shook his head slowly, defeated.

"In that case, Mrs Delvecchio is free to go where she pleases, including the bathroom."

Sarah stood up, scrapping the chair back as she did so. As she left the room, she could not resist smiling victoriously at Robbins.

"Jesus! Pregnant women!" He said under his breath.

It was loud enough for Rico to hear and he looked up sharply. "Pregnant? She's pregnant?"

Robbins grinned like he now had the upper hand. "You know nothing about that? So does that mean she is lying?"

"I don't know about that. Maybe they just hadn't got around to telling anyone. My main concern is your treatment of her, especially in light of what you have just said."

"She was treated with respect." Robbins sighed wearily.

"Really?"

Robbins shrugged. "You know we can arrest her for withholding information."

"Information that you don't know that she has. It's just your fantasy."

"I know she knows something and enough for us to get a grip on Marco Delvecchio. I'll bring her down with him if I have to, pregnant or not."

Rico sat back and put the lid on his Cartier pen. "Robbins, you know nothing and you have nothing. You followed her around waiting for her to be in a vulnerable position before picking her up. If you really had something you would have come to the house with the law on your side instead of praying on her naivety and hoping she would tell you anything that you wanted to hear. Just like last time when you allegedly made this deal that no-one on the planet can corroborate. Marco Delvecchio is an honest business man and your harassment of him and his wife will land you in trouble. You have no proof of any wrong doing, just suspicions because of my clients Italian ancestry."

"In my experience, that is often enough."

"His taxes are filed and up to date. He donates considerable amounts of money to worthy charities and he employs a good many people."

"A real pillar of society." Robbins sneered.

"If you have issues with Mr Delvecchio, perhaps you should talk to him and straighten them out instead of badgering his wife. However I must warn you that your behaviour will be reported to your superior if it should continue." Rico knew of Robbins' previous trouble on this 'case' and he knew the remark would be enough for the Agent to back off a little.

They eyeballed each other until the door was opened and Sarah appeared at the doorway.

"Mrs Delvecchio, we are leaving now. Agent Robbins has detained you long enough without cause." He stood and turned away from him.

Robbins let out a huge sigh knowing for the moment at least, he had lost the battle. He drummed his fingers on his desk as Rico and Sarah walked down the corridor. He knew plenty about the Delvecchios but had no physical proof. Testimony was hard to come by as witnesses were often eradicated, too scared to talk or paid off. Again, no proof because the Delvecchios were damned good at covering their tracks.

Robbins stood up and walked around the desk pondering his next move. He kicked the waste bin in frustration, scattering the contents. He decided he would call his team together for a brain storming session rather than just go back to old fashioned surveillance but he knew that it would eventually boil down to that.

Rico pulled into a rest area off the highway after they had been travelling for about half an hour and had put Miami firmly behind them. Marco and Sarah were in the back, holding hands but not a word had been said while they had been in the car. As the car rolled to a stop, Sarah turned to her husband in confusion, having a frightening sense of deja-vu. Her mind flashed back to the Everglades.

"Marco?" She questioned him.

He smiled reassuringly and squeezed her hand. "It's okay. We just need to talk somewhere safe."

Sarah looked around and saw all of the trucks and drivers in the vicinity and her mind settled. Knowing her fears had been ridiculous, she climbed out of the car and followed Marco and Rico over to a picnic bench, the roar of the traffic a distant hum. As Sarah sat down, Rico went over to the 7-11 shop and brought a couple of drinks. Sarah hadn't realised how parched she was until she started to drink the fizzy orange drink. Rico sat opposite Sarah and Marco sat to her right, straddling the bench and facing her. He had his hand on her thigh.

Rico finally loosened his tie leant towards Sarah. "Tell us what happened, beginning with when Robbins picked you up this morning."

Sarah cast her mind back to the start of the morning when she, Rosa and Grace had been interrupted in their shopping spree. She recounted the journey to the FBI office where she had sat in the back of the car, locked in but not handcuffed. There had been no conversation then between herself and the Agents. No-one had really said anything much when they entered the FBI offices and surprisingly politely searched her bag. When she got to the part when Robbins entered the room to begin to question her, Marco interrupted.

"What did you tell him?" He asked with impatience. His fingers were drumming on the bench in agitation.

"Nothing! Give me some credit!" She snapped back.

Marco opened his mouth to retaliate but Rico held up his hand to silence him and take control of the conversation.

"What we mean, Sarah, is what answers did you give to his questions?"

Sarah took a deep breath and thought about her conversation with Robbins.

"He asked me why I came back to Florida. I told him I wanted to be with my husband." At this, she looked at Marco and smiled, harmony restored. "He queried why I left in the first place and I told him it was none of his business, just marital differences. Then he asked me about being shot." She looked at Marco again. "I told him that I'd just said it was you because I was angry and wanted Grace."

"What did he say to that?"

"Not much. I was just trying to stall him until you got there."

"Is that all? Anything else we should know about?"

Sarah shifted uncomfortably on the concrete bench. "Well, I may have said that you will kill him…" She looked uncertainly at Marco.

He laughed. "I will, given the chance! I don't think we need to worry about him any more, he's just fishing. He'll leave us alone now we've embarrassed him."

Sarah was not so sure. "Rico, can they make me say anything?"

He shrugged. "Do you know anything?"

"I know lots but nothing about Marcos businesses apart from the fact he is successful. Besides, how could they prove that I know anything?"

"They can't. We have nothing to worry about. Let's get home." Rico stood and walked towards the car, with Marco and Sarah following behind him.

Marcos assurance at being left alone by Robbins and his team were a little premature. Sarah became increasingly aware over the next few weeks of shadows following her, cars in the rear view mirror and suits on street corners. When she collected Grace from school there was usually a dark coloured car nearby watching her, once or twice taking photos of her. She informed Marco and Rico of every incident, getting more and more anxious as each event happened.

CHAPTER TEN

Things appeared to quieten down for the next few weeks. The FBI presence seemed to slacken off a little, at least a noticeable difference in Sarahs eyes. Sarah settled down to Palm Beach life quite nicely and her friendship with Andrea blossomed although Marco asked that she keep her pregnancy secret for just a little bit longer.

Sarah's first hospital appointment was due in the middle of April. Marco was eagerly looking for ward to seeing his child on the black and white grainy screen, something he had missed out on with Grace. But although Marco had promised to go with Sarah to the appointment, something came up and he let her down at the last moment. Feeling a little spiteful, Sarah went against Marcos wishes and told Andrea that she was pregnant. She wanted her friend to accompany her to the hospital if her useless husband couldn't or wouldn't. Andrea, delighted at the news agreed to go at short notice. As cross with Marco as she was, Sarah was all smiles and determined that he would not ruin this special moment as she saw her baby for the first time.

The scan revealed a healthy baby and a due date of 24th September. With a photo of the baby, it suddenly felt real for Sarah and she couldn't wait to start telling people. Other than the last few days of morning sickness and an ample bosom, she showed no signs of being pregnant so this made it real.

As she and Andrea left the hospital filled with excitement, Sarah still had the photo scan in her hand. She saw a Ford Taurus parked across the street in a tow zone and knew it would be Robbins's cronies. In mid-sentence, she stopped talking to Andrea and strode purposefully over to the vehicle.

Leaning down against the drivers door, she saw Robbins in the passenger seat. The driver was not someone that she was familiar with, an attractive African American female in her early thirties.

Sarah banged on the window and it was automatically opened by the female driver. "Hey Robbins! You wanted proof that I'm pregnant, here it is." She flashed the photo in his general direction.

He glanced at the black and white and then returned his gaze at Sarah.

"Congratulations but that's not what I want and you know it. I want the baby's father – I guess that is Delvecchio, right?"

Sarah snarled at him. "You are despicable, do you know that? If I see you following me again, I will sue you and the FBI for harassment, do you understand?"

The window was wound up, signalling that Robbins didn't care about her threats and the conversation was over.

Sarah stormed back to her car to where Andrea was waiting for her. She was hopping mad and wanted Marco to do something about it.

Arriving home, she calmly walked into Marcos office and told him what had happened with the FBI at the hospital.

"I'll sort it out, I promise." He told her. "How did the appointment go?" He smiled, trying to placate her.

"Like you care." She said sulkily. She was still upset with him that he had ducked out of the appointment in the first place.

"Of course I care but something came up that was unavoidable." He walked round to the other side of the desk and put his arms around his sullen wife.

"Us having this baby is unavoidable, Marco. I thought you were happy about it. You missed out on Grace and I just hoped that you would take an interest in this one."

He dotted kisses on Sarahs face to win her over. "I do care. I love you and I'm sorry."

Sarah pulled away from his embrace, unconvinced. "You are

supposed to protect me from this kind of shit, Marco. I do not need the aggravation of the FBI following me around and my husband missing important appointments with me. I wonder what Don Miotto might say about it!"

"Are you going to throw that at me every time we have a row or a disagreement?"

"Maybe. Just get this sorted." She scowled at him and left him to contemplate her words.

The harassment appeared to slacken off over the next few days. She still saw the Taurus parked up from time to time but it did not follow her around and there were no more confrontations between Sarah and Robbins.

That was probably why Sarah was confused when Marco introduced her to Harry Pilgrim. She was sat in the sun by the pool with a magazine when she heard her husband talking to someone in a low tone as he walked down the path towards her. She looked up from the magazine and saw the stranger with her husband. He was marginally taller than Marco and quite skinny lending him a slightly lanky look. His hair was a light coloured brown and he wore trendy sun glasses that sat on his hawk like nose. He was a very strange looking man. He smiled at her as he noticed her looking at him showing off uneven teeth.

They came and stood next to Sarah and she squinted up at them both, somewhat blinded by the glare of the sun.

"Sarah, sweetheart, I want you to meet Harry."

Harry leant down and offered Sarah his hand. "Pleased to meet you, Mrs Delvecchio." came the English accent with a slight cockney twang.

"Nice to meet you too, Harry. Where about in England are you from?" She enquired politely.

"I used to live in East London but moved to Cornwall before I came out here."

"Are you here on business?"

Marco glanced at Harry with a 'here we go' kind of smile and sat down on the sun-lounger next to Sarah. Harry remained standing.

"Sarah, I want you to get to know Harry real well. He's going to be around for quite a while. Especially around you and Grace." He had not been looking forward to having this conversation with Sarah since he had made the decision a couple of days ago. She could be feisty when she wanted to be.

"Well, I'm sure Harry is very nice but I'm not sure that I understand."

"Harry is going to be looking out for you and Grace. He's going to be responsible for yours and Grace's safety and well-being."

Sarah looked up at Harry and then back to Marco. It dawned on her. "You mean like a bodyguard?"

Marco nodded slowly. "Yes, kinda like a bodyguard."

Sarah looked back at her magazine. The conversation was over as far as she was concerned. "Well, I don't need a bodyguard. You can give Harry something else to do."

"Sarah, this is not negotiable." Marcos voice took on one of authority. "There is more shit going on than you realise and I need to know that you and Grace will be safe when you are not with me or in the house."

The authoritative tone was not lost on Sarah. She knew how far she could safely push him. She would have to find another way of ditching Harry.

"Fine. Whatever." Her tone told Marco that it was anything but fine. "I'm sure Harry will be thrilled with my routine which starts now, Harry, with picking up Grace from school." Angry, she stood, leaving Marco still sat on the sun-lounger and flounced up to the house.

Once in possession of her car keys, she slammed the front door shut. Harry was already stood waiting by her silver Mercedes SUV and tried a friendly smile.

"Do you want to drive Harry or am I still allowed to do that?" Without waiting for an answer, she got into the drivers seat and started the engine. Harry clambered into the passengers seat and strapped himself in as Sarah floored the gas pedal and kicking up dust and shingle from the drive, headed for the gates. She shouted at the poor unsuspecting men at the gate house for them to hurry up and open the god damn gates before she opened them with the fender of her car.

Harry watched her with something close to amusement as she

drove along, her face flushed red with anger.

"Sarah, why are you so angry?" He asked calmly.

She ignored him, determined to make his life miserable so he asked for another assignment from Marco.

"Sarah?" He prompted not about to give up.

On arriving at the school, Sarah parked up and then turned to Harry.

"I'm angry because he doesn't trust me" She paused. "Do you know our history, Harry?"

He shook his head. "That's not my concern. I'm here to ensure that you and Grace don't get hurt."

Sarah laughed. This man didn't look like he could protect himself. "And what are your credentials, Harry?"

He took a deep breath. Marco had warned him that she would probably give him a hard time. "I have been working for Marco for the last three years doing various things for him. He trusts me. Before that, I was chief of security for one of those big cruisers out of Miami Port which was how I met your husband. I did that for ten years and got sick of booting drunken Americans off my ship. I wanted something a bit more…meaty."

"Well, you'll certainly get that working for Marco. Have you ever fired a gun, Harry? Have you ever killed a man?"

Harrys green eyes bored into Sarahs. She was much calmer now but he decided a dose of the truth might still be in order.

"How much do you really know, Sarah? How much has Marco told you? You see, I don't think you are in touch with the world in which you live in. I'm going to tell you some things now that I shouldn't but as you are behaving like a spoilt kid, I think it will be in your best interests to know. Your brother in law, Joe? He's off the rails. He's way out in space. He's building his own little empire around his drugs world that doesn't include your husband, your daughter or that new baby of yours. He is certainly no fan of yours. Then there is the little matter of the FBI who seem determined on tramping over you to get to Marco. Now then…" He looked across the front of the car to Sarah who was now completely calm but had a very frightened look about her. "Are you going to stop with the hysteria and allow your husband to protect you, through me?"

Sarah nodded slightly, feeling chastened. She was still trying to absorb Harrys words. She looked across at the school gates and saw the kids begin to spill out of the classrooms. She got out of the car and let Harry follow her. As they stood waiting for Grace to be released from class, Sarah looked at Harry.

"Joe wants to kill us all?" She asked quietly.

Harry put a hand on her shoulder. "We haven't had any specific threats but Marco, rightly, doesn't want to take the chance. It may all be nothing, but until the threat goes away, you and I will become inseparable."

Sarah laughed nervously. "Will you be sleeping at the bottom of my bed?"

Harry dared a smile. "I'm not that kinky. You just need to let me know any time you leave the grounds."

Sarah soon got used to having Harry around. Despite his gawky appearance he had a very authoritative air about him and Sarah felt safe having him around. Most of the time, he was just a shadow in the background, inconspicuously tailing Sarah when she went shopping but disappearing as soon as Sarah arrived back to the safety of her home. At the beginning of June, Rosa gave birth to a girl. She and Sal named her Adina after his mother. Sarah enjoyed being an aunt and it made her look forward to the birth of her own baby just another three months away.

Grace celebrated her sixth birthday in style by inviting her entire class to the house for a pool party. Sarah insisted that some of Marcos employees were around to act as lifeguards as twenty six year olds in a pool was asking for trouble. They had a barbecue after wards and the entire event passed off without incident.

Sarah's thirty-first birthday was just after this and she wanted to keep it low key with her advanced state of pregnancy. She wanted a girls night out with Andrea, just a dinner and a pleasant evening. Andrea had recently befriended a woman by the name of Beth Rogers which Sarah was happy to invite along. She didn't have many close friends or people she could trust. Most people were friendly to her because they were scared not to be because of Marco.

Sarah agreed to be the designated driver so with Harry sat in the back of the car, she drove to Andreas house to collect her and Beth. They then drove to Pompano Beach to a restaurant on the shore that she and Marco had been to a couple of times before. Once they had arrived, Harry made himself scarce by sitting at the bar. He was out of earshot but still in visual contact with Sarah in case he was needed. He sat on a bar stool drinking club sodas and chatted up the bar maid, a blond bombshell with bosoms to match.

The women chose to sit outside in the fresh air near a patio heater. It was mid June but unusually chilly and they were glad for the outdoor heater and the warmth it gave off. The day had been hot and wet but when the sun had set, it became cooler and was more noticeable after the heat of the day.

Andrea and Beth ordered a bottle of white wine and Sarah just a lime and soda. After the waiter had taken their food orders, Beth began to open up a little. She had only known Andrea for a short time since meeting at the Country Club and neither woman really knew a great deal about her.

After her second glass of wine, she moved on to the touchy subject of her scoundrel husband.

"Luke is a great guy when he's not drinking. I keep saying to myself that I'll leave him but when he's sober I love him so much and can't bear to be without him. He keeps promising me that he'll get help and give up the drink and for a while, he will abstain. Then something will happen, a bad day at the office or something and he will have just one little drink. That leads onto another and then another. That's when he gets nasty and won't let me leave him." She stared into space and took another mouthful of wine. She then looked at Andrea and Sarah in turn, waiting for some disapproving words or a frown. Both of these women had perfect marriages at least on the outside and couldn't possibly know what she was going through. They would never understand what made Beth stay.

"Men can be very persuasive, Beth. They all promise to change. Some do but most, invariably don't." Andrea answered.

Sarah reached for Beth's hand across the table. "You have to do whatever you think is the right choice for you. Not for Luke, for you." Sarah insisted as she glanced over Beth's shoulder briefly. Harry was still on his bar stool and seemingly making in-roads with the bar maid. She was smiling flirtatiously with Harry but Sarah guessed it was just part of the job description.

Their appetisers arrived and Sarah dived in. She was ravenous as always. She would have a hard time shifting the extra weight after the baby was born.

"So what made you and Marco get back together again?" Beth asked.

"He promised to change and it would appear that he has." Sarah said, simply. "I guess I'm lucky."

"Why did you split up in the first place?" Beth pursued it.

Sarah began to get a little edgy discussing her relationship with a near perfect stranger.

"Just a difference of opinion." She answered, unwilling to say more. It was in the past as far as Sarah was concerned, no need to bring it up or even think about it. She glanced over at Harry again who was being poured another club soda.

Andrea saw this and threw in a new direction for the conversation, aware that Sarah did not want to talk about Marco with Beth.

"So Sarah, tell us about Harry then." Her eyes sparkled as she spoke.

Sarah put her fork laden with mozzarella and tomatoes down on her plate and she couldn't help but smile. "Harry." She mused. "I don't know an awful lot about him really. He's English, he's funny, he's great." She shrugged. Despite her early opposition to his presence, they were becoming friends.

"How do you know him?" Beth asked.

"He's worked for Marco for a number of years, apparently. He is a bit of a mystery to me really, but I do know that he used to be head honcho for security on the cruise ships out of Miami Port."

"Why do you need the security?" Beth asked, fascinated by Sarah and Marco's life.

Sarah shrugged. "It's just what Marco wants at the moment." She felt a presence at her side and looked up.

"Well if it isn't my dear sister in law! I thought it might be you."

"Joe. What do you want?" Sarah asked flatly.

"I came here for a quiet dinner. After all, it is my neighbourhood. And I find you here. What a treat!" His sarcastic tone intimated that it was anything but. He hated this woman with a passion that he had never felt before, an over-riding feeling that not even the best cocaine could dull. He dreamt about her. Not sweet dreams, but dreams where he was ending her life in the most painful way, tormented and drawn out. He looked down at her now and imagined he was slitting her throat and he would watch as the dark almost black blood he felt sure must run in her veins ran down her neck and dripped into a pool on the floor. Joe smiled to himself as he heard the heartbeat of her unborn child slow down and eventually stop. A double whammy.

One day.

Smiling sickly sweet and wanting him to leave, Sarah said, "Well, I'd hate to keep you."

"You don't keep me and neither does my brother. I see you are both polluting the world with your brats again?" He smiled malevolently. He was wired.

His words brought a reaction from Andrea who had been until that moment trying to stay out of the conversation. Cliff had told her a little bit about the trouble that was brewing within the Delvecchio family.

"Joe! That is an evil thing to say. That is your flesh and blood!"

He laughed. "So you aren't convinced of my brothers paternity either. It does seem strange that the first day she lands back in Florida, she claims to get pregnant with my brothers child. Believe me sweetheart, that thing has nothing to do with me." He patted Andrea on the head in a very condescending manner.

Andrea snatched his hand away and scowled at him.

Sarah once again looked over Beth's shoulder wondering why Harry wasn't here to sort this out – that was what he was paid very handsomely for. With dread, Sarah saw that Harrys bar stool was empty along with the glass that he had been drinking from. She knew she would have to deal with this herself.

"Joe, I think you should just go. I don't want to talk to you and you don't want to talk to me."

"You're right." He sneered. "I don't want to talk to you. I don't want to see you. I want you dead. I want at the very least, for you to leave Palm Beach and Florida for good taking all of your dubiously fathered brats with you. Maybe then I can reconcile with my brother."

"Your falling out with Marco has nothing to do with me as you well know." Sarah was starting to get extremely agitated and she could feel her blood pressure rising. Short of asking a waiter to move Joe on she wasn't sure how she could get rid of him. The waiters in this restaurant didn't look as though they could move their bowels let alone a determined Joe Delvecchio.

"You just keep telling yourself that Sarah, if it makes you feel better."

Sarah looked down at her unfinished Caprese and felt a small wave of hopelessness and something akin to fear wash over her. It was then she saw the shadow fall over her plate. She looked up and with relief that almost turned into tears, she saw Harry stood in front of her, next to Andrea, his arms cross defiantly as he stared at Joe. "So, you must be the unwanted brother." Harry asked calmly.

Joe turned to Harry and appraised the smart but casually dressed and strange looking man talking to him. Despite his mawkishness, Joe liked what he saw and was somewhat intrigued. "I guess that would be me. And you must be the bodyguard." He spoke with a casualness as though he were addressing an old friend. "I heard my gutless brother had put someone on his slut of a wife. Too cowardly to do it himself."

Harrys interest piqued. "You heard?"

Joe realised his slight faux-pas and ignored the question. "So are you going to ask me to leave then?" He challenged Harry, smiling slyly.

Harry shook his head. "No. I'm going to tell you leave. I will escort you out forcibly if necessary and I don't care about causing a scene." He eyeballed Joe almost daring him to defy him, still smiling coldly.

Joe stood down after assessing his options. He'd taken a strange kind of shine to the Englishman and wanted him to drop his guard. There would be other times.

"Anything you say." Joe half bowed in a mocking way. Still grinning, he walked through the centre of the restaurant terrace with his male dinner companion in tow and out through the gates that went out through the garden to the parking lot.

Sarahs pulse rate began to return to normal. Harry squeezed her shoulder and asked if she was okay.

"I'm fine. Joe wouldn't try anything. Not here, in public anyway."

Harry nodded but inwardly, he wasn't so sure. When Joe was high as he so obviously was then, he'd think he was invincible and capable of anything. He left the women to their meal, returning back to his perch at the bar and ordered another club soda from Erin.

"So are you a knight in shining armour to all women?" She asked playfully as she mixed his drink.

He shook his head. "No. Just to that one. Her husband pays me well and one day, I'm going to enjoy roughing up that guy." He smiled happily showing off his crooked front teeth.

After dropping Beth and Andrea off at their respective homes, Harry drove Sarah back to the mansion. She was subdued after the events at the restaurant and spoke very little on the journey. It had brought home what Marco and Harry had been saying all along, that Joe did have ideas of his own that didn't include her and it scared her.

Harry waited out of sight in Marcos office and allowed Sarah to tell Marco her version of events of the evening, knowing the boss would want to talk to him after he was through with his wife.

He was right. After Sarah had gone upstairs to bed, Marco came into his office to find him. He poked his head around the door and told Harry to walk with him. They wandered slowly around the gardens to talk while Marco did his spot checks.

"What concerns me the most Marco, is someone has apparently told your brother that you've hired me."

Marco nodded in the dark. "Sarah did not pick up on that. Do you think we have a mole?"

Harry shrugged. "It's something to be mindful of." The thought had been going through his mind all evening but didn't really worry him. It was a commonplace event. The Delvecchios had moles planted in various places, including government offices.

Marcos mind was in overdrive as he thought about the consequences of his brother planting a spy in his camp. He had too much to lose if Joe stumbled across something he shouldn't and knew he must find out who was betraying him and eliminate the problem.

"We need to look into this, Harry and route out the problem. We'll talk tomorrow." He left Harry in the garden by the mostly unused tennis court and went to find Gabe.

Despite several attempts to ascertain the source of Joe's information, it was six weeks down the line before they were discovered. Marco and Gabe had let unimportant snippets of information be passed to several of his men in turn and then followed it up see if anything came of it. Marco had spoken in passing to Karl Shepstone, one of his lower echelon soldiers that Sarah had her final hospital appointment and was giving him grief for not being able to make it. It was a plausible explanation as Marco had missed all of her appointments, much to his detriment in her eyes. It was just four weeks before the baby was due and Sarah was actually having lunch at Andreas. Grace was at school and to Sarahs puzzlement, Marco and Harry drove Sarah to Andreas before driving off in her Mercedes SUV saying they needed to take it to the garage.

In reality, they drove it to the maternity wing of Colombia Hospital and parked the car towards the rear. Turning off the engine, they sat back to wait behind the blacked out windows to see what might happen.

After half an hour, Marco was beginning to get fidgety when he saw the beat up Camero he knew belonged to Joe cruise up and down the lines of parked cars. He and Harry watched it as it turned around and began to slowly crawl towards the SUV with it's blacked out windows. Marco knew Joe had several beat up cars for his nefarious business transactions as he felt it would not be so obvious as his BMW that he usually favoured.

The black wreck slowed almost to a halt as it drove past the SUV that Marco and Harry were sat still in and then it speeded up slightly. It eventually found a parking space one row over and five cars down which it fronted into, allowing it's occupants a good view of the front of Sarahs vehicle.

Harry slowly crawled onto the back seat of the SUV. He had to make it appear as though the car was empty and not to rock it. Very slowly, he opened the tailgate and jumped outside, closing the door quietly behind him. He sneaked along the rows of parked cars towards the Camero so as not to let it's occupants see his advance. With great stealth, he circled around and double-backed to the ageing vehicle. Coming up behind it, he pulled his gun from his waistband ready and with a satisfied grin on his face, he knocked on the passenger side front window.

After a brief moment of hesitation in which the cars occupants weighed up their limited options, the window was wound down with a screech of glass that really did not want to budge.

"Ah. Mr Delvecchio Junior." Harry said, knowing his choice of title would just infuriate Joe. "What a pleasant surprise." Harry was enjoying his work.

"What? What do you want?" Joe demanded, pissed off that he had been found out.

"I was just passing when I saw your run-around. What happened to your BMW?"

"This is a good car but I don't need to explain myself to you."

"Of course not. But tell me this. Why are you in the maternity wing of a hospital?"

A pause. Then, "Like I said, I don't need to explain myself to you." Joe turned from Harry and looked straight ahead. He had not seen Sarahs SUV pull out of its space and head around to where he was parked.

Harry shrugged. "Okay then. Well, I have to go. I have a living to earn and no time to waste sitting around ogling pregnant women or their husbands." Harry couldn't resist. He'd heard about Joe's tendencies. He laughed at his own humour and Joe growled an obscenity at him that made Harry laugh a little bit more. He walked backwards to where Marco had pulled up waiting for him, grinning at his own humour but not taking his eyes or attention off the volatile Joe.

"At least we know where the leak has come from." Harry said as he climbed into the car and settled back onto the black leather seat.

Marco nodded but said nothing. He'd already called Gabe and told him to reach out for Shepstone but not to alert him. Marco wanted to deal with this himself. It was personal.

Sarah was sat in the kitchen drinking tea. She'd felt unwell shortly after arriving at Andrea's house – the two year old David running riot did not do much to ease Sarahs nerves. Andrea dropped her home less than half an hour after she had arrived. Sarah decided that with just four weeks to go before baby number two arrived, she really should take things easy.

Flicking through her copy of the Palm Beach paper – it was better than any gossip magazine – the door to the kitchen opened and Karl Shepstone walked briskly in. He stopped short when he saw the Boss's wife sat at the breakfast bar supping tea.

"Hey, Mrs D. I thought you had a hospital appointment." He ventured, unsure.

Sarah shook her head and put her paper down. "No. I'm all done with those until Junior here puts in an appearance." She looked down at her huge belly and put her hand protectively on the bump.

Karl looked confused. "I thought Marco said…" His voice trailed off. He WAS confused.

And concerned.

"Karl? I'm glad you are here. I'd like a word please. Now." Marco had entered the kitchen from the hallway and stood looking very austerely at Shepstone. His voice was full of malice although his tone was level. Harry stood behind Karl by the French doors that lead to the garden. They had effectively blocked all escape routes for Karl.

Karl stayed where he was while he thought about it and centred himself. There was a possibility that he was in deep trouble but if he stayed calm, he might be okay. He thought this day would come eventually ever since he had come to work for Marco just under a year ago. Not long after, Joe had approached him and offered him money if he were to report certain things back to him. He also offered Karl a more senior position that could take him years to achieve while working for Marco. He was fairly new to the business so he was also using this time to make his bones and take his experience to Joe's crew when the time was right. He knew though, that if he played it calm and got himself out of this mess, Joe would take him now.

"Sure Boss." He went for the subservient option and walked slowly towards Marco who now held the kitchen door open for him to pass. Harry followed the two towards the office. As the trio, lead by

Shepstone walked into the cavernous hallway, Karl looked to the front door but found it guarded by two men both with their guns on show. His options were shrinking by the minute as he was now at the door to Marcos office and he knew he was running out of time to conjure an exit. He glanced towards the living room, it's hallway door wide open and just beyond that, Karl could make out that the French doors that ran along the outside wall were all open to let the hot August air in. Karl was only nineteen and in much better shape than his ageing boss or his side kicks and Karl realised that if he could get to the doors and make it to the back entrance, he might just have a chance. He'd go straight to Joe.

Without thinking for a second more, Karl made a break for it. Marco shouted out behind him but he didn't run after him. Instead Harry dashed through the sitting room in pursuit of Karl. Marco doubled back and walked calmly back into the kitchen passed a perplexed Sarah. The two men on the front door dashed behind him like a whirlwind, causing Sarah to start in surprise and spill her tea.

"Marco?" She queried.

He ignored her and walked out of the door and onto the patio, following along at a leisurely pace.

With several men shouting and hot tea in her lap, Sarah felt close to tears for unknown reasons. She felt like she was a spectator in a fox hunt. She saw Scott run down the path and past the pool towards the back gate which lead onto a lane and eventually to the beach. His gun was drawn. Whoever was trying to evade capture was obviously headed that way. She assumed it to be Karl as he had just been summoned personally by her husband.

Thankful that Grace was spending the day at a friends house, Sarah left her paper and what was left of her tea and went upstairs to change. She could hear the dogs barking as they were let loose to scent out Karl. Sarah lumbered up the stairs and along the hallway to her bedroom. From the relative safety of the balcony, she watched as men swarmed over the grounds looking for Karl, searching the pool house, the sheds and the shrubs. Occasional shouts from the men rang out as orders were dispatched from Gabe downwards.

A shot rang out quickly followed by another. She thought she heard a man call out in agony, perhaps having had been hit by a bullet.

It all seemed to ring around Sarahs head and she wondered again what sort of lifestyle she had chosen. But chosen it she had and she would not run away again. She knew she was safe from harm whatever may happen around her.

With a cool flowing dress on, Sarah headed back downstairs. The fuss would surely be over soon and peace would be restored, of that she was sure.

At the bottom of the stairs, she hesitated, thinking that perhaps she might be safer upstairs where she could at least lock the bedroom door. Deciding that upstairs would be better, she turned around, holding the banister rail to balance her. She felt very unsteady on her feet.

From out of nowhere, a hand grabbed her arm from behind and another snaked around her neck, covering her mouth before she could react or scream. Sarah was wrenched backwards so her enlarged belly protruded even further. Terror gripped her and she felt she might be bent in two. She felt a cold hard object thrust up into her neck and she realised that it was a gun.

"Not a word." A menacing voice spoke quietly in her ear.

It was Karl.

The hand across Sarahs mouth was slimy and tasted metallic. He began to pull Sarah across the marble hallway, her feet slipping on the smooth surface, barely able to stand upright. From behind her, Sarah heard a door slam shut and a clatter of many feet. The feet skidded to a halt as Karl spoke in that same menacing voice he had used on Sarah just moments before.

"Let me out of here and she'll be fine." He spun Sarah around with a force of strength that surprised her. She was acting as a shield between him and the guns that were now trained on him. With his back to the wall, he slowly moved across the hallway towards the front door. His hand was now removed from her mouth, no need for silence anymore. Karl had one arm around her throat and was pulling her not too gently along while his other hand had the gun in it, now rammed in her side, pointing downwards as if towards the baby.

Marco saw the absolute terror in his wife's eyes as she was pulled across the hallway, her feet entangling in one of the rugs. He felt a complete hopelessness as he watched her being edged towards the front door, terrified for her life and that of their unborn child.

Marco put his loaded gun down slowly on the floor and instructed the men stood behind him to do likewise. He did not want any accidental shots being fired. He felt the anger build in him that this should be happening in his own home. He would hold onto that anger for when the time was right.

Karl had now reached the door and was mentally working out what to do next. He manoeuvred his hands so one had the gun pointing point blank into her neck and the other held her arm pinned up behind her . Running through his mind was the thought that if he killed Sarah Delvecchio and also Marcos child, Joe would be in his debt for a long time. It would leave Marco devastated and his businesses would suffer, leaving the door open for Joe.

His now free hand had blood dripping down on it from an upper arm wound and Karl groped for the door handle leaving a smear of blood on the door and the handle. He found it and looked into the black raging eyes of Marco, his ex-boss's lip snarling with the intense anger he felt as he watched Karl slowly open the front door. Karl smiled, feeling victorious.

"Slow." He warned Sarah. He glanced behind him to check if anyone was waiting to ambush him but saw no-one. They backed out into the sweltering August early afternoon heat.

"I need the keys to one of those cars." He instructed, his confidence building. "I want one of you to open the doors."

Marco gestured to Harry, who turned and went into Marco's office to get a set of keys. He grabbed the first ones he saw which happened to be to Sarahs Mercedes and then returned to the scene in the hallway. He slowly walked by Shepstone and his terrified captive to the driveway. As Harry walked into the sunshine, he looked around and saw at least six men with their weapons trained on the front door. He shook his head discernibly and the men stood down. Harry didn't want a trigger happy man playing the hero and a gun going off in the direction of Sarah.

Harry unlocked the door to Sarah's SUV and put the keys in the ignition ready. As Karl and Sarah approached, Harry took a few steps away from the vehicle and smiled encouragingly at Sarah. He watched helplessly as Karl got in the drivers side and then practically dragged Sarah in while he sidled across to the passenger side, the gun still rammed in her neck.

"Let's go." He demanded, a smile playing across his lips as he realised he was almost home and dry.

Shaking and near to tears, Sarah started the engine to her car up. She put the vehicle into drive and looked up and directly ahead.

Almost in the same split second, three things happened. As Sarah looked up, she saw a sniper gun aimed in her direction and she screamed. Sarahs scream startled Karl who had dropped his guard just a fraction thinking he was almost free and he fumbled the gun dropping it into Sarahs lap. Before Karl could react, the windscreen shattered as a bullet tore through the glass and into Karl's throat. Glass shattered and Karl's blood spattered across the cabin of the car and covered Sarah as she sat there screaming, her hands over her ears to shut out the terrifying noise around her. Karl was gurgling next to her, clutching his wound with both hands as if to try and stop the blood. His face was suddenly terrified as the reality of impending death hit. The drivers door was suddenly yanked open and Sarah practically fell into the arms of her husband. He pulled her out and held her to him, trying to shield her from the scene of the dying man in her car. Sobbing, she held onto him tightly.

"Keep him alive!" Marco shouted as he saw Karl drowning in his own blood. He hurriedly walked Sarah into the house to sit her down on the sofa.

"Please don't leave me!" She begged as she collapsed on the soft leather suite.

Marco crouched down in front of her, gently squeezing her hands in his. He kissed her blood spattered cheek trying to soothe and calm her shattered nerves.

"You are safe now. Karl is in no state to come after you. I have to deal with this and then I'll be back. I'll send Harry in." Marco promised, kissing the palm of her hands in turn.

By the time Marco had returned back outside, Karl was dead. His glassy eyes stared straight ahead through the shattered windscreen from where the bullet had been fired. His once white shirt was soaked in his blood as it had gushed down from his neck wound. Marco pulled Gabe away from the open passenger door and looked inside at the mess. Blood was everywhere. One of Graces dolls was on the floor of the front seat and was now covered in liquid crimson drying in the heat. He picked it up and stared at it for a moment, ponderous, angry and sick.

Gabe put a hand on his shoulder. "You want me to deal with this?" He asked. He knew Marcos sensibilities where Sarah was concerned and was happy to finish off this piece of business for his boss.

Marco turned to look at him, the man who had fired the snipers gun and had most likely saved his wife's life.

"Sure, Gabe. Thanks a lot." He said quietly.

Gabe just shrugged. It was all in a days work for him and was no big deal although with Sarah life being on the line, it could have turned out much worse. Thankfully, Gabe had been trained to act now and think later, that was why he was a success at what he did and why Marco held him in such high esteem.

"Report the car stolen." Gabe instructed his boss. The car would never be found. The Delvecchios knew a car wreckers in the next county and no questions would be asked. The ML320 would be driven there under cover of darkness before the police received the call about the loss.

Marco looked at his right hand man. "Are you going to cut him up?"

Gabe smiled. "Not this time, I don't have the stomach for that today. Besides, a couple of the guys are going fishing tonight. I thought Karl might like to go along." The smile turned sadistic as Gabe looked at his boss for approval, which he received with a slight nod of the head after a few moments thought and Marco turned to go back inside to see to his wife.

CHAPTER ELEVEN

The aftermath of the Shepstone incident was light, at least as far as Sarah was aware.

She never saw her silver Mercedes again but two days later, there was a brand new one sitting on the driveway, dark blue in colour. It again had the blacked out windows as Marco insisted all of his cars had. It even had a new car seat for Grace.

Sarah was badly shaken for several days by what had happened and half expected to go into early labour. Each day it did not happen, she was thankful.

Other than Karl himself, Scott Wolfe was the only other person to have suffered any injuries. The second gunshot Sarah had heard had been Karl returning Scott's fire, both of them hitting the other. Karl had been hit in the fleshy part of the upper arm while Scott had had his ribs grazed as the bullet just nicked him. The family doctor, Dr. Sturgess had given him the once over and bandaged him up. Marco had assigned him to light duties around the house for the next week or so.

Grace had shown great concern that Scott had been hurt, although she was told that he had broken a rib playing sports. She followed him around the house always offering to get him a drink or a newspaper or telling him to sit down and rest.

One particularly hot afternoon, Sarah was sitting inside while Marco stood at the window watching his daughter shadow Scott.

"Isn't she a little young to be having crushes?" He growled to his wife.

Sarah stood and went over to her husband to watch her daughter with him. "I wouldn't worry too much about it, darling. I think it's quite amusing though. Scott seems concerned that the Boss's daughter has a thing for him."

Marco shook his head. "I didn't think I would have to worry about such things at six years old. What am I going to do in ten years time?" He seemed genuinely concerned.

Sarah wrapped her arms around his waist. "If you get too overprotective, she will rebel. I was always told not to do this or that but I did it anyway. You must let her find her own way and guide her."

He kissed her. "I will. I will just kill any man who hurts her."

"Yes and with an attitude like that, our daughter will have lots of secrets that she will be too afraid to open up about. I would say that her surname is enough of a guarantee that the boys won't mess with her."

Marco looked at her and smiled. "At least when our boy is born, I can let him get on with it."

Sarah snortled. "Who's to say it's a boy? Besides, boys are far more trouble. You are testament to that!" She jested.

"It's a boy." Marco seemed convinced. "There have been enough females born in this family lately and it's time to redress the balance." He looked at Sarah's shocked face. "Come on, sweetie. I'm Italian – I need a male heir!" He laughed again.

Much to Sarahs amusement and Marcos satisfaction, his son and heir to the huge Delvecchio fortune was born amidst a terrific September Florida thunderstorm that threatened to knock out the power for miles around. The storm raged outside as Sarah brought Giorgio Alessandro into the world after a relatively easy birth, if there ever was such a thing. As the furore outside died down, she held her swaddled son close and looked at his angelic face. She felt a renewed hope as she stroked his face gently that perhaps the world wasn't all bad.

Despite the war in the Middle East, suicide bombers and world poverty, perhaps life could eventually change for the better with the birth of new innocents. Sarahs thoughts turned to Joe and how Graziella had one day held her infant son to her with much the same thoughts. Sarah was glad in a way that Graziella was not around to witness the downward spiral of destruction that her youngest son was on. She would have had her heart broken by him and what he was capable of. The men guarding Sarahs hospital door was testament indeed to that.

Tears began to fall unbidden down Sarahs face and that was how Marco and Grace found her moments later.

Marcos smile disappeared as he saw his wife crying and rushed over to her side, the huge bouquet of flowers discarded on the floor. His thoughts were that something was wrong with the baby.

"What is it?" He ran his hands through Sarahs hair in an attempt to calm her.

"What sort of world have we bought this child into, Marco?"

Relief flooded though him and he smiled at her. "A world where he will be very much loved. He will have parents who cherish him and the best of everything." He looked over to the door where Grace was still stood a little unsure. "And a big sister to look out for him. Isn't that right Grace?" He held out his hand to encourage Grace to come forward.

She rushed over to the bed and clambered onto her fathers lap to get a good first look at her baby brother.

"He looks funny." She frowned.

Marco laughed. "He is only an hour old. He'll soon be a very handsome boy."

"What's his name?"

Sarah told her and her frown remained.

"That's a funny name."

"Giorgio was my fathers name and we thought it would be nice to call him after your grandfather. You are named after your grandmother, my mother." Marco explained. Grace accepted this and reached out to touch the baby.

A few weeks later, Sarah was sat at home in the newly decorated and kitted out nursery. She had just fed Giorgio and was lulling him to sleep on an antique rocking chair. The nursery was next door to what was once known as the Yellow Room, now Graces permanent room and decorated in pinks and lilacs, her colour of the moment. Harry had gone to collect Grace and they were expected home at any moment. Grace was not liking school one little bit since they had started the new school year and Sarah suspected that Giorgio's arrival had not helped.

Just as Giorgio had drifted off, Grace came storming into the nursery and slammed the door. The noise made the baby jump and he awoke and began to scream.

"Grace!" Sarah reprimanded her daughter.

The little girl stamped her feet and burst into tears.

Sarah took a deep breath as both of her children's wailing reached a crescendo. She knew Marco was in an important meeting downstairs and this racket would surely reach him. Sarah put Giorgio in his crib to cry – he'd be okay. Grace needed immediate attention.

"Come with me." Sarah said calmly and took hold of her daughters hand.

With a trembling lip, Grace followed her mother out of the nursery and down the hallway. Still sobbing slightly, she went across the stairs and into her mother and fathers bedroom. Sarah sat on the edge of her huge bed and lifted Grace up beside her.

"Tell me what the matter is, Grace." Sarah said softly as she wiped her daughters tears away with a tissue.

Choking back the sobs, Grace spilled her hurt.

"Everyone at school is picking on me. You and daddy don't love me anymore now that you have got a new baby. Even Auntie Rosa doesn't want me now she had her smelly baby!"

Sarah pulled her little princess onto her lap.

"Grace, there isn't enough room in the world to hold the love I have for you. That will never ever change. Daddy is the same. You will always be his princess." Sarah kissed the top of Graces head. "Giorgio and Adina are very small and need all of our help. They can't play on their own or feed themselves or do anything. He especially needs all the help he can get from his big sister."

"So you won't be sending me away?" Grace turned to look at her mother with something close to fear in her eyes.

Sarah held Grace close. "Of course not! Whatever made you

think such a thing?"

"The boys at school. They said that when Daddy doesn't like someone anymore, he sends them away. To heaven."

"That's just stories Grace. Your father loves you more than life itself. Now, will you help me to stop your brother crying?"

Grace sniffled again and nodded.

Friday afternoon, with Giorgio fed, content and sleeping, Grace and Sarah were reading a Cinderella story after school. They were in the living room to escape the mid-October heat and planning a swim very shortly.

The front door slammed and Sarah tensed slightly, still feeling the effects of the trauma of the Shepstone incident although she was loathe to admit it. She heard her husband call out for her from the hallway and she relaxed considerably. His footsteps could be heard pounding along the hallway towards the living room and he threw open the door in dramatic fashion.

"Daddy!" Grace squealed in delight. She got off the sofa and ran towards him.

Marco scooped her up in his arms and whirled her around.

"How are my two favourite girls?" Marcos face was radiant and grinning.

Unusually so.

"Good. We did some writing at school today." She informed her father.

"You did? What did you write?"

"Mostly about Giorgio and how we have to look after him. Then at lunch time, I had to run really fast."

"Run?"

"Uh-huh. Two boys were chasing me and wanted to kiss me. I had to run with Darcy to get away."

Sarah burst out laughing. She had been watching Marcos face throughout this conversation and it had gone from being the soft one of a devoted father to a hard one of one who wanted to commit murder.

Marco set Grace on the floor. "Grace baby, why don't you go upstairs and get ready for the pool. We can all go swimming."

Grace cheered and raced off upstairs to find her bathing

155

costume.

Marco came and sat down beside his wife on the soft white sofa.

"Did you hear that? She is just six years old." He sounded defeated.

Sarah nodded. Given their conversation just a few weeks ago, she was disheartened that he was still feeling like this.

"She's gorgeous. What do you expect? Besides, how old were you when you first started chasing skirt?"

"It's not the same." He shook his head and took Sarahs hands in his own.

"Sweetheart, please don't fret about it. She is just a child – let her stay a child for as long as possible. There will be time enough for her to grow up and understand the evils in the world. As I have said before, no-one in their right mind would trifle with her and as she just said, she can run fast!"

Marco smiled at last and buried his face in her neck, breathing in the warm smell that got his heart racing just that little bit faster. He brought his arm around her waist and pulled her closer, his breathing becoming heavier. Very gently, Marco encouraged Sarah to lie back on the sofa as he kissed her neck so she barely felt it although it sent every nerve in her body jangling. He undid the top two buttons of Sarahs blouse and his kisses got lower.

Sarah groaned softly. "You know we can't. Not here and not now."

Marco stopped kissing her and looked at her. She brought his lips to hers and kissed him passionately. "It doesn't stop me wanting you though. It's been weeks."

"A week before our son was born – do you remember?" He grinned as she blushed.

She kissed him again to hide her embarrassment that memories of their love making should cause her to redden.

"Grace wants a swim. You need a cold shower." She told him. "I'll see you in the bedroom at nine o'clock tonight. Do not let anything at all get in the way, no emergencies, no phone-calls. You are off duty by then, do you understand, Mr Delvecchio?"

"I love it when you are dominating, Mrs Delvecchio!" He

grinned like a school boy and walked rather strangely out of the room to cool off before taking his daughter for a swim.

Sarah finally got Giorgio settled by eight forty-five that night. She looked in on Grace on her way through – she was practically comatose and was unlikely to rouse again until at least six the following morning, she was a heavy sleeper.

For all of Sarahs earlier posturing, she was exhausted. She had only fifteen minutes to get ready for her date with her husband and she secretly hoped that some emergency would arise and Marco would be late.

Once in the bedroom, she drew the drapes closed, leaving the French doors they covered open for the air. It was still very warm outside for October. She unpinned her hair and stripped as she headed for the en-suite bathroom. As she stepped under the hot needles of water, she once again prayed that Marco would be held up. She was beat but had promised her husband a night of passion and she would not fail him. She hated the thought of pre-planned sex and if Marco was sufficiently late, she'd be in bed and asleep by the time he turned up.

The hot water began to revitalise her.

Sarah felt the door to the double shower slide open and before she could react, Marco had walked in and put his arms around her, sharing the water. He pushed his lean body against hers and his hands slipped to her post-natal belly.

"Marco, don't please." She pulled his hands away and turned to face him. He looked hurt.

"Why?"

"I'm just...I'm not.." She looked down at the swirling water unsure what exactly to say to him. The suds were being sucked down the drain. "I just feel unattractive. I was hoping to be under the covers and in the dark by the time you showed up. You're early, for once!" She half laughed.

Suddenly, he understood. He put his arms around her again despite her slight protests. "You are the most beautiful woman I have ever known and I want you with a voracity I have never felt before. You may be a little bit bigger than you were nine months ago but you are still beautiful to me. You being the mother of my children turns me on more than any stick insect you may care to name." He cupped Sarahs chin in his hands and forced her to look at him. "Or is it that you don't find me attractive anymore?"

Sarah laughed. Nearly every woman in the county wanted a piece of her husband and here he was on a plate waiting to be devoured by her. She needed no second invitation.

They were dozing for the second time when the baby monitor by the side of the bed flickered to the dark green light and slight snuffling noises could be heard, indicating that Giorgio was stirring, hungry again.

"You want me to go?" Marco volunteered, half asleep.

"No, you stay here. You don't have what he needs. You have about an hour before I'm back for what I need." She kissed his lips and smiled. Marco nodded softly and closed his eyes again drifting peacefully and satisfied into a deep sleep. Sarah suspected that would be the last she would see of him that night.

At a quarter to one, Sarah closed Giorgio's bedroom door tight and walked back along the hallway. The house was dark and peaceful, just the odd howl of a guard dog in the black Florida night. Her silk dressing gown flowed out behind her as she passed the huge picture window at the top of the stairs and saw Scott Wolfe, back on active duty walking up the drive towards the gatehouse. Since the shooting, Marco only permitted a few of his most trusted men inside the house.

Quietly, she opened the bedroom door so as not to disturb Marco and was surprised to see him sat up in bed with the light on. He smiled at her as she closed the bedroom door behind her and softly padded over to the bed.

"You're awake!" Her astonishment was evident.

"Of course. Sit here." He patted the bed beside him for her to sit. She did as she was told bemused by the order. Her dressing gown gaped open.

Marco cleared his throat, distracted by what he saw. "I have something I want to give you."

She raised an eyebrow in jest.

Marco chuckled. "You are an insatiable minx!" He took her hand in his and put his serious face on. "I don't think you realise just how important you are to me, or how much I love you."

"Marco…" She tried to interrupt. He silenced her by putting his hand up.

"The best thing that ever happened to me was you returning to Florida to be with me, as my wife. Having Giorgio has been the icing on the cake as far as I'm concerned and it has made me complete. I know words are just words and I will do whatever I can to make you believe me. I want you to be the happiest woman on earth, whatever it takes." He reached over to his side of the bed and pulled open the top drawer of his bedside cabinet. He brought out a little blue velvet box and passed it to Sarah.

She looked at him. "Whatever this is, it's not necessary."

Marco shrugged and folded his fingers around hers surrounding the box. He opened the box and Sarah gasped.

Inside was a blue sapphire ring, emerald cut sat plainly but very majestically on a platinum setting. The stone was about half an inch long although not it the least bit ostentatious, just very classy.

"Blue sapphire to represent the first boy to be born into this family in quite some time." Marco continued. He meant since Joe but did not want to spoil the moment.

Sarah just sat looking at the ring speechless. Marco took the ring out of the box and placed it onto her finger next to her wedding ring. It fit perfectly as he knew it would.

"You never had an engagement ring, there wasn't enough time. I didn't want to wait and had to get a wedding ring on your finger. We weren't together much after Grace was born so an eternity ring never entered the equation. This is to make up for all of that. To make up for it and to shower you in jewels. Hell! I shouldn't need an excuse to shower my wife in jewellery but I know you'd just object."

Sarah just stared at the beautiful deep blue stone on her finger not finding any appropriate words to say. Marco continued.

"I want you to get used to receiving and wearing beautiful things. I don't want you to cry with happiness every time." He reached across and wiped away a errant tear.

Sarah finally found her tongue. "You want me to be ungrateful?

To expect such beautiful things? I'm not like your associates wives and I wasn't born into this rich lifestyle. I grew up on a council estate in South London and if I got a sapphire ring every day for the rest of my life I would still never take it for granted. Or you." She leant over and kissed him passionately.

Marco chuckled again. "I knew you'd say that. That's why giving to you is such a pleasure and that's why I want to spoil you."

Sarah lay back in her husbands arms and could not take her eyes off the ring. She slipped off her dressing gown and relaxed into his embrace. "I'd never take you for granted, Marco." She paused. "That's not the same as being manipulative though, is it?" She asked slowly.

"Manipulative?" Now relaxed, Marco was drifting back to sleep, his voice heavy with drowsiness.

"Yes. You know, to work you, for my own ends."

He managed a sleepy laugh. "Isn't a one hundred thousand dollar ring enough for you? What do you want?"

"Shooting lessons."

Marcos eyes flew open. "What?"

"You know, to learn how to handle a gun, how to fire it, how to protect myself."

"You have Harry for that."

"Sure, but what I want is to do it for myself and to protect my children. Do you have any idea how defenceless I felt the other week in my own home?"

"About as impotent as I felt watching it happen in front of me and not being able to do a damn thing?"

"Maybe?"

"Even if you had been a sharpshooter, you wouldn't have been able to draw a weapon in the position you were in."

"I know, but for next time…"

"No!" Marco was adamant.

Sarah smiled and threw the covers of him. "Do you think that you are in any position to say no to me with that?" She pointed towards his groin.

"Bribery?" He was incredulous. "If I don't give you what you want, we don't have sex?" He had to smile at her resourcefulness even if he was against the idea.

"Not bribery. Just manipulation." She covered his mouth with hers and kissed him long and hard, enough to start the arousal again. "If you say yes, I say yes and we both get what we want. You can get me a licence and a WPB gun club membership, I know you can." Her hand slipped lower and he groaned.

"That's so unfair." He moaned. She worked him a little bit longer before she withdrew her hand and smiled at him.

"Well?"

"Okay! Okay! Just finish what you've started!" He grabbed her hand and put it back. She was right. He was in no position to say no to her.

CHAPTER TWELVE

"*So how does my* husband know you?" Sarah asked the leggy blond at West Palm Beach's private gun club a week later.

Kristina, the leggy blond dressed completely in white smiled tolerantly at her. She had always had a thing for guns and loved working in the swanky club where Florida's rich and famous residents came for lessons.

"Purely professional. He sends me people who need to know how to shoot and I teach them. I hope we are not going to have a problem." Kristina replied in her drawling South Carolinian accent.

"No problem, Kristina. It's called an ice breaker. Let's just stick to the lessons." Sarah replied frostily.

Kristina smiled almost apologetically and passed the gun to Sarah. It was a Magnum, a revolver with a repeat action cylinder, that all the 'newies' started out with. It felt heavy and deadly in Sarahs hands and she felt a sense of power wash over her that she wasn't completely comfortable with. She turned it over in her hands as Kristina began her tuition. She talked about the various parts of the gun, how to hold it and how easy it was to fire it. They walked over to a lane at the far end of the firing range and Kristina showed Sarah how to fire it. Sarah already had the protective goggles and earplugs on and watched with awe as Kristina fired off the six rounds and then stood back to reload it for Sarah. The shots rang out much louder than Sarah had anticipated.

"Take a couple of shots and see how you go" Kristina suggested as she handed the gun back to Sarah.

Sarah mimicked Kristina's stance, feet apart, arms raised shoulder level and aimed for the paper target some forty feet away. With her adrenaline running at the max, Sarah squeezed the trigger and felt the recoil that made her take a backwards step. Repositioning herself, she fired off another shot and was ready for the recoil that time so it did not displace her.

With all the bullets fired, Kristina pressed the red button at the beginning of the lane and called for the paper man to be returned to the front so the two women could see how Sarah had done. Four of the bullets had hit the paper but not within the black circles on the target.

Kristina reloaded the Magnum - she said Sarah would learn that later – and explained how better to hold the gun to aim for the target.

By the end of the first forty-five minutes Sarah had hit the target within the circle five times. It was an excellent start and Kristina commented on the fact.

"I'll see you same time next week?"

"Sure Kristina, thanks very much." Sarah felt very pleased with herself as she took off her goggles and gave them back to her tutor.

Sarah went into the café where Harry was waiting for her and then they headed off towards home. She was about half way home when her cell phone rang. She looked down at the caller ID and saw it was Andrea. She answered the call with a cheery greeting. Andrea, however, was not so cheery.

"It's Beth. It looks like Luke beat her up real bad this time. We're at the hospital."

"What?" Sarah did not want to believe it. "I'm on my way."

Sarah cut the call and made a U-turn in the highway ignoring the prohibiting signs in the road. She headed back towards Palm Beach downtown to where Colombia Hospital was, Harry urging her to slow down all the way. Just a few minutes later she had arrived at the Emergency Room and squealed to a halt next to the ambulance bay.

"Harry, I need you to go and collect Grace from school. Rosa is home with Giorgio and Adina, please take Grace to her and I'll be home as soon as I can." She instructed.

"But Sarah…"

"Harry, DO NOT argue with me. Grace needs you more than I do at the moment. I'll be fine. Just go!" Before Harry could remonstrate further, Sarah charged into the Emergency Room, leaving her illegally parked car with Harry.

Sarah rushed into the chaos and noise of the Emergency Room looking for Andrea. Looking around, she could not see her friend among the many people that were waiting in the chairs. Sarah hurried over to the reception and waited a little impatiently behind a man yelling at the receptionist to tell him where his brother was.

"A doctor will see you soon, Sir. Please take a seat and they will be with you as soon as possible. Yes, ma'am?" She looked behind the man to Sarah.

"My name is Sarah Delvecchio and I'm here to see Beth Rogers."

"Sure. Hey, Samuel!" She called out to an orderly who happened to be walking by. "Can you take this lady to Mrs Rogers?" She went on to the person in the queue behind Sarah.

Sarah followed the orderly through the hectic corridors of the ER and eventually they came to a curtained off cubicle that he gestured to. Sarah pulled back the curtain and saw Beth laying on the bed in a hospital gown very bruised and battered.

"My God! What the hell happened?" Sarah rushed to Beth's bedside and took her hand.

"Luke." Andrea spat with a quiet fury.

Beth's bruised eyes began to swell up with tears as she began to recount the story.

"He stayed out all of last night. When he came home this morning at eight o'clock he was still high and still drunk. I should have just gone to work but I stupidly tried to start a fight."

"Beth, this isn't your fault." Sarah urged quietly.

"Maybe, but I didn't help the situation. I should have left him alone and talked to him when he'd sobered up. Instead, I demanded to know where he had been all night."

"What did he say?"

"He started to shout and said it was none of my damned

business. I began to get angry and felt it rise up inside me until I exploded. I yelled at him, telling him what a worthless scumbag he is. I followed him through the house, screaming like a demented woman at him. He grabbed me and pushed me against the kitchen table, forcing me backwards. I thought he was going to snap me in two." Her voice began to break again and she looked at Andrea for support. Andrea had already heard Beth's story and nodded for her to tell Sarah.

"Tell her everything." She urged.

Beth looked back to Sarah and a fresh batch of tears fell. She lowered her eyes in shame. "He raped me." She whispered.

"What?" Sarah felt sick.

"I know he's my husband but I didn't want him to. I tried to get away and begged him to stop but he just ignored me and went ahead." She choked back a sob. "I stopped struggling thinking it would be easier but he still hurt me, he was so rough." She began to cry violently as the memories gripped her. Sarah stroked her hand in an effort to calm her. She waited silently until Beth got control of her sobs and was able to continue.

"When he was done, he laughed at me and called me awful names that I can't repeat. I lay there a moment hoping he would just leave and then I could go. But he starting to make coffee like it was a normal morning, and then I guess I came to my senses. I got up from the table and went upstairs intent on getting my suitcase and walking out. I didn't say a word. I hadn't realised that he'd followed me upstairs and when I pulled the case from under the bed, he asked me what I was doing. I didn't speak and I couldn't look at him. He asked me again and I told him that I was leaving him, he would never see me or hurt me again." She took a deep breath and ran her hands through her hair. "He called me vile names again and forbade me to leave the house. I just ignored him and carried on packing some bare necessities. I guess my silence infuriated him again because he grabbed me and spun me around. He punched me square in the face." She gestured towards the cuts and bruises in her once pretty face. She looked out of the window at the beautiful sunshine outside. "He began to tear at my clothes again, I guess the violence was turning him on but I struggled and managed to get away. I got to the top of the stairs before he caught up with me and he punched me again. I remember falling down the stairs but that's it until I woke up. He'd gone but I was naked so I reckon he had another go at me." Beth kept staring out of the window unable to look Sarah or Andrea in the face.

Sarah didn't know how to respond to such a monstrous tale.

"Beth?" Andrea prompted.

Beth turned her gaze from the outside to Andrea her face looked terrified. After a few moments, she turned to Sarah as if resigned to having to tell the rest of her tale. "I also found out I was pregnant." She said quietly.

Sarah frowned. She didn't think it was necessarily good news. "Was?" She had picked up on Beth's use of tense.

"I was bleeding and in terrible pain in the ambulance on the way over here so with luck, I'm not any more. I don't want that mans baby and be tied to him for the rest of my life. They are going to do a scan soon so I'll find out soon enough but hopefully it's gone."

Sarah stroked Beth's hand again. "Have you spoken to the police?"

Beth shook her head. "It will only make things worse with Luke. I just want to get out of here and go back to New York." New York was where Beth lived before she came to Florida.

"Why don't you come and stay with us for a while, while you get your head together." Sarah suggested. She saw Andrea frown out of the corner of her eye.

Beth shrugged. "Marco won't like it." It was well known that Marco did not like anyone in his house.

"You leave Marco to me. He's putty in my hands." Sarah smiled but knew it would be a difficult task.

The curtain parted and a hefty nurse entered the closed off cubicle. "Hello Beth, I'm Shirelle. I'm going to do your scan and then we can get you something for the pain. We'll get you admitted and moved somewhere comfortable and private." She smiled warmly at Beth.

Sarah stood up. "Beth, I have some things I need to attend to. I'll be back later this afternoon and I'll bring you some things to make you comfortable." She patted Beth's lower arm and stared intently at Andrea before leaving the treatment area.

Sarah grabbed a waiting cab outside the hospital and with a

rage boiling up inside her went home. She could not understand how somebody could make such an unprovoked and vicious attack on a woman they purported to love.

The cab drew up by the fountain at the front of the house and in her blind fury, Sarah gave the driver a hundred dollar bill, more than twice the amount it should have been even with a tip. She stormed into the house.

"Marco?" She yelled at the top of her voice as she slammed the heavy front door behind her. Her voice echoed around the seemingly empty house. She called out again but it was just silence of the substantial house that greeted her. She headed towards Marcos office and burst through the door without knocking. Marco was sat in his large black leather chair behind the large cherry wood desk and he looked up sharply at the intrusion. Gabe stood to his left and two strangers were sat opposite him.

Unperturbed, Sarah interrupted. "I need to talk to you."

"Sweetheart, I'm in a meeting."

"Now!" She would not be denied and her eyes were blazing with the fury she felt inside.

Marco looked at her for a moment before coming to the conclusion that she would not wait. Sighing, he looked at his guests. "Gentlemen, please excuse me for a moment." He stood up and walked around his desk and grabbed Sarahs arm. He pulled her along the passageway until they reached the kitchen.

"I was in a very important meeting!" It was Marcos turn to feel anger as he glowered at his wife, waiting for an explanation.

"This cannot wait. I have just come from the hospital. Beth has been admitted."

Marco softened a little. "Is she okay?"

"Not really. She has been beaten up and raped by her husband. She may have had a miscarriage and she didn't even know she was pregnant until she started bleeding."

"Nice guy. He makes your husband seem like the Arc Angel Gabriel!"

His attempt on humour was not appreciated by Sarah. "This is not funny, Marco. Beth is going to come and stay here for a while when she is discharged, just until she gets her head together."

"Oh no, Sarah. You know I can't have that."

"Yes I know, but Beth is not a stranger. She is my friend and she needs refuge from her abusive husband."

"Can't she go to a woman's safe house or something?"

"Probably but she's not. She is coming here for as long as she needs and that's an end to it." She glared at Marco daring him to defy her.

Marco ran his hands through his dark hair. He really was unhappy with the situation but one look at his wife's face and he knew that he would have to give in. He would set down his own rules for Beth's stay later. "Okay." He acquiesced. "Can I go back to my meeting now?" He turned to go.

"That's not all." Sarah stood her ground.

He turned back to face her. "What else?" His impatience was returning.

"I need…" Sarah was unsure how to say what was on her mind. "Someone has to deal with Luke."

"Deal with him?"

Sarah nodded.

Marco laughed. "Do you think I own Rent-a-Thug or something? Maybe you should go and visit a bar in Miami downtown and put the word about, make some contacts. A couple of hundred dollars should cover it." He laughed again and shaking his head, he began to walk away.

Sarah hung her head. "Marco, Beth was repeatedly raped by the man who promised to love and cherish her. He as good as pushed her down the stairs in the home they shared, probably killing the child they created in the process. Don't you think you could at least talk to him?" He voice was calm and quiet.

Marco had stopped and walked back to her. He stood in front of her and said nothing for a while. She looked into his impassive face for a clue as to what he was thinking. This was his business and he was an expert at it despite his earlier protestations. He nodded very slightly. "You want me just to talk to him?" He finally said.

Sarah shrugged. "Do what you have to do. I have to get back to the hospital."

Beth was discharged from hospital the following day and as Sarah was settling her into the guest suite, Gabe took Eddie, one of his young associates to Beth's house. They waited outside in the car a few doors down where they could keep an eye in the comings and goings of the Rogers' house. Gabe sat smoking his cigarette, relaxed. This was an easy assignment. Eddie was playing patience on his cellphone as they both waited for their quarry to arrive.

At just before four, Luke arrived driving erratically down the street in his Ford Explorer. He left the car at the kerbside and skipped up his pathway as though he didn't have a care in the world. Gabe flicked his cigarette out of the window and blew the smoke from his lungs.

"Let's go."

Eddie switched off his game and put it in his jeans back pocket. He got out of the car and followed his immediate boss. They walked four houses down to where Luke now lived on his own.

Gabe knocked on the door and waited.

Luke answered the door abruptly. He scowled at the strangers on his doorstep.

"Luke Rogers?" Gabe asked sourly.

Luke appraised the man who had just spoken. He was tall and muscular and very severe looking. He considered his options. "You cops?"

Gabe pushed his way passed the surprised home owner and into the house followed by Eddie. "We are your worst nightmare. We're here to talk about Beth."

Luke followed the two men into his kitchen.

"Is this where you raped her?" Gabe asked. Eddie stayed silent; he was just back up muscle.

Luke snorted in derision. "Rape? I don't know what you're…"

Gabe shook his head. "You are scum, you know that? You know you killed your own child?"

This shocked Luke. He'd had no idea. "What?"

"Beth was pregnant but thankfully she miscarried."

Luke sat down on the kitchen chair shocked by what he had just heard. "I have to see her. Where is she?" He looked up at Gabe imploring him to tell him where Beth was.

"She doesn't want to see you, buddy."

"I have every right..."

"You gave up every right when you beat the crap out of her."

"D'you think you scare me? What are you, some kind of hired goon?"

"Beth doesn't know we are here. We are here at the behest of Sarah Delvecchio. You know that name?"

Luke shook his head.

"I suggest you look into it. Meanwhile, stay away from Beth. Our next visit won't be so friendly."

"You don't scare me." He should have been scared.

"We are not here to scare you. I just want you to stay away from Beth. Do we have an understanding?"

Luke shrugged. He was not scared just a little concerned at who these goons were. And where had Beth got to? What had she been saying?

Two days later, Beth felt well enough and brave enough to get out of bed. She felt wobbly as she stepped out of bed and out on her new dressing gown that Sarah had purchased for her. She made her way down the stairs of the quiet house and into the large galleried hallway looking for the kitchen. It was her first visit to the house and she didn't know her way around. She walked towards a door that she thought might take her into the kitchen - she was in desperate need of coffee. As she put her fingers on the door handle, it was opened from the other side. Marco stood there surprised at seeing her.

"I was looking for the kitchen." She said, a little awkwardly.

"Oh. Well, I was just headed there. It's the other side of the hallway." Marco came out of his office and strode across the hall. Beth followed him meekly.

Marco put on some fresh coffee while Beth sat quietly on a stool at the breakfast bar watching him.

"It's good to see you up, Beth. How are you feeling?"

"Better thanks." She felt uncomfortable being here barely dressed with Marco. "Is Sarah around?"

He smiled as he produced two cups for the coffee and grabbed the sugar. "She is at shooting lessons. I just can't say no to that woman." He smiled at Beth.

Beth shifted in the stool. "Marco, I know that you are not happy with me being here and I promise that I'll be gone as soon as I can."

"Beth, it's okay."

"Maybe just a few days more and I'll feel ready to face the world again. I'll get myself a job and somewhere to live."

Marco went over to her and put a comforting hand on her shoulder. "There is no hurry. Take your time. Besides, " He looked off into the distance behind her. "I may be able to find you somewhere to live." He looked thoughtful.

The coffee maker gurgled to a stop and he poured the black liquid into the two cups and handed a cup to Beth.

"Nowhere fancy, Marco. I doubt I'll earn enough money to pay for anything sumptuous."

They walked to the kitchen door. "Don't worry. Just leave it to me." He opened the door for Beth to pass through.

The front door opened and Dominic Russell walked through searching for Marco. He waved as he saw him coming out of the kitchen. His smile widened as he saw the young girl in the dressing gown beside Marco.

"One of your guys said it would be okay to come in." He told Marco.

"Sure. You want some coffee? We've just made fresh."

Dom nodded and Beth volunteered to go and get him some.

"Who's your friend?" Dom asked as Beth disappeared back into the kitchen.

"A friend of Sarahs needing sanctuary. I swear that I sometimes feel like I'm running a missionary for lost souls!" He laughed lightly as they headed for Marcos office for their meeting.

Beth brought Dom's coffee through shortly after and he smiled flirtatiously at her as she handed it to him.

When Sarah arrived home from the gun club later that afternoon, she found her husband in the pool splashing about with his daughter. Beth was sat on a sun-lounger nearby, watching the goings-on and laughing with Giorgio on her lap and Sarah felt a pang of jealousy at this joyous family scene that she had not been part of. She plucked her son out of Beth's arms and called out to Marco.

"Isn't it a bit cold to be swimming?" It was mid-November and not particularly warm. She only hoped Marco would have had the foresight to switch on the pool heater.

"Tell that to Grace!" He called out before Grace ducked his head under the water from her vantage point of being seated on his back.

Sarah wondered to herself who the adult was as she walked inside with the baby, intent on coming back outside with some warm towels for Grace. Part of her was glad that Marco was spending time with his daughter. He'd been so busy lately and he was rarely home. When Sarah returned, Grace was already out of the pool and shivering slightly in the cool air. Sarah shook her head disapprovingly at Marco who had remained in the water. With Grace wrapped in the large fluffy towel, Sarah asked Marco what his plans for the evening were.

He pulled himself out of the water and dripping wet, advanced towards his wife. He embraced her with the sole intent of soaking her and she squealed out her protest as Grace giggled at the sight of her parents larking about. Sarah handed Marco a towel.

"I have to go out tonight and I won't be around for dinner. I won't be too late home but don't wait up." He began to towel dry himself off.

"Do you want an early dinner?"

Marco kissed her cheek. "Don't worry about me, I'll get something later."

Sarah thought he looked troubled as he turned to go inside the house to shower and change before he later left the house with Gabe and Eddie.

Marco arrived back home late and tired. The house was silent and dark as he took of his jacket and put the keys to the Lexus away in the safe. Marco had checked in at the gatehouse and all was well and he knew he should make the rest of the security checks but he was beat. Gabe had known that Marco was done for the night and he volunteered to do those checks for him and the dogs were loose so if anything was amiss, he'd know from their wild and menacing barking.

Wearily, he climbed the stairs and went along to check on the children, a habit he'd had since Giorgio had been born. Grace's deep breathing was comforting to him and he tucked her back into bed. She'd kicked her covers off and would get cold in the chill night air soon. He kissed her forehead gently so as not to wake her and brushed a stray lock of hair away from her eyes. Smiling to himself, he left Grace's bedroom and went next door into Giorgio's nursery.

His son was sleeping soundly in the pale blue room which overlooked the rarely used tennis court. Marco stood at the bottom of the crib and watched the rise and fall of the baby's chest, the only movement he made. Marco felt a sense of peace flow through him that he thought was missing and would never return. Yawning, Marco decided it was time for him to turn in. He left the baby's room quietly and headed back down the hallway towards his own bedroom and his wife. The moonlight came into the house through the huge picture window that his mother had loved so much. He could almost see her standing at the bottom of the stairs looking upwards and out of this beautiful glass pane. She always said that it looked as though it was the doorway to heaven and he often looked through it in search of her or his father whenever he felt the need.

Like now.

Marco sighed. Things seemed to be spiralling out of his control and he was trying to reign it back in, to curb the problems. Tonight, Marco had made a start. He had taken the first few steps on the long road to achieving what needed to be done. He looked through the large window again, his face illuminated by the full moon outside and searched for his father and his guidance. Giorgio Delvecchio Senior had been only in his mid fifties when diagnosed with prostate cancer and hadn't been left with much time to teach his eldest son the finer points and less desirable ways of running the family business. Mercifully, a heart attack had claimed Giorgio before the cancer became vicious just after Grace had been born. Marco had ascended to the family throne before he was really ready and perhaps made some bad judgement calls. That was why things had turned out as they had. He knew many of his decisions had left some people in doubt as to his ability to be the boss of the family, even if he was the eldest son.

Things were all going to change from now.

He crept along the hallway towards the bedroom and quietly opened the bedroom door. A slight squeak was heard as he pushed the door open and he cursed under his breath. The room was quiet and dark apart from the sliver of moonlight that spilled across the room. Marco could make out the sleeping form of his wife in his bed. Stealthily, he slipped off his shoes and had begun to unbutton his shirt when Sarah stirred.

"Marco?" She sounded groggy from sleep.

"Yeah. Go back to sleep." He replied softly.

Sarah had picked up the strain in Marco's voice despite her sleepy state. She sat up in bed concerned. "What's the matter, darling?"

The trousers were discarded on the floor and Marco slipped into bed beside her.

"Just stuff." He toyed with the idea of confiding with Sarah. He'd often told her things in the past, important things pertaining to his business that other men in his position would not dare tell their wives. Their four years of separation were proof enough that Sarah could keep things to herself.

He snuggled up to her, her skin soft and warm against his. He closed his eyes and breathed deeply, relaxing his entire body and praying for sleep. He was exhausted.

"If you need to tell me anything, that's okay." Sarah whispered before she kissed his stubbly cheek goodnight.

"Not now, sweetie. I'm beat."

"Okay. Sleep well." She pulled his head into the curve of her neck and let him fall asleep. She drifted off again before her son cried out for her.

Within three days, Beth had moved into her new home. The Delvecchio Family owned several properties around town that were available for the single men in Marcos employ to use. One of them, a town house on South Ocean Drive had a vacant room with an en-suite bathroom that Marco thought would be ideal for Beth. It was rent free for her and only Eddie lived there currently and he would make excellent in-house security for her. Marco had warned him that she was off limits to any advances he might make. Beth was delighted with the arrangement and promised Marco that as soon as she had a job, she would either pay him rent or look for a place of her own.

"I might be able to help on the job front too." He smiled brightly at her. He handed Beth a business card which she took with a frown. She looked at the card and the name emblazoned in gold lettering across the middle.

"Dominic Russell? The name sounds familiar." She mused it over in her head.

"You made him coffee last week. Give him a call, he may have something for you." He took a few steps away from her towards the door thinking their conversation nearly over.

Beth smiled coyly. "You've been so good to me, Marco. Why?"

Marco paused as he shrugged. "You are Sarahs friend."

Beth paused. "Is that all?" She asked pointedly as she took a step closer, her eyes toying with him.

Marco stared at Beth for about five seconds. "Are you coming on to me, Beth?"

Beth moistened her lips lavisciously, her heart rate having just increased.

"Maybe." She replied. "Would you be offended by that?"

Marco took three strides towards her and with his face just inches from hers, he put her straight with a level tone.

"Know this. You are here for as long as Sarah wants you to be. She has done plenty for you in the last few weeks and you will do well to remember that." He half turned away from her before adding, "For the record, no, I'm not offended but I'm sure my wife would be. She trusts you but I don't think I do. Watch your step." He warned.

Beth had barely breathed while Marco delivered his discourse. When he had finished, she took a moment to snap to. She apologised. "Just an error in judgement. It won't happen again and I'm sure you'll agree that Sarah doesn't need to know."

Marco grunted his agreement and left the townhouse.

CHAPTER THIRTEEN

Thanksgiving went by in a blur as did Christmas in the Delvecchio household. Sarah insisted on having as much a traditional English Christmas as was possible in eighty degree heat and she threw herself into it like she hadn't been able to do in many a year. Her mind went back to where she was last Christmas and she would never have believed anyone then if they had told her how her year was about to pan out. As she watched Grace 'help' Giorgio open his presents on Christmas Day morning she was thankful she had taken the chance in returning to Palm Beach.

As the family walked back from church in the early evening sunshine, Sarah turned to her husband. "It's been a great day but we'll have to spend Christmas in Aspen next year. Let the children have snow on Christmas."

"Ah." Marco replied with regret in his voice. "We don't have the chalet there anymore. I sold it about two years ago."

"Okay. We'll have to book a lodge or something, just for the four of us."

Marco nodded. "I think you and I need a vacation. In a few months time, when Gio is a little bit older and can be left for a week or so. I also wondered what you thought about getting a nanny."

Sarah felt affronted. "Don't you trust me with your children then?"

They had reached the gatehouse and after being let through the side entrance, Grace was released from Marco's grip and ran on ahead, eager to get back to her new toys. Marco stopped Sarah by putting a hand on the stroller she was pushing with her son sleeping inside.

"That's not the issue and never even contemplated. I know you love the kids but I just thought you would like some time to yourself now and then to get out and see your friends. I don't want to keep asking Rosa and besides, she and Sal are moving out into their own house in the New Year anyway. I thought if our kids had someone regular and trusted, they would be happier to be left behind so you and I can go away together. I think that's important."

Sarah smiled and pushed on. "It's easy to see how you are so persuasive at work." She jested. "That was some speech. Do you have anyone in mind?"

"No. I thought we should interview together after last time."

The last time. Molly.

Just before Grace's first birthday, Marco had been arrested and indicted for tax evasion. He had been refused bail as he was considered a flight risk. He was looking at eight to ten years just on that and the FBI were still digging. All of his bank accounts and assets had been frozen by the IRS until at least after the court case and inevitable sentencing, which had rendered Sarah penniless for as long as Marco was in prison. That was when Vinnie Bonnetti had entered their lives. Marco had told Vinnie to do whatever was necessary to get him out of jail and to keep his family safe from harm. Vinnie decided that while this mess was being rectified, it would be in Sarahs best interests to leave the country with Grace and they headed to England, bankrolled by Vinnie. This was when Sarahs betrayal of Marco had taken place but worse still, the Delvecchio nanny had turned out to be an informer.

Sarah and Grace were living in a one bedroomed suite at the Landmark Hotel with Vinnie ensconced in a suite across the hallway. Vinnie was usually busy all day either with people coming and going from his suite or he was out on the streets of London doing whatever it was taking to free Marco. Sarahs boring but daily routine was habitual. Every morning after breakfast in the suite, she would take her one year old daughter for a walk through the busy streets, stop for a coffee and then back to the Landmark for Graces afternoon nap. All of this included Molly. Molly was Sarahs only friend and confidant through

these troubled times and they would walk and talk about pretty much everything
.   One particular morning, Sarah was feeling very low after having spoken to Marco in jail the night before. He had seemed very angry with her and Sarah knew now that it was probably because of the drugs he was taking at the time. Molly suggested to Sarah that she take Grace for a walk on her own to give her time to go to the leisure club for a swim, a Jacuzzi or just some time to herself. Sarah was plain wore out and she assented, heading for the leisure club before Molly could change her mind. She had done forty laps of the pool and was heading for the sauna when Molly came tearing into the club shouting hysterically for Sarah. Sarah turned to where the shouting was coming from and saw Molly alone.

"Where's Grace?" Concern was starting to hit Sarah.

"I turned my back for ten seconds to buy a can of soda and she was gone. Two men took her out of the stroller and ran into the crowd. They got into a car - I didn't see it but they were all gone!" The young girl seemed quite distraught and was wringing her hands in fear. She had just allowed Grace Delvecchio to be taken from her care.

Sarah thought her world had just collapsed. Her precious baby girl was missing. her husband was in jail and she was penniless and miles from home.

What she didn't know was that Marco had insisted to Vinnie that his wife and child were never unaccompanied and so Enzio had been following Sarah and Grace whenever they left the hotel. That included today. He had seen Molly hand Grace over to two guys in casual clothes and watched as their blue rented Ford sped away but not before Enzio had taken the registration plate. While Molly was telling Vinnie her made up story, Enzio had spoken to a female acquaintance in the British traffic police and had found out the car was a hire car belonging to Avis. He had spoken to the car rental company and struck lucky on his fourth telephone call before anyone would divulge anything. He persuaded the girl at the rental desk to give out the address of the renter, he was full of charm and grace when he needed to be.

He took a cab to the house in Ealing, West London and brazenly walked up to the door and rang the bell. There was perhaps unsurprisingly, no answer. Enzio looked through the letter box and found the place to at least look empty. He cupped his hands over his eyes as he looked through the front bay window searching for any sign of life. Enzio sneaked through the side gate and surveyed the back of the house. As far as he could make out, there were no occupants inside.

Enzio smashed a small back window and made his way inside. The place had been lived in until recently, perhaps since when Grace had been taken, but the occupants decided a move to be in order. The only thing that remained were several empty take out cartons and a take away menu from an Indian restaurant. It was Enzio's only clue so he staked out the restaurant.

Meanwhile, Sarah had been heavily sedated after receiving a phonecall from the kidnappers. They had told her to tell the Delvecchios to stay away from the family of a Bahamian banker, who was the chief witness against Marco. The Bahamians were scared and threatening to withdraw their testimony against Marco. The FBI knew that without this, their case would fall apart. Enzio wasn't convinced that the FBI had taken Grace, most likely it was someone hired by the Bahamians so they would feel protected.

Fortunately for Grace, whoever was behind it were novices at the games the Delvecchios were experts at. After two nights staking out the Indian restaurant, Enzio spotted one of the two guys he'd seen on Marylebone Road taking Grace and he followed him. The kidnapper had his hands full of Indian take away and his mind was not on the job which again proved to Enzio that the FBI was not behind this. Enzio followed the man to his house and then in the dark, he peered through the windows. He heard a few snippets of conversation that convinced him this was the right place. He called Vinnie to say that he thought he had tracked them down but wasn't sure if Grace was in the house. He'd soon find out.

He quietly walked into the house through the back door and smashed guy number one across the face with his gun, knocking him out cold as he plated his takeaway and before he realised there was an intruder in the house. The second man did not go so quietly or quickly and Enzio took several punches to the abdomen before he was able to overpower him. Quietly, he stalked through the rest of the small, unkempt house until he found Grace asleep in a dirty bed. Without waking her, he picked her up and walked out of the house, calling a taxi as he did so.

Back at the hotel, Grace was reunited with her joyful mother while Molly had been kept in the dark on the latest advancements. Enzio took Molly out 'for a walk' and coerced her to a quiet ally near the Embankment and proceeded to beat her to within an inch of her life. It sent the Bahamians a 'do not mess with us' message. By the time Molly was fit again, the Delvecchios were back in Florida although Molly would never tell anyone what had happened, only that she was set on by two drunken men. She headed back to her home town of Dallas when she was well enough to. Sarah was only ever told of Molly's involvement with the disappearance of her daughter, not the retribution she suffered.

So, after the New Years Eve party at the Palm Beach Country club, which Sarah found easier to bear than last year, Marco and Sarah set about looking for a nanny for their children. The task was long and arduous, Sarah not really convinced that it was right for her or the children. Beth helped Sarah with the original list and narrowed it down to four, which Sarah and Marco then interviewed. After whittling it down to just two, Sarah introduced them separately to Grace. Grace got on straight away with Jenny Ellis, a nanny in her late twenties. She had been employed by the same family in Atlanta for the last eight years and wanted to move to the Miami area. Grace wanted her as her nanny and so after Marco had made extensive checks on her background, Jenny was employed and moved into the mansion near the children's bedrooms.

Jenny looked after the children while Sarah and Marco, Rosa and Sal and Andrea and Cliff all went out one Friday night to celebrate Marcos birthday. He was starting to feel his age and felt apprehensive at approaching forty so wanted to go out somewhere and pretend he was twenty-something again. They all went to Carlottis for dinner, which Marco now owned fifty-one percent of. Cliff owned a part share in a night-club on the outskirts of West Palm Beach so they all decided to head over there after dinner. The wine had been flowing all evening and they were all merry by the time they tried to get into the night-club. The security man on the door did not at first recognised Cliff or Marco and they were all in danger of being refused entry. Sarah barged to the head of the party and went up to the security man.

"Do you know who these guys are?" She purred as she put her hand on his chest, feeling the body armour beneath his jacket.

He looked at her and then at the laughing Cliff behind her. "Drunks?"

Sarah sniggered. "That..!" She pointed to Cliff, "is your employer. That.." She gestured towards her husband. "is Marco Delvecchio. Now, are you going to let us all in?"

He looked at the men again, both grinning like drunken idiots. Sarah was surprised that Marco was not throwing his weight around. The security man was still having none of it.

Cliff's club manager walked by just then and recognised the party. "Hey, boss! " He greeted him genially. "You all up for night out with the ladies?" He walked up to Cliff and shook his hand. This completely threw the bouncer who could only stand aside and let the party in.

The manager, Tom, led them to a brown leather-bound semicircular seat around the table and sat them down. He discovered it was Marcos birthday and offered to buy them a bottle of champagne. He knew the benefits of keeping the local Don on his side. Cliff thought it would be a good idea to start telling jokes.

"Have you heard about the dyslexic devil worshipper?"

A shake of heads all around.

"He sold his soul to Santa!" Mass hysteria all around.

When the laughter had subsided and the drinks had been replenished, Cliff tried another one.

"Two parrots sitting on a perch, one said to the other, do you smell fish?"

This one took a few moments before the punch-line sunk in. Rosa got it first and burst into laughter which quickly spread around the table. When they had got their breath back, Sarah decided she wanted to dance. She had not been clubbing since her premarital days when she lived in a flat share near Reading in England. She had the hunkering for a dance. She squeezed past Sal and Rosa who were sat on the outside and skipped towards the dance-floor alone. The others were too busy laughing at her to join in. She was happy to dance alone, she felt liberated and carefree for the first time in a long time. It was as though she had no cares in the world despite the fact that her brother in law probably wanted her dead. She chose to forget that fact tonight.

Before too long, Marco joined her much to her astonishment. He was quite an agile dancer although he was no John Travolta. The drink had emboldened them both and their moves became quite seductive. Sarah put her arm around Marcos neck and began to gyrate quite close to him, smiling foxily at him.

"For an old man of thirty-seven, you got the moves, babe!" She pulled his head towards her and kissed him on the lips.

"Age is irrelevant. I feel like an adolescent every day you are around." His arm slipped to her waist and he pulled her close joining in the gyrations until they were in time. Sarah began to burn inside.

"Is being an adolescent a good thing?"

He looked directly into her eyes. "Oh yes. It allows you to do irresponsible things."

"Like?"

He smiled. "Come with me." He laced his fingers in hers and she followed him off the wooden dance floor. Puzzled, she followed him, glancing towards her table. The remainder of the party were engrossed in another of Cliffs dreadful jokes and didn't see Marco and Sarah disappear.

Marco lead her away from the loud music and towards the back of the club. They stopped at a door which was strangely leather bound with pewter studs and Marco punched in a number into the key pad at the side. The door made a clicking sound as the unlocking mechanism kicked in and Marco turned to Sarah and grinned. He pulled her without much resistance into the room beyond. With a wicked laugh, she followed him and released his intertwined fingers from hers.

"Marco?" She queried as she twirled around and looked round the room, dizzy with delight.

"Cliff owns a quarter share of this and I own a bit more. " He said slyly, not wanting to divulge much information. "This is where Cliff carries out his meetings that he cannot do from his downtown office. It makes a nice hideaway for me too." He grinned as he caught her and pulled her in close.

Sarah looked over his shoulder as he began to smooch with her to the distant music permeating from outside. The office was just that.

It had a desk with a chair either side and plenty of storage space. She spied a dark grey velour sofa against the wall. Her earlier desires were beginning to get the better of her. She stopped dancing and slunk over to the sofa. Laying back seductively, one leg bent over the arm and the other planted firmly on the floor, she smiled at her husband.

"Come here. I need you." She held her arms open and watched as he grinned and hurried to her. He fell into her embrace and began to kiss her with a passion fuelled by alcohol. His hand began to snake up her thigh covered by her scarlet dress and was surprised when he encountered no underwear.

"Well, it is your birthday." She explained.

He laughed. "How the hell did I survive four years without you?"

Her rely was to caress his neck with her lips and manoeuvre herself so Marco was on the sofa and she was astride him. Just how she liked it. She tantalised him by ruffling her skirts in his face and laughed as he groaned from the tease.

"You can be such a bitch!" He murmured.

"Yes, but you love it!" Her fingers found their way to his zipper and with a heavy sigh, she unzipped him and freed him. "No underwear either?" She mused.

"It's my birthday. I was hoping to get lucky." He clasped his hands around her neck and pulled her to him, contriving to put himself back on top. Sarah was having none of it and pushed him down, sliding down slightly so she could ease herself onto him. Marcos face was one of relief as he pushed into her and knew that she was not just going to tease him, although as she quite rightly said, he loved to be teased by her.

It was hot, sticky and passionate and over for both of them in just a few moments after a lot of groaning and grinding. Sarah disentangled herself from Marco, who lay on the sofa with a daft look on his face as though he had just had sex for the first time. Sarah kissed him and then began to readjust her clothing.

A knock on the door startled Marco and he jumped up off the sofa and began to stuff himself back into his trousers.

"Marco? Sarah? You okay?" Cliffs voice could clearly be heard from the other side of the locked door. With a slight buzz, the door opened just as Marco zipped himself back up and without saying a word, both he and Sarah walked by an astounded Cliff and back into the noise of the club.

With a laugh, Cliff let them by and closed the door to his office. He was astounded by the change in Marco since Sarah had returned just over a year ago. Gone was the austere unbending Marco Delvecchio who liked to dish out his own form of justice. He had been replaced by a man who was calm and fair although he could still be the judge and jury when he had to be. Cliff knew it was down to Sarah and that Marco's private family life had finally been put back on track.

Some five weeks later, Sarah knocked sheepishly at Marcos office door. He had decided he was working from home today, he just had a few things to deal with that meant he wouldn't have to go all the way to his marina office. Sarah knew he was alone as the door was slightly ajar. She pushed the door open a little and peered her head around the opening. Marco smiled as he looked up and saw her flushed face peeking round.

"Do you have a minute?" She asked timidly.

He nodded and put his pen down.

Sarah came in and strode around to his side of the desk. She perched herself on the desk in front of him.

"Do you remember your birthday?"

He smiled at the memories although most were fuzzy. The important things were vivid. "Of course. The best one in years."

"Good. Well I have a belated present for you."

He began to rub the inside of her thigh but she pushed his hand away. "I don't need any presents from you. You're present enough and you needn't go to any trouble."

"It's no trouble. But it won't be ready just yet."

Marco frowned yet smiled at the same time, puzzled.

Sarah sat forward on the desk, her legs either side of the chair that Marco was seated on. His eyes flickered downwards at her approaching hips. She leaned forward and put her arms around his neck. "It would seem, Mr Delvecchio that your antics in the night-club has landed me in a whole lot of trouble. If we weren't already married,

I would insist on a proposal."

He looked up at her face, smiling and yet a slight look of worry in her eyes.   Realisation hit. "Another baby?" Marco laughed.

"Every time you get me drunk, I get pregnant so once this one is born, no more drinking for me!" Sarah smiled. "I feel exhausted at the very thought of another baby, nanny or not!"

Marco shook his head in happy disbelief. Life was pretty good for him.

A couple of weeks later at the beginning of April, Sarah was sat in bed reading a holiday brochure on Hawaii. She had not forgotten Marcos Christmas Day half promise of a holiday. She was trying to convince him to take her to the Pacific Islands, she had always had a hankering to go there and laze on the beaches and see the glorious volcanoes but he claimed he was too busy at the moment. Sarah intended to work on him.

Marco came out of their bathroom and sighing, he climbed into bed beside her.

"What's the matter?" She asked of him, putting the holiday magazine down on her lap.

"I'm just tired, that's all." He lay back on the plump pillows and turned his head to the left to look at his wife who had a sly smile on her face.

"Well, I'd say you need a vacation. A week lying on a beach next to your nymph of a wife!" She teased. She thrust her magazine under Marcos nose.

He pushed it away. "Now is not the time. I've told you there is too much going on, too much to be done and I can't leave right now." He was irked that they were having this conversation again.

"Oh, please yourself then! I just thought a holiday would do you some good." The holiday magazine was thrown on the floor in petulance. Sarah leant over and kissed Marco on the cheek goodnight. She looked away towards the balcony doors. "Did you want the doors closed?"

Marco looked over at the French doors that lead onto the private balcony from the Master suite in the house. The drapes wafted around in the slight breeze brought in from the April night. He sighed and threw the sheet from him. "I opened the doors earlier, it was too hot in here." He got out of the bed and walked over to the open double doors. "Its got a little cooler now."

"That's because YOU are Mr Frosty." She chided softly. "Marco?"

He turned his head towards her, his body moving very slightly. At the same time, he cried out and slumped to the floor, barely moving.

Sarah screamed and leapt out of the huge bed towards her prostrate husband. He had a huge expanding flower of crimson on his chest and he was heaving and gasping for every breath. His eyes reflected terror that he had never felt before as she knelt down next to him. Sarah reached out and grabbed the first thing that came to hand, a discarded item of clothing, a shirt that she had bought for him just that week and pressed it hard against Marcos chest.

"Shit!" He grimaced against the pain.

"Darling, I have to call 911. This is too serious!" She told him before he could protest against people in his home. Sarahs hands were shaking and she felt very nauseous at the sight of the blood seeping from Marcos body. Grabbing his hand, she forced it to pressure the material to staunch the flow of blood before standing up and running to the bedroom door.

"Someone call 911!" She shouted at the top of her voice. She knew Gabe and Scott were downstairs and she heard shouts below as they galvanised into action. Before she had even knelt back down beside her husband, Gabe had crashed through the bedroom door behind her.

"Jesus!" Gabe muttered as he pulled his cellphone from the attachment on his belt and called for an ambulance. He then called the gatehouse and told them an ambulance was on its way and to let it through and give them every assistance. He also told them effective immediately, the estate was on lockdown. Scott appeared at his shoulder and peered at the scene with Sarah frantically trying to help Marco. He echoed Gabe's earlier sentiments. "Scott, go outside and let the dogs loose. Whoever did this must still be in the grounds. I want them found." Gabe instructed.

Scott just nodded and after taking a final look at his distressed boss, he disappeared, practically flying down the stairs.

Sarah meanwhile was sat on the bedroom floor with Marcos head on her lap. Anguish showed on her face as she gently stroked his cheek with one hand while desperately trying to stem the flow of blood with the other. Marco himself was extremely pale and agitated. He was sweating from the effects of blood loss and shock.

"You'll be okay, darling." Sarah tried to soothe him although her insides were in knots.

"Sarah, I love you and I always have. Remember that." He murmured. His eyes flickered.

"And you had better always love me. We have another baby coming." She reminded him as she choked back sobs that were threatening to overcome her. "Stay awake, sweetie." She looked at Gabe for help. She didn't know what else to do. Gabe had squatted beside Marco, unsure himself of what exactly to do. He shrugged helplessly.

Sarah heard the dogs go loose outside yapping at the black night. In the near distance, she heard the faint yet welcome sound of the emergency services on their way. It was music to Sarahs ears. "They're coming, sweetie, stay awake!" She said more forcefully as his eyes threatened to close. She slapped his cheek, almost imperceptibly to bring him back from the oblivion that beckoned.

"You always were a ruthless woman!" He whispered. "I feel like shit and you are slapping me around." He again grimaced with the pain emanating from his chest.

Sarah managed a small laugh and she kissed his tacky forehead. Outside, the blue and red lights of the ambulance reflected from the driveway and Gabe rushed off the lead the paramedics to Marco.

They gave him oxygen and something for the pain while they assessed the wound. They packed the wound tight and wrapped his chest in bandages before putting him onto the gurney and wheeling him out to the top of the stairs. As Sarah followed behind, she saw Jenny peering sleepily from her bedroom door.

"What's going on?" She asked, fear in her eyes as she saw Marco being carried downstairs.

Sarah raced over to her, still in her night-gown. "Jenny, I have to go with Marco. Can you stay on duty until I get home? I know you are meant to be off tomorrow but I will make it up to you." She pleaded.

"Of course. Don't worry about the children, it seems as though you have enough to worry about." Her head gesticulated down the stairs to where the gurney was now being righted to wheel straight to the ambulance.

Marco was still conscious when Sarah had reached the bottom of the stairs. She tried to get into the ambulance beside Marco for the trip to Columbus but Marco said no.

"You aren't dressed and I need to speak to Gabe."

"But..." She tried to protest.

"Don't argue with me Sarah. I'm not in the mood."

She nodded reluctantly as the ambulance doors closed on him and she blew him a kiss. The sirens wailed off into the night.

"What's happened?" Harrys voice appeared out of nowhere over Sarahs left shoulder. He had just seen the ambulance pull away, lights flashing.

"I have to get dressed." She turned to go back in the house and Harry followed. "We were in the bedroom and out of nowhere, Marco was just shot. Just like that." Her voice began to break and she choked back the tears that wanted to overwhelm her. Harry put a hand on her shoulder to comfort her but she shrugged it off and went inside. "Can you take me to the hospital, Harry?"

He nodded as if he would have never considered anything else.

Harry waited with car keys in his hand while Sarah threw on some clothes and then joined Harry in the hallway. Harry drove to the hospital while Sarah called Rosa on her cellphone.

"Rosa, I'm sorry to call so late." She began.

"Sarah, I heard. Someone just called Sal and told him what happened. We've been told to go to the house. Can Jenny take Adina? I want to be at the hospital with you."

"Sure Rosa, Adina will be fine. I'll see you at the hospital. Please hurry, I don't want to be on my own." She pleaded.

"I'll be there as soon as I can." Rosa promised.

Sarah disconnected the call and choked back another sob. The shock was beginning to set in. Harry reached across the seat and took her hand in his as he drove.

"Marco will be fine, Sarah. He's a fighter. They'll patch him up and he'll be back home bellowing orders before you know it!" He assured her, squeezing her hand.

"I hope so, Harry. I don't think I could get by without him. Not after everything that we've been through. We're having another baby." She smiled across to him through her tears that were now free falling.

Harry laughed. "That's fantastic! There is no way that he will let this thing get the better of him now!"

"It is." Sarah said quietly, unable to find the same joy that gripped Harry.

They drove in silence the rest of the way to the hospital. Harry dropped Sarah directly outside the Emergency Room before he went off the park the car. Sarah ran inside and saw Gabe in the waiting area. A Doctor was talking to him and Gabe held up a hand to stop him as Sarah approached.

"Sarah, this is Marcos doctor. He wants to operate." Gabe informed her.

The doctor lead Sarah and Gabe to a private waiting area with comfortable chairs and a coffee machine. "I'm Doctor Pitchford and I'm the surgeon in charge of Marco's treatment. He lost consciousness shortly after arriving here and he has lost a lot of blood. We need to operate to remove the bullet and repair the wound but we need the consent form signed." Doctor Pitchford held forward a clipboard with several sheets of paper attached to it."

Sarah sat down on one of the comfortable chairs as a young nurse entered the room. She looked across at Sarah, pale and scared looking and walked over to her.

"Will he be okay?" Sarah asked to no-one in particular.

"The doctors will do everything possible for your husband." The young nurse assured her. Her name badge advised anyone who was interested that her name was
Melanie.

Sarah stood and walked over to the Doctor. She took the clipboard from him with shaking hands and signed the form that allowed near strangers to hack away at her husbands chest. Thanking her, the doctor sprung into action and left the relatives room. Melanie stayed behind.

"He's in good hands." Melanie told Sarah as she walked over to the patients worried looking wife. "Doctor Pitchford is the best in Florida."

Sarah was by now completely overcome and unable to hold back the flood of tears that had been threatening since Marco had fallen. She felt the room sway and if it wasn't for Harry rushing to steady her, she would have been in a heap on the floor.

"Can I get you anything, Mrs Delvecchio?" Melanie asked. "You look very pale." She sat Sarah down on the sofa.

"I'm fine. This is all just a little bit much for me." She smiled shyly at Melanie.

Melanie smiled back encouragingly. "Well, why don't you stay here and take it easy? I'll go upstairs to the O.R and see how things are getting along. It will be a while before there is any real news though so don't expect me back too soon. Meantime, please try not to worry."

Easier said than done, Sarah thought as Melanie left the comfort of the relatives room in search of news.

Harry came into the room and Gabe went over and spoke quietly to him. After a few words, Harry gave Gabe the keys to Sarahs car and gave him brief directions on where he had just parked the SUV. Gabe left and Harry came over to sit beside Sarah without saying a word, he just held her hand and squeezed it tightly.

Gabe walked out into the cool night air. Before Marco had lost consciousness, he had given Gabe clear instructions on how he wanted the situation handled. Gabe was to call the Chief of Palm Beach County Police, James A. Davis. The Chief was on the Delvecchio's payroll and Marco wanted him to be inside his house when the inevitable investigations began. There would be Crime Scene Investigators all over the outside of the house by this stage and Marco did not want them inside his house. He also told Gabe to call Chicago.

Rosa arrived at the hospital a short time later and while Sarah filled her in on what had happened so far, Harry took his leave and went outside. An armed policeman had appeared and was stationed at the door of the relatives room, no doubt his arrival instigated by Chief Davis. Harry was desperate for a cigarette and stood by the ambulance bay puffing away watching as people were brought in various stages of life and death. His thoughts drifted briefly to the possibility of Marco not pulling through and he knew that Joe would inevitably take the reins should the worse happen. Joe's plans would not include Sarah or the kids and the idea put the fear of god into him.

Harry took another long drag on the cigarette and looked at his watch. It was just after 2 a.m. He was beat but the evening was not even close to being over for him. Erin was waiting for him in his apartment and on any normal night, he would have been cosying up to her and her ample bust by now.

His mind drifted back to the problem at hand and he sighed deeply. Another ambulance pulled up and in a rush of colours and shouting, a gurney was pulled out from the rear of the vehicle. A grey looking old woman was on the gurney and with the medics trying to pump life into her chest, they disappeared into the ER Harry pulled on the cigarette and threw the remaining third of it away. He went back inside to the bright lights of the hospital building.

Just before 4 Am., Melanie walked quietly into the relatives room where Sarah was now sleeping on the chair with her head on Rosa's shoulder. Rosa in turn had her head rested on the top of Sarahs also sleeping lightly.

Melanie knelt down in front of Sarah and gently shook her shoulder to rouse her "Mrs. Delvecchio?" She spoke softly. "Sarah?"

Sarah jumped awake, waking Rosa in the process. As she sorted her thoughts Sarah grabbed Rosa's hand and braced herself for bad news.

Melanie smiled. "The doctors will be back down soon to see you but everything has gone well. Your husband is in recovery and I'll take you up to see him shortly."

Sarah choked back a sob of pure relief. She thanked the nurse through her tears for all her kindness and then turned to Rosa to hug her. Harry handed them an instant coffee from the machine. He was happy that Marco seemed to be okay.

Doctor Pitchford came into the room just a few minutes later and stood in front of Sarah. "As Melanie has already told you, your husband is recovering. The bullet missed everything major and chipped the underside of his scapula before settling into a fleshy part of the shoulder, hence the bleeding. We have taken the bullet out and the police are in possession of this. We have repaired the site of the bleed and although he is very weak from the heavy blood-loss, we expect Marco to make a full recovery."

Sarah nodded enthusiastically. She just wanted to see Marco now.

"I'll wait here with Harry while you go up." Rosa informed Sarah.

Sarah just nodded again, too tired and emotional for any real conversation. She followed Melanie down the hallway to the elevators and they went two floors up to the ICU. As soon as Sarah and Melanie stepped out of the elevator, Sarah knew where Marco was with the armed policeman at the door. She shrugged, almost apologetically at Melanie. Melanie let Sarah go in alone.

Marco was lying propped up in the bed. He looked very pale and vulnerable in the bed with a sheet drawn up to his waist and was hooked up to a heart monitor as he was fresh out of surgery. As Sarah sat in the chair next to the bed, Marco opened his eyes and turned to look at her.

"Hey!" He managed a weak smile.

"You okay?" She asked as she wrapped his hand in hers. She looked at the bandages strapping his shoulder and most of his upper body, a little extreme for a superficial wound in Sarahs view. She wondered what the doctors weren't telling her.

"I will be. I guess I have you to thank for saving my life."

"What?" Sarah thought he was rambling now. The drugs, perhaps. "For sticking your new shirt on the wound?"

He shook his head very slightly, the effort causing him pain. "Don't you remember? You called out to me. I turned my head to look at you. If I hadn't moved, the bullet would have hit me plum in the heart. No chance of surgery and no second chances."

Sarah sat back in the chair, unable to take it in. It didn't seem possible. Marco had been a little terse as he got out of bed to close the French doors and she was aware that it had been down to her mithering him about the holiday. She had undone the front of her dressing gown as she sat in bed to give him a flash and to make him smile. Was he saying that was what saved his life?

"It's fate, Sarah." With an effort. he bought her hand up to his lips and gently kissed her fingers. "Have you seen Gabe?" He asked her.

"No. He left just before you went for surgery."

"Can you tell him that I need to see him?"

Sarah stood up and bent down to kiss his clammy forehead. "No. I'm in charge now for the foreseeable. You are going to rest and get stronger. You have one cop on the door and the other will be here as soon as we leave and Harry informs me that they will be here for as long as you are, twenty-four-seven. The only people allowed through that door will be family. And I mean BLOOD family. Me, Rosa and Grace."

He shook his head. "Not Grace. I don't want her to see me here like this."

Sarah shrugged. "Fine, but no business or help me god! I'll shoot you myself. Do you understand me?"

He smiled. "You are so much like my mother and you would have liked her. The scary thing is, my father used to obey her every word, much like I do with you. Just twenty four hours though, there is much to discuss."

Sarah kissed him again, this time on the lips. "Sure. You get some sleep and rest up. I'm going home to see to the kids and then I will be back. Do you want anything specific from home?"

He shook his head as his eyes began to close. Sarah left the room and once out of earshot and eyeshot, she collapsed in a flood of tears. The shock, stress and relief had all set in simultaneously.

"You want to argue this with me, Gabe? You really want to start a fight with me that you won't win?" With a cold hard stare, Sarah looked at Gabe as he tried to tell her that he had to see Marco immediately. She had returned home from the hospital, had showered, wanted to catch a few hours sleep and see the children. Jenny had agreed to stay on for the rest of the day so Sarah could return to the hospital later.

Gabe tried to stare her down. He had, out of courtesy, enquired after Marco and just vaguely mentioned that he would leave for the hospital shortly as there were things he needed to talk over with the boss. "Come on, Sarah! You know roughly how things work. I have to get in and see him - I need to know how Marco wants this thing handled.

"Yes, I know how things work and we both know who is responsible for my husband lying in a hospital bed right now. He's not going anywhere and when he is fit and well, he can tell you then. Aren't you suppose to be his second in command, or something? Make some executive decisions."

"No, I'm not. I've just assumed that title since Joe left, it was always him before that. Anyway, I'm not supposed to discuss this with you. Just let me see Marco."

"Chill out, Gabe. I'm not that stupid and I know how things are! The upshot of this is. You are not talking business with Marco at least until tomorrow night. If I have to, I'll tell those cops outside his door that it was you who shot him. That will put you in jail for at least forty-eight hours and away from Marco." Sarah crossed her arms in glorious victory as she faced down Gabe in the hallway by the front door.

Gabriel snorted in derision. He looked at his boss's wife and thought that perhaps, she might just be mad enough to go through with it. "You'd do that?"

Sarah nodded. "If I have to."

Gabe threw his arms up in the air in defeat and resignation and walked through the front door to head for home. He needed some sleep for when he was permitted to see Marco. The hard work would start then.

After taking Grace to school, Harry escorted Sarah back to the hospital. Enzio was left at the school to sit and watch out for Grace but Sarah knew she would be safe there.

Marco had rested well after his operation and that, coupled with a blood transfusion had brought colour back to his cheeks. He looked much better now than when Sarah had left him at four-thirty that morning. His eyes were closed as she quietly entered the private hospital room and she assumed he was sleeping. She sat quietly in the chair next to his bed. She entwined his fingers in hers.

Marco sighed deeply. "That feels good. I hate not sleeping next to you at night." He opened his deliciously brown eyes and looked at Sarah.

"Did I wake you?" She asked apologetically.

He shook his head. "I was just resting my eyes. I've been awake for a while. It's hard to sleep with all of these pretty nurses flitting in and out raising your pulse rate!" He jested. He looked hard at her. "You don't look too good." He looked concerned.

Sarah smiled weakly. "I'm okay, just a bit tired. I didn't sleep very well. It's kind of hard to sleep when your husband is in a hospital bed fighting for his life."

"That's a bit dramatic. I'll be out of here in a few days."

"And then what happens, Marco? You and I both know who did this - where does it end?"

He shook his head. "That's my problem."

"It's also mine. Do you remember when we were first married and someone took a pot shot at me? I was just shopping, I didn't even know your business then. We'd only been married a fortnight and most people didn't even know we were married but someone decided it would be a good idea to try and kill me. With your nefarious business and your enemies, who's next? Grace? Gio? Are we going for a family tradition of bullet scars?"

Marco shook his head slowly. "That's not how it works."

"I don't give a shit how it you think it works! I know how it is and your brother does not care who he gets next!" Sarah was enraged at the thought her innocent babies could be hurt like this.

"If it's business, it's kept within the business, if you know what I mean."

"No, I don't know what you mean so why don't you explain it to me? Mind you, I'm not sure I even want to know!"

"Good because I can't discuss it here, it's not safe. Please just trust me that you, Grace and Gio are safe." His eyes took on a pleading look.

"Really?" Sarah asked, not convinced.

Marco nodded.

"So why do we need Harry?" Sarah played her trump card.

"To stop the FBI hassling you. Do you see Robbins around anywhere?" It would seem as though Marco had an answer for everything.

Sarah sat back in the chair unable to think of a reply. She looked away from Marco and stared out of the window. She had the violent urge to hit out at her husband but she fought it. Where was the challenge in striking an injured man?

"Sarah, don't go all quiet on me. I would rather you scream and shout at me than go silent."

She turned her attention back to him. "How long are you going to be in here for?" She chose a safer path to track.

"A couple of days. What have you said to Grace?"

"Nothing. What am I supposed to tell her?" Her voice had not lost its petulance. Marco picked up on this and was weary of it.

"Why don't you go home and catch up on your sleep? Come back when you're less irritable." His words were like a tinderbox to dry grass. Sarah stood up and screamed in her frustration, then left the room without saying another word.

Marco was discharged from hospital four days later although he brought home with him plenty of painkillers and antibiotics. He still tired easily and more or less went straight to bed on his arrival at the house. He was to hold court in his office later on in the day and all of his senior members of staff had been told to be available. The press were camped out at the bottom of the drive and Ugo and Pino were having a hard time keeping them in check. Rico had been summoned to sort it out legally.

Beth arrived at the house around teatime and was pleased to be let in the grounds. "What a circus back there! Ugo smuggled me in through a hidden gateway when he saw my car. Thank god! I wouldn't want my picture in the paper entering this den of iniquity!" She laughed as she embraced her friend. "I'm sorry I haven't been around before, it was impossible to get past the little Hitlers at the gate."

"The house had been on total lockdown since Marco got shot. Even the phone calls have been routed through Rico." Sarah handed

Beth a cup of coffee.

"Do you know who did it? "

Sarah looked up sharply at her friend as she thought about her answer. She knew Marco did not want certain things made public knowledge. "The police are still looking into it all. We know that whoever it was, was inside the grounds. They must have been on the pool-house roof as it pretty much looks straight into our bedroom and with bullet used it wouldn't have had the range to be fired from outside. That's what the police are saying. Whoever it was must have been sat waiting up there for an opportunity. They are combing the area and I'm sure they will have some answers soon."

"Are you scared? I mean, what if they come back again?"

Sarah shrugged. "Unlikely. Marco has stepped up security, as you know so we are safe enough here. So how is your job going?" Sarah wanted to get off the subject.

Beth had recently been employed by Dominic Russell as yet another secretary to him. He had taken a shine to Beth when he first clapped eyes on her and was a prettier picture than his cheap tart of a wife. As far as he was concerned, Beth made it worth his while going to the office in the morning. Beth liked working for Dom but was refusing his subtle advances because of her history with Luke. She liked Dom well enough but he was her boss and she was keeping well away from men.

The following day, Sarah took Marco a light lunch into his office. He had been working until quite late last night and was up and at it early again this morning. He was sat with Gabe and looked tired when Sarah knocked on the door and went inside without waiting for an answer.

"I thought you might want some lunch." She said to her husband as she put the plate down in front of him. It was just a tuna fish sandwich. Gabe took the hint and left the office. He had been secretly impressed with Sarahs show of defiance against him the other day and his estimation of her had increased.

Marco looked up at her and smiled his appreciation. "Thanks. I've been feeling a little hungry." He yawned. "I may go upstairs for a snooze after this. I'm still a bit tired."

Sarah snaked one arm around Marcos neck and kissed his cheek. "You need to take it easy." She chastised him gently.

He took a bite of his sandwich and chewed it. When he had swallowed it, he looked up at her. "You can be so tough when you want to be."

She smiled at Marco and poured him a coffee saying nothing.

"Do you want to go out for dinner tonight?" He asked casually.

She frowned. "Wouldn't that be over doing things a bit? You are only just out of hospital and you said yourself that you are tired."

"I'll be okay after a snooze. Besides, it's only dinner and I do need to eat. We'll be home by ten and I'll stick to mineral water." He promised.

Sarah leant down to kiss his cheek again. "Okay. Leave it to me and I'll organise it in the proviso that you do no more business today and go upstairs and rest."

Marco took a gulp of his coffee. "I love it when you boss me around. If only I had more energy, I'd let you take me upstairs for a spanking." He grinned, ever hopeful.

Sarah kissed him passionately on the lips which would have to suffice for now.

The family were still on a high security alert so while Marco and Sarah went to Carlottis for dinner that evening, they could not have their usual table. Their table was outside on the deck overlooking the sea and it was too much in the open for Gabe and Scott to be able to protect them. They sat inside the restaurant about halfway back in a little nook that was very private. Gabe and Scott sat a few tables away out of earshot but so they could see the door and the couple in the nook.

Marco was finishing his appetiser before he dropped his bombshell.

"There is something that I need to discuss with you away from the distraction of home." He put his shrimp fork down on his empty plate and pushed it away slightly. He looked at Sarah, blossoming in her third month of pregnancy. She looked stunning in a simple black linen trouser suit. The sides of her long dark hair were pulled up and held in place with a clip with a red silk rose adorning it. He felt the luckiest man alive being married to her.

"I thought there would be something." She replied knowingly. "You are still not well enough and yet you insist on coming out tonight." She reached over for his hand. He was still quite pale and looked exhausted and Sarah wished she had made a stand against him and they had stayed in.

"I'll be fine. What I have to say needs to be said and without histrionics from you."

Sarah took a deep breath. "I'm not sure I like the sound of this."

Marco shrugged. He knew what he had to say was not going to be welcomed by his wife. "It's not something that I wanted to happen just yet. Events have taken over my plans in the last few days and I have had to bring things forward and take drastic action."

"What is it?" Sarah urged.

"Vinnie."

Sarah felt a chill go down her spine and it wasn't the cool sea breezes coming in through the open windows. She felt a bit dizzy. "What about him? Surely you don't think I have any feelings for him?"

Marco laughed. "No, not at all." He reassured her. "Rico, Gabe and I have been discussing the options and I have come to a decision. Since this thing with Joe kicked off some months ago, I have needed someone I can trust. Rico and Gabe are both loyal to me and good at what they do but they aren't family. Excluding Joe, Vinnie is the closest thing to family I have that I can call on."

"What do you mean by family?" Sarah asked.

Marco ignored the question and continued. "I've asked Vinnie to come to Florida and help me out." He put his hands up to stop Sarahs protests before they started. "It was going to happen at some stage anyway but with this attempt on my life, it's going to be sooner or later."

Sarah sat back and threw her napkin on her plate, her appetite suddenly failed her. "I thought you wanted to discuss this with me. It sounds to me like you have already made your decision."

"With regard to Vinnie joining me, yes, I have made up my mind. Sarah, there are things going on that you don't know and I can't tell you."

She looked away from him, tired if hearing the same old story with regard to protecting her from his secrets. She wished he would just tell her, however horrific and repulsive she may find it.

Marco continued. "It's just a short term thing until things with Joe settle down. Vinnie is my brother and I need him here."

"I just don't understand your need of him, Marco. First Rosa and then the business deal that went wrong, not to mention my mistake with him. What makes you think you can trust him? Why have you suddenly forgiven him?"

Marco shrugged again with effort to his shoulder.

The waiter came to take their empty plates and the conversation ended while the waiter hovered. When he left their table, Marco answered her. "I don't know. He knows he has more to gain by being with me than against me. His advancement in Chicago has slowed and he would be better off financially here. He has a child now and he needs to think of him."

Sarah thought back to the letter she was asked to type to the child's nanny and smiled. She could not imagine him as a doting father. "What if he sides with Joe?" She asked.

"I can keep an eye on Vinnie here. Joe would never be accepted as head of this family, despite what he brags about. Vinnie would never live to help him achieve status."

"It seems as though you have it all worked out."

Marco sat back. "Pretty much. It's just you that I have to convince."

"And Rosa." She added. "But if it's what you want, you don't need my blessing. I'm surprised that you even discussed it with me. I'm just concerned that it may cause a rift between us as I'm sure Vinnie and I will meet at some stage."

Marco shook his head. "There should be no need of that. He's looking at apartments in Boca. He wants to be by the sea for James benefit but away from the problems that we seem to attract here."

Sarah sighed. What did it really matter to her anyway? She had cemented her relationship with Marco and hopefully he would realise where her loyalties lay. She had made it clear to Vinnie while she was still in California that there would be no future for them so surely there would be no problems?

Although Sarah didn't see him, she was aware that Vinnie had made the move to Boca within the week with the flurry of activity that it created. She tried not to let it play on her mind although it made her feel strangely vulnerable as she knew what she had to lose if Vinnie got any peculiar ideas and tried to ruin it for her. Rosa stayed clear of the house, she still did not want to run into Vinnie even though her life had moved on considerably since her time with him.

Sarah had ideas of her own of how to fill in her considerable free time. One beautifully warm, sunny morning in early May, she went to the Family townhouse to collect Beth. She was still living there, Marco said it was fine for however long she needed it and she said she felt safe being there with Eddie and his cute butt. After picking up Beth, the two women drove off to West Palm Beach to meet a real estate agent who claimed to have on his books exactly what they were after. An old school house in much need of repair on the outskirts of town and within the price range that Sarah had stipulated.

They arrived at the address and laughed as they saw the rundown building. Not put off, they got out and went to meet with Gavin Chettle, the realtor. He smiled warmly at the women and shook both their hands in turn, Sarah first as he knew she was the one with the money. With Gavin prattling on about what they could do with the building, they took a good look around the outside. The garden was very overgrown and had rusted school playground equipment hidden amongst the grass. The back of the building looked fairly solid with just the windows broken. It had three stories, but the top floor was probably just an attic room. Eager, they went inside.

The inside looked like a typical school building. It had a large entrance hall with five rooms that were once classrooms coming off. Down the hallway there was a large ancient kitchen with its disused and rusted appliance still in place, and two bathrooms, one for boys and one for girls. Going up the concrete stairs were four more rooms and what looked to be an old office. Gavin explained that this would have been the teachers room, confirmed by the presence of a small bathroom with one stall and a small hand basin off the room at the back.

As Sarah walked through the building, she began to image how it would look once the builders were in and interior designers put their hand to it. There was plenty of parking outside and lots of scope for what she and Beth planned to turn it into.

"So what do you ladies think?" Chettle asked as they returned to the front gate.

"It's fine." Beth enthused.

Sarah was a little more reserved. "I would have to think a little more on it. We would, presumably, need planning permits?" She looked at Chettle who was slightly perplexed. He didn't think permits would be a problem for the Delvecchio's. He didn't voice this opinion of course, he merely smiled his smarmy realtors smile and skated over the question with one of his own.

"When will you be able to let me know? I have another party interested but I thought you'd like first refusal."

"Just a few days, Mr Chettle and I shall call you." Sarah promised. She had her husband to convince first.

Gavin Chettle walked back to his hire car with a faint hope of reprieve. Ironically, Sarahs brother-in-law was pressing him for money from loan repayments he claimed Gavin owed him. The bastard had already blown up his precious BMW, hence the hire car. Joe Delvecchio had given him until next week to pay up or Chettle would probably pay back with blood. With any luck, this deal would go through in time.

As Sarah pulled up outside the front of the house, she looked across to Marcos office window. She saw the blinds were closed which usually meant he was at home and hiding from the rays of sunshine. She had no recollection of him having planned visitors and decided she should take the chance that he was available. She needed to talk to him before Grace came home from school and before Jenny started her night off. There would be no chance of sensible adult talk once Sarah was taking care of her children.

She went inside the cool hallway and strode purposefully towards the closed office door which normally meant he was in a meeting. She knocked anyway and opened the door, peering around tentatively. He was alone but on the phone. He looked up and smiled when he saw who it was and beckoned her in. Sarah silently walked in, closing the door behind her while Marco continued his telephone conversation in an animated fashion. She sat on the desk to his side while she waited for the call to reach it's conclusion. He was obviously wound up by whomever was on the other end of the phone and Sarah wondered if now was the right time to ask him such a huge favour.

The phone was slammed back into it's cradle with a show of temper from Marco, causing Sarah to jump slightly. Marco took a deep breath and smiled up at her, caressing her lower leg which was dangling beside him. His shoulder was beginning to ache again now that the painkillers were wearing off.

"Are you okay?" She could see his eyes were clouded with pain.

"I need some stronger drugs. These ones don't last five minutes." He rubbed the area that the bullet had torn into him, healing nicely but still lightly bandaged and painful.

"Perhaps you should just slow down, sweetie. The doctor said that anything stronger can be addictive."

He nodded. He understood Sarahs concerns with him and drugs of any type. "I'll be okay. What are you doing in my domain?" He asked with a wry smile.

"Just making sure that you are okay. Do you want some coffee or anything?"

He nodded. "Let's go outside in the sunshine. I used to be tanned and good looking and now look at me!" He laughed.

Sarah leant over and kissed him firmly on the lips. "I still fancy you. I'll meet you outside with the coffee in a few minutes." She jumped off the desk and headed for the kitchen.

Once outside in the May sunshine, Marco relaxed and relished the thought of spending a few minutes alone with Sarah, who in turn was looking for an opportunity to raise an important question. He sat on the silver patio chair and turned his head towards the bright sunshine.

Sarah came out with a tray of coffee and some of Marcos favourite cookies. She poured his coffee, black and sweet and handed it to him. As she poured her tea, the demand tumbled from her lips.

"Marco, I need to borrow some money."

He looked at her over the rim of his coffee cup. "Sweetheart, you don't need to ask. The money is there and it is yours as much as mine. You don't normally ask or care judging by this months credit card bill. Just help yourself."

Sarah took a sip of her hot tea. "I know but it's more than just a few dollars. Also, you might want to know what I need it for."

He raised an eyebrow, intrigued by her words. He put his cup down and decided to humour her. "Okay, I'll bite. How much do you need?"

"About four hundred. To start with."

He picked his cup up again and took a sip of the syrupy Italian coffee.

"Thousand." She finished.

Marco choked on his drink. Sarah rushed around the table to slap his back and when he had caught his breath, he looked at her through watery eyes. She went and sat back down in her chair. "Four hundred thousand dollars? To start with?" He was incredulous. "What the hell for?"

"It's all legal and above board." She assured him.

"I should hope so!" He was still shocked.

"Darling, just hear me out. Don't say anything until I have finished explaining. Beth and I want to open a centre for victims of drug abuse." She held up her hands to stop his interrupting. "Not drug users, but people like Beth who have been in some way a victim from an actual abuser. To give them someplace safe to stay while they get back on their feet." Sarah pulled her chair around to her husband so she could be closer to him and watch for a reaction. "We've found the perfect place although it does need a lot of work. The loan is to get the place up and running and then we will rely on charitable donations to keep the place open. Andrea is good at fundraising and we'll eventually be able to pay you back with interest."

Marco looked over Sarahs shoulder while he digested this hair-brained idea. Scott Wolfe was wandering around the back gate. Marcos eyes dropped back to the pleading eyes of his wife. "How long have you been planning this?"

"Since Beth lost her baby. I haven't said anything before now as we hadn't got anywhere with the plans or even found a property."

"And now you have?"

"And now we have." Sarahs eyes lit up with the excitement of the project. "We've found the perfect place that will hold about twenty people once we have developed the property. We'll have professional but voluntary counsellors and advisors."

Marco crossed his legs, aloof as though he was dealing with just another business associate and not his wife. "What about your family? You'll soon have three children, not forgetting your very demanding husband."

Sarah shifted over to sit on his lap. She put her arms around his neck and kissed his cheeks and nose. "And you will always come first, I promise. My role will mainly just be the start-up. Once it is up and running, I'll just help Andrea and Beth with the fundraising and lend our name to help that along and make it marketable. The children will never suffer and I would NEVER neglect you." She nibbled at his earlobe, trying to manipulate his decision.

He allowed Sarah to continue, he was enjoying the sensation although he had already reached a decision.

"Here's what I'll do." He said softly. "I'll have Rico look into it. The finance, the viability, all of it. If, and only if he is happy with it, I'll give you Carte Blanche for the entire project."

Sarah squealed with delight and peppered his face with kisses. "Thank you, darling, thank you. I love you so much!"

He laughed. "You always do when you get your own way."

Sarah slapped him playfully, kissed him sincerely and then went to collect their daughter from school.

Beth called several times a day for the next three days while Rico was doing his research. She was desperate to know if Marco had made a decision yet and Sarah promised her that as soon as she knew, she would call Beth.

On Friday afternoon, Sarah was just taking Giorgio outside on the patio for his nap when Cliff went to find her. He found her just as the baby was drifting off and Sarah sat back in the chair to rock the pram back and forth to soothe him.

"Sarah? Do you have a minute? Marco wants to talk to you."

Sarah looked up at Cliff, puzzled. Marco didn't usually send anyone to find her, he usually showed her more respect than that and came himself. For a split second, it occurred to her to say to Cliff that she was busy and Marco would have to wait. When she realised how childish she was being, she smiled at Cliff and checking Giorgio was sound asleep, she followed Cliff to Marcos office.

Marco was, as usual, sat down behind his huge cherry wood desk finishing off a phone call. Rico was leant against the window sill clutching some important looking papers. As usual for him, he was impeccably dressed in a tailored suit, white shirt buttoned to the top and a dark tie - the epitome of a successful lawyer despite the ninety-five degree heat outside. Cliff, the family accountant, was casually dressed in light coloured chinos and a cotton button through shirt open at the neck and a sprinkling of dark hair peeking through. He looked flustered and hot as he pulled a chair round for Sarahs use opposite Marco and then sat on a vacant chair next to her.

No-one said a word or moved a muscle until Marco had finished his telephone call. Once completed, he sat back in his chair and smiled at Sarah.

"Rico and Cliff have been looking into your proposal." He informed her without preamble.

Sarah sneaked a sideways glance towards the window at Rico but his face was impassive and gave nothing away. He had barely moved since she had entered the office. She turned her attention back to Marco.

"And?" She prompted when it became apparent that Marco was stalling for dramatic effect.

"Rico has advised me that planning permits would not be a problem. He has recently been dating a young lady at City Hall in the planning department and we have assurances that as long as we don't build any higher, your plans will sail through." He leant forward. "Cliff has similarly assured me that Andrea is a fantastic fundraiser and is very much looking forward to 'getting stuck in' as your English brethren might say." His eyes were twinkling as Sarah began to get the impression that he was going to green light her.

"My only concern as I've said before is your participation in it all. Our family name gets a lot of bad press and I'm a little troubled that this will add fuel to the fire. People will question our agenda."

Sarah nodded. "I can understand your reservations. What I don't understand is why you are all of a sudden concerned about what people think. This is a good thing for our stuck up community and my only agenda is to help people less fortunate and less privileged than ourselves."

Marco smiled. Sarah was right. He usually didn't care about what people said behind his back and no-one would dare say anything to his face. He looked her in the eye and nodded. "Okay."

A grin crept across Sarahs face as he gave her the go ahead. She knew he would expect copious amounts of sexual favours for this but it would be worth it. They locked eyes for a few moments not saying anything before Sarah took her leave. As she closed the door, he was still looking at her, smiling. She mouthed the words 'thank you' to him and closed the door behind her to leave the men to it.

The following day, Sarah, Beth and Andrea met for lunch to discuss their plans for the school house. Cliff had made Gavin a perfectly acceptable offer on the property which had been accepted and the Rico got to work on the legal side of things. The School House would be a Delvecchio possession before Graces seventh birthday next month and they hoped to have the centre open before baby number three came along in early October.

Andrea had already booked the function room at the Country Club for her first fundraiser and she was planning on bringing in a top chef from London, an old friend of hers to organise some top notch catering and charge the rich of Palm Beach through the nose for it. The women also thought an auction would be a good idea if they could get some of the designer stores on Worth Avenue to donate something of value. Andrea would be the persuasive one and promised she would drag some items of value out of them.

CHAPTER FOURTEEN

Two days before Graces birthday, Sarah and Beth went to collect the keys for the school house from Gavin Chettle. He met them outside the building and was in possession of a new black BMW. He'd managed to pay Joe what he was supposed to owe him and had some left over to get himself some decent wheels. He was leaning against it as Sarah and Beth pulled up in Sarahs SUV.

"Hello Mrs Delvecchio, Ms Connor." Beth had gone back to her maiden name. Chettle smiled broadly at them both as they got out of the car and walked towards him.

"Mr Chettle, thank you for meeting us here." Beth spoke calmly although her insides were in knots. This centre meant a great deal to her.

"I understand the money has been wired to your account?" Sarah was all business.

"Yes, ma'am, thank you. Here are your keys." He handed them to Sarah and she felt a flush of pleasure course through her as she turned the keys over in her hands.

"Thanks Gavin. We can get the builders and architects in now." The party turned and walked up the pathway towards the front door.

"What are your plans?" Gavin ventured. The whole neighbourhood was buzzing with ideas on what the Delvecchios wanted with the property and Gavin would love to be the one to tell.

"I'm sure you'll know soon enough. " Was Sarahs mysterious

reply. "This is Palm Beach after all! Come on Beth, lets get inside." Leaving Gavin none the wiser, Sarah and Beth went inside through the red painted wooden double door. This brought them to the large hallway and they wandered around what was going to be the reception area, their footsteps echoing around the long abandoned building. Both of them visualised how it would look when the remodelling was complete and Jake Shaw, Beth's friend and interior designer had put his mark on everything.

Sarah wandered into one of the old classrooms, full of dust and cobwebs. The building had not been used in about eight years. The area had grown too small for the school house and had had a new school built two blocks away, very modern and much bigger. Nothing had been done with this magnificent building until now. Beth meandered up the stairs, the railings rusted and broken in places while Sarah stayed downstairs. She strolled to the rear of the building and wiped the one remaining but filthy window pane clean to peer outside. The playground had weeds sprouting through the concrete but she could still just make out a hopscotch grid marked out on the ground. This would be a glorious haven for the guests of the new Stamford Centre while they got their shattered lives back on track.

"Are you happy now?" A gentle male voice behind her startled her slightly. Marcos arms slipped around Sarahs ever expanding waistline and his hands settled on her swollen belly.

Sarah relaxed into his embrace, grinning. "For now." She teased. "This is going to be such a positive thing, Marco. It will quell the voices of dissenters in town who are convinced that you are just an evil monster."

"Well, not too much, I hope. I like having a bad reputation, it's good for my business." He jested.

"Maybe. Now my name is on the deeds, Andrea is stepping up the pace for the fundraising. She has confirmed the evening at the Club for next week. All the invites have gone out and she has had a good response so far."

"Do you need me there?"

"Of course!" Sarah was surprised he even asked. "Just for the opener. I won't expect you to attend all the functions, I know it's not really your thing."

Beth had entered the room, unaware that Marco had arrived. She hadn't seen him since her attempted pass at him.

"Oh hi!" She said, somewhat nervously.

Marco just glanced at her. "Sweetie, I have to be getting back now." He said to his wife. "I'll see you at home later." He kissed her cheek and glaring at Beth, he walked out.

Sarah was still too excited to notice the strained exchange between her husband and her friend.

On the day of the charity event, Sarah, Beth and Andrea met at the club mid-morning to supervise the final arrangements. The party planners had already arrived and were hard at it, putting the banners up, laying out the large floral arrangements on the tables and with Andreas help, making some small adjustments to the seating plan for dinner. The caterers were in the large kitchens and Beth had gone straight in there to supervise. Sarah, meanwhile had seated herself at the bar and was going through the running order of the evening, which was due to start at seven-thirty. Gifts for the auction were still arriving so Sarah added them to her list and made a note in Andreas speech to thank the donators.

Sarah left the club with Harry in tow at twelve thirty to meet Marco for lunch for one at Carlottis. Again, Gabe was sat at a nearby table and Harry went to join him while Sarah and Marco sat inside the restaurant. As Sarah approached, Marco stood to greet her and kissed her hello. He felt himself fall in love with her all over again.

"You got a busy afternoon ahead?" He asked as he perused the menu, although he already knew what he would be ordering.

"Yes. Hair salon, getting ready and I hope to put the kids to bed before we go." She sighed. Although it was partly her idea and she was enjoying it, she was weary and would have liked a rest at some stage before the hectic social evening began. "Why?"

"Oh, I just felt like spending the afternoon in bed with you, that's all." He replied, peering over the menu with a wicked glint in his eyes.

Sarah grinned. "Any other day and I would jump at the chance. But tonight is important and it needs to be just right. After this function is over, I will take a back seat and let Andrea and Beth take the reins. I promised you that this would not impact on our lives and I meant it."

"So, can we spend tomorrow afternoon in bed?" His wicked glint had not disappeared.

Sarah found his leg under the table and intertwined it with her. "I insist on it. And tonight…" She had a sultry look as she made this promise.

Sarah met up with the girls at seven fifteen to begin welcoming in their guests and their wallets. Marco had already gone off to mingle with his co-horts; he didn't want to be too involved with what was going on and wanted to keep some distance. Andrea and Beth had already had a few glasses of champagne and were laughing as Sarah was handed a glass of orange juice.

Mrs Delvecchio was receiving lots of admiring looks from both the male and female guests. Her sun-lightened hair had been straightened and fell seductively to her shoulders. She wore a simple silver top which was gathered under her ample bosom and fell loosely to her hips with a satin trim. Under this, she wore simple black trousers and low heeled silver pumps. She wore her favourite diamond necklace, the one that Marco had given her on their first New Year back together.

Beth looked equally stunning in her pink and black lace corset style dress. She drew her fair share of lustful glances not least from Dominic Russell. She looked radiant and rebuffed most men's half hearted advances, something that as a natural flirt, she found hard.

Andrea tried to keep her friends in check. By no means a drudge in her gold slinky dress, she nonetheless thought it her duty to keep her friends away from Palm Beach's finest male tarts.

The most famous tart of all, now tamed came over to Sarah unable to stay away any longer. He had been watching her from across the room, smiling flirtatiously to make men part with their hard earned money for the sake of charity. He took her hand in his which made her start. She looked at his handsome features, serenely looking around the room at all the people who had come here for her. Sarah smiled at her husband and kissed him, unable to refrain. He looked ravishing if casual in his stone coloured suit and black shirt, no tie.

"This is all down to you, sweetie. You did this." He murmured in her ear. He swept his hand around the room, swirling the neat Jack Daniels in the glass he was holding.

"I wish I could take the credit. It's your money, Andreas hard work and Beth's idea. I just used your sexual favours to get it off the ground."

Marco turned to her. "You used me?" He was jocular.

Sarah kissed him again. "I sure did. I'd better mingle." She gave him that seductive look again as she moved away through the crowd.

The dinner went fantastically well. All the guests who had paid well over the odds for their meal enjoyed the feast that was laid before them. Between each course a few of the delectable items were auctioned off raising hundreds of thousands of dollars. The piece de resistance was a ladies Cartier watch donated by a jewellers on Worth Avenue. Marco was a good customer of the French proprietor of Worth Jewels and had been only too happy to donate the magnificent timepiece. They estimated that they had recouped at least half of Marcos initial loan and if he hadn't been so drunk, he might have been happy about it.

As the evening wound down, Sarah found herself talking to a bunch of people she barely knew. She had met Jerry Stone once before - he was the owner of the marina and had drawn her into conversation. Unfortunately, Shelley Russell was also there, looking spiteful and catty. Sarah eyed her suspiciously knowing that she had a thing for Marco. It was well known that she and Dominic had somewhat of an open relationship and Sarah hoped Shelley would not reach higher for Marco.

"So, Sarah. When is your baby due?" Shelley asked with a fixed and unfriendly smile on her plastic face.

"October."

"That's quick work. Don't you already have a young child?"

"Giorgio, yes. He's coming up to a year old. We decided to have another one straight away and besides, I don't have much else to do." She tried to make her words sound light-hearted. Her audience had suddenly expanded.

Jerry put in his dimes-worth. "What about the Stamford Centre? That's what we are all here for. Aren't you getting involved with that?"

Sarah turned slightly to face Jerry. "Only as a fundraiser, Jerry."

"So what's the real story behind it all?" Jerry's wife piped up.

Everyone was really curious about the entire project. The whole town knew that Joe Delvecchio was an addict, knew about his refineries and dealers and most wondered silently if the Stamford Centre was just some kind of smoke screen.

Sarah pressed on choosing her words carefully as Marco had instructed her. "We really just want to help people less fortunate than ourselves and we see this as an opportunity to do just that. That's it."

"That's it?" Someone Sarah didn't know queried.

She nodded. "We are just the financial backing behind it. I don't have any qualifications to be a counsellor or anything."

"So get qualified." Jerry told her as if it were that simple.

Sarah stared at him and hesitated for a second. "That's not really possible." She stammered looking for a way out now.

Marco had wondered over with another fresh glass of Jack Daniel's and was watching the group and listening to the conversation pan out. He did not like where it was going. He had told Sarah that people would be suspicious.

"Why not?" Shelly asked, unaware that Marco now stood behind her.

"Because she has a husband and children to care for, that's why not!" His eyes blazed as he looked around the small group of people and dared them to retort. One by one, they slowly broke off and wandered away.

Sarah had felt her face grow hot with shame and her eyes dropped to the floor, unable to look at anyone. As the crowd dispersed, Marco took Sarahs elbow and lead her over to a safer circle of friends. She shook him off.

"What?" He asked innocently.

"YOU!! How dare you come into my conversation and behave like a caveman?" She shoved him in the shoulder, the one with the bullet wound in it and he scowled as the dull pain spread at her rough touch. Sarah turned from him and walked into the lobby where a few people turned to look at her in what appeared to be sympathy as she stormed by.

Peter was waiting outside in the cool night air with the Lexus and she asked him to take her home. "Marco is staying on a bit longer but I'm tired." She sat back in the leather seats as Peter closed the passenger door behind her and walked around to the drivers door. When he had started the engine and got under way, he looked at her flushed face in the rear view mirror and asked if she was okay. She looked near to tears.

"Fine. I'm just tired." She snapped back.

Peter knew when to and when not to pursue a conversation with an angry woman and he drove Sarah home in silence.

Once home, she locked the bedroom door making it quite clear that her boorish husband would not be welcome in their bed that night. She couldn't bear the thought of him sleeping next to her and she knew that he would get her to forgive him too quickly with his gentle touches and kisses. She was a sucker for him but she wanted him to be really sorry for embarrassing her like that.

When Marco arrived home around an hour later, he tried the door and softly called her name a couple of times. She lay there quietly in the dark before he got the message and went away, presumably to sleep in one of the guest suites.

The following day after dropping Grace off at school, Sarah decided to head for the beach. It was a beautiful day and she was still avoiding Marco. He was not a beach person and would not look for her there.

Harry, as ever had to accompany her and the three of them sat on a blanket under a large parasol just feet from the gently lapping waters of the Atlantic. It was early September and the heat was still forbidding so Sarah and Giorgio mostly stayed in the shade. Harry was happy to sit in the sun and top up his tan.

Sarah asked about Harrys love-life as she took Giorgio to splash about in the water. He was trying to walk and not happy to sit all the time.

Harry confessed that he was still seeing Erin.

"The cocktail waitress?" She asked, surprised.

"She works the bar in Pompano, yes." Harry smiled. "We both work strange hours and it suits us both."

"You want to make the most of an uncomplicated relationship while it lasts. Before you know it, marriage and kids get in the way."

Harry shook his head. "Not for me. I have too much living to do for all of that."

Sarah smiled as her son tried to stand and succeeded in landing with a bump on his butt. "There's no better feeling in the world than kids with someone you love. Even if he is a pig..." She said the last sentence under her breath but Harry got the gist of her words.

"Marco means well."

"Don't make excuses for him, Harry. He has very old-fashioned ways and he needs to move with the times. His behaviour may have been suitable for his father but not in this day and age." Sarah looked up at Harry and in the distance she saw her husband coming down the beach. Sarah had to stifle a snigger at his appearance. He wore a red and yellow Hawaiian shirt and baggy white shorts which was very unbecoming. He had his usual sunshades on rarely going outside without them.

"Hey sweetheart!" He called as he approached. "I've been looking everywhere for you." He plonked himself on the blanket beside his son. Harry made a discreet retreat.

"I've been hiding out from you." Sarah replied quietly. "And I'm still not speaking to you after last night, even if you do look ridiculous in those clothes."

He looked hurt as he gazed down at his get-up. "You don't like them? I borrowed them from Sal. I don't have any beachwear. And why aren't you speaking to me? Why did you lock me out of the bedroom last night? You promised me a night of passion."

Sarah shook her head in disbelief. "How much did you have to drink last night? You behaved like a Neanderthal and humiliated me, don't you remember that?"

"Oh come on! It wasn't that bad." He looked at Sarah for a response and was met with a cold hard and unforgiving stare. Marco backed down a bit. "I'm sorry if I upset you." He finally said.

"I don't think you are. You are never sorry for anything that you say or do so why should now be any different? Besides, a public humiliation requires a public apology."

He tried the humour track. "So me wearing this crap doesn't do it for you?"

Sarah shook her head. "You need to start treating me differently from your cronies. However you may be with them, I am your wife, your equal and I won't put up with your crap, however well meaning or drunk you may be." She said sternly.

"My crap?"

"Yes, your crap. Your father may have got away with the nice Italian wife who stays at home, produces kids and is blindly obedient. To a certain degree, I am blindly obedient and I want to be but I am also more than Sarah Delvecchio wife and mother, I am a person in my own right and want to be recognised as such."

Marco shrugged. "Okay. You know I can't say no to you. I really am sorry and I will make a public apology to make it up for you. Can we go in now for lunch, it's getting too hot out here." Giorgio had also started to get tired and testy so without waiting for an answer, Marco picked up his son and headed back across the sand towards his house, leaving Sarah and Harry to collect up the rest of their belongings.

Marco stayed around for lunch. He had a late appointment in Miami so had time to spare and appease his wife. They were about half way through lunch when the housemaid, Enza knocked on the dining room door and peered her head around.

"Mr Delvecchio, I am sorry to disturb you but you have a visitor."

Marco looked at his watch in puzzlement. Neither he nor Sarah were expecting anyone and the gate house would usually call down and announce arrivals. Marco put his cutlery down and went outside into the hall to see who had interrupted their lunch with Sarah waddling behind him.

"Joe!" Sarah was more surprised than Marco to see her brother-in-law standing there with his hands in his pockets. He looked just as ill and was obviously still a user despite Marco requesting he clean up his act.

Joe smiled unpleasantly at the sight of the couple and showed his black and rotting teeth. He had no idea they were expecting another brat, he'd had no contact with his family for quite some time.

"How did you get in here?" Marco growled.

"It's my family home too, you have no right to keep me out."

Marco made a mental note to hurt whoever was on the gate

and let this monster in the house where his child was sleeping. "What do you want?"

"I'm sorry I didn't beg an audience with you. You being my brother I thought I'd be welcome."

"I told you before Joe, you get yourself clean and you are welcome to be at my side."

"Clean." He mused the word as if it were a foreign language. "Where's the fun in that? So I'm here now. You got five minutes away from your game of happy families?"

Disgusted with Joe, Sarah turned away and walked outside. She had lost her appetite and didn't want to finish her lunch. Jenny was in the pool doing her daily lengths while Giorgio was sleeping in his baby carriage in the shade near the poolhouse. Sarah went over to look at her sleeping adored son, his hair tussled from sleep and his thumb wedged firmly into his mouth. Smiling to herself, Sarah went and sat on the edge of the pool and slipped off her shoes to dangle her feet in the cool water. It was a hot and humid day and being six months pregnant only increased her body temperature. It was two-thirty in the afternoon and they'd be due for a thunderstorm soon - you could set your watch by Florida storms in the summer.

Jenny swam over to Sarah at the side. "Would you like me to collect Grace from school?" She asked

Sarah thought about it. She was too hot and too tired so she nodded.

Jenny pulled herself out of the pool with the agility that Sarah no longer had and wondered if she would have so again. Her life was pretty perfect although she wished she hadn't got pregnant again quite so soon. She barely had the energy to appreciate the two wonderful children she had.

She heard angry stomping footsteps coming down the path from the house behind her. Jenny said hello to Marco as she passed him and got no response, unusually so. Sarah turned her head to see Marco come thundering down the path towards her and as he stopped behind Sarah, her feet still in the pool, she looked up into his face and saw anger raging in his eyes.

"Sweetheart, what's the matter?"

He paced the path up and down behind her unable to communicate in his wrath.

"Is it Joe? "Sarah persisted.

Marco squatted down beside Sarah so he was on the same level. "The bastard wants his share of the business!" He spat the words out.

Sarah waited for him to continue. He rarely, if ever, talked business with her and she wasn't quite sure of what to say or how to react.

"He seems to think he's owed something other than what he has." Marco pressed on.

"Have you spoke to Gabe about this?" It was a safe enough question.

"He's not around at the moment." Marco sat down next to Sarah and took off his socks and shoes. He let his feet dangle in the water to try and cool off his raging blood. He reached for Sarahs hand and took it in his and felt his ire begin to subside. "I've told Joe that I want nothing from him, no proceeds from what he is involved in."

"Drugs." Sarah stated.

"Drugs." Marco confirmed. "Christ knows there is enough money in that alone to keep him rich for a long time but he still wants more."

"So what did you say to him?"

"I told him to go fuck himself!"

Sarah couldn't help but smile. Marco never swore in front of her and it was testament to his outrage. It still sounded a strange word coming from his lips.

"Anyway, that's my problem. This latest confrontation will doubtless exacerbate the situation with my brother. I know you don't anyway, but please, please don't leave the house without Harry."

"I won't." She promised him. She looked across at the baby's pram which had started to rock slightly with the movement of the waking child inside. Marco followed his wife's gaze and felt the remaining anger leave him as his thoughts turned to Giorgio. He stood up and padded across the pool area towards the pram, leaving a trail of wet footprints behind him. Giorgio recognised his father and began to giggle, causing Marco to pick the child up, his Miami meeting and confrontation with his brother all but forgotten.

CHAPTER FIFTEEN

Sarah and Rosa took to the shops on Worth Avenue a few days later, all children left with Jenny. Sarah had recently been feeling a little bit low and Rosa decided she needed to spend an obscene amount of money to cheer herself up. They spent a couple of hours in the beauty salon, which Sarah emerged from with ruby red tints in her hair and bright red talons to match. Rosa had a hot stone treatment and a facial and they then felt ready to face the boutiques on Worth.

In Saks Fifth Avenue, Sarahs favourite department store, Sarah fell in love with a dark brown soft leather Prada handbag with a small price-tag of nine hundred dollars. To redress the balance for the payer of the credit card, she bought Marco a Cartier tie pin with three studded diamonds encrusted on it. He didn't like too much bling and this would suit him perfectly.

Harry then drove them to the Breakers for lunch. He had seen the dark blue car following them around all morning. It had stationed itself outside the salon while Sarah and Rosa were inside and knew Jack Robbins was back on Sarahs case. They had done a disappearing act for quite a few months and Harry wondered why the sudden interest again. He was unsure whether to call Marco. He decided it could wait until he dropped Sarah back home. Harry was good at keeping Joe away with a show of strength and arms but he was fairly powerless with a government official.

"Mind if I sit down?" Robbins asked as he did so anyway. Rosa and Sarah had just been seated in the restaurant of the Breakers Hotel and were deciding what to eat. The FBI agent had just strolled through the restaurant flashing his badge as he made a beeline for Sarah.

"Long time no see, Robbins. What do you want now?" Sarah asked as she put her menu down in front of her and looked up at him.

"You are still on my mind, Mrs Delvecchio. You know it's just a matter of time until we get him and we'll get you then too."

"I'm pleased for you."

"Think about your children. Both parents in jail. A mad uncle out to get them."

Sarah shook her head. "You're still clutching at straws then. Does that mean that you have nothing new?"

Robbins said nothing but continued to stare at Sarah.

"I'd like you to go, Robbins. I'm trying to have lunch with my sister-in-law."

Robbins stood to leave. He looked at Rosa and then at Sarah. "We'll meet again very soon Sarah, mark my words." He grimaced as he walked away and Sarah knew that he was just hassling her to intimidate her again.

"That man needs to get a life." Sarah said to Rosa as they watched him walk out of the restaurant and join up with a colleague. They both turned around and stared at Sarah again before leaving.

"Isn't Harry supposed to keep that man away?" Rosa asked.

Sarah shook her head. "The FBI would only arrest Harry if he tried to stop them talking to me. Harry is around more for Joe's sake than anything."

Rosa shifted uncomfortably in her chair. She hated the huge rift between her brothers and knew it was irredeemable although what had caused it remained a mystery to her. The two had always got along and had been really close when they were growing up but the last four years or so had seen a dramatic change in their relationship. Rosa guessed it was a difference in opinion with the family business but neither Marco or Joe ever confided in her. She knew she would have to do some investigating if she wanted to now the truth.

Over the next few weeks, the work at the Stamford Centre

was nearing completion. The remodelling had been completed and Beth's interior designer friend Jake Shaw was back to make the inside look modern and calming. Jake had spent several days in Florida from New York looking around and getting ideas of what was required. He suggested that all the bedrooms should be painted in neutral colours and to have vibrant colours in the fabrics as a contrast. He was very enthusiastic in their meetings and was never downhearted when his ideas were declined. He often arrived with great swathes of sample materials and colours. When the paint for the walls was decided, Jake supervised the decorators with flourish.

Jake also arranged for his studio in New York to send some furniture catalogues so the ladies could match furniture with fabrics and get a better feel for it. Once they had arrived, he met with Sarah, Andrea and Beth at the Delvecchio house.

"I love this place, Sarah." He had been here before when he redecorated Graces bedroom but he was still very enthusiastic about the house.

Sarah took him through to the dining room where the fabric swatches and catalogues were laid out on the solid wood table. Jake declared his love for the item.

"Where did you get all of this stuff?"

"This is my husbands family home and it's probably been here for years. The only thing I've changed here is the bedrooms."

"I would love to have a good look around here. The design is fabulous!"

Sarah smiled steely at him. "That won't be possible. Let's just get on with the job in hand, shall we?"

Once the furniture was chosen and ordered, the curtains, bed linen and everything else right down to the cutlery was decided on and orders were placed. They would be going over their original budget but Marco was happy to extend their credit line. The pace of the work at the centre was making Sarah feel extremely tired and Marco kept hinting at her to relinquish responsibility of the grand opening. Beth seemed reluctant to manage the final few things on her own and pleaded for Sarah to keep her hand in. Jake knew what was required and was happy to stay on to the completion before heading back to New York.

One particularly hot late September afternoon, Sarah stood

on the balcony from her bedroom watching a torrential downpour. Lightening flashed out to sea as the storm made it's way land-ward and the thunder crashed along with it. The rain was lashing down and from the undercover balcony, Sarah watched as the rain hit the hot pathways and turned to steam, rising skyward. The thunder crashed overhead and Sarah turned back inside to get Giorgio ready for the school run. The little boy had just celebrated his first birthday with all the pomp and splendour due Marcos first born son.

Jenny was in the nursery playing with him and she had made him ready for the journey prior to her going off duty until the following morning. Sarah often wondered how she managed without her. Sarah picked up her heavy son with a groan and kissed him. His hair had so far remained fair even though Sarah thought it might go dark. From the pictures of Graziella that she had seen, Sarah knew fair hair ran in the family. Giorgio had the chocolate brown eyes identical to his father and sister and he had the same flashes of temper that Marco had even at one year old. He kicked out now and went rigid at the inconvenience of being taken away from his noisy toy train.

"We're going to get Grace." Sarah told him and he smiled immediately at the mention of his adored older sister. He showed off his newly cut bottom teeth and they said goodbye to Jenny and went downstairs to find Harry.

As Sarah struggled down the stairs with her child, she called out to Harry who came out of the kitchen almost immediately with car keys in hand. Over the months he had become used to Sarahs routine, such as it was.

"Here, let me." He rushed over to Sarah and took Giorgio from her. They went through the front door with Harry tickling Giorgio and making him scream in delight. By the time Sarah had caught up with them, Giorgio was safely strapped in his car seat and ready to go. They trundled down the drive splashing through puddles from the recently abated storm. The gates were opening as the car arrived and the man at the gate - Sarah didn't know his name - waved them through. She turned left onto the rapidly drying streets; the sun was so hot that in just a few minutes one would never know the storm had been so heavy.

As the gates locked behind her, Sarah saw Robbins car parked across the street, it's darkened windows closed even in this heat and humidity. Sarah glanced across at Harry who just shrugged so Sarah floored the gas pedal. Looking in her rear-view mirror, she saw the car hadn't moved. Harry was looking behind through the wing mirror at the stationary vehicle.

"He must be after Marco." Harry suggested.

Sarah laughed. "He'll have a long wait. Marco isn't due out until late tonight." She looked up at the dissipating storm clouds and watched the sun burn through. "I hope he fries in that car." She muttered with malice.

Harry stayed with the SUV as Sarah went inside the school gates for her daughter. As Grace climbed into the car, Gio kicked his legs with a frenzy of excitement. He adored Grace and giggled in that beautiful baby way as Grace spoke to him.

After just a few minutes of driving back home, Sarah noticed a truck behind them. It appeared to be following her so she made a couple of quick turns and sure enough the truck made them too.

"Harry?" She said quietly and calmly.

"I've seen it. I think it's one of Joe's guys."

"Joe?"

"Yeah. I've seen one of Joe's guys in that truck before. I doubt it's him in there now though."

"What shall I do?" Sarah looked in her rear-view mirror at the children in the back seat. Grace was reading Gio a story from her school book and was oblivious of anything going on around her.

"Head for home, same speed, most direct route. I'll call ahead and let them know we have a problem." Very calmly so as not to alert the children, Harry pulled out his cell phone and called Gabe. Gabe reiterated what Harry had said to Sarah.

Sarah slowed down and kept to the speed limit, keeping a nervous eye on the tailing vehicle. It did not speed up or try to do anything but follow Sarahs Mercedes but she was still relieved when at last she made the final turn onto her road. She could see the gates already open and two men were stood visibly, yet still on Delvecchio land with their weapons drawn. Sarah quickly made the turn into the driveway and then slowed. She watched as her pursuer slowed the truck considerably to assess the situation. Seeing the two guards ready for them, they did not like what they were seeing and so sped up quickly and disappeared in the direction of the marina. The iron gates slid behind her and the locking mechanism kicked in. The guns of the gate guards were holstered and Sarah breathed normally again. She floored the gas and sped up the drive kicking up the dust.

The scare made Sarah realise that she must put aside the plans for the Stamford centre and leave it in Andrea and Beth's capable hands. She decided she must concentrate on her self defence lessons. Her shooting practice had taken a back seat lately.

Marco and Sarah had invited Andrea and Cliff, Rosa and Sal for dinner that evening and Sarah decided over dessert to make her announcement.

"I'm taking a step back from the Stamford Centre now." She said, putting a hand across her swollen belly as though that were all the explanation necessary.

Andrea was a little surprised. Like Beth, she had hoped that Sarah would continue until they were open just over a week away. The grand opening was next Friday. "Will you be there for the Grand Opening?" She asked.

"Of course. I just can't be so involved anymore. I have other things to attend to." She smiled at Marco. "I also want to take up my shooting lessons again."

Marco stared sharply at her. He put his cutlery down and propped his chin on his palm, unhappy. "I don't think that's such a good idea."

"Why not? After yesterday, I think it's a perfectly plausible idea."

"Sarah, you are pregnant!"

She looked down at herself in mock surprise. "So I am! How did that happen?" This drew chuckles from their guests which flared Marcos temper.

"You can't go shooting guns off in your condition!"

"Why not?"

"It might upset the baby."

Sarah laughed.

"I mean it! I do not want you to do this until after the baby is born!"

"But it won't hurt the baby..." Sarah protested.

"Marco, I'm sure it's fine.." Rosa tried to placate her brother.

He banged his clenched fist on the table. "You are not to defy me on this Sarah. Do you understand?"

Sarah stared at him in disbelief that he would behave like this yet again in company. She threw her napkin in disgust on her plate and stood up.

"Fuck you!" She replied to the astonishment of everyone in the room. She left the dining room slamming the door behind her.

Andrea put a calming hand on Marcos lower arm. "Let her go. You both need to calm down. Rosa and I will tidy away." She said quietly.

Marco thanked her and sat quietly at the table fuming inside.

Sarah walked out through the kitchen and out of the rear door. It was dark and late but with the security lights on, she could make her way down the path towards the newly enclosed swimming pool, its waters still and inviting. She continued towards the back entrance to the estate where Gabe was sat smoking a cigarette. He stood as he saw Sarah approaching, discarding the remains of the cigarette.

"Are you going somewhere?" He asked efficiently.

"Just for a walk." Her voice was short.

"You need Harry if you leave the grounds."

"Harry is off tonight. I won't be long, Gabe."

"Sarah, I can't." He apologised. It was more than his life was worth.

"Then you come with me." She desperately wanted to get out of the estate.

Gabe shook his head. "I can't leave here until Scotty gets back in an hour or so."

Sarah sat on Gabs vacated seat. "This is worse than being in prison." She moaned, despair taking hold. She struggled to hold back tears.

Gabe snickered. "This is no prison, believe me." He should know. He had spent eight years in jail for nearly killing someone when he was in his early twenties. He'd been careful to stay out of jail since then. "What's the matter? Why do you so desperately want to leave?"

"My pig of a husband! I swear, sometimes I wish I'd stayed in

San Francisco. I'm just trying to protect myself and my children but he won't let me take up my shooting lessons until after this baby is born."

"Well, that is just a few weeks away and the firing of a gun may startle the baby."

"Not you as well, Gabe. You are just like him. Do you really think that I would do anything to harm my child?"

"Of course not! What do I know about babies? But this is something that you need to discuss with Marco, I can't get in between you two." He handed her a tissue. The tears had begun to escape.

She took the tissue and thanked him. "Do you mind then if I just sit here for a while?"

He shook his head. He'd be glad of some company.

CHAPTER SIXTEEN

Sarah slept in one of the guest rooms that night. She could not bear to sleep in the same bed as her pig of a husband. He barely spoke to her as he came into the kitchen the next morning while Sarah, Grace and Giorgio were having breakfast. He grabbed some coffee to go, kissed his children and left.

While Sarah was changing and dressing Giorgio, she made her mind up. He may be someone important in his male dominated world and he might be able to order people around under pain of death but she'd be damned if he thought he could do the same to her.

She asked Jenny to take Giorgio for the morning while she took Grace to school and then did a bit of shopping. Harry, as ever, was to accompany her.

"All you ever do is shop!" He jested to Sarah as they pulled away from the school gates.

Sarah said nothing but instead headed to West Palm Beach.

Harry was confused as Sarah by-passed Worth Avenue and headed away. He said nothing, thinking perhaps she'd found a new place to shop. When she pulled up outside West Palm Beach gun club, he frowned.

"I thought you were shopping?"

"I changed my mind." She replied tersely and got out of the car.

Harry followed her into the cool of the building and went to the cafe for a drink.

Sarah showed her membership and proceeded through to the indoor range. She was just being handed a gun and some ammunition when Kristina came up to her.

"Hi Kristina, I thought I'd get some practice in."

The tall blonde woman smiled awkwardly. "I'm afraid that won't be possible." She gently but firmly took the gun from Sarah and handed it back to the man in the cage.

"Why not?" She was confused but handed her clip back.

"Mr Delvecchio called this morning and told us that he doesn't want you here at the moment." Kristina watched as Sarahs eyes clouded with anger.

"What?"

"I'm sorry but we have to respect his wishes."

"His wishes?" Sarah repeated. "Don't you mean his orders?"

"Call it what you want, Mrs Delvecchio. The bottom line is that I will have to ask you to leave." She put a hand on Sarahs arm to lead her outside. Sarah shook it off in anger.

"Don't touch me! You are all the same, you people." She walked herself out to where Harry was just stirring his coffee.

"Are we going?" Harrys confusion remained.

Sarah said not a word but walked out to her car with as much regal poise as she could muster, Harry quickly following. He had only just belted himself in when Sarah floored the gas and took off with her tyres squealing.

Sarah said nothing as she headed for her destination and Harry didn't question her further. He was used to her mood swings now and decided to go with the flow.

When Sarah pulled into the Marina and headed for the parking lot, Harry began to get worried. Still she said nothing as she pulled up beside Marcos Mercedes and then got out of her car. Harry followed her towards what appeared to be a ramshackle two storey warehouse on the waters edge. Sarah opened the door from the car park and surprised a middle-aged man who was sat on a stool inside the door, standing guard.

"You can't go in there." He informed her gruffly as he tried to block her entrance.

She stared in defiance at him and pushed him out of the way. The man had recognised the Don's pregnant wife and hurried up the stairs after her, closely followed by Harry calling her name.

At the top of the wooden stairs was another door with black paint peeling away. Sarah stormed through and looked around the smoky room. There was a large open room with several old chairs and a kitchen table in the middle and a small window to the side. Several men looked up from what they were doing in surprise as she entered the room with Harry and the guard calling out behind her and making a commotion. Opposite the wall with the window was a closed door and Sarah headed for this. One of the men pre-empted her move and got between Sarah and the door.

"Get the fuck out of my way!" It was the first words she had uttered since leaving the gun club.

The man blanched at the vile words that Sarah had uttered but stood firm. Her face was ugly with rage and Sarah tried to get the man out of her way. He pushed her gently away, not knowing who she was.

"Hey, Hey!" Harry rushed to her side to protect her. "Do you know who this is?" He scowled at the man. "I suggest you let her pass."

"No can do. The Boss is in a very important meeting and cannot be disturbed." The man didn't even care who this woman was.

"What the hells the noise out there?" Marcos booming voice suddenly resounded around the room making everyone else hush.

Sarah took the opportunity to pass the guard. She threw open the door and saw Marco with the Chief of Palm Beach Police Jimmy Davis. Both men turned to stare at Sarah in disbelief. Sarah never bothered Marco here but judging by the murderous look on her face, it could not wait.

"How dare you?" She shouted at Marco.

"Sarah, I'm kinda busy..."

"Sit down and you listen to me for a change." Chief Davis stood to leave, a movement Sarah caught out of the corner of her eye and she turned her wrath on him. "And you! Sit down and don't move!" He sat. She turned her attention back to Marco. "I am not one of your hired hands that you can order about and I will not come to heel!"

Marco sat back forward in his chair and leaned his elbows on the desk. "What is this about?"

"I went to see Kristina today."

He nodded. "So you went behind my back? After I told you last night?"

"Yes but I'm not one of your lackeys and I won't tolerate it anymore. I'm sick of being told what to do and when to do it. I can't go out on my own and I feel like a prisoner. You are not the boss of me, do you understand?" Sarah exploded. She banged her fist on the desk as she leaned towards Marco from the opposite side of the desk.

"Can we talk about this later?" He looked around the room and saw all the men trying to look as though they weren't listening.

"Why? So these people don't realise what a fucko you are? New flash, Marco – they probably already know but are too afraid to tell you."

"Harry? Get her out of here!!" He shouted.

Sarah laughed as she turned to go. "Sometimes I can't stand you. You are a pigheaded self centred boar and you will NOT order me around."

"Harry?" Marco had had enough of the screaming harpy in front of him and he wanted to get back to business.

Sarah left the office without assistance from Harry. She managed to get back to the car just ahead of Harry and she locked him out. Laughing, she took off alone feeling elated at her sudden freedom.

Harry ran back inside to grab a set of car keys to follow her but by the time he had returned, Sarah was long gone.

She drove South, the beaches and towns flying by until her temper fizzled out and Sarah found herself in Boca Raton. Suddenly feeling emotionally exhausted, Sarah pulled over into a car park and sat for a while just breathing as she thought about what she had done and how furious Marco would be with her. Her cell phone had rang almost continuously on the journey to Boca, Marcos number flashing up as the caller but she had ignored it.

Now she had pulled over she looked at the thirty eight missed calls and was even now reluctant to call him back. She had nothing to say to him at the moment and she didn't want to be found.

Sarah got out of the car and followed the path down to the

beach. She paid the cabana boy for a sun chair and sat and watched the world at play. It was hot and still and the beach was packed. With some degree of envy, Sarah watched the slim young women play beach volley ball while appreciative young men looked on, whistling and cheering. The girls were jumping lithely and laughing out loud as they missed easy balls. With all of her obvious privileges, Sarah could not remember the last time she had laughed and had proper fun.

At around two o'clock, Sarah was beginning to feel the heat and get burnt. She thanked the cabana boy and headed up the beach towards one of the numerous beachside cafes. She sat and had a long cold drink and a tuna steak with salad while her cellphone rang furiously. She looked down at it and saw it was Harry's phone calling. She connected the call but said nothing in case it was Marco trying to trick her into answering.

"Sarah, where the hell have you been?" It was Harrys frantic voice.

"Just out. I needed to be alone."

"Marco has been going ballistic! Where are you?"

"Having lunch and enjoying the freedom. Don't worry about me, I'm fine and I'll be home tomorrow when his Lord and Master stops treating me like his slave." She disconnected the phone and switched it off, not wanting to keep hear it ringing. It was getting annoying.

After lunch, Sarah walked along the beach road and noticed the sea was strangely calm. She checked herself into the Ocean Lodge and was looking forward to chilling out and having some time to herself. When she got to her room overlooking the sea, Sarah had a long hot bath using the complimentary bath gels supplied by the hotel and then crawled into bed for a nap.

When Sarah awoke, it was getting on for six thirty and nearly dark. She felt hungry so as soon as the sleepiness had left her, she headed out for something to eat. As she passed the front desk, the receptionist ask her if she had seen the news that day.

"No, I've been a little preoccupied. Why? What's happened?"

"Nothing yet, but there is a tropical storm heading in this general direction. It's not hurricane strength and they don't reckon it will be too bad. It's due to hit the North of the state so there is no evacuation order yet but it's advisable to keep an eye on the Weather

Channel."

Sarah thanked the girl for the information and headed out anyway. It was very calm outside and Sarah knew from experience that that wasn't necessary a good thing. She also knew that it could be several hours before any sign of the storm hit.

Sarah awoke at just after midnight and was aware of very heavy rainfall and lashing winds outside. She got out of bed and headed over to the French window that led out onto the balcony. Opening it very slightly, the rain poured through the small gap soaking her and the carpet at her feet. The sea beneath her was crashing up onto the beach throwing up bits of debris. It was just the beginning and would get much worse.

Sarah closed the door and switched on the T.V. before getting back into her bed to watch it. It occurred to Sarah to call home but she knew that her children would be safe in Jenny's care.

The eye of the storm was headed for the Southern coast of Georgia so Florida would only get the intense winds, rain and storm surges. The Georgia coastline had been evacuated and the Panhandle had battened down the hatches while everyone just waited it out.

She drifted off the sleep again with the T.V still on softly in the background. At just before six, Sarah awoke with a start at a sudden noise from the television, or so she thought. She opened her eyes and saw it was still dark outside and the storm was still raging. She dragged herself out of bed to go to the window and check on the weather situation through the window. She opened the door very slightly and heard the rush of the wind roaring through the gap. Even in the dark, Sarah could make out the angry sea below her window throwing white florescent foam onto the beach. The sea had advanced closer to land and water was crashing up onto the hotel gardens, dislodging the shrubbery and washing away the patio furniture that had been by the pool. Sarah closed the door to protect herself and the carpet from the elements and that was when the first contraction hit.

Thinking it must be the practice contractions, Sarah refused to panic but went and sat on the edge of her bed once it had passed. It couldn't possibly be for real, she still had another three and a half weeks to go. She gave it another few minutes and convinced herself that it was a false alarm. She clambered back into bed and pulled the sheet up to her chin and tried to go back to sleep. She wouldn't be going home until the storm abated so a sleep-in would be permissible.

The second wave of pain woke her up. It was six-thirty. Realisation hit her with horror that this was not a practice run, that she really was in labour and the baby was going to be born far too early.

When it had passed, she grabbed her cellphone and called Harrys number. She'd be hanged if she would give her husband the satisfaction of a phonecall. There was no connection, probably due to the storm. She redialled, called the house number but that too was dead. The phone lines were usually the first to go when these storms hit.

By nine Am., the contractions were coming every fifteen minutes. Still unable to reach home and still unwilling to call Marco, Sarah dialled '0' for the front desk. She asked them to call an ambulance for her explaining that she had gone into labour early. The lady receptionist volunteered to come and sit with her while they waited for the ambulance. The storm was still too bad for her to leave the hotel even though she was now off duty.

Dorothy sat with Sarah and made her a cup of tea. The storm seemed to be getting much worse - it was due to hit landfall at midday and the experts predicted that it would then tail off much as they usually did after leaving the power of the ocean.

The ambulance took its time arriving at the Ocean Lodge because of the atrocious conditions outside and by this time, Sarahs labour had speeded up. After examining her, the paramedic decided that she was too advanced to be transferred to the hospital and she would have to deliver in the relative safety of the hotel room.

At just after nine forty-five, baby number three was brought into the world. With no assistance but gas and air, Sarah was in a whole lot of pain and her screams could be heard even above the roar of the storm outside.

"A beautiful baby boy!" The paramedic announced and he handed Sarah her son. "We need to get you both to hospital as soon as possible. The baby will need special care as he is a bit early." There was no panic as he said this, just matter of fact.

"But he is okay?"

"He seems to be. He's small as you'd expect and there is an increased risk of infection in prem babies so we just need to be cautious."

Dorothy had put together Sarahs few belongings and put them into her handbag. As the paramedics wheeled Sarah and the baby down the hall and into the elevator, Dorothy followed behind. She volunteered to call someone for Sarah but Sarah declined the offer. Dorothy stopped as they reached the locked doors of the hotel. She did not want to go outside into the maelstrom. She handed Sarah her bag and wished her well.

As the ambulance headed off to Boca Raton's hospital, Sarah asked the driver of the rig if they could take her to Columbus in Palm Beach. She would feel happier with her own doctors around her. She offered extra payment.

"We need to admit you to Boca Raton and then arrange for you to be transferred. The weather is still pretty bad and I can't risk you or the baby on a long journey." He apologised to her.

Sarah was too tired and too much in shock to really care one way or another.

At the hospital, baby Delvecchio was taken to the special baby care unit and put into an incubator. His breathing had become a little shallow on the short journey in. Sarah was admitted and although exhausted, she was in good health.

"Can we call anyone for you, Sarah?" Her assigned nurse asked again as Sarah lay back on the plump pillows.

She shook her head sadly and looked out of the window. She had no inclination to see Marco. She drifted off to sleep soon after.

Sarah woke up in her hospital bed some two hours later and she was aware of someone sat beside her even before she opened her eyes. She turned to her left and opened her eyes, seeing Marco waiting patiently for her to awake.

"Were you going to call me?" He asked gruffly.

She shook her head. "Not today. I'm still very angry with you and this is all your fault."

"I thought it might be." He tutted. "Is the baby okay?"

Sarah nodded. She turned back to look out of the window. The storm had abated but water was still streaming down the outside of the window. "How did you know I was here? Did the hospital call you?"

"No. Vinnie was waiting inside the hotel in a room on the ground floor. He followed the ambulance here and called me."

"And why was he in a room in the Ocean Lodge? Happy coincidence?"

He sighed as though she still didn't get it. "I had all the cars fitted with a tracking device since this trouble with Joe started. He was closest and checked in just after you did. It didn't take long."

"A tracking device? Unbelievable." Sarah muttered.

"It's for security." His tone was measured and patient.

"No, it's not. You just don't trust me. I can't go anywhere without you having to know exactly where I am. That makes you a control freak and I don't know how much longer I can take it." Tears of frustration began to fall down her cheeks and she furiously wiped them away.

Marco stood up and perching himself on the side of her bed, he wrapped his arms around her. "No, that's not it. I just couldn't bear it if anything happened to you. You are still under Alessandro Miotto's protection and he has sanctioned these measures and I happen to agree with him. If we ever get over this problem with Joe, things will be different and less restrictive." He promised.

She pulled away from Marcos embrace despite feeling comforted and secure by it. "I want the baby transferred to Columbus today. Can you go and see to it please?" She turned her back on him and closed her eyes again, evident to Marco that their short conversation was already over and she was still very angry with him.

Sarah released herself from hospital the following day and accompanied her baby son to Columbus Hospital in Palm Beach in the ambulance. Once there and the paperwork had been completed, she spent most of the day with him, just sitting with him and talking to him. He was being fed through a drip at the moment and so there could be no bonding like there had been with Grace and Gio. The only way he would know who she was would be through the sound of her voice.

At the end of the day, Sarah called Harry to come and collect her. She had two other neglected children at home that she must get back to, even though leaving the baby, small and vulnerable almost broke her heart. She promised him she would return early the next morning.

Grace was thrilled to see her mother again and excited to hear the news on her new brother.

"What is his name?" She asked dancing from one foot to another.

"Adam." Sarah had decided without consulting Marco.

"When is Adam coming home?"

"I don't know, darling. He is very poorly and needs to stay in the hospital until he is better. Why don't you come with me to the hospital tomorrow and see him?" Sarah suggested to Grace.

CHAPTER SEVENTEEN

Adam grew steadily stronger over the next few days and the nursing staff were extremely pleased with his progress. Sarahs mood lifted considerably at this news although she was still sour with Marco. He had been sleeping in the guest suite for the past few nights and they had barely spoken two words to each other.

Beth and Andrea convinced her to go to the opening gala of the Stamford Centre on Saturday night. Sarah said she would put in an appearance and would try and get Marco to do the same. When she curtly asked him later that day, he said he would try but Sarah could see from the look in his eyes that he had no intention of going anywhere near the place on Saturday night. She gave up trying to convince him.

The night before the grand opening, Sarah knew Beth was at the Centre on her own doing some paperwork and going over a few things before the guests began to arrive early next week. Sarah had no desire to sit in the house on her own - Marco was locked away in his office with Gabe.

"Come on, Harry. Let's go for a drive." Sarah poked her head around the lounge door where Harry was sitting reading an English newspaper, anxious to keep up to date with the news from home.

Harry smiled wearily - he'd had a long day and was keen to go home and sleep. Nethertheless, he put his paper aside and followed Sarah out to the front of the house. She was already seated in her car which had not been put away for the night after her hospital vigil with the baby that day.

They drove through the darkened streets, a busy Friday night with people going out for a night on the town although it was not quite eight o'clock. There was still debris scattered on the roads from the storm last weekend even though the city workers had cleared away much of it. The people of this neighbourhood did not like to see their streets in a mess. Sarah pulled her car into the small parking lot to the side of the Stamford Centre and looked at the darkened building.

"Do you want to wait here?" Sarah asked Harry, although it was more of an order than a suggestion. "I'll only be a few minutes. I just want a quick look around to make sure everything is okay for tomorrow."

Harry yawned. "Okay. Don't be too long or I'll have to come looking for you."

"Half an hour, tops." She promised him as she opened the car door to leave.

Sarah walked along to path newly cleared of the weeds and headed to the brightly painted red front door. She let herself in calling for Beth as she did so. The whole building seemed to be in total darkness and if Sarah hadn't seen Beth's car outside, she would have been convinced that the building was devoid of human company. Sarah switched on the desk lamp on the reception desk and it cast a surreal glow across the lobby. It was eerily silent and Sarah called for Beth again.

With no reply forthcoming, Sarah headed down the hallway to where the communal lounge area was with the large squishy sofas and light wood furniture. She flicked on the ceiling lights as she entered and saw the room was empty.

"Beth? She called again.

Still no answer.

Puzzled, Sarah switched off the lights and headed back to the lobby. She walked behind the desk and opened the door to the office behind. Finally, she saw Beth sat in the chair behind the desk, her head bowed looking down at some paperwork with the desk lamp on.

"There you are, Beth. I've been calling you. Have you been hiding out?" Sarah smiled as she saw her friend.

Beth looked up slowly and Sarah smile froze as she saw Beth

had been crying, her black mascara in rivulets down her cheeks. She had silver duct tape across her mouth and it seemed that her hands were tied behind her. Before either woman could say a word, Sarah was grabbed from behind, a hand stifling her instinctive scream.

    Harry tried to smother another yawn with his hand. He was fading fast. Sarah spent most of her days with the baby at the hospital which meant he had to be at the house much earlier and stay much later than was usual. His girlfriend, Erin was keeping him up most of the night with her insatiable sexual appetite so Harry never seemed to sleep much anymore. Thoughts of her young supple body kept him going when he thought he would keel over from exhaustion.
    His cellphone rang and he pulled it out of the inside pocket of his black leather jacket. It was Marco.
    "Is Sarah with you?" No pleasantries. Harry was used to that just lately. There had been a thick atmosphere in the House of Delvecchio for the last week or ten days.
    "Yeah." Harry half lied. "We're at the Stamford centre. Sarah wanted…"
    Marco exploded with the force of a volcano. "You're where?"
    "We'll be on our way back soon."
    "Can you see Sarah now?"
    "No, but.."
    The phone disconnected.
    Harry shook his head at Marcos crazy mood swings. He had them worse than any woman he had ever known and there had been quite a few of those. He lit a cigarette and wound down the window to let the smoke out and some air in to keep him awake. He really hoped Sarah would not be much longer, he needed to catch up on some sleep. Erin was not staying over tonight.
    As Harry exhaled the third drag on his cigarette, he could have sworn he heard a scream coming from inside the building which was almost in total darkness. From the side where Sarah had parked her car, he could just make out the glow of a single light coming from the back of the building throwing its pale yellow light across the rear patio. Harry held his breath a moment and waited, holding his breath looking towards the old school building, his tiredness suddenly forgotten.

Harry threw the remains of his cigarette out of the open window, the orange tip glowing in the darkness. He opened the glove box and felt for his gun. After checking it was loaded, Harry got out of the car and leaving it unlocked, he walked along the path that Sarah had taken just fifteen minutes before.

Putting his ear to the door, it seemed the building inside was deathly silent. He quietly opened the door and then heard low voices coming from the office, the same yellow glow emanating from the crack under the door. He heard a soft thump, followed immediately by another. Harry crept forward, his adrenaline running to the max. He heard his blood pounding in his ears. He knew what the two thumps he'd just heard had meant.

Peering through the small glass window in the door, Harry saw two men he recognised. Without any prior warning, one of the men fired his weapon directly at the others head and the second man crumpled, dead before he hit the ground. Harry flinched. The first man grinned, obviously happy with his work and stood to aim the gun at something on floor level. Harry waited no longer and rushed into the room, firing in the direction of the assassin. The man in the office had a split second head start, hearing the door crash open and turned to run. Harry had hit him in the shoulder, not a fatal wound, just a fleshy one, blood finding the floor immediately. He returned Harrys fire as he took off through the back door. The bullets missed Harry but still he was unable to move and go after the fleeing man, so sickened at the scene that faced him in the office.

As he tried to compose himself, he became aware that Marco and Scott had come into the room behind him. Scott ran through the room after the wounded assassin, following his bloody trail while Marco stood behind Harry, his brain not computing what his eyes saw.

"Sarah?" Marco spoke softly. The sound of shouting and gunfire could be heard at the back of the building. Gabe had gone round the back and had probably met the killer as he fled. Marco struggled to hold his dinner down as he looked down on the three motionless bodies of Andy, one of his soldiers, Beth and his wife. The two women had been tied and gagged, one had blood streaming from an open head wound, grey matter spattered on the carpet around her where half a skull had been blown away.

Harry gagged and had to look away.

Marco came to his senses and his instincts took over. He went to Beth first but she was so obviously dead, her long dark hair matted with thick blood escaping from what was left of her once pretty face. He stepped across her body, slipping in Andy's blood as he did so and headed to where his wife lay.

Sarah lay with her hands tied behind her back, a strip of silver duct tape across her mouth. Marco untied her hands and lifted off the tape. She had blood streaming down her face from a deep cut above her eye where she had been pistol whipped. He untied her feet bound at the ankles and gently picked her up in his arms.

Gabe and Scott came back into the room. Gabe nodded at Marco to confirm that they had killed the runner. "It was Mikey." He added.

"I need to get Sarah out of here." He told them, taking control of the situation. "My footprints are in that blood, this place needs to be spotless."

Gabe knew what to do. He'd done this before. "You get Sarah out of here, we'll get this place organised." He promised as Marco turned to leave through the back door.

"I need you back at the house as soon as possible." Marco called over his shoulder. He carried his wounded wife out of the building and gently laid her on the back seat of her car, discarding the child seats into the trunk. Harry drove home while Marco sat in the back with the still unconscious Sarah in the back. He stroked her hair, cradling her head in his lap as he wiped away the blood from her face with his handkerchief.

He called Vinnie.

"Vinnie, I need everyone back at the house. Call Sal and get Rosa and the baby over to the house and tell him not to take any shit off my sister!" He disconnected.

Marco knew he couldn't take Sarah to the hospital. He needed to be in control of the situation and that could not happen in a place as open as the hospital. He called the family doctor and told him he was needed at the house straight away.

As Harry screamed to a halt outside the front of the house,

Doctor Sturgess was just behind them. He rushed out of his car and followed Marco as he took Sarah upstairs, protesting to Marco about her condition.

"Marco, she should be in a hospital!"

"No can do, Doc. You'll need to treat her here." Marco laid Sarah gently on top of the bed and took her shoes off as Doctor Sturgess began his examination of her. "Do what you can. We cannot go to the hospital." He insisted.

Looking at Marco in consternation, Doctor Sturgess looked through his black bag to see what he needed.

With Sarah still out cold and under the care of Doctor Sturgess, Marco stormed downstairs to his office. The hierarchy of the Delvecchio family had been hastily assembled except for Gabe and Scott who were using their cleaning skills at the Stamford Centre.

Marco shut the door behind him with a quiet fury. With his hands on his hips he spoke without looking at any one person in particular.

"Will someone tell me what the hell just happened?"

No-one spoke. No-one dared.

Marco continued. "This was supposed to be an easy hit." His voice was still quiet. Marco walked over to where Harry was standing. "Perhaps you would like to tell me what the hell my wife was doing there and how she got involved."

Harry looked surprised. "Sarah wanted to check on things before the opening tomorrow." He said simply. Sarahs involvement was accidental.

"Did you not think to check with me or Gabe before you took her out there tonight?" Marcos voice was getting louder as his anger intensified.

Harry shook his head. "I don't normally. Are you telling me that something was going down?"

Marco stared at him for a second before turning away without answering.

The door opened and Gabe came in quietly shutting the door behind him. He'd put Scott on patrol close to the house. "The place is clean. The plan is back in motion." He confirmed to Marco.

"What plan?" Harry was exasperated. He was in charge of Sarahs security and he got the distinct feeling that he had been left out of the loop of something significant.

Marco looked back at Harry. "We found out that Beth had been planted by the FBI - our friend Jack Robbins." He told Harry who looked stupefied by this news. "She'd been fishing for anything illegal since day one. It had all been an elaborate hoax, even her being beaten by her so-called husband who was actually an Agent assigned to protect her. We all got sucked in."

The door opened again and this time Vinnie walked in. He'd come as quickly as he could from Boca Raton after Marco had called him from the car. He stood at the back of the now crowded office.

"What happened?" He asked anyone who could supply an answer.

"Sarah decided to go to the Stamford Centre tonight." Marco told him.

Gabe picked up the story. "Andy and Mikey are both dead. They killed Beth as planned but then decided to try and hit Sarah too. We got to Mikey before he died, painfully and slowly." He grinned at the memories. He loved to inflict pain and death to deserving people. "It seems that they were working for Joe and after telling him of the situation and our plan to deal with it, Joe paid Mikey and Andy a hundred grand to kill Sarah too."

"Not Andy. I saw Mikey kill him." Harry piped up.

Marco and Gabe looked up sharply at this new piece of information.

"Well, we'll never know." Gabe would brief Harry properly later. Harry had not known of the plan but might be able to shed some light on the events that had earlier taken place. Gabe had said all along that Harry should be informed about what was going to happen but Marco had said no, the less people that knew about it the better. Gabe would not bring it up now, Marco would not appreciate being admonished in public "Are we sure it was Joe?" Marco knew deep in his heart that his brother had indeed, finally taken the opportunity to strike back at Marco but was saddened all the same that the rift between them was now irreparable.

"So you planned to hit Beth tonight?" Harry was still trying to get his head around everything.

Gabe nodded. "We wanted it to look like a botched robbery at the Centre." He paused and looked across at Marco. "You know, Boss, this actually tidies things up quite nicely. With both the shooters dead, there are no witnesses. We can blame the whole show on Joe."

Marco nodded. He was silently coming to the same conclusion just as Gabe had said it out loud. "I think we need to speak to the Chief."

Sarah woke up sometime later in a dark room. She had no idea what time it was. The windows were open and she was glad of the cool air coming in, she was so hot. She tried to sit up but it felt like a sledgehammer bounced off the base of her skull. She groaned and lay back on the soft pillows. A gentle hand reached out of the darkness and put a welcome cold cloth on her forehead.

"Marco?" Sarah asked trying not to vomit.

"Stay quiet." Rosa whispered. "Just lie still and stay quiet."

Sarah felt so very tired that before she could say another word, the welcome blackness washed over her.

As soon as Rosa was sure Sarah was asleep again and would be for some time, she crept out of the bedroom and down the hallway to the top of the stairs. She walked along to the nursery to where she had put her daughter to sleep in her travel cot a few hours previously. Adina was sound asleep next to her cousin Giorgio. The room was cool with the air conditioning on and Adina had kicked her sheets off so Rosa carefully tucked them back in causing the child to stir slightly. When she had settled down again, Rosa went next door to ensure Grace was okay. After convincing herself that all the children were fine and undisturbed, Rosa walked back down the hallway to go downstairs for some coffee. She was beat but it would be a long night. As she passed the picture window, Rosa saw the reflection of car headlights coming down the drive. There was much going on that she didn't know about so she decided to linger to see if she might overhear anything.

The huge front door below her opened and she heard low male voices, their words indecipherable. She leant out over the banister to try to at least find out who had just arrived. She saw the Chief of Palm

Beach police disappear into her brothers office. He was dressed in plain clothes so it was obvious to Rosa that he had been summoned from home. She knew then that whatever was going on was very serious indeed.

As a child, Rosa would often hide out in the passageway that lead to the basement. She could overhear her fathers business meetings that he conducted in what was now Marcos office, although at the time she had no idea of the significance of the conversations that she had overheard. Rosa knew that if she were to go to the passageway now, she might be able to learn something. The basement was only accessible from inside the house and no-one had ever bothered to make the inner walls to the office soundproof but she would have no cover story if she was discovered. The only things she was aware that was kept in the basement was Marcos extensive and expensive wine collection. She hoped the men would be too busy to go the basement and doubted anyone would be much in the mood for a drink.

Treading very lightly for fear of her intentions being discovered, Rosa crept into the kitchen and put the coffee machine on, that way she would have an excuse for being in the kitchen at least. She tried the door to the basement and found it was unlocked. Grabbing a flashlight instead of putting on the ceiling lights, she scurried along to the point on the wall where she knew the office began and pressed her ear against the cold wall. The first voice she heard belonged to Jimmy Davis.

"Marco, what's going on here? You can't just summon me in the middle of the night - it will arouse suspicion."

"Call it brotherly love, Chief and yes, I can summon you at any hour. That's why I pay you." Marco replied dryly.

There was silence and a scrape of a chair. Rosa assumed Davis had reluctantly sat down. "What happened?" He asked, calmer now.

"Joe had Beth killed and he tried to kill Sarah too. She has been badly hurt." Marcos voice was matter of fact.

"Jesus!"

"Relax, we can sort it."

"Sort it how, Marco? A young woman has been killed! I can't just brush that under the carpet!"

"You underestimate me, Jimmy. We have friends in lots of places and they will all conclude that Beth was killed while disturbing a robbery. Our security men were rounded on by the robbers as they went in to investigate gunshots and shot the killers in self defence. No wasted police man hours looking for killers, all nice and tidy."

"And Sarah?"

"In bed with depression after having the baby early until she is recovered."

"It's all too neat Marco. Someone somewhere is bound to ask questions."

"Well it's your job to make sure they don't."

There was another prolonged silence as the men in the room digested the situation. Then Rosa heard a chair scrape again and she assumed someone had stood up.

"I guess it will work." Davis concluded.

"It had better, Chief."

The door to Marcos office squeaked open and then closed again as Jimmy Davis left the room and Rosa pulled her ear away from the wall. She was shocked to the core by what she had heard. Her brother Joe was sick with his addiction but surely he would not kill innocent people? The three Delvecchio siblings had been close as children and youngsters but since Joe had taken up his habit, the closeness had dissipated but he was still Rosa's brother. She wanted to help him but didn't know how to, it was beyond her comprehension as to what he was going through and why he had got himself into it. What Rosa did understand was the world that her brothers lived in. She knew there would be retribution for this night and that scared her to death.

When Sarah awoke again, dawn was almost breaking and a faint light appeared around the closed drapes. She could hear the dogs lose in the gardens barking furiously at something. The sprinklers emitted a low soothing noise below her window but other than that, Sarah could not detect any noise. Rosa sat in the chair next to the bed, her head back in slumber.

The nausea had subsided for which Sarah was grateful. She tried to sit up but found it was still too painful to move her head and she groaned slightly with the stabbing pain and the bright lights that exploded across her eyes. The noise stirred Rosa and she opened her eyes.

"Hey. Are you feeling better?" Rosa asked sleepily.

"Not really. My head is pounding. What happened?" Sarah had no recollection of the previous evenings events.

"I'll go and fetch Marco. He wanted to know when you woke up." The younger woman left in search of her brother who walked into the room just a few moments later, during which time, Sarah had sat up with a monumental effort. Doctor Sturgess followed dutifully in behind Marco.

"Hello Sarah. I just wanted to check on you. Do you mind?" He asked in that gentle doctor way he had.

She shook her head forgetting the pain it caused her when she moved. She groaned again.

"Do you feel sick?"

"Not so much now, thankfully."

Marco perched himself on the opposite side of the bed from which Doctor Sturgess attended his wife, watching his every movement. Sarah lay back on the soft pillows afterwards as the medic put his implements back into his bag.

"Marco, she really needs to be in the hospital. Sarah has concussion and I think her cheekbone may be fractured. You can see for yourself the bruises. Apart from that, she only gave birth just over a week ago and is fragile."

Marco nodded. "I know but we have discussed this. Sarah must stay here. You have x-ray facilities at your private surgery, right?" The doctor nodded. "I can get her there but that's the best I can do for the moment." He stroked Sarahs hand and then spoke to her. "You understand that, don't you?" It was almost a plea but Sarah nodded anyway. She really had no idea what was going on.

Doctor Sturgess shook his head in consternation as he left the room. He'd bought Marco into the world and was not afraid of him. He knew the circles this family moved in and had some idea of what was going on - he'd seen the news that morning and had struggled to get passed the press that was camped outside the gatehouse. He believed Marco when he told him that Sarah needed to be in the house. He didn't like it one bit, but he understood it.

"Marco, will you tell me what happened?" Sarah asked. "I remember being with Beth and ..." Her thoughts drifted as the memories clouded.

"Don't worry about it for now. The kids are fine." He changed the subject and his tone was upbeat. Anything to get her off the subject of Beth. Marco didn't think she'd be strong enough for that now. "Can I get you anything?" He kissed her bruised face, his touch gentle and soothing.

"Some tea would be nice and some iced water. Then I must get up."

"No, you need to stay here for at least the rest of the day."

"But it's the opening night at the Centre." Sarah protested weakly.

"It's been postponed until you are better. We can't not have you there!" He smiled, kissing her again.

Sarah relented and settled back down under the sheets.

While Marco was making fresh coffee and some tea for Sarah, Vinnie swaggered into the kitchen.

"Morning. You get any sleep?" he asked.

Marco shook his head. He'd need another shot of coffee soon.

"Is Sarah awake yet?"

Marco nodded. "She doesn't remember what happened yet."

"Were she and Beth close?"

"Fairly. That will change when she finds out Beth betrayed her. I will tell her the truth sometime but at the moment, the robbery story is the best one to tell her. She isn't strong enough for the truth."

Vinnie agreed. "Do you want me to go and see Joe? He'll be scanning the papers for news of his handiwork this morning."

"No, I'm going." Marco told him forcefully. "This is far too personal to send anybody else."

"Marco, I'm not sure that's a good idea. I agree with you that it's personal but you are way too close to this thing. You have also been up all night and your reactions and perceptions will be slow."

Marco slammed the milk carton down on the worktop, spilling some of the white liquid. Angrily, he asked Vinnie what he wanted him to do. He couldn't just ignore his brothers participation in the events.

"Of course not. I'm not suggesting that you do. Let me go to Joe. I'm on the outside here and not personally involved. Besides, Joe will never be expecting me." He grinned slyly.

Marco mopped up the spilt milk while he thought about Vinnies proposition. He nodded. "Okay. But you just talk to him today. We need to do this by the book." He looked at his brother to ensure he understood the gravity of his words. Vinnie looked at him with his emerald green eyes and Marco knew that he was on his side.

Without saying another word, Marco took the tray of refreshments up to Sarah. As he opened the door, he noticed that she had fallen back asleep so he put the tea tray down on the table beside the window and decided to crawl into bed with her. He was beat and he wouldn't be missed for a couple of hours.

Joe knew that he would be receiving a visit from Marco before the day was out. He'd had a phonecall late last night from Jerome, the guy who was supposed to be driving Mikey away from the Stamford Centre. Jerome had told Joe that something had gone wrong. He had seen Sarah go into the club as expected but Harry had waited outside which was not expected. Harry had stayed in the car for about fifteen minutes before he suddenly dashed inside with his gun drawn. The door had barely closed behind Harry when Marco, Gabe and Scott arrived, their car screeching to a halt by Sarahs car. Jerome had watched Gabe go around the back of the building while Marco and Scott had gone through the front. There had been lots of shouting and shots had been fired before Marco had come out of the back door with a limp form in his hands. Jerome knew it was Sarah but couldn't tell if she was dead or alive. It was obvious that Mikey and Andy were beyond help so Joe had told Jerome to leave the area and get out of town for a few weeks.

And so Joe waited.

Joe knew Marco would lay the blame at his door. He chuckled to himself as he thought how Sarah would feel when she found out that it was her husband who had ordered the murder of her friend and not her evil brother-in-law. He'd heard ten days ago from a source that Beth was an FBI plant and that Marco had found out. Joe's source had told him of the plan to get rid of Beth and Joe knew that this was his opportunity. He hated Sarah with a passion and if he could get rid of her, Joe knew Marco would crumble and be unable to carry on as head of the family. His allies in San Francisco, who still had Sarah under their protection, would lose all faith in Marco. He would have no option but to put Joe in charge. Joe knew he deserved to be head of the family. He'd be able to lead the family to where it should be, as one of the most influential in the country. That would never happen as long as his brother stayed in command.

Joe smiled as the buzzer to his front door resounded around the apartment. He stubbed out his cigarette and then rose to answer the door. He was quite looking forward to hearing what his brother had to say.

He got quite a surprise when he opened the door and saw Vinnie and Al standing in front of him looking smug. He chuckled again to hide his surprise and bowed mockingly and allowed the two men to pass into the apartment. They walked into Joe's living room and looked around the luxurious apartment. Joe had an up to the minute home entertainment system that took up most of one wall, a huge plasma screen dominating the room. Vinnie had a good idea what Joe watched on the screen. There were two red leather sofas around a coffee table that had evidence of a recent fix of cocaine. The small amount of white powder on the glass top announced that Joe still had his dirty habit.

Joe swaggered in after his surprise guests and sat down on one of the sofas. He lit another cigarette and offered the packet around. Vinnie and Al both declined.

Vinnie guessed that Joe had not been up long - he was wearing an emerald green Chinese smoking jacket and by the looks of it, nothing underneath. He looked ill, the usual traits of an habitual cocaine user. He was much, much thinner than Vinnie remembered him.

"Vincenzo! I was expecting a visit from the master himself. I should have known he'd be too much of a coward to come over. Won't you sit down?"

Vinnie and Al ignored his invitation. "You were expecting Marco? Why is that?"

Joe shrugged.

"Actually, Joe, Marco was all for coming over here but I stopped him. I'd thought I should come and give you a chance to save your miserable life. What the hell happened to you?"

Joe blew out a lungful of cigarette smoke. "My brother and

his wife happened. The head of this Family is a snivelling spineless weakling, you should be made aware of that."

Vinnie again ignored his words. Al stood silently by the door. "Do you want to tell me what happened last night?"

"I really have no idea what you mean."

"You already said that you were expecting a visit from Marco."

"I just heard a rumour that someone hit Sarah last night and I knew that I'd be in the market for the blame."

"Is that so?"

Joe nodded and he continued smoking.

"So are you going to ask how Sarah is?"

Joe laughed. "Everyone knows how I feel about her. Why pretend?" He looked up at his half-brother standing above him, his hands casually in his jeans pockets, a light blue and white checked shirt outside his jeans. Joe thought that if they weren't related, he might take a shine to him. Not that being related had stopped his stupid bitch of a sister.

"Do you have any idea of what you have started?" Vinnie wanted to know.

Joe just shrugged again. "You can't pin this one on me. If Marcos operation went wrong, that's down to his bad planning. You should take that up with him."

"We know it was you. Harry saw Mikey kill Andy after Beth was killed. Andy was very loyal to us and would never betray Marco, whatever the cost. I caught Mikey and he told me that you'd offered him a hundred grand to kill Sarah at the same time you were both told kill Beth. It would have all worked out quite nicely for you if Harry hadn't have got in the way and stopped Mikey from shooting Sarah."

Joe had had enough and he tried to stand up to get these two goons out of his home. Al stepped forward and pushed him back down onto the leather suite.

"You know damn well that I had nothing to do with Beth!" He snarled. As much as he might like to take the credit, killing innocent females was not his style.

Vinnie shrugged and pursed his lips as though in sympathy with Joe although he felt none. "It's not a question of what I *know*. You need to think about things *look*. Our whole world knows your feelings towards Sarah. Who's going to believe you were not behind last night?"

"The whole world knows YOUR feelings towards my sluttish sister in law." Joe muttered.

"Old feelings, Joe. That's why I am here now. To make up for what I did to Marco and to help him in any way I can. That's why I make this vow to you - I will kill you."

Joe laughed. "You'll have to get in line, brother dear!"

Vinnie was walking towards the door to leave. As he approached the door, he turned round to look at Joe again. "I have just jumped to the head of the line. And you are no brother to me."

Joe just laughed again as Vinnie closed the door behind him. He stood up and walked to the window to wait for Vinnie and Al to reappear. He liked a man with a tight butt and Vinnie possessed just that. He smiled to himself as the two men reappeared and walked towards their car. Just as the car pulled away, Vinnies lunchtime appointment arrived. Joe had taken a liking to a twenty year old guy called Drake and had called upon him a couple of times. With his thoughts still on Vinnie, Joe turned from the window and went to his personal stash of coke to get ready for his party for two.

Sarah awoke and felt the strong comforting arms of Marco tightly around her. She moved her head towards him without the dizziness this time and saw he was sleeping soundly next to her. She lay in his embrace feeling secure and safe whilst trying to remember what had happened to induce this state of vulnerability. She could remember going into the Stamford Centre and looking for Beth while Harry waited in her car. Her mind went fuzzy after this and she strained to recall the events. With a jolt to her heart, memories of Beth being tied up in the office chair, her mascara staining her pale cheeks, fear evident in her eyes. Sarah recollected being grabbed from behind, being forced down onto the floor before being blindfolded, bound and gagged, the smell of new carpet almost choking her.

Marco stirred in his slumber and Sarah stayed motionless, not wanting to awaken him and disturb him. He snored very softly in her ear and she knew he could sleep for a while yet. Sarah suspected he had been up until very late last night trying to punish whomever had hurt her and Beth. She wondered again where Beth was - Marco had been vague earlier when she had tried to quiz him.

Rosa brought a tray of coffee into the room sometime later. Sarah gently roused her husband and the three of them sat on the large bed talking. Rosa told Sarah and Marco that the children were okay. The hospital had called sometime earlier that morning asking after Sarah as she had not shown up to see Adam. Rosa told them that Sarah had a slight cold and did not want to bring an infection onto the ward. The nurse told Rosa that Adam was fine, he'd had another good night and the doctors were going to be having a confabulation as to when he might come home.

"Is he safe there, Marco?" Sarah was worried that her baby was defenceless at the hospital.

"Relax, someone has been there with him since he got there. He's fine or I wouldn't have left him there." Marco assured her.

"So will you tell me what happened? Where's Beth?"

Rosa and Marco exchanged glances. Rosa made her excuses and left with the empty coffee tray and left the room. As soon as the door closed behind her, Marco took hold of Sarahs hand.

"Sweetheart, what do you remember about last night?"

Sarah stared off into the distance as she tried to remember. She shook her head. "Not much, really. I went inside the Centre looking for Beth. She was in the office and she'd been crying. I think she was tied up. Is she okay?"

"Do you remember anyone else being in the office?" He ignored her last question.

Sarah thought long and hard about it but didn't know for sure. "How is Beth?" She asked again.

Marco paused. He knew he would have to tell Sarah the awful truth sometime and hoped she'd be strong enough. He took a deep breath. "Beth is not good. She was shot."

Sarahs hands flew up to her mouth in dismay. "Is she going to be okay?" Her voice was shaking.

Marco shook his head very slowly. "Beth died last night before we could get an ambulance to her." He looked intently at her, searching for a reaction.

Sarah said nothing for a while. She was sorting through her thoughts. "Was it Joe?"

Marco nodded very slightly.

Sarah sat back against the pillows, pulling away from him. "What are you going to do about it?"

It was not the instant reaction he had expected. "It's being dealt with." Was all he had to say for the moment, to Sarah at least.

"I want to be the one to kill him, Marco. He has killed my friend and he has caused me nothing but trouble since I've been back. I want a cyanide bullet to rip through his heart."

Marco was disturbed by Sarahs vehement words. This was not like her at all and he put some of it down to grief for her friend. It occurred to him to tell Sarah the whole truth about Beth, thinking it may lessen her grief for the dead girl. However, Sarah had had enough shocks for one day.

"There are procedures, Sarah that we must follow." He told her simply.

Sarah nodded and looked out of the open window at the blue sky outside and thinking how unfair it was that Beth would never see another sun setting.

Vinnie had returned and was sitting in Marcos office drinking coffee. He poured Marco a Jack Daniels, neat, as he came into the room. He looked as though he could do with it.

"Joe denied it, as I thought he might." Vinnie updated him.

Marco said nothing as he slugged his drink and poured another. He knew for the most part what had happened. The only cloudy part was how much Andy was involved in it. He always thought Andy was loyal to him and with Mikey killing him, it more or less confirmed to Marco that Andy knew nothing of the plot to kill Sarah. It seemed that if Harry hadn't burst in the room when he had, Mikey would have killed Sarah next. Harry said it looked as though he was aiming for Sarah, unconscious on the floor, when he had fired at Mikey, causing him to flee.

"It doesn't matter what he denies, it's what people believe. I've set the wheels in motion and there is no way back for Joe."

"This has worked out well." Vinnie seemed pleased with himself.

Marco shook his head. "No. We have to make the most of a bad situation. It is done."

"I'd like the job, Marco."

Marco looked up at his half brother while he thought over the request. "We have to have approval first."

Vinnie nodded. "How long?"

"I don't know. It's being considered so just a few days. If we get the go-ahead, I want it done before Christmas. We need to set a plan up so we are good to go when we get the okay."

Vinnie smiled. "It will be my pleasure. I have already promised Joe that he's a dead man."

CHAPTER EIGHTEEN

The next few days were very quiet at the mansion. Sarah was up and about like nothing had happened and was doing a very good job at masking her grief. Her face was still bruised but some good foundation hid most of that. The cheekbone that Doctor Sturgess feared broken was thankfully intact but quite tender to the touch. She went to see Adam every day after dropping Grace off at school, hidden behind dark sunglasses which were standard issued in Southern Florida anyway and so did not arouse suspicion. She came home at lunchtime to be with Giorgio. The hospital had given Sarah the good news that Adam could come home on Friday. He'd be two weeks old by then at it cheered Sarah up immensely.

Sarah took it upon herself to arrange Beth's funeral. She knew of no immediate family that Beth had to take on this heavy burden and she did not want to find Luke. She didn't think he deserved the opportunity.

Sarah went with Harry and Enzio to the funeral home where Beth had been taken. It was the first funeral that Sarah had ever had to arrange and to have to do it alone was harder still. Marco had told her that Beth must have family somewhere and that they should be the ones to do it. Sarah had ignored him as she ignored most of what he said lately and went ahead anyway. The funeral was arranged for Friday morning prior to collecting Adam from the hospital.

Friday morning arrived after an interminably long week and Sarah felt that she could barely rouse herself. She suddenly felt old and anxious as though she had the weight of the world on her shoulders. She wanted to hide under the bed forever. Marcos behaviour of late was not helping. He'd become very petulant last night, saying that he wouldn't go to the funeral after she had refused to have sex with him. Sarah couldn't care less one way or another if he went or not but he had spent yet another night in the guest suite.

After she had showered and dressed, Sarah went downstairs for a cup of tea. Andrea and Cliff had arrived at the house but there was no sign of Marco.

Or Harry.

"Where's Harry?" Sarah asked Cliff. She didn't really care about the absence of her husband.

Cliff shook his head, not knowing the answer. "Gabe had been trying to raise him for an hour. He'll be here. Marco said he'd meet us there."

Sarah shrugged. Marcos presence was of no consequence to her.

Harry didn't show so Peter drove them to the cemetery in the Mercedes unaccompanied. As the three mourners dressed in black got out of the car, Sarah noticed a considerable press presence. She was surprised by this given the official line of Beth's murder. But then, Mob funerals, however remotely connected were always newsworthy. She saw Jack Robbins and a few of his colleagues gathered around at a safe distance and was surprised to see him here. Robbins had been keeping his distance for some weeks now.

Sarah and Andrea sat on the chairs gathered for the mourners, Cliff stood behind them. Just as the service began, Marco arrived out of nowhere and stood next to Cliff. He placed his hand on Sarahs shoulder for comfort and she was grateful for the contact, reaching up and placing her hand on his. Sarah saw Dominic Russell sat on the opposite side of the coffin. Sarah had heard rumours of Dom and Beth embroiled in a hot blooded affair that had started up after she went to work for him. Dom being here added weight to the gossip.

As the service went on, Sarah sat with her head bowed and thought about Beth. She wondered to herself why she couldn't cry for her friend. Her heart felt like lead most days and everything seemed a monumental effort but she hadn't yet shed a single tear. She felt almost numb, unfeeling and uncaring even now. Even the sight of the coffin had not moved her to tears. She wished she might even feel anger towards the people who had put Beth in her grave.

But nothing.

The service drew to a close and Andrea was sobbing freely next to her. Sarah hugged her closely and she then stood to leave, strangely irritated by Andreas grief. She and Marco wanted to be away quickly to get to the hospital for Adam. They were both eager to get him home and find some semblance of normality again, whatever that entailed. As Sarah turned to Marco she noticed he was staring straight ahead with a look of incredulity on his handsome, unshaven face. Sarah followed his gaze behind her and saw her brother in law placing a red rose on top of Beth's coffin amidst a sea of white flowers. Joe's gaze drifted from the angry stare of his brother to the hatred filled ones of Sarah, his face locked in a sadistic grin. As the crowd of mourners began to drift away, Joe winked at Sarah before he walked away amongst the throngs of people. Marco took Sarahs arm and began to lead her towards the car. They walked silently but before they reached the waiting car, the couple were accosted by Dom.

"Sarah, I have to talk to you." He called after them with a pleading tone, causing Marco and Sarah to pause.

"What is it, Dom?" Marco asked.

"The papers, what they are saying isn't true, is it?" His eyes were welling with tears as he searched for the truth.

"What do you mean?" Marco posed the question trying to avoid Sarah having to talk to him.

"Beth wasn't a random victim of a robbery gone wrong, was she?"

"This is twenty-first century America. It happens."

"I was there, Dom, I saw it happen." Sarah assured him, the lie tripping neatly off her tongue.

"Really? So how come of the four people in that building, you were the only one to survive?"

"Dom..." Marco warned. He did not like where the conversation was headed and they turned to walk towards the car.

"I just want some answers, Sarah! I want the truth!" Dom shouted out.

Scott had been waiting in the front of the car and had seen the confrontation between Dom and Sarah and Marco. He left the car and walked hurriedly over to the couple with Dom still trying to talk to them. Dom had grabbed Sarahs arm just to get her attention but Scott was having none of it. He fairly flew at Dom and pulled him away, while Marco was pulling Sarah in the opposite direction. Scott pushed Dom away none too gently until he got the message. When Scott knew the Boss and his wife were safely in the car, he released Dom.

"I'm sorry, man. Beth was not what you thought she was." He said without thinking and walked back to the car.

A photographer from the local press and seen all of this play out and had taken some snaps. The only ones he was going to publish were of the confrontation between Scott and Dom. It would make for a very one sided story in the paper the following day.

As Sarah and Marco attempted to relax in the back of the car, they put their thoughts to bringing their baby son home. At least, Sarahs thoughts were. Marcos were more on the state of his wife's mind.

"Why did you call the baby Adam?" Marco had had no say in the naming of his second son.

"I like it. Do you mind?"

He said he didn't mind. It was just a name after all but the atmosphere between them had once again descended in the back of the car.

"Sarah, we have to talk." He reached for her but she shrunk away.

"About what?"

"A lot of things but I'm concerned about the state of our relationship right now."

"Why? Because I wouldn't have sex last night?"

Marco let out a big sigh. It was an issue with him - their sex life was normally very healthy and barely a day went by without some form of sexual activity between them. But this was not the time for petulance. Knowing there was more at stake then just sex, Marco took the tactful way. He took a deep breath.

"No. We don't talk about anything and you are bottling

everything up. You haven't shed a single tear over Beth and I find that very disconcerting."

"There'll be a time to cry for Beth after her murder is avenged. How is that coming along, by the way?" She asked sweetly.

"You know I won't discuss that. Not with you anyway."

"You just carry on shutting me out like always and maybe that's the problem."

"Not this again!" Marco groaned. "You know that I don't have a regular job and most of what goes on, I can't talk to you or anyone about. You know all of this so why won't you just accept it?"

"Because some things affect me, too. I don't want to know everything, Marco, believe me. But I'm not as naive as I was when we got married, or when I came back from California and I had hoped that I would have proved myself to you by now with my loyalty to you and not just as your wife. I don't know what else I can do. I want to be a part of your life. All of it - good and bad. "

They sat in silence for a while as the car journeyed closer to the hospital. Both of them stared out of the window watching the world go by. The car rolled to a stop outside the hospital and as Sarah clicked open the door from the inside, Marco informed her,

"I have approval to take out Joe." He too, was opening the car door and did not break stride as he told her of this information. He got out, closed the door and walked around the back of the car and took her hand. She did not blink but allowed herself to be lead inside the hospital building.

"Thank you." She breathed the words as they walked swiftly into the I.C.U to collect their son.

Grace was thrilled to have Adam home and it was Gio's turn to have a fit of jealousy over sharing his parents. Marco had told everyone that he was not to be disturbed for the rest of the day unless a dire emergency reared up - he wanted to spend this time with Sarah and his children.

Grace and Gio were put to bed while Adam slept in the living room in his Moses basket. He was currently waking for a feed every three hours. He had a very healthy appetite and was growing stronger by the day.

Between feeds, Sarah and Marco sat down to a steak and salad dinner that he had prepared and were enjoying spending time together. Sarahs mood had improved considerably since he had brought her up to speed with his plans and Marco pondered yet again if he should tell Sarah the truth about Beth but was loathe to spoil the moment. It could wait for another couple of days although the longer he left it, the harder it was becoming.

After dinner, Marco cleared away and then went upstairs to check on his sleeping children while Sarah put on one of her favourite DVD's - Gone With The Wind. As he was coming back down the stairs, Gabe came in through the front door.

"What?" Marco asked. He knew from the severe look on Gabe's ashen face that something was very wrong.

"It's Harry." Gabe spoke quietly. They were in front of the open doors to the sitting room. The O'Hara family had just arrived at Twelve Oaks for the Bar-be-Que. Marco walked into his office and Gabe followed him, closing the door behind him.

"I've been calling Harry all day to find out why he never showed up this morning. I couldn't get hold of him so I sent Enzio over to his place." Gabe hesitated.

"Just tell me!!" Marco hissed through clenched teeth.

Gabe hung his head. "Harry's dead. He was in bed with Erin. She's dead too." He couldn't look at this boss.

Marcos hands flew to his head and he ran his hands through his hair in disbelief and shock. "Fuck!"

"They were both shot and it looked like, maybe..." Gabe started to tell the story but couldn't finish.

"Looked like what, Gabe?"

He shrugged. "Maybe we should wait for the autopsy."

"It looked like what, Gabe?" Marco repeated.

Gabe hesitated unsure how to say it. "It's just, the way Harry was, it looked as though he had maybe been raped." Gabe looked as though saying the words would make him choke.

Marco swore again. Loudly and repeatedly. Gabe said nothing while his boss got it out of his system.

"It has to be Joe." Marco was pacing the floor, very distressed, muttering to himself. "Harry always said he had a thing for him." He paused as a thought hit him. "Was he alive when it happened?" Marco felt sick.

Gabe shook his head. "There's no way to know until the autopsy has been carried out. I've set Lois Jordan and her team on it. She'll see Harry right but will stay discreet." Gabe knew Lois Jordan was on Delvecchio payroll and although she would never lie or compromise her integrity, it was handy to have someone from the crimelab on their books for special favours.

"This has to end, Gabe. Call Vinnie in now. Tell him we need to bring it forward. I have to go and tell Sarah."

Gabe had been trying all morning to raise Harry. As he saw Marco's limo pull away from the front of the house to go to the Rogers girl's funeral, Gabe began to get a nasty feeling in the pit of his stomach. It was not like Harry to let Sarah or Marco down. He'd known Harry for five years now and the Englishman had always been one hundred percent reliable and willing to do anything Marco asked him to do. Gabe knew Harry had a girlfriend that kept him up most of the night but still Harry was never late. He went looking for Enzio and found him at the gatehouse.

"Enzio, I want you to go over to Harrys apartment and get him out of bed. I haven't been able to contact him all day. Do it now!" He ordered without giving away his fears to Enzio.

Enzio nodded and took his car keys out of the drawer of the small desk in the gatehouse. He checked his gun was loaded as he always did before he left the estate grounds and opened the sliding gates. Carlo waited inside the building and closed and locked the gates after Enzio had driven out.

Enzio drove his Mazda through the rich streets of Palm Beach towards West Palm Beach where it was slightly more affordable to rent and most of Marcos employees had apartments there. Even though Marco paid well, not many could justify the huge fees demanded by landlords in the rich suburb. He drove over the Flagler Memorial Bridge and looked at the beautiful blue waters of Lake Worth below him. It was another fine day in Southern Florida. After seven minutes or so, Enzio pulled into the parking lot for Harrys apartment building. It was a dark red brick building and reminded Enzio of an old fire station. Harrys apartment was on the second of four floors. He got out of the car, careful to lock it behind him and strode purposefully towards the building. As was usual for this type of apartment, there was no concierge in the lobby so Enzio headed straight for the stairs, not being an elevator man.

The building seemed very quiet. It was eleven o'clock on a Friday morning so Enzio guessed that most people would be either at work or making the most of the weather on the fine beaches that Palm Beach County had to offer. As he arrived at the second floor, Enzio noticed that Harrys front door was slightly open. He walked straight up to it and called Harrys name through the slight crack in the door.

There was no answer. Enzio slowly opened the door further and peered around the gap. It was silent inside and Enzio's internal warning system began to toll. He put his hand on his hip to the reassuring bulge of his gun and slowly walked into the apartment.

He cleared the first room, the kitchen and proceeded to walk down the hallway to the living room. It was untidy. Harry barely had time to keep his place in order and there were empty pizza boxes strewn on the floor and a couple of empty beer cans. The stereo system was on but not playing. The C.D had long since stopped playing. The curtains were drawn making the room very dark.

Quietly, Enzio headed for the bedroom. The door was open ajar and a light was on. The closer he got, the stronger the musty smell became and Enzio's heart began to beat fast in dread anticipation of what he might find.

His worst fears were confirmed as he peeked around the open door into the bedroom. Enzio saw both Harry and Erin dead on the bed, naked, blood covering the bed-sheets. Erin had been shot between the eyes and her glassy eyes stared up at the ceiling, seeing nothing. Her long, blond hair was loose around her shoulders and she was covered to the waist with a sheet, her ample bosom that Harry crowed about bare for the world to see.

Harry was lying next to her on his front. Enzio could see that he had been beaten, there were red welts across his back where he had probably been punched or kicked. His hands were tied to the bedpost in front of him and he was face down in the pillows. As Enzio looked down his body, he could see red marks around his anus and although he was no expert, Enzio guessed the reason for that. Harry had a gunshot wound to his temple, which had obviously killed him. He hoped he was dead before he was attacked but Enzio had a hunch which sadistic bastard had carried this out and knew that he would have wanted Harry to suffer.

He came to his senses and called Gabe.

"You'd better get over here." He said when his boss answered the phone.

Tuesday afternoon, Sarah was wheeling Adam around the grounds in his pram while Gio was tottering along beside her. She was not allowed outside the estate now, she had no bodyguard since Harry had been killed. She was numb to the pain of losing two close friends in such a short space of time and wanted to spend time with her children – they were her only source of peace right now.

Sarah laughed at something Gio did - a babyish stomp of his foot on a bug in the luxuriant grass and as Sarah looked up again, her laugh died in her throat. With Gio's babyish gurgling below her, she looked up into the eyes of Vinnie.

"Hi." He smiled at her. "I was hoping I'd bump into you sometime." His green eyes sparkled.

Sarah tried to ignore him and walk on with the pram, geeing up Gio.

"Sarah, we can't ignore each other forever. With all that is going on, I'll be staying here pretty much permanently and will be around the house a lot more."

Sarah stopped and looked at him. "What do you want me to say, Vinnie?"

"Just for things to not be awkward would be a start."

"Okay, let's leave it at that then." She took a few steps forward from him.

"Are you worried about what Marco might say? Are you in doubt about your feelings for him?"

She turned on him. "Absolutely not! I love my husband and coming back here was the best thing I ever did. He is kind and wonderful and I have no regrets at all. I just don't want to give him any doubts by me talking to you."

He nodded. He understood that. "I think you made the right decision. So why is he so unhappy right now?"

Sarah laughed in derision. "Let me think! Could it be that his brother had gone on a murderous rampage? Perhaps that he is afraid for the life of his young children? You really are a stupid shit!" She was very angry with Vinnie and his lack of sensitivity.

"No. I think his worries are closer to home. The Joe problem has been sorted, it's just a matter of time."

"What do you mean?" Sarah was curious. Her apathy to life had suddenly reversed ever so slightly.

Vinnie thought about his words for a moment. He knew he couldn't say too much but he wanted Sarah to be at peace with everything, to have that innocent look she once possessed but had been lost since he last saw her. "Joe has about twenty fours hours to live. He will be taken out tomorrow night at the Blue Star restaurant in Jupiter Beach tomorrow night, nine o'clock - but you haven't heard this from me."

"Why are you telling me this?" Sarah continued walking to keep up with Gio as Vinnie spoke to her.

Vinnie paused. "Maybe because I'm sick of looking at my brothers miserable face. He has enough going on without problems at home."

"What has he said?"

"Nothing. Just that you and him aren't much on speaking terms."

Sarah nodded and wondered if that was all. She knew Marco was a bit of a closed book and didn't talk about his problems, marital or work related to anyone but Vinnie was his brother even if what they discussed was shared pleasure.

"What is he doing this afternoon?" She asked.

"I was hoping you might be able to answer that. Perhaps spending some quality time with his wife before he leaves for a business trip?"

Sarah knew then that her reticence in the bedroom had been spoken about between the two brothers and she felt a flush of embarrassment. Vinnie looked long and hard at her to see if she understood the implication of his words and that was confirmed by the red flush to her face. He turned to leave.

"Vinnie?" Sarah called out. He faced her again. "Thank you for what you have said. I'm sorry for the way I treated you in the past and I'm glad you are here for Marco and I hope you and I can get over this."

He nodded. "Be good to him, Sarah. He loves you very much."

"I know." She whispered as he walked back up the lawn towards the house.

CHAPTER NINETEEN

Marco raced up the stairs two at a time. He was already running late. He wanted to grab a quick shower before heading out for the airport where his private plane would fly him to Grand Cayman for forty-eight hours, mainly for an alibi for the events of the next few days.

He threw off his clothes leaving them in a pile on the floor, as was his wont, for the maid to clear away when she came in tomorrow. Sarah would be pissed that he'd done a disappearing act but she was constantly angry with him these days and a little more would make very little difference. He hoped they might be able to patch things up soon, once things calmed down.

The water hit him like hot needles of glass shards and he felt his mood begin to lift. He knew two days away from Sarah would do them both good. She had been like an ice queen since before the baby had been born and he was feeling more than a little bit tense and frustrated. He had been faithful to Sarah since the day she had reappeared back into his life nearly two years ago, albeit unexpectedly, but he was unsure how much longer he could keep that up. The good thing about Grand Cayman were the bronzed skinned beauty queens that were always willing and more than able. Perhaps if he was a little less permanently horny, he might be able to look at the situation with Sarah a little more objectively. A solitary liaison would not do anyone any harm and Sarah would not find out. It was harmless and totally unlike the last time.

He switched the running water off and slid back the screen door, shaking the water from his hair and reached for a towel.

Sarah tried not to smile as her husband stepped from the shower. He looked up as the last few loose drops of water fell from his dark hair and almost took a step back in surprise. Sarah was sat on the vanity unit with a glass of champagne in her hands and wearing very little. After speaking to Vinnie earlier that day, she'd grabbed Enzio as company and had been to the lingerie department of Saks, buying a very sexy black and pink Basque that her post natal breasts were squeezed into above the matching panties. Her slim legs were encased in black stockings, knowing Marco went mad for a suspender belt. High heels completed what there was of her outfit. Sarah was leaning back against the mirror with one leg propped against the towel rail. She raised her champagne glass to him.

Marcos reaction was almost instantaneous and he managed to raise more than a glass. He smiled almost gratefully as he walked towards his wife, still dripping water from his recent shower. Sarah pulled him to her fuelled by a passion she had not felt in some months. She kissed him long and hard before slipping down off the vanity unit and pulling Marco into the bedroom.

"Is that better?" he asked a short time later.

Sarah smiled, her eyes still closed. "I needed that!" She sighed deeply.

He stroked her hair tenderly, relieved that he would not have to seek out a local girl in Grand Cayman "Give me ten minutes and we can go again."

Sarah laughed and rolled on top of him, kissing his stubbly face. She had not given him a chance to shave earlier. "Don't you have to go out tonight?"

He sighed with the pleasure of her nibbling his ear. "I was but I've missed my take off slot now."

"Take off? I thought you were going to Jupiter Beach..." She trailed off knowing she had said too much.

Marco shot up, throwing Sarah off him. "What do you mean?" His face took on one of anger, changing from one of a satisfied man in seconds.

"Nothing. I..." She didn't know what to say.

"Who have you been speaking to?" He demanded.

Sarah reached for her housecoat, knowing their lovemaking was over for tonight at least. "Vinnie just said..."

"Vinnie? " Marcos face was angry, jealous and confused. "Why have you been talking to him?"

Sarah sighed. She knew the minute Marco had told her that Vinnie would be moving to Palm Beach that the jealous fits would happen sooner or later. "We just ran into each other in the garden today, that's all." She headed for the bathroom. Marco followed her.

"Today? Is that why the sudden complicity with me then? You have been pushing me away for weeks and yet the day you run into Vinnie is the day you behave like a whore with me?" His voice showed the hurt and anger that he was feeling.

"Marco, get over yourself. Vinnie just gave me a wake up call, that's all. I had the feeling that as your *wife* and not your *whore*, you would be pleased I made an effort. I see it was a wasted one." She turned in the bathroom doorway to look at him, still sat on the edge of the bed. He looked lost and alone but Sarah had no inclination to go to him and massage his ego anymore. She closed the bathroom door and hit the shower.

CHAPTER TWENTY

At six forty-five the following night, Sarah slipped out of the back door. Jenny was on duty tonight and so the children would not miss her for the few hours that she needed. Feeling like an errant teenager, Sarah sneaked down the path by the pool and on towards the back gate. She knew this would be the be-all and end-all of her plan and she hoped that she might be able to get by whoever was at the back gate.

As usual, it was Scott who sat on the large stool with his back against the wall for support. Sarah waited close by in the Oleander bush and thought about how she would get by him. Knowing someone was always stationed there, she had given a great deal of thought as to how she might get by but had come up with nothing as yet. She thought about throwing a stone to distract Scott and hoped he might walk away just long enough for Sarah to make a run for it. That was supposing that the gate wasn't even locked.

If Sarah ever doubted that she had a guardian angel, he came to her then and his name was Gabriel. Gabe appeared out of the darkness, his presence known by the orange glow of the tip of his cigarette. He called for Scott to go with him for a moment, the gate would be okay for five minutes and the young man followed his boss up the path.

With a small skip of joy, Sarah left the cover of the Oleander bush and hurried to the gate. She tried the latch and found to her delight that it lifted. Lady Luck was on her side that night, at least, so far. The gate opened without even a squeak and she left the safety of the estate and rushed out towards the beach.

Walking at a fast pace down the lane, she came across an abandoned car, a plain generic car, some kind of small dark Ford and hurried over to it. The keys, as planned were on top of the back offside wheel and she grabbed them, opening the door to the wreck with the black leather gloves that were hidden with the keys. The engine started on the second time of asking and Sarah carefully put it in gear, something she was not used to doing and slowly drove up the lane towards the main road.

Knowing time and circumstance were against her, Sarah drove with extreme care. She did not want to get pulled over in a car that was not hers and that she had no insurance for, much less the stolen weapon under the passenger seat next to her. Marco had secreted a number of weapons in the roof eves of the summer house that only he and Gabe were supposed to know about. Sarah knew far more than she would ever let on to her husband. She had carefully selected the weapon for the job that morning. It wasn't too dissimilar to those that she was used to firing at the Gun Club and so felt confident about using it.

The drive to Jupiter Beach took less time than she had planned for and she pulled up in the almost deserted parking lot of the Blue Star restaurant sooner than she had anticipated. She had about one hour before Vinnie arrived and she wanted to have got the job done and be back home again before he showed up. She had no desire to see him, much less for anyone to know she had been at the restaurant.

Sarah took hold of the gun and checked it was loaded in the way Kristina had often shown her. The serial number of the weapon had long since been shaved off and was now untraceable. She left the car unlocked and walked over towards the restaurant. Her heart was pounding but she felt no fear of what she was about to do or of being found out. She felt no emotion at all.

Peering through the window of the salubrious establishment, she saw her quarry, surprisingly with his back to the door in a careless disregard for his own safety and his dinner companion, a young man of twenty or so facing the entrance. There were no other diners and just one waiter. The waiter seemed to be edgy and looked towards the main door continuously. He served what looked to be antipasti and then left the dining room to go into the kitchen. Sarah took her opportunity.

Vinnie arrived at the house just as Sarah was leaving through the back gate. He was looking forward to carrying out this deed he was about to perform for his much wronged brother. He was however, surprised to see Marco in the house and not in Grand Cayman.

"Why are you still here?" He asked, puzzled.

Marco scowled at him. "I understand that you have had words with my wife today? I told you to stay away from her!"

"Whoa, Marco! It was a pure accident and I just told her that she should be more appreciative of you."

"Really? So how does she know about tonight?"

Vinnie shrugged. "She needed to know that Joe would not be an issue for much longer. I didn't tell her any details. " Vinnie half-lied.

Marco grunted, not entirely happy. He was the one who decided what Sarah needed to know and when.

"Listen, Marco, I'd better get going. Timing is crucial tonight. I'll call you on the way back."

Marco nodded and allowed Vinnie to go, gathering Al on his way out.

Vinnie drove towards Jupiter Beach with his most trusted man beside him and felt strangely relaxed. He knew after tonight there could be something of a backlash but things would eventually settle and remain calm. Marco was a good leader of this family and Vinnie wanted to be by his side. It was what he had always wanted despite the distractions along the way.

He pulled into the car park and saw it was almost empty as planned. Something tugged at his conscious.

Almost empty??

Sarah walked into the near deserted restaurant with her gun drawn and trained on the back of Joe's head. She crept in crab-like as she had seen the cops do in so many movies, both hands firmly on the gun.

"Joe?" She spoke quietly.

Joe turned his head and looked around. He saw Sarah with the gun in her hand and laughed. "What the fuck is this?"

Sarah was about six feet away to the side of him. "You have

caused me and my family nothing but trouble since I got back here. It ends tonight." She said with a quiet and determined fury.

Joe laughed again. "You? Don't make me laugh! You playing at being a gangsters moll now?"

"This is no game, Joe. This is for Beth and for Harry." She aimed the gun at Joe's head and paused.

"Beth?" He snickered. "Sweetheart, as much as I would like that one under my belt, it had nothing to do with me. You need to look closer to home." He put another mouthful of olive oil soaked bread into his mouth, oblivious to the gun trained on his temple.

"What do you mean?" Sarah asked, still eyeing him up through her gun sight.

Joe looked at her with an amused look on his disgusting face. "Oh! So he hasn't told you yet? Beth had nothing to do with me. That was all your precious husbands idea." He laughed as he saw her face clouded with confusion. Sarah dropped her aim.

"Don't talk such rubbish! Why would Marco want to kill Beth?" Sarah looked at his companion who seemed calm and was continuing eating and drinking the expensive red wine on the table.

Joe shrugged. "If I told you, it might make me complicit in his plans."

Sarah strode up to him and put the gun against his temple point blank. "If you don't tell me, it will make you a dead man."

Joe still seemed rather amused at his sister in law playing at being a gangster but decided to humour her. "Well, it would seem that your dear friend Beth was planted by the FBI. She was in deep with another friend of yours, Jack Robbins, I believe his name is and with her having connections in Palm Beach County, Robbins thought it would be good fun to put her in your way and see what happened. I bet he wet himself when you made friends with her."

Sarah took a step back, not wanting to believe what Joe was telling her. Surely if Marco had known, he would have told her. She shook her head in denial.

"Believe it, baby, it's the Gods honest truth." Joe continued. "Marco found out, how I don't know – you'll have to ask him that, he never did confide in me. The little I knew, I had to find out through Mikey."

"So Mikey *was* working for you! What about Andy?"

Joe took another mouthful of the delicious bread that the Blue Star served and chewed it before continuing. "Just a sucker who got in my way." He shrugged.

"And Harry?" Her voice began to break.

Joe smiled laviciously. "Never have I experienced such pleasure in killing a man."

"You're sick!" Sarah whispered. "He was a good man."

Joe nodded. "He was good for me. I love it when they put up a fight, it makes the pleasure so much more intense. I didn't want to kill him, I asked him to come and work for me but he felt that he couldn't betray you or my shit-breath brother."

Sarah aimed her gun again, this time so much closer to Joe. She took a few steps back, wary of the blood spatter and carefully eyed him up down the barrel of the gun.

Joe's face suddenly clouded with fear but Sarah hesitated for a moment. She knew that there would be no going back. She became aware of the door opening again and someone walking in. She knew she would not be able to look around to see who it was for if she took her concentration off Joe, he would undoubtedly draw a weapon and kill her. However, she knew she could not have any witnesses. She trusted Marcos ability to quash witnesses as he had done countless times in the past Sarah squeezed the trigger.

"Sarah, NO!" She heard Vinnies voice behind her.

Joe laughed nervously. "This should be interesting.'

Vinnie walked over to a hesitant Sarah and reached for her weapon. She slapped his hand away.

"I have to do this Vinnie. If not for Beth, then for Harry and all the times Joe has threatened me and my kids." She spoke with a quiet force.

"This is not your concern, Sarah. Leave it to me, please." Again, he tried to reach for her gun. She pushed his hand away.

While this little battle was occurring, Joe's dinner companion Drake had slowly and imperceptibly drawn his own small gun from his ankle holster and passed it under the table to Joe. At the last moment, Al had seen some movement under the table and aimed his gun at the youngest man.

"Hands on the table, buddy!" He shouted, his Chicago accent thick and recognisable.

Drake hesitated a moment too long and Al, taking no chances, fired his weapon, the bullet smashing through the soft skull of Joe's dinner companion. He slumped backwards, his mouth open in surprise as Death took him and his eyes stared unseeing at the blue painted ceiling.

Joe cursed at seeing his favourite piece of ass dead on the chair opposite him. He turned his blazing eyes to Al and brought Drakes small gun up to aim. His last thoughts were to kill Vinnie, knowing it would have more of an effect than killing Al. He aimed for Vinnie.

Sarah was stood to the side and had been all but forgotten. She had perceived the danger and aimed for Joe's head just as Joe had aimed for Vinnie. She knew that if she had the courage to go through with this, it would make everything better. Without thinking for another second, she squeezed off two bullets, straight and true. They had smacked into Joe's brain but not before he had fired one bullet aimed for Vinnie. As Joe died from Sarahs bullets, Vinnie fell to the floor. He had been hit square in the chest.

Calmly, Sarah dropped the gun to the side and surveyed the damage. Joe was dead by her own hand and she felt absolutely no remorse, just justice for Harry and immense confusion over Beth. She looked over to where Al had rushed to Vinnies side.

"Call an ambulance, Al." She instructed, taking control.

"You dumb bitch! There will be no response to any 911 calls from here for at least half an hour!" Al was ripping his shirt off to stem the blood flow currently pouring from Vinnies chest.

"What? Why?"

"Marco arranged it, just in case."

Sarah looked around frantically at the mess in the restaurant. Two dead bodies and another very nearly. Vinnie could not die, Marco needed him.

"Then we have to get Vinnie to the hospital."

"And say what?" He looked distraught.

Sarah wondered to herself what kind of man Al was. He was completely panic stricken and almost entirely useless. "Get him in the car!" She ordered taking control again.

With a grunt and a groan, they lifted Vinnie between them and got him into the back seat of the car he and Al had driven to Jupiter Beach in. Sarahs junk car had been picked up from the wreckers yards and untraceable. The car was clean of her prints, she was certain. Sarah drove Vinnies car to the hospital with Al playing nursemaid in the back with Vinnie.

After Vinnie had left, Marco went in search of Sarah. They needed to sort things out and an afternoon session in bed would not suffice. He looked in the bedroom, still untidy after their furious lovemaking earlier that day but he found she was not there. He went down the hallway, passed the picture window to the children's nursery. Jenny was in the room reading Grace and Gio a story while Adam slept. Grace leapt up as her father came in the room and raced over to hug him. He picked his beloved daughter up and kissed her while asking Jenny if she had seen Sarah. She answered in the negative.

After a few minutes, Marco made his excuses and putting Grace down, he left the nursery and went downstairs. She was not in the kitchen or the sitting room either. He shouted for Gabe and went into his office. Marco poured himself a Jack Daniels, a recent habit of late and waited for his right hand man to arrive. Gabe arrived barely moments later.

"Have you seen Sarah?" He asked.

"No. Not since..." He hesitated. "I don't actually know when I last saw her." He shrugged. "Would she have gone shopping?" It was a standing joke among Marcos employees of his wife's ability to shop for Florida.

"At this time of night?" Marco snapped.

Gabe just shrugged. It was not his responsibility to keep tabs on Marcos wife. However, seeing the angry state Marco was in, Gabe thought he should make some kind of effort. He picked up the phone and dialled the gate house. Carlo was there but he assured Gabe that Mrs Delvecchio had not left through the front or side gates that evening. Gabe put the phone down without thanking the man and decided to go to the back gate and speak to Scott.

Scott similarly assured Gabe that he had not seen Sarah leave and he had been there all night except when Gabe called him away for a few minutes to check on the broken lock to the summer house. Both men hesitated as they put the two events together. Could it have been possible that Sarah had sneaked out during those few minutes? Gabe rushed back up to the house to find Marco.

He was pouring himself yet another drink.

"Marco, what does Sarah know about tonight?"

Marco shrugged. "Nothing that I told her. Why?"

Gabe sat down without invitation. "I was walking by the summer house earlier today and noticed the lock was broken. It had been forced. Earlier tonight, I pulled Scott off the back gate to check the stock in there. One of the Berettas is missing and two rounds of ammo for it." He looked up at Marco, hoping he would make his own conclusions.

He struggled with it for a moment. "And you think Sarah took it and somehow sneaked out of a well guarded house?" He snickered looking down into Gabe's face.

Neither man said anything for a while. Marco was recalling the time when he had told Sarah that Beth had been killed and her vehement words as she swore she would kill Joe. She'd had a lot of shooting lessons and Kristina had told him that she was a natural. Marco put his empty glass down on his desk. "We have to call Vinnie and call this off tonight. There will be other nights but I can't take the chance with my deranged wife out there somewhere."

Gabe picked up the phone and dialled Vinnies cellphone. It wasn't quite eight thirty so Vinnie would still be on his way to the restaurant and there would be time for him to turn around.

The phone was eventually answered by Al who sounded breathless and edgy.

"It's Gabe. We have to halt the proceedings."

"It's too late."

"What?"

"The Don's wife was already there when we arrived. She's killed Joe and Vinnie has been shot in the chest. We are on our way to the hospital now."

Gabe looked almost fearfully across at Marco with the phone still to his ear and he listened to Al's hysteria down the line. Gabe had no idea how to tell Marco that his wife had killed his brother with an illegal firearm.

"We'll meet you there, Al." He said quietly and put the phone down.

Marco was watching him intently. "What's happened?"

Gabe breathed deeply. He had worked for Marco for a long time and his father before him and they had known each other since childhood. He had never before been so reluctant to say what he had to say as he was right then.

"Gabe?" Marco prompted, his temper beginning to rise.

"Well, the good news is, Joe is dead."

"Already? Why so early?"

"That's the bad news. When Vinnie and Al arrived, Sarah was there. It seems that she did indeed get hold of the gun and she has in fact, killed Joe."

Marco nearly smiled with disbelief, thinking it was a joke. He saw Gabe was not laughing with him and realised it was the truth. "Sarah? She killed Joe?" Marco could not and would not believe it. His wife hated violence and it was one of the reasons that had driven them apart the first time around. She deplored the violent lifestyle that sometimes came with the job he had and even though she'd had lessons, he didn't believe she was capable of killing someone in cold blood. He shook his head.

"Marco, we need to get to the hospital and sort this out."

"Why the hospital?" Marco looked up sharply.

"Vinnie has been hit pretty bad by the sounds of it. Al and Sarah are on their way in the car. I'll call the Chief en-route and tell him of the change in plan."

"No!" Marco said sharply. "Let him think it was Vinnie." He did not want his wife to be known as a killer, if indeed, she had carried out the killing.

Gabe picked up his car keys and they headed out of the door.

Sarah screamed to a halt outside the emergency room. A Doctor was standing against the wall having a cigarette break. Sarah shouted at him to come and help, that her brother in law had been shot. The Doctor called for a gurney and some assistance and he ran to the back of Vinnies car. The back seat was covered in blood as was Al and Vinnie looked very pale to the point of death.

"What happened?" The doctor asked.

Sarah shrugged. "Just help him!" She insisted as a couple of nurses pulled her out of the way to get to Vinnie. With effort, they managed to get the unconscious muscular man onto the gurney and wheeled him into the ER Sarah moved the car while Al went inside to give the Doctors any information they needed. She knew Marco and Gabe would be here very soon and she was dreading the confrontation. It had gone slightly awry in her mind, she should have killed Joe and left. She should have killed him straight away instead of stopping for a chat with the evil monster. No-body would have known it was her and she would have been back home now having dinner and trying to appease her husband. Instead, she would probably never get his forgiveness.

After parking the car, Sarah went inside to find Al. He was sat in the chairs with his head in his hands. She went to the coffee machine and bought two cups of the cheap tasting liquid, handing one to Al.

"He'll be okay." She assured him calmly.

"Are you not bothered by what you have done?" He asked without looking at her.

She shook her head. "Why should I? I'm sorry Vinnie got hurt but that wasn't my fault. You have to expect casualties."

"Your husband will hit the roof." He said quietly.

"I know." Her words were just as quiet.

Marco arrived half an hour later. Even in this time of immense crisis, he still looked immaculate with his navy suit and blue shirt on, not a hair out of place. Sarah couldn't help but smile as she saw him come into the E.R even though he had a thunderous look on his face and she knew she would be in for his full wrath.

He saw her and stormed over in her direction. He grabbed her by the elbow and forced her to walk with him. He didn't say a word as he looked for somewhere quiet to shout at her. He found an empty treatment room and threw her inside, slamming the door behind them both.

"Marco..." She began.

He looked down at the floor, unable to look at her without

wanting to strike her. His hands were on his hips to control them, his jacket flared out behind him. "What the *fuck* do you think you are doing?" He managed to look up at her, his eyes blazing with intense rage.

"I told you I was going to do it. You should be pleased."

"*Pleased?* Why should I be pleased? I have a brother about to die and a wife who is a cold blooded murderer! What is there to be pleased about?"

"I got the job done. Joe was going to die anyway, does it matter who did it?"

"Yes! Yes, it does! Your DNA will be all over the scene and the police will come looking for you. Do you know we have the death penalty in Florida?" His anger started to dissipate and Sarah knew he was calming down.

"My DNA is not all over the restaurant any more than Vinnies. I had lunch there yesterday and plenty of people saw me so if anyone finds anything, I have an alibi."

"And what of your alibi tonight? Why were you there?"

She thought about it for a moment. "I was meeting Vinnie for dinner. We were going to discuss a surprise holiday for you."

Marco laughed although there was no humour in it. "You think you have all the answers, don't you? This is not a game, Sarah and I do not appreciate your encroachment into my business!"

Sarah looked down in penitence that she knew Marco would expect of her. "I'm sorry Marco but I did it for Harry and I'd do it again."

Marco said nothing for a moment. He put his arm around her and led her out of the office. "Come on, let's go and see how Vinnie is doing."

They walked back along the corridor to the loud, chaotic E.R, full of panic stricken and hurt people. Al and Gabe were sat together not talking and looked up as Marco and Sarah approached.

"How is Vinnie?" He asked them both.

They both shook their heads.

"Have the police been around yet?"

Again, they both shook their heads.

Sarah sat next to Gabe, while Marco stood above her. "Was

anyone ever going to tell me the truth about Beth?" She asked.

Gabe and Marco looked sharply at her.

"Joe told me." She answered their unsaid question.

"I didn't know when the right time would be." Marco said quietly, barely audible in the din.

"How did you find out?"

Marco sat on the empty plastic chair next to Sarah and took her hand in his. "When she was in the townhouse. I'd done a few basic checks on her but only found out what the FBI would want me to, like her fabricated history and her made up marriage. She made a pathetic pass at me and warning bells began to ring so I carried out a full check on her. I know someone at the West Palm Beach FBI office who made some investigations on my behalf. He said Beth had been arrested on fraud and embezzlement charges by Robbins over a year ago. He offered her a way out if she could get to me. Her whole story was a lie. She was never married to Luke, he was her protection, her back up plan. She'd been mugged the night we all thought she'd been raped and used the situation to get closer to us."

"Did you ever confront her?"

Marco shook his head. "No. She would have denied it and then run. She lied to all of us, especially you."

"But what about the Stamford Centre? That was her idea."

"And what better way to get to know my finances and business dealings?"

Sarah shook her head. "I'm sorry, Marco. I really am."

He squeezed her hand in encouragement.

The four sat in silence for the next half an hour until a doctor came over to the group.

"Hello. I'm Doctor Pitchford. I'm treating your..." He was unsure exactly of the relationship.

"Brother." Marco confirmed for him.

"Mr Bonnetti is in a very bad way. The bullet has lodged in his heart and he has lost a huge amount of blood. We have stablised him enough to operate on him but he is very weak. His chances are not good, I have to prepare you." He looked very grave. "We are taking him up to the O.R now and I'll send news as soon as I have some but it maybe a few hours if all goes well."

"Thank you, Doctor." Marco looked up at him. The Doctor nodded and walked away.

No-one said anything for a while.

"Vinnie has a child." Sarah said after ten minutes or so. " A son, I think. Is he in Florida?"

Al nodded. "He came down with Vinnie and his nanny. They live in Boca. Should I call the nanny?"

Marco shook his head. "Not yet. Let's wait until we know anything."

The time passed very slowly and one by one, the group stood up and walked around. Gabe and Al went outside together for a cigarette at some stage, leaving Marco alone with Sarah.

"So what are we going to tell the police?" She asked her husband.

He shrugged. "You seem to have all the answers. Perhaps you can come up with something."

"Maybe the truth would be best. About everything." She tested him and he bit.

"You'd do that?"

"No, of course not. I have more to lose than you do although I'm sure Robbins would offer me a similar deal to last time. He wants you!" She jested. She would never tell anyone of her husbands criminal activities.

"We'll think of something tomorrow. I can't think about anything but Vinnie at the moment. Gabe has called Jimmy Davis and we won't be questioned about it tonight.

"What about Joe?"

"It's fine, Sarah. Just leave it for now, please." He leaned his head back and closed his eyes.

Sarah did as she was told for once and stayed silent.

Gabe and Al came back into the building shortly after and everyone tried to get comfortable for the long wait ahead. Sarah watched the people come and go in the E.R as her only source of amusement.

Eventually, Doctor Pitchford came back. Sarah nudged Marco in the ribs to wake him from his gentle doze.

The Doctor had a smile on his face. "We have removed the bullet and repaired the lining of his heart. He may need future surgery but for the moment, Vinnie is stable and recovering from the operation. We will keep him in a coma until we know the heart is strong enough and we won't know that for a few days. You can go and see him if you like, but he is hooked up to several machines and you may find it distressing."

Marco stood and shook the Doctors hands for saving his brother life, at least for the time being. He wanted to go and see him.

"You go, Marco. I'm going home. I'll see you back there later." She kissed his stubbly cheek goodbye and went out into the car park to find the car. She realised that for the first time in months that she was free to go wherever she chose without fear. She just wished Harry was still around to enjoy the freedom with her. At the thought of him, Sarah began to cry. She had not shed a tear for him or for Beth but now the tears fell freely down her face as she drove through the darkened streets onto the US-1 and she began to sob for Harry until she felt her heart would break. She remembered all the wonderful things he had done for her, the times he had made her feel safe just by being around. The children had loved him too, in fact they often saw more of Harry than they did their own father. She remembered how he would always make the children laugh with a new game when they were in the car. She had only met Erin once but Harry was in love with her and she did not deserve to die the way she had. Sarah tried to calm her sobs as she pulled up to the gate house and Carlo came out to see who was in the car.

"Mrs Delvecchio, the Boss has been looking for you." He told her.

"I know, thank you Carlo. We've caught up with each other." She told him politely. She just wanted to get home and crawl into bed. Carlo disappeared into the small white building and pressed the button that released the sliding gate to the mansion grounds. Sarah thanked Carlo again and crawled slowly up the drive. It was past midnight and she did not want to disturb anyone.

Sarah had a quick shower as if to wash her grief for Harry and her intense feeling of betrayal over Beth. She understood now why Marco behaved the way he did around people he did not know one hundred percent. It would make her more wary of making new friends and acquaintances in the future.

Sarah crawled into bed. As soon as her head hit the pillow, unconsciousness rolled over her and she slept.

She became aware of movement in the bed beside her sometime later. She raised her head to look at the clock beside her bed and saw that it was just after two. She had only been sleeping for an hour but it was such a deep sleep that it felt to Sarah like it had been a whole day. Marco was settling down beside her.

"How's Vinnie?" She asked sleepily as he curled himself around her.

"No change. The hospital will call if there is any news."

Sarah lay her head back on the pillow and felt his breath on the nape of her neck.

"Marco, I am sorry I went against you."

"Uh-huh." He was unconvinced and knew she would do the same thing again given the chance. As Marco had sat by his brothers bedside, he knew what a monumental thing Sarah had done for him. She had crossed a line tonight, by killing a man and Marco was strangely turned on by that. That the dead man had been his brother did not concern him for as far as Marco was concerned, Joe had died a long time ago. He knew that Sarah was no longer the innocent woman he had married what seemed a long time ago but one that demanded as much respect as he was given with his title.

"I love you, you know that." She whispered.

"I know. Perhaps now though, you will do as I ask of you. You can be a right pain in the ass sometimes."

"I know but you wouldn't have it any other way. People don't need to know it was me, do they?"

Marco laughed softly at her hypocritical attitude. "No, they don't." He agreed. "Gabe and I have decided that Vinnie is to take the credit for tonight. Our original plan stays in effect, despite your best efforts to land us all in jail." He kissed her neck. "Good night, sweetie."

Sarah lay awake as she felt Marco drift off into a deep and almost untroubled sleep. He was right, she was a pain but he still put up with her. Sarah put up with all of his foibles too because she loved him unconditionally. She had some kind of hold over him that she really didn't understand no matter how much he was revered in his male dominated world. He was an ordinary man to her with a less than ordinary job and take on life but that was how Marco did things.

    E malavita.

Printed in the United Kingdom
by Lightning Source UK Ltd.
136233UK00001B/253-255/P

A LIBERAL
VOCATIONALISM

A LIBERAL VOCATIONALISM

Harold Silver
and
John Brennan

METHUEN
LONDON AND NEW YORK

First published in 1988 by
Methuen & Co. Ltd
11 New Fetter Lane, London EC4P 4EE

Published in the USA by
Methuen & Co.
in association with Methuen, Inc.
29 West 35th Street, New York NY 10001

© 1988 Harold Silver and John Brennan

Typeset by Boldface Typesetters, London EC1
Printed in Great Britain
by J.W. Arrowsmith Ltd, Bristol

All rights reserved. No part of this book may be
reprinted or reproduced or utilized in any form or by
any electronic, mechanical or other means, now
known or hereafter invented, including
photocopying and recording, or in any information
storage or retrieval system, without permission in
writing from the publishers.

British Library Cataloguing in Publication Data

Silver, Harold,
A liberal vocationalism.
1. Vocational education
I. Title   II. Brennan, John
370.11'3   LC1043

ISBN 0-416-09262-4

Library of Congress Cataloging in Publication Data

Silver, Harold.
A liberal vocationalism / Harold Silver and John
Brennan.
p.   cm.
Bibliography: p.
Includes index.
ISBN 0-416-09262-4 (pbk)
1. Technical education – Great Britain. 2. Business
education – Great Britain. 3. Vocational education –
Great Britain.
I. Brennan, John, 1935– . II. Title
T107.S56   1988
607'.1041 – dc19

Contents

Acknowledgements

Part One: Frameworks 1
1 Confuse or clarify? 3
2 Stigmas and dichotomies 18
3 Preparing students for employment 34
4 The language of policy 53

Part Two: Vocationalism – A project 69
5 Concepts, courses, and institutions 71
6 Engineering education: a background 77
7 Engineering education: courses and explanations 93
8 Engineering education: a note on the United States 137
9 Business studies: a background 144
10 Business studies: courses and explanations 157
11 Business studies: a note on Europe 184
12 Environments 194
13 Institutions 215

Part Three: A liberal vocationalism? 231
14 A liberal vocationalism? 233

Appendix 254
Bibliography 257
Index 270

Acknowledgements

This book grew out of a project supported by the Council for National Academic Awards, and our thanks are due primarily to the CNAA for that support. The original project was one of three it supported simultaneously under the umbrella title of Higher Education and the Labour Market (HELM), with a project committee chaired by Sir Bruce Williams until the summer of 1986, and then by Professor Gareth Williams. We are grateful to them and to the rest of the committee for their active support and help. The work benefited considerably from experience shared in seminars with colleagues from Brunel University, North Staffordshire Polytechnic, and elsewhere – including the CNAA itself.

We would also like to thank the Commission of the European Communities for the grant which enabled John Brennan to visit a number of European institutions during the work. There are too many people in the British, American, and European colleges and universities which we visited to whom we owe major debts for their help and co-operation for us to be able to list them all here. We would only say that wherever we went we met with uniform willingness to collaborate. This was particularly important in relation to the four British institutions which we explored in some depth. To the people named at appropriate places we record a particular debt.

At different stages in the research and in its elaboration into its present form two other people, Pamela Silver and Jolanta Pieniazek, have made major inputs. Although their names do not appear on the title page, they have contributed substantially to the work on which the book is based. We are deeply grateful to them both. Finally, we would like to thank Jackie McDermott for preparing the index.

Harold Silver and John Brennan
April 1987

Part One
FRAMEWORKS

1
Confuse or clarify?

'If it's easy to start an argument about transport', commented the Duke of Edinburgh in 1961, 'it is just as easy to start a riot about education and training' (Edinburgh 1962: 293). Wherever the entry is made into such educational vocabularies, the riot follows. Education and training, theory and practice, the liberal and the vocational – the polarities have centuries of turbulent history, mounting as the concepts and the processes have become explicit elements in social and economic pressures and conflicts. The focus of this book is on the vocational and, as Margaret Thatcher underlined, as opposition spokesman on education in 1970, when she wrote about the fledgling polytechnics: 'they have tended to provide training for specific jobs; in modern jargon (which often seems to confuse rather than clarify) the courses are vocationally motivated' (Thatcher 1970: 16). The aim of the book is to rescue a usable interpretation of the vocational.

Confusion is not eliminated by definition, or bypassed with negatives. What the vocational is has no stable meaning, and it cannot be established by simply listing the things it is not. The elements of social processes exist only in relationships, and the discussion here can focus on the vocational only by adventuring into the relationships in which it is held. From Aristotle to modern technological policy-making the 'liberal' and the 'vocational' have been in tension – though through most of that history it is the voices of the liberal that have been most heard. One of the purposes of this book is to hear and to interpret the sounds of institutions, courses of study, and teachers now commonly perceived as vocational – to listen to other voices.

How deep the confusion surrounding the vocational and the liberal has been in this century can be best illustrated from Monroe's *A Cyclopedia of Education* published in the United States in

1914. In it John Dewey wrote a piece on 'Liberal Education', outlining its trajectory from Aristotle's definition as associated with knowledge in the context of leisure and the cultivation of mind by a leisured class freed from the preoccupation with practical matters of slaves, serfs, mechanics, or tradesmen. The distinction was between a liberal education as an end in itself, and professional training as a means for practical ends 'beyond itself'. Dewey emphasizes the basis of the distinction between liberal and servile education in Greek class distinction, and the complexities later introduced by the rise of natural science, and the claims of vernacular languages, literature, history, and other disciplines. In a society which bases its constitution on class distinctions it is 'comparatively easy to assign a distinct content and a distinct purpose to liberal education', but modern changes – including 'the democratic ideal' – make that increasingly difficult:

> Liberal education becomes a name for the sort of education that every member of the community should have: the education that will liberate his capacities and thereby contribute both to his own happiness and his social usefulness. . . . In short a liberal education is one that liberalizes. Theoretically any type of education may do this. As matter of fact, all of them fall much short of accomplishing it.
>
> (Dewey 1914: 4–6)

Just as any type of education may liberalize, so any may be illiberal if it is excessively narrow and restricts the imagination.

In the search for clarity one then turns to the brief editorial entry under 'Vocational Education', which begins:

> In a certain sense, all education is vocational in that it aims to prepare one for the more efficient and satisfactory performance of the activities of life. Even liberal education is in a sense vocational, for in its various forms it has aimed to prepare for the life or calling or 'vocation' of a statesman or man of public affairs, of the gentleman, of an ecclesiastic, or whatever the particular social concept of the liberally educated man may have taken.

> In 'ordinary usage', however, vocational education is differentiated from 'the more general stages' of education by being chiefly concerned with 'the practical application of knowledge acquired in early stages of the educational process and the

education of selected or differentiated groups. The reader is therefore directed to other encyclopedia entries under 'Theological Education', 'Technical Education', 'Agricultural Education', 'Teachers, Training of', and so on. The brief discussion ends by underlining the fact that 'the vocational aspect of education is becoming a topic of very general importance, and is discussed in its theoretical aspects, in addition to the above topics, in the articles on Education; Art in Education; Citizenship and Education' (Monroe 1914: 740). It is unlikely that the search for clarity would end with Dewey's assertion that any education may be liberal or illiberal, set alongside the view that 'in a certain sense, all education is vocational'. Across the two interpretations the analysis relates to social structures, subject content, happiness, social usefulness, stages of education, preparation for professions, the application of knowledge, theories, and ordinary usages. It is not only modern jargon which may confuse rather than clarify.

We are concerned in this book predominantly with the nature of the vocational as it is perceived in, and in relation to, higher education. Another set of relationships is implied by such a focus – including the relationships with social structures, social processes, and the economy that have become increasingly close and intricate internationally in recent decades, but also relationships with other levels of education. The exploration of the vocational in higher education relates on the one hand to industry, manpower, social service, and the professions, but also on the other hand to secondary schools, full-time and part-time educational opportunities beyond the secondary school, access, and in-service and continuing education. Focusing here on how the vocational is perceived in relation to undergraduate education, the discussion is continuing a prolonged historical debate about the purposes of such an education, and echoes of that debate. The participants in that debate have always, however, had to have in mind – with one degree or another of explicitness – the total process of producing the 'educated person', including the assumptions that can be made about prior learning experience, and what can be assumed about later learning. The curriculum of the secondary school, and its appropriateness for what society conceives to be desirable goals for this stage of education; the existence of postgraduate routes into the professions and therefore the opportunity to delay certain subject content or specialization;

the existence and nature of apprenticeship; 'second-chance' entry into the educational process: these and other features of the total educational picture are not ultimately separable from a discussion of undergraduate education. It is a question here of focus, and of the specific directions in which illumination is being sought.

The point of entry into the discussion of vocationalism in higher education is therefore the undergraduate course of study, and in some of the investigation conducted here two limitations have been placed on the field. The first has been to look mainly, but not exclusively, at engineering and business studies as exemplars of the areas of study which have been most labelled or discussed in terms of vocationalism (though in different ways and with different chronologies). The second has been to focus on the 'public sector' of higher education in Britain – though with a strong interest in associated international developments. The public sector – as the polytechnics and colleges and institutes of higher education in England and Wales, and the central institutions and colleges in Scotland came to be called – grew out of, and were identified with, local authority traditions. For England and Wales the 1987 White Paper *Higher Education: Meeting the Challenge* rightly pointed to the misnomer, since university funding was equally 'public', and it referred instead to the 'polytechnics and colleges sector'. The public sector, as it is still most commonly termed, however, has been specifically identified with vocationalism in higher education since the late 1960s, and probing its meaning and implications in the public sector has been a means of exploring a difficult and often passionate public debate at its most self-conscious and explicit. In broad terms the public sector has often been seen to have what the Americans call a 'mission'. That part of it which from the 1960s was validated by the Council for National Academic Awards has had to define its institutional and curriculum purposes in public ways not familiar in the university sector. The national peer-review system developed initially by the National Council for Technological Awards from the mid-1950s, and then by the CNAA from 1964, led to documented and accessible views about course intentions and procedures, debate and judgement about course content and purposes, the review of experience within institutions, and comparative analysis across institutions and within subject areas and disciplines. The 'new higher education' in the landscape has been a way into vocationalism in relation to policy and practice in a period when the vocabulary of vocationalism has become more widespread and more strident. It has been, again, a question of finding a focus which makes the currents of debate most visible.

As the references to the Monroe encyclopedia illustrate, the elements of the debate are neither insular nor new. The nature of 'a liberal education' for 'the liberal professions' has been one important historical thread, and the growing accountability (suasive as well as structural or financial) of higher education for its service and economic roles has relentlessly in the nineteenth and twentieth centuries confronted the defensiveness of the traditional liberal educator with the demands of the scientific, the technological, the professional, and the economic. T.H. Huxley, in a discussion of technical education in 1877, was anxious to set technical skills alongside other ends not to be forgotten, including 'the end of civil existence, I mean a stable social state without which all other measures are merely futile, and, in effect, modes of going faster to ruin' (Huxley 1899: 430). The converse of this mode of going faster to ruin was, of course, the failure to develop science, technology, and other modern studies adequately to ensure economic survival, and the pressures were therefore increasingly strong in the late nineteenth century and into the twentieth century to incorporate such studies into the university curriculum, or to develop appropriate parallel institutions. These competing demands on the curricula of higher education and on the very conception of a university or college were presented differently, and had different outcomes, in Europe and the United States, and the tensions and accommodations involved have different national resonances. In the resolution of the conflicts that took shape different hierarchies of values were established in the different countries, and cultural and social traditions weighed differently in determining the status of subjects, institutions, and graduate employments.

In Britain, the eighteenth and nineteenth centuries saw accommodations with mathematics and science, but with enormous ambiguities about industry-related and professional studies laying claim to a place in university provision from the late nineteenth century. In a famous passage of an inaugural address at St Andrews in 1867, John Stuart Mill laid down guidelines that were to be followed widely in thinking about university education. The university, in his stentorian phrases, had a proper and well-understood function:

> It is not a place of professional education. Universities are not intended to teach the knowledge required to fit men for some special mode of gaining their livelihood. Their object is not to make skilful lawyers, or physicians, or engineers, but capable and cultivated human beings.
>
> (Mill 1867: 4)

There was good reason to have schools of law, or engineering, or the industrial arts, but separate from – although perhaps in the same locality as and under the general superintendence of – 'the establishments devoted to *education properly so called*' (our italics). The hierarchies of knowledge and institutions are here clearly delineated, and the inclusiveness or exclusiveness of conceptions of culture are equally clear:

> What professional men should carry away with them from an University, is not professional knowledge, but that which should direct the use of their professional knowledge, and bring the light of general culture to illuminate the technicalities of a special pursuit.
>
> (Mill 1867: 5)

The professional – that is, the new professional – claimants to university positions faced the dual obstacle in late nineteenth-century Britain of having neither easy access to the universities, nor high-status specialized institutions of the kind that had become common in France, Germany, and other European countries. In the second half of the century the new university colleges, the University of London, the Scottish universities, the newly created polytechnic institutions, were available for such purposes to varied extents, but there was a dominant set of 'liberal values' which continued to determine the conditions on which the professional and the technological were admitted, and the resistance which continued to operate.

An important contextual statement of the position for the discussion here was the equally famous analysis that Cardinal John Henry Newman offered in the 1850s. Newman's view was in one important respect almost identical with Mill's – professional or scientific knowledge was not a 'sufficient end of a University Education'. Newman was not hostile to either, and accepted that a university could teach specific branches of knowledge, but there was an important distinction to be made between the teaching of law, medicine, geology, or political economy inside and outside a university. Outside a university, there was a danger of narrowness, of giving lectures 'which are the Lectures of nothing more than a lawyer, physician, geologist, or political economist'. In a university, on the other hand, a comparable lecturer

> will just know where he and his science stand, he has come to it, as it were, from a height, he has taken a survey of all knowledge, he is kept from extravagance by the very rivalry of other studies, he has gained from them a special illumination and largeness of mind and freedom and self-possession.
> (Newman 1852, 1943 edn: 104–6)

Newman's entire argument rests on the identity of a liberal education as pointing to these last-named qualities, the worth of knowledge in itself, irrespective of results: 'not to know the relative disposition of things is the state of slaves or children'. A liberal education, in this view, is 'useful' – Newman explicates the concept at length – in that it is an instrument of good. The cultivated intellect was 'in a true and high sense . . . useful to the possessor and to all around him; not useful in any low, mechanical, mercantile sense, but as diffusing good, or as a blessing, or a gift, or power, or a treasure'. The whole position Newman adopts, and one which was to remain at the heart of twentieth-century discussions about higher education, is contained in one simple statement: 'I am prepared to maintain that there is a knowledge worth possessing for what it is, and not merely for what it does' (Newman 1852, 1943 edn: 157–60). The distinction between *is* and *does*, the different senses of 'useful', the in and out of the university, the concept of what is 'sufficient' or 'special' – all of these are echoed in the modern debates and practices.

The relationship between the 'cultural' and 'professional' purposes and processes of higher education has been subjected to long nineteenth- and twentieth-century debate in the United States. From the mid-nineteenth century, but particularly from the turn of the twentieth century, Americans have had a major preoccupation with the nature and purposes of a college or university education. The nature of the college curriculum, the role of the liberal arts, accommodations to technological and economic change, the expansion of access, the zigzags of institutional competition and strategies for survival in hard times, the impact of the system of electives at the undergraduate level from the end of the nineteenth century, and the relationships between a college education, professional preparation, and the employment market have all been hotly debated. They have at times had direct implications for the shape and the existence of institutions.

The acceptance, much earlier than in Europe, of undergraduate studies in subject areas like business and forestry, and the history from the 1860s of the growth of education in agriculture and the 'mechanic arts' in the 'land-grant' institutions, present quite a different trajectory of discussion and development from that in Britain and Europe. Within these American frameworks of concern and action questions of breadth and narrowness, specialization, the nature and purpose of a liberal or general education, the role of a liberal education as a preparation for the professions, and the sequencing and structure of study in secondary and post-secondary education, have been subjects of profound academic and public concern. In the pre-industrial United States, as in Europe, it was, as Dewey stressed, comparatively easier to assign a 'distinct content and a distinct purpose' when the class constituencies and their social and professional aspirations were clearly understood. In the 1790s Bowdoin College included 'useful and liberal arts and sciences' in its Charter (Sills 1944: 401). Following the Morrill Act of 1862, Massachusetts – like other states – looked to its new Agricultural College 'to teach such branches of learning as are related to agriculture and the mechanic arts, in order to promote the liberal and practical education of the industrial classes in the several pursuits and professions of life' (Massachusetts 1863). The former presents the 'useful' in association with the liberal arts and sciences within a confident understanding of overall purpose. The latter presents the liberal and the practical ('without excluding other scientific and classical studies, and including military tactics') in confident juxtaposition, and in the American context it was not to be difficult to argue the case for the incorporation of the useful and the practical into the developing pattern of higher education. As one commentator has put it: 'The utilitarian tradition has deep roots in American life. A continent had to be developed' (Mosely 1971: 38).

The intrusion of the utilitarian into higher education curricula did not go without resistance and controversy, but the struggle over the reconciliation of the two threads in American higher education – its relationship to work and careers, and a liberal preparation for life (Newman 1979: 51) – took place in different circumstances from those of nineteenth-century Britain. Many historians and educationists have commented on the uniquely American persistence of attention to the problems of a 'liberal' or 'general' education, and the battle to move curricula towards or away from a greater integration of the liberal/general and the professional has been a significant feature of higher education in the United States. It penetrated, much more explicitly than in Britain, the debates surrounding engineering education, for example, and the much more articulate American general education movements of the nineteenth and twentieth centuries have at times gone much further than in Britain in addressing the curricular issues of breadth and specialization, the nature and balance of professional and pre-professional studies, the virtues and dangers of vocationalism, the role of the liberal arts as 'tool' subjects for professional curricula (Sanders 1954b: 8), and the possibilities of interpreting and shaping professional courses as a liberal education. The nineteenth-century juxtapositions and antitheses, and attempts at reconciliation, have therefore been projected firmly into late-twentieth-century American debate. In the 1940s, Van Doren was arguing around the alleged contrast between the liberal and the useful, and the confusion that abounds between the useful and the utilitarian, ending with a plea for liberal education to move closer to the technical arts, and for technical education to be more intellectual (Van Doren 1943: 166–7). Meyerson, a quarter of a century later, was emphasizing that the universities had always been centres of professional education and specialization, and was arguing for a creative tension between the pure and the applied, the concrete and the theoretical, the rationalistic and the empirical (Meyerson 1969; 1974).

By this stage the argument both in the United States and in Europe was no longer about what subjects should be admitted to the university, or to 'higher education' as it had now become, but about the modalities, about control, not only about creative tension, but also about the specific elements of the tension, and who decides the contents and processes within the tension. Accountability, planning, economic responsiveness, had moved into the equations. As in Snow's *The Two Cultures and the Scientific Revolution* (1959), the debate was now about claimants to cultural identity and acceptance, about obstacles to understanding in a particular national context; and in Ashby's *Technology and the Academics* – published the previous year – the debate was about particular historical paths in relation to science and technology, debate which assumed increasing prominence in Britain as its international economic position continued to weaken. Some of these tensions have been less pronounced in other countries, but they have surfaced strongly elsewhere at different times, as some of the discussion in this book will illustrate. Lynn White's defence of a technological culture and rejection of an old 'aristocratic humanism' is one American version of the continuing cultural contradictions and failure properly to understand and absorb engineering and technology (White 1968).

Attempts in the 1960s and afterwards to remodel French higher education and its curricula are another illustration and one which, as in Britain, points to the importance of looking beyond the universities in search of the practical and vocational in higher education. The development of short-cycle higher education in the *Instituts universitaires de technologie (IUT)* reflected a suspicion by the state that the universities were too preoccupied by theoretical and academic concerns to respond positively to a need for greater practical and technical training (Cerych and Sabatier 1986). Not dissimilar sentiments have surfaced from time to time in discussions about the role of the English polytechnics and the German *Fachhochschulen*.

Looking further across Europe, we find in Poland a longstanding tradition of state ambivalence about the universities and a relatively early establishment of a strong system of non-university institutions. The Polish polytechnics and other monotechnic academies had already been developed prior to the outbreak of the Second World War and they enjoyed and continue to enjoy considerable prestige. Their emergence and their relationship to the universities have to be seen in relation to the historical role of the Polish universities and intelligentsia (and in particular their role during the period of partition), their prestige, and their relative cultural autonomy from prevailing political authority. Today, while the planned socialist economy gives a strong central direction to both higher education and the economy, and therefore in principle much greater potential for achieving a close match between the output of higher education and employment needs, the curricula of Polish higher education, in universities and non-universities alike, reveal the legacy of the historical role of the universities in Poland's divided past. Curricula in all subject areas are broadly-based and emphasize the theoretical foundations of knowledge.

Central planning of employment for graduates may not ensure that they are adequately prepared (Brennan and Pieniazek 1984).

Although the main focus here is on Britain, these international resonances of the issues cannot be ignored. While the concept of the vocational is often used with confidence, therefore, it is surrounded by historical and operational ambiguities. Science was reluctantly accepted in Victorian England into the canon of a liberal education, but is today often listed in vocational categories. There is frequently confusion arising from difficulties over what constitutes a course of study or a subject. Chemistry, for example, came to be regarded in Victorian England 'as not only useful in a vocational sense', but also widely accepted 'as part of a liberal education' (Bud and Roberts 1984: 166) – but was it *itself* a liberal education, an education, in Mill's phrase, 'properly so called'? What, similarly, *is* an engineering education, when some curricula include subject areas – such as economics or business, social studies, and the humanities – *within* the definition of engineering education, some regard them as useful extras, and some ignore them completely. The specialist discipline-based honours degree of the recent English tradition places such debates in a different context from the broader and longer courses found in other places and at other times. Clearly, definitions and operations are responsive to national traditions, the pressures of the market place, changing public priorities, changes in knowledge frontiers and statuses, fashions. What is said about an education is also responsive to what needs to be heard – for purposes of recruitment, funding, development, or self-protection. People have to be persuaded. A concept like the vocational becomes a political counter, more amenable to the taking of positions than to the reaching of understanding.

The central purpose of the discussion in this book is to try to pin down some of the implications of the vocational in terms of precise courses and precise institutions. We are not, as is explained in greater detail in a later chapter, examining student *experience* of such courses and institutions. The emphasis is on intentions, explanations, claims for content and procedures. The important general consideration to be borne in mind, however, is the long continuity of the dilemmas inherent in the discussions. There is still, for example, a considerable ambiguity that surrounds 'vocation' and the 'vocational' (and in American usage the equivalent ambiguities of the 'professional'). Dewey encapsulated the vocation/vocational distinction in 1917, pointing out that the meanings

> vary from the bread and butter conception which identifies 'vocational' with an immediate pecuniary aim to a conception of the calling of man in fulfilling his moral and intellectual destiny. With the first idea it is not difficult to attack the growing trend toward the vocational as the source of all our educational woes; with the latter, it is easy to glorify this trend as a movement to bring back the ideal of a liberal and cultural education from formal and arid by-paths to a concrete human significance.
> (Dewey 1917, 1980 edn: 151)

There have been attempts along these lines to rescue the concept of vocation for the 'bread and butter' activities of vocational education, but the two poles are not easily brought together, and the attempt may cement rather than resolve the confusion. A British example, from a Conservative Party document on education during the Second World War, illustrates the point:

> it is impossible to overstress the importance of personality and vocational ability in the teachers, and the necessity of so revising the conditions of recruitment and training for the teaching profession, that training becomes a supplement to vocation rather than a substitute for it.
> (Conservative Sub-Committee on Education 1942: 91)

The difficulties arise from the complex historical legacies, the unresolved conflict of value systems.

Newman's attempt to define acceptable professional studies in university terms, and Mill's attempt to bring 'the technicalities of a special pursuit' into the 'light of general culture', did not, in fact, come near to resolving the conflict, which could only intensify as the processes which they resisted grew stronger. What the twentieth-century protagonists attempted, therefore, was some kind of reconciliation between the polarities. The most famous version of this reconciliation was A.N. Whitehead's, first published in 1917 and then more influentially in *The Aims of Education* in 1932. Here Whitehead explored the exaggerated claims, the defects, the strengths, and the future needs of a 'liberal' education and a 'technical' education. The core of his argument lies in the emphasis on action: 'the insistence in the Platonic culture on disinterested intellectual appreciation is a psychological error.

Action and our implication in the transition of events amid the inevitable bond of cause to effect are fundamental' (Whitehead 1932: ch. 4). The separation of the intellectual and the aesthetic from event and effect points to 'the decadence of civilisation'. He concludes: 'essentially culture should be for action'. The goal of scientific curiosity is 'the marriage of action to thought'. From that argument to the rejection of the separation of literary, scientific and technical cultures is a short step, resulting in one of Whitehead's most quoted passages:

> The antithesis between a technical and a liberal education is fallacious. There can be no adequate technical education which is not liberal, and no liberal education which is not technical: that is, no education which does not impart both technique and intellectual vision.
>
> (Whitehead 1932: ch. 4)

Dewey, Van Doren, and many others have battled with the same 'fallacious antithesis', and the proposals for curricular reforms of many kinds that have surfaced frequently in higher education since the 1950s in particular have often reflected such arguments. In the new universities of the early 1960s, in evidence to and recommendations of the Robbins committee on higher education, in the degree structures developed by the polytechnics in the late 1960s and 1970s, in the debates within the CNAA about course balance and sandwich courses, and in the views of the professional associations on education and training there are constant echoes of the struggle to define how the marriage of the liberal and the technical or vocational can be effected. In Britain, as in the United States and elsewhere, the focus of debate has frequently shifted – especially in relation to curriculum issues – from Newman's distinction between *is* and *does* to Whitehead's emphasis on the marriage of action and thought. American debates, particularly in the 1980s, about the rescue of a liberal education from overwhelming pressures towards 'bread and butter' vocationalism, indicate that older tensions remain and that complexities have not been eliminated in the shift of debate.

In Britain, as we shall see, vocationalism has – notably in the 1970s and 1980s – become a central concept in policy-making and in public debate about education, and the confusion that Margaret Thatcher saw in the term has if anything deepened. Short-term demands on the educational system for correctives to national economic inadequacies have, in particular, brought the concept into sharp focus. In higher education this has meant the taking of positions on the structure of higher education itself, as well as on the balance of its curriculum, and on the status of and relative support for specific subject areas and employment-related courses of study. A major theme of such discussion has been the relationship between the universities and the 'public sector' institutions on the one hand, and industry on the other. In Britain this relationship was growing in many instances (Sanderson 1972) just as the views of Mill and Newman and others were making their main impact. The form and content of such relationships have been controversial ever since, and the discussion of vocationalism in relation to policy pronouncements in Chapter 4 suggests how difficult in British conditions it has been to achieve clarity on the nature and extent of higher education's responsiveness to public needs and political and economic overtures. The slow emergence of a 'binary' system of higher education in the late nineteenth century and early twentieth century, crystallized in the creation of the polytechnics in the late 1960s, has been one feature of the difficulty. On each side of the 'binary line' claims and assumptions about what is distinctive and what is common have been expressed and refuted.

Peter Scott, in charting the transition from the 'liberal university' to the 'modern university', emphasizes that the development has been in response both to external pressures and to the 'internal momentum, even dynamism, of knowledge and its constituent academic disciplines' (Scott 1984: 61). In the university sector itself the balance and shape of the responses have varied considerably between kinds of university and individual institutions. Amongst and within rough and ready categories – the colleges of advanced technology which became universities after the publication of the Robbins Report, the new greenfield or cathedral-town universities of the 1960s, the late nineteenth-century provincial university colleges-become-universities, Oxbridge – there have been differences of curriculum structure and interpretation, as well as common features. Within the public sector, similarly, there have been major differences of range and aspiration between the polytechnics and the colleges of higher education, and equally significant differences within each of the categories. In Britain, as in Europe and North America, the outcomes of debates about specialization and breadth, both within the traditional areas of liberal education and in the new areas of preparation for the professions, differed widely across institutions in the late-nineteenth century and during the twentieth (Ben-David 1977: ch. 3). As we shall see, it has not been easy in those situations to assert distinctive purposes and locate the vocational within them. Dewey saw the ease of assigning 'a distinct content and a distinct purpose' to education as having gone with the disappearance of society which was explicitly and constitutionally committed, as in slave or feudal society, to formal class distinctions. It has certainly been clear in the conditions of the nineteenth and twentieth centuries that purposes, including vocational purposes, have been made massively more difficult to define and to agree by competing pressures and priorities, as the institutions themselves and others have struggled to interpret them.

It is against these backgrounds that we attempt in the following chapters to look at the British and international versions of vocationalism, and to retrieve a usable concept for discussion and action. We consider a typology of courses and look in depth at some of them. We record the views of people whose voices on the subject of the vocationalism ascribed to them have been little heard. We try to assess, in the realities of the late twentieth century, where we now are with a cluster of concepts and processes that has had, in changing circumstances, centuries of scrutiny.

2
Stigmas and dichotomies

In a lecture on 'The place of the engineer in society' in 1966, Lord Snow expressed his surprise that engineering had not 'become more of a humane education', and that engineers were not more respected and active in the decision-making processes of government, parliament, and the civil service. British social history had to explain why other countries in the nineteenth century had paid more attention to the engineer and engineering education, and England had done the reverse: 'if we had put one tenth of the effort into engineering that we put into the Indian Empire, we should now be a very prosperous country' (Snow 1965–6: 1,260–1). There is no need here to examine in detail the particular British, not just English, historical complexities surrounding the difficulties over the vocational to which we have referred. It is important, however, to emphasize further the difficulty that nineteenth-century spokesmen for a liberal culture and values had in adjusting to the new realities of an industrializing society. Newman's defence of knowledge as 'its own end' and Mill's defence of the universities against preparation for the particularities of professions and livelihoods were simply the most eloquent thrusts of the debate. In spite of the critically important new dimensions brought by the establishment of London University and later by the provincial university colleges, the public voice of the English universities contained strong, if varying, degrees of concern about the position of technology and professional or 'modern' studies in the liberal canon. Scotland, by and large, did not find it difficult to incorporate and to justify these components of a university education.

Martin Wiener's persuasive argument is that Victorian England, while building an industrial economy, inherited a strongly entrenched suspicion of technology, a desire to evade the realities of industrialism, the gentrification of the new industrial and professional classes, and the taming of the industrial spirit as not 'truly English'. The economic crises of England from the 1970s onwards were, in his words, preceded by a 'century of psychological and intellectual de-industrialization' (Wiener 1981: 5-19, 81, 157). The anti-industrialism of what Wiener terms a 'gentry ideal' became an integral part of late nineteenth-century models of culture. A liberal education continued to be associated with 'certain privileged callings', and science, technology, business, and other aspects of modernity had to struggle to enter, or to acquire status in, the standard-bearing institutions of what we now know as secondary and higher education. In the early 1930s Sir Michael Sadler was arguing that a liberal education was 'not a veneer of culture', but that commerce and industry had so far failed to establish a secure place within it: the 'connection between a liberal education and business life became strong in Scotland sooner than in England' and the rest of western Europe and the United States had moved more rapidly (Sadler 1932a). The relationship between 'intellectual de-industrialization' and the schools has been widely documented and analysed. Discussing the nineteenth-century public schools, Bamford describes the least favoured employment outlets as being science, engineering, and medicine, 'where the attitude of the schools amounted to a virtual boycott until the 1860s; even then the increase was largely confined to Rugby'. Science and engineering were almost ignored by the public schools until the end of the century (Bamford 1967: 213, 221). Wilkinson's study of *The Prefects* suggests that the late nineteenth- and early twentieth-century public schools bred complacency, over-confidence, and lack of imagination (contributing to the military mistakes of the First World War, and the failure to resist fascism), and the continuing process of 'gentrification' was one of the obstacles to the mastering of the problems of industrial and economic change (Wilkinson 1964: 87-90). Even English and modern languages had a difficult time penetrating the ancient English universities (Lucas 1933).

While Germany, France, the United States, and other countries were establishing different forms of scientific, technological, and 'modern' studies in their secondary- and higher-education systems in the nineteenth century, Britain made slow and sometimes painful adjustments to the changes being thrust upon it. In the late nineteenth and twentieth centuries British higher education had to respond to international competition, pressures from professional, commercial, and industrial organizations, the changing role of the state in the promotion, management, or control of educational and other institutions, the manpower demands of the increasingly vociferous state or employers, the pressure of new clienteles. As Moberly pointed out in 1949 (and Trow in the United States was to demonstrate in detail as the process accelerated in the 1970s), 'these changes in the provenance and character of their students naturally affect the universities' own aims and methods. They call into question older ideals, whether christian–hellenic or liberal' (Moberly 1949: 48).

Although, as commentators underlined with particular vigour in the 1970s (James 1971; Watson 1973; Edwards 1977), the nation and its higher education were in continuing identity crisis, the underlying features of the crisis were of long standing. Hanson located them in 'ambiguities', 'contrasts', and 'dichotomies' (Hanson 1957: 117), and many of the university colleges went through sharp versions of these contrasts at their point of establishment, or as they developed. Many of the late nineteenth-century colleges, their founders, patrons, and staffs, agonized over an appropriate curriculum and its range. Even after the First World War colleges were surrounded by disagreements about their curricula and purposes. In Leicester, for example, there were public expressions of view that the college should specialize 'on the kind of training needed for our local industries' and help to enable Britain to keep up with foreign competitors, but also that for the institution to 'do real university work it must be done on broad lines, and with high ideals, giving foremost place to the humanities' (Simmons 1959: 70–1). Such debates stretch back into the nineteenth century and before.

The dichotomies were expressed in many forms. Faced with the demands of technology, industry, commerce, and the professions, English liberal education could not decide – particularly from the 1850s – whether it aimed to produce experts or amateurs (Haines IV 1959). Given the long tradition of vocational education for the church or the law, and the long nineteenth-century debates about the place of science in a liberal education, universities were torn between a version of the vocational and various (mainly European) models of mental training or objective enquiry (Fores 1972: 13; Edwards 1977: 4). Whatever the accommodations with science, those with technology were more difficult to make. The authors of *Science Versus Practice* demonstrate that tensions surrounding Victorian chemistry handed on a legacy of mistrust of the practical, and in general that 'as in modern industry, the relationship of science to technology in mid-Victorian Britain was problematic' (Bud and Roberts 1984: 149, 165). Whereas Europe in general, and Germany in particular, had by the end of the nineteenth century largely removed the 'second-rate stigma' from its technological institutions, Britain had failed to do so (Ahlström 1982: 82-3), and had neither sufficiently adapted its existing institutions nor established adequately recognized and resourced new ones. Technology continued to be perceived in Britain, as the Finniston Committee was to lament, as a subordinate branch of science (Committee of Incuiry 1980: 25). The same tension had existed in the United States in the decades following the Second World War, as attempts were made to bring technology back from over-identification with abstract science and mathematics, to rescue it from a position as hand-maiden to science (Truxal 1986: 12; Kanigel 1986: 22) and to assert its independent cultural identity. In Britain particularly, however, whether inside or outside the university, technology was widely feared by the proponents of a liberal culture as 'inhuman' (Redwood 1951, I: 97-8; Nuttgens 1978: 9).

Adjustments to this changed world might rest on a number of premises. New subjects might, for example, be admitted if they were sufficiently abstract (Engel 1983: 293), and therefore sufficiently distanced from the world of work, and indeed some of the arguments in favour of university science were posed in such terms. There might, on the other hand, be seen to be virtue in admitting 'professional' subjects in order to render them, as Newman argued, useful in the sense of tending to the public good, rather than as practical preparation for employment – to be judged in relation to the corpus of university knowledge, not in relation to the world of work. Sir Joshua Fitch extended the argument at the turn of the century, in a form which revealed the major changes that had already taken place since the 1850s. Universities, he argued, were not places of useless learning, but providers of 'instruments of culture and intellectual power'. Their traditions needed to be enlarged in order to harness them to the new needs of society, and one such tradition was that of ennobling and liberalizing 'the higher employments of life', as had long been the case with law and medicine. He therefore recommended that the universities should add English, chemistry, electricity, architecture, textile manufacture, agriculture, banking, and commerce to their provision – and he used as his model the London School of Economics, which was 'broader and more comprehensive than any academic institution hitherto known in England' (Robertson 1980: 174–5).

By this stage, of course, enlargements of the tradition were already in train. The provincial university colleges accepted some of these broader areas of study – and some were established in order to provide them. The beginnings of an 'alternative' system of higher education had been made with the creation of the London polytechnics in the 1880s and 1890s. The older order of a liberal education as conceived for much of the nineteenth century was already being undermined by the emergence of a conception of professionalism as service. Such a conception, accelerating in the final decades of the century, set the idea of the professional man against that of the business man, that of service and duty against that of profit. Rothblatt describes the professional ideal as an emergent solution to the Victorian crisis of university and society (Rothblatt 1968: 86–93; 1976: ch. 12; 1983: 133–6). By these means various kinds of skills and approaches to them were being admitted into the curricula of the universities and what, later in the twentieth century, was to be seen as the system of 'higher education'.

The processes we have described are, of course, not the only ones at work in the twentieth century's inheritance of various forms of anti-industrialism, but they are the ones which most directly affected education, and higher education in particular. They are also the ones which provide the most obvious and important framework for a discussion of attitudes in the recent past and in the present of the 'vocational' content of higher education. They help to explain the ways in which universities from the late nineteenth century distanced themselves from the technical colleges, and contributed to a continuing definition of culture which many expanding areas of study, notably engineering, found it more difficult to enter than was the case in many other advanced industrial countries. Lord Eustace Percy pointed out in 1950 that the field sciences had only just begun to be accepted as 'instruments of general education', and laboratory-based sciences were still not accepted as being similar in status to archaeology – and he foresaw a future in which industry might

Stigmas and dichotomies

recruit its administrators from among zoologists as well as arts graduates (Percy 1950: 55). While important, if belated, changes had taken place by the 1980s, a polytechnic director could still, in 1985, consider that 'the climate was now *more propitious* for the acceptance of engineering as an integral part of the British culture' (J.M. Illston, reported in Reid and Farrar 1985: 3; our italics). Finniston, speaking to an international audience in 1984, compared the lack of public understanding in Britain of what professional engineers do with their position in France, Germany, Japan, or the United States, and hence their lack of public recognition and status in Britain. 'In my country', he commented crisply, 'engineering falls into a category of public ignorance' (Finniston 1985: 4).

A 'category of public ignorance' sums up part of the story of engineering in higher education, as it does to some degree the later story of business education. It is also applicable to the position of the institutions which have most recently entered the category of higher education – the polytechnics and the colleges and institutes of higher education. This tripartite typology of higher education appears simple, but is in fact, as we have noted, overlaid with complex considerations of function and status, within as well as amongst the categories. Having launched the binary system, Anthony Crosland as Secretary of State for Education and Science explained in 1967 that the new polytechnics were to be 'distinctive from the universities', more comprehensive in their student intakes, but not divided by 'too rigid' a line from the university sector. He defended the policy against the criticism that 'we are preserving a privileged position for the universities by deliberately trying to create inferior institutions outside' (Crosland 1974: 217–19). One of the threads in considering the nature and categorization of courses of study and their legacies is also the nature and categorization of the institutions with which they are most closely identified. The struggle for public recognition of the range of institutions entering higher education in the 1960s and 1970s has been as much concerned with 'public ignorance' and long-standing stigmas as has that of the subjects of study which acquired their vocational labels in the nineteenth century. The binary development in Scotland has been different from that in England and Wales, with its central institutions having been prevented from developing liberal arts courses as in the polytechnics, and the 'practical arts' having greater historical recognition in Scotland. The Scottish Tertiary Education Advisory Council (STEAC) review in 1985 proposed that this historical divide between the central institutions and the Scottish universities should continue, but, as we shall see, the apparently clearer dividing line leaves questions about vocationalism in courses and institutions as salient as elsewhere in Britain (STEAC 1985: 55–6).

Apportioning 'blame' is of direct interest to the policy-maker, given the pressing need in the policy process to abandon or change a direction, and justify the choice. A brief account of the cultural context of industry, commerce, the professions and their educational analogues has to be concerned, however, not with apportioning but with hearing the messages of blame. In contemporary debate Britain's industrial and economic 'failures' are discussed in terms of unionism and mangement, the direction of public and private endeavour, public need, and private choice. It is not so much these contemporary public debates as the dominant signals of blame that they have transmitted in the recent past that have influenced the discussion of vocationalism in higher education. When the Engineering Employers' Federation responded to the Finniston Report in 1980, for example, it believed that 'the extent to which professional engineers may be regarded as responsible for the economic situation in the UK is overstated' (Engineering Employers' Federation 1980: 1). If it is not the engineers who are to blame, the answer must be elsewhere, and the Director General of the Engineering Council suggested the answer in 1985: 'The cultural attitude fostered by succeeding generations of academics has been one of the most powerful forces contributing to the decline of our industrial base' (Miller 1985: 13). We have seen, however, in Wiener's analysis, that the 'academics' themselves inherited the Victorian legacy of a 'gentrified' approach to industry and commerce shaped above all by the successful middle class acquiring gentry values and gentry ideals. Wiener presents the debate around vocationalism in education in the precise form of divergent attitudes in British conservatism. Bamford and others blame the public schools.

The problems surrounding the meanings of vocationalism, and attitudes towards it, have to be situated in that context of controversy, misunderstanding, and confusion of value and judgement. That historical context also provides some essential explanations for rescue operations, or important innovations or curricular changes that have taken place in answer to the decline in the industrial base, or in recognition of weaknesses in inherited educational processes and their outcomes. An example would be the requirement of the National Council for Technological Awards from the mid-1950s that courses for the award of its Diploma in Technology should contain a component of 'liberal studies', the precise nature of which was to be left to institutions, but which should ensure a measure of curriculum breadth. The 'liberal-studies' movement in technical and higher education related to government policy which favoured curriculum breadth and saw the addition of studies of this kind as one important way to 'liberalize' the technical curriculum. From 1964 the CNAA took over this emphasis and the early history of the Council contains an important emphasis on the need for 'complementary or contrasting' studies in its validated courses. When the CNAA's newly created Business Studies Board, for example, held its first meeting in 1965 it had 'liberal studies' as an item on its agenda, in the context of the procedures that the CNAA had inherited from the National Council for Technological Awards. The minute reads:

> The Board discussed whether it was necessary for Liberal Studies to be included as a specific subject in a business studies course. . . . Some members thought that particular reference to it was not required, and others considered that the course as a whole should be so balanced that it was liberal in its entire conception. . . . It was finally agreed that the Board would expect to see in a business studies course some provision for the student to gain an appreciation of a contrasting discipline to those already covered in the course.
> (CNAA 1965: 2–3)

The hesitations and decisions recorded here in the emergent area of business studies are explicable only in terms of the prior failures of the university system, and the colleges of advanced technology and other technical and further education institutions, to establish coherent and widely acceptable twentieth-century understandings of what was meant by an education 'liberal in its entire conception'.

The Council itself continued to grapple with the need to establish such an understanding for the new public sector of higher education, specifically with regard to the qualities that a CNAA degree course should promote in students: 'all courses must include studies which by complementing or contrasting with the main subjects studied will help to provide a balanced education'. It should be possible to convey to students that scientific method ('in the sense of a critical and sceptical approach to enquiry and a readiness to test hypotheses') is important in arts subjects, and that the activities of the scientist and technologist involve 'speculative enquiry, the exercise of creative imagination and the capacity for making value judgments' (CNAA 1969: 2). The CNAA was faced, as had been Whitehead, Snow, and many others, with the outcomes of generations of isolation and mistrust across cultures and institutions. The liberal studies approach was intended to mend or at least compensate for the break, and overcome some of the limitations imposed on various kinds of curricula by the hermetic structures and attitudes that resulted from a particular set of social and cultural traditions. 'Modern' studies were still having to be negotiated, not just to meet new circumstances but also to contend with profound, unresolved disputes and difficulties of the past.

The dominant, inherited dichotomy has been that between the liberal and the vocational, but there have been many others in attempts to address different versions of the issues, or to evade the difficulties of the liberal–vocational divide. It should be emphasized that the vocabularies are not uniform even across English-speaking countries, and the meanings are by no means stable across either time or space. The modern American usage of 'humanist', for example, has not been domesticated in Britain, and 'further' education does not carry in America the implications of its British or Australian usage. The problems of pinning down the social and educational resonances of the terminologies are, however, international.

What the nineteenth century did for the concept of the liberal, as contrasted with the vocational, was to impose on it an association with gentlemanliness, leisure, and privilege, of learning for learning's sake, the cultivation of detachment, the attainment of qualities of character, and 'the intellectual and moral cultivation in academic-preparatory schools, colleges, and universities reserved for the male children of a country's social elite'. It was these qualities, not those of a specific training or preparation, which pointed towards the church and the bar, politics and (later) the civil service, colonial service, the professions, and the role of the country gentleman: 'these positions in life were, after all, considered to be the proper rewards of a liberal education' (Herbst 1980: 32–4). Herbst includes industry and commerce in the above list, but these can be included in the British analysis only with the reservation that their status remained somewhat different from the remainder of the list, and those employed in them had to learn to display the characteristics thought proper to those other callings. Vocational education was therefore readily identified with preparation for socially inferior occupations, stripped of its historical association with 'vocation', as understood to apply to the priest or the barrister. The vocational acquired the sub-meaning of specific low status and related to the servile operations of industrial, commercial Britain. It also became associated with narrowness and practicality, and came as a result to be contrasted with breadth and the academic. These were not semantic distinctions, but reflections of attempts to define social hierarchies: the academic ranks above the practical (Hawkins 1973); knowing (science) ranks above doing (technology); higher honour is paid to the academic than to the technical (Harvard Committee 1945). Liberal comes to denote general or unspecific – and therefore free-ranging and superior to the vocationally and directly 'useful' (Cheit 1975: 3). The vocational therefore comes also to be reserved for the 'less talented', which – whether explicitly or not – acquires the implication of 'lower class'.

In American terms the essential dichotomy in the nineteenth and twentieth centuries has been that of general and professional education. Although the concept of a liberal education has remained a central feature of the vocabulary of American education, it is the shape of a general education, and of its opposites, amidst the growing complexities of knowledge and of social and economic demands that has been the important parallel focus to the British discussion. Subsumed in the American debates have been such familiar tensions as those between the scientific and the classical, narrow professionalism and broad requirements and choices (Thomas 1962). General education has been promoted (and there have been scholars who have spent their lives interpreting and promoting the concept and its various models of implementation) as an antidote to narrow-gauge professional preparation, as an alternative to the patchwork of electives that developed from the end of the nineteenth century, as a battering ram against the dominance of departments and specialization, and as the common foundation which enables students to go on to an understood and flexible professionalism or vocationalism. As the demands for increased vocational content to undergraduate studies have grown in the 1980s, the general education idea has been increasingly seen to be in distress or disarray, and further reinterpretations of the general and the liberal have been urgently sought. An essential difference, however, between the American and British attempts to understand and bridge the various dichotomies involved has been the existence of a much more massive postgraduate superstructure in American higher education. Arguments for delayed specialization, and for the extension into undergraduate education of the general education insufficiently provided at secondary-school level, have been persistent American themes. The extensive foundation or preparatory programmes of American colleges and universities, and the expansion of remedial components as new constituencies of students have entered higher education, have been possible within that structure, and the vocational/liberal or professional/general tensions have to some extent been constantly pushed further up the educational system.

Different emphases are attached to essentially similar debates in Europe, where longer undergraduate programmes of study can more easily accommodate 'liberal breadth' with 'vocational specialism'. A first two years of broadly based 'general education' can, as in France, provide the base for subsequent professional specialization. Not unrelatedly, employers in many parts of Europe make much more sophisticated use of educational qualifications in recruiting staff. Posts may require the possession of specialist qualifications in subjects such as business studies where the British employer would be content to recruit 'generalist' arts graduates, although preferably from one of the prestigious ancient universities. Such recruitment practices themselves raise questions about how far British employers are persuaded of the vocational possibilities of higher education.

Central planning of both education and employment provides yet a further context for these questions. In Poland there is a sense in which all higher education exhibits a vocational purpose. For all fields of study the planned economy ensures a high degree of certainty about what graduates will be doing after graduation and an expectation that they will have been prepared adequately for doing it in their higher education. All courses of study follow a state-imposed curricular pattern consisting of three main elements – theoretical subjects, vocational/professional study, and social sciences and state ideology. Courses take between four and six years to complete, but incorporate elements which would be reserved for postgraduate study or in-company training in Britain.

Longer courses located in a different kind of labour market can attempt different things. More precise delineation of institutional function (for example the German *Fachhochschulen* and universities, and the French *grandes écoles*, universities, and IUTs) can alter the form and the vehemence of debates about the vocational/liberal and professional/general tensions which arise in all systems of higher education.

We are not at this point concerned directly with the various attempts to break down such antitheses inherited from long battles of this kind. To address these issues would mean exploring the many attempts, for example, to define general and vocational education as a combined entity, and the explicit movements to bring together the twin traditions of liberal and utilitarian purposes. It would mean looking at the attempts to combine liberal learning and career education, strategies based on a denial in modern circumstances of any separation of education from the workplace. Such a consideration would take in John Dewey's efforts to promote the abolition of barriers between school and work, by reforming the school in response to the changing, increasingly technological dimensions of work, and more recent similar emphases – suggesting that a liberal education has to address the reality that work has a 'powerful impact . . . on our lives. Confronting this reality should be a central concern of the common core curriculum' (Boyer 1977: 150). The discussion would encompass the cycles of attention paid to the liberal arts as an integral component of professional training, and of the citizenship towards which all education should point. Some of these analyses and strategies will be visible in later discussions of specific programme areas in higher education.

In British terms such a discussion might, for example, take in attempts in the 1920s to overcome curricular distinctions between hand and brain, manual and academic, in the schools (Silver 1983: ch. 7). In higher education it would examine Sir Walter Moberly's 1949 discussion of a threefold typology of traditions – Christian–Hellenic, liberal, and technological and democratic, together with such 'spurious remedies' as scientific humanism. More important for our purposes is the range of structures, curricular devices, and processes which appeared at various points in the twentieth century, and notably in the 1960s and 1970s, in order to address the institutional, subject, and career differences and statuses of a rapidly changing social and educational environment. The liberal could no longer be automatically associated with the general, and liberal 'narrowness' – particularly in its classical and literary guises – came under attack. Breadth could be seen as fragmentation. The vocational, in higher education, could be seen as broad. The pejorative version of 'vocational' could be confronted as 'narrowly vocational'. There were many who argued from the mid-century that the boundaries between the vocational and the non-vocational had been either blurred or removed. Proponents of technology as a 'third culture' saw it not as a bridge but as the fusion, if properly translated into the right educational processes, of the two main traditions. There were attempts to rescue vocational meanings of an older kind for the modern use of the vocabulary, and, broadly interpreted, there were calls for *more* vocational relevance of certain kinds in types of education which had previously been considered as exclusively liberal.

Littered across this historical wasteland of vocabularies are other dichotomies which have left imprints on contemporary British education – specialist and non-specialist, specialist and generalist, academic and practical – many of them more directly relevant to secondary or further education. Some of these dichotomies, or 'tensions' in an interpretation by George Tolley have had major implications for public-sector higher education well beyond the discussion of 'liberal', 'complementary', and 'contrasting' studies to which we have referred. In 1982 Tolley looked specifically at the way he saw sandwich courses, combining college study and industrial placements, bringing these tensions – of which he identified four – into relief. The first was between teaching and learning: 'In sandwich courses there is an intrinsic recognition of the need to base learning upon experience and to provide opportunity for ordered reflection upon that experience' (Tolley 1982: 67). This, in Tolley's formulation, reflects long-standing traditions of debate about the nature of the university's guardianship of knowledge, about the priority to be given to 'experience', and the power to decide on its relationship to the acquisition of essential knowledge. It is a tension which emerges in various guises in the interviews and discussions later in this book.

Tolley's second tension is between 'abstraction' and 'application': 'All knowledge must have a base of abstraction. . . . But abstraction without application . . . cannot sustain the real world or the aspirations of most students.' This tension, again, is widely reflected in our discussion, and has relevance to the analysis of differences between subjects, between courses, between institutions. The third tension is a version of these first two – that between 'detachment' and 'involvement'. Tolley acknowledges that an environment in which detachment is possible is 'one of the necessary attributes' of an institution of higher education, but 'if detachment becomes an end in itself, then education becomes both suspect and lacking in purpose'. Involvement enhances 'learning and competence'. The history of higher education is not without frequent debate about just such a tension. The public sector has been particularly anxious to define and strengthen its forms of 'involvement', its purpose of securing student competence, and its identity as against what it has seen as the relative 'detachment' of the universities.

Tolley's final tension is that between 'generality' and 'particularity'. In all of the previous three cases he sees the sandwich course as making at least a distinct and unmistakable contribution towards resolving these tensions, and in this fourth case the same is true:

> Most teachers in higher education . . . seek to enlarge the territory which their specialism occupies in a course. But there is always a contrary pull – towards the generalisation of concepts. The sandwich course emphasises the particular, set within the context of application, so that the limit of generalisation may be explored and defined.
> (Tolley 1982: 67)

Tolley summarizes the implications of this analysis of sandwich courses for vocationalism as a basis for a discussion of the future relationship between education and work:

> If sandwich courses are vocational (as indeed they are) then their vocationalism may be said to relate to and be founded upon, not a preparation for a career but to the characteristics

of emphasis or bias in resolving or maintaining in balance these four tensions. The bias is towards learning, application, involvement and the particular.

(Tolley 1982: 67)

Similar arguments for the virtues of effectively combined work experience and academic study are to be found in the United States. Hawkins, for example, in arguing for undergraduate study to be based on prior work and other experience, is picking up the tradition of 'co-operative' education (that is, mixing college-based and employment-based experience) pioneered by colleges like Antioch (Hawkins 1973). Although most of the courses explored later in this book are of the sandwich type, we are not concerned specifically with the sandwich-course role in relation to these tensions. None the less, Tolley's analysis is germane. It indicates, first, forms in which traditionally expressed dichotomies can be and are reinterpreted in modern terms; secondly, the nature of the vocationalism highlighted by the development of a non-university sector of higher education; and, thirdly, the possibility of shifting the emphasis in a discussion of vocationalism away from a vague notion of preparation for a career towards the various structures and balances represented by courses of study, as well as their precise relationship to the world of work. All of these tensions and dichotomies are present in some form in the discussions which follow.

In terms of higher education, the contemporary echoes of older debates have become louder as the economic and political uncertainties and pressures have sharpened conflicting views and made institutions more introspective. The movement towards greater public, or at least explicit, accountability, and towards central intervention in the name of manpower and other economic goals, has compelled institutions, and the universities in particular, to relocate themselves in contexts and relationships established largely by government and public authorities and agencies. The distance travelled by the 1980s in revising meanings and assumptions is illustrated by a response from the London School of Economics in 1984 to an enquiry by the University Grants Committee, amidst continuing anxieties about funding, and with a pressing need for self-explanation and self-defence: 'In a civilized society there is no conflict between academic excellence and vocational or more generally practical usefulness. It is by insistence on quality that one avoids the pitfalls of a narrow and badly-defined "vocationalism"' (London School of Economics 1984: 1). What this and much of the debate of the 1980s reveal is the extent of the changes in attitude towards the vocational (and in the LSE document what is termed a 'humane professionalism') in the academic community, as well as the political strength of the 'narrow and badly defined "vocationalism"' against which this comment is directed. In the arenas of politics and policy-making, public discussion and academic attitude- and decision-making, there was neither consensus nor common understanding around these issues, whether in terms of what higher education could and should provide, or what the curriculum of secondary schools should contain. A report by the American business community in 1985 reflected another version of the same set of difficulties over using a vocabulary that had accreted ambiguous or unacceptable overtones. Discussing school-level vocational programmes, the committee concerned recommended that

> the term *vocational education* should be limited to those programs specifically designed to prepare students to enter a particular field upon graduation (from high school). All other forms of nonacademic instruction should be identified by a different term to avoid confusing them with programs that impart specific job skills.
> (Committee for Economic Development 1985: 8)

The committee did not suggest what the different term should be.

3
Preparing students for employment

We shall return to these considerations, but it is important at this point to look at the possibility of breaking down the global vocabulary of the vocational in higher education into more manageable components in the discussion of higher education specifically. Vocationalism, as we have seen, has commonly come to imply deliberate preparation for employment, but in the higher-education system of the late twentieth century, after considerable institutional and course diversification, such preparation can be seen to relate to employment with different degrees of directness and specificity. To examine these differences is to approach the dichotomies and ambiguities we have considered from another direction.

Ways of delineating the relationship between higher education and the labour market, or segmented labour markets, have been of increasing interest in the 1970s and 1980s, notably in the United States. In that context there have been various attempts to describe the processes and functions concerned. In Scotland, Burnhill and McPherson have suggested that the universities engage, broadly speaking, in five sorts of 'vocational preparation'. 1) Preparation for employment in the subject disciplines themselves, especially in research. 2) The vocational preparation of professionals, 'explicit, purposive, and planned in relation to a segment of the labour market'. 3) Vocational preparation by the non-professional faculties, with a 'largely fortuitous' connection with the requirements of employers, in spite of attempts at manpower planning. The vocational significance of such courses 'often stems from what the student makes of the fortuitous connections between the specifics of the course and the labour market'. 4) A form of vocational preparation 'characterised by the "generalisability" of skills and fundamental, theoretically-mastered knowledge'.

5) A form of 'general preparation' which sees the graduate as 'a person with a set of values, skills, personal dispositions and habits of thought that make him or her valuable to employers irrespective of the particular contents of the university courses followed' (Burnhill and McPherson 1983). What this typology does is extend the discussion of the vocational beyond what has been traditionally labelled as such, in order to describe relationships between courses and potential employment, relationships which appear in this list in descending order of specificity and explicitness in the design and presentation of courses.

The American analyses of such relationships have often attempted to categorize the knowledge base and content of courses, as they relate to their potential use by students graduating and entering the labour maket. Geiger, for example, describes the content of college courses as divisible into 'general, disciplinary or instrumental knowledge':

> General knowledge would encompass both basic skills, acquired or refined, plus the diverse bits and clumps of information that are picked up during the course of undergraduate studies.... Disciplinary knowledge is the most problematic. Academic disciplines provide the infrastructure of American colleges and universities ... disciplinary knowledge ... serves the special purposes of the discipline that engenders it. It is only a partial reflection of the real world.... Instrumental knowledge, by way of contrast, exists for an ulterior end.
> (Geiger 1980: 17-18)

The problem faced by institutions in offering and designing programmes is therefore to package these kinds of knowledge to satisfy the particular balance institutions wish to achieve between their own definition of academic propriety and the perceived needs of students and the wider society. These perceptions, again, are open to categorization, and in the United States Martin Trow more than anyone has attempted to address the problems of doing so in periods of rapid changes in social needs and values, and in institutional scale, opportunity, and responsiveness to pressures from many directions. He portrays higher education, for instance, as performing three types of functions for the occupational structure of society:

> *First*, it selects and forms intellectual and governing élites ...

creators of knowledge, the scientists and scholars; professional leaders . . . teachers in universities and elite secondary schools; politicians and civil servants. This is done through a combination of what might be called a higher vocational training . . .

Second, there is another kind of function, and that is to train large numbers of highly skilled people, not only the institutional leaders, but also the rank and file, of the professions and semi-professions, both technical and managerial. . . .

Third, there is another set of functions of a large and comprehensive system of higher education, and that is to educate a whole society to be adaptable to rapid social and economic change. . . . These, in broad terms, are the central functions, respectively, of elite, mass and universal access higher education.

(Trow 1974: 35–6)

The vocabulary of functions and their particular features as Trow presents them, as well as the deductions for higher education that might be drawn from them, are less important here than the fact that Trow reflects the need of systems and institutions of higher education to define their relationships, or combination of relationships, with the occupational structures which they serve. Accountability pressures from the society and state have made that need increasingly felt.

The American analysis, in the context of a larger and more diversely funded and defined higher education system, does not precisely fit the British situation, but it points towards the same need to be more specific about the ways in which institutions and their courses, students and their intentions, and employments and their changes, all interrelate. Irrespective of where they may fit into a liberal/vocational dichotomy, academic qualifications of all kinds are being used to regulate entry into employment. The international implications of the 'qualifications spiral' have been vividly described by Dore and a further dichotomy of certification/education has been introduced into the vocabulary of the vocational (Dore 1976). The social functions ascribed to educational qualifications are many and varied and are frequently contradictory: they are the mechanism of equality of opportunity, they legitimize social inequality, they ensure the social exclusiveness of the professions, they provide a 'screening' service for employers. Whether they also reflect an educational experience of the slightest relevance to actually doing a job seems almost immaterial!

The widening of access to higher education coupled with the increasing levels of unemployment in society makes a growing instrumentalism in students unsurprising. Most students need and want to get jobs after they graduate and they expect, and most higher education institutions promise, that their degrees will help them. The promise of a 'meal ticket' is only partly dependent on the nature of the courses offered. The currency of the resultant qualifications in the labour market is what ultimately matters. This currency can be considered from two points of view: (i) the power of the qualification to regulate entry into employment; and (ii) the extent of the occupational training which has been delegated to higher education by employers.

A degree as a regulator of entry into the labour market gives higher education a role in employee selection. From the employer's standpoint, a degree in a particular subject is essential, desirable, or irrelevant for selection. Although the recruitment process is dependent on decisions made by the graduate (to apply for a particular job) and by the employer (to offer a job to a particular person) the actions of both employer and employee will be constrained by the level of professional closure of the occupational field (Saks 1983). It is the effects of these constraints on the recruitment process which are of concern here.

The following uses of degree qualifications to regulate entry to employment can be identified. They reflect declining determinacy in the employment outcomes of a course.

(i) A specified degree as sole regulator

(a) Output matched to employer demand: entry to a specific field of employment is regulated by a specified degree qualification and numbers in training are controlled effectively and matched to employer demand. The specified degree is thus both necessary and sufficient to gain entry.
(b) Imbalance between output and demand: entry requires a specific degree qualification, but numbers in training are not controlled effectively with the possibility of shortage or oversupply. Possession of the degree is necessary, but it may not be sufficient to gain entry.

(ii) A specified degree as partial regulator

(a) Output matches demand: entry can be achieved by a number of routes, some but not all of which require a specified degree qualification. Numbers in training (graduate and non-graduate) are controlled effectively. Although not necessary to gain entry, possession of the specified degree should be sufficient.

(b) Imbalance between output and demand: where numbers in training are not controlled effectively, possession of the specified degree is neither necessary nor sufficient to gain entry.

(iii) An unspecified degree

(a) In the graduate labour market: an unspecified degree is a requirement for entry. As numbers cannot be controlled, possession of a degree is necessary but not sufficient to gain entry.

(b) In the general (non-graduate) labour market: a degree qualification is not required; it is not necessary and it is not sufficient. (It might be of considerable 'market value' in securing employment, but the market is not 'fixed' in favour of graduates.)

In regulating selection for employment, the above categories represent a movement from a very high degree of closure to an 'open market'. They also represent a movement from minimal employer and student freedom (regarding whom to employ and where to seek employment) to a very high degree of freedom. Category (iii) is the classic 'keeping of options open'. Vocational objectives may characterize courses in all categories, but where courses in (i) and (ii) seek to prepare students for quite specific employment, courses in (iii) must necessarily be concerned with more general and transferable knowledge and skills.

A further dichotomy in the vocabulary of vocationalism to which we have so far made relatively little reference is between education and training – a dichotomy of particular importance also in discussions of British further education. It is a dichotomy full of resonances. In the present context of the currency of educational qualifications in the labour market 'training' is being used neutrally and perhaps rather loosely to refer to any process of preparation, formation, or socialization for employment. As

Preparing students for employment

understood here training will involve changes to a person's knowledge, skills, and attitudes in a direction useful to employment. Higher education's contribution to training for employment will vary in scope and significance and in the employer recognition attached to it:

(i) Initial occupational preparation completed. The graduate is fully qualified to 'practise', e.g. medicine, education, social work. (In some cases a period of post-qualifying work experience may be necessary before full professional status is obtained.)
(ii) Initial occupational preparation partly completed. Further training is required (within higher education or in-company), but graduates may be exempted from the full training programme, e.g. accountancy, law.
(iii) A necessary educational base for training. Subsequent training assumes the base of a specified degree, e.g. psychology.
(iv) An optional educational base for training. Employment relevance is claimed but subsequent training does not presuppose it, e.g. business studies.
(v) No explicit employment relevance is claimed.

At one end of the scale the employer has entirely sub-contracted the initial training function to higher education. At the other end the employer retains full responsibility for and control over the training process. It should be emphasized that the above is not making any assumptions about the efficacy of training. Whether undertaken in higher education or in employment it may be done well or badly. The distinctions introduced are intended to refer to the location of responsibility for training, to the formal recognition that, in full or in part, training has taken place.

Underlying the regulation of entry and occupational training roles is a consideration of the diffuseness of the employment outcomes from a course. A medical education is intended to lead to a specific occupational role. A course in geography can lead to employment in a wide range of occupational fields. In so far as there is vocational intent in the design of a geography degree it is to provide the graduate with knowledge and skills which are usable in a variety of employment settings. Unlike the example of medicine, there is no one-to-one relationship between the course and a specific occupation. The design of the medical curriculum is informed by what a doctor is thought to need to know and to be able to do. Such direction is less easily available to the designer of a geography degree because there is much less clarity about what the graduate will do and what he or she will need to know in order to do it.

In summary, a course's relationship to employment will be specific or diffuse and will vary in the nature and degree of selection and training which is undertaken. Empirically a strong relationship between specificity, selection, and training can be expected. Occupationally-specific training both requires a specific employment referent and helps to legitimize the use of the degree qualification in the regulation of entry.

None of this necessarily indicates the ease with which graduates from particular courses will obtain jobs. Employers may reveal preferences in the 'open' labour market for graduates of particular types (e.g. Oxbridge historians) so as to produce strong empirical relationships between particular courses and particular employment. Such cases of selection and strong regulation of entry may entail no explicit training at all. The degree is used as a 'screening mechanism' whereby graduates with certain individual attributes – such as personality, social background, 'A'-level scores – can be identified by virtue of the criteria and effectiveness of the selection procedures which have been used in regulating entry to higher education.

We have used the dimensions of selection and training in a formal way to imply regulation and control by a professional body or statutory agency. In the absence of formalized regulation and control, course–employment relationships will be determined by market demands and preferences. Strong relationships might still occur, but these will be contingent on the recruitment policies of individual employers and on the job applications of individual students. For example, the value which individual employers attach to degree qualifications in business studies is an empirical question, whereas health authorities have no choice but to attach validity to medical qualifications (and to deny validity to others). Similarly medical students will be quite clear about their employment destination whereas business studies students will be more uncertain.

In the case of diffuse relationships, different levels of training relating to different occupational destinations may be achieved within a single course. For example, a law degree represents both a partial completion of professional training and a general base for a wide range of other forms of employment. Such examples are not uncommon although they raise questions of the extent to which a course can both perform a highly selective role for one occupation and successfully develop more diffuse relationships with others. The perceptions and expectations of both employers and graduates are likely to associate the diffuse relationships with failure to achieve professional goals.

Figure 1 summarizes the dimensions and indicates the kinds of empirical variation which can be found. Two clusters of course types are indicated, reflecting respectively specific and diffuse employment links. The justification for the two exclusive clusters is: (i) that specific occupational training must assume a specific and identifiable employment outcome; and (ii) that selection must assume specific and identifiable characteristics in those selected which are not possessed, or not possessed to the same extent, by those who are not selected.

Eight different types of course–employment relationship are indicated. Some courses may straddle types and the precise classification of individual courses is not attempted here. The rest of this section considers the eight types in general terms. The main characteristics of each type are set out, their problems and advantages are indicated, and some examples of the type are suggested.

When courses are directed towards preparation for a specific employment category, the possibility of the over-supply of graduates for a finite number of jobs must necessarily arise. The consequences of this situation are considered separately for courses of each type.

Type A: Sole regulation and completed training

This provides the perfect manpower planning model of higher education. Graduates have no difficulties in securing jobs for which they have been explicitly prepared in higher education. Their initial training is complete; they represent the only source of manpower to the employer.

In view of their absolute dependence on the output of higher education and their preparedness to sub-contract the whole of initial training to it, employers may be expected to be heavily involved in course design and operation. Academic autonomy over the content of the curriculum will probably be limited by professional body control and regulation. Many courses of this

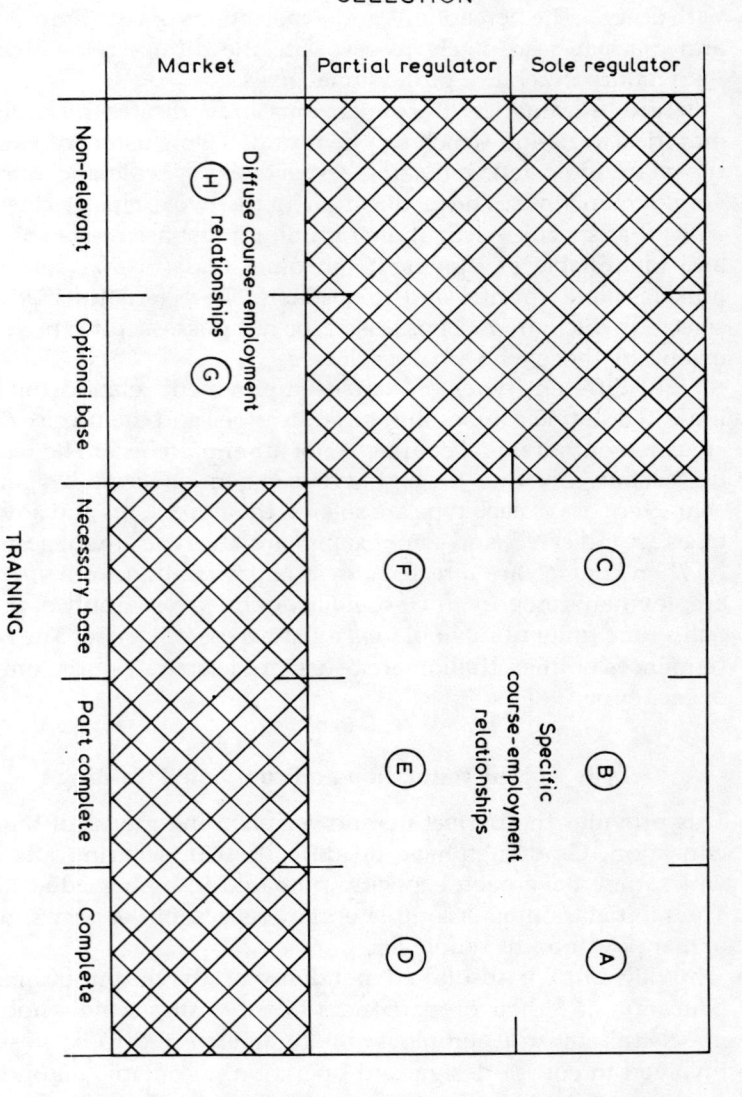

Figure 1 Relationship between degree courses and entry to employment

type will contain substantial periods of work experience, although in some occupational fields practical work in the laboratory or studio will be an effective substitute. The academic staff who support such courses will normally have substantial 'professional' experience and will maintain continuing links with 'practice'. The constraints imposed by employers' needs and professional bodies' requirements will limit both their opportunities for innovation and the amount of individual and institutional variation in course design and teaching.

For students, occupational choice has taken place before entry to higher education and there will be a high level of commitment to the vocational objectives of the course. Higher education is occupational preparation and socialization for these students. They are likely to identify more with the professional group to which they aspire than with the general student body. Their involvement in student affairs and commitment to student 'culture' will be limited. They will expect to find 'relevance' in their studies and will evaluate them primarily in these terms. Examples: medicine, pharmacy.

Over-supply

The manpower planner's model of higher education runs into difficulty as soon as a course's exclusive supply of manpower is met by inadequate employer demand. The assumptions of all parties – teachers, students, and employers – will be undermined. If over-supply of graduates is large, considerable disillusion will arise among students whose vocational motives may be replaced by academic or other sorts. Over-supply enables individual employers to be more discriminating in their recruitment and systematic preferences for the graduates of certain institutions may exacerbate the problems for students from lower-status institutions.

Where they exist, external control mechanisms are likely to be used as soon as possible to reduce the over-supply, either by closing courses or by restricting student numbers. Either way the morale of staff and students will be low as they face uncertain futures.

Type B: Sole regulation and part-training

Exhibiting many of the characteristics of type A, courses of this type share the initial occupational preparation of graduates either with postgraduate courses or with in-company training schemes. The degree is not itself a licence to practise. This division of labour allows greater scope for the 'academicization' of the curriculum by teaching staff not all of whom will be professionally qualified. There may be less emphasis on work experience as part of the course as this can be reserved for the post-graduation phase of training. Employers will be less involved in and prescriptive about the content of courses when they have opportunity to remedy failings in in-company training.

Students will be no less vocational in their motivations, but may less readily perceive the relevance of the course and be impatient for the beginning of genuinely professional work. Occupational socialization will be less powerful. Completion of the course does not represent 'qualification' in professional terms. All of these factors may lead to some students changing track into different occupational fields at the end of their course. This 'wastage' represents a weakening of the course–employment relationship. Example: engineering.

Over-supply

As the graduates are only part-trained for an occupation which is over-supplied, the 'shock' of encountering difficulties in obtaining employment will be less severe. In such circumstances, a rather more academic approach and looser employment links may actually be of benefit to students. A logic of justification in terms of broader educational values will be more acceptable to students and to employers both of whom will recognize that a degree in the subject does not necessarily, logically, or empirically entail professional practice. Thus, employment outcomes in non-professional fields will not be equated with personal failure. Indeed, the two-stage process of preparation for employment will facilitate the 'cooling out' of students before the final professional and qualification stages and thus provide a more effective means of regulating entry.

Type C: Sole regulation and the educational base for training

Courses of this type display similar but heightened characteristics of type B. There may be a greater discontinuity between the academic world and the professional field. Many teachers will not be professionally qualified or experienced and will relate primarily to an academic research culture rather than a professional work culture. The motivations of students will be more varied and there will be a danger that some students will confuse the academic subject with the professional field and, as a consequence, find their vocational objectives frustrated. As the course itself may not emphasize the occupational role model, students are more likely to develop in different directions, in particular towards the researcher/teacher role models provided by their lecturers. Rather more graduates from this type of course will be retained within higher education, taking research degrees or masters courses. Employer interest in and professional regulation of the curriculum is likely to be minimal with higher education performing primarily a selection rather than a training function. Example: psychology.

Over-supply

The above characteristics are positive advantages when professional outlets are limited. Students have made relatively little progress in acquiring professional role models so that a forced change in occupational direction is more easily accommodated. The construction of such courses primarily according to educational rather than occupational criteria will more easily meet the needs of students with a multiplicity of motivations. Nevertheless, there is a danger that intending students will perceive courses as leading to employment destinations which few in fact will reach.

Type D: Partial regulation and completed preparation

These courses will share most of the characteristics of courses in type A. The important distinction is that selection and training are shared with other entry routes – for example, there may be non-graduate entry or non-relevant graduate plus professional training routes. Employers are thus faced with a choice between different types of occupational preparation and they may reveal systematic preferences for the output of one type. Certain entry routes may come to be associated with and/or be monopolized by leading employers. In this potentially competitive situation, the status of the specialist graduate training route will be crucial for the career prospects of students. Consequently there may be considerable 'status insecurity' among students who are likely to make particularly strong demands for relevance in their courses in order to give themselves an advantage over competitors from different routes.

As such courses have no monopoly over selection, employers may be less interested and involved in the design of curricula. If dissatisfied with the product they can turn elsewhere. Where there are multiple entry routes into an occupation, these sometimes relate to differentiation within the occupational field. Thus the BEd entry route into teaching has become particularly associated wth primary education and the less academic parts of secondary education. Examples: education (BEd), social work (degree + Certificate of Qualification in Social Work), physiotherapy, dietetics.

Over-supply

Employer 'route' preferences will be crucial for the success of these courses. Students may well perceive themselves to be 'better qualified' than the competition, but unless such perceptions are shared by employers, disappointment and disillusion will be particularly high. However, where their standing with employers is good, such courses can be as successful as any other vocationally specific course.

Type E: Partial regulation and partly-completed training

Compared to the previous forms of vocationally specific preparation, courses of this type represent decreasing 'value' to students. They provide a route to a specific job, but training is not complete and there are other, and possibly more desirable, routes to the same occupation. In large and differentiated occupational fields, other routes may be associated with more prestigious destinations.

Nevertheless, students who are vocationally committed and have made an early career choice will be attracted to such courses, particularly where other routes are more competitive and outcomes less certain.

Employer involvement in and professional control over course design will be variable. Some occupations will place great emphasis upon the specialist graduate entry route as a means of enhancing professional status. In cases where professional control over recruitment is affected by other means – for example, professional examinations in accountancy – there is likely to be much less interest in higher education in general and ambivalence towards specialist undergraduate programmes in particular. Examples: accountancy, law.

Over-supply

When jobs are difficult to obtain, the nature and standing of the competing routes will be particularly important. The degree represents an element of employee training which would otherwise need to be undertaken by the employer. The employer has to balance the relative quality and costs of higher education and in-company training, the wage costs associated with different routes, and the calibre of recruit from different routes.

Type F: Partial regulation and educational base for training

The conviction with which such courses can claim to provide specific employment outlets for students is unlikely to be high and their vocational intent might be more accurately described under types G or H. The exception is where the competing routes are unpopular with employers or potential employees in which case a situation approximating to that found in type C will pertain. Type F courses are most likely to be associated with expanding occupations which are undergoing rapid professionalization.

The characteristics of type C will appear in accentuated form. There may be no 'professionally' qualified teachers and professional considerations will not be significant in the design and delivery of the course. The professional field and the academic area will share a common subject matter that will ensure a basic relevance to students with vocational motivations. But perspectives on that common subject matter are likely to be very different and emphasis on critical academic values may even be subversive of vocational ends. In such cases vocationally motivated students may be 'converted' to academic values, may be 'turned off' the course, or may successfully come to inhabit the multiple realities of academic and professional worlds. Because of the potential conflicts, some employers may actually be antagonistic to graduates from this sort of course who will be knowledgeable without having received any occupational training or socialization. Recruits of this kind would be well placed to be critical and disruptive of existing work practices.

Such courses would be attractive to students with weak vocational interests. The course would commit them to little, but might provide them with useful information on which to base a subsequent career decision.

An example of a type F course might be those social science courses which, although not engaged in the preparation of social workers, are recognized as 'relevant' to those purposes and permit access to accelerated professional training.

Over-supply

The relatively slight investment by students in professional preparation when coupled with difficulty in obtaining jobs will quickly lead to students seeking alternative occupational outlets and the 'diffuse' employment relationships described in types G and H will be approximated. Nevertheless, there are some important differences in so far as some students are attracted to the courses out of specific vocational considerations and may then have to cope with the non-achievement of career ambitions.

Diffuse links with employment

Courses in this general category have a complex relationship to the labour market. Their graduates enter an open labour market which is not 'fixed' in their favour by professional bodies or by statutory control mechanisms. A degree is but one attribute which they bring with them into the market. Even at the end of the course, major career choices remain to be made, and employment outcomes are potentially diffuse and indeterminate.

Much of higher-education provision is to be found here. It would be a considerable mistake to regard it as non-vocational. Although there may not be explicit preparation for a specific occupational role, courses in this general category may contain curricular features of relevance to employers over a wide range of fields. Examples of employment-related competencies which can be acquired are computing skills, modern languages, quantitative methods, and skills in report writing and in oral presentation, analysis, and synthesis. The major distinction to be made amongst courses of this sort concerns the explicitness with which they attempt to prepare students for employment. (It should be noted that it is not meaningful to refer to 'over-supply' in relation to these types of course. There is no clearly-defined area of employment to which a concept of over-supply could be said to refer.)

Type G: Open market and employment-relevant educational base

An increasing number of courses set out to produce graduates who will be useful to employers over a wide occupational field. Curricula are devised in relation to perceived employment needs. Although graduates will enter an open employment market, the designers of such courses hope that they will be particularly well-equipped to compete in that market. Their studies will have been 'relevant'.

The aims of these courses are to lay a foundation for work, to transmit knowledge and develop skills which are transferable, at least within broad occupational fields. Students will select these courses out of general, if ill-defined, vocational concerns. Lecturers will possess a commitment to employment relevance although the diffuseness of employment outcomes will make relevance difficult to achieve. The problematic and diffuse links with employment are nevertheless central to the justification of the whole enterprise and considerable staff time will be given to developing them. The preservation of a compulsory period of work experience may be zealously guarded for similar reasons.

The employability of such graduates is very much an empirical question. However, some studies have suggested that where they are able to recruit in a relatively open employment market, employers are more interested in individual attributes than in types of course (Gordon 1983). Much will depend on the 'quality' of students recruited to the courses. Unless this is at least as high as that of other 'open market' courses, the claims for a relevant curriculum may be of limited advantage to graduates. In so far as they reflect differences in student quality, institutional differences may be more significant than course differences in effecting links with employment. Nevertheless, the potential advantages of this sort of course are considerable. Graduates are not tied to the market demand in specific fields but are equipped – in terms of knowledge, skills, and disposition – to be mobile across a wide range of employment contexts. Examples: business studies, public administration, computing, hotel studies.

Type H: Open market and non-relevant education

Sometimes thought of as non-vocational, graduates from these courses – which include most humanities and pure science courses – may possess many characteristics which are of value to employers. However, curricula are not designed primarily in relation to employment needs, nor are students attracted to the courses from vocational motivations.

In so far as employers believe that graduates possess qualities which are not generally found in non-graduates, courses of this type will provide access to a restricted graduate labour market. However, the expansion of higher education has outpaced any growth in this market and an unknown but almost certainly large number of graduates compete for jobs in a potentially open (non-graduate) labour market.

Courses of this type will be designed in relation to educational considerations. Teachers will have little or no experience of non-academic work and may have very little knowledge of what their graduates actually do after leaving higher education. Until they leave, the students may also have little idea of what they will do.

The uncertainty and potential diffuseness of destinations prohibits explicit preparation either in terms of knowledge and skills or attitudes and values. The transition from higher education to employment may be difficult.

For those employers who wish to take full control of employee training and selection, graduates from such courses have much to offer. Employers will be looking for abilities – intellectual or other – which have been identified by and/or developed in higher education. However, given the absence of restrictions on employer choice in this particular labour market, the graduate will need to demonstrate attributes of value to employers in addition to the possession of a degree.

Given that precise career aspirations have not guided their choice of course, students' involvement in and satisfaction with their experience of higher education will be impervious to employment considerations. Difficulties in obtaining employment will not be relished but there is less reason to suppose that they will influence the student evaluation of higher education.

What we have tried to do above is to consider the likely implications for the vocational of the different kinds of currency which degree qualifications can possess in the labour market. This currency provides an important context both for the designers of the courses and for the students in pursuing their educational and career objectives. The context is of course a changing one. Professionalization has increased the importance of educational qualifications in both selection and training. The growth in higher education and the numbers of graduates has inevitably affected their position in the labour market. Growth has been accompanied by diversification – of institutions, courses, types of student. The eight kinds of relationship to the labour market described above illustrate this diversification.

The labour-market context for course planning is not a fixed one, but nor is it directly amenable to control by educators. Employers, professional bodies, government, all have interests in the role of educational qualifications in the labour market. At the extremes, these interests can have a crucial impact upon the educator. High levels of interest are likely to be accompanied by statutorily enforced controls on the content of curricula, admission of students, length of study, form of assessment, and pedagogy. At the other extreme, a situation of almost complete lack of interest may obtain where the problem for the educator is how to get the employers to 'take notice'.

What the model presented in this chapter suggests is the susceptibility of the whole range of higher education courses to interpretation in vocational terms of one sort or another. An important part of the history of public-sector higher education has been the introduction of new, vocational, fields into the curriculum and the attempt to secure their acceptance, both by the academic world and employers. They have had varying degrees of success. But what a significant part of this growth has entailed is a 'reaching out' by higher education to form a partnership with other interests to raise the currency of particular qualifications in particular fields of employment. Partners have been more or less willing, but clearly the structure, and in particular the diffuseness, of particular labour markets can have a considerable effect on the success of the endeavour.

In Part Two, we shall be looking in particular at two major fields of study which occupy contrasting positions in the model presented above. In engineering, degrees have an established position in the structure of qualifications which regulate entry and provide training in the profession. Business studies has no equivalent professional structure, and business-studies degrees are relative newcomers to the employment scene. Engineering degrees have a longer history. Both relate to employment fields which are large and diffuse. In terms of our model, engineering is probably an example of category (b), sole regulation of entry and part-training, and business studies is an example of category (g), open market and an employment-relevant educational base. The importance of the typology to the discussion in terms of engineering and business studies is its demonstration of the range of perceptions available in higher education of relations with the world of employment, and therefore of course purposes and contents, responsibilities to students, and accountabilities to a variety of constituencies. The interviews conducted reflect how those responsible for courses situate themselves in the traditions and diversities that we have outlined.

4
The language of policy

The primary focus of this study is on the definition, description, and interpretation of courses and institutional aims and activities. Before we turn directly to a consideration of these, it is important to set both the analytical model we have propounded and the views of those engaged in the processes on the ground alongside some British policy statements which illustrate the debates to which all of this relates, and to which in many respects it is a response. Perceptions of course and institutional goals are conditioned by public expectations and rhetoric, and by financial and political considerations, as well as by the academic and professional logics of the courses and institutions themselves.

The tension between dichotomous expressions of the liberal–vocational, liberal–technical elements in education has run through the policy formulations of recent decades, particularly where technical and technological expansion and manpower planning to meet national 'needs' have been concerned. One of the early policy documents which encouraged the development of 'liberal studies' in technical colleges, many of which later graduated to higher technological status, was a Ministry of Education circular in 1957, which stressed 'the importance of introducing a liberal element into technical education', and outlined various ways of 'liberalising a technical course' (Ministry of Education 1957). British traditions and assumptions about technical education, science, and the nature of the liberal were different in this respect from those of Europe and the United States, where underlying assumptions and social, cultural, and educational processes and structures were translated into different post-secondary and higher-education curricula. In the reverse direction, seeking not to make the vocational more liberal, but the liberal more appropriate to future careers, the process assumed greater urgency in Britain with increasing economic difficulties and sharper competition for graduate employment in the 1970s. One of the earliest policy expressions of this concern was in the White Paper, *Education: A Framework for Expansion*, issued in 1972 by Margaret Thatcher as Secretary of State for Education and Science:

> The Government have sympathy with the sincere desire on the part of a growing number of students to be given more help in acquiring – and discovering how to apply – knowledge and skills related more directly to the decisions that will face them in their careers and in the world of personal and social action. This is what is meant by 'relevance'.
> (Secretary of State for Education and Science 1972: 31)

Developing from such a concern in the late 1970s and 1980s was to be a mounting emphasis on the 'relevance' not only of emphases within and help relating to particular courses of study, but also the importance to the nation's needs of those courses of study themselves. The relevant and the vocational could be interpreted in relation to individual needs and career aspirations, the changing structure of the labour market, and estimates of manpower needs and national futures.

In 1983 the Secretary of State invited discussion and advice on the future of higher education in the next decade. What followed indicated the extent to which the language of vocationalism had become central to debate about higher education, and the ways in which the system was responding to the pressures from political and economic directions. The first paragraph of the response to the Secretary of State from the University Grants Committee contained the explanation that 'the universities provide the bulk of the country's science and engineering graduates and research workers, as well as qualified graduates from medicine, law, architecture and numerous other professions'. The UGC went on to accept that there would be a shift towards the sciences and engineering, but underlined a need for additional resources 'if there is to be a significant increase in places for science, engineering and other vocationally relevant forms of study' (UGC 1984: 4–5). The emphasis on science as 'vocationally relevant' raises questions about both the interpretation of science, and the extent of the 'other' forms of study – likely to be considerable when science in such a general formulation is included.

On behalf of the public sector, the National Advisory Body for Local Authority Higher Education responded more fully on this area of debate. It issued a consultative document in 1983 addressing some of the issues directly. It defended the sector against accusations of not being as responsive to employment needs as it should be: 'it is difficult at the system wide level to discern clearly what these needs are'. It defended the sandwich system as an important route for the 'qualified professional', experiencing college-based study integrated with practice, suggested that in various ways the system had been responsive to manpower needs (directly in medicine and teacher education), and pointed to reports and pressures over the years from industry and commerce asking for higher education to be 'more immediately vocationally specific'. The questions the NAB asked of the institutions, therefore, included: 'what should be the balance between general courses, and more specifically vocational ones?' (NAB 1983: 2, 5, 10). By the time the NAB issued its final advice to the Secretary of State the following year, it had formulated answers to some of its questions. It continued to emphasize that the sector was concerned 'primarily with serving professional and vocational needs', but, with a firm and explicit dismissal of the passage in the 1972 White Paper, it realized how difficult was the terminology:

> Vocationalism is an imprecise term which has led to a confused debate. The notion of relevance as set out in the 1972 White Paper 'Education: A Framework for Expansion' is even less helpful. What lies behind both these terms is the view that the higher education experience should equip students with the skills and abilities to enable them to meet the economy's need for highly qualified manpower. . . . The economy will not be well served by providing too narrow a specialist focus in initial higher education provision. A policy which identifies one side of the binary line as more vocational than the other is neither accurate nor helpful.
>
> (NAB 1984a: 24, 39)

In an important joint statement by the NAB and the UGC, these questions of skills, narrowness, and the qualities needed by future contributors to the professions and the economy were addressed directly and in the context of defining the purposes of higher education generally. The statement warned against emphasizing 'specific knowledge', which quickly becomes outdated. Initial higher education:

> Should therefore emphasise underlying intellectual, scientific and technological principles rather than provide too narrow a specialist knowledge. The abilities most valued in industrial, commercial and professional life as well as in public and social administration are the transferable intellectual and personal skills.
>
> (NAB 1984a: 4)

The statement included among such skills the ability to analyse complex issues, to identify the core of a problem and the means of solving it, to synthesize, clarify values, make effective use of numerical and other information, work effectively with others, and communicate clearly: 'a higher education system which provides its students with these skills is serving society well' (NAB 1984a: 4). Although in other respects the binary division between the universities and the 'public sector' remained strong, there were emphases and claims regarding purpose and student attributes and learning that were visibly common to higher education as a whole.

When, following this consultation, a Green Paper was produced in 1985, the dominant themes were set in the context of Britain's poor economic performance since 1945, and the higher rate of production of qualified scientists, engineers, technologists, and technicians in competitor countries. The paper warned against 'anti-business' snobbery, underlined the importance of the 'entrepreneurial spirit', and called on higher education to 'foster positive attitudes to work' and to strengthen links with industry and commerce. It attached special importance to vocational qualifications, and castigated employers for recruiting graduates 'by reference to general ability and leadership qualities', without providing 'clear signals of the importance they attach to competence in science and technology'. Employers needed to make a greater effort 'to persuade more youngsters to opt for the relevant subjects'. The paper, in a final paragraph in the section concerned with subject balance, recognized that employers value broadly based personal skills, and stressed the importance of providing adequately for the arts – although the proportion of arts placed in higher education 'can be expected to shrink'. The dominant emphasis in the paper, however, and one

The language of policy 57

to which the paper drew clear attention, was not left in doubt: 'In higher education the Government believes it right to maintain a distinct emphasis on technological and directly vocational courses at all levels' (Secretary of State for Education and Science 1985: 3–9). Higher education in both sectors maintained that it already worked with industry in ways urged by the Green Paper, and widespread objection was voiced to the dominant tone of the document. Its 'vocational' emphasis provoked a good deal of adverse comment, as did the general thrust and many of the specifics of the argument. Sir Keith Joseph found himself having to defend the paper against what he considered an unfair reading of its message. Speaking to the Committee of Vice-Chancellors and Principals he reaffirmed his recognition of the importance of the humanities in higher education, and in its response to the Green Paper the UGC welcomed that recognition and made a broad, clear statement to the Secretary of State:

> As you said, the training of the mind provided by an arts course is highly valued by industry in its own right, and in this sense the humanities generally are no less vocationally relevant than the sciences. Vocational relevance is not confined to courses preparing students for a limited number of specific kinds of employment.
>
> (UGC 1985: 4)

The UGC statement was broad and clear in its interpretation, though it indicates how diverse the use of the term 'vocation' could now be.

Sir Keith offered another defence against accusations of 'espousing the "new vocationalism" which seems to mean an excessive concern with the immediately useful to the neglect of wider cultural values'. He told a conference on the Green Paper that he had always believed in the humanities as ends in themselves, and rejected the 'alleged philistinism' perceived in insistence on the contribution of higher education to wealth creation. He saw no dichotomy in higher education combining the pursuit of learning for its own sake ('the contribution of higher education to a humane and civilised society') with preparation for employment. There was also no incompatibility with emphasizing science and technology in higher education, when economics and demography made it necessary. He referred in passing to some subjects outside the sciences and engineering as 'highly vocational', for example modern languages and business studies, but reaffirmed his commitment to 'liberal intellectual traditions' (Joseph 1985: 2-3, 12-19). In 1986 he was reported as regretting his inattention to technical and vocational education (he was not here referring specifically to higher education) in his early days at the Department of Education and Science, again reasserting his support for the tradition of liberal learning for its own sake, and emphasizing the need for a workforce that was not narrowly skilled, was versatile, and had the ability to respond to change and use a range of personal skills (Joseph 1986).

What some of this debate indicated was a continuing lack of clarity about what to include in any definition of liberal or vocational, and the difficulty of sustaining a discussion about either without constantly separating off the 'sciences and engineering' from the remainder of higher education. A commitment to the liberal could easily be translated into a commitment to the arts or humanities. A discussion of the relation between higher education and employment, particularly in a period of higher education's self-defence against a variety of accusations and pressures, could easily ascribe wide, indeed universal, meanings to the term vocational which made it unrecognizable from the term as it was being used by critics or opponents.

Those difficulties become more apparent as the range of policy statements is widened. The STEAC report on the future of higher education in Scotland, following on the heels of the Green Paper, supported the Government's 'wish to see a higher proportion of students studying subjects of vocational relevance', but at the same time considered it essential for Scotland's broadly based educational tradition to be protected: 'we would moreover caution against the sole pursuit of industrial and economically "relevant" subjects, vitally important though they are' (STEAC 1986: 48-50). The very use of the vocabulary of vocationalism produced attendant reservations and cautions.

It would be important, for a full consideration of the problems we are identifying, to look beyond higher education, for example to the definitions of vocational objectives, work-related courses, and occupational considerations at other levels – including some of those discussed by the Business and Technician Education Council (e.g. BTEC 1983), and in relation to the Technical and Vocational Education Initiative in secondary schools, launched by the government through the Manpower Services Commission in 1982. Here, however, it is possible only to remain within the various constituencies of higher education itself.

Without reference to the same vocabularies, the Finniston report on engineering took care to warn against the 'narrowness of outlook' about which many employers had complained. The report drew attention to the neglect of skills and understandings which contribute to 'the whole engineering dimension', or, as was reported from regional engineering conferences, 'neglect of the human and creative aspects of engineering' (Committee of Inquiry into the Engineering Profession 1980: 78, 84–6, 188). Finniston himself, in the years following the report, stressed the importance of widening engineering education, enabling engineers to understand and relate to other people, and even making an engineering education broad enough to point towards other forms of employment (Finniston 1984: 63; 1985: 5). The direction of breadth and versatility, however, was not the one in which the DES was prepared to go in permitting new courses to be mounted in the public sector. Its circulars sought a precise match between courses and employment needs. New courses would be approved only if they could 'be demonstrated to be of clear value in meeting the needs of industry for skilled technical, technological or scientific personnel, or otherwise essential to meet the operational needs of industry, commerce, the professions or other employers' (DES 1982). The National Advisory Body, in the meantime, was stressing the ambiguities of the vocational discourse. In its commentary on the conclusion of its 1984/5 planning exercise the NAB commented that there had been a shift of balance 'into the more technological and directly vocational programmes', and these were listed as engineering, science, mathematics, and business-related courses. The most obvious question raised by the list is: if mathematics is directly vocational, what is not? If mathematics is included, presumably English should be? Vocational is beginning, in such discussions, to equate 'usable skill' or 'applicable knowledge' (NAB 1984b: 1).

It is revealing to pursue this discussion at a different policy level – that of institutions. The polytechnics have in the 1970s and 1980s had to try to define themselves in positive terms as a group of institutions, and as compared to the universities, given the late-comer's need to justify the incursion. Both of these elements of definition are visible in the way the polytechnics present themselves and their courses in their prospectuses (and we shall subsequently see how they do so in other ways). British institutions of higher education do not adopt 'mission statements' as do American institutions, but prospectuses (and to some extent the institutional review documentation of CNAA-validated colleges and polytechnics) indicate, however crudely, the institutions' interpretation of their policy positions regarding courses, recruitment, and a variety of other matters. Not all the polytechnics – to which the discussion at this point is confined – offer an explicit statement about themselves, and in their recent prospectuses Birmingham, Kingston, Newcastle, Wolverhampton, and Thames polytechnics do not do so. All of the others describe themselves, either as individual institutions, or as part of a sector, or both, in terms which indicate how they view their curriculum balance or their relationships with the labour market. Many of them are anxious to identify what is 'distinctive' about the polytechnics, and most of them include some reference to their vocationalism.

The interpretations of the vocational roles of the polytechnics vary in these statements, either explicitly or in the apparent assumptions on which they are based. Some describe their courses as 'realistic' or related to 'real-life situations'. Some refer to the wide range of their courses, the different levels at which they operate, or the variety of their modes of teaching and of their students. In some cases the concept of vocationalism is closely identified with that of interdisciplinarity. The most common explanations of the polytechnics' vocationalism, however, relate to their commitment to prepare students for employment – sometimes with references to 'general' or 'specific' preparation, and this is occasionally contrasted with 'traditional' or 'purely academic' courses (with the implication that these are more likely to be available in universities). There is frequent reference to the close relationship between the polytechnics' courses and industry, the professions and commerce – to which 'the community' is sometimes added. Some examples will illustrate the range of interpretations.

In 1984 Brighton Polytechnic explained that 'some specifically vocational qualifications are offered only by polytechnics', and reprinted on the first page of its prospectus a statement by the Committee of Directors of Polytechnics proclaiming the polytechnics to be 'distinctive in having a clearly defined role combining the closest relevance to industry, commerce and the professions, the widest range of studies at all levels, and the greatest variety in the age, background and interests of their students'. A polytechnic provided 'a unique learning environment'. In subsequent years, Brighton omitted this CDP statement and substituted a description of its own 'corporate goal':

> To provide a teaching and learning environment which can foster the personal and professional development of young people . . . and the continuing recurrent education of men and women of all ages having particular regard to the need for courses which aim to improve national productivity and which aim to improve social and economic conditions. To provide educational leadership to the community. . . . To provide the resources and opportunities for the advancement of knowledge.

To achieve these ends, the polytechnic needed to 'attempt to preserve an academically well-balanced institution'.

Bristol Polytechnic, in a statement entitled 'Polytechnic Jargon', explains that the majority of its courses require study 'closely related to the needs of a profession'. Many of them cover more than a single discipline and provide the 'cross-disciplinary education which is increasingly demanded by employers. . . . It is in this vocational bias and the frequent interplay of disciplines that polytechnics provide an alternative form of higher education to the universities' (1983/5). Huddersfield Polytechnic contrasts its range of courses – from doctorates to certificates – with that of the universities, adding: 'We also tend to preserve the traditions inherited from our constituent colleges and provide courses which are strongly vocational' (1984/5). Liverpool also points up the difference between universities and polytechnics:

> It is clear that more and more people are aware of the tangible differences between the education offered in the University sector and the Polytechnic and for many the latter, with its vocational emphasis, is becoming an increasingly attractive proposition at a time when career prospects are a prime determinant of education choice.
>
> (1984/5)

In considering such claims alongside, for example, the National Advisory Body's insistence that the university and public sectors are not divided along vocational lines, the nature of the respective statements and the audiences addressed have to be borne in mind. It is not easy to explain to students or the general public the distinctive features, if any, of a polytechnic in a way that will influence student choice. Those who compile prospectuses, like those who write 'rationales' of courses, have to identify the distinctive, persuade, and judge what customer or critic may wish to hear, as well as what to display or to underline.

Some features of the polytechnics, their histories and present identities, are commonly presented by all or many of them. The comprehensive nature of the polytechnics is one such feature that is widely stressed. Oxford Polytechnic provides a 'more comprehensive range of levels of courses' than the universities, offering vocational, technical, and traditional degree courses (1985/6). Middlesex Polytechnic offers one of the most 'richly varied' range of educational opportunities in the country: 'some courses are traditional in their approach; others are unusual and even unique' (1984/5). Portsmouth Polytechnic describes its vocational courses as useful or necessary for particular careers, but stresses that not all its courses are directly related to careers in that way. This does not mean that graduates from 'non-vocational' courses have no jobs available:

> Graduates and diplomates are sought by many employers on the assumption that higher level study in any subject will develop the general abilities to enquire, to argue, to analyse, to criticise and perhaps to produce original ideas. Most employers will also be interested in an applicant's personality, ideas, manner, appearance, ability to get along with people and willingness to be trained and to work hard. These factors will often be more important than the subject or level of qualification.
> (1983/4)

Sheffield Polytechnic likewise describes its courses in 'academic subjects', but also its 'less traditional courses . . . which give realistic vocational and professional preparation for careers in the modern world' (1984/5). On the other hand, Scotland's central institutions, unlike the English polytechnics in being prevented from offering liberal arts courses, which are the preserves of the Scottish universities, have no difficulty in presenting their courses. Robert Gordon's Institute of Technology in Aberdeen, with an emphasis typical of these institutions, explains that 'the majority of courses at RGIT are vocational or career-oriented and we at the Institute undertake to provide you with the necessary education and training for you to commence your career in your chosen profession' (1983).

These institutional statements, which are policy statements only in their continuing announcement that their chosen or designated direction is the one they intend to pursue, have over the years been paralleled by institutional and course statements for validation purposes as submitted to the CNAA. Since the CNAA has taken a direct interest within the validation procedure in the employment prospects of graduates, such submissions have – increasingly in the late 1970s and 1980s – addressed the question of vocational definition and content, particularly in subject areas sensing themselves to be at risk in the prevailing climate. A 1983 BA resubmission in Social Sciences repeated an earlier formulation of aims which included the following:

> The provision of a sustaining undergraduate education for those who expect to be engaged subsequently in activities for which an understanding of social relations, institutions and organisations is essential. The view is taken that this understanding is made feasible from a basis of academic analysis which is related to the contemporary world but which is strongly informed by theoretical, comparative and conceptual approaches. The programme is vocational in the important sense that it lays the foundation on which subsequent professional, postgraduate, in-service or post-experience vocational education and training may build; and that it equips its graduates with the means of coping with a world of change.

More succinctly, but less clearly, another Social Science submission (1983) describes such an undergraduate course as providing 'a broadly relevant education which covers many of the aspects to be found in postgraduate, vocational and professional training'. A 1982 BA resubmission in Modern Studies describes the structure of the course as 'directing students towards areas of vocational or postgraduate study'. Another CNAA-related institution, discussing vocationalism in its 'progress review' documentation (1985), accepts the need to respond to economic and technological demands. Though vocationalism remained the dominant goal of its courses, 'increasingly determined by manpower planning objectives', it threatened to 'swamp the traditional liberal concept of education beyond Advanced level. . . .

The need to preserve these humanising pursuits will become greater during the next decade'.

Crucial features of the polytechnics and similar institutions in the United Kingdom are highlighted in some of these examples. Their work relates to the technical and further education traditions from which they derive – though we shall return to a discussion of the adaptation of these traditions. They have felt it essential to present themselves in sharp and distinctive vocational terms. The meanings of their expressed vocationalism embrace the employability of graduates (an ingredient which pushes the concept ever wider across the curriculum); the relationship of institutions and their courses to future employers (including, and especially, relationships through sandwich structures and the part-time students already in employment); the expectations of employers (including personal attributes, and interdisciplinary experience). Even where no direct vocational content or relationship is claimed, as with the social science courses quoted, it has been felt necessary to indicate their relevance to possible future vocational intentions. To what extent such indications represent an interpretation of course goals and realities, or a response to the needs of the market or the validator, or some combination of the two, is an underlying question of institutional policy analysis, and is part of the concern of this and related discussion.

In all of these self-scrutinies, the polytechnics and other public-sector institutions have had the distinctive feature of operating within the validation procedures of the CNAA, the universities, and other professional bodies. Of all these the CNAA, which has been the central validating body for all of the polytechnics since their designation at the end of the 1960s, has had the most explicit requirements, and has been most public in its responses to the policy formulations likely to influence its own operations and those of its related institutions.

In its own policy statements, regulations, and principles, the CNAA has addressed directly, though not always in detail, the curricular issues raised in this discussion. In its early years the CNAA was operating in subject areas seen as vocational, and its efforts to encourage broader studies, complementary and contrasting courses of study, discipline-based enquiry, and the integration of academic study and practical work through sandwich courses, pointed towards a generous definition of its essential vocationalism:

The language of policy 65

77% of all courses approved by the Council are sandwich courses and most of these are designed to meet a vocational need, whether it is in industry, business or the professions; this is not to say of course that the content of the courses is narrowly vocational.

(CNAA 1967-8: 10)

A decade later the CNAA was considering the margin of difference between the courses in its institutions and those in universities, and was describing the complexities involved in making the comparison or contrast:

> Generally speaking, Council's degrees cover the same range of subjects as those of universities (except for medicine, dentistry, veterinary science and forestry), though a greater emphasis may be given in many CNAA courses to vocational or practical work. This is particularly true in the technology-based courses where a significant number are in the sandwich mode of study. However, the CNAA is not unique in this respect as several of the technological universities offer courses which incorporate the sandwich concept. The CNAA also approves degree courses in subjects which are not normally taught in universities, such as art and design and creative and performing arts.

(CNAA 1979: 19)

In the 1980s the Council emphasized the range of its validated courses of study:

> some programmes will seek to prepare students for a particular profession or vocation; some will seek to develop a student's general problem-solving skills; some will seek to promote a student's artistic development; some will seek a breadth of subject coverage, while others will encourage specialisation and yet others will transcend traditional boundaries of knowledge.

(CNAA 1983a: 22)

A primary aim, however, had to be the development of the student's 'intellectual and imaginative skills and powers. . . . The direction of the student's studies must be towards greater understanding and competence. . . . A programme of studies must stimulate an enquiring, analytical and creative approach.' Against the background we have considered, therefore, the CNAA tried to portray an approach to learning that would militate against narrowness:

> The student must be encouraged to appreciate the nature of attitudes, modes of thought, practices and disciplines other than those of his or her main studies. He or she must learn to perceive his or her main studies in a broader perspective. As part of this process he or she must be enabled to develop an informed awareness of factors influencing the social and physical environment.
>
> (CNAA 1983a: 23)

These formulations had given the CNAA some difficulty from the beginning: the 'informed awareness of factors' had taken the place of the aim to 'give the student an informed awareness . . . of the contribution they can make . . . in widening man's imaginative horizons and his understanding of his culture and environment'. That formulation, adopted in 1974, was itself considered by one commentator to be a watered down version of a more splendid aim: 'to give the student an understanding . . . of the contribution they can make . . . in widening man's imaginative horizons and his understanding of the universe' (Smith 1978: 341; see also Oxtoby 1972).

The Council remained attentive to the issues, but did not go further than the brief statement in its Principles in elaborating a categorization of its courses. In its response to the Finniston Report in 1980, it accepted the thrust towards more broadly-based, more application-focused engineering degrees, considering that many 'vocational broadly-based courses' were nearer to the Finniston goals than single-discipline courses. Equally important, however, were those 'general engineering degree courses with vocational slants meeting specific needs, such as Engineering with Business Studies' (CNAA 1980: 15). In its response to the 1985 Green Paper, the Council emphasized the existing close links of the public sector with the world of work, with 'a strong emphasis on applied studies and a willingness to respond to changing employment needs'. Given the range of public-sector higher education many of the courses validated by the CNAA did 'not fit into the simplified categories of arts or science, liberal or vocational, pure or applied'.

The CNAA's view was that, although higher education existed

to serve society, its duty was not 'simply to respond to society's perceived needs; it should help to shape the expression of those needs through critical discussion'. Flexibility was a question both of provision and of the graduates themselves, whose adaptability, 'analytical communication and interpersonal skills' were welcomed by all employers. In 1986 the CNAA emphasized, as did the UGC, the relationship between arts courses and employment:

> As the Green Paper says, rigorous arts courses prepare students well for many types of employment. We believe that public sector arts, humanities and social studies courses are particularly effective in developing both general and specific skills relevant to employment.
>
> (CNAA 1986a: 2-5)

The need to move away from rigid boundaries between the vocational and its perceived opposites was a theme picked up in a variety of contexts by the CNAA in the mid-1980s. When the Review of Vocational Qualifications (launched by the government in 1985 through the MSC and DES) was taking place, the CNAA wrote to suggest that 'one of the factors that has led to the difficulties currently being experienced is the rather arbitrary distinction made between "vocational" and "academic" qualifications and the higher status generally accorded to the latter' (CNAA 1985). A CNAA working party on long-term developments expressed the view that the public sector had a 'creditable record as far as the provision of vocational courses is concerned', but it was anxious that the concept of 'vocationalism' should not be interpreted in a narrow sense. It agreed that it was desirable that 'any course of higher education should give the graduate the kind of intellectual grounding which will stand him in good stead for performing a responsible role in a number of walks of life' (CNAA 1983b: 7). In its evidence to the STEAC inquiry on higher education in Scotland, the CNAA acknowledged that one of the characteristics of the public sector in general was that 'its courses mostly have a vocational orientation' and that this was markedly so in Scotland 'where it has been deliberate policy that the public sector degree work should complement rather than compete with that of the universities'. The CNAA's point in the evidence was that the significant contribution of these public-sector courses within Scottish higher education had not always been fully appreciated (CNAA 1984: 3). In its 1986 response to the STEAC report itself, the CNAA had a different point to emphasize, one that reflected its response to the Green Paper concerning England and Wales:

> While the CNAA recognises and respects the SED policy that the central institutions should concentrate on courses with a specifically vocational orientation, the CNAA believes that well designed arts and humanities courses also provide a valuable preparation for a wide range of occupations.
> (CNAA 1986b: 3)

What the CNAA's own discussions, and wider debates throughout the system, had highlighted by this time was the diversity of possible responses to known needs and political and other pressures.

From its creation in the mid-1960s the CNAA had sought to evade the pejorative associations of 'vocationalism', adopting it with wide connotations, guarding against its identification with narrowness and training implications unacceptable in higher education. Increasingly in the late 1970s and 1980s, as economic and manpower-planning pressures mounted, government and national bodies of various kinds also adopted the vocabulary and its associated extensions of meaning, in attempts to alter or defend the structures and practices of higher education. What exactly vocationalism was, in the new conditions of the late twentieth century, and how palatable it was as an alternative to traditional 'liberal' higher education values, or as a version of that tradition, were not questions to which there were simple or unequivocal answers. If policy has to do with both intention and strategy, the language of policy is both future-oriented and burdened with the meanings which may have remained unchanged or unquestioned as the realities it attempts to reflect have undergone important changes. Vocabularies, locked into attitudes and procedures, are some of society's most immovable and intransigent objects. Policy at national strategic levels and at institutional levels remains buttressed by terms whose uncertainties and ambiguities have been constantly probed in the past, but need to be subjected to fresh controversy and situated in new understandings.

Part Two

VOCATIONALISM – A PROJECT

5
Concepts, courses, and institutions

It is in the context of the history and policy frameworks described in the previous chapters that the institutions of the maintained sector have developed to become the major providers of undergraduate higher education in the United Kingdom. As we have seen, a vocational content and purpose has been an important feature of the way these institutions have seen themselves and have been seen by others, including the CNAA.

As the validating body with responsibility for the standards of the majority of degree courses in the maintained sector, the CNAA agreed in 1983 to support a project which would inquire into the meaning of 'vocationalism' held by those who had worked and were working in 'vocational traditions'. In agreeing to support the project, the CNAA was acknowledging that a concept central to the stated objectives of many of its courses was in fact subject to considerable ambiguity and confusion. The project proposal stated that:

> The importance of this proposed exercise in clarification lies in the largely unexamined assumptions about vocational education in judgments made from outside it, in the unspoken or unheard assumptions of those engaged in self-declared vocational activities, and in the often confident assumption that there is a consensus of meaning around the concept. The usage is in fact most confused and ambiguous, including by institutions offering CNAA degrees, in what are sometimes announced as specific or general areas of vocational study. The ambiguities include different assumptions about course content, about the nature, level and timing of vocational elements, about teaching methods, about students' and employers' expectations of professional relevance, about the assessment

of work-oriented learning, and the viability and acceptability of vocationally relevant content within the institution, and by the various constituencies involved.

The project was to attempt clarification of these issues by exploring them with polytechnic and college teachers who were closely involved in the design and teaching of courses widely regarded as – in some sense – vocational study. The objective was to explore the congruence of understandings and interpretations of teachers with the wider perspectives and vocabularies in which policies at national level were being articulated. This was to be achieved through a series of interviews with 'insiders' – experienced academic staff who had made their careers in fields generally regarded as vocational.

As we have already noted, the vocabulary of vocationalism has been drawn into discussions of courses in virtually all the subject fields. The interviews were to concentrate on only two of them, but two which have considerable importance in the profile of public-sector higher education – engineering and business studies. All of the English polytechnics have degree courses in these fields, as do most of the Scottish central institutions and a number of colleges and institutes of higher education in England. The broad areas of business, science, and technology accounted for 49 per cent of CNAA-registered undergraduate students in 1985. The two subject fields are important to the sector and important to any explication of the nature of the vocational. Engineering education has a long history in the United Kingdom and has received considerable public attention in recent years. The growth of business-studies degrees has been an important feature of the development of public-sector higher education over the last twenty years, where it exists as a distinctive kind of course not found in any numbers in the universities.

The selection of engineering and business studies was important to the aims of the study, however, for reasons other than size. In terms of the typology described in chapter 3, they occupy almost opposite extremes in the spectrum of the vocational. Engineering degrees play a crucial role in the regulation of entry into a highly professionalized occupation. Employers and professional bodies impose explicit requirements upon undergraduate curricula as an important stage in the process of occupational training. In contrast, business-studies degrees possess little regulatory force in a diffuse occupational field characterized by a multitude of entry routes at different educational levels. Business-studies graduates face an essentially open labour market in which they must compete with graduates from other subjects and in many cases with non-graduates. As there is little consensus among employers about what a person entering business needs to know there is relatively little external constraint upon the undergraduate curriculum. For the teacher of a business-studies course, there is a smaller degree of certainty about the employment destinations of students.

The interviews based on engineering and business-studies degrees took place in four institutions: Humberside College of Higher Education, Leicester Polytechnic, Napier College, Edinburgh, and Oxford Polytechnic. The issues in which we were interested were live ones, however, in many other subject fields and for this reason we took the opportunity to investigate a limited number of other courses at the four institutions. Those were architecture (in two institutions), estate management or land management (in two institutions), and planning (in one institution).

Although the relevant literature of the professional institutes and other bodies was scrutinized, the focus for the interviews was specific courses in specific subject areas in specific institutions. The starting point for discussions was the course descriptions, contained mainly in initial and review submissions to the CNAA, prospectuses, handouts to students, and some internal documentation, all of which were obtained in advance. These provided the basis for an initial analysis of changes in courses and their expressed purposes. The interviews focused on the aims of courses and units as laid down in this documentation, the strategies and concepts most salient in the definitions and presentation of courses, and the applicability and implications of 'vocational' definitions as offered and perceived (or avoided or rejected) by the courses and their leaders. In a small number of cases deans of faculties or heads of departments with direct experience of a course or courses were also interviewed. In addition, we interviewed the directors of the four institutions in order to explore institutional 'missions' and associated interpretations of their 'vocationalism'. Since two of the directors concerned were engineers with important profiles in public-sector higher education engineering, they were interviewed twice, once as a preliminary to the work on engineering, and once later as directors of their institutions. Given the basis of the interviews in course and institutional documentation, interviews could only be loosely structured, and they varied according to the course or institutional history concerned. Where an interviewee placed emphasis on a particular concept or process (for example, interdisciplinarity or problem-solving) the topic was allowed to assume some priority in the interview.

In addition to the main body of interviews in United Kingdom institutions, the project recognized the relevance of international parallels and the need to go beyond Britain for usages and meanings of the vocational. The project proposal suggested that

> British attempts to use and understand some of these definitions have international parallels, but also that there are difficulties in borrowing other countries' experience. The United States has a longer history of admitting – and more extensively admitting – vocational subjects (such as accountancy, business, forestry . . .) into the university curriculum. European – notably German, French, Swiss . . . – specialized institutions have a longer and more prestigious history than their British counterparts – even where British counterparts exist. In spite of such historical and structural differences it is important to establish the range of meanings of the vocational as developed in other countries, and to take account of the institutional and curricular differences in which they are visible.

It was therefore decided to include European and American dimensions in the study. In the United States a number of state colleges (in the process of being redesignated state universities) in Pennsylvania were included with particular reference to their business, engineering, or pre-engineering courses, and American engineering education was looked at more broadly. The European study included a consideration of business education as conducted by those institutions in France and West Germany working in tandem with British colleges and polytechnics in the promotion of 'European business studies'. A special study of relevant dimensions of higher education in Poland was also commissioned in order to provide opportunities to contrast a society with different labour-market conditions and different principles of social organization.

Although reference is made to these dimensions of the study, detailed accounts are not included here. Our central concern was to focus on the British interviews and investigate how conceptions of the vocational enter into the everyday practices of teachers and the courses they provide. We were well aware that statements about course intentions did not necessarily describe the realities of courses as experienced by students. Indeed, many of the people we interviewed were at pains to emphasize the discrepancy between intentions and realities. Formal statements of course objectives have frequently been framed to meet the perceived preferences of particular publics, including potential students, institutional managers, funding bodies, and – particularly important in CNAA-validated institutions – the appropriate subject board of the CNAA. More generally, the policy context described in the previous chapter forms a part of the work environment of all those who are responsible for the design of courses. The way in which they describe their courses publicly will partly reflect the messages they hear from the wider environment, but as we have seen the messages from outside are ambiguous and vague. What do staff working at course level make of them?

In the following chapters we describe the concerns of those involved in designing, managing, and teaching degree courses in the areas of study concerned. In the main we present these concerns in the words of the people involved who – unusually for a project of this kind – agreed that their comments need not be presented anonymously. Before we turn to the interviews and to preliminary chapters outlining something of the background of the fields of study, it is important to ask the question – what sort of clarifications might a study of this kind be expected to offer? The hope was not the unrealistic one of resolving controversy or ambiguity, but simply one of making unexamined assumptions more explicit. Such a process is essential if policy at any level – government, national accrediting and validating bodies and other national agencies, local authorities, institutions – is to remain in touch with the realities it purports to represent. Research may affect policy in a variety of ways, according to what it sets out to do, how it does it, and how its procedures and outcomes are interpreted. Research knowledge does not accumulate and have its impact, if any at all, in uniform and predictable ways. It may or may not be listened to – and is therefore itself part of the fluid processes it investigates. What it may do is affect public life 'through its effect on global, diffuse and hard-to-control systems of knowledge and belief'. It influences 'broad assumptions and beliefs underlying policies, not particular decisions' (Cohen and Garet 1975: 38–40). The research on vocationalism, therefore, is concerned not with decisions but with discussion and direction.

Into the discussion came voices which have been heard only infrequently in debates about the vocational. They are informed voices, and it is important that they be heard in deliberations about the purposes of institutions and their courses, about the education and training of students, and about their preparation for entry into employment.

6
Engineering education: a background

The growing nineteenth-century concept of the 'professional' as playing a service role developed also into one of the 'expert'. The marriage of the two produced a relationship and a tension: service, good practice, and 'professional' attitudes were increasingly allied to specific skills, knowledge, and 'mastery' (Jarvis 1983). Preparation for such professions ran parallel with that for engineering, although the problems were not the same. Engineering was perceived as being 'merely' about mastery, about information and skills, about techniques and manipulation. While European and American engineers came more and more to be seen as needing other attributes – personal, academic, and professional – for which preparation and training of some kind were necessary, Britain was slower in the twentieth century to recognize these extensions as possible or relating to the basic processes of higher education. The 'liberal studies' developments of the 1950s and 1960s were an attempt to find a new definition not so much for engineering as for the curriculum which contained engineering. They were almost an acceptance that engineering and the engineer were established, stable entities to which something needed to be added. Engineering was often 'larded with management and liberal studies' (National Council for Technological Awards 1964: 5). Eric Robinson ridiculed attempts to liberalize courses (in technical colleges and universities) by 'adding capsules of culture in the form of literary, artistic and social studies – almost anything will do provided it has nothing to do with science and technology' (Robinson 1968: 77).

The role and status of liberal-studies courses in programmes of engineering education were controversial and their weaknesses evident. Throughout the 1960s and 1970s there was anguished debate about their content and propriety. There were those who thought that *any* subject might be liberal, as long as the *breadth* of a liberal education was being achieved (Adams 1963: 274–8). Some institutions, including Brunel College (as it then was), rejected the 'special subjects' approach to the liberalization of technology, and attempted to construct programmes in which liberal education would be carried by the staff as a whole, including the technologists (Jahoda 1963). If engineering education was too narrow or too instrumental, the questions to be addressed included whether that was necessarily the case, and if so what constituted appropriate balance or breadth? Was a broader scientific or technical base the answer? If complementary liberal studies were the answer, why was the United Kingdom the only country which, in a survey of engineering education covering seventeen European countries and the United States, used the concept of 'liberal studies' in that way (Conference of Engineering Societies 1960: 44–5)? Not that the problem, whatever the vocabulary, was uniquely British. Proposals to marry professional and liberal education in the United States included approaches which recommended 'peppering the curriculum with value courses. By adding courses in ethics or religion or morals, it is presumed, a countervalence to a value-free curriculum is achieved' – an attempted remedy for student disillusionment with 'the skill-oriented, value-empty training so predominant in professional schools' (McCinnes 1982: 214). The widespread inclusion of humanities in technological and engineering courses had led, in one analysis, to the problem of 'transvaluing', of bringing humanities faculties to an acceptance of technology to the point at which a reconciliation of different value systems could take place (Scally 1976).

The range of answers to such problems was visible in the ways in which institutions responded to the greater 'flexibility' introduced by the CNAA in 1971. Some polytechnics, like Sheffield, laid stress in their prospectuses on engineering as a 'generalist' course – civil engineering, for example, being both 'academic and practical' and 'broadly based'. Such a course, including both communication and technology and society, makes no obeisance towards the conception of liberal studies as it emerged under CNAA auspices in the 1960s (Sheffield City Polytechnic, prospectus 1984/5). Lanchester Polytechnic, on the other hand, not only remained within the CNAA definitions, but continued to use them in its prospectus to explain the presence of liberal studies in some full-time and sandwich courses in applied science and engineering. The liberal-studies scheme was intended to introduce students to 'subjects outside the scope of their main subject offered in sufficient depth to provide a basis of knowledge for continuing interest', and 'to provide an opportunity for students from different courses to study together and thus to integrate the educational community' (Coventry Lanchester Polytechnic, prospectus 1984).

Many prospectuses, in introducing combinations of engineering with other subjects (for instance languages, business studies, or economics) emphasize that these subjects are not peripheral to the course, and – particularly following the Finniston proposals – have defined industrial engineering practice, management, and other components as part of the 'engineering dimension'. The prospectus of Brighton Polytechnic is indicative of the group of polytechnics which moved away from the liberal-studies-as-breadth approach to engineering education. The Faculty of Engineering and Environmental Studies introduces its courses as 'unashamedly specialist in nature right from their commencement'. The degrees in electrical and electronic engineering provide 'a design-orientated professional training'. The main aim of the mechanical engineering course is to educate engineers who can overcome the problems of change: 'this course is unashamedly "vocational". . . . social, economic and environmental consequences of engineering decisions are considered sufficiently important to justify the inclusion of a subject entitled The Engineer in Society throughout the course' (Brighton Polytechnic, prospectus 1984). The important point is the emergence of parallel interpretations of engineering education in terms of breadth and specialism.

The range of views and the extent of change over two decades can be illustrated by two statements. An inaugural lecture by E.W. Parkes as Professor of Engineering in 1961 looked in detail at what should constitute the education of an engineer. Parkes's analysis of the features which distinguished the engineer from his fellow scientists included an interest in design and the time spent on decision-making (both of these being continuing emphases in the 1980s). The background to the latter was not simply technological, since it required economic and social factors to be considered. Nor were the results simply technological. The conclusion was that to complete the education of the engineer 'we must take him outside the faculty of science and expose him to the faculties of arts and social science as well'. Such teaching was 'essential to the engineer's education, and it is his courses in arts and social science, rather than those in his own faculty, which stamp him as an engineer, and distinguish him from a mathematician or natural scientist' (Parkes 1963: 17–18). This is an extremely strong statement of the 'liberal-studies' case, but it represents the aspiration of the engineer to a form of completeness which was rarely achieved in practice in the decades which followed.

Twenty years later W.A. Turmeau, Principal of Napier College, was wrestling with the same implications of the preparation and impact of the engineer that Parkes had considered. The ends he postulates are the same: 'society today is affected by problems associated with energy, transportation, communication, manufacturing industry, pollution and with the environment, and engineering education must embrace all these areas of concern'. It is no good, however, 'adding fragments of the study of the humanities or the social sciences to the curricula of existing engineering courses'. Engineering education has sought to provide a broad technological base, and to introduce students to industrial methods and to relevant sociological and economic factors, adding the study of the humanities and social sciences: 'the changes, however, have been perfunctory and fragmentary'. Turmeau's remedy, therefore, has a different emphasis from that of Parkes: it is not just a question of exposing the engineer to courses in other faculties, but rather one of achieving an integration within engineering education. His emphasis, using the experience of Napier College, is on 'integrated non-technological studies'. Whether the solution is this degree of integration, or affirmation of design-based, project-based, unashamedly vocational or specialist courses, it is clear that for at least some engineering educators and institutions the terms of the debate have changed significantly since the 1960s (Turmeau 1982).

Sir Gerald Nabarro, MP and engineer, told a conference on engineering education in 1973 how he had entered engineering untrained, knowing nothing of any engineering process: 'it was all self-taught, at a time when higher education was not readily available. Engineering is, after all, only commonsense' (Goldberg 1973: 6). His definition of engineering, little more than a decade old, would not be credible anywhere inside or outside engineering. Other definitions might stress its scientific base, its manipulation of the physical environment, its outcomes, or the use of resources of 'men, money and materials' (Isaac 1982: 51; Ministry of Technology 1977: 1). As the engineer and engineering assumed a more critical place in economic consciousness, more attention was paid to defining them both. Isaac's portrait of the good engineer, in 1982, included a knowledge of engineering science, an enquiring mind, a creative technical imagination, an ability to communicate, an informed and sensitive view of the environment, and active interests outside engineering (Isaac 1982: 49). Many aspects of available definitions came under attack – with the Finniston Report, for example, criticizing 'the misleading national tendency to regard engineering as a subordinate branch of "Science"' (Committee of Inquiry 1980: 25).

Like teacher education or business studies or town planning, engineering is not a 'discipline'. Courses of education and training 'have been called into being by a professional need, rather than having developed out of the inner structure of a subject' (Lane 1975: 60). The search for an appropriate identity, between the nineteenth-century university world with its emphasis on knowledge for 'its own sake' and the needs of a modernizing society, lies at the heart of dilemmas regarding course structures in engineering education in Britain or the United States. The crucial tension is that between the theoretical (or fundamental, or scientific) and the practical (or applied, or instrumental) which the 'liberal university' had sought to evade or to exclude. In different forms this tension has governed the shapes of engineering and other professional curricula in Britain, as elsewhere, in recent decades and has been at the core of discussion about the vocational (although traditionally liberal areas of the curriculum have themselves also been subjected to considerable change). The engineering curriculum has in addition been pulled in a variety of ways towards and away from a comprehensive view of the social responsibility of the engineer. A presidential address to the Institute of Mechanical Engineers in 1970 echoed the 'common complaint that the applied scientist is made to work so hard that he has no time to think of wider issues', whilst 'in some other faculties the undergraduates seem to have so much spare time that . . . they devote an inordinate amount of it to a consideration of the imperfections in the world around them' (Morrison 1970-1: 54-6). Whatever the difficulties, much attention has been paid to the question of the engineer's 'wider role', and to the position of these 'contextual' insights in the curriculum – as *extensions* of engineering or as *part* of engineering.

The mounting interest in the engineer's social role runs through the literature of engineering education since the Second World War, accompanied by attempts to translate the interest into undergraduate curricula. In 1967, for instance, Thring, discussing the chartered engineer of the future, talked of 'the engineer's responsibility to mankind', and his role in helping to 'steer civilization in the right direction' (Thring 1967: 10-12). In 1975 the Council of Engineering Institutions underlined that training develops abilities which can respond to 'technical, economic, financial, commercial, social and other relevant factors' (Council of Engineering Institutions 1975: 8). By the 1980s there was increasing stress on this range:

> the real challenge for engineers is to optimise the use of resources whilst continually enhancing the quality of life ... the functions of design, manufacture and use of engineering systems need to be established not just as respectable intellectual fields of study but as a corner-stone of engineering education.
> (Turmeau, Grant, and Rankine 1982: 47)

A basic tenet for the Engineering Industry Training Board was that students should be helped to 'develop an appreciation of their wider role in the engineering industry and in society' (Engineering Industry Training Board 1983: 6). One of the most detailed analyses of the content and aims of engineering education, reporting in 1983, confirmed the view of the majority of engineers and those who worked with them that what was needed was a broader, less specialized education (Beuret and Webb 1983a; 1983b).

Debates around such issues fed complex pressures back into the curriculum. There were other considerations – preparation for leadership in industry or in the wider society, for example, raising the question of how early potential for a leadership role in engineering itself could be identified. The Engineering Employers' Federation, for instance, contested the 'streams' proposed by the Finniston Report, and argued that it was not possible to recognize leadership potential as early in courses as Finniston suggested (Engineering Employers' Federation 1980: 2–3). The concept of leadership itself involved ambiguities. Leadership in *engineering* pointed towards mastery and specialization, with concessions to broader contexts; leadership in *industry* raised much wider concerns. The engineer's aim of improving the product, the process, and the profession competed with other professional, commercial, and industrial aims.

The most obvious issue arising from these concerns was that of the range and shape of the undergraduate engineering curriculum. The diverse pressures involved have been recognized throughout the century (White 1906). Possible components in addition to the central core of science and mathematics, have included the 'practical arts' interpreted in various ways, industrial practice, the social and economic sciences, communication, management, design, languages, and other borderline or contingent subjects. Various patterns of training, more or less 'generalist', have emerged in recent decades, reflecting one or another interpretation of student motivation or professional or industrial needs. Within accepted subject areas – for instance materials science – content and purpose have changed, and subject boundaries have become blurred (Diamond 1970). Demand for the inclusion of new subjects has raised the difficulty of omitting or pruning the old. The debates around the Finniston Report have indicated how imprecise have been the aims, and therefore the content, of engineering education. The report underlined not only that technology had in Britain become too synonymous with science, but also that some of the deficiencies in engineers and engineering had to do with qualities under- or unrepresented in the traditional curriculum. In discussions with employers the committee found that shortages 'were sometimes more concerned with the experience and personal qualities they sought than with absolute numbers of engineers'. The committee received evidence of the 'poor communicative skills' of engineers and engineering students, and of their 'narrowness of outlook'. The traditional university emphasis on fundamentals as preparation for future flexibility resulted in students graduating with a knowledge of engineering science and analytical tools, 'but they usually have little experience and skill in their application to engineering tasks as they occur in practice: they are also often without an understanding of the constraints under which engineering work is conducted in practice'. Students therefore needed to have early contact with engineering practice 'within the working environment' in order to identify them with the profession and provide a more coherent base for future activity (Committee of Inquiry 1980: 25, 54, 77–84; Finniston 1984).

Responses to the committee's interpretations and suggested strategies reflected some of this range of pressures, but pursued the target of an acceptable modern definition of engineering education and its goals. A national conference to consider the report expressed the view that there was support for a new system of engineering formation 'which includes teaching courses more comprehensive than present ones, and which recognises that engineering is not merely science applied, but a fundamentally separate activity with its own intellectual framework' (quoted in Battersby 1983: 17). A polytechnic conference to discuss post-Finniston strategies reviewed the basis on which they were to be decided. A paper presented by two officers of the CNAA not only attempted to present the desirable attributes of the engineer but also underlined how courses stultified them. It considered the 'intellectual skills' of the engineer (the ability to communicate, interpret, analyse, solve problems, make decisions, work with others) and their 'activity skills' (project management, market design, production planning,) and suggested that the overall aim should be the 'Citizen Engineer role . . . evident on the Continent' (Warren and Reid 1981: 43–7). Engineering education was being debated in terms both of specialism and of broad range, curriculum shape, and intention.

In recent history, Ashby points out, specialization has come to be associated with science and technology, but, as he rightly points out also, there is no particular or necessary association between specialization and subject (Ashby 1963: ch. 4). The British sixth form and university traditionally produced the single-honours student and supporting structures which the Robbins Report sought to undermine. Suspicion of specialization emerged slowly in the immediate post-war years, but accelerated under the impact of expansion and institutional diversification. In 1954, the Chancellor of the University of London told the graduates that 'having obtained the specialised education which this University offers it is your business to obtain a general education' (Harris 1955: 53). The concept of specialization has aroused controversy and passion. Engineering, some have argued, is no more or less a specialization than anything else (Christopherson

1967: 4). Robinson and others have argued that the really narrow specialization occurs in some of the traditionally liberal areas, and that creative thought is exercised most emphatically in science and technology (Robinson 1968: 72–3). The Duke of Edinburgh carefully teased out the role of specialist training in a broader framework for the engineer:

> The qualities of imagination, enthusiasm and compassion are present to a greater or lesser extent in all of us. It needs the process of a general and liberal education to give them point and direction. Specialist training can give people the ability to make sweeping technological innovations but it needs a broad and liberal education to enable people to foresee the effects of those innovations.
> (Edinburgh 1962: 298)

Most of the discussion about curriculum breadth in engineering in recent years, certainly in the United States, would probably accept as a frame of reference the argument of Lewis Mumford that

> specialised knowledge must be treated as only a part of organised human experience. . . . Instead of over-stressing subject matter and forgetting relationships, we must stress orientation, and make it possible for the student to find his way from any given starting point to every other relevant part of human experience.
> (Mumford 1946: 54)

This is where the argument for breadth has normally pointed. While the starting point for concern about the curriculum may be the product or the industrial or economic need, it leads on to consideration of the 'engineering personality'. In some versions this has led to resistance to specialization (or to over-specialization or narrow specialization) as undesirable or ineffective (Edington 1969; Runge 1963), in others to the promotion of the wider range of curriculum content and outlook. The Engineering Institutions agreed unanimously in their submissions to the Robbins committee in the early 1960s that such breadth was essential, and the Federation of British Industries said the same, seeking to marry vocational education with broader understanding (Committee on Higher Education 1963: pt 1, vol. B, evidence of Institution of Production Engineers and FBI; vol. D, Joint Advisory Committee on Engineering Education). The Royal Aeronautical Society, the UGC, and a host of others have weighed in at various times with similar arguments and demands (Royal Aeronautical Society 1964; UGC 1964). Engineers themselves, it is clear from the Goals of Engineering Education project, share views of this kind: they and their colleagues, the research showed, believed that engineers needed to see engineering in a broader business context, to express themselves, to chair and take part in meetings, to reflect several disciplines – all based on a more practical engineering education. Without proper attention to human purposes and the wise application of skills, engineering would retain the low esteem it had enjoyed since the late nineteenth century, engineering education would remain a poor preparation for the real roles of the engineer, and the personal qualities would be lacking that would enable engineers to play a serious role in the policy process (Beuret and Webb 1983a: 9–14, 22–4; 1983b: 6–8). Engineers were fairly critical of their education, and two comprehensive demands followed:

> The broad direction of change sought is away from a specialised theoretical, academic treatment and towards a more thorough vocational preparation for the profession of engineering. This is expressed as a demand for a broad general preparation for the full range of abilities required of an engineer.
> (Beuret and Webb 1983a: 64)

The important emphasis here is the contrast between specialized and vocational – to practise the profession requires a certain kind of breadth.

Related arguments are legion. Breadth is necessary for flexibility and to cope with the unknown (Committee on Higher Education 1963, pt 1, vol. B: 406, evidence of Institution of Chemical Engineers). Breadth and relevance in training are essential because of the half-life of specialized knowledge (Turmeau, Grant, and Rankine 1982: 48). Skills and knowledge rapidly become obsolete, and should therefore be left to industry (Pearson 1972: 189; Porrer 1984b: 5). Too much stress on 'relevance' may lead to 'spurious vocationalism' (Porrer 1984b: 5), and the emphasis should therefore be on transferable skills (National Advisory Body 1984: 4). The job the engineer does rarely requires those highly specialized skills (O'Flaherty 1969: 5).

In engineering as in other areas of study – and many of the

above arguments might equally apply in, for instance, teacher education, business studies, or architecture – the problem has been how to achieve the breadth, and what to sacrifice in order to achieve it. There have been, in business studies, the same appeals for wider understandings and the elimination of narrow and fragmentary approaches (Fairhurst 1982: 126–7). In this case also, there has been the question not just of over-loaded curricula in a technical sense, but also of what constitutes an appropriate preparation for the 'full range of abilities required', in the context of the human personality and experience. In engineering as elsewhere the question has often revolved around the notion of 'fundamentals', interpreted differently within different traditions of engineering education. The 'engineering science' approach – identified for the Finniston committee by the Engineering Professors' Conference as the one associated with the universities and better students (Engineering Professors' Conference 1978: 30–1) – has priorities different from those of the 'professionally oriented' approach. Many employers, as the Finniston committee found, were critical of engineering education as too theoretical and scientific (Committee of Inquiry 1980: 83), although a report to the British Association for the Advancement of Science in 1977 had emphasized what it saw as a trend in all countries towards a 'fundamental education in engineering', including an agreement that the first half of a degree course should be 'non-specific and designed to give the student a broad base in engineering science' (British Association 1977b: C39). In the 1970s there were analyses of engineering education and engineering science which strongly emphasized the role of the undergraduate degree as an introduction to scientific thinking, resisted the inclusion of the practical and the managerial in the first degree courses, and considered the possibility of 'engineering education' becoming postgraduate, based on a broad undergraduate curriculum of pure and engineering science (Chilver Committee 1975: 26–7; Calderbank 1973: 60).

Questions of range and balance therefore break down into curricular sub-questions subject to debate and controversy. One example is that of relevance. Here, as in other areas of higher education, the concept has been commonly used but elusive. A number of studies have shown that in recent decades there has been a strong undercurrent of student expectation that higher education will have direct or indirect relevance to career intentions (Marris 1964: ch. 2; Silver and Silver 1981). Disentangling the dimensions of relevance has, however, never been easy. Oakley pointed out, for example, in relation to the planning of specific polytechnic courses, that relevance has to be considered differently in 'academic', 'vocational', 'interest centred' or 'project based' courses (Oakley 1973: 14). Course relevance relates to the activities of the engineer, or to roles as perceived by employers – and it is clear that industrial employers have a variety of interpretations of what they consider relevant to their operations, basing their recruitment on criteria often far from those associated with immediate relevance (Pearson 1984: 35; Roizen and Jepson 1984). In 1984 approximately one-third of all vacancies for graduates were described by employers as being for 'any subject' – and the percentage was increasing (Central Services Unit 1984a; 1984b; Porrer 1984a). Relevance, within the engineering curriculum and elsewhere, remained a difficult concept to handle, and its utility in analysing the vocational has been doubtful.

A second example is the pressure in engineering towards the inclusion of management and business in the curriculum of undergraduate engineering students. The argument has frequently been in terms of postgraduate management courses, but the demand for an undergraduate contact with management, economics, or related areas has grown. Sir Denis Rooke stressed 'the importance of teaching technological and basic business skills as an integrated experience of undergraduate studies (Rooke 1982: 128). The Finniston Report was cautious about them, and critical of the new, enhanced engineering courses as including 'a substantial component of business topics and engineering management plus some required experience in industry rather than the extension of engineering practice which we wish to see' (Committee of Inquiry 1980: 86-7; Jobbins 1980: 8). The Institution of Mechanical Engineers had three years earlier expressed the view that business studies should be included in training – but with two conditions: they should be presented by practising mechanical engineers from industry, and they should not be at the expense of basic engineering studies (Institution of Mechanical Engineers 1977: 56). In these as in previous respects the wider world was intruding into the curriculum and altering the basis on which engineering had been defined in the past. The vocational, as it applied to engineering education, was being reinterpreted.

The curriculum solutions sought for engineering education have included ones of central importance to any discussion of its 'vocational' or 'liberal' or other characteristics. Not least has been the attempt to emphasize engineering as essentially a problem-solving activity. One of the motivations for finding new approaches to the curriculum has been the persistent criticism of existing courses as incapable of promoting some of the qualities required in the inventive, imaginative engineer, the 'citizen engineer', the 'humane technologist'. Alongside the critique have run parallel and urgent analyses of the needs. The authors of *The Humane Technologist* pointed out that technology has depended on 'the juxtaposition of imagination, free-ranging curiosity, and inquiry' and 'disciplined implementation of patterned instruction' (Davies *et al.* 1976: 151). The classic American statement of technology as action, driven by those kinds of forces, was Lynn White's *Machina ex Deo*, which more than any other analysis of recent decades has highlighted the humanistic function of engineering, designating engineers as the chief revolutionaries of our time, who promote new humanistic concerns and give to established humanists as much as they take from them (White 1968). It has not been easy for engineering education to respond to such imperatives, but the accent on problem-solving has been one response, and a related emphasis on project work has been another. The problem-solving approach developed particularly strongly in the 1970s, partly as a way of encouraging students to operate both as specialists and as members of an interdisciplinary team. In some institutions the project became the grand finale of the various learning processes, in others it was an early and regular introduction to the realities of engineering problems. A General Education in Engineering Project report on projects was critical of early attempts at liberal and complementary studies, and emphasized instead the range of skills and knowledge and integrating activities involved in project work, promoting engineering not only as a professional study, but also as an 'exciting, worthwhile and useful education' (Goodlad 1977: 3–8; Armstrong *et al.* 1982). There were those who were critical of projects as exercises for assessment, riddled with weaknesses of preparation and analysis (Harding 1973), but at the University of Bath and elsewhere there were committed attempts to define the objectives of project work, to plan it, to enable students to see what were the challenges, the constraints, and the purposes (Black 1975; Cowan and McConnell 1970). The intention was to promote such attitudes and skills as initiative, co-operation, communication skills, awareness of the organization of knowledge, and sense of responsibility.

The shape of the curriculum, the content and nature of the education, and the recruitment of students, have been clearly determined by the image of the engineer. The low status of British engineering has to some extent related to the image of engineering as torn between science and craft (McCulloch *et al.* 1985: chs 8 and 9). The portrait of the engineer as 'homo faber' has been a particularly British one (Glover 1980: 27) and the components of his activity as traditionally seen in Britain have been either unflattering or misunderstood, or a combination of both and more. Nabarro's engineering as 'commonsense' is a view from the inside mirroring a longstanding view outside the profession. Attempts to recast the curriculum have gone alongside attempts to enhance professional status by widening the role of the engineer in industry and society (Turmeau, Grant, and Rankine 1982: 47).

The image of the engineer has therefore been governed by old notions of the craft identity of his work, on which more recent versions of competencies have been superimposed. The image as widely perceived has contained little of the exciting vocabulary of the Duke of Edinburgh's or the GEEP project's characterization. Personal development aims have not been accepted as serious components of an engineering education (Jenkins 1983: 7). Yet employers and others have complained of the weakness of graduates' interpersonal skills, and various research analyses of employed engineers' reflections on their undergraduate experience underline their and their employers' concern about the lack of emphasis on personal qualities (Laycock 1978). One reflection of the felt need for such an emphasis is to be found in a recruiting leaflet issued in 1980 by the Institute of Civil Engineers. It contains a set of guidelines regarding the 'O' level examination base that school pupils should consider acquiring:

> English, mathematics and physics are obviously essential; chemistry and a foreign language desirable, and because a civil engineer has to understand the world around him, geography, history, art, economics, and environmental studies are valuable extras. Sport, music, and drama can help you to get on

with other people as team work is an important feature of civil engineering.

(Institute of Civil Engineers 1980: 7)

Similarly, at university level, the early efforts of Birmingham University's electrical engineering department to promote discussion groups and the like were aimed at producing 'a certain calibre of man' (Tustin 1950: 267). Here, as elsewhere, the nature of an engineering education, its school base, its undergraduate components, its assumptions about the appropriate characteristics of an engineering graduate, were being redrawn. Beuret and Webb found a considerable emphasis on human and social skills (Beuret and Webb 1983b: 8), and the concepts of personal skills and personal relations appear frequently in the engineering literature of the 1970s and 1980s (Council of Engineering Institutions 1975; Engineering Industry Training Board 1983).

Related to such concepts have been many of the elements discussed above – communication, social and economic studies, professional responsibility, for example – and particularly the project as a method of undergraduate work, a way of approaching what the authors of *The Humane Technologist* discuss in terms of interactive skills, the ability to motivate colleagues, and perceptive interpretation of large numbers of people as citizens and customers (Davies *et al.* 1976). The implementation of strategies to promote such characteristics and skills is complicated by the characteristics of students on entry. Past definitions of engineering have tended to build on the known personal characteristics and quality of entrants. In 1977, the Institution of Mechanical Engineers considered that student quality in Britain was lower than that in the United States and other EEC countries (Institution of Mechanical Engineers 1977: 57), and there has been widespread discussion in recent decades about the reasons why engineering has failed to attract the higher-quality students. The nature and quality of students, their school experience, their personalities and expectations, do not define the purpose of an education, but they do help to explain some of the intentions of those who have designed and run engineering courses, and the characteristics of the courses themselves.

Some of these issues, raised in the literature of engineering education and reflected in the history of engineering in Britain, were explored in this study by examining course histories, and in the interviews which related to them. Although some of the courses studied contain the word 'technology' in their titles, and some of the discussion relates directly to the study of technology and its implications, it is with the range of courses generally understood as 'engineering' that we are concerned here. Many of the issues discussed in terms of vocationalism in engineering courses point also to questions of concern in business education and in other areas, and are followed up in those further discussions in later chapters.

7
Engineering education: courses and explanations

Humberside College of Higher Education

Engineering

A part-time BSc in Engineering started at Humberside in 1980. Four years later the course was approved for honours also, and became a BEng. The 1984 submission, agreeing with the Finniston, GEEP, and other findings, underlined that many new graduates, trained to enter careers in research and development work, were in fact employed in the application of engineering in industry, transforming ideas into hardware or services, operating within the constraints of 'scientific knowledge, engineering techniques, available time, cost limits, problems of manufacture or construction, the state of the market and the competence and willingness of the work force'. There was an insufficient number of degree courses 'with a broad engineering approach which reflects the needs of many practising engineers'. The college therefore defined as the major aims of the course:

(i) to provide a sound academic education in the fundamental principles of electrical and mechanical engineering;
(ii) to provide a knowledge and understanding of present practice in electrical and mechanical engineering;
(iii) to develop initiative and imagination in the solution of engineering problems;
(iv) to develop the applications skills required by a professional engineer;
(v) to develop an understanding of the role of the engineer in industry and society.

The vocabulary of this statement will recur throughout the course histories and interviews – 'fundamental principles', 'practice', 'imagination', 'skills', and the 'engineer in industry and society' – and particularly 'problems' and 'problem-solving'. Recent submissions to the CNAA, prospectuses, and statements by the engineering institutions and the Engineering Council echo concerns with application, a broad, basic foundation, and an awareness of the engineer in the wider world.

As elsewhere, Humberside also itemizes in its statements some of the characteristics it seeks to promote in engineers and the relationship between its own endeavours and the future employment of its students. The sandwich element, the industrial training, built into the course (in this case during the second and third years) is seen as a particular vehicle for the development of the student's 'personal abilities and skills, e.g. self reliance, judgement, the ability to communicate and work with others, confidence, and sense of responsibility'. It introduces the student to the world of work, helps to develop interests, and provides a clearer picture of career opportunities. The 1984 course description emphasizes the roles of 'design and manufacture' and 'engineering systems' as integrating subjects, the importance of a 'cross-disciplinary approach', and the development of 'a systematic, logical and creative approach to the solution of applications and problems'. Breadth, an 'economic and industrial framework' through 'management and organization', and the aim of coherence through specific topics and especially the project in the final two years of the four-year course, are all emphasized. Attention is paid to teaching methods, with the earlier years conforming to 'traditional tried and tested methods revolving around lecture, tutorial and laboratory sessions' – given the need to transmit information efficiently, to reinforce understanding and to teach facility in analytical techniques. The 'supportive' and 'coercive' (the word is in the submission) relationships are then relaxed, and the number of case studies and problem-solving assignments increases. Students on the honours course are faced with less well-defined problems, require greater skills in problem identification, and have to accept greater responsibility for the learning process.

THE COURSE LEADER (DR TATE) thought that the aims of promoting initiative, imagination, and an ability to solve problems were achieved particularly through the course in design, which was 'the subject that helps to integrate the rest of the course', and those subjects, notably in the final year, in which students were asked to solve real problems derived from local industry and consultancy work: 'We tend to wrap our course around real problems and case studies'. *Given the high information content of the course, when do students begin to think for themselves?* 'Right from year one. We try not simply to concentrate on the information content of the course. The syllabuses are really very flexible, in that we attempt to incorporate the information required to solve the problems set.' *How do the students react to the stress on problem-solving right from the beginning?*

> They are generally speaking very 'anti' at the beginning.... During the first term they are very anti-experimentation which is a problem-solving exercise, unlike traditional laboratory work.... The students are given a very basic statement of what is required, and freedom to use and adapt the equipment available. In effect they are thrown in at the deep end, and often get upset and frustrated. They are not led, but encouraged to question 'What is?' and 'What if?'... generally speaking, they are made to think for themselves, which they do not like.

He thought that the students settled down by the end of the first year and enjoyed it, and by the end of the final year they appreciated the importance of the experience.

Given the breadth of the course, there was a problem about achieving what the submission describes as a coherent course, 'not a collection of isolated Electrical and Mechanical Engineering topics'. The course tended to be coherent amongst small groups of lecturers (experimentation feeds into design, materials technology into design . . .). By the third year the student began to feel it was all coming together, after the industrial placement, which puts 'everything into perspective'. The project was crucial in this respect, together with the assignments in the final-year subjects: 'if somebody does an assignment on control, then it will tend to pull in some design and some electronics for example'. The project embraced all aspects of the course.

Does the problem-solving pull against the 'coercive' information needs? The question had to be seen in the light of the quality of students who were relatively weak when compared with those attending universities and some polytechnics. This made remedial English and mathematics necessary for a number of first-year students. Their knowledge and understanding of physics might not be at an appropriate level, which could cause some problems. Confidence was, however, built up, and a BTEC student, for example, who previously had been used to 'spoon-feeding', could experience an initial shock, but by the second year he would have learned how to learn. Importance was attached to developing learning skills, and attention was paid to teaching methods, 'though not all staff seem to appreciate the need'. Although discussion of teaching methods did take place, there was no formal, college-wide scheme of support: 'I came from Oxford Polytechnic, which was my first teaching post, and I found that the Education Methods Unit there... was excellent, and very supportive towards staff. We do not have a similar system.'

Do the course content and contact hours mean that criticisms of engineers as 'narrow' people (engineering students had little time to do other things) were true? 'I still think it's very true. Sad.' *Do employers worry about that?*

> Some employers do, some not.... The issue that concerns me is that some professional bodies like the Institution of Mechanical Engineers emphasize the importance of schoolchildren being culturally well provided for, yet suggest substituting technological subjects for humanities.

How much discussion is there by students, how much questioning? At the end of lectures, he felt there was little feedback on anything other than engineering. Within the lecture theatre, the laboratory, the workshop, the amount varied according to the lecturer. He personally tried to take account of current events, preferring not to give a 'straight' lecture, and welcoming opportunities to develop discussion.

The industrial placement helped. Students were prepared for the placement with discussion, advice, check lists, documentation, and in many parts of the course lecturers made use of the experience afterwards. Those teaching operations management, engineering appreciation, design, found it 'difficult to work without it'. *In what sense, then, can the course be described as 'vocational', given that the term is often used to imply narrowness, a lack of critical ability?*

> It is a vocational course which is broad based, and emphasizes the 'application' of engineering.... However, it is not as

all-embracing as I would like to see it. Engineering is not simply about problem-solving, but should take into account the wider implications of what we do.

The 'engineering appreciation' unit was important in this connection, and every member of staff teaching on the course was responsible either for giving a talk or finding an external lecturer (for instance, a lawyer on industrial law). Some of the desired change that would 'more meet the needs of industry than our present course' was, he underlined, constrained not so much by the CNAA as by the Institution of Mechanical Engineers, and the information requirements it imposes.

Against the background of nineteenth- and twentieth-century debate about the purposes of higher education, and the long time it took for engineering to be accepted as a legitimate higher education (interruption: 'It's still a question as to whether it's been accepted') *what is the purpose, the justification of the course?*

> I look at it from this point of view – how can I justify engineering as a career for a prospective school leaver? ... I am frequently asked by parents about engineering as a career ... and it takes time to explain the wider view. At the present time, schools of engineering place emphasis on the traditional subjects, rather than trying to assess engineering ability at the point of entry, although this is beginning to change. It is important ... to enrol the more able, all-round, student, which may be possible if the subject range, considered to satisfy entry requirements, is widened, as is often the case for other professions.

THE PRINCIPAL (DR EARLS) commented on engineering in general, not on engineering at Humberside specifically. *Where is engineering now in a discussion of traditional liberal/vocational dichotomies? Do engineers see engineering as a modern liberal education, or as essentially different from a liberal education?*

> I think quite a few people who organize engineering courses would like to think that engineering was a fairly liberal type of education. I don't think it's easy to defend that position ... it's taught very much as a linear progression from one set of circumstances to another set of circumstances, where it's deductive, it's reasoned, it's progressive, it's hierarchical, and so on,

and I think one of the deficiencies of engineering education is that it doesn't have the ingredients of lateral thinking.

Nor, he believed, did it have some of the 'unbounded environment' of the social studies, where there are multiple solutions to a problem, the most *appropriate* depending on another set of circumstances which are 'political, economic, sociological, cultural, and so on'. The engineer tended to be brought up to think there was one good solution and the rest were inferior – his job was to find the good one:

> if he is careful he will progress inevitably, inexorably, towards a good solution. So in that sense I don't believe it's a good liberal education.... An engineer tends to have what he assumes are a set of given, valid facts and he doesn't have to, if you like, question his starting point.

Pressures on engineering education included demands – from Finniston and GEEP for example – for more intellectually able people, and from industry for graduates to be more immediately useful. The more generalized courses of the 1940s and 1950s had been supplemented by new courses more narrowly technical, covering a narrower range of concepts (electronic as against electrical engineering, control and instrumentation as against electrical, and electrical as against engineering science):

> This produced graduates who have narrower horizons, in a sense ... their intellectual versatility has been reduced in some ways, although the content in a depth sense has become much higher ... a deeper attack in a very much narrower spectrum. ... In some curious ways this has maybe been appropriate because the students who do courses at polytechnics are as a piece intellectually less able than students who go to universities, in terms of 'A' level scores, and I think many of us believe that the narrow course is the one for them, the less able student, and the broader course is the one for the more able student.

Britain had not followed the American route of postponing a lot of the specifics to postgraduate courses, partly because the narrower focus had suited many colleges and universities, and partly because of the lack of a strong tradition of postgraduate education.

The fact that more able students taking, for example, engineering science had a more versatile base was a commentary on the type of student rather than the course. One attempt at 'liberalization' was the CNAA's 'Principle 3' (which had required a balanced programme of studies aimed at 'the development of the student's intellectual and imaginative skills and powers') and its attempt to introduce 'contrasting or liberal studies', which had been 'a terribly artificial way of meeting an identified problem: it was a totally inappropriate and singularly, catastrophically inappropriate method of ... patching on something that might be called liberal education'. Few engineering courses in fact, tackled the social role of the engineer ('they might make a passing gesture by trotting in a sociologist'). The problem was partly the people doing the teaching – 'they are themselves enthusiasts about their own technology or their own specialism' – so the system was trying to produce a type of product that could not be produced from the available ingredients. The danger of producing culturally or intellectually isolated people was not greater than in the case of, for example, mathematics or zoology, but

> I think you have to go back to the type of people who study engineering. They tend by and large to be the more introverted type, the type with a narrower range of interest.... You mustn't always simply look at the process as being at fault, you must also look at the raw material.

Where does engineering stand in relation to the curriculum of higher education, which has accepted mathematics and science into its cultural definitions, but not so readily engineering? Dr Earls found this unacceptable, since the 'non-vocational' was taken to include law and medicine, which in fact pointed directly towards careers: 'I don't believe that the curriculum of a lawyer or the curriculum of a medic yields that much wider a view of role than would be true of the curriculum of an engineer'. There was no difference in purpose between the curriculum of an engineer and that of the scientist or mathematician, or even the theological curriculum – though it might be wider. There could not really be any significant difference from that of the dentist, the vet, the medic. Discussions of the differences between a vocational and a liberal, a general or a professional education were 'fairly substantially' about differences amongst students rather than curricula ('that doesn't mean that the curriculum couldn't be improved').

Leicester Polytechnic

Engineering Technology

The polytechnic submitted a scheme for a BSc/BSc (Hons) in Technology in 1978 and it began in that year. The 1983 proposal for a renamed course, a BEng and BEng (Hons) in Engineering Technology, set out the general aims of the course with only minor adaptations from those defined in the earlier submissions:

> To provide initial preparation for professional work as an Engineering Technologist in industry with specialist knowledge in one of the four areas defined by the Post Foundation programmes.

> To provide education in problem identification and solution, where problems may involve science and technology, human factors, economic and social factors and communication, but without requiring early specialisation.

> To provide an environment conducive to personal development.

The second of these aims echoes some of the Humberside terminology, with a more explicit reference to 'communication', and spelling out professional and personal goals which are implicit in the Humberside statements. The more detailed objectives set out by the Leicester course relate to a variety of attitudes, skills, and knowledge, including the 'ability to think logically, in quantitative and conceptual terms, to analyse situations and problems critically and objectively, to postulate solutions creatively and to make independent judgements'.

The 1978 submission talked of its being a 'problem-solving education', and built in to the 'broad based technological course' a measure of specialization in one of four 'vocational activities': engineering design, operational engineering, systems engineering, and energy utilization. A degree of coherence was to be achieved by a scheme of 'integration studies' and 'project work'. 'Balancing studies' included human geography, the English legal system, economics, and sociology. The more recent course has dropped the 'balancing studies', partly because the original structure, which incorporated a diploma in higher education and sought to attract students without the usual science 'A' levels, has been changed, after a disappointing response. The programme now includes 'balancing modules' for all students, including 'industrial organization and administration'. Foundation studies include 'industrial economics' and 'integration studies' which, taken together with other studies, 'are believed to satisfactorily provide for the realisation of the general education and integration aims at this stage'. The general-education role continues to be supported in later stages by studies 'requiring broad multi-disciplinary approaches'. The course aims at 'a graduate who possesses technological competence with an appreciation of the complexities which surround the application of technical knowledge in the real world' – in the spirit of the issues highlighted by the GEEP project (which was based at Leicester Polytechnic). Projects, case studies, and a variety of teaching methods are emphasized in the submission.

THE COURSE LEADER (MR RUE) explained that the Leicester commitment from the beginning had been to applications. Beginning as an external London degree, part-time, the course had been based on engineering science. It was then transferred to the CNAA, which was re-examining engineering degrees and emphasizing their vocational aspect:

> We were very keen on that, having seen that the London-type degree worked well with our part-time students because they'd got industrial experience, but would not be really appropriate to the student we wanted to produce. So we started off with the idea that as far as we could, recognizing that you've got a core of engineering science that you have to cover, we based the whole thing on applications. And we actually started at the output end. . . . We started off by saying – what sort of jobs were our students going to do? That defined our four programmes . . . actually vocational areas. . . . It was far easier than we envisaged to develop a core base of a year and a half, and then still allow them to diversify into their vocational areas for the final year and a half [the Leicester degree is not a sandwich course].

With falling demand for specialists for research and development departments in industry, the course had sought to produce graduates who were 'much more vocationally orientated, but had a broad perspective, who . . . knew something about design or knew something about the total field of operations, rather than perhaps the narrow field of production engineering'. The course had been designed with specific exercises in mind to develop logical thought and abilities connected with problems and solutions, but it had also set out ('somewhat glibly') to permeate the course with them: 'you have to get an attitude developed in the student . . . one of the main philosophies of this course was to broaden students, to get them more flexible'.

Not all students were responsive and motivated on entry, he thought, but some developed increased motivation, even as late as the third year. Many coming on to the course needed a year or so to 'realize what's going on'. The problem,

> ironically, is that we made the entrance broader to try to attract the broader student. The trouble with the broader student is – he's taken his broader 'A' levels because he doesn't quite know where he's going, so you almost have to accept that some of the broader students are not quite as well motivated as those that have decided they're into technology at sixteen.

One of the difficulties of discussing teaching methods and their effectiveness was that 'we're having the same raw material . . . the output might change but you have to recognize that you're working with the same raw material'. The students have acquired the same type of 'A' levels, been through the same sorts of teaching situations. Now they had to acquire more information (the BEng had meant the incorporation of more material), and changes, albeit slow ones, were having to take place: 'we do role playing for instance, we do much more computer aided, we use the computer where we can to demonstrate things'. There was a slow swing towards student-centred activities – but in terms of 'A' level points and previous experience, however desirable it might be, 'you can't radically change your basic material'.

Attempts had been made to ask if there was a different way to present information or reduce material, but unfortunately, and even with the modern technology, 'there is a very hard core of scientific, basic knowledge that students have to know in engineering . . . it's a slow, drip drip process. . . . There's also a number of very hard conceptual things that you need to know before you can ever approach any real engineering problem.'

Contact hours were longer than desirable. *If students have little or no time for other things, is the course inevitably producing narrow engineers?* That, he considered, was one aspect of the situation, but there was another:

> This student has been brought up on not doing art and geography and history and the things that get them out. They've been brought up on maths and physics and chemistry, where you sit in a lecture room, and you sit with your apparatus ... you don't need to mix with people, and I'm quite convinced that the average student in technology has gravitated towards technology because he doesn't like people – that's an extreme statement but there is something about our students that discourages them from taking part in student union activities for instance – one is time, but I think the other is character.

In some cases students worked in pairs on projects, in others individually. In the former case they were teamed on the basis roughly of one student who had come through the 'A' level route with one via technician courses, in the hope that this would have some educational benefit. Group case studies brought students into exercises with local industry – energy surveys of buildings, swimming pools, factories, robotic surveys – within given, broad briefs, but involving original thought. Individual projects required students to show depth in an area, but especially the ability to see the particular problem in context – and they give a twenty-minute 'presentation' before a group of at least three people (supervisor, second reader, industrial contact) but possibly other staff and students. Throughout all of these projects and case studies there was explicit emphasis on written and oral communication skills. *What, then, is the answer to the accusation of narrow vocationalism?*

> I realize that we are missing out on some areas of 'education' in inverted commas. . . . I as course leader would not like to think that the course is totally geared to mass-producing people for engineering, full stop. . . . I run this thing called 'integrated studies' . . . and while I won't say we go as far as going to archives and things, we do try to force them slightly broader, and certainly into social interactions.

Does 'force' mean there is student resistance?

Oh yes, again, students don't want to know about the environmental effects of what they're doing, for instance. The role playing we do is a public inquiry ... centred on something basically technological – we're doing the Channel Tunnel this year, for instance – it will be concerned with the technicalities of it, but it will also be concerned with social implications, environmental implications, transport, economics, ethics. ... In a way I don't have to force students to do that, that they find quite interesting. ... I've brought in sociologists and others to talk, and it is difficult for us, without quite a bit of working together, to see each other's viewpoint, because we do seem to be in different worlds.

Students did not argue and question a great deal, however, because in a sense there was little to argue about, and the students' background was such that they did not debate a thing because 'a) you don't know enough about it, and b) factually, you can't debate it'. There was some constructive debate while students were working on group projects, particularly in design. The proportion was different: on many other courses 70 per cent of what students did might be debatable. In a subject like economics students could be faced with questions like: 'You can prove anything by statistics, can't you?'

That obviously infers that they've had discussions about this sort of thing. Our engineer's answer to that would be: 'yes sometimes'. Full stop. Because he wouldn't think it was worth discussing it any more. He knows what numbers are. He knows what they can do. He's not philosophical. In our courses we spend 70 per cent of the time taking factual information down. So it's the proportion, it's what the students are used to.

It was a sad fact that students might sometimes be discouraged from discussing because there was material that they had to get through.

Is the course vocational, and if so, in what ways?

I think in two ways. One is that it reflects what actually goes on in industry, as opposed to what goes on in a textbook, and secondly it does impart certain manual skills that can be directly applied on the first appointment in industry. ... In that way it does fall in with the arts definition of vocational, because they say that their courses are all vocational because they finish up with manual skills.

The difference was in the industrial applications.

Textile and Knitwear Technology

Leicester Polytechnic's BSc and BSc (Hons) course in Textile and Knitwear Technology took its first students in 1971 on a course which had a modular structure. The reorganized course approved by the CNAA for a 1977 start was structured around a series of 'subjects common to all students', plus 'additional group studies' with an industrial placement in the third year of the four-year sandwich course. The aims of the course as defined in a 1985 course document were:

(i) to develop in students ability to retrieve and correlate information; think critically and logically; make informed decisions; and communicate clearly;
(ii) to provide a sound education in the fundamentals of textile and knitwear technology and to make students aware of the scope and limitations of the methods employed;
(iii) to sustain and stimulate the interest of the student in order to provide a firm basis for continuing education and to develop the ability to adapt to changing circumstances.

One of the 'general objectives' of the course was defined as the provision of a 'well-balanced vocational education through the study of knitwear and related technology', with an emphasis on literacy and numeracy, with a specialism in scientific, managerial, or aesthetic appreciation, and with an ability to appreciate 'the dynamics of industry with the thrust and flexibility to adapt and innovate'. 'Introduction to the textile industry', one part of the course, touches not only on the industry itself and its social and economic importance, but also on its history, the sociological context of fashion and textiles, the psychology of colour, and the roles of the technologist and designer. Many of the components of the course have a substantial information base, some – chiefly 'management science' and 'industrial organization and administration' – emphasize a case-study approach, and others underline the importance of investigation, problems, and projects. The final project is described as 'an extremely important part of the course and enables the student to apply the techniques and knowledge gained during earlier study'.

THE COURSE LEADER (MR WILLMORE) saw the first aim (correlating information, thinking logically . . .) as informing the course generally. The basic science, maths, and statistics – including textile science – were presented in the first semester, and the applications of that knowledge became a natural progression throughout the course. Students found it easier to establish a participatory, questioning role if a good 'class identity' was established. Since they were all together during the 'induction semester' they felt 'sufficiently relaxed to ask questions and participate'. By the end of that semester 'they know where they're going . . . perhaps they've even changed their mind' and people commented on the change in their confidence.

How easy is it for students to be responsive, given the heavy information load and time demand?

I suppose that depends on the style of lecturing. . . . If you just fire facts at them with very little discussion then there is no time, but we try and have a tutorial system, tutorial back-up. . . . I like to, and certainly other classes . . . try and stimulate discussion, and to talk around a subject . . . the way to get through the work is to give them some printed handouts, and then talk through the handouts, and I guess most other people use a similar kind of system.

Is there dialogue, questioning, as in many other subjects?

Yes. It would be rather different of course because we have a very high practical content, and a lot of this dialogue perhaps would take place in the practicals. Some of it would take place in class . . . we try to design it so that [the practical] runs more or less in parallel with the theory classes, and of course that's the ideal opportunity because the students then are totally relaxed.

The course submission talks about a 'well-balanced vocational education' – what is the significance of 'well-balanced'?

I think to some extent some of these terms are quite nebulous, but I suppose well-balanced in the sense that it contains all the elements of textile technology . . . this is why we do the textile science in the first year, so even those students who don't have a scientific background know what polymers are, and how polymers lead on to yarns, yarns lead on to fabrics, fabrics lead on to garments, finishes, clothes, design, and so on.

The specialist options dealt with other areas – personnel management, industrial relations, plus management economics, finance. Under the previous, modular structure students have found the course more fragmented, and it had now tried to become more integrated – the same member of staff, for example, teaching textile testing, textile fibres, and maths and statistics.

The emphasis on the practical, he indicated, meant that students were not just in theory classes and were not just seeing machines demonstrated; they were rolling up their sleeves, getting the spanners out, and using the machines. They actually produced something which was all their own work. Students could spin yarns, they could enter competitions for fancy yarns. They had a design project to complete at the end of each academic session, something they presented and had externally examined. In the first semester students working in groups of three (ideally a design student, a management student, and a technology student) had a design project to solve and had experience of working together and learning from one another's strengths. The word 'communication' in 'design/communication studies', implied the intention that students

> actually talk to each other, but also that they communicate what they achieve to us. They write a report, where they first of all summarize what they attempted to do, whether they did it and how successful it was . . . but also how they communicated with each other.

There was also a formal component of communications: in all subjects there was a course work element – a case study, a report, a practical dissertation, or a seminar. The topic of their final-year dissertation was negotiated during their third, industrial year. Whilst on placement during that year, they gathered information, explored possible questions, sought advice on worthwhile topics. By the beginning of their fourth year they pretty well knew what they were doing – it was something they were interested in and it became 'a joy, or it should be a joy to actually try and achieve something in that area'. By becoming an expert in the area they were also enhancing their career prospects:

> I think that it is a better reflection of a student's ability to first of all set out right at the beginning with an idea and see that idea reach fruition and along the way there are all the peripheral things that are involved in the project – they've got to liaise with members of staff, secretaries, they've got to meet the demands and the deadlines.

Are these students any different from others in higher education?

> I'm not necessarily looking for high academic flyers. In fact you could almost say that high academic flyers and practical ability are almost mutually exclusive. People that are good with their hands, are able to be both creative and also able to translate those ideas into positive end products are quite rare . . . a rare breed. Obviously there is a minimum set of grades that I'm looking for . . . people that have an interest in textiles . . . that shines through at the interview.

All the students entering the course were motivated to enter the industry, 'virtually in every case. There's perhaps one or two who want to be textile teachers maybe ultimately'.

There has been discussion for 150 years about higher education being for self-critical members of society – does this course match the criteria for that sort of higher education?

> An education rather than a training, I take your point. . . . I think it's got to be a combination, ultimately we've got to supply industry with graduates that can do the job, that's what the students want, they want to get meaningful jobs in the industry, that's what industry wants, and I guess it's our responsibility therefore to meet the demands of industry, and to some extent they say, 'we want people who know the technology, not that just know the principles . . . [know] what the machines are capable of doing, what the limitations are'.

Is the course, therefore, a vocational course, and is it what some people might term 'narrowly vocational'?

> We're trying to educate our students. We're trying to say, 'these are the facts, these are the limitations, these are the capabilities, these are the parameters in which we would ask

Engineering education: courses and explanations 109

you to work, now go away and think about how to relate these things, how to improve it possibly, what your comments are, what are the limitations that *you* think are implicit or explicit'.

Unlike students on arts courses, he emphasized, these students were relating information to an industrial environment: 'we are not encouraging them to go away and be metaphysical'. In some respects the process was the same, though in this case the message was: 'it's vocational'.

Napier College, Edinburgh

Napier College was the outcome of a merger in 1974 between the Edinburgh College of Commerce and the Napier College of Science and Technology, and it transferred to Scotland's central-institution sector in 1985. It is not unlike other Scottish non-university institutions of higher education in being debarred from developing courses in the liberal arts, and in concentrating on 'vocational courses' (STEAC 1985: 55–6). The college reported to the CNAA at its institutional review in 1981 that it had continued 'to develop vocationally orientated degree courses, with inter- or multi-disciplinary curricula'. The sentence, 'most of the courses at Napier College are vocationally orientated', is a permanent feature of its prospectus. Although the courses discussed below are comparable with the ones in the English polytechnics and colleges, it is important to remember that Scotland has different traditions and structures of schooling and higher education, and in particular that Napier and similar institutions operate in a different institutional and policy framework.

Communication and Electronic Engineering

A BSc in Communication and Electrical Engineering was approved by the CNAA for a first intake in 1976. Proposals to add an honours component were approved to begin in 1981, and the degree was converted to a BEng as from September 1985. The 1980 submission, for implementation in 1981, described the programme of studies as being designed 'to provide for the development of the intellectual and imaginative skills and powers of the student and to stimulate an enquiring, analytical and creative approach'. Three aims were specified for the degree:

(i) to provide an education in Communication and Electronic Engineering at degree level based on a broad foundation of fundamental principles of Electrical Engineering Science;
(ii) to give some insight into the behaviour of industrial organisations in a changing environment;
(iii) to produce graduates who are attracted to a sector of industry which can offer relevant and rewarding employment.

The honours degree would provide students 'of appropriate calibre with a deeper and more rigorous understanding of subjects particularly relevant to the Communication and Electronic Engineering industry ... to have a greater awareness of the applicability of the subject matter and to demonstrate conceptual abilities of a higher order'. Different parts of the programme stressed the broader context (organization studies), final year 'investigations' (in which students faced, among other things, the need to curb excessive enthusiasm and apportion their time judiciously), and the importance of communication.

By 1985 the three stated aims had been extended to five, with the additional aims of providing an educational foundation 'on which a progressive and continuing education may be built during the student's career after graduation', and of providing 'a programme of engineering applications which enables new graduates to make an immediate and lasting contribution to the solution of engineering problems in industry'.

What was presumably an error in the earlier submission had now been corrected: graduates were no longer to be *attracted* to a sector of industry, but *attractive* to it. The application to transfer to a BEng degree recognized the emphases in the Finniston Report on applications, management, and organization as a contribution to 'the engineering dimension', and communication, and all of these were given greater prominence – as was design.

THE COURSE LEADER (MR RAE) described the course as broad (in engineering terms) at the beginning, becoming fairly specific, with the accent on communications and a supporting role by electronics. For a student to address the problems of communications adequately, it could not be 'diluted' in a general degree. A student was not a fully-fledged engineer by the end of the fourth

Engineering education: courses and explanations

or fifth year: but through the course and its supervised work experience what he obtained was 'a good idea of what's going on ... how to apply the stuff that they do here'. Since 1980 the aims had become more elaborate and specific:

> What's happening is we're demanding more of ourselves and the students, trying to do it in the same amount of hours – which is one of the problems ... in the BEng submission a lot of emphasis was on applications. ... What we've tried to do is move it, keep some of it in the syllabus content, but also move it more into the laboratory. ... They've got to make more decisions.

Students did have to get to grips with a great deal of very specific information in a broad field, some through lectures, some through documentation, and in tutorials, laboratories, and engineering applications. Lecturers from industry took seminars on practical problems, their solutions, and the technology. Students were active, involved in decision-making in the laboratories. On a design exercise they had specifications, 'work in groups, talk among themselves, come to a decision ... get all the detailed information and they just carry it through'. On different kinds of projects they worked alone or in groups. The group experience was important and was deliberate, knowing that it paralleled what took place in the work situation, and

> pressures are on us from the outside bodies to look at group behaviour as well ... one of the problems of group work is identifying what the individual's doing ... you don't have to get the groups to be too large, because you're always going to worry that somebody's going to sit back and not bother. ... On our mini-project our largest group would be four. Doing lab work ... an exercise must be done in three hours, we hope to work with groups of two. ... With the mini-project which lasts a few weeks someone might be responsible for putting together some drawings for it, and you might not need to do anything until the second week ... but you must listen in in the first week ... and there might be somebody who's going to build it, and somebody else is going to test it ... you're learning from the group activities what actually goes on

Is fostering of 'intellectual and imaginative skills' a responsibility of the whole or specific parts of the course? Students might not be expected to be creative in all subjects, he stressed, but they needed to be 'enquiring and analytical' throughout. While exposing them to all the fields, you might expect them to be creative in some. In lectures they were encouraged to question, 'find out why we're saying something'. The analytical basis lay in students' being set problems and having to solve them. Creativity came in an area like a project, which they enjoyed doing and wanted to be creative in.

Is the emphasis on the creative and the analytical the answer to outsiders who think engineering and technology are 'narrowly' vocational?

> As an outsider I could say that all you do if you go into history is history.... You try first of all to expose them to the field ... that's the first objective of the course ... to get them to understand what the actual field they're in is about ... you must tell them what's there and why it's there and get them to do dissertations and background reading to try and find out why something occurred in a certain manner ... when it seemed obvious it should do it another way ... and then from that expand it into techniques that hopefully when they come to an unknown they can apply ... to try to solve the problem.

Communication was an integral part of the course, and had been adjusted in the new programme 'to try and meet the requirements that Finniston was asking in a course outside the sort of skills required of what you'd call the standard engineer'. Exercises like case studies, projects, and assignments of various kinds helped students to pull things together, especially in the later years – including the work on the major project which is

> a technological project.... We expect them to be able to take this specification and produce working models ... design, hardware, software ... collate and produce a report, and put it all together in a report ... he also gets interviewed during the first term [of the final year], and he presents a talk in the second term on it, to his peer group plus members of staff.

He believed problem-solving occurred in various ways, but explicit preparation for problem-solving and decision-making was a minor part of the course at present, with attempts being made to integrate it into management and organization and elsewhere.

How much questioning and challenging do students actually do? They challenged in class and seminars, they did discuss. It was not a matter of writing on the board and saying 'take it all down'. The trouble was that other fields of knowledge required questioning and challenging as 'a prime function of their mind':

> The prime function of a lawyer is to be inquisitive and analyse and look at the background information. . . . I'm not saying that for an engineer that's not a prime function, but he's got a lot of other things to take over in his actual work than the major decision-making role. . . . When an engineer leaves a course, should he walk into an industry, take major decisions, etc? I don't think he can . . . in the early years it's very difficult, because they're frightened to say in front of people . . . it's in these years that you're trying to convince them – you must ask. If it's a stupid question – it's not stupid if you didn't understand it.

Is there discussion about the role of the engineer? Not as a syllabus. In communication systems or digital transmission, for example,

> when you look at the syllabus it's all technology, the words are all to do with engineering. However, when I'm in the class – now this is where the difficulty comes in – saying what the course is actually *doing* . . . discussion that's taking place is the implications of what we're actually talking about, the implications of sort of foisting technology on people, and looking at the role they could play.

What did not come out in the documentation about the course was the 'flavour of engineering' that was present, which was being aimed at while still 'satisfying a special need' and course-content requirements.

Is the course vocational, and if so, in what sense?

> I think I've got to say *yes*. It *is* a vocational course, it's satisfying a specific need in industry. I would say the vast majority, I can't say all . . . get jobs in communications, in communication engineering . . . the point about the vocational aspect is that it is seen to be directly satisfying a specific need, that's the point. That doesn't stop you using all the other techniques that other courses use . . . to be enquiring . . . what you're doing is channelling what the enquiry's about.

Is students' time so committed that they can't do other things?

I think that's still a problem on engineering courses. It was a problem when I was at university. There was nobody in engineering when I was there who got involved with anything to do with the students' union or extracurricular activities . . . most of our lads get involved more in sports than the other activities. . . . I don't hear anybody complaining that they wish they had more time to take up a particular interest.

Energy Engineering

A BSc in Energy Engineering was approved by the CNAA in 1980, and converted into a BEng unclassified and with honours in 1984. The 1980 scheme was not unlike the Communication and Electronic Engineering degree in its broad aims – to produce an engineer with an 'enquiring, analytical and creative approach to problems', with a knowledge of the fundamentals and applications of mechanical, electrical, and control engineering, understanding the economic structure of industry and 'financial methods of measuring performance', taking a wide view of the energy implications of an engineering project, and acquiring the skills necessary to analyse and design complete plant energy systems. There was an emphasis on skills and creative problem-solving, the broad base of energy engineering, 'which crosses the boundaries of established disciplines', and the importance of different approaches to learning. An important change in the definition in 1984 was to extend the aim of 'an enquiring, analytical and creative approach' to problems to one of 'problem definition, analysis and solution', involving a more explicit reference to 'an awareness of the commercial and business objectives of an industrial company', and 'an awareness of the role of the engineer in society'. The addition of honours meant the inclusion of a project in the fifth year. The move to greater laboratory and practical work led to an emphasis on continuous assessment.

THE COURSE CO-ORDINATOR (MR BANNISTER), on secondment to the Scottish Vocational Education Council (SCOTVEC) at the time of the interview, confirmed that the change to BEng had meant only a slight change in the philosophy of the course, especially in its later years, though the course had already been oriented towards engineering applications, as witnessed by the group assignments towards the final year: 'the emphasis is very similar to what it was originally'. It was a broad course, 'not an easy course', and the students had some difficulty piecing together at the beginning what it all meant:

> We spend a lot of time at the beginning... trying to tell them what the course is about, and invariably out of maybe 30 or 40 students you get one or two who find they're on the wrong bus as it were... sometimes they get this impression of energy being alternative energy – looking at solar energy, wave energy and things like that, and this course is not about that.

The ones who were on the 'right bus' still found it difficult at first:

> because even when you get through to the second year, and sometimes even in the third year, they're still saying – 'Why are we studying such and such a thing? What's the relevance of this?' – you have that on a lot of the courses anyway. On interdisciplinary courses you do have that problem. It takes a while for them to get the idea, some catch on quite quickly – the ones that have sort of a broad view of life catch on quite quickly.

'Energy studies' was included in the first year with the specific aim of giving students 'the broad picture':

> They look at all the energy sources, and they look at the wider view of where energy is used... where you can get energy and what you can do with it... an interest generator... the first year we had that in the course we overdid that... they were tending to get carried away with that subject and leave the others.

Energy studies was taught by a combination of engineering and business-studies lecturers, including an economist. *Do the students see economics as part of the course, or as something separate?*

> The economic side of it is emphasized throughout the engineering side. We keep emphasizing the point that it's all very well making this thing technically feasible, but it's got to be economic... reinforced in all the other subjects... What we're leading up to is a project in the final year.

How much note-taking is there, how much information from lectures?

He thought there was a tendency to less note-taking, 'in fact we're getting off this business of note-taking', though some lecturers used old-fashioned techniques. The trend was towards 'letting them find out', and he believed students really did get to grips with the problem-solving that was emphasized in the course aims at the end of the first year. Before students went out on their skills training period they did a skills project. Even in the first year they designed and made something. The 1984 scheme emphasis on solutions was reflected in work the students were doing in the first year, and in the later group project. Project work, with students working in groups of different sizes and alone, was spread across all years of the course. Right from the start they were not merely absorbing information, but designing and making, working on complex energy analyses, demonstrating creative ability.

Where do they develop their communication skills? 'This is a big problem. They should pick this up all the way through, in all the lab work they do. . . . There isn't a subject called "communications." They did written and oral reports, particularly in the third and fourth years, did group assignments, role played – for example with the staff acting as a parent company and the students as a board of directors – and they had to report: 'so it's a sort of traumatic event for them, having to speak in front of their colleagues and in front of the staff'. In the fifth year under the new scheme it was intended that the project would make a major contribution to bringing everything else together.

Do students argue with each other and staff, engage in dialogue . . . ? Not so much, he felt, in the first year when they were in need of guidance, though they did in the period of preparation for the skills training.

> In the third and fourth years this comes out more than in the first and second years. . . . Particularly after their industrial training period they'll argue. That changes them. After they've been out in industry . . . they've been in the adult world, and they've had to argue with adults. In fact if you go and visit them in industry, you're liable to get – 'This place is a load of rubbish, they're doing this wrong and they're doing that wrong'.

Is that confidence one of the strongest arguments for sandwich courses? Some people said that the students went out as boys and came back as men. He did not think it was quite like that, but there was in fact a tremendous change. *And are students too occupied to take part in other things, as in the past?*

> It's still the same, I'd reckon. Very few of them – there's the occasional odd one that'll take part in the students union . . . but not like the arts student. They tend to have their heads down in lab reports. I don't think they want to, and they're not that way inclined. The political scene they want to avoid . . . sport – that's okay, but union activities . . . very much less than arts students.

Students even had to have their arms twisted to attend lectures on engineering by outside speakers.
Is it, then, a 'vocational' course?

> A difficult question. . . . It depends what you mean by vocational. Does it suit them for a particular job? If you take vocational as that, and he does have this feeling in his mind that he's not only getting a job, he's getting a worthwhile place in society.

Do you use the word 'vocational'?

> No, I tend not to, in fact, because it tends to be a sort of in-word educationally, but . . . I would use it in the sense that he's going to get satisfaction out of this job, he'll get respect from – well, he may not, engineers don't get respect from the rest of the community. . . . He'll be doing a worthwhile job in society . . . and fulfilling for himself. . . . We're very conscious that we educate them for a job and a position in society.

A 'liberal' education once implied a gentleman, and a 'vocational' education dungarees – are you arguing that division no longer makes much sense?

> That's right. One of the things we try and emphasize is that when you solve engineering problems you've got to be careful that you don't just create other problems . . . you've got to be aware of what an engineer would call engineering and society. . . . There are certain ethics, right and wrong, of the result of your engineering skills.

But students did not really talk about these issues, only some of the 'far-thinking' ones. *People argue that you don't get enough of those?* 'That's almost like saying you don't get enough *good* students'.

Technology with Industrial Studies

The BSc degree in Technology with Industrial Studies was approved by the CNAA for a 1975 start, was approved for honours four years later, and as a BEng in 1984. The 1979 submission emphasizes the aim of producing graduates who, 'through studies of both technology and industrial studies, will be able initially to take up technological positions in the fields of engineering and manufacture and a wide range of management services and who will be capable of proceeding at a subsequent stage in their careers to positions in management'. Society increasingly needed people 'qualified by the nature of their inter-disciplinary studies to deal effectively with the implications and consequences of technological, sociological and economic changes', and the course set out to produce graduates responsive to those challenges, and adaptable to the career changes they would face – to be flexible enough to cope with 'new responsibilities, new functions and new jobs'. The thematic subject of 'manufacture' was introduced in that year as the principal means of 'ensuring coherence and integration of the degree curriculum', and an 'integrating assignment' in the final year furthered the same end. By 1984 the aims of the course were being itemized along the lines followed by other Napier courses – an 'enquiring, analytical and creative approach encouraging independent judgement and critical awareness', a broad course of study, encouraging the ability to reason logically, communicate clearly, and read critically, understand principles and their application, understand 'financial, commercial and business objectives', and appreciate industrial relations and industrial and social change. For honours students there were greater intellectual demands and the need for original and creative thought.

THE COURSE CO-ORDINATOR (MR GLEN) underlined engineering applications as the main change in the translation to a BEng degree. It was difficult not to treat these as discrete and a lot of effort was being made to spread these activities across the curriculum, including design. An attempt was made in the first year to relate the industrial studies and technologies, which began by seeming remote from each other. The interdisciplinary emphasis was difficult to achieve in the student's early years:

> What we do in the final years (the existing BSc in this is similar to the BEng) is to run student-centred activities called course weeks, and this is where they get a typical industrial problem. They work as individuals or in teams and it's not just the technology they have to sort out – they have to sort out the economics, the costing, marketing.

There were two of these in the final year, one emphasizing the technology, the other biased more towards management and economics.

Contact time, he indicated, was quite high, but students spent much of it in effect working on their own, with total hours per week falling to about fifteen in the final year. The students' main problem was the management of their work load, 'whether to concentrate on their course work or concentrate on lecture and tutorial material, to consolidate that – sometimes there's a conflict'. Students were presented with real problems, often quite open-ended and 'requiring a good depth of analysis'. *Do students understand the interdisciplinary, integrating aims?*

> What is happening really (remembering the BEng is still only in its second year) is that on the mainstream courses like maths, computing, manufacture and technology, we're still building these up as skills. In design we're making an attempt to use these subjects in an integrating role.

Students did a product assessment and analysis, looking for example at hair driers of different qualities and price ranges, dismantling them, looking at the technical points, at the marketing and retail outlets, and trying to get figures on sales. The project (replacing 'integrating assignments') served the same purpose. *How does the course actually stimulate creativity, independent judgement...?* On traditional university courses in engineering, which are or used to be engineering science oriented, engineering problems came late, if at all. That way, students developed skills of analysis and synthesis, but creativity was not developed at all – hence the importance of the course on design,

> where we do very little lecturing ... because all the foundation work has been done in other subjects so what we're saying to

> them is that we're giving them open-ended problems, and this is broadening the outlook ... think as broadly as possible about all possibilities and then focus in on a solution to the problem.

He explained that there was nothing in the course labelled 'communication', but groups had to make presentations to the whole class, often using overhead projectors and slides. They were retrieving information, using a library, learning to work in groups. Preparing to go out for a period of 'skills training' they were asked to design something, to do proper drawings ...

> They do all the design activity here, all the paper work ... in a way performing an engineer's role, because this is what an engineer does in industry, he talks to other people, he comes up with ideas ... the machine shop chap will say 'we haven't got a machine that can handle that size of material. . . . ' This is what they get used to until they come up with something that they're actually going to make, and they make it ... they find that very often they have to make modifications.

In this way students realized that the different parts of the course belonged together.

In tutorials in some subjects there is a lot of discussion and debate – is this true of students on this course?

> In fact the industrial studies people make a very strict point of that – they want tutorial groups of round about eight ... to get this dialogue. . . . In design this goes on all the time ... there's a lot of work to be done by the student there and tutorials as such are more guidance to ... help think through the problem. . . . Each subject has its own methodology. . . . They're questioning all the time, very much so.

Is there a difference between these aims and those of a traditional 'liberal' higher education?

> We're trying to get some sort of balance between being too focused in on the technologies at the expense of the broader issues, the sociological implications, the economic considerations. . . . Engineers should not be simply concerned with solving technical problems, they should be much broader based and be in charge of the money for a change – to see where the funding should go.

Some of the words used to describe course aims were 'terribly general' – so that when CNAA visiting panels came they asked: 'What exactly do you mean by that? How are you going to implement that?'.

Students gained confidence and breadth by, for example, facing a viva with the dean of the faculty on their project, by their experience of industry on their placement, and by the research work taking place which 'rubs off on the students, as it should'.

THE PRINCIPAL (DR TURMEAU) had previously published views about the ability of engineers to comprehend the position of modern man, perhaps even better than those in the arts and humanities. There was a particular logic, he explained, about the engineer and the way he thinks that was very different from social science, for example, often 'without any cognisance of what's going on in the outside world'. If, however, the engineer could be taught

> to recognize the outside and the consequences of what he is doing ... which is what we have done with a lot of our courses, to bring sociology and psychology, ... accounting and management into the courses, if one can do that ... if one can have this precise logic and, if you like, mechanical mind – it is a mechanical mind, a very logical, sequential type of thought process – if you can have that as the centre piece which is capable of appreciating all the sociological and economic and psychological aspects, I think that provides a very, very sound management capability or decision-making capability ... a very sound basis for somebody who can aspire to higher positions. ... That has not happened in the UK, it has happened in other countries.

What some courses have tried to do was simply add 'a bit of management' on the end of the final year.

Would the word 'liberal' be a description of these engineering courses?

> No, I wouldn't use the word 'liberal', I don't like the word 'liberal'. ... The word we've been using is 'broad-based' – it's not a very good word. ... A lot of people would argue that we should give them the mechanics of the course here and they'll then go out into the outside world and learn all these things, but I don't think that's the case. ... It took me a long time to

> get to the stage where I realized that ... people were more important than machines, that the human being was by far the most complicated machine of the lot.

Is there really a difference between an engineer aware of the social implications of what he does, and someone in the humanities who becomes, say, a teacher?

> Yes, the reason I think the engineer ... can sometimes give a more balanced opinion than fairly traditional people ... [is that he has] a more balanced view and can come back to the nub of the problem. ... Sociologists and economists get carried away ... and they don't know where the centre is. ... The engineering mind or the radical mind for that matter, or even the scientific mind, can always home in and usually see what the problem is.

Finniston, he thought, went too far in the stress on practice, which was fine in the shape of sandwich experience after two or three years of a college environment, but was a waste of time at the beginning: 'Young people need to work out, I find, some kind of self-discipline, they've been under the control of a school, ... of parents, they find quite a change when they come here.' A later industrial placement could influence the teaching, because by then they could benefit from the experience, they would know something about the jobs they would be doing in the future, know how to talk to people.

One of the advantages of a college like Napier was the ease of crossing department boundaries – in universities departments were 'all-powerful'. If engineering in the college wanted service from a department of economics, for example, it got their top-line people.

Are there critics saying 'vocationally oriented' undergraduate education is not really a higher education at all?

> I know the argument and it's one that I would not accept, it's one that we don't accept here. You can use all sorts of vehicles for education, you can use the liberal vehicle and you can use the vocational vehicle as well – that's the one we happen to think is best ... an educational process can go along many tracks ... the vocational one, where the education can benefit and widen the person's mind, give them new horizons in terms of thought and learning ... but at the same time provide

Engineering education: courses and explanations 123

them with a background of information which could be useful to society, not just themselves . . . and that would be our definition of vocational.

Some might argue that a liberal education points towards a diversity of employments?

We've had students who've gone into the publishing business, into public relations, all sorts of things – and not necessarily going straight into engineering jobs. In that sense the education is being used as a basic education. . . . I think the reason that engineers tended to become engineers is that . . . they're fairly dedicated people.

People use the word 'vocational' disparagingly: is the liberal/vocational distinction at all useful?

I don't think it is very useful. The words don't mean anything any more, and they're used so much that I think they've become meaningless. Certainly, they've changed their meaning over the years. . . . Liberal studies is a dirty word around most educational establishments. Vocational tends to be used in the wrong context . . . vocational in our sense . . . is an education which recognizes the way the world operates.

Oxford Polytechnic

Engineering

A BSc in Engineering was approved by the CNAA for a 1974 start, and replaced a BSc (Eng) honours degree of London University. The degree was extended to honours in 1978. The course was redesigned and resubmitted in 1981 and 1983, and again in 1985 as a BEng, unclassified and with honours. In 1974 the aim of the course was described as being 'to produce graduates having a broadly based education who are prepared for professional careers in electrical and mechanical engineering and can qualify as professional engineers without further academic study'. The course had been designed 'to develop the student's interest in the technological and sociological aspects of engineering'. Creativity, the formulation and solution of problems from real situations, communication and the 'role of engineering in the development of civilisation', and of the engineer in society and industry, all featured in the statement. Design, manufacturing processes, management, and 'the professional engineer' were part of the curriculum of this three-year, non-sandwich course. By 1983 the aims were stressing breadth ('a firm foundation for a variety of careers in engineering'), a critical approach to studies, basic principles, the 'management of the financial and human considerations in engineering', the applications of knowledge, communication skills, and 'an awareness of some of the present and future problems facing engineers'. Analytical skill and competence in solving engineering problems were stressed. The 'sociological' aspects were now de-emphasized, and engineering practice was more strongly emphasized, broadly reflecting the aims of engineering applications as defined in the Finniston Report. Here and in the application to transfer to a BEng there was a commitment to 'engineering awareness', as well as to the knowledge base, skills, and competences needed by an engineer. A course report covering 1982–4 included among the changes 'the formal presentation of Engineering Awareness lectures to first year students by industrial speakers', and emphasized that 'various elements of the course aim at integration of subject matter and relating the different areas to each other through design studies, project work and application exercises'.

THE ACTING HEAD OF THE ENGINEERING DEPARTMENT (DR BREMBLE) stressed the escape from past traditions of engineering courses which had gone down an 'intellectual route', relying on the measurement of students' intellectual ability, degrees, and qualifications. It was now important to understand how to make use of knowledge and intellectual capacity to tackle open-ended problems in the real world: 'in the past we have asked people to solve problems, now we are asking them to formulate problems at the same time and then to solve them, and that's probably more difficult'. Historians, for example, might also be concerned with strategies and techniques, but they were not producing solutions in the real world. Project work, case studies, design, were integrative elements, pointing to connections which in the past had come up only accidentally:

> We really do go down the route where we do say it's vocational, we do tell people that 'you're going to be engineers at the end of it', but we really shouldn't be saying that. We

should be saying that 80 per cent of our students are going to be engineers at the end of the day, but it really is a tremendous training to do other jobs as well. . . . If you've trained as an engineer you'll be able to handle yourself better in the real world than if you've trained as a historian.

When students *apologized* if they had decided not to go into engineering then they had got the wrong impression, 'we really ought to try to break out of that straitjacket'.
Has the BEng narrowed the course, with more emphasis on producing engineering automata?

No, I don't think that's right at all. I think it's broadened out their perspective and it's broadened out staff's perspectives in that we are having as staff to talk to . . . other disciplines so that we can interact and interrelate with them, and we are also giving students much more freedom to pursue problems in the way that they would want to pursue them.

Laboratory work in the past, he suggested, had required students simply to back up theories and write a report, but open-ended design-focused problems make students think a lot more and work together. *Some courses in the earlier programme have been dropped – is that repackaging, does the material get followed through in other ways?* 'Communications' had been dropped in the first year, on the assumption that it was happening in other parts of the course – that had been a mistake, and it might be reintroduced. 'Engineering and civilization' and the civic role of the engineer, also dropped, were probably not being picked up enough in other parts of the course, and it had probably been narrowed down to some extent in that respect. Too much time was still spent in communicating information, but 'I have a feeling that it is changing, and that we need to cause it to change more so'. Conditions and funding were forcing a change in the direction of less formal approaches to teaching, but there was still a fair way to go: 'we're a very entrenched, very conservative bunch of people'. *Some people might not expect engineering students to disagree, argue, engage in controversy as much as students in the arts and social sciences – would that be true?*

That's an overstatement, I think of the situation. It does happen, and it's happening more, as we cause more open-ended problems to be tackled, as we cause students to define their

> own problems.... I accept that by and large they will go down the direction in which I will direct them.... One of the basic problems, one of the basic constraints, is that we are looking ... at a science where we are producing artifacts at the end of the day, and the opportunity for argument is less, I would have thought, than it is in other areas where people have opinions.

The course had to satisfy the CNAA and the profession, two pressures for slightly different things. The conservatism of the profession itself said 'you can't be an engineer unless you know this, this, and this'. The Engineering Council had pointed to the existence of a lot of obsolete material which was not necessary, and had urged more computer-assisted learning and self-teaching packages. An advantage of working through the CNAA was that

> we have to sit down with people from other departments when we have our various visits and we push each other along. ... I am becoming more and more convinced that [peer review] has tremendous value and it worries me that if we don't have that sort of thing happening, if you like from the CNAA, we won't do it very well for ourselves.

Are you doing something 'vocational'?

> I'd say yes, we are doing something basically vocational, and 80 per cent of our students would see that we are doing something vocational.... The aims of our particular course are fairly broad. ... I have just been looking at another course ... where they are much more specific about identifying the particular role of the engineer that they would be producing, and they make no bones about the fact that they are producing engineers at the end of the day.... We had the Institutions in fairly recently, and they said 'it would be easier to see what the aims of your course are if you were more specific about the particular role that you see your students undertaking when they go into industry', and I ... would be inclined actually to ... argue against that, and say 'yes, it's vocational: we are really wanting to produce people who can go into a variety of jobs within engineering.... We are wanting to make them think ... at the same time as providing them with the opportunity of moving into a career outside engineering. Basically we are vocational.

But not 'narrowly vocational'? The course did not explicitly prepare people to go in other directions, but that was something that was happening, and needed to be addressed. And it was not true of students going into engineering jobs: 'we are producing people who are better able to expand into engineering. I don't think there's any question about that'.

Civil Engineering

The CNAA approved a BSc in Civil Engineering Construction in 1977. In 1983 this became a BSc, undifferentiated and with honours, in Civil Engineering, and in 1985 a BEng. The 1977 submission pointed out that the preparation of graduates for both design and production roles had become more difficult as a result of technological advance and increased design complexity, and the Oxford course was therefore primarily concerned with the preparation of students for the production sector:

> It aims to develop mathematical and scientific abilities, and an informed and creative approach to the technological, economic and managerial aspects of construction work. It also aims to develop the student's awareness of the impact of construction work on the physical and social environments and his capacity for making informed environmental judgements in the ordering of his professional activities.

Communications and surveying featured in the first year, 'environmental and integrative studies' in the second, and the latter continued, together with a project, in the fourth year of this sandwich course.

The general aim defined in 1983 was 'to provide a sound education in the fundamentals of civil engineering with an emphasis on the process of civil engineering construction', based on a thorough understanding of scientific and technical principles, human resources, organizations and systems, and the legal, economic, social, and political environments in which organizations operate. The specific aims included an understanding and experience of engineering design and construction, an understanding of the principles and techniques of management, the development of the power 'of logical argument, an imaginative, open-minded and questioning approach to problem solving and an enthusiasm for independent learning', and an awareness of the need for good communication. In 1984 the Joint Board of Moderators of the Institutions of Civil, Structural, and Municipal Engineers was told that a discrete subject of 'communications' had disappeared, but that the material was covered by construction practice, in which communication skills were to be developed in relation to topics 'directly related to civil engineering, at an early stage'. Environmental and integrative studies had been redesigned and reduced, but continued to play a vital role. Ninety-five per cent of the graduates entered civil engineering on completion of their course.

THE HEAD OF DEPARTMENT (MR MORRIS) indicated that transition to the BEng had made little change, given that the course already had a higher practical content than many traditional courses. The four-year course was a preparation, and the Institution would not expect any graduate to be 'fully formed'. Employers, however, liked graduates to be as useful as possible from the start – and how much so depended on which side of the industry:

> The contractors, who actually build what's been designed, like graduates to be immediately useful . . . normally that relates to site skills with instruments, and so on – the capacity to read drawings and interpret them . . . and transmit information. . . . Consulting engineers, on the other hand, expect a certain basic quality of academic understanding. . . . A lot of consulting engineers, I think, take the view that in that highly professional environment, where a graduate is surrounded by seniors who've gone through the same processes, the in-house learning is easily accommodated. But with contractors, I think very often a graduate engineer may be the only graduate on the site.

The sandwich experience made a great deal of difference: 'they're only too keen to graduate and get back into a job that's permanent'. At graduation students felt themselves to be 'partially formed engineers', which might not be true of non-sandwich graduates.

'Construction practice' now included much of what had been 'communication', but it added to it an element of introductory material on the industry and on certain technological processes. Students learned communication skills within the groups in which they worked and they had leadership roles to act out.

Within the department there was a general belief that all subjects in the first year, and in subsequent years, needed to be vehicles for enforcing communication skills. In the past,

> students felt that the first year of the course . . . was too wholly academic, that it was to do with engineering science. It was to do with materials science . . . mathematics, statistics, computing, and the only really practical skill that they started in that first year was surveying, and they couldn't really identify what they were doing as having any great significance for the profession they aspired to.

In the second year, 'engineering and the environment' (replacing 'environmental and integrative studies 1') brought together a variety of historical, technical, and professional material, and in the final year an 'integrative studies project' brought together the main core subjects 'in an interlocking manner'.

The course aims use words like imagination, questioning, open-minded – aren't those aims for all students on all courses?

> I think what we've suggested there is probably the general view now in most engineering courses . . . whereas I doubt whether it was even considered as being a sensible aim of the course thirty years ago. . . . There was a fairly rigorous view taken that they had to extend their skills, in certain numerate subjects particularly, and then develop them in discrete packages, and then go out into whatever job they were going to do and make use themselves of those packages. In fact you can't begin to integrate subjects of the sort on our course in civil engineering without introducing some historical background as well, which is liberal in a sense, and without relating the problem-solving they might do to technical subjects. . . . Some staff are fairly rigorous tunnel-vision engineers who have no vast imagination but a lot of knowledge of their subject. . . . But we have a fairly good team of engineers in this department, several of them are liberal.

Students normally had good motivation, and they needed it – first because the course was demanding academically in terms of time ('engineers are second to medics I suspect') and they had to commit themselves to a lot of time in lectures, labs, practicals, and seminars compared with 'some more liberal studies'. They had to get stuck in quickly – 'there's no honeymoon period'.

Secondly, construction was not as profitable an industry to work in as it had once been: 'the palmy days of the fifties have gone and the old days of the Raj have gone as well'.

Laboratory-based students did not have as many opportunities to take part in other activities. At Cambridge, on a 'narrowly mathematical' course,

> we were booked for twenty-four hours a week, 9 till 1, Monday to Saturday (plus work in the drawing office).... Partly because of room availability I suspect... we couldn't practically programme [our students] to have all their lectures, say, in the mornings... the only free afternoons are Wednesdays ... most of them then probably feel they've got project work to do.

The important period for the project was the final year, with experimental, laboratory-based inputs and a substantial report. The 'integrative studies project' was one for which the scenario was generally but not always produced by the staff, this year looking at a redevelopment scheme for a town-centre car park site, which at one time used to be a canal basin. Students visited the site, examined historical photographs and drawings, and role-played at different stages of the development project over two terms.

THE INTEGRATIVE STUDIES TUTOR (MR SMITH) explained that in the normal traditions of an engineering discipline students had studied subjects in relative isolation from one another:

> One of the purposes is to try to integrate these through the project, so that they can actually see the interaction between the different subjects they have studied. Another is to practise potential engineers in the planning, design, and construction of a project from its inception through to completion. So in one sense it's a design project... in the very broadest of senses.... We try to include at least one external person to be involved with the subject each year... usually it's a civil engineer but this year we had a city planner.... They are taken through week by week with specialist staff... putting the students in a position of having to respond... we commonly adopt role playing.... To be honest, there are a few who find it tough – those few tend to be the ones that are

Engineering education: courses and explanations 131

less imaginative and perhaps whose industrial training experience didn't give them the breadth of view that one would have liked.

This experience included the writing of reports and letters, feasibility studies, and obtaining information. Most of them enjoyed it, 'because they can see the reality of it'.

Do you use the word 'vocational'? The head of department agreed that they did:

Yes, we use it. Not always happily because of certain inferences, but it's inevitable it's going to be used in the institution, as is the concept that there are pure academic courses in the arts and sciences, and there are also within the institution vocational courses like architecture, estate management, town planning, civil engineering.

The course has the necessary breadth for the field, but is it also limiting in certain ways?

Yes, necessarily so, though sadly. I think students are now required to be more prepared for employment than our generation was. Even so this course is less narrow than mine was, but it would be exciting to broaden it still further. But would it then attract students, I wonder?

Commentary

The interviews focused on a number of areas which suggested how the concept of 'vocationalism' related to courses, their content and purposes; students and their characteristics; teaching strategies; the influence of the world outside – employers, the engineering institutions, the CNAA, the recommendations of the Finniston Report. Comparisons emerged with other subject areas and with university practice. The strengths and limitations of courses were visible. Against the background of the extensive course documentation (in addition to CNAA submissions there were course handouts and outlines, statements for accreditation purposes, publicity material) the concern with course aims and their implementation was prominent and explicit.

One range of explanations which produced variations of emphasis was that which was concerned with the students themselves: with the particular characteristics, backgrounds, and limitations of engineering students; the qualities required of engineers and the nature of an engineering culture; the career patterns of graduates – their immediate and longer-term needs and roles; the students' 'cast of mind', capacity for logical thought, creativity, and imagination; their willingness and opportunity to take part in debate and controversy; the nature of any differences from students in the arts and humanities.

A second area of interest, in the context of CNAA and professional body requirements, was the emphasis on practice, real problems in a real world, the ultimate outcomes in terms of artifacts and designs and professional involvements, and therefore – in terms of courses – the emphasis on experience and applications, problem-solving and decision-making (and the formulation of problems, and the particular importance of open-ended problems). There was often a feeling that Finniston had made less impact on the public sector than on the universities, because in terms of problem-solving, applications, and the 'engineering dimension', the public sector was already well down that path.

The aims of courses as set out in submissions for validation and in explications by staff related generally to the promotion of desirable qualities and skills, as well as to preparation for employment – normally interpreted with a breadth which included some aspects of the civic role of the engineer, some aspects of management or economics or business, social and psychological considerations, and environmental and ethical issues. The pattern of involvement of these aspects, alongside technological and 'engineering science' (rarely in these cases called that) and other competence-related areas, was not uniform, and in many cases there was an expression of regret that a course did not do more in these respects – or in the field of communication. Older, discrete approaches to some of these topics had in many cases been abandoned for more diffuse forms of 'permeation', and almost always with an eye to integration across the wide range of subjects included in these broadly based, interdisciplinary courses. Integrative strategies (which also called for student qualities of independent work and judgement, and frequently the characteristics needed to work in groups) have been assuming greater importance – for example with the use of case studies, individual and collective projects and assignments, and the clearly articulated importance of design. The sandwich element of those courses which were constructed to contain such an extended period of industrial placement is presented as not merely an important experience in itself and as clarification of employment opportunities, but also as contributing to final year teaching and learning strategies.

The limitations which some interviews underlined in terms of student previous learning or personalities also entered the discussion of staff/student contact hours, and the willingness or ability of students to take part in activities outside the engineering course. That they rarely did so (with the occasional exception of participation in sport) was seen as a result both of the course and its demands and also of the students' personalities and commitments.

Generally speaking, the dichotomy expressed in the past in terms of liberal *vs* vocational won little support. 'Liberal' was used only sparingly in interviews to indicate a measure of breadth beyond the traditional frontiers of engineering. 'Vocational' was used to suggest preparation for jobs, but in all cases without accepting an inevitable implication of narrowness or a closed mind (though one interview did strongly underline the narrowness of students and the course as at present described – with relatively poor-quality recruitment and the need to remove some constraints on course structure). Many of the interviews rejected 'vocational' as a useful or usable term, and those that did accept it often drew attention to the difficulties of using it. The overwhelming impression given by those interviewed was of a conception of vocationalism interpreted as an education which takes account of 'the way the world operates'. It is that recognition which dictates the interdisciplinary nature, emphases, breadth-with-a-view-to-integration, problem-focused. employment-conscious shapes of courses. The courses are diverse in many ways, but they also display many similarities in their histories and definitions, in the explanations they offer of their distinctive purposes (and the distinctive features of engineering in the public sector generally), and in the intentions and attitudes expressed in interview.

It is important to remember here, as at other points in this study, that we are concerned with vocationalism and related concepts such as intention, interpretation, and understanding. There is no attempt, as we have indicated, to evaluate these intentions and their embodiment in course and programme design as they are experienced in practice. There was no attempt to follow students and staff through lecture theatre or classroom, laboratory or workshop, or to elicit responses to teaching processes or sandwich placements. Those discussions of higher education which suggest that any subject or topic can be taught 'liberally' or 'illiberally' point towards quite different analyses of teaching methods, student learning, and the broad and complex experience of higher education itself. While aspects of the higher-education experience in those terms are touched on in this study, they are not the focus. The analysis of the course histories and the framework of the interviews were concerned primarily with prevailing understandings of purpose and explanation, in order to see the extent to which those most actively involved in this segment of education responded to past and present emphases in public debate. In that respect, what the engineering interviews themselves most uniformly and clearly indicated was the explicit and considered nature of that response, and the awareness of the academic and professional contexts within which it was formulated.

One comment made was that the professional institutions took the view that 'you can't be an engineer unless you know this, this, and this'. Therein lies the dilemma for the engineering educator. In our typology of the vocational described in chapter 3, we located engineering in category (b) – 'Sole regulation and part-training'. Engineering degrees play a key role in the regulation of entry into the profession. Employers and the professional institutions expect that a large proportion of professional training or 'formation' will have been completed during an undergraduate course. Consequently, there are quite explicit external expectations and requirements concerning the content of training.

Employment outcomes are specific. Few graduates will move out of engineering, at least initially. Many courses, however, had even more explicit target outcomes. In addition to the major branches of engineering – civil, electrical, and mechanical – we have looked at courses in textile and knitwear technology, in energy engineering, and in communication and electronic engineering. In the words of one of our interviewees, courses are under pressure to 'supply industry with graduates that can do the job'. And those are jobs which have a high knowledge content and require the possession of particular skills. There is a lot that the 'practising engineer' needs to know. As we noted in chapter 3, courses which possess such a central role in selection

Engineering education: courses and explanations

and training for employment face external pressures and controls over the curriculum which severely limit the autonomy of educators.

Nobody we spoke to wished to dispute this essential vocational goal of an engineering education. The problem was rather how it was to be achieved for the distinctive kind of student that engineering degrees recruited. Tensions were apparent between 'immediate usefulness' and longer-term career needs. Such tensions were picked up in the range of external pressures that courses faced. Employers, the professional institutions, Finniston, the CNAA – all provided different emphases, different models for the goals of an engineering education, but engineering educators themselves possessed some distinctive views.

Differences in emphasis could not disguise an overwhelming consensus that engineering education should be vocational but should avoid being 'narrowly' vocational. There was a near universal aim to achieve application and breadth with a consideration of context. There was concern to 'broaden' students, to provide a 'balanced' curriculum, but to do so in ways relevant to the 'needs of practising engineers'. The constraints were the high information content of the courses and the students themselves.

The students were the products of specialized, some would say narrow, sixth-form educations. They had specific career intentions and higher education provided the route, the only route, to achieve them. In three years of college study, plus in most cases one year of professional placement, the detailed requirements of professional formation had to be accomplished, with whatever elements of a general education could be achieved in the time. Objectives which in other national and subject contexts might require several stages of education, moving from the general to the professional over four or five years, had to be achieved in England in three. Little wonder that several of the interviewees felt that engineering students tended to 'lose out on an overall education'.

A major concern of engineering educators was an attempt to combat the external pressures towards narrowness. Staff tried to get students 'to think for themselves', to be creative and flexible. There was substantial evidence of concern about study methods, partly in the context of what some saw as the poor quality of the students, but also as a way of achieving extremely ambitious course objectives. Students therefore experienced a range of teaching and learning methods with much emphasis placed on projects and practicals as ways of 'letting them find out'. Students were expected to 'make presentations', and could be subjected to vivas. The industrial placement had a key role to play.

The development of students as individuals and their formation as engineers were not held to be contradictory. Most staff appeared to believe that a broadly based but practical course would achieve both ends, within the constraints of the requirements of the professional institutions, the students themselves, and shortage of time.

The starting point for the design of engineering degrees was 'What sort of jobs are our students going to do?' This was known with some confidence. Getting a job was not the central problem. However, in moving from a knowledge of employment outcomes to the construction of a suitable education for that employment, staff had to work within tight constraints. As we shall see, this situation was very different from that faced by their colleagues working in business studies.

8

Engineering education: a note on the United States

One reason for taking a side glance at engineering education in the United States is that a series of major inquiries before and since the Second World War have made it the most visible undergraduate curriculum in the United States, and probably anywhere. As elsewhere, American engineering education has been scrutinized in terms of balance amongst science, technology, the position of engineering in contemporary world society, and the range of studies and activities necessary for the ability to synthesize required of an engineer. More perhaps than any other aspect of American undergraduate education, engineering has been the subject of persistent experiment, with colleges and universities like Carnegie–Mellon in Pennsylvania, Harvey Mudd in California, and Worcester Polytechnic in Massachusetts promoting a range of experimental engineering programmes. The American Society for Engineering Education, the journal *Engineering Education*, and the professional associations of specific branches of engineering have sustained throughout this century an acute interest in the content and direction of engineering education, and – particularly since the Mann Report of 1918 – have regularly surveyed curricula, students, and the profession: 'quite possibly no other professional group has studied its own curriculums in greater detail and with more enthusiastic criticism than have the engineers' (Griffith 1981: 488; Walker 1971: 823). All such experiments, and all the reports on the deficiencies of engineering education, start somewhere close to Lynn White's 1960s comment about the professional that 'only by being more than a specialist can he remain an adequate specialist' (White 1967: 145). Not many analysts of engineering education from the inside could match the passion which White devoted from the outside to his interpretation of technology:

> As [engineering schools] modify their educational structures to meet the newer professional needs of engineers, they will feel increasingly the shift towards common human concerns, and this in itself will promote humanistic attitudes. When this happens, engineers will wake up to the fact that engineering has humanistic functions of the highest order.

It was the responsibility of engineers to understand themselves as engineers and to share that understanding with the rest of society, to be conscious of their own history, to build bridges towards humanist scholars, especially in the history of technology and science, to transform technology itself into a fully-fledged humanism: 'the study of technology as one of the forms of the creativity of mankind is as yet little developed' (White 1968: 146–7, 167). It has been with some sense of the potential of engineering as a new culture, as well as with the requirements of the market, in mind that many experiments in engineering education have taken place, frequently with an eye to interdisciplinary new subject areas attempting to marry engineering functions with socio-humanistic concerns (the hybrid term is commonplace in the engineering curriculum), with human studies of various kinds, with management, and with ethical, historical, and other studies. They have had an eye also to teaching methodologies, to the processes of problem-solving, and to developing in often conservative, job-oriented engineering students the ability to handle uncertainty and ambiguity and the wider demands of non-instrumental elements in the curriculum (Holloman *et al*. 1975: 42–7).

Carnegie–Mellon University exemplifies the aspirations in these processes. The Carnegie Institute of Technology, one of its constituent parts, sought to make its engineering science courses 'culturally balanced' and a 'liberal professional education'. In the 1940s and 1950s it was trying to prevent the 'humanistic–social' part of the programme from being 'a thing apart – a decorative misletoe'. An effort was made to bring the humanities and social sciences into the 'self-reliant learning and problem-solving' mode which was to be the feature of all courses. The problem-solving focus, which was to become a motto for engineering education widely, had a specific intention of combating some existing features of engineering courses:

> Problem solving is the main task of the engineer, and when

Engineering education: a note on the United States 139

employed in the right way, is one of the most important activities in engineering education. It can do much to remedy the lack of a critical understanding of the engineer's tools of thought, and it is a means of preparing the student to deal with new problems, of equipping him to answer questions that have not yet been asked.

'Social relations' and other courses were to underpin this ability to deal resourcefully with problems (Smith 1954; Smith et al, 1957; Teare 1948). The 'Carnegie Plan of Professional Education in Engineering and Science', a product of the 1940s and promulgated by the Institute in a variety of ways, made a simple distinction between training and education:

> The aim of professional education at Carnegie Institute of Technology is to equip students to go on learning after graduation and to grow throughout their lives in professional and personal stature and in usefulness as citizens. Carnegie does not seek to *train* students to *be* professional practitioners at graduation, but rather to *educate* them so that they will *become* professional men of full stature.
> (Carnegie Institute of Technology 1954)

The pursuit of that aim continued. A University 'program in technology humanities', begun in 1975, aimed to develop courses which would 'stimulate interest, teaching and research in the relationship between technology and society' (Tarr 1980: 1). In 1981 the Professor of Civil Engineering and Public Policy was retracing the Carnegie–Mellon 'unique tradition of liberal professional education'. In the late 1960s Robert Hutchins, proponent of the Great Books approach to a core undergraduate curriculum, had spoken on the CMU campus advocating the abolition of all institutes of technology, but 'if he had looked carefully beyond the Great Books, he would have discovered that the leading institutes of technology were in the forefront of promoting a well-rounded general education in our technological society' (Au 1981: 2).

In places such as Carnegie–Mellon that search for a redefinition of aim and practice has been consistent across decades, and with less invention in many other institutions preparing engineers. The pressures to redefine have come through the requirements of the professional institutions and the processes of accreditation.

The extent and form of the incorporation of the 'socio-humanistic stem', for example, has been explored and constantly reinterpreted in past decades by committees of the American Society for Engineering Education and regularly debated at its conferences and in the pages of *Engineering Education*. The Accreditation Board for Engineering and Technology lays down 'the equivalent of one-half year as the minimum content in the area of the humanities and social sciences' (ABET 1980: 3). Institutions themselves also define core requirements that engineering students, like all others, have to meet.

Given the breadth of engineering courses, therefore, it is not surprising that there are claims – perhaps more credible in some American institutions than in Britain and elsewhere – that engineering is the model of a modern liberal education (Harrisberger 1984: 139). It is also not surprising that there are equally strong criticisms of the failures of engineering education, resulting from incremental approaches to the curriculum, its distance from practice, and in many cases a failure to implement the grand designs and rhetoric of institutions' public statements and accreditation claims.

The trajectory of American engineering education from the late nineteenth century was one of growing attempts to detach it from identification with craft pursuits, a process of transition that has been described as a shift 'from experience to science' and an attempt to supplant *experience* with *understanding* as a basis for engineering education (Seamans and Hansen 1981: 24). Science had been the instrument used to transform engineering 'from what had often been considered a craft to what was increasingly called a profession' (Haber 1974: 267). It was, as we have underlined, a movement of the 1970s to bring engineering more widely and systematically back towards a problem-focused engagement with technology. The time sequences, models, and curricular structures have been different in the American case from that in Britain, but some of the issues emerge in similar terms, and the overall attempt to locate the engineer amidst the many academic, professional, and wider public demands suggests similar questions, if not solutions. The comparison, to be complete, would need to probe more deeply not only the histories of engineering and its comparative academic and social statuses, but also the histories of secondary-school curricula, the processes through which students enter engineering programmes, and the quality and characteristics of the students who do so. One mechanical engineering instructor summarizes engineering students as

> a multi-faceted challenge to the educators. They represent a diversity of academic backgrounds, preparedness, motivation skills and attitudes. They also are rather unique among college students, being better prepared, more career orientated.
> (Brillhart 1981: 119)

American engineering educators, certainly in recent years, have in public discussion been reasonably satisfied with the quality of students being attracted to engineering, and have often seen their graduates as 'better prepared' and more widely educated, and the products of an important blend of a general and a professional education.

Engineering educators with whom we discussed some of these issues operated comfortably amongst these competing models, pressures, and requirements. At Pennsylvania State University, for example, the head of the department of mechanical engineering saw undergraduate curricula conforming to the ASEE view of engineering as the application of science for the benefit of mankind, and saw the programme as responsive to the implementations of that definition. The department's course is presented in its publicity as broad in range and career opportunities. Like all degrees in the College of Engineering at Penn State emphasis is placed on the 'application of engineering method', and

> all majors include a social-humanistic stem which extends throughout the eight semesters and gives the student a knowledge of social and human relationships and duties of citizenship, as well as an appreciation of cultural interests outside the engineering field. The stem includes a required course in economics and electives to be chosen from the fine arts, humanities, and social sciences.
> (Pennsylvania State University, Bulletin 1985/6)

As with some of his British counterparts the head of department counterposed engineering with its applications in the real world to the arts and humanities which did not. The accreditation board, ABET, insisted on only restricted professionalism at the undergraduate level, though the aim in the future was likely to be greater specialization. The design courses were where qualities of imagination and innovation were most encouraged. One required course in the seventh semester, for example, in engineering design, aimed at 'synthesis, analysis and evaluation procedures in creative mechanical and thermal design, integrated with engineering fundamentals through authentic design projects' (*Curriculum Information and Planning Manual* 1985). In this, he indicated, students could work in small teams, identifying needs – for example, that of a hospital for inexpensive machines to solve particular problems of handicapped patients. This presented students with the need to evaluate ideas, produce models, work together, make oral presentations, and confront real human problems. As a result of such experience a small proportion of students, perhaps up to 10 per cent, was tempted to graduate work or conversion programmes in disciplines other than engineering – including law, sales, and medicine.

The acting head of the electrical engineering department at Penn State discussed a curriculum contained within the same regulations as other engineering curricula in the College of Engineering, meeting the same university requirements and similar accreditation requirements, feeling there was no difficulty in satisfying both. Most graduates did enter electrical engineering, but a small fraction used their experience in other directions – concerned, for example, with patents in law firms. The engineering faculty discussed their own teaching methods and ways of learning – including strategies for encouraging students to plan 'self-learning'. Design skills were taught in lecture courses and in laboratories. Some courses were inevitably more concerned with fundamental principles and theories than others. The amount of laboratory instruction was extensive, and was presented to students as a course of assignments with a series of objectives, the final one of which was 'the growth in your justified *self-confidence*, knowing that even quite unfamiliar assignments can be tackled by you and moved toward successful completion' (*The EE Stem laboratories* 1986). In addition to these assignments there was stress on the importance of projects in the final two years, and overall on engineering as problem-solving.

It is doubtful whether American educators in engineering or other vocational or professional areas would claim to have established an entry into a new technological culture quite of the order promulgated by Lynn White. What Americans do present is a well-grounded, if still confused, debate about issues of vocationalism more explicitly detailed than is often the case in Europe.

Engineering education: a note on the United States

Given the scale, diversity, and career orientation of American higher education it is not easy to detect patterns of interpretation except through accreditation requirements, and in the similarities of structures induced both by accreditation and by state-wide consultation and planning amongst state institutions. Where student expectations and experience are similar across the American system it is as a result of those processes, and of the general influence of particular professional bodies. The difficulty of drawing clear and rigid distinctions between the vocational and the liberal emerges particularly sharply in that situation, where the system, institutions, educational processes, and presentation of knowledge are subject to rapid change and constant reappraisal.

9
Business studies: a background

Compared with engineering, business studies is a relative newcomer to higher education in Britain, and its development has been accorded less public and political attention. Within the overall expansion of higher education in the last twenty years, undergraduate business education has been a significant growth area. It has been so in both public and university sectors although the growth has been on a different scale and taken a different form in each. The universities have introduced courses in banking, accountancy, industrial economics, and business studies. In the public sector, the four-year sandwich degree in business studies has predominated. By 1980 there were forty-one such degrees with a total enrolment of nearly 8,000 students. Today, about 5 per cent of all CNAA courses are in business studies, accounting for about 7.5 per cent of all CNAA students. In addition, there are courses in accountancy, secretarial studies, business economics, and specialist degrees such as retail marketing. However, it is the four-year sandwich degree in business studies which is the focus of this chapter. Every polytechnic has one and there are several in colleges and institutes of higher education. They attract large numbers of applicants and, as we shall see, their graduates appear to be much in demand in the labour market. On all kinds of criteria they have been a success story in the growth of public-sector higher education. But a success of what sort? It is this question which we shall seek to explore in this and in the following chapter.

We are here concerned with some of the contextual factors, both inside and outside higher education, which affect undergraduate business education in Britain. We shall outline some of the debates which have surrounded the development of business-studies degrees and chronicle some of the changes which

Business studies: a background

have occurred in them since their emergence in the mid-1960s. The chapter which follows will report on a series of interviews which we conducted with staff who are closely involved in the running of these degrees. We shall also in a later chapter draw some comparisons with the approaches to business education found in other countries.

In a foreword to the proceedings of a conference on 'values in business education' held in 1982, the then Chairman of the CNAA Committee for Business and Management Studies wrote: 'it is not clear whether the underlying concern of staff and students in those courses is a study of business or a study for business' (Graves 1983: 5). George Tolley was here making a distinction which recurs in the discussions about the growth of undergraduate business education. As he was undoubtedly aware when he made the statement, course philosophies and aims have been overwhelmingly on the side of 'for business' with the full support, even requirement of, the CNAA subject board. What Tolley may have suspected was that the educational reality of the courses was sometimes rather different.

If there has been a fairly unambiguous employment-related purpose in the business-studies enterprise, a major problem for its realization has been the diffuseness of the occupational roles to which it is directed. There is no profession of 'businessman' with clear job specifications, career structures, entry routes, and qualification requirements. You do not need to be a graduate, still less a business-studies graduate, to become a businessman. A degree in business studies carries with it no special professional status. It may facilitate exemptions from some professional examinations in business and commerce but then so do qualifications in other subjects. For most jobs, business graduates face open competition from graduates from other disciplines and, in many cases, from non-graduates. According to a variety of surveys (Gordon 1983; Roizen and Jepson 1985) and public statements, many employers appear to prefer the competition, that is, they seek graduates from traditional disciplines from traditional universities.

However, although they face a potentially very open labour market, business-studies graduates appear to do remarkably well in it. Whether on the basis of the First Destination statistics or the results of the CNAA graduate survey (Brennan and McGeevor 1987), a comparison of business-studies graduates with other graduates reveals the vast majority of them entering employment immediately on graduation, obtaining jobs which are at graduate level, and after three years being among the highest salary earners of polytechnic graduates. Another feature of their employment, and one which contrasts with university business graduates, is the high proportion who enter industry rather than commerce and the significant numbers who enter manufacturing industry.

If obtaining a relevant job is to be taken as a measure of successful vocational higher education, then business-studies degrees appear to be doing a good job 'for business', even if it is one which employers do not always recognize. It does however appear to be recognized by school-leavers who form the vast majority of business-studies undergraduates (there are very few mature students on business-studies degrees). A survey by Horner (1982: 15) revealed the vocational motivations of most business-studies students. The three most popular reasons for choosing a business-studies degree were (a) they wanted a career in commerce or industry, (b) they would find it easier to obtain employment with a degree in business studies, (c) their final career choice would be easier because of their experience of industrial placement.

Practical success but lack of formal recognition in the labour market marks the short history of CNAA business-studies degrees. A consequence of this lack of formal recognition is that business-studies graduates will find themselves working alongside graduates from a wide range of other disciplines. Except where in-company training is highly individualized, this means that employers will not be making any special assumptions about the knowledge and skills of their graduate intakes. How can they if they have no special requirements in recruitment? One of several consequences of this lack of formal recognition by employers is that course designers are not constrained either by the requirements of external professional bodies or by less formal but clearly articulated wants of employers.

At the admissions end, course designers are also free from external constraints imposed by specific pre-entry qualifications. The subjects of 'A' level study are largely immaterial for admission to a business-studies degree. Some subjects, for example economics or mathematics, may be desirable but course designers and teachers can never assume that all of their students will possess them. Thus, in seeking to provide an education 'for business', staff in institutions have neither a specific academic foundation on which to build nor a set of professional/employer requirements to meet. Being in the public sector, however, their courses have to be validated and for that reason it is important for us to give some attention to the role and approach of the CNAA subject board for business studies. Before doing so, however, and before looking at the curriculum of business-studies degrees, there are some further contextual factors which need to be recorded briefly.

One consequence of the relative newness of degrees in business studies is that very few of the staff who teach on them have themselves taken business courses as undergraduates. Typically they are graduates in disciplines such as economics, law, sociology, or accountancy or, in some cases, with completely unrelated first degrees but with substantial practical experience of business. They do not therefore possess inherited models of what a business-studies degree should be like. They do not even necessarily possess a detailed knowledge of all its constituent parts. Business-studies degrees, as we shall see, adopt a generalist approach to business education but are dependent on discipline specialists for teachers.

We have seen that the concept and curriculum of business-studies degrees are not heavily constrained by professional or employer requirements. Such degrees are not dependent on a particular academic base provided by 'A' levels. Their teachers have not themselves experienced such a course as undergraduates and may have only a partial knowledge of its content. There are, however, other sources of influence on business-studies degrees which derive from other models of business education available in the United Kingdom and we should refer briefly to them before turning in detail to the business-studies degree itself.

The CNAA business-studies degree is the major form of degree-level undergraduate preparation for business. But it is far from being the only educational route into a business career. We have noted that graduates from many disciplines embark on careers in business. Although their business education may begin with in-company training, for many it will lead to a postgraduate course of some sort. The main postgraduate qualifications are the Master in business Administration (MBA) and the Diploma in

Management Studies (DMS). Both are post-experience and accordingly have rather different goals from those of the undergraduate business-studies degree. Nevertheless, potentially they provide a major source of influence on the undergraduate curriculum. How far that potential influence is realized is open to some doubt, however, because a peculiar characteristic of business education in Britain is the organizational separation of initial undergraduate education and training from post-experience education and training. Indeed they are frequently called different things, 'business' referring to initial education and the term 'management' being used for post-experience education. The university business schools are exclusively post-experience, postgraduate providers and even in the public sector management departments are frequently organizationally distinct from business studies.

The other major source of education and training for business is provided by courses leading to the certificates and diplomas awarded by the Business and Technician Education Council (BTEC) and its Scottish equivalent (SCOTVEC). These courses are offered in England and Wales by most polytechnics and many other further and higher education colleges in the public sector. The growth in courses and in student numbers has been considerable and has paralleled the rise of the business-studies degree. The BTEC courses are relevant to our interest because BTEC has attempted to impose on them an educational philosophy which has undoubtedly had some carry-over effect on degree courses in recent years. BTEC courses are intended to be practical and problem-centred, and to eschew the teaching of academic disciplines and the traditional forms of cognitive skill which accompany them. The focus is upon the practice of business and the development of those practical skills which will assist it. BTEC course philosophies, however, do not always sit comfortably in the conventional academic milieux of polytechnics and institutes of higher education. The implementation of the courses is frequently at odds with their philosophies. Nevertheless, BTEC has undoubtedly provided a fund of often radical new thinking about curriculum, pedagogy, and assessment in the field of business education. Many teachers on business-studies degrees teach also on BTEC courses. There can be little doubt that there are reciprocal influences in play between the two levels of course.

Business studies: a background

These, then, are the main institutional and educational/professional contexts in which business-studies courses are located, and we can now examine their nature in general terms before turning to the case studies in the next section.

All of the full-time courses are four-year sandwich degrees (there are in addition sixteen part-time business-studies degrees) with in most cases a 'thick' sandwich – that is, a single block industrial placement of at least forty-eight weeks, usually located in the third year of the course. The first referent for discussions about the curriculum of business-studies degrees is usually the Crick Report of 1964, produced for the National Advisory Council on Education for Industry and Commerce. That report saw the degrees as essentially multidisciplinary, stating that 'the courses should be firmly grounded on a few basic disciplines, the essentials of which the student would need to grasp so as to be able to use their modes of thought and tools of analysis in tackling business problems' (National Advisory Council 1964: 10). The main disciplinary candidates for this role, according to Crick, were economics, accounting, law, and sociology. The first ten years or so of the history of business-studies degrees saw course teams attempting to work such a formula. The disciplinary essentials could safely be left to the discipline specialists as far as the inner logic of the disciplines was concerned but could not be so left if their essence was to be determined by the practical needs of business. A search for relevance, in curriculum selection and organization, ensued in order to identify precisely those bits of disciplines which would have most to contribute and to put them together in such a way as to create a meaningful whole for students.

In 1981 a report from a working party of the CNAA Committee for Business and Management Studies found that

> although the core disciplines outlined in the Crick Report continue to form the academic base for business degrees, changes have taken place in their treatment and location within the curriculum. In very general terms, curricula have come to be organised on the basis of business rather than disciplinary themes and categories. Although most degrees continue to provide a disciplinary foundation in year one, there is an increasing tendency to introduce the study of functional areas of business at a relatively early stage of the course.
>
> (CNAA 1981: 2)

The main functional areas examined in business-studies degrees have been finance, marketing, and personnel and all but two of the degrees running in 1983 included provision for specialist study of these and other functional specialisms as part of the final year. The time accorded to specialist study varied considerably between courses. Notwithstanding the provision for specialization, business-studies degrees continue to profess aims which are general in character, seeking to produce graduates who are knowledgeable and competent in all areas of business activity. The prospectus descriptions of business-studies degree courses in the mid-1980s have expressed these aims in varied yet similar terms, and with emphases important to our discussion here. A course would provide 'a general education in business related subjects of sufficient breadth to offer students a range of career opportunities in industry, commerce, the professions and the public sector' (Liverpool Polytechnic 1984/5). A course would be 'broadly-based' in the 'major business associated disciplines so as to equip its graduates to contribute immediately to the day-to-day functioning of the organisations which first employ them. It is an intellectually demanding course that seeks to develop in its students a constructive yet critical approach to business and industry' (Teesside Polytechnic 1983). The aim of a course was to provide a broad education which prepared students 'for a business career that can evolve as tastes or circumstances change' (Manchester Polytechnic 1984/5). The sandwich element assumes considerable importance: 'As a sandwich course it integrates academic knowledge and practical training' (Hatfield Polytechnic 1984/5).

The subject basis of business-studies courses in the 1970s and early 1980s is still visible in some of these definitions of aims, but so also are the practicality and the broad career-relatedness. Trent Polytechnic spelled out the position clearly at that point in the development of business studies courses:

> Although most graduates will follow careers in finance, personnel work, marketing, production, or the public service, it would be a mistake to assume that the courses offered in the department are just narrow training for specific occupations and professions. For instance, the honours degree in business studies involves a close study of the underlying business disciplines of economics, mathematics, sociology and accounting,

with the emphasis on the application of these subjects to business problems. To achieve this educational objective great stress is placed on participatory teaching methods such as case studies, business exercises and group tutorials.

(Trent Polytechnic 1984/5)

Many of these elements surface again in the interviews in the following chapter, with an emergent emphasis on the study not of disciplines but of business functions. Whatever the curriculum balance, the overall declared aim – whether or not the vocabulary of vocationalism was used – in polytechnics and colleges offering business-studies degrees was invariably in tune with the succinct Middlesex statement: 'The course has been designed to provide an academic education in a vocational context, thus enabling graduates to succeed in a dynamic business environment' (Middlesex Polytechnic 1986/7). Achieving the desired balance and connections amongst the components of these courses, however, was not a simple matter.

A problem identified by the 1981 CNAA report was the difficulty of achieving 'a cumulative integration which was both academically sound and vocationally relevant' (CNAA 1981: 5). This is invariable seen as the task for the final year and is a twofold problem of (i) integrating the academic elements of the degree, and (ii) integrating the academic and placement parts of the degree. Project work, integrating courses in business policy, business-organization or decision studies, a shift of emphasis from business structures to business processes, are all potential solutions which have been tried. The CNAA report concluded 'that considerable progress has been made in the integration of disciplines but that significant problems remain in relating the placement to the academic programmes (p.6).

Where then are business-studies degrees going? Compared with courses in many areas there have been considerable changes to curricula in their relatively short history. Reflecting current preoccupations, Roy Bailey has commented that business studies is 'about doing something, not simply about knowing something' and advocates continual movement away from concern about 'academic problems' to 'problems of action, of choice and decision' (Bailey 1983: 22). Noting the increasing rejection of academic disciplines as the basis for the organization of business-studies curricula, David Brown has examined the epistemological problems which this throws up. Both the disciplinary model of Crick, with its view of disciplines as tools to be brought to bear on the underlying reality of business problems, and the BTEC-influenced approach which attempts to tackle that reality more directly through use of case studies and practical problem-solving, are for Brown examples of an educational model of business studies which emphasizes a 'practical reality which should be mastered'. Such a model is essentially conservative, aiming to produce people 'who can work within the organizations in the way they are now' and regarding change as 'immanent in the system and beyond rational human resistance' (Brown 1983: 26) or, for that matter, control. In contrast, Brown advocates a model drawing on Kuhnian approaches to science which sees business as 'some sort of language community' and business education as 'teaching people the languages which are used' (p. 27). Thus Brown has provided two very contrasting ways of looking at what business-studies courses are doing. In our view it would be wrong to look directly for the curricular consequences of Brown's 'phenomenologist' model. In the same way as we need to be alert to different 'realities' of business, so too may there be different 'realities' of business-studies degrees. What we need to look for is the ways in which teaching staff are tackling the design and delivery of their courses when the Crick disciplines no longer provide the organizational framework for the activity. The same questions of intention, interpretation, and explanation that we have considered in the case of engineering then come into play.

In chapter 10 we consider the views of people who have responsibility for business-studies degrees, and an important context for their activities is the role and views of the relevant CNAA subject board. We noted the relative absence of formal external constraints on the development of business-studies degrees. Yet despite this, an analysis by Anthony Saul reveals a very considerable homogeneity among business-studies courses (Saul 1983). The requirements, real or perceived, of the CNAA represent one source of influence which may bear some responsibility for this homogeneity. The formal position of the CNAA subject boards is that they are not prescriptive. Consequently, BTEC-type guidelines on philosophy and curriculum do not exist. Nevertheless, the views of CNAA board members as they interact with each other and as they respond to course developments up and down the country throw out potentially powerful messages to teaching staff in the institutions. Most usefully for our purposes, the Undergraduate Courses Board of the CNAA Committee for Business and Management Studies recently tried to make explicit its own thinking about business-studies degrees. The board's discussions indicate some plurality of perspectives but also some underlying points of consensus. A distinctly 'for business' definition of business education has been provided by the board's chairman, R.J. Bull, and appears to have received broad endorsement by other members: 'Business education is the personal development of the organisational, administrative and management skills which draw upon relevant knowledge and analytic skills to facilitate the education process' (Bull 1985: 5). Bull goes on to identify the components of (i) understanding of context, (ii) understanding of business process, and (iii) 'the development of an individual's managerial and inter-personal skills needed to transform knowledge and cognitive skills into practical action'. Thus, although business studies accommodate the familiar academic skills of 'the acquisition and application of ... knowledge and cognitive skills', these are not seen as ends in themselves but as a vehicle leading to capacity for 'practical action' and requiring the development not only of cognitive but of *effective* skills – managerial, administrative, and interpersonal.

Similar sentiments are echoed by other contributors to the board's debate. Fitzgerald observed that 'skills and knowledge bases are simply the instruments to subject effectiveness. More important are the attributes of mind and attitudes created by study' (Fitzgerald 1985: 4). McKenna sees 'a desirable outcome of the business studies course [as] the blending of relevant knowledge and practical experience. This overall process contributes to cognitive development, as well as the enhancement of interpersonal and communication skills, in the better programmes' (McKenna 1985: 7).

What emerges is the view that the aims of vocational business education may be achieved less through curriculum content – that is, what business graduates know – and more through the development within graduates of dispositions and capacities for practical action in business settings. And as Bull indicates, this has as many consequences for pedagogy and assessment as it has for the content of the curriculum. What these are can only be answered by looking at courses. However, it is worth observing that these debates within the CNAA reflect some dissatisfaction with business-studies degrees. The reasons for it are not difficult to find. They reflect the lack of recognition accorded to business-studies degrees by the business community. As Fitzgerald puts it: 'Business employers time and time again say that they do not consider business studies graduates preferentially at initial recruitment point' (Fitzgerald 1985: 2). For these reasons, there is considerable emphasis in debates about business-studies courses on the need for innovation and change.

The apparent indifference of employers may well be overstressed by business educators. After all, they do seem to employ business-studies graduates in ever-increasing numbers. Each year, nearly 2,000 students are found placements in industry. Yet a sense of marginality to the professional education of the business community pervades the debates about undergraduate business education, notwithstanding the very significant success of the courses in establishing themselves as a major force within public-sector higher education.

Business activity is diverse. It contains many functional roles and occurs in varied organizational settings. It remains unclear for which roles in which settings an undergraduate business qualification is relevant preparation. This is a question which appears to have little troubled the business community.

The failure to answer it, however, creates problems for business educators. Graves has commented that curricula tend to assume large-scale organizational contexts for business activity (Graves 1983). Bull complains of the relative neglect of public-sector organizations (Bull 1985). How transferable are the knowledge and skills acquired from a business-studies degree? How interchangeable are a business-studies degree holder, a BTEC diploma holder, a history graduate, in terms of what they can do in what kind of role in what kind of organization? The lack of any consensus about the answers to these questions creates an underlying uncertainty about undergraduate business education.

In terms of the typology introduced in chapter 3, business studies occupies the position of an open market and employment-relevant educational base. It operates at the diffuse end of educational–employment relationships, its awards are not used systematically by employers to regulate recruitment, and although employment relevance is claimed for the curriculum subsequent professional training does not presuppose it. Some of the problems which arise for vocational work in higher education in such

Business studies: a background

circumstances have been illustrated by the preceding discussion. Yet there are also advantages. Business education does not have to struggle to free itself from the requirements of professional bodies or the interference of employers. We do not find, as in other employment-related fields, the concern to protect educational values against the instrumental goals of occupational training. This kind of debate has scarcely been heard in business studies. Business educators have been far more concerned to attempt to persuade business of the vocational value of business-studies degrees than they have been to protect their educational value against instrumentalist pressures from outside. This may be because the pressures are not there but it does mean that the educational nature of business-studies degrees has received relatively little explicit attention. However, one or two points can be made.

In the early days of business-studies degrees, the placement appears to have carried most of the work preparation load. The taught curriculum was a multidisciplinary attempt to provide a relevant academic base to that preparation. Its academic strengths were those of its constituent disciplines and the academic breadth of the curriculum meant that accusations of professional narrowness were never seriously made. After all, if economics, law, accountancy, and sociology could each separately constitute an honours degree, there could be no need to further broaden a programme which contained all four. However, as the visibility of disciplines has declined, so the educational qualities of the programmes have been recast. Educational purpose is no longer defined in narrowly academic terms. The claims of business studies to provide a broad, liberal higher education rest not just on the breadth of knowledge acquired, but on the challenge of application, of doing as well as knowing, of the interplay of the cognitive and the effective in Bull's terms, although, as Bull himself points out, course-assessment methods have not been developed to test these claims fully. But, it must be remembered, in so far as such educational values obtain, they exist in order to serve an overriding value of the effective preparation of students for careers in business.

The predominant concern of business educators has been and is to gain acceptance and recognition for business studies as a vocational qualification of value in the business world. Its value within the educational world has not been problematic. Speaking to an international audience of business educators, an assistant chief officer of the CNAA summed up the achievements of the CNAA business-studies degrees:

> there has been a determination on the part of course teams to make their courses more relevant to the world of business, to link discipline areas to business concerns and business problems, to produce curricula organised on the basis of business rather than academic disciplinary themes and categories.
> (Goldman 1984: 4)

The success of their endeavours can be judged by the enormous demand from school-leavers for course places and the success of graduates in the labour market. The absence of professional regulation and closure has not prevented the achievement of vocational goals.

10
Business studies: courses and explanations

Humberside College of Higher Education

Humberside's four-year honours degree in business studies was approved by the CNAA in 1977. It runs alongside BA honours degrees in Accountancy and Finance, and in Secretarial Studies, which – unlike the degree in business studies – are not sandwich courses. Accountancy and Finance has operated since 1978, and Secretarial Studies since 1980. All three share a common first year, and were resubmitted for approval by the CNAA in 1983. An honours degree in Business Information Systems was also approved in 1985.

The aims of the business-studies degree were described in 1977 – and reaffirmed six years later – as being that the programme should have

> both an educational and vocational aim. We see the differences between these aims as being matters of emphasis rather than of kind. It is intended that the student should acquire habits of mind, through critical analysis and evaluation of all that he, or she, studies, which are a prerequisite for a successful career, whether in the field of business or elsewhere.

The degree therefore needed to explore the world of business, but also the way in which 'it reacts with a dynamic environment'. Alongside a balance between 'vocational and educational' elements and considerations of business in the present and its likely changes, the course sought to improve the students' prospects of employment, 'inter alia by developing their potential as individuals'. The 1983 review of the course reported student criticisms – in a generally approving framework – that the course was too 'theoretical and abstract'. The review made suggestions for 'improving the vocational content' of the course. Two types of integration were aimed at: the integration of academic work and business activity (mainly through industrial training and a project or dissertation), and integration amongst a range of academic disciplines (including through experiential learning techniques). The course was self-consciously interdisciplinary and various means of achieving integration had been tried: studying in depth 'an area of activity relating to business for a full week' was a current approach. The final-year project more than any other element in the course 'enables students to display qualities of originality, independent thought and initiative' – and it was proposed in 1983 to introduce assessment based on projects in the second year also in certain units of the course. The first two years of the course, largely 'Crick-based' in the 1977 submission, now contain only one of six units which is a 'Crick' discipline.

THE COURSE LEADER (MR CUTTS) emphasized that the wide variety of employment opportunities mentioned in the prospectus was a range of business and administration employments, with many students going back to jobs in companies where they had had sandwich placements, jobs in retail management, and public utilities, and a few – when the college was training secondary teachers in business studies – into teaching, either in schools or further education after a PGCE. The vast majority of the graduates went into business 'in the broad sense', and were motivated to do so on entry to the course. *Is the reference to 'an educational and vocational aim' still applicable to the course?*

> Yes. One of the reasons it's in that particular document, one of the reasons we laid more stress on the vocational element is that if you looked at the original submission (in 1977) there was more emphasis on the educational side than there was on the vocational side, and the faculty as a whole in terms of its ideology has been moving more towards an applied form of business education.

> *There is reference to students acquiring 'analytical and evaluative skills commensurate with degree level higher education' –what sort of skills are these mainly?* That applied, he considered, to most of what happened in the fourth year. In the original submission there had been too much of 'this is the answer' and not enough of 'what is the answer?'. One aim now was to get the students

to do the searching, to identify the characteristics of a particular business situation, giving a hint of 'what kind of answers are likely to be best in a commercial sense'. There had been a move away from 'the gospel according to the staff': this had been the first degree course put up by the newly formed college in 1976, and inevitably it had been conservative. The later version embodied a 'more taxing way of teaching'. A course like 'The state and the economy' changed as personnel and attitudes changed – it was designed to be as contemporary as possible, and the content therefore changed according to what was happening, particularly in Europe and in national politics. The intention was to give students an understanding 'of the political-economic factors which affect businesses'.

Some parts of the second year were designed to prepare students for the industrial placement. Students on placement were often required to produce company reports: they had originally been producing 'academic essays' on the course – and the two did not match. There was now more case-study work, therefore, in the second year, and students were more used to writing reports designed to say: 'this is the best way for the company to go'. Student assignments in marketing, labour studies, and operations were in the form of a long case study, perhaps comparing and contrasting two companies and making recommendations about their marketing. *How much use, then, is made of the industrial year when they return for the fourth year?*

> To be honest the answer has to be – not as much as we would like.... [People who teach on the fourth year] have encouraged the students to relate their own practical experiences to the theory they are being taught in the fourth year.... One of the things that students are undoubtedly coming up with is ... that some of the theory just doesn't match their practical experience.

The interdisciplinary links were difficult to establish, though a full week's discussion of a theme like the nuclear power industry (with a visiting America professor to introduce a discussion of Three Mile Island) and its ramifications did manage to cut across the economic, political, and other boundaries – important particularly for the younger students. Students, particularly straight from school, found it difficult to respond to an injunction to remember that 'business is about everything and we just find it convenient to teach it in terms of law, economics, or behavioural studies, and you need to think across discipline boundaries'. In the first year the Crick model of separate disciplines still operated, but the course was moving away from it and had already done so in the second year. A 'business environment' or similar component was under discussion for the first year.

Projects were produced in second-year courses – students might work together but had to produce 'an individual response' to a problem and were encouraged to get help from staff in such things as research methods. The dissertation in the fourth year was intended to be much more 'academically rigorous' and benefited from previous experience of that kind of operation. Topics were selected by students, in consultation with a dissertation supervisor.

Is there any way in which a higher education in business studies is different from a higher education in other subjects, such as geography, history, economics . . . ?

> With some university education I think the answer would be yes. . . . My own university education was in law – essentially the kind of requirement which the university put to me was knowledge based. . . . 'Can you tell me what the legal position is? . . . ' There was no attempt to train me in skills of advocacy, for example. I would argue that a business-studies degree, if it's going to be successful, explicitly or implicitly must actually train its students in skills which they can apply to business situations. In other words I don't believe that knowledge in itself is sufficient in business.

Some people would argue that you're shifting the balance away from a 'real' higher education?

> This is not the first time that this accusation . . . has been put to me in those terms. . . . You have to look at the market place. This is probably very much a business-orientated approach. I believe that ultimately *one* of our responsibilities . . . is that we must produce people who are capable not only of getting employment but of getting employment and being valuable in that employment.

The argument might continue – humanities courses induct students into an approach to knowledge which includes critical abilities, judgemental ability. . . . *Are your students critical and judgemental, or more passive recipients of information and learning skills to survive in business?*

> If you'd asked me that question five years ago I would have had to admit that they tended to be passive. The answer to it now is that they are becoming much more judgemental. . . . I don't know whether the difference is that the students have changed, or whether they have changed because the course has changed . . . probably a combination of both.

There was now, he emphasized, more competition to enter the course, students were more motivated. In the fourth year, students did discuss and dispute – very much so, in the second year quite a lot, and in the first year not very much. The most significant change was 'the gap between year 2 and year 4'. He had no doubt that the year in industry had 'an incredible effect on them. They come back far more mature, far more worldly wise'. But even the second-year students were beginning to question. There had also been a change in teaching styles. *Is yours a vocational course?*

> The answer has to be yes. The inevitable follow-up is . . . what do you mean by vocational? . . . One of the things we're trying to do is to give students an awareness of the overall operation of business, both internally and externally, so that they can feel comfortable in any form of commercial activity – and by commercial activity I'm including things like charities which are not profit-making necessarily. I would say that was one of the ways we seek to be vocational. . . . They can actually understand the pressures . . . which affect the operation of any organization. Those pressures will obviously be environmental, they will be legal, they will be economic. Equally they will be personal factors, because one of the things that I think students learn . . . is that internal politics in a company may actually have as much effect as external politics, that power sources are important.

You are not accepting that your students do none of the things that form part of the traditional defence of a liberal higher education?

> No, I'm not. . . . I wouldn't have said that the university degree that I undertook was particularly successful in producing these kinds of qualities in me. . . . My criticism of that kind

of approach is that . . . I suspect it tends to produce in the student a rather theoretical view of life . . . also quite an egocentric view of life. . . . One of the things that is alleged to occur is that you get self-awareness. I suspect that the self-awareness is rather isolated. One of the things that we are trying to do is emphasize that people operate in a community . . . a business community, I make no apology for the fact.

Social psychologists and others might also be solving problems in the real world, but they did not set out explicitly to do that. *Are students on the course good at identifying and solving problems?* There was no doubt, he believed, that 'their facility for identifying problems and for realizing those factors in a problem that are crucial and those that are peripheral improves over time. Like anything else, you get better with experience'. The dissertation was a point at which students were particularly identifying problems and summoning evidence, and some became quite excited about it, and could produce systematic and original work, making very specific recommendations. A good dissertation was a 'more than adequate justification' of the degree.

Leicester Polytechnic

The BA Business Studies degree was launched in 1969, with an honours level added in 1973. It was resubmitted to the CNAA in 1979 and 1984. The broad aim of the course was described in 1979 as being to 'equip students with the basic knowledge and ability to analyse business problems and the approach to decision making. The course deals with activities related to the marketing, human, and financial aspects of business, within the public sector'. These general aims were amplified in 1984 to include the following goals:

 (i) to create a critical awareness of alternative forms of analysis which are of use within the business environment;
 (ii) to provide knowledge and skills which are relevant to problem-solving in business;
 (iii) to provide studies which are of vocational relevance;
 (iv) to ensure students encounter material and techniques on the course which reflect changes in business practice.

The course contains a number of 'core subjects' and options, the core subjects including 'Reasoning and communication in business' in the first and second years, 'Functions of business' in the second year, and 'Business organization and decision-making' in the final year. The final-year project is described as 'a sustained piece of work on a specific topic', and through it 'students will develop and practise the ability to research, sift and evaluate evidence at a detailed level... the project encourages an integrative approach to problem-solving'.

THE HEAD OF THE SCHOOL OF ECONOMICS AND ACCOUNTING AND COURSE LEADER (PROFESSOR BARON) thought that there had been no intentional major change of aims in the previous five or so years, though there had been an attempt to make them somewhat more specific in terms of individual courses. There had been a renewed belief that the course was about 'doing business rather than about describing business' – something difficult to reflect in course descriptions. This did not necessarily mean a shift from the Crick model based on disciplines – economics, sociology, psychology, and law were still there: the course had moved about half way in the spectrum of business-studies degrees. Some areas had been linked, and an innovation was the 'Reasoning and communication' course. The course was not as 'Crickish' as some or as 'integrative' as others were trying to be.

The prospectus has always described the course as an 'advanced, general education for business' – how is that to be interpreted?

> At an advanced level, but not being industry-specific, not being functional-specific.... [Changes have involved taking on board] micro-computing.... It has had to reflect that there are significant changes in... the legal and political environment in which industry works, business works, the social structure in which it works.

'Reasoning and communication', he emphasized, was a rigorous course:

> We try and look at the basis of analysis that people have for the thought process... as well as being a communication course.... The driving light behind it is an accountant... supported by somebody in economics... [with a background in] the philosophy of economic thought.

Students were well motivated, though that was not ascertained by interview (there were at the time 3,500 applicants for eighty-five places). *Do students find it a bit bewildering at first, faced with seven subjects in the first year, including 'Reasoning and communication'?*

> Some do, yes. They find that course particularly bewildering because they're asked to do things that they've never been asked to do before.... On the whole they tend to enjoy it in the end.... They're willing to accept what's thrown at them a bit more than they used to be.... I suppose they might rationalize it saying 'this is what we've got to suffer to get a degree at the end of it . . . it doesn't make much sense to us at this stage, well, let's wait and see....' They're not docile, they're more motivated, they have a target.

Is there dialogue and debate as in some other subjects? They were to be found in a different way – less so in lectures because of the large groups, more so in seminars.

Has there been a change in status of business studies in the academic world?

> I would argue there has widely been a change of status, and there certainly has within this School.... It will add Business to the title next year.... Business studies, business-science degrees have a status that is higher than it used to be. That naturally follows when you use those crude indicators . . . like applicants for a place, employment rate, salary when they leave the institution.

The course was seen as a success story within the department, the majority of the work being with the degree, the part-time degree, and the diploma. Status with employers had not changed as much as 'people try to portray', in that they did not necessarily look for business studies graduates:

> Employers tend to want people who win out at interview in terms of personality, presence, and ability to communicate, and have demonstrated by a degree . . . they've got some ability, can put some hard work in. If they want that kind of person, all well and good. Business-studies students on those grounds compete just as much with, say, an economics or a history graduate. But when it comes to interviews they've got

the great advantage that they've worked for a year, they have studied in relation to the environment in which they're probably applying for a job. . . . [A 1983 study shows] business-studies graduates start at about a thousand a year more than an economics graduate.

Have there had to be any changes in teaching styles, methods, responsiveness to changed situations . . . ? The credibility of the staff was also important, and staff development, he felt, had become more important. Part of the problem was that staff were 'beaten down by the resource pressures on us', a high staff-student ratio, larger classes, lecture and seminar groups. The strategy was to ensure that enough resources could still be deployed for the supervision of sandwich placements and projects, with individual attention. There was an increased problem of keeping up to date. Staff discussed the problems of teaching methods, in course teams, in specially arranged seminars.

Is the business-studies degree a vocational course, and if so what does that mean?

What is a vocational course? . . . I don't think I have a satisfactory answer to that. My personal predilection would be that a vocational course is one that has some element of training in it and is a total area of study leading to some kind of specific employment. Before I came here I ran a course in agricultural and food marketing, now that was industry-specific in other words and it was easier to argue that it was vocational than with a business studies degree which is not industry-specific. I think it is still vocational though because its focus is actually on doing something when a person goes out from here. . . . In that sense it is vocational very broadly described, because business is not a profession and is a long way off becoming a profession.

Defenders of a 'liberal' higher education in the nineteenth century would describe it as an education in which people learned to be aware, critical, and self-critical. *You're not saying that your students don't acquire such characteristics?*

In no way. . . . I made the point that they would be able to do something [on graduation] at the starting level. Our real aim, in addition to that, and why we call it a *higher* education, is that we believe that for many of them this will be the last opportunity when they do get time to sit down and to develop those

> self-critical faculties, the ability not just to be self-critical but to be critical of the system in a positive sense of generating questions that should be asked of it and finding answers to them. ... If they hadn't had a higher education they would be more likely to accept the everyday and commonly accepted practice. ... My challenge to the old liberal-studies approach in this country – and until very recently to things like economics degrees – is that it taught them to be critical, but an aspect of being critical is to be able to implement the positive remedies and alternatives. But what British liberal education did was produce ... very critical individuals, very descriptive individuals, with absolutely no answers.

THE DEPUTY COURSE-LEADER (MRS GORE), discussing the supervised work experience in the third year, explained that placement supervisory staff conducted small groups seminars in the second year in preparation for the industrial placement. There was also a one-day session on interview techniques, and following examinations at the end of the second year there was a week of pre-placement activity, with speakers from industry, and others. There had been an effort to ensure that the experience of the placement was drawn on in the final year. A recent development had been to require that one-third of the report they produced on their placement had to be a case study of a decision or a decision-process within the firm. The core course for all students in the final year was concerned with decision-making, so that students could draw on their experience to the benefit of that course, and tutorials in the first term of the final year related to the placement experience. *Do students actually contribute?*

> Oh yes. It depends on their analysis. The core course heavily links into it. We have had a staff seminar the year before last ... a discussion of the work experience year. ... All staff agreed that it was very important to try and ensure that the wealth of experience gathered in that year was utilized in the course.

Problem-solving and decision-making are referred to in submissions – is this a thread through the course? This had been successful in the previous course, she pointed out, and it had been retained in the current course. The course tried to achieve a balance between 'general issues in management' and 'functional areas' – the latter in the final year, after the work experience.

Is there a problem about creating 'critical awareness', in the words of the course submission, at the same time as handling the range of courses and materials?

> Yes. . . . In the previous scheme teachers in the final year sometimes felt that that was the main weakness – not so much the problem-solving because that can be dealt with by a method of teaching in tutorials . . . presenting them with case studies and problems . . . critical awareness was more of a problem. To try and build up this approach throughout the degree and not just leave it to the final-year tutors we incorporated in the new scheme a course called 'Reasoning and communications'. . . . [Students'] reaction is very good. They like to think that there is a course there that pays particular attention to thought . . . and the industrialists that we've talked to have been very keen on that. . . . It's early days yet, and in honesty I don't think it's proving to be quite as popular as we had hoped.

How did it work? It varied, she explained. The first year included things like the elementary skills of report writing, and there were some more philosophical aspects to it. In the second year, it was very much a question of students communicating. *How much dialogue is there, in that or other classes?*

> You'd find it in the classes I teach, particularly in the final year. . . . Our students are orientated to making sure that there are applications, and if they can think up something that doesn't suit what you've been saying you'll hear about it . . . not quite the same sort of atmosphere perhaps that you'd find in a university. Particularly after work experience, students have a rather different approach. . . . On the old course there had been a feeling that the parts, particularly of the second year, were too separate. 'Functions of business' on the new course had been quite successful in the second year in pulling the course together. There was still a worry about the first year, when they did a lot of courses and topics – these would probably be reduced in the future.

The project was where the students worked individually and exercised independent judgement but 'like students everywhere they start off with enthusiasm, read for too long, are reluctant to actually start putting pen to paper, then panic at the end, but get it straight eventually'.

Is there anything distinctive about business-studies students, are they different in any way from other students?

Different from other students in the polytechnic, yes. They have, by the time they're leaving anyway, a particular set of values, partly because of the work experience. They've been working in management and they've tended to pick up the management ethos. We also as staff, I think, take a fairly tight approach – we regard ourselves in a sense as their bosses . . . and expect them to be on time, hand their work in on time, and take a business-like approach to their work, whereas in other academic disciplines one might say, 'well, it's the idea that's important . . . ' [Some other courses] are not as general as our business-studies degree is. . . . Although we're 'general' we have a fairly academic approach to our studies, and that comes over in the type of student we produce.

Some people might argue that your course distorts the purpose of higher education, is too restrictive, too geared to the market place – how do you respond?

You mean it's too much of a training, and not enough of an education . . . that might be true in some business-studies approaches, but I feel that ours is very much an education, very much training people to think, and use high-order skills – critical evaluation, logical presentation.

Those would be characteristics of many other students – is there something special about your students? 'Yes, they will have been taught them within the business environment . . . they will already have developed those skills within the appropriate framework'. *Is yours a vocational course of study?*

In a very narrow sense of a vocational *training*, no, we're not orientated to vocational training. What we provide is an education with vocational relevance and usefulness. I do believe that the things we teach are usable and relevant and provide the general-education high-order skills. . . . If you think that industry wants high-order skills, then it becomes vocational. If that is what industry wants, then you're providing what industry wants . . . and I think that is what industry does want. It wants people to think clearly and argue clearly, as well as . . . the business methodology and so on.

Napier College, Edinburgh

The BA in business studies was approved by the CNAA in 1975, and the honours extension was introduced in 1980. A revised course was approved for a 1982 start. The overall aim defined in 1975 was

> to give students a general education relevant to a career in industry, commerce or public service through an academic study of business. It will produce graduates who will have developed the ability to identify and evaluate issues and who will be able to meet the rapidly changing demands of industrial society.

The aims and purposes of each of the four years were to provide a foundation course in the basic disciplines and to introduce the student to the nature of the business environment; to introduce the student to some of the functional areas of business; to develop an analytical approach to business problems; to enable the student (on industrial attachment) to recognize that practical knowledge and understanding of industry and commerce is a learning process reflecting academic studies; and to consolidate and integrate previous studies through activities in which the complexities of business problems are analysed and solutions proposed, and to make a choice when a number of decisions are possible. The five-year honours course outlined in 1980 also emphasized a general education relevant to careers in industry, commerce, or public service, and the need for students to be prepared to meet rapidly changing demands during their working life. The honours course specifically aimed to develop 'the greater capacity to recognize the existence of a problem, define it and propose solutions, more ability to integrate the subject areas of the courses, conceptual abilities of a higher order'. In the final years courses were included in 'business policy' and 'behaviour in organizations'. In 1981 the submission proposed major changes in aim and content, underlining that the course reflected the background of the Scottish educational system, 'where entrants have a broadly based education at school covering both arts and science subjects'. Emphasis was on the management of 'financial, human and physical resources', a 'generalist' degree combining theoretical and practical aspects, a sound academic foundation linked with an emphasis on problem-solving, reaching decisions and analysing their effects, and operating effectively as a member of an interdisciplinary team. The study of 'the academic and applied aspects of business and its environment' would enable the student to develop the qualities needed for business:

(i) a command of the basic business disciplines and a knowledge of the factors influencing the social, economic, and political environment of business;
(ii) analytical, problem-solving, and decision-making skills;
(iii) social skills and a critical personal awareness which will encourage a creative and positive response to dynamic situations.

These characteristics were included in the 1983 'Guidance notes for students'. The submission emphasized synthesis and an interdisciplinary approach, movement away from the Crick structure and the focus on 'functional areas' of business. A variant of the degree on a part-time basis (not discussed here) aimed in 1982 to 'provide a balance between the educational and vocational aspects of the course'.

THE HEAD OF THE DEPARTMENT OF BUSINESS STUDIES AND FORMERLY COURSE CO-ORDINATOR (MR MCINTOSH), AND THE COURSE CO-ORDINATOR OF THE PART-TIME DEGREE (MR VETTESE) were interviewed together.

> M. In the last submission we endeavoured to reduce the number of discrete disciplines. . . . One of our objectives was to make it an interdisciplinary course rather than a multidisciplinary course. . . . We tried to break down some of the stark distinctions between the likes of economics and accounting, maths and information technology, and to make the focus of the course – the core of the course – business studies, business organization.

This was an attempt to escape from the Crick model. The course was becoming less broad, the number of discrete subjects had been reduced, contact hours had been reduced, and the number of options increased (some functional areas, some 'almost discipline based'). *How long does it take the student to get a feel of the connectedness you are trying to establish?*

> V. It takes in some ways right to the end of the course. . . . Pious notions about interdisciplinarity and catch-all connections

between the disciplines are not available in the early stages of the course.... The course is built so that tutors know where the links are, but integration is an event that happens in the mind of the student towards the end of the course, and virtually cannot be planned for.

M. I think the very existence of a strong subject area ... in business studies, business organization, really helps to integrate the other subjects.... The strength of the previous course was the strength of other departments ... economics .. accounting ... behavioural science. No one was telling them anything about business studies, business organization, business at large. [Now] they are at least aware from day one what sort of a subject it is they are are going to study.

The ability to analyse and synthesize built up after the initial concern with knowledge and comprehension. 'Business policy' encouraged integration through the use of case studies, which appeared in some form in some subjects from the first year:

V. ... within 'business organization' ... a somewhat shorter form of real world business histories, for example ... where the firm came from, so you're not teaching economic history but the history of business, of real businesses they can identify with. In the first year they can set off to do their own little business histories and bring them back to tutorials, so that this approach to individualizing the learning process starts in the beginning.

M. 'Business organization and information systems', 'behavioural science' as well in the second year, is highly analytical, relying on case studies. That's not to say that the other subjects aren't using case studies.

How do you promote creativity in students, as emphasized in the 1981 submission?

M. Along with critical self-awareness I think maybe over the last twenty-four months or so this has given us more food for thought than anything else. I think we would have accepted two years ago that we weren't achieving it particulary well, that we weren't introducing the whole idea of problem-solving in a dynamic world. ... we designed an outdoor development programme ... and we take students away to Glenmore Lodge

> near Aviemore in the first half of their second year, and we do a bit of role playing... problem-solving, through management games... to emphasize the importance of group dynamics in decision-making, to expose students to each other.

Communication skills were approached through seminars and essay writing, and preparation (in the second year) for industrial attachments – including interview practice and the writing of reports: there was no formal assessment. *Are all the students employment-oriented?*

> M. Five years ago a large percentage of students coming on the course would state explicitly that they wanted to go into education or the public sector. A further large minority would say they didn't know what they wanted to do... [leaving] their options open as long as possible. Another large majority would simply say it was an alternative to unemployment.... Perhaps increasing numbers now have an attraction for industry. We don't have the same number who want to teach... [or] go into the public sector. I think students are more business motivated... many come on the course because it is a sandwich course, and they get the opportunity to taste the job before going in.... Some of the students do come on the course because they perceive the subjects involved to be interesting and exciting... yet have some reward at the end of the day.

Questioning and discussion took place in tutorials, in the treatment of case studies, always with some more keen to participate than others.

How defensive does one have to be about business studies as a higher education? They believed this not to be necessary at Napier. One problem was the association of 'business studies' at school level with shorthand and typing and the use of the word processor. The course had established a 'business-studies philosophy', and the subject was becoming more involved with other areas – notably engineering. Whereas in the past technology-related areas would have been 'topped up' with 'liberal' or 'general' studies, they were now turning to business studies for that sort of input.

There was a senior lecturer in the department with the responsibility for teaching and learning methods:

M. It's a faculty cost but it's within the department. and that's a demonstration of the seriousness with which we have approached [teaching methods] – perhaps that was lacking, lacking new learning methods four or five years ago – to break down some of the traditional views of teaching and learning in the college, to make learning more effective.

V. And I think as a disseminator of modern thinking on teaching and learning methods . . . scan educational journals, look at new methods that use audio-visuals, and so on.

Projects were an opportunity for students to demonstrate skill in business evaluation, integration, and other things. Topics were selected in consultation with tutors, mainly whilst on industrial placement. Students often became obsessed with the project late in the day, during the second half of the fourth year – it was difficult to stimulate interest in an academic project while they were on attachment. Students were prepared for the placement – employers and students currently on placement were invited in, and students were told what employers and the college expected. Students were also encouraged to find their own placements. However,

V. . . . there's virtually no way of compensating for an effect that will always be there, that they've been in an academic, college environment for two years, and there's quite a few myths that they may have collected along the road that will be exploded by the shock. . . . That's part of the exercise, they're going to learn from that.

The choice of honours or unclassified route lay with the student, after much counselling and guidance. Some students disappointingly opted for the unclassified when they would have made good honours students:

V. . . . their track record shows that, they know that. They already have . . . a very strong vocational bias, and they say: 'I don't perceive taking an honours degree as helping me with my work. I want to get out there as soon as possible and get into management'.

Is yours a vocational degree course?

M. Yes, all students won't perceive it that way . . . not all students come on the course with a clear vocation in mind, that they're going to be marketing managers, or personnel managers . . . none the less, within the degree we have fairly clear career paths. . . . There are areas the students can choose to study which are not purely vocational. The degree itself is designed for a vocation in business management.

v. Because it's vocational, a BA degree in business studies, ordinary or honours, is an excellent passport to interviews . . . it's vocational in the sense that its graduates are employable. . . . If that was the only element of 'vocationality' . . . that was built into the course I would be disappointed, because I think that would be denying the rigour of the course. But we know that graduates . . . change jobs . . . three or four times in their first five or six years . . . and I would hope that then, after five or six years, the educational content of the business studies degree scores, that is, I hope it is vocational in the sense that it will make them good managers.

Do the students share some of the characteristics of higher education in general, perhaps described as a liberal education?

v. Scotland in particular does have a profound tradition of liberal education, and if I thought we were releasing graduates who . . . had not during the course seen the spirit of criticism in that liberal sense then I would be quite disappointed. I wouldn't say that the degree is overly vocational or anything like that.

M. At times I've actually been accused of doing an anti-business-studies degree. We seem to spend a lot of time criticizing what's going on in business, doing critiques of marketing and personnel relations. . . . I do get concerned at times that as part of what I would perceive to be a wider trend we have backed off from some political issues. The students themselves are to some extent politically neutered when they come on the course . . . I think at times we've got to give ourselves a shake and say: 'right, what's in the course that's reflecting wider society?'

That did happen, they indicated, in specific cases – the study of multinational organizations, for example, raising international and social responsibility issues: 'I wouldn't underestimate the impact of moving away from the old Crick formula in this' (M).

Oxford Polytechnic

An honours degree in business studies began in 1974, was replanned and reapproved in 1979, and was re-presented for a progress review visit in 1982. The 1974 submission contained as options finance and accounting, and manpower studies, and marketing was added the following year. It is a four-year sandwich course. The aims of the course as described in 1974, and not subsequently changed, were to produce graduates 'with an understanding of business and business problems and activities'; to develop the ability to 'think logically and communicate clearly, whether in numerical or verbal form, and to learn from situations met during and after formal education'; to provide an 'intellectually satisfying and coherent education through the integration of disciplines', enabling students to 'appreciate the interdependence of technological and socio-economic factors in society'; to 'extend students in the exercise of their critical and analytical faculties, judgement and creativity', and to equip them for a 'wide range of careers', to make a contribution 'to society and to the business world'. Also added in 1974, and later dropped, was the expressed belief 'that these differing aims can be achieved together by providing a broad vocational education'.

In 1979 an emphasis on 'business systems' and 'marketing' was intended to integrate other studies, and other changes in the course were designed to 'aid student motivation, prepare better for the industrial year, and produce more rounded business graduates'. Problem-solving and decision-making were features of some of the courses, including for example 'business systems' in the first year, which aimed 'to develop problem-solving skills in business contexts'. Emphasis was placed on the value of the industrial year, and on project work. The 1982 review explained how the balance between disciplines and practical materials and contexts was seen:

> Our method of avoiding discontinuity between disciplines and business functions is to include some of the functional studies with disciplines in the first year and to gradually increase the proportion of functions. Even in the final year some discipline studies remain.

THE COURSE TUTOR (MR PENDLEBURY) described the course as intentionally broad: even in the final year – when students specialized

– the common core still accounted for half the course. The course was both general and sufficiently specialized for students to obtain exemption from various professional bodies – a subsidiary, but important objective. Pejorative attitudes towards business studies were no longer in evidence: 'that sort of criticism was around more before there were many business graduates about. Now that industry has seen business graduates, you don't hear much of that'.

Humanities courses may argue that they produce students with 'critical intelligence'. Does that apply to business students? 'Certainly, and I think the fact that they have to integrate to a large extent the different studies they do during the course of the degree emphasizes this. Certainly there is very little spoon-feeding.' *Does the course as a whole, or do particular parts of it, 'extend . . . critical and analytical faculties, judgement and creativity'?*

> I don't think it's so much special parts as the fact that students come here from a variety of academic backgrounds, and in the first year this is to some extent conversion to get them into the business-studies subjects, so there is not so much of [that aim] in the first year, but as the course develops there is more and more of it.

Students did take part in discussion in tutorials – though this would vary from subject to subject (generally a tutorial had no more than four students). A common pattern for tutorials was for students to submit essays for discussion with the tutor and fellow students. Students did have a significant amount of information to master: 'I think the fact that they are dealing with six subjects is a big factor here, and typically four would be new to them when they come on the course'. *How difficult is that for students?*

> It is very difficult to generalize. We have particularly geared the course so that the first year is not as hard work as the succeeding years, because a lot of people are starting subjects from scratch, and it may be we have gone a bit too far in that direction.

Problem-solving and decision-making were in fact firm threads through the course:

> It's important to remember that the third year of the course is

the year out in industry, and they are then going to be faced with real problems. Therefore we need by various techniques to get them used to problem-solving in the first two years of the course, so that they are ready to make a good contribution in year 3. We feel that we want to give students to industry who will be worthwhile to them in this third year.

Across the course there were some common approaches to problem-solving, but accountancy, for example, was different from behavioural sciences, 'so we can't expect too much commonality between them'. Case study was probably the most common strategy, but in problem-solving and decision-making 'we don't have a special Oxford Poly approach'.

The final-year project was not compulsory but most students opted to produce one (they were at risk in final assessment if they did not), and its educational value was seen as being very high. Students came into college during the industrial year for briefing on the project.

[An advisory note to students whilst on their placement explains: The student is responsible for the project, not the tutor... the tutor's role is sometimes misunderstood. The tutor should aim to give equal help to those who ask. But specific advice of what to do is limited to ideas for projects, suggestions of sources/comparisons to look at, and advice on lay-out and on the structuring of the argument being presented. (June 1985).]

Most students were enthusiastic and saw the project as an important part of the course. Students were viva'd on their projects.

He felt that the course was still in the Crick mould, but in replanning for a 1987 review 'we are looking to a degree that is much more skills and functions oriented'. *Are projects and such strategies a means of escaping from the discipline-based structure?*

That's not unusual. We were doing that right from the start. I think most people were doing it, in the early 70s anyway.... We'll be looking not so much at economics, behavioural science, law, but business context and business operations, and so on.... We'll be making more use of the sandwich... and bring it more into the final year.

There was already a weekly session throughout the second year with the industrial-year supervisor, discussing applications to firms and bringing in specialists to talk about jobs in industry.

Does a course like this come out of the traditions of the universities and out of those of the colleges from which institutions like Oxford Polytechnic emerged? 'Yes, and I think we are an amalgam, hopefully, of the best of both.'

Commentary

The business-studies courses share many of the same or similar aims in the student qualities they aim to develop, the kinds of knowledge, understanding, and skills they seek to promote, and the interpretations of an appropriate higher education they put upon the courses and their outcomes. With an extremely high demand for places they are able to recruit good-quality, highly motivated students, committed to the courses and to future employment in industry, commerce, or the public services. Some of the interpretation of the course aims and vocational implications is therefore conditioned by the commitment and intentions of the students, with fewer of them entering employment outside commerce and industry, even where they did so a few years ago. Course teams do not, therefore, have to concern themselves with those students who might be treating the course purely as an end in itself. Even though 'business' is a disparate field and students' *precise* job intentions may not be clear at the beginning, courses can be defined on the basis of certain coherent assumptions.

The aims of the courses, none of which goes back beyond the mid-1970s, point uniformly to the habits of mind they hope to develop in students, with emphasis on critical analysis, critical self-awareness, logical thought, and ability to identify and solve problems, and to relate constructively to dynamically changing conditions. Students are expected to be, and apparently are, responsive to the challenges of active teaching and learning situations, and are prepared for the most part to question and discuss (or in some cases to 'suffer' puzzlement for the sake of the degree to which they are motivated), and confront problems of the match between theory and experience.

Staff are often preoccupied with the problems or weaknesses of teaching strategies, have often made major changes in course structures, and are critical of their own courses. The particular, discipline-based ('Crick') structure of the courses established under CNAA auspices has provoked constant anxiety about the nature, balance, and future shape of business-studies degrees. There is constant definition and redefinition of courses on an axis between completely discipline-based and completely function-based, with a sense of movement away from the Crick mould, from description to doing – although the disciplines remain in place to one extent or another. One of the problems of the discipline-based (multidisciplinary) course has been the difficulty of pursuing 'integration', with the earlier techniques of project and integrative topics being supplemented by new courses, role playing, case studies, and residential programmes. A number of strategies emerge as of central importance. The industrial placement is one of these, with constant reference to its importance, the ways in which preparation for it takes place, the ways in which it feeds into the final year (or in the case of Napier two years) of the course – with some self-criticism about successes in doing this. The dissertation or project is another crucial integrative experience, and often related to the industrial placement. Emphasis throughout is on the acquisition of knowledge and skills in a business environment, in course units concerned with the (interdisciplinary) issues of 'business policy' or 'business organization', or in the days or weeks set aside for major case explorations. Although the strategies for improving communication skills differ from course to course, these are of constant concern, both as preparation for the continuing demands of the course itself, or as preparation for the entry into employment – including the interview, when 'personality, presence, and ability to communicate' are often being sought.

In all cases the courses are seen as vocational, with a positive connotation though not always with the same interpretation. Courses are seen as offering a rigorous form of higher education, but one which related to employment in a 'wide range' of jobs *in* commerce and industry. Although courses are seen as containing various training elements, the courses are not held to be vocational training. The vocational outcomes of the courses include critical, responsive roles in the business community and in society, and not only the obtaining of employment but also being valuable in employment. Some of the educational outcomes may not become apparent until career points some years after graduation. Neither the course nor future employers want students who have merely learned routines; students are expected to be 'businesslike', but also to be able to generate questions and suggest answers. Whatever the differences between a business-studies degree and other degrees, there are skills and qualities involved that business studies shares with higher education widely. The courses are defended as appropriately vocational – that is, as the right vehicle for learning the operations of business in its wider contexts – and as a legitimate and good higher education.

We described in chapter 3 the employment opportunities for business-studies graduates as constituting an 'open market' for which their courses provided an 'employment-relevant educational base'. Unlike engineering, a business-studies degree does not regulate entry into a specific profession or set of professions. Consequently it does not have its curriculum constrained by the requirements of professional bodies.

A business-studies degree is not industry-specific and it is not functionally-specific. We have seen it described as the study of 'business in a broad sense', as 'vocational, very broadly described', as a qualification which would help graduates to obtain employment and which would be valuable in it. The interviews produced little discussion of the *content* of the curriculum as distinct from its broad structural features. Unlike engineering there is not a large knowledge base that must be transmitted. This enables the business educator to place his emphasis on 'doing' rather than on 'describing'. This gives rise to concerns about the development of skills, about the relationship between different parts of the curriculum (integration), about the establishment of values (a management 'ethos', or the capacity for judgement amidst dynamic change). No less than the 'liberal educator', the business educator is concerned to develop the 'whole person', but development is in a different direction. For some it was described as 'skills in frameworks', for others as 'a business-like approach'; others talked of a 'particular set of values', and others spoke of 'critical people' who can produce 'answers'.

Business-studies degrees have undergone considerable changes since their inception in the early 1970s and the widespread adoption of the formula of the Crick Report. Changes have been mainly in the direction of a greater emphasis on skills, on problem-solving, on making courses in some sense 'more vocational'. The focus on 'doing' has led to the construction of course units in areas such as 'reasoning and communication'. Goals which would be familiar in the 'hidden curriculum' of the liberal educator increasingly achieve explicit curriculum attention from the business educator.

The pressures for these developments in the business-studies curriculum have not come from employers or from professional bodies. The picture here is not one of pressure but of relative indifference. What then has been the impetus for change? Two contributory factors should be noted. One that has been referred to earlier is the carry-over effect of the philosophy of course developments promoted by the Business and Technician Education Council. Another might lie with the students. The demand for places on business-studies degrees is high. All of the staff interviewed appeared satisfied with the ability and motivation of their students. Developments which have required a more participatory involvement of students have been possible because of the quality of students recruited. Moreover the quality of intakes may have assisted the improvement in status of business studies within institutions. This in turn may have given staff greater confidence to move away from conventional academic norms.

Business-studies degrees of the kind described in this chapter are very much the property of public-sector higher education. They have not developed on the same scale or in the same form in the universities. Their success in recruiting good-quality students and in building on their motivation for careers in business has ensured that business-studies graduates have been well-equipped to compete in an 'open' labour market. As we were reminded, 'business is not a profession and is a long way off becoming a profession'. Thus, the courses are not training professionals in the sense that engineers are trained. Business-studies courses appear to be geared to the production of a 'type of person', characterized by a set of skills, values, and aspirations that are largely transferable across the business community but which are intended to ensure success within it.

An extended American comparison in the case of business studies – in the US more commonly called 'business administration' – would indicate some of the features we have previously noted in relation to engineering, including the role of the liberal arts in an undergraduate business course. The longer American experience of commerce and business programmes has, again, presented some of the same underlying issues as in Britain, though similar reservations about the educational system, curriculum assumptions, and institutional requirements have to be made as in the case of engineering. In the United States there have been similar discussions of what business leadership requires – such as an analytical mind, problem-solving ability, imagination (Jones 1985) – and the available strategies for achieving these and similar characteristics, including the importance of a broad culture and the combination of theoretical understanding with specific skills (including those of measurement). Some universities and colleges – the University of Maryland, for example – have experimented with liberal-arts courses directed specifically at business careers (not liberal studies additives to business-administration courses). The Maryland course, entitled 'Liberal arts in business', was a response to an awareness that business was beginning to hire liberal-arts graduates in the early 1980s, and that these could benefit from a curriculum which combined the aims of a humanistic vision with the skills and analytical abilities required for business. The course is explicitly a combination of the traditional values of a liberal-arts education, and the preparation of students for a career in business (Kenny 1984; University of Maryland 1984). Those institutions with a more traditional programme in business administration – such as those state universities (until recently colleges) in Pennsylvania where we had discussions – are bound (and feel themselves bound) by accreditation requirements, which are intended to ensure that curricula are not too vocational, and include a proportion of liberal-arts courses to provide an appropriate balance. The American Assembly of Collegiate Schools of Business lays down that the 'professional' courses should be concentrated in the last two years of the four-year programme; so as to provide in the first two years a foundation 'in those academic areas necessary for an appropriate combination of descriptive and analytical approaches to the study of business administration. Such foundation work would normally include courses in mathematics, social sciences, humanities, and the natural sciences', and across the whole programme the target is 40–60 per cent of time spent on business administration and economics (Slippery Rock University, *Requirements for BSBA Degree*, undated). The 'distribution requirements' for business administration as for other programmes at Bloomsburg University of Pennsylvania, for instance, feature lists of courses in humanities, social sciences, and natural sciences and mathematics, the aims of which are presented to students in terms of effective communication, analytical, and quantitative thinking, the ability to make independent and responsible value judgements, an appreciation of the arts, the physical and biological environments and society, and other explicit goals (Bloomsburg University, *Undergraduate Catalogue*, 1983/4). Slippery Rock University (or State College, as it was at the time), also in the Pennsylvania state system, defined the objectives of its business administration programme in 1974 as supported by a curriculum designed to enable 'a successful business person ... [to] possess an understanding of all aspects of life. The ... program continues to place emphasis on liberal arts, sciences and humanities as well as requiring a thorough understanding of economics' (Slippery Rock State College, *A Proposal to Establish an Undergraduate Program*, 1974).

An essential ingredient of these American examples is their assertion of a broad preparation for active and understanding roles in business. With different emphases this is true of the British counterparts. The explanations and justifications in the British course descriptions and interviews are in no way defensive. They suggest that the courses are aiming to provide an important new contribution to higher education and to the employment market, and are not merely responsive to it but are creatively determined to meet needs not always understood even by employers themselves. Course leaders therefore do not feel 'constrained' by the labour market, but have the benefit of buoyant student demand, and shape courses which foster many of the qualities and characteristics which they conceive to be common to higher education in general. As in the discussions of engineering, a binding theme is preparation for and involvement with the 'real world', its problems and needs. In British terms, therefore, interpretation of the vocational in such courses indicates an attempt to balance an awareness of the possible employment outcomes with the traditions and interpretations of a quality higher education. Here again, the process has been highly explicit, constantly open to review and amendment, always aware of the role of the CNAA and peer judgement, and permanently sensitive to the basis on which courses operate, the goals they seek to attain, and the contexts to which they relate.

11

Business studies: a note on Europe

A feature which undergraduate business education in the United Kingdom shares with its counterparts in several other European countries is its location mainly outside the universities. In West Germany, the *Fachhochschulen* have developed business studies as one of the main planks of their exclusively vocational curricula over a period that roughly parallels the growth of business-studies degrees in the English polytechnics. In France, business education has formed a part of the élite *grandes écoles* sector of higher education for a much longer period of time, and French business schools with their close links with the *chambres de commerce* provide a privileged route into employment with top companies. More recent developments in France have seen the introduction of courses in business as part of the two-year short-cycle education provided by the *Instituts universitaires de technologie* (*IUT*). Once again, the universities were bypassed: 'viewed as too preoccupied with theoretical studies in the arts and sciences, too divorced from job markets outside secondary education, and too dominated by the Left to provide such technical training' (Ce333 and Sabatier 1986: 163).

Reflecting the opportunities for mobility of labour within the EEC, a number of business courses have been designed to equip students to operate effectively in a European rather than a national employment context. The courses are offered collaboratively by institutions in two or more countries. They recruit students from the participating countries, and they divide their studies between two institutions and in several cases receive two national qualifications. We visited several of these joint courses in England, France, and West Germany in order to gain first-hand knowledge of European experiences of providing courses with explicitly vocational objectives, and to draw out similarities and contrasts in relations between institutions and employment in the achievement of a 'practical' curriculum and in the opportunities for graduates.

There was no doubting the popularity of the courses with students. The prestige of the French *grandes écoles* is a major attraction to students in its own right. However, in Britain and Germany staff reported that the 'European' courses attracted more well-qualified applications than did equivalent national courses. We spoke to students from all three countries, and they emphasized the attractiveness of the courses in terms of the 'use and extension of languages', the 'year abroad', and the improvement of job prospects. In respect of the last, the German students in particular spoke of the considerable demand for and recognition of business-studies qualifications by German employers. These perceptions, which were supported by the lecturers in the *Fachhochschulen*, suggested a more explicit labour market currency for the German *Diplom-Betriebswirt* or *Diplom-Kaufmann* than exists for the English BA Business Studies. The French students were confident of the standing of the DESCAF and of the employment opportunities which it would open up for them.

All of the institutions visited made claims for the practical nature of their courses, of service to business, and of meeting industrial needs, and frequently contrasted their approach with what was regarded as the more theoretical and academic nature of the universities. That said, the differences between the institutions were large and are summarized in Table 1.

The distinctiveness and prestige of the French *grandes écoles* is widely recognized. They recruit the best qualified students mainly from professional middle- and upper-class backgrounds. In so far as employers use higher education as a screening mechanism – to identify potential employees with highly desired attributes – French employers make use of the *grandes écoles* in much the same way as English employers make use of the universities of Oxford and Cambridge.

Business graduates from the English polytechnics and the German *Fachhochschulen* are not destined for the same levels of seniority in employment or positions in society as the *grande école* graduate. Consequently, preparation is for a rather different kind of occupational role.

Although the distinctiveness of the *grandes écoles* is clear, several commentators have pointed to the considerable similarities

Table 1 *Comparison of polytechnics, Fachhochschulen, and grandes écoles*

	Polytechnics	Fachhochschulen	Grandes écoles
1 Course provision	Comprehensive	Limited subject range and levels	Monotechnic
2 Site	Large	Medium–large	Small
3 National prestige	Low	Low	Very high
4 Staffing	(a) Appointment mainly on academic criteria, not regulated by statute	(a) Appointments: new staff must have doctorates or equivalent, and at least five years of industrial experience	(a) Appointments: dual criteria of academic and business experience
	(b) Staff on full-time teaching contracts, emphasis on research and consultancy variable	(b) Staff on full-time teaching contracts, emphasis on research and consultancy variable. Some part-time teaching by industrialists	(b) Majority of staff on part-time contracts: consultancy required but research optional
	(c) Mainly university educated	(c) Must be university educated	(c) Mainly *grandes écoles* educated

5 Student admissions	Identical formal requirements for university and polytechnic	Different (lower) formal academic entry requirements from universities plus work experience requirements (although this varies between the *Länder*)	Different (higher) academic entry requirements from universities
6 Qualifications	Terminal qualifications identical for university and polytechnic	Different terminal qualifications	Different terminal qualifications
7 Length of course	Same as university	Shorter than university	Non-comparable
8 Finance and control	Public	Public	Private (Chamber of Commerce)

which exist between the polytechnics and *Fachhochschulen*. There are certainly similarities in terms of institutional ideology and in status relative to universities. But the differences are also important. To summarize them, the work-related practical ideology of the *Fachhochschulen* is reinforced by a range of statutory measures which have shaped the form of educational provisions to accord with that ideology. Measures related to staff appointments, student entry requirements, length of courses, terminal qualifications, and areas of study have achieved a clear differentiation between *Fachhochschulen* and universities. The differences between universities and polytechnics in England are nothing like as clear-cut on any of these factors. Differences in curricula were not marked between the three countries, with all courses moving from disciplinary foundations at the beginning of the course to greater emphases on functional specialism. There were differences, but these were institutional as much as national, a function of the approaches of different lecturers. Students identified the most practical elements of the curriculum as computing, languages, and functional specialisms in areas such as finance and marketing.

All courses pursued the practical and sought applicability to the real problems of industry and business. Yet national differences in approach were marked. Given the broadly common curriculum content, differences appeared to reflect pedagogic style and the role of work experience.

Almost all students found the German courses most 'academic', most discipline-based. Indeed, many German staff and students use the term 'economics' or 'business economics' when referring to the course. Student learning was essentially independent and passive, 'reading books in the library'. Although the German courses were described as 'academic', several students felt that the English courses were more theoretical. For example, the English treatment of accounting was described as 'more theoretical', and concerned to present 'a true and fair view'. The German approach was 'more practical', 'more legalistic', and more related to the operation of rules and procedures which once learned could be applied in a semi-automatic fashion. Both English and French staff criticized the German students for an over-concern with 'right' answers – with 'knowledge' rather than 'understanding'.

The French course was seen as being very practical and this

was achieved through a predominantly case-study approach. The students were heavily taught and heavily dependent on lecture notes for the acquisition of information. Foreign students found the academic level very high but the teaching approach 'more like secondary school'. Contact hours were high and attendance compulsory. Assessment was frequent and by a wide range of methods. 'The style of teaching is very strict, it is like the school system. You have to do homework and the teachers control you closely. [In Germany] you have more freedom. They have more tests, every few weeks, the control is harder' (German student studying in France). The students did not read, their institutions hardly possessed libraries. Apart from the lectures (the essential lecture notes are frequently journal articles) the students often worked in small groups of four or five. Case studies taught a 'system of approach' (as opposed to general theoretical principles). The case studies had a 'general relevance'; 'you learn how to think about a problem', but the focus was on 'the solution' rather than on the problem. This was what the course was about, not the acquisition of information: 'teachers sum up all the information. There is no need to read'. The essence of the French approach was that the teachers provided students with the information as economically and efficiently as possible. The student's job was to *use* the information in exercises and case studies to find solutions to practical business problems. It was the confrontation with practice which provided the intellectual challenge rather than the mastery of a body of knowledge.

The main contrast between the English and French approaches to the use of work experience lay in the degree of integration with the college-based part of the course. In Britain, the placement was frequently described as 'useful but separate' from the academic part of the course. The final-year placement was described by one French graduate as 'clearly the most intellectually demanding part of the whole programme'. It lasted eight weeks and was closely integrated with antecedent and subsequent academic study. A French lecturer described the final placement in this way:

> We ask them to go in a firm, they work in groups of two or three students, analyse and solve a problem pertaining to personnel or marketing. That's a lot of work and they invest a lot. They are most interested and the results are very good.

The French final-year placement was intended to be an executive traineeship with precise objectives. It had to serve the interests of the students and the firm. Students were given specific tasks to achieve and their success in achieving them was closely evaluated.

Business education in the polytechnics and *Fachhochschulen* exhibits many of the features characteristic of higher education to be found in the university systems of the two countries. The emphasis is on the *acquisition* of knowledge, whether theoretical or practical, and on the student's own responsibility for that acquisition. Although there are clear differences in pedagogy between the two countries, the courses are part of conventional academic work and share its norms and values. French students must also acquire a body of knowledge, but for them the process of acquisition is something to be achieved as efficiently and economically as possible and this gives rise to methods of teaching and learning which would not be regarded as consistent with the conventions of higher education in other institutions. The real emphasis of the French approach is on *application*. Fifty per cent of a business-studies course at the École Supérieure de Commerce in Toulouse was devoted to case studies and exercises and the intellectual challenge of the course was seen to lie in these.

The Director of the École in Toulouse described the ways in which he attempted to achieve practical relevance in the work of the institution. First, in the appointment of staff particular emphasis was placed on professional experience. Secondly, the Director was himself an entrepreneur. Thirdly, many practising managers were involved in the teaching and examining of the courses as well as in placement supervision. Fourthly, the staff of the École were encouraged to engage in professional work and many were on part-time contracts.

It was estimated that approximately half of the Toulouse staff had significant amounts of work experience prior to appointment. However, French practice emphasized continuing relationships between business enterprises and the work of the École, and this was achieved in a number of ways. First, executives from local industry provided some of the teaching on the course (between 10 and 15 per cent of the curriculum in the first year rising to 40 per cent in the final year). Secondly, most of the 'full-time' staff were employed on part-time contracts (of between 40 and 80 per cent) to facilitate continuing business activity, often in the form of consultancy. Thus, most staff were engaged in consultancy or industry-based research. In addition, there was the inevitable liaison with industry which arose from the organization of student placements and also from employers' recruitment practices.

In Britain, institutions attempt to appoint staff with business experience although most appointments are full-time and there are relatively few teaching inputs from the business community. Some staff, particularly in professional fields such as law and accountancy, may engage in consultancy although there does appear to be some difficulty in arranging industry-based secondments. There is considerable contact through placement organization and supervision. Industrial experience was a prerequisite for appointments to a post in a *Fachhochschule*. There was the possibility of study leave for staff to update their industrial experience, although the take-up of this was not great in the institutions visited.

In all countries, business graduates will possess practical experience of business activity although this will not necessarily have been obtained within the course. The timing of the work experience has implications for its function. The English sandwich placement appears to be designed to achieve a level of personal growth and maturity which is obtained through admission policies in Germany. In France, the final-year project/placement is designed to fulfil specific professional and academic objectives.

For all students the most important relationship with employment is obtaining a job at the end of the course. Most students were confident of their future employability and the statistics of graduate employment tend to support them. The English students would have to use their qualifications in a relatively open labour market. Lecturers at the British institutions regretted the relatively low recognition given to specific business qualifications by British employers. That the students were nevertheless successful in the labour market was to be attributed in large part to the attractiveness to employers of their personal qualities and the realism of their occupational aspirations.

German employers make much more sophisticated use of the structure of educational qualifications. Holders of the *Diplom-Betriebswirt/Kaufmann* could expect to apply for jobs which made specific demand for their particular qualification. Both British and German students appeared to use newspaper advertisements plus speculative writing to firms as the main sources of job applications.

In Toulouse, the jobs came looking for the graduates. At the time of the visit, the École had received requests from firms for personnel in the following fields: purchasing/sales (119 posts), export (20), finance (85), information technology (11), and general management (63). By graduation, it was expected that each student would have an average of four jobs on offer. The availability of such information and the publicity given to it illustrates the commercialism of the *grande école* enterprise. Detailed information on employment, including salaries, is collected and published, and constitutes, for the Toulouse Director, a prime means of course evaluation.

It is also evident that *grandes écoles* graduates are destined for top management jobs which will not be reached by the majority of polytechnic and *Fachhochschulen* graduates. The latter will face some competition from university graduates and are more likely to have to settle for middle-management positions in less prestigious companies.

Vocational higher education inevitably contains the potential for tension between business and academic values. One way of looking at business education in the three countries is as a playing out of these tensions.

A presupposition of vocational higher education is that there is a knowledge base to the related professional area. Questions are then raised as to defining what it is and deciding who shall provide it. The answers to both questions lead on to a consideration of the use made of educational qualifications by employers.

Adopting the terminology of the model of higher education–employment relationships described in chapter 3, a particular qualification may be necessary and/or sufficient to gain entry into a particular career. Looking at business education in France, Germany, and Britain in these terms, it would appear that possession of the Diplôme d'études supérieures commerciales, administrative et financières (DESCAF) is both necessary and sufficient to gain entry to élite business careers. This cannot be said either of the *Diplom-Betriebswirt/Kaufmann* or the BA Business Studies, but both have a currency at middle-management levels in business. In Germany, for many jobs the possession of the graduate business qualification is indeed necessary in so far as many employers specify its possession when advertising posts. This is very rarely true in Britain. In both Britain and Germany, the sufficiency of the qualifications to gain appropriate employment is very dependent on labour market fluctuations, given the absence of effective manpower planning in both countries. The likelihood of sufficiency is much less in Britain because business graduates will be in competition for jobs with graduates from a large number of other fields. Given the emphasis placed by British employers on personal attributes, it is upon possession of these that the business graduate may be specially dependent.

With regard to training, courses in higher education can be distinguished in terms of the proportion of initial job training that is completed. In only loosely professional fields such as business this may be difficult to discern because there is no agreed consensus among employers of what constitutes basic competence in an employee. However, the heterogeneity of the graduate recruits into British business is such that employers are not able to assume that any pre-entry training has taken place. (This does not of course prevent larger companies from mounting differentiated in-company training schemes which can take account of variations in knowledge base.) By their more rigid use of specialist qualifications, French and German companies can, if they so wish, make assumptions about the knowledge and competences of the graduates they recruit. Thus, because of their greater use in selection, the DESCAF and the *Diplom-Betriebswirt/Kaufmann* are able to claim a larger role in training for their respective occupational outlets.

How much pre-entry training do employers want and expect? Even within the *grandes écoles* there was an acceptance that job-related skills are best learned on the job. If so, what is business education intended to achieve? It can aid selection by identifying candidates who have demonstrated some degree of commitment/interest to a business career. It can provide a basis for subsequent training by transmitting attitudes and values compatible with business activity and by providing knowledge and experience of basic business functions. It can also be used as a surrogate for other factors relevant to employers, including intellectual ability or social background. Each of these uses has rather different implications for the content and organization of courses. Employers' wants are conditioned by tradition, by prejudice, by personal experience as much as by a rational appraisal of employment needs, the same kinds of factors as determine student preferences in choosing their higher education.

Despite similarities in the content of curricula, the courses studied all revealed significant national differences in approach. Perhaps most noticeable were the differences in context. Differences in the background of student intakes and differences in the currency of the business qualification in the labour market are crucial to an appreciation of the characteristics of courses. There are also practical differences. The polytechnics and *Fachhochschulen* are relatively low-cost institutions recruiting students of average ability. It is by no means certain that the pedagogy of the *grandes écoles* could be implemented effectively in these institutions.

Entry into a career in business follows a different route in each of the three countries. The characteristics of courses reflect the social and cultural significance of these routes as well as differences in the broader educational traditions in which they are located. The meaning of the vocational is bounded by these contexts which heavily influence the character of particular courses.

12

Environments

In order to provide some additional points of reference and comparison, in three of the British institutions studied some attention was paid to one or more courses in some aspect of the 'built environment' or a similar area. (Napier was not included, not having undergraduate courses in this general area.) These courses offer further indicators of interpretations of the vocational in public-sector higher education, in subjects which point largely to specific professional outcomes.

Architecture

Humberside College of Higher Education

Humberside's degree in Architecture (1979, submission for honours approved 1985) is 'design-project-based', projects being carried out in 'workbases', 'charged with teaching design methods, theory and practice', each different in approach and all providing opportunity for student initiative. The aim is to provide students with 'a wide spectrum of the process of designing' in all its stages, an understanding of the 'interrelationships between many of the various facets of design', a degree of 'self reliance and responsibility for their own education', and an appreciation of the relevance of architectural design to the quality of people's lives.

THE BA COURSE LEADER (MR JONES) stressed the uniqueness of the project-based approach, its arts orientation, and the student choice of workbase to join at the beginning of the second year and at intervals thereafter (with staff and students 'contracting' their responsibilities). It was intended that the honours version of the degree, beginning in 1986, should dovetail the theory and technology courses into the project work better than had been the case so far. A framework of progression enabled half of the history/theory work to relate to projects and at any given point in the course it was known roughly what area was being covered by projects. Some students, particularly in the second year, found the challenge to chart their own course and to adopt an exploratory mode difficult, but it was an essential element of being an architect, and they did get better at it. The final-year project was an opportunity to do things very well: some were doing exceptional things – but the demands of the third year were very heavy. A small number of students dropped out and returned for the third year, but it was not a sandwich course, and students were not encouraged to do that.

A case study (a technical project) was spread across the whole of the second year, involving the detailed study of an existing building. A large percentage of students stayed on after the degree to complete the diploma, and very few went into jobs other than architecture. Each student was selected carefully, including by interview, to ascertain that the student 'has some kind of initiative. . . . We're not at all interested in O and A level . . . we're more interested in how that student performs at interview. . . . We're looking for the creative side of architects'.

In the CNAA submission you never use the word 'vocational' about the course, but is it?

> Yes, I think it is. . . . This is a course for architecture, for people to become architects. . . . It's not a general arts degree . . . but it's not narrow. . . . The thing about the architecture profession is that it's as wide as anything. There are so many different ways of practising architecture . . . working in the community . . . on expensive Middle Eastern hotel blocks. . . . Wide arts degrees are in some ways, I think, a failure. We are, if you like, interested in products as well as process. At the end of the day we're interested in the person, his cognitive powers, his powers of initiative, reasoning . . . being developed . . . [but] we want to see the product, which is a sound and sensitive building, so it is vocational in the sense that that's what we want them to produce.

A workbase, with up to seventeen students, operated like a seminar with discussion, papers by students, argument, and debate – inevitable, given the crisis in architecture. *Is what you're doing adapting an old 'liberal' tradition – being critical, self-critical, situating oneself in 'the human condition' – to a new situation?*

> I think it's a curious mixture. There's that element . . . but also there's the old element of the master–apprentice situation. . . . At the time the student is in your workbase you're saying, 'look, this is what *I* do, you've chosen to join me, so think along my lines for a bit'.

He thought it was a little like – in say, the 1890s – sitting at the feet of the master and learning that way. But students needed to get to the point where they were asking where it had come from, why there was this building, who these people were, who was going to live in it. . . . American architecture courses tended to look at aesthetics and objects, while this course tried to look at concepts. There were professional constraints: the professional institution in architecture (the Royal Institute of British Architects) was 'incredibly moribund', and one should at all costs 'as far as I'm concerned, avoid their inputs'. They had a particular role, to do 'with a particular type of practice', but it was not one that 'this School wants to be associated with', though at the moment the course had to be approved by the RIBA, on the basis of the same kind of documentation as that submitted to the CNAA. The RIBA were willing to approve the course, however, in their own present difficult situation.

> The main thing about the course is that we're trying to provide . . . a bespoke education . . . we're trying to make it fit the particular individual . . . let the individual develop at his own pace . . . we try and get rid of the peer-group comparison as much as possible. . . . We're very aware of the danger of imposing one stylistic view on students.

Oxford Polytechnic

Oxford Polytechnic's BA in Architecture was approved by the CNAA in 1972, approval was renewed in 1976, and it became a BA honours in Architectural Studies in 1981 – a change of title responsive to a perceived CNAA 'steer' in an academic direction. The 1976 statement of aims was confirmed in 1981 as:

> to produce a graduate who can perform well as an intelligent, knowledgeable and creative designer. . . . It aims at completeness and self-sufficiency up to the threshold of a career in

architecture in that it serves for the majority of students as a plateau of achievement for advancement to architectural and related studies after a break for professional training. For others who elect to enter industries or professions in which an understanding of architecture will be of value it provides a liberal education.

The core of these aims was reformulated 'more precisely' in 1981 as: to produce a broadly educated honours graduate who has an understanding of the human, environmental, and technological factors bearing upon the design of buildings, and of the nature of design itself; and who has developed the ability to participate in the design process. Greater attention has been paid in recent years to verbal expression, to 'investigative and discursive skills', and to the problem of students not oriented 'confidently on the vocational route to the architectural profession'. Consideration has been given to 'the possibility of non-vocational routes through the Course', but this was abandoned in favour of greater flexibility for the individual student.

THE ACTING HEAD OF THE DEPARTMENT OF ARCHITECTURE (MR BENNETT) emphasized the role of the design project in developing student skills and qualities, the project and inputs to it constantly changing as technological, social, and other changes took place. Since the majority of the students wanted to become architects, they wanted their minds trained 'through the vehicle of the professional subject in which they are hoping eventually to be employed'. *There is reference in the documentation to 'vocational' and 'non-vocational' elements – is that vocabulary acceptable?*

I would want that word to be very carefully defined. If a vocational course is a course which is capable of being used as a basis for professional life, or even if it means a course which fulfils certain necessary requirements for entering into a professional field . . . that's one thing. But if by a vocational course one means a course whose educational potential is in some way limited as a result of its being those other things, then I would very much want to question the definition of the word. . . . I would question it in relation to our course. It does not seem to me that there is any correlation between the ability of the course to satisfy professional requirements and the ability of the course to satisfy general education.

Students entered the course enthusiastic about entering the profession, and their single-mindedness 'undoubtedly has an effect on the whole life and thinking of the department'. There was a range of separate courses for the student to package, but

> we have always believed that the main intellectual demand which is made upon the students is not in the understanding, still less in the actual absorption of facts and figures of those individual lecture courses, but in the application of them simultaneously to design projects. That is what it is difficult to achieve . . . necessarily we make our inputs as simple as possible, without losing the necessary rigour.

Students were not presented, as might be the case on many 'traditional academic courses, with a body of information which they were expected to understand and critically assess and use for tasks like writing essays'. A student was presented with a design problem 'in fairly broad terms', and had to define the problem more precisely and solve it within a large number of constraints. That was a considerable, and transferable, skill. *Is that not what people traditionally consider a 'liberal' education?*

> It probably is not. . . . I'm not absolutely sure . . . whether there is in fact somewhere stored up in heaven an authoritative definition of what a liberal education is. I rather suspect that a liberal education is anything that you happen to want it to be from time to time. . . . I don't know what the opposite of liberal is – I hope it's not 'illiberal'. . . . One of the things one notices about certain traditional, academic courses is that in order to introduce rigour they often introduce professionalism . . . they tend to train the classical scholar as if he or she was going to become a teacher of the classics or an editor of the classics.

If you take two traditions – liberal, nineteenth-century meanings, and twentieth-century accreted vocational meanings – do you reject both as simple descriptions of your course, but you might maintain you are drawing on both?

> Yes, and I would want . . . to ask what all these words are about. . . . If 'liberal' means making you aware of great ideas and so on of your culture, or the history of western civilization, questions of ethics or politics, and so on, then . . . these matters also come into our course, because we see them as

fundamental to the practice of architecture. The history of architecture comes in, we discuss the professional role of the architect, the function of a building, the way people use buildings, the symbolism of buildings, semiology ... none of those things makes sense except in some understanding of the culture and civilization of the architect.

Does a simple liberal/vocational dichotomy not stand up?

I don't think it does at all. There is another distinction which I think is worth making between ours and other courses. . . . We tend to be rather distinct from other 'vocational' courses, such as engineering . . . [which] has only fairly recently become project-based, and I think the project-based nature of architecture courses is always regarded with some suspicion, not to say contempt, as being a kind of apprenticeship, and the project system of teaching as opposed to the lecture and the textbook system of teaching to which I was subjected, is now regarded from the point of view of teaching techniques and so on as extremely OK, but at one time it was regarded as a kind of sitting next to Nellie experience.

Land management, estate management

Leicester Polytechnic

Leicester Polytechnic's BSc in land management took its first students in 1973 and for honours in 1979. The course was developed 'for the prime purpose of preparing graduates whose aim is corporate membership of the RICS (the Royal Institution of Chartered Surveyors)'. The aims were described in 1981 documentation for CNAA reapproval as being 'to assist undergraduates to become broadly educated individuals who have a significant understanding of the nature and philosophy of Land Management and the particular skills and ideologies appropriate to their selected areas of concern'. The honours programme was concerned particularly to achieve:

(i) the pursuit of excellence in terms of the development of intellectual, vocational, and communication skills;
(ii) the provision of an appropriate foundation to enable the honours graduate to proceed to post-graduate studies and/or research;

(iii) to prepare the honours graduate so that in due time he or she may take their place as leaders in the practice and government of his or her profession.

The course had 'both academic and vocational aims'. Land management seeks to explain the relationship between man, society, and land, particularly the social system by which interests in landed property and natural resources are 'allocated, managed, used or misused'. There are two routes through the course. Estate management is concerned with the 'management, appraisal, supervision and control of "interests" and "estates" in landed property'. Estate development is concerned with the social system by which ownerships and uses of land are developed, allocated, or controlled, including 'the evaluation of development schemes, the making of decisions . . . determining the most satisfactory means of achieving the implementation of development, redevelopment, conservation or rehabilitation of land'. Students are encouraged to acquire a 'rigorous systematic and scientific approach' and to use a 'goal seeking/problem solving approach'. Also encouraged are 'a healthy scepticism and the questioning of conventional wisdom'.

THE COURSE LEADER (MR LAND) explained that the course prepared students for only two of the seven divisions of the RICS, but even within one of those – the General Practical Division – the vocational opportunities were 'so wide that we couldn't hope to "train" anybody to go and practise in any one of those divisions'. The course was therefore preparing people for a wide variety of vocational opportunities (estate agent, professional department of bigger agencies, institutional investors . . .). The course had to 'properly educate' the student, so as to be able to go in any one of those directions. 'Training' took place in employment. Nearly all students were on entry to the course motivated to reach a professional outcome of that kind: 'we try to "stretch" them on the honours course, and only a small proportion opt off it: they have to face up to the educational objectives of the honours programme when they make the choice in the second year'. There a was substantial information content throughout, but the final, third year was more of a synthesizing year, with a problem-solving basis, applying and questioning previously acquired information. Students were encouraged to raise questions throughout the course. They might expect to be spoon-fed in the first year, but they would find that they were not: 'a very great deal of the work has to be done for themselves'. There was a plan to reduce the amount of teaching in the final year.

Will students, say half way through the second year, be found arguing, debating, questioning? Certainly – 'We rely fairly heavily on a tutorial system and in the tutorials it is the students who are expected to do most of the talking.' Students prepared papers, and these provoked discussion and criticism. In this, students were, he considered, operating like students elsewhere in higher education. The submission talks about a 'healthy scepticism' and at other points raises ethical and other issues. *Does this in fact run through the course?*

> Yes, because I suppose one could argue that the majority of the students come from a middle-class background with some fairly well pre-conceived ideas, hence the promotion of a healthy scepticism.... Chartered surveyors are perhaps not particularly well educated – historically they tend to do things because that's the way it's done.... We like to raise the question.

The documentation talks of honours students focusing more on problem-solving and the non-honours students having more of a vocational core – is that how it works out? He thought that distinction was not in fact clear. At one point, for example, the degree students did something as 'demandingly problem-solving' as anything the honours students did: since the course was tailored to honours the degree students were probably stretched more than was originally intended. Since the RICS was 'multivocational' there was a broad range of subject content to the course. It was 'multidisciplinary': the land manager 'has got to be a planner, he's got to be a lawyer, he's got to be a valuer, he's got to be an economist'. Subject titles would in future tend to disappear in the final year, in favour of a more 'cohesive' estate management context, though it would not be easy to do. The problem with the final-year project was the difficulty of finding more than fifty different titles each year, and there was a wide variation in the quality of the projects produced. There was no one point in the course where students were being encouraged to be independent, self-motivating: students matured, there was an accumulation of experience, they discovered in the first year that they had to become more independent, they had to demonstrate a capacity for self-researched work in the second year, and the third-year project was intended to be a synthesis of all that. There was considerable discussion about teaching methods, and 'one of the things we want to achieve is a very much more integrated approach', so that students did not see topics in isolation.

How do you explain your course against the background of what people in the nineteenth and twentieth centuries have claimed a liberal higher education ought to be?

I am not what most people would look upon as an academic. I am an ex-practising professional . . . having spent twenty-five years practising the profession about which I now talk. . . . I didn't go to university. . . . My professional qualification was earned . . . as an articled pupil in a professional office. . . . I would now designate that very much as training. . . . It's very much the master–apprentice situation. . . . Here we are preparing our 'apprentice' to be not aping his master, but to be better . . . he has time to think about what practice does rather than simply being tied to earning a living. . . . There wasn't time to think – is there a better way of doing this, you ruddy well did something as you were told. Here we've got to be vocationally orientated – the course wouldn't exist if it wasn't, if it was just broad education for the sake of education. . . . A large proportion of the people who teach on the course are ex-practitioners . . . students are educated to know that there are different approaches to a given problem.

Some people use 'vocational' pejoratively, meaning merely or narrowly vocational – are you using the term in a positive sense, to mean producing people who can think for themselves? 'Absolutely right. We think that our generation of chartered surveyors is going to be a very much more thinking generation of chartered surveyors than the generation that came before, pre-full time education.'

Oxford Polytechnic

Oxford Polytechnic's BSc in Estate Management admitted its first students in 1975, with its first honours programme beginning in 1986. Like the Leicester course, it prepares students for exemption from examinations of the RICS in the General Practical Division, and to a lesser extent the Planning and Development Division. The aim, described in a 1984 submission to the CNAA, is 'to produce graduates who have had a rigorous academic training in the disciplines constituting Estate Management whose intellectual calibre, ability and education will enable them to apply principles in the resolution of problems arising in that field'. Honours graduates would need to demonstrate a higher level of academic attainment:

> analyse problems; propound solutions and demonstrate their ability by a high level of communicative skills. Students must understand that estate management is a coherent, integrated discipline which whilst having its origins in separate related studies can stand alone . . . graduates must be capable of devising new approaches to problems as they arise. . . . We aim to produce graduates who are aware of the limitations of their own knowledge and who are prepared to continue their education after graduation.

THE COURSE LEADER (MR BOOTH) thought that, although students were faced with an array of subjects,

> by the end of the three years what started as a series of quite distinct educational packages has been integrated into a single study . . . and all they wait for is the professional experience, the first few years of their practice experience, to make that a professional reality, so they are poised when they go from here to make a reality of the ideas.

Students had clear career intentions: 'that is what we look for . . . and that is bound to be so in 80 per cent of the cases'. It required a degree of commitment to cope with the course, and those without it often withdrew. *How much are the students acquiring information, and how much are they learning how to learn?*

> I would say that this course is not a highly 'academic' one, even with the new honours degree. The honours degree undoubtedly promotes the academic element, but one of the reasons why this course has proved over the years to be attractive to employers is because we have developed techniques of a fairly narrow professional focus, and we supply information that is related to that focus. I wouldn't say that we have hitherto, whatever our aspirations for the future, concentrated much on learning how to learn. That is a deficiency I think we have been aware of, and in the new honours course we go a considerable way to remedying that deficiency. The emphasis from now on is going to be

considerably more on learning than on teaching. . . . Teaching techniques are going to have to change.

In some parts of the course new types of staff would be needed, for example in financial management and marketing, which the profession had not concentrated on in the past. Students' capacity 'to think and analyse is going to be far more attractive to us in reviewing applicants'.

Is yours a vocational course?

Yes. What makes it vocational is that the staff here have a clear idea of where the students are going to go when they leave here. . . . The profession itself quite clearly recruits from courses such as this, and the students when they come in have a very clear idea as to what is going to happen to them when they go out – so there is a tripartite understanding about career. . . . The fact that such a course as this exists doesn't exclude the possibility of, for want of a better word, a more 'liberal' course being available elsewhere. . . . Because it is a narrow vocational course doesn't exclude the development of the personality and the development of ideas – it's just the matter, the substance of the course is different. We're playing with ideas surrounding the land and the way that it is utilized, often in a very broad way. People are invited to speculate, to cast about widely for new ideas. . . . I'm accepting that it is narrow, but I'm not accepting that in terms of intellectual development it is constraining. The narrowness relates to the commitment to the vocation. The subject area covered by the course is, however, wider than most other disciplines.

He described one of the exercises – a 'professional practice examination' – which took place in the final year, in a different location away from Oxford each year, requiring the involvement of surveyors in the town selected. Students carried out commissions presented as letters of instruction from 'clients' and related to real properties, providing an opportunity for students to apply their knowledge, and acting as a 'sort of bridge between the course and practice'. Students had to show that they had mastered the elements of law, evaluation, building construction, and so on, and could display certain personal qualities in negotiating successfully and in carrying the process through to completion. They produced a case file for each aspect of the work, made an oral presentation of the case, which would involve staff, external examiners, and people in the profession, and they produced a report.

Might some people not criticize a course like this for being too close to the professional bodies, too amenable to outside pressure?

> I am not aware of any particular anxiety or conflict . . . We have a number of people who come here as graduates in other disciplines . . . arts subjects . . . liberal degrees, and they have decided they want a professional qualification . . . they have had to submit to the disciplines imposed by the professional in trying to achieve the necessary competence.

The criteria applied by the CNAA could be different from those applied by the RICS, and those had had to be reconciled: 'at the end of the day we have to satisfy the CNAA'. Not that this was a problem because many of the CNAA Surveying Board were members of the RICS, so it was not really a juggling act 'because of the commonality'.

Planning studies

Oxford Polytechnic

Oxford Polytechnic's three-year BA honours course in planning studies was introduced in 1977 and reviewed and modified in 1981. The BA and the one-year diploma course which follows, taken together, qualify a student – after appropriate practical experience – to apply for membership of the Royal Town Planning Institute. A 1984 course handbook, based on the 1981 submission to the CNAA, presents the principal aims of the course:

(i) to produce a broadly educated honours graduate who has an understanding of the nature and philosophy of planning and the particular knowledge and skills appropriate to a selected area of planning;
(ii) to provide a sound basis of vocational education which can be continued after graduation to a full professional level in a fourth-year Diploma course.

The course has 'both academic and vocational aims', preparing students for a career in town planning, but also for further specialist courses, research, and a wide range of graduate employment. The course aims to increase the student's 'knowledge of society's environmental needs' and the problems of satisfying them, skill in formulating, presenting, and implementing solutions to environmental problems, and 'sensitivity to the values and needs of different groups in society'. There are four main areas of study: a core (planning history, theory, and method); a foundation (basic methods of the contributory disciplines and their application to planning); concentrations (selected from six areas); and options (lasting one term, in the second and third years).

THE HEAD OF THE DEPARTMENT OF TOWN PLANNING (MR GLASSON) underlined that students had broad interests on admission, and the course itself was broadly based, becoming more specialist towards the third year, with the graduate diploma as the 'sharpest and most professional related' part of the package. The word 'studies' was important in the degree title, since although there was a strong vocational element in it the course was in itself not enough for students to be able to practise as chartered town planners. After three years,

> I'd hope students would say, 'I've been through a foundation period in this course and I've acquired a variety of foundation knowledge in the social sciences, in design, in planning theory and planning techniques and I've acquired relevant skills, and then for the last four terms I've been applying that knowledge and those skills to a specialist area'.

Skills, he explained, included technical skills (e.g. graphics and information technology), skills in communication, verbal and visual skills – all important, but taking no more than 20 per cent of the student's contact time. It was difficult to quantify the amount of time spent on conceptual knowledge, and to separate it from skills: project work – 'learning through doing' – combined both.

Is what you are describing very different from what an arts student might experience?

> I think there's a fundamental difference, say, comparing a planning student with a geography student, and that is the problem-solving approach, actually producing solutions to problems. I did a degree in economics and geography. It was ... analytical ... but not particularly prescriptive. It did not evaluate alternatives, did not necessitate putting your head on the block and saying – this is my proposal. ... One of the main points we would argue in favour of planning education is the problem-solving skill which students have when they come

> out and I think that is particularly attractive to employers. . . . You may pick that up with some other courses, but it's rarely the central part of the education, I would say, whereas here it is.

Students had to come up with solutions which worked for people, which made financial sense, and which could be politically acceptable. Planning education up to about five years ago had produced designs, now the accent was more on implementation – simulation exercises, negotiation techniques . . .

In the prospectus the course is described as one of a group of 'broadly based professional courses', and in the submission it is described as providing a 'sound basis of vocational education' – is it a vocational course?

> Yes, but it's also one with good academic standards. We want students to come out not just to do something mechanically but to think what they're doing, why they're doing it. . . . Planning education can . . . provide a student with many outlets, in that it produces students who can think for themselves, are well organized, independent, can put together reports well. . . . In particular, planning education equips students with knowledge and skills which they can apply in certain professions. . . . We find that our students are being called in to other professions because they offer particular skills and knowledge. . . . What planning education does in particular is put together various dimensions, various aspects, economics, sociology, politics, design management. . . . You only get partial coverage if you just do economics or just do sociology. . . . In our foundation years . . . we are focusing on those parts of those disciplines which are particularly relevant for planning education.

A variety of teaching techniques was used, including individual and group projects. Students were exposed to 'all types of planning theory' and a lot of it was controversial – which was inevitable, he thought, 'if you're planning in a pluralist society'. High academic standards, in such ways, reinforced 'good vocational education'. To explain its operation you 'almost need a hybrid phrase'.

In this field and others there are tensions between the 'academic' and the 'practical'. The broad and the specialized, generalists and specialists – and these debates take place in the professional arena outside. *How much do you have to listen to those resonances?*

> We do this a great deal, though we try to avoid the mistake of

reacting to short-term trends. You've got to have a course which is robust for a number of years. You get over that by having courses which do have flexibility within them and can adjust.... We listen in many ways. We have a foot in practice, through consultant research. We have major research programmes in the department.... We're very much in tune with practice with our short-course unit.... We're in touch via the branch of the RTPI.... We meet planners on a regular basis there. We're involved in all kinds of other ways as well.... But the debate (about the shape of courses) mainly takes place in this department, with staff and students.

THE DEAN OF THE FACULTY OF ARCHITECTURE, PLANNING AND ESTATE MANAGEMENT (DR HEALEY) is also associate head of the Department of Town Planning. She has written about polarities in the planning field between the professional and the academic, understanding and skills, vocational and academic, academic and practitioner. *How prominent are these tensions in designing courses?* 'Pretty prominent', she thought:

Major course design work was done in the 1970s.... We're now confronting a new round of course design... how we're going to do that... I'm not quite sure where that's going to go.... Because planning has been trying to develop a kind of academic status from a very unacademic base, perhaps they have been more exposed than they might have been where it would have been recognized that there was more of an academic contribution.

Generalist/specialist tension had as much to do with 'a bid for control of particular sorts of work' as with academic concerns. Tensions between practitioners and course designers were not about course design. The professional institute went along with the idea that you needed a core, around which students could then specialize. British (more than American) planning education was linked into what the job market was interested in: 'They want people who've done economic development, industry and commerce... urban conservation and urban design... transport questions, and the range of specializations that gets selected reflects the world of work out there.'

Is planning different in these respects from other multidisciplinary courses, like social work or teacher education?

> Probably not . . . it's interesting what makes one multidisciplinary course different from another. . . . [In architecture] you do need a long time . . . the range of things that have to be brought together . . . a pretty robust technological understanding of structures and materials and construction, with a good grasp of the social and economic context of buildings, with a good idea and knowledge of management, how you actually manage a building project, with a good grasp of what all that means for the design of the project. . . . In planning it's not quite so much but it's still quite a lot.

Planning involved a mix of public-policy questions and spatial arrangements, development, and the physical environment. It entailed a knowledge of the social sciences, form and design, good verbal reasoning and quantitative reasoning, and the ability, when they had put all that package together, to go out 'and write coherent reports about things'. Courses therefore had to bring practice 'into the mainstream academic discussions. . . . The CNAA has been quite important in pushing that'. Public-sector higher education had been 'a more creative force for change, it has picked up new ideas' which had changed very rapidly since the early 1970s. New staff had been appointed to the polytechnics rather than the universities. The polytechnics had made the running. The debate in the academic community had changed, the universities were changing and 'coming along behind'.

Are courses like this at Oxford and elsewhere a 'vocational higher education'? Planning studies on the Oxford Polytechnic model was, she thought, 'on its way to being a vocational higher education' – the diploma was needed on top of it. The multidisciplinary course focused increasingly towards the end on applying knowledge in practical situations:

> We have always said that there was no fundamental incompatibility between the academic and the applied . . . intellectually challenging if we got the mix right. . . . We don't . . . claim that at the end of the three years people could go out and immediately have all that they needed as an initial training for a vocation.

Not until the diploma year were questions tackled regarding professional attitudes and ethics or the specificities of law.

We are trying to produce people who have expertise which is useful, know what putting that to work means, know both the technical and the ethical questions in putting that to work, and if that means vocational then I'll have a vocational label.

The difference between that and a traditional 'liberal' education, she believed, was that 'it's putting knowledge to work in organizational situations, in relation to someone else's definition of the problem rather than your own'.

Would it be true that in this and similar courses you are drawing on two traditions – the 'liberal' tradition with an emphasis on independent thought and flexibility, and another tradition concerned with employment destinations and the application of knowledge? 'I would think that's very interesting, actually. The liberal tradition I recognize, the other tradition I am not sure that I have seen articulated. . . . I think that would be the case.' Students, she emphasized, were 'vocationally oriented' on entry. They came because they were 'interested in the environment', a lot came because they wanted 'a job at the end' and their parents had told them it was a professional education and 'a good thing'. That was less strong than in estate management, but was still very strong indeed. There was a problem:

You have to show them that planning is a political and institutional process, as well as a set of concerns one might have about things, as well as a set of skills and techniques you can apply – and some students have great difficulty with that, and they get quite depressed because they think after a while that you can't do anything because of the institutional problems.

By the end of the third year most students had established a sense of coherence, appreciated 'the meaning of the range' of work, and there were 'sense-making devices'.

From the late 1960s the educational community had strongly influenced the professional body. Course designers had been 'forced because of the CNAA to be clear why we were proposing certain things, and why we thought that they met the objectives of the practice community, the proper objectives of the profession'.

Commentary

In all of these areas stress was laid on the pre-professional (or even pre-vocational) nature of the undergraduate courses, which required further study and qualifications and/or experience for students to be eligible for membership of the appropriate professional body. In all cases the course had an eye to the requirements and role of the professional institution, with which relations varied but which, in estate or land management and planning studies, were almost an integral part of the professional lives of the tutors concerned. The professional body, being coterminous with the employment field or fields for which students were being prepared, was accepted in these two cases as a body of peers, and one which did not impose 'outside', unacceptable constraints: it was indeed amenable to dialogue and influence. The longer history of the architecture profession, and the nature of its established roles and recent internal controversies, perhaps explain the different perception of the RIBA in the one interview where it was discussed.

The aims of the courses as expressed in the documentation echo many of the elements apparent in engineering and business studies, including student qualities of independent thought and self-reliance, with understandably stronger emphasis on willingness to undertake further education, and with greater emphasis on the application of knowledge and skills at the expense of detailed reference to 'coherence' and integration. The relationship between the academic/vocational content of courses and their rigour was followed up in the interviews.

The interviews brought out in all cases the importance of the breadth of the course as an aspect, even though differently structured in the different courses, of the complex practice of the future professional, feeding – with different rhythms on different courses – into the student's own engagement with practice, with projects, and with problem-solving, goal-seeking, solution-proposing activities. Course structures, the previous experience of staff appointed to teach them, and the commitments of course planners indicated the importance attached to the incorporation of practice into the courses themselves, not as discrete elements but as pervasive contributions. The emphasis everywhere was on active student learning (or on movement in that direction in the one case where it was felt to have been inadequately achieved). In essentially design-based courses the project had a high profile, but in all of the courses there was an emphasis on case studies, simulation, or other interdisciplinary or self-motivating strategies. Even references to a master–apprentice situation were intended to underline how quickly students were expected to take an independent stance, to develop at their own pace, and to question and challenge.

Courses were accepted as 'vocational', but with a range of explanations. In many instances there was the proviso that the course pointed to a variety of occupations or employments within the field, with students motivated, but not precisely motivated, towards such employment from the outset. The breadth of occupational opportunities in estate and land management and in planning was reflected in the breadth of the courses. The position in architecture was different, though the 'architectural studies' course was seen as a liberal education for those few students who did not opt for the 'vocational route'. Even where the narrowness of the vocational preparation was concerned, it was strongly denied that this implied any intellectual constraint. Courses were not only in general not educationally limiting, they were in fact seen as at least as challenging as traditional liberal-arts courses, the difference lying in the organizational and professional contexts in which the knowledge and skills acquired were to be applied. It was not that 'liberal' (the meaning of which was strongly questioned) education was missing from these courses – it was being supplemented, a 'healthy scepticism' was being combined with positive proposals, and participation in dialogue and debate with induction into the processes of putting knowledge to work. The essential context was a tripartite (student–staff–employer) understanding of the range of likely employment outcomes, and in all cases the interviews emphasized the educational opportunities and aims the courses were designed to exploit within that broadly and positively conceived framework.

Such polarities as liberal/vocational, specialist/generalist and academic/professional were therefore not seen as having, expressed in these forms, meaning or relevance, and the courses were either drawing on or reconciling in practice the discrete threads that those polarities may have once represented.

All of the courses were located at the vocationally specific end of the typology set out in chapter 3. They offered a part-training or an educational base for training for occupations which, as with engineering, were characterized by regulation of entry by a professional body.

A division of labour between undergraduate education and

postgraduate training, whether education-based or employment-based, was important for the educational purposes of all of the courses. We noted in chapter 3 that this could allow greater scope for the 'academicization' of the curriculum. Indeed, we did find a 'steer in an academic direction' in architecture and a movement towards 'academic status from a very unacademic base' in planning. But a greater visibility of the academic was not in opposition to but provided a redefinition of the vocational task, described for us in the case of estate management as producing 'the thinking generation of chartered surveyors'.

The specificity of employment outcomes and the clarity of the routes to achieving them seemed to have encouraged a confidence of purpose about the courses. All were multidisciplinary but the disciplines remained more in evidence than in business studies and disciplinary problems were not seen as necessarily distinct from professional problems. Attracting good students and without the professional pressures towards curriculum overload, the courses did not appear to be faced with the kinds of pedagogic problems evident in engineering. The educators seemed to have a secure role *within* the profession and were in many cases seen as providing a key impetus towards professional change and development.

13
Institutions

We have seen earlier some of the ways in which institutions in the public sector have, particularly in their prospectuses, indicated to some degree the philosophy on which they seek to operate. British colleges and polytechnics do not normally have publicly disseminated 'mission statements' on the US model, though documentation for CNAA validation purposes – particularly for institutional reviews – has always suggested institutional aims, as well as the kind of course aims which we have discussed. As Davies has pointed out mission statements can have a variety of purposes – inspirational, the assertion of institutional or sector differentiation, justification for autonomy... (Davies 1985), whereas prospectus statements are directed to students or constituencies which influence recruitment. They have to persuade.

The realities of institutions are not easily discernible in national policy statements which, whilst appearing to be prescriptive and in fact imposing constraints, nevertheless leave or create many of the ambiguities we have previously discussed. The 1956 *Plan for Polytechnics and Other Colleges* talked of

> a strong and distinctive sector of higher education which is complementary to the universities and colleges of education ... the object will be to develop them as large and comprehensive institutions offering full-time, sandwich and part-time courses of higher education at all levels.
>
> (DES 1966: 9)

Within that broad definition the polytechnics – and those subsequent colleges of higher education like Humberside with a similar range of courses and levels of provision – have tried to project a 'mission' which is 'vocational', 'applied', and employment- and community-orientated. The courses we have discussed, whether in long-established areas such as architecture and engineering, or in more recently defined forms of professional preparation such as business studies, estate management, and town planning, have developed their identities within institutions themselves establishing identities. In the four institutions with which we have been mainly concerned it was important to have this wider context and perspective of the director or principal.

Humberside College of Higher Education

Director: Dr J. Earls

The college prospectus contains phrases common in public-sector prospectuses – 'relevant courses', many with 'a strong vocational bias'. Do those define what the college is about?

Very much so. If you take courses like fishery studies or industrial food technology, then demonstrably these courses have fairly specific, industrial, career aims, which are reflected in the syllabuses and in the curriculum. Of course at the same time we wouldn't want to argue that vocationalism is necessarily a very narrow education, so that the curriculum does have other ingredients, hopefully which will have a wider applicability and make the students reasonably mobile.

How does that differ from what the universities do? Are their courses not designed in the same way?

They're not designed in the same way. It's hard to compare any one institution with another, but generally I think it could be said that the courses at the colleges have a much more obvious and demonstrable industrial connection. . . . Quite a few of our courses, especially business studies, are sandwich . . . so that we would say that our courses have a more immediate articulation with industry, and they're much more responsive to the perceived needs of industry, whereas I think in general for the university sector one might say they are . . . more concerned about their own institutional objectives.

Presumably some university courses do what you're doing, and some of your courses don't do that?

That's indeed true, and I think that the university sector and the public sector are overlapping sets, and I think if you went to Salford or Loughborough you would find that their courses would be very similar . . . if you went to possibly Exeter you would find that their engineering courses were very different from engineering courses at Humberside.

What is it that makes your courses vocational?

I think it's three things. One, it's the content of the course. Also to some extent it reflects the aspirations of the students – clearly the students come in to do certain things and they believe that what they're going to do is going to be relevant and immediately helpful to them. . . . But thirdly, I think it's the attitude of the staff, and the things the staff do. . . . The staff in an institution like this are much more intimately involved with and understanding of industry . . . their research work is generally applied . . . and it's the consultancy and the applied research that inform the curriculum and the content.

How do you meet the objections of people who say that it isn't what higher education is about – it ought not to be serving the needs of industry?

I suppose the classical mode is to do PPE or Greek and Latin – and that's an education, and doing industrial food technology is not. I think again that's untrue, they are overlapping sets . . . if you do industrial food technology there can be as many intellectual demands and the student can develop in the context of a course like that as well as in PPE. [In] areas like design or business studies . . . some of the problems are just as intractable and intellectually demanding as they would be if you were translating a Latin text or writing a dissertation on Iranian architecture.

He explained that there had been debate in the college in recent months about 'learning to learn', based on a paper prepared by himself and the student counsellor, examining in the faculty boards the scope for more 'student-centred' learning, the need for staff development and a 'general change in the attitude of students to the way they learn'. [This discussion was preceded in 1984 by a director's paper on 'academic priorities', picking up some of the Leverhulme discussion on the aims of undergraduate courses, pointing towards breadth, balance and personal skills not particularly knowledge-related. The director's paper underlined the wide range of subject specialisms in the college, with their different educational emphases – 'creative, discursive, analytic, synthetic, professional, social, numerate, linguistic'. A central question was the possibility, through good teaching/learning practice and other measures, of making 'what is taught' subordinate to 'how it is taught', of establishing a common purpose and process, a 'style', producing graduates with an 'educational "water mark" '.]

In addition, he thought, part of any academic structure reorganization under consideration should redefine courses so as to make students more mobile (perhaps through a modular structure), but also in order to help 'to bind the college together', give the student more choice, and enable 'people from outside the college to come in and take elements of the work of the institution, which . . . they can't do when the courses are defined in a monolithic fashion'. That constraint had in the past been partly due to 'CNAA's preoccupation in the early days with coherence and progression' – and these now had to be partly sacrificed in favour of continuing education and other advantages.

Is the antithesis between the liberal and the vocational breaking down?

> I do think so . . . primarily for the reason that employers, especially over the last five or ten years, have become very much more interested in the affective qualities of the students, their attitudes, their enthusiasm, their commitment, and while they may want an electronics engineer or an industrial food technologist they also want a person who is enthusiastic, commited, flexible, responsive.

Arts students have traditionally had time to develop these qualities by doing other things, such as music or politics. A criticism of students on 'vocational' courses is that they don't have time to do that?

> I'm sure that's true. If you take a typical engineering course then probably the minimum number of hours in any one week is about twenty, compared to an arts student's twelve. I think you now have to look at what that twenty consists of . . . things like group projects, mini-projects, syndicate studies. . . . There's

a drift from one towards the other. The curriculum is still longer for the typical vocational student.

Some might argue that the public sector is too open to outside pressures?

That's fair. Employers will tend to think very much in terms of their short-term needs . . . whereas we've got to be minded that our graduates are to be in employment for the next thirty to forty years. . . . I think employers have to realize the imperatives that educational institutions have to face in terms of standard, content. . . . Any completely subservient role between the college and the employers would be wrong, but it's quite understandable and quite proper for students to feel that their course is informed by what industry believes to be important.

In relation to the 'mission' of the college how useful, finally, is the concept of 'vocationalism'?

My impression is that it's becoming less important to talk about being vocational. I'm not sure that it means too much to school leavers or . . . to school teachers for that matter, and certainly a lot less to parents by and large. I think what I would want to emphasize is that the college has courses of a kind that is related to the needs of industry, but which develop the student as an individual and create in him or her the qualities for good career progression. You could do these things, achieve these objectives by doing a course in Iranian architecture or by doing a course in industrial food technology, so I would say that vocationalism is something I am less wedded to now than I would have been ten or fifteen years ago.

Leicester Polytechnic

Director: Dr D. Bethel

You don't use the word 'vocational' in your prospectus, but if you look at all the courses that is the impact. Is that in your view what is distinctive about the polytechnic?

Certainly. The emphasis is on the application of knowledge, and I would say philosophically the emphasis is on the idea that people learn best when they understand how the courses can be applied to real life. So the difference is not just the aim – the application of knowledge – but the actual learning process must be different if that is your aim.

There are some courses in the polytechnic which might not fit that, and some courses in a university that might. Is it that the majority emphasis is different?

I would argue this. . . . I believe one can draw up a model of a classical university and you will not find one of the universities in the UK which fits that model entirely. . . . A number of courses at Oxford and Cambridge are entirely vocational, for instance the architecture course. . . . However, the teaching of it is very different from the way we teach architecture here. . . . If you turn to the polytechnics, let me give you an example I love to quote – our degree in the history of art. There are only five degrees in the history of art in the public sector, and they're not all alike. I think the one at Leicester is unique in so far as its origins were in the police, insurance companies and banks, wanting to recruit . . . people who were probably graduates in art history, but who understood the valuation of artifacts, and who could tell the difference between a good copy, a fake, an original, a reproduction, and so on. So our history of art degree was formed on the basis that we would produce such people. The universities were not producing anyone capable of doing the job without further specialist training. . . . In addition to the normal scholarship [our graduates] will have a scientific training.

Such students, he believed, could use techniques to attribute, could watch the market value of art, make valuations for collateral purposes for banking, and for insurance purposes, and give accurate descriptions to the police and Interpol – all of which illustrated the difference between similar courses in a university and a polytechnic.

A spokesman for the liberal tradition of higher education might retort that such a person will do a good market job, but is that higher education?

I'm not in the business of defending [our approach] – the defence has to be on the other side. . . . The people to whom you refer lived in an entirely different world, where, for example, everyone was in a class and knew what that class was

> ... whereas today everyone has expectations ... of all kinds which can only be met by, I believe, a different kind of education. ... I would argue that what is intellectual stimulating today is quite different from what was intellectually stimulating 150 years ago. There is no doubt in my mind that for a majority of the people ... technology and its applications is intellectually stimulating. ... Higher education cannot be graced by that term unless it is intellectually stimulating and a training of the mind.

Having a course with employment outcomes in view did not, he insisted, remove those stimuli and 'to some extent it ought to concentrate them. ... With luck and good teaching you may even discover better stimuli', better ways of 'producing an enquiring mind'. This was the argument for sandwich courses and project work. How actively does the polytechnic engage with questions of teaching methods? Probably, he suggested, in three main ways:

> through our staff development programmes ... detailed discussions between the individual and his head, the head and the assistant director in charge of staff development, working out what is best for the polytechnic, the school or department, and the individual. ... The second one is, we have a Centre for Educational Technology and Development, and people are seconded there, particularly when they first come into teaching ... to learn about the importance of how people learn. ... When preparing resubmissions ... of courses, staff invariably are seconded for a while to this Centre to be assisted in questioning what they are doing. ... Thirdly, in our promotion strategies we rate development in teaching and learning strategies highly.

Is there a problem about students in the kind of courses we are discussing not having the same opportunities for extra-curricular activities, because of heavy contact hours? The students in the polytechnic with the longest curriculum hours, he pointed out, were in art and design, whose interests did go beyond art and design, but whose reading time was limited:

> The technology/science people have more time ... art and design students do about twenty-nine hours a week, science and technology about sixteen, very few people do less than

> that.... When we have the kind of general interest lectures that we do put on for town and gown purposes, we get a very poor attendance from the polytechnic as a whole, staff and students.... When we have music, drama, dance, recitals, we don't get queues of polytechnic people.... I don't believe it's to do with the way they're taught or what they're taught, I do believe it's about the much much longer ingraining tradition.

Polytechnics had a stronger 9 to 5 tradition than universities, with their residence and stronger sense of community. Some countries might think we are producing rather narrow people, in the technologies and other areas: would they be right?

> I think we do. It doesn't start here, it starts in the sixth form, or even before that of course, with the narrowing down of the curriculum.... Uniquely in this country the professions can distort higher education, certainly limit it, by insisting on certain things being put in the curriculum ... in any of those subjects with a professional body which, in our terms, validates along with CNAA or in addition to CNAA ... does constrain what should be in the curriculum.... The Engineering Council now ... are *insisting* that curricula be broadened both in univesities and in polytechnics, and in a sense going counter to the professional bodies who in the past dominated engineering education.... One can blame to some extent the influence of the professional bodies.

Polytechnics were more accountable than universities to other bodies in society, but:

> I don't object to this accountability.... We have a range of consultative committees, and voluntarily we put our curriculum and curriculum changes ... to our consultative committees for their comments, advice. We don't *have* to take their advice, we don't necessarily take the advice, but ... it gives an input from practising people to academic life, and it allows academics to argue with practising people about the practice of education.

Do you use the word 'vocational'?

> No. I don't, because I think it's misleading. It has connotations of narrowness, and of technician level, neither of which is what vocational education need be about. The traditional

vocations of law and the church and medicine for example. ... I leave [that vocabulary] aside. ... I wouldn't want to use the word while it still had connotations which are not helpful.

Napier College, Edinburgh

Principal: Dr W.A. Turmeau

How do you interpret the strong 'mission' that Napier has, and affirms in its prospectus and documentation, of 'vocational relevance', as part of the tradition of this college, and given the way Scotland organizes its higher education?

In Scottish public-sector higher education,

> colleges such as this are, shall we say, advised by the Scottish Education Department to do vocational types of courses, and not to do social sciences and liberal arts, so to that extent I suppose we're directed. On the other hand, we have done the types of courses within that framework that we think are required by industry and commerce ... a slightly limited framework, but we do what we think is right within that framework.

As CNAA, SCOTBEC, and SCOTVEC courses they clearly had 'positive career prospects'. A course could not be mounted without SED approval, and they needed to be sure that there was a demand for the course, and a need for graduates from the course. Within that framework courses were designed on the basis of the college's expertise.

The prospectus, academic plan, and other documents stress that courses are vocational and interdisciplinary. Is that a strong connection as perceived by the college?

> In the early days certainly interdisciplinarity had a very high profile – it still has a high profile. I think we feel that courses that are going to be vocational in nature must inevitably provide the student with a relatively broad band of disciplines, a broad band of education. A student in engineering obviously should know something about business and management. ... We feel it's to the advantage of students to have a relatively wide range of knowledge. ... It's not a case of interdisciplinarity ... so the student has a well-rounded education which is

going to be useful. We realize that we're not just educating people for a job this year, next year, or the year after.... We're trying to educate them for... a career.... We do feel it necessary or important to give the student a reasonable breadth, though we do have some relatively single-discipline courses.... Our BA Business Studies may sound like a BA Business Studies at a university, but in fact our business studies degree has a sandwich element, it does have options, it does have a wide base and vocational aspect. It's different from a traditional university degree. In some ways the universities have been copying us as far as business and management type courses are concerned.

An accusation from some people working in 'traditional' fields might be that courses of the kind you describe tend to become narrow, unquestioning, information-gathering?

We wouldn't concede that at all. There are still discipline-oriented subjects within the courses.... [On] a single-discipline course you may learn a lot about that but not much about anything else.... It's important to know how one discipline impinges on other disciplines. An engineer may be a wonderful designer... but if he can't equate the impact of that design on society, and the cash flow concerned with that product, then there may not be much point in designing the marvellous product in the first place.

The implications of those types of courses for teaching methods were discussed in the institution, in boards of studies, and achieving integration was not easy. All boards of studies were concerned with how the different elements of courses interconnected. The staff teaching courses did get together – this was not a 'cafeteria system'; the courses were coherent, and that was their strength, and the strength of the students by comparison with those who might have done a 'pick 'n' mix' course. There was a staff development committee, and each faculty had a staff development responsibility, carrying out the policy of the staff development committee (or academic board). As much as possible was done to encourage staff to take higher degrees and attend seminars and conferences, and there was an 'inherent' staff appraisal system in the departmental structure.

Historically, in England 'vocational' has had a pejorative usage, and implied low status; has that been true in Scotland?

I don't think so. It hasn't had the same connotation attached to it, I wouldn't have said. Scottish universities have turned out MAs and broad-based degree courses for a long time. . . . I suppose you could have called them vocational, so the word doesn't have the same 'dirty hands' concept it might have in England . . . it doesn't raise any eyebrows and suggest second-class quality.

The concentration of vocational courses in the central institutions (CIs) and colleges had not, he felt, been narrowly interpreted. What had happened in Scotland where the CIs had been under Scottish Office control had been a concentration of vocationally-oriented courses in the CIs

> to the extent that there aren't any arts courses, liberal arts, or anything like that in the central institutions, which *has* happened in the [English] polytechnics, but I think this has worked to their advantage . . . provided it's properly looked after and properly controlled. . . . At least we are seen as different – I think we are seen as something slightly lower than the universities currently. . . . That can be changed, and will be changed as a result of the STEAC report. Nevertheless, we are seen as different . . . providing a different function . . . career orientation . . . sandwich courses . . . different types of courses. Where the polytechnics in England, some of them, have been seen to be in competition with the universities. If they try and compete I don't think the polytechnic's going to win.

Napier was not competing with Edinburgh University and only peripherally with Heriot-Watt (the three principals had meetings, knowing the institutions were going 'down different lanes'), and

> I think that with the vocational orientation that we have, and with the background that we have, the sort of public recognition that we have, I would certainly see us coming up in the field . . . because we have gone along that road . . . the higher that profile the more funding we will get, and eventually I hope we will get equal funding.

There was nothing wrong with being interpreted as being 'a service station'. The basis of a community depended on industry and commerce and service industries:

There is . . . the counter argument that we should be allowed to do liberal arts and things of that type. I think maybe even the time will come when we might do that . . . the market right now is doing the things we're doing. When we've done well, even better, in that field . . . we would hope actually to get university status within five years or something like that. . . . There was a fairly strong faction within STEAC which was for a University of Scotland. I still think that is on the cards . . . we certainly don't rule out the possibility of doing liberal arts, but it would be ridiculous to do it now when we have something like eight applicants for every vacancy we've got on vocational-type courses. . . . I go along the line for example, that engineering is just as good an education for life as a course in the liberal arts. Education doesn't have to be through liberal arts or social sciences or something like that, it can be through any course, provided that it's the right type of course. . . . A scientist or an engineer is getting just as good an education, provided it has the wide base we're talking about, as the other types of education.

Oxford Polytechnic

Acting director: Mr V.T. Owen

The polytechnic prospectus talks about providing 'vocational, technical and traditional degree courses'. Is it easy to discriminate amongst courses described in that way?

Certainly if you look at my subject area which is history/international politics, you can argue that is totally non-vocational in the strict sense of the words – if you just think of engineering or business studies, let's say, as vocational. I would argue that correctly studied, in the sense that one's mind is flexible enough to move around various areas, I think that almost any subject can be vocational, in what I would term the *real* sense of the word 'vocational'. I think in many ways that probably is a bit out-dated, setting degrees out like that . . . distinguishing so rigidly between areas, especially since we offer as our major degree course the modular course, which does spread across virtually every discipline we have here, and which does combine the 'vocational' courses with the 'non-vocational' – someone can read history with computer studies for example. I think everyone would say that computer studies was vocational, but perhaps not everyone would argue that history was, but I think that history combined with computer studies is most certainly vocational.

If the distinction is slippery within the institution, the prospectus also claims that the polytechnic sector is complementary to the universities. Do you think the distinction is slippery across the boundary as well?

Yes, I do. . . . That is certainly not a terminology I would wish to stick by. . . . I think in certain areas we are complementary, and in certain areas we overlap, and quite considerably actually.

Are most of the courses designed to direct people into fairly specific forms of employment?

No. Some most certainly are. If you look, for example, at the faculty of architecture, estate management and town planning, I think that the majority of students who go through that are directed most certainly into a definite line of work . . . they will probably work within the area of architecture, town planning, or estate management, whereas someone going through most of the other faculties could go into totally diverse kinds of work.

So what defines the content and quality of a course is not necessarily that there's a job at the end of it?

Not necessarily that there's a specific job at the end of it. I think there has to be a job at the end of it, otherwise we're really wasting our time and theirs. But I don't think we should say: 'right, when you complete your three years or however long it is you will go into business or profession X, Y, or Z'.

Some people out of traditional 'liberal' backgrounds would accuse courses like town planning, engineering, business studies, of narrowness, producing robots rather than thinking people. You're not accepting that kind of argument? 'No, I'm not. I think that certain subjects obviously allow one to use one's mind in different and broader ways than others, naturally, but having said that I think any subject taught properly must allow an element of that.' *At your own two previous polytechnics and here at Oxford has there been much discussion about what 'being taught properly' means?*

It's a subject that increasingly gets on to the agenda. I think in the early days one was much more concerned with getting courses approved, getting recognition, and lifting the institution away from being a technical college or whatever it was. I think as we perfect our courses and as we gain experience we do tend to look much more at the ways we teach and how we can improve that teaching. Certainly here at Oxford there is a great deal of emphasis placed on the teaching aspect and the way we teach.

Some subject areas are more information-oriented than others – engineering for example. Does that raise anxieties?

Yes . . . but I'm pleased to say that . . . in the eighteen or nineteen years that I've been in the game the engineering subjects, for example, which, when I first came into this sector of higher education, were taking twenty-eight or twenty-nine hours a week teaching, class contact, have now reduced that to something like twenty. It's not marvellous, but it is going in the right direction. At the end of the day I think they will always argue that there is a certain amount of information which must be put over, but I would also argue that there is a certain amount of information which a student must absorb whether he is reading English, history, or mechanical engineering. The distinction is – how do you do it? Do you expect the student to learn and absorb information for himself under guidance, at home, or in his study, or must we insist on actually teaching him, lecturing to him, giving him notes? I would prefer the former approach, even in a subject like engineering.

There was still a difference between the amount of time arts students had for extra-curricular activities and, for example, engineering students with laboratory commitments. The distinction had diminished

but it's still there. There is still a reluctance on the part of some institutions and, I think, the older style teacher, to abandon the need for this very close contact. It has improved, there is no doubt about that, and it is improving. And I think that it will also be forced to improve more rapidly as our resources diminish.

One of the things people say about 'vocational' courses is that they place institutions under pressure from outside sources – professions, industry, commerce – including on the content of courses. Have you, particularly during the last four years at Oxford, had any anxieties about such pressures?

> On the contrary, my anxiety is that we don't use the world outside enough. I think the world outside *should* be consulted, *should* be involved in the design and the furtherance of all our courses. I think that the days of producing a sort of 'ivory tower academic' are gone forever, and I am rather pleased that's happened. . . . I would argue that for all our courses. I think the greater the outside involvement we can find the better. . . . I wouldn't really call it interference, I'd call it assistance. . . . There's been quite a wind of change in the universities in this respect.

How useful is it to use this word 'vocational'?

> My view is that it is one of the most misused words in the English language. If it could disappear for ever I'd be terribly pleased, because it does confuse people. People's interpretation of the word 'vocational' varies to an incredible extent . . . from the very narrow definition of coming with blinkers in one channel tunnel, looking for one job at the end of the day, to the sort of vocationalism which I would expound, namely that if you are learning properly, in the sense that you are equipping yourself for a whole area and series of jobs . . . [that] is much more vocational in the long run, because the world is forever changing and will continue to change even more. How one gets away from [the word] I don't know: I really would like to see it totally removed.

Part Three

A LIBERAL VOCATIONALISM?

14
A liberal vocationalism?

Throughout our discussion it has been apparent that the concept of the 'vocational' is in a number of ways defensible as a legitimate and even central process of higher education, and that the concept of a 'liberal' education therefore requires reappraisal. One of our interviewees talked of the need for a 'hybrid phrase' to describe what has emerged in the public sector since the 1960s. Such a concept would straddle the older tradition of liberal values and the younger tradition of more explicitly employment-oriented courses, across a much wider range of employments, than would have been acceptable to spokesmen for the 'liberal tradition' in the nineteenth century. The concept would need to indicate the extent to which, in the conditions of the late twentieth century, these traditions as embodied in the profiles of sectors and institutions have been made to combine or to overlap. Our discussion suggests the need to recognize the importance of bringing the discussion of higher education away from extreme positions in defending liberal and vocational traditions, and towards a conception that, with many of the reservations and conditions we have discussed, comes into an academically, professionally and socially defensible central position.

An extensive discussion of these 'traditions' would necessarily involve a more sustained analysis of these sectorial and institutional characteristics and statuses than has been possible, as well as of their implications for the educational system more widely. It would involve an examination of what is changing in the universities, and across a much wider range of disciplines than we have addressed. It would entail an examination of the impact of modern technologies on higher education curricula, and the responses of higher education – internationally as well as in Britain – to the imperatives of economy-led policies. Although those directions have not been followed here in detail, it is clear that the voices of those we have heard in 'vocational higher education' in no way echo the certainties and assumptions of national policy vocabulary and syntax of recent years.

The 'hybrid phrase' which seems to us most convincingly to reflect the discussions we have heard and our interpretation of the processes and intentions involved is a 'liberal vocationalism'. Some of our interviewees have looked to a 'broadly based' or some other generously defined form of the vocational, though breadth does not always seem to summarize what they are seeking to establish or to preserve. The concept of a liberal vocationalism arises not out of theory, or out of policy intention, but out of the historical realities of course development in the contexts and on the bases we have described. If we are concerned in this respect with change in the relationship between abstract 'values' and the impacts of politics, economics, and the labour market, we are concerned with courses, with the expressed aim and design of courses, with the delivery of courses in the shape of teaching methods and technologies, and with the evaluation of course effectiveness. We are concerned also with the mix of students to whom courses are delivered and who in return – by their own characteristics and activities – help to shape the courses. We are concerned with the nature of the institutions and profiles of higher education within which the courses are designed and implemented. We have therefore in this study focused on courses, and we do not believe that any other focus is possible for a serious analysis of vocationalism and its implications.

We have chosen to look at courses through the eyes mainly of those who are responsible for designing and running them. They have been anxious to defend or explicate what they are doing, while at the same time being realistic about the problems. As we have emphasized on a number of occasions, the reality of courses may be different from intentions, but this would be as true of the 'conventional' single honours degree in any institution as it is of the applied 'vocational' degree.

Everyone with whom we discussed these issues was hesitant about the label of 'vocational', unless it was clearly defined or its implications were made explicit. Most rejected dichotomies based on conceptions of 'liberal' and 'vocational', few were prepared to reject completely the applicability of 'liberal academic' values to their own courses. Yet everywhere there was a sense that we were talking about a distinctive kind of higher education, shaped by diverse influences, but sharing common characteristics. The following features were present in virtually all of the courses we have been looking at:

(i) curricula selected from several disciplines;
(ii) curricula related to 'real world' problems;
(iii) an emphasis on breadth – of courses and of outcomes;
(iv) a concern with long-term employment needs;
(v) a concern to produce questioning and critical graduates (while conceding that this was not always successful);
(vi) an openness to external – 'industrial' – influences.

Courses in many of the fields we examined were in the process of shifting their emphasis from 'knowing' to 'doing', and looking for new methods of teaching and learning through which to achieve it. Among the main differences which we detected in this process were, first, the volume of information to be transmitted and its implications for the achievement of other course objectives (in particular, in engineering); secondly, concerns about the quality of student intakes (again in engineering); thirdly, some indications of changes in the professions resulting from changes in their educational basis for recruitment (for example, chartered surveyors). The subject areas we looked at differed in the role performed by their qualifications in the labour market, and we considered some of the likely consequences of this in chapter 3. Where qualifications have the greatest power to regulate entry to jobs, educators are likely to face more explicit external constraints on the curriculum. This was most evident in engineering where the information load was great and in conflict with the achievement of other educational aims. In fields where there are alternative routes of entry and a structure of qualifications outside of first degrees, the constraints of information requirements are much less. So in planning, with a clear structure of postgraduate training, the approach to what a degree was about was held to be distinct from the more explicit vocational preparation of a professional course. The position was similar in business studies, where we saw a lessening of concern about what a business-studies graduate needs to *know* and increasing interest in what he or she needs to be able to *do*.

The role of educational qualifications in the labour market is continually changing. In some employment fields, a relevant first degree may come to assume much greater importance in regulating entry than in others. In such cases, courses may come under pressure to do different things as employer expectations adapt and become more explicit. However, with the possible exception of engineering where there are conflicting signals from professional bodies and employers, external interference was not considered to be a problem. Indeed, the view was often expressed that more involvement by employers would be welcomed as an effective means of bringing the 'real world' into courses.

The map of higher education is gradually changing as more fields of employment become linked to relevant undergraduate degrees. We have not mentioned courses in catering, home economics and hotel management, nursing, health studies, and pharmacy, or recreation, sport, and human-movement studies. Courses in these and other fields are making a new kind of contribution to the labour market. They enable more and more students to select courses for career-related reasons and to use higher education as an explicit preparation for work. Whatever the precise set of educational and personal objectives achieved, these courses provide an educational experience which denies boundaries between academic and real-world knowledge as well as between knowing and doing.

And yet 'traditional' university courses continue to attract the best students and to draw the top employers. We do not know with any certainty how far the curriculum map in the universities is changing. As we have seen in our interviews with heads of institutions, there has been a clear attempt to make public-sector higher education distinctive from that found in the universities and to build on technical-college and further-education traditions. Notwithstanding the very considerable overlaps which exist, there seems to be little doubt that the two sectors have different educational profiles.

One consequence of the growth of more courses with specific employment links is that the size of the 'open' labour market for graduates might eventually be reduced. At present, careers in many fields are achievable by a variety of different routes, some involving higher education, some involving specialist degrees. In so far as the specialist degree route becomes the more favoured, or even obligatory, the career options open to the 'generalist' graduate are reduced.

New graduates with qualifications from the public sector are likely soon to exceed the numbers coming from the universities. But it will be twenty years or so before their full impact will have been made on the labour market. Most of the people we spoke to talked of long-term employment needs. Given that at least some of these graduates become the graduate recruiters of tomorrow, we may begin to see changes in the attitudes and expectations of employers, bringing further changes in the role of educational qualifications, further opportunities for course development, and further erosions in the boundary between 'academic' and 'real' worlds.

The issues reflected in our interviews and analyses are not, of course, a monopoly of the subject areas we have explored, nor of public-sector higher education associated with the CNAA. The discussion could have revolved similarly round courses in institutions whose work has been validated by universities, or courses in subject areas such as the performing arts. The self-explanations of those institutions and those courses can point in similar ways to preparation for a career or a variety of careers. Debates about a 'retreat into specialised uselessness' as against 'educating for capability' in architecture (Nuttgens 1986: 1) are not confined to that area of professional preparation, or to the others we have discussed. The universities have also not been exempt. A consultant called in to investigate the policies and running of Stirling University in a crisis of the 1970s recommended the addition of some 'vocationally biased' subjects to the university's curriculum in order to contribute 'a sense of motivation and a certain down-to-earth common sense', and new areas of study at Stirling were in fact to include ecology, management science, business studies, and film and media studies (Young 1973: 14).

In the institutions and the subject areas we have considered, and in these wider circles of institutions and subjects, there is a concern to understand and make explicit the implications of the pursuit of knowledge, not for its own sake but in relation to its applications. What we have found, as Barnett underlines, is a sustained, explicit justification, or at least explanation, of the roles of the polytechnics and other institutions in the public sector, a denial of past attempts by philosophers and others to establish clear or self-contained definitions of what constitutes 'education' and 'training' (Barnett 1978: ch. 4).

It is important in considering these issues to emphasize that the polytechnics and colleges have had the dual need to define their distinctive roles, and to establish themselves in public awareness. They have had to define, explain, and persuade – and convince themselves, and meet varying degrees of outside pressure and expectation. They have had to satisfy the CNAA and other professional and accrediting bodies. In any analysis of institutional or course statements, therefore, there is the difficulty of evaluating the balance of messages, those which express a core commitment, and those which are responsive – in reality or rhetoric – to outside signals. One of the virtues of the public sector's development in these decades, as we have underlined, has been the explicitness of its intentions, but part of that history of explicitness has to be understood in terms of the requirements of the CNAA and other bodies, including those which in the 1980s determined the priorities of higher education in the public sector – the Department of Education and Science and the National Advisory Body for Local Authority Higher Education. As the discussion has indicated, a major difficulty of the public sector has been the level of public acceptance of the universities but the need of the public sector constantly to explain and to justify its activities. There has been a fundamental difference in what becomes public and explicit in the two sectors.

In our earlier discussion of policy formulations we saw ways in which the CNAA and its related institutions had expressed their commitments to vocational or employment-related course contents, while at the same time confronting issues of breadth and balance. It is important in this respect to remember the scale of the growth of public-sector higher education since the mid-1960s, and in particular the scale of the CNAA's responsibilities for institutions, courses, and students across the following two decades. By the academic year 1983/4, the numbers enrolled on full-time advanced courses in the universities and in the public sector were almost equal at 268,000 and 266,000 respectively. The addition of part-time students swung the balance firmly in favour of the public sector. First-degree courses validated by the CNAA have accounted for by far the largest part of the student population in the public sector. Although the history of the sector can be traced back to the nineteenth century, its development to the point where it rivalled the universities in the scale and comprehensiveness of its undergraduate provision had been accomplished in less than twenty years. By 1985 there were 1,335

CNAA first degrees with a total student population of 167,926, of which 38 per cent were enrolled on courses in science and technology, 11 per cent in business and management, 11 per cent in art and design, and the remaining 40 per cent spread across arts, social studies, and education courses. These broad subject categories in fact disguise the character and distinctiveness of individual courses. Thus, for example, of the 45,913 students enrolled on arts and social studies courses, only 12,901 were taking what could be described as single-honours degrees in conventional academic disciplines.

The combination of the scale of the CNAA's provision and the explicitness of its concern over recent decades with what constitutes acceptable standards, and the processes of ensuring and evaluating them, placed the CNAA in a salient role in relation to the discussion of vocational education. Its validation processes involved detailed consideration of many of the components of vocationalism that we have addressed – course content and its justification, teaching methods and staff development, the employment needs and expectations of students, relationships with the employment market, the pressures and demands of other professional, accreditation, and examination bodies, the quality and nature of student experience, and the operation of institutions. The CNAA and its institutions have also had to respond increasingly to the vagaries of the graduate employment market and to the statuses of subjects (and the resources allocated to them) in the pecking orders established outside higher education itself. Those we interviewed, particularly in engineering, also raised sharply the particular pressures on thinking about the curriculum from the quality of student recruitment (unimportant in business studies, with its buoyant recruitment and lack of real university competition). One element in determining the shape and character of curricula is the way in which those who design courses perceive the quality of students at entry and their expectations of the learning process and the characteristics considered appropriate for employment.

The educational goals pursued in the courses which we have considered were without exception ambitious ones, though there were some doubts expressed about the extent to which they were achieved. However, in the main there is very considerable demand for these courses and in some cases students with very high entry qualifications are being recruited. Courses which provide students with sustained challenges clearly have major impact upon their personal growth. Interesting and exciting courses recruit the most able students who are stretched and developed into the kinds of people employers want to hire. Thus the liberal goal of the education of the whole person is expressed as part of rather than in opposition to the pursuit of the vocational. As some of those interviewed suggested to us, staff take part in the wider debates in the profession or the industry, and are sensitive to the representations of employers or professionals, but the decisions are made 'in the department'. The CNAA, the public sector in general, the directors of institutions and leaders of courses that we have considered and encountered have not been resistant to these outside pressures – indeed have in many cases been explicit in welcoming them, in describing the mechanisms for recruiting their experience, and would wish to strengthen them.

We have seen how conscious course leaders are of the prior school experience of their students. Differences between British and American or European higher education also relate, as we have seen, to differences in school structures and curricula. Similarly, any discussion of the nature of vocationalism in higher education must take account of the changes in schools and in further education (from both of which the courses we have considered recruit students) that have taken place in recent years. In the 1970s and 1980s considerable attention has been given to the relationships between school and work, bringing schools closer to industrial as well as to other community processes, and to the nature of work-related further education – all of which have been the subject of national policy debate. One of the diffuse concerns is about when, at what age levels, for what groups of pupils or students, the vocational should become explicit. This is in fact two sets of questions.

First, how is the educational system structured for different constituencies and, at different stages, sub-constituencies? At what point, within compulsory or post-compulsory education, do choices occur? How are choices differentially distributed according to educational and social criteria – academic ability, social class, gender, race, culture, geographical location, or physical handicap? How does the curriculum at a given stage reflect these differentials and anticipate the relationship between that phase of formal education and the needs and expectations of the labour market? The vocational as an issue of debate has to be located within those structures, that phasing, and those relationships with or perceptions of social differentiation and the labour market.

Secondly, no less complex are related questions of what becomes explicit. While all education necessarily serves as preparation for something, or more accurately in advanced societies tangles of somethings, at what point does or should education not only serve but also aim to serve as preparation for specific, notably occupational, outcomes? How responsive, and at what stages, should educational processes be to the overt, but often contradictory, requirements and pressures of the wider society? At what points should education itself take part in defining common or diverse civic and other roles for its clienteles? How do relationships between the different stages of education (and their priorities and statuses) dictate the acceptance of vocational targets at any one of them? Within what power structures – systemic, professional, community, economic – are public decisions about the vocational made at different stages of educational provision?

The complexity and difficulty of such questions correlate with the degree of pluralism operating in the society, and answers will depend on national traditions, level and type of economic development and change, cultural norms, assumptions about the processes of human growth, the detailed structures of the educational system, and the operation of the labour market. The history of 'liberal education' in national and international contexts has depended in the past on the stabilities and continuities seen to be at work and to be protected, and vulnerable to the sorts of change these questions reflect – especially since the late eighteenth century in Europe and the mid-nineteenth century in the United States. What is understood by and acceptable as vocational in secondary education, for example, therefore differs between countries and across time, and varies according to the availability of higher education, access to it, and its component institutions and sectors. It differs, similarly, according to the priorities and statuses allocated in the society to the occupations to which it points, and the definition of competencies, skills, and credentials required not only for entry to those occupations, but also for access to different levels of within-occupation status and authority. Assumptions and decisions about the vocational at any stage in the system are therefore a point of intersection between complex educational structures on the one hand, and complex political, economic, and social realities on the other.

We have seen ways in which different national responses at these points of intersection have been heavily influenced by strong historical pressures in given directions. Traditions of gentrification or the relative statuses of knowledge differ and have in recent decades operated differently on national educational policies. Throughout the nineteenth century there was in the conditions and concerns of the United States a considerably more explicit attention than in Britain to the public service purposes of the university: the Rockfish Gap report of 1818 defined for the University of Virginia what it considered the essential aim of higher education: to form statesmen, legislators, and judges (Commissioners for the University of Virginia 1818: 4). That explicitness runs through the state and institutional attempts to define and redefine purposes throughout the nineteenth and twentieth centuries, from the University of Virginia at one stage for instance, to the West Virginia Institute of Technology at another – where 'virtually every degree field is career oriented either by design or opportunity' (West Virginia Board of Regents 1979: 33). That tradition, as we have seen, has not gone uncontested, but as a sector or tradition in higher education it has produced a constant discussion of the meanings of technology and engineering, business and the professions or semi- or minor professions, within definitions of culture and higher learning. It is of supreme importance in the American case to note that within those different constraints and lack of constraints the discussion of engineering and technology in particular has had quite a different resonance from its British counterpart. From the 1940s there has been a mounting public assertiveness of the 'cultural', 'humanistic', or 'liberal' connotations of engineering and technology. In the 1940s and 1950s it was the 'cultural value' of engineering subjects (Sanders 1954a: 18–19), or the possibility of teaching 'professional or specialized subjects in a liberal manner' (Hancher 1954: 359). In the 1960s it was technology and science as integral to the human adventure and as part of the democratization of culture, and the engineers as the 'chief revolutionaries of our time' (White 1967; 1968: 149). In the 1970s it was enthusiasm for Eric Ashby's conception (probably more influential in the United States than in Britain) of the 'technological humanist'

A liberal vocationalism? 243

(Hazzard 1971: 6), and for technology and its history as a 'clear humanistic study' (Friedman 1979: 32). In the 1980s it was the development of such emphases as the Sloan Foundation's 'new liberal arts program', based on quantitative reasoning and technology, and technology as a lever for changing institutional culture (Morison 1986), as a way of thinking to enable all students to 'feel in control' (Edgerton 1986: 5), and as a branch of moral philosophy (Murchland 1982: 301, citing Paul Goodman).

Views of this kind have neither totally refashioned American culture nor produced the widespread curricular and learning outcomes often hoped for, but there has been a continucus exploration of the nature of specialization and a general education within the historical and structural frameworks we have indicated. There has been a longer concern with these issues and the nature of work-oriented education as a reality to be addressed than has been the case in Britain, both in broad terms and in relation to specific areas of study such as architecture or medicine. It has been easier to argue the case in the United States for dispelling the false dichotomy of the useful and the liberal, given that there was clearer and more consistent evidence in the United States that 'liberal studies were from the beginning eminently useful even if they were not specific in their focus'. The difference between a liberal subject and another was more visibly a difference in emphasis – on 'cognitive skills, rational analysis, the stuff it took to be communicative', as against the 'liberal' emphasis on contemplation, and the assessment and reassessment of self and society (Rudolph 1984: 15–16). Out of this tradition came Schön's interpretation of 'the reflective practitioner' and a form of professionalism based on 'reflection in action' (Schön 1983). The thread was not absent from British higher education and discussions of the meaning of culture in modern terms, but it was never as pronounced as in the American case.

The result in Britain, throughout this century and particularly in the 1980s, has been a periodic lurch towards or away from a consideration of the 'service' or career-oriented or employment-oriented functions of education at different levels. One such lurch was the debate about vocational education at the secondary level which took place in the late 1970s and 1980s, compelling participants to consider how specific a definition they were willing to attach to the concept in terms of the school's curriculum and its aims for all pupils or groups of pupils. The technical and vocational education initiative, whatever its other aims and effects, compelled this attention more than any other curriculum development since the first decade of the century. Education authorities and schools bidding – or declining to bid – for the first rounds of TVEI funding under this Manpower Services Commission scheme to promote vocational elements in the secondary curriculum had to define their own educational commitments and values in the light of political, social, and economic changes which could be seen to relate to the scheme. When the Society of Education Officers also pursued the notions of 'education for enterprise' and 'general vocational preparation', they were confronting the technological pressures of a decade, and the political expression of those pressures that had surfaced in Callaghan's Labour administration in 1976-8, and had become explicit and headlong under the Thatcher Conservative administration from 1979 (SEO 1983). In one form or another, concepts like 'general vocational preparation' were becoming prominent, most frequently for instrumental reasons, but also as a new humanism, or as a mix of both, for two main reasons: they were responsive to a society preoccupied with unemployment, and they were 'general' – including such concepts as human relations, imagination, and other skills and characteristics not unlike the traditional values and targets of the curriculum. In some respects what the move towards more explicit vocational content, general or otherwise, in the curriculum indicated was a failure to reconsider the validity of the 'liberal' secondary curriculum that had been in place since the ending of the 'higher grade school' experiments with the *Regulations for Secondary Schools* of 1904, and the failure of the debates of the 1920s to reconcile the 'liberal' and the 'technical' or 'vocational' in terms of the school curriculum (Silver 1983: ch. 7). British educational policy across these decades had failed to confront the challenge to established values as embodied in school as well as higher education curricula, and had failed systematically, and much less systematically than in the United States, to explore the cultural and educational impacts and meanings of modern technology, industry, commerce, and other aspects of society subject to rapid change. The door was therefore left open for crude or panicky attempts to influence or direct the curriculum towards apparently immediate needs.

The uncertainties and ambiguities inherent in the concept of vocationalism therefore point discussion in a variety of directions, both within and outside higher education itself. Throughout our interviews and analysis the focus of response to the concept of vocationalism and the vocational has been 'Yes, but . . . '. There has been a desire to accept the major implications of the concept, but on condition that it is defined in broad or generous or otherwise more acceptable terms than are implied in its common usage. Yes, but it depends what you mean. Yes, but we must be careful to define. Yes, but it is important to emphasize the positive virtues. Yes, but not *narrowly* vocational. Yes, but that does not mean the rejection of many of the traditional qualities of higher education. *Yes, but* could well have been the title of this book. What the reservations underline strongly is the 'hybrid' nature of the defence of the concept. A broadly-based or general vocationalism, incorporating all the different employment-related emphases visible in the interviews and in our typology, is one which seeks to escape from the vulgar and damaging versions often present in popular or policy usage. It is also one which attempts, in the public-sector context we have explored, to marry traditions and to preserve and to project forward new interpretations, often still bound by conceptual ambiguities and the limitations imposed on exploration by economic constraint, student recruitment, or lack of public understanding or recognition. The defence of the vocational in the terms most encountered in this study is one which opposes simplistic responses to the short-term and interpretations purely in relation to technology and industry-specific courses. The CNAA, in its response to the 1985 Green Paper, underlined that

> the flexibility that is needed in higher education is not constant change attempting to meet short-term needs for particular specialisms, but the creation of a flexible product – graduates who whatever their subject discipline have the ability to learn new skills, and who have developed the analytical, communication and interpersonal skills that all employers welcome.

Public-sector provision in the arts and humanities was seen as an essential part of this policy framework and government policy should

> recognise explicitly that it is not only science and technology courses which can contribute to the improvement of economic performance . . . that even courses in subjects which are

studied primarily for their own sake can be a valuable form of vocational preparation.

(CNAA 1985: 3–4, 11)

A 'liberal vocationalism' seems to encompass much of what was presented in the subject areas, institutions, and wider discussions we have considered. Such a concept would have a distinguished, if – as we have suggested – not a dominant, British tradition. It would relate to some of the defined purposes of the late-nineteenth-century university colleges: the campaign for a university college in Liverpool, for example, in the late 1870s had the dual objective of providing an education of quality in the arts and sciences, and a technical institution serving ends 'of immediate value' (Fiddes 1937: 82). Sir Michael Sadler's view of a liberal education in 1932 (offered in a lecture on 'liberal education and modern business') was one in which were blended 'freedom and strict discipline; drudgery and diligence; the education of the body and the education of the mind; training by others and self-training; science and letters; questioning and awe, preparation for livelihood and for leisure' (Sadler 1932a: 9).

Although in this study our concern has been with the vocational in higher education and the reinterpretation and extension of liberal traditions, any examination of recent developments in these liberal traditions, at least in the public sector, would have come across many other examples of their extension to incorporate, if not always the vocational, at least the applicable. In some cases this will have taken the form of extending the range of subject choice – for example, the arts 'major' who can take a science or business 'minor'. In other cases it will have involved bringing together new integrated subject combinations, for example in communications where a blend of literary, social science, and technology themes takes place. Even in what might be described as the conventional single honours degree, examples can be found of the curriculum being reshaped to emphasize application and relevance to employment. The blurred edges and distinct overlap of formerly discrete categories become apparent from whichever end of the spectrum one begins. The Leverhulme study of higher education found 'an infinite gradation between the most academic higher education and the most utilitarian further education' (Leverhulme 1983: 2).

We have emphasized the central importance of the courses

themselves in considering the nature of the vocational. The implications of that consideration reach out into policy and practice in many ways, and particularly for the roles and positions of the staff engaged in these kinds of courses in these kinds of institutions – the very people whose views we have reported. The concept of a liberal vocationalism has a bearing not only on curricular policy and provision at national and institutional levels, but also on interpretation in practice by teachers and students. The staff with whom we have discussed the issues have terms of reference, and work within opportunities and constraints, resulting from their position as 'vocational educators'. The vocational educator has emerged into more publicly recognized roles as pressures for altering the curriculum and recruitment balance of higher education have increased in recent years. Given the historical circumstances in which technological and professional education, and many of the institutions with which they are identified, have grown in Britain, it is obvious that there is a profound ambiguity in the position of the staff who teach in these areas in their institutions. The vocational educator is often caught between the demands and values of the academic community and those of the world of practice whose manpower and other needs there is a strong imperative to satisfy. The vocational educator is part of both worlds, and there is a danger at least in some areas of the academy that the duality will not be understood and will not be appropriately rewarded. In some established or economically and politically well-supported areas of study this may be less of a problem, especially where the status of the staff concerned is buttressed by traditions of research. The engineering and architecture educator will in these respects have somewhat different positions, and both will be different from the teacher educator or the health visitor educator.

The courses we have discussed and the polytechnics and colleges where they are taught do, however, present important common features for vocational educators. They are inevitably more concerned than 'academic educators' with the relevance of courses and experience to employment potential and characteristics. They relate closely to practitioners in the field, and see students as prospective practitioners also. They feel comfortable, as we were told in interviews, in the immediate and wider professional environments in which they work, and which form their predominant points of professional reference. They share, however, the tensions and ambiguities of their position in traditional academe – that is, in the total community of higher education. Their territory is a focal point of internal and external influences, often considerable and powerful. Their legitimacy in the professional arena is not easily matched by academic status or, in many subject areas, financial rewards. While the public sector has done much to establish the importance of the teacher role, of successful student learning, of sound course planning and review, the vocational educator is still often constrained, in terms of advancement, by the traditional measures of staff competence. Surrounding both the vocational educator and the public-sector institution are suspicions that they are not involved in 'real' higher education, and those we interviewed understood and responded to those reservations. The gentry ideal that Wiener underlines in his interpretation of British traditions is strongly embedded in thinking about higher education, but there are inevitably changes occurring as patterns of economic and social activity change, and as the structures of higher education change. Many traditional areas of higher education have become the most vulnerable. Academe has had to learn how to respond not to the expansion of industrial society but to the implications of 'post-industrial society', the information society, the penetration of all aspects of academic life by new technologies, and the emergence of new hierarchies of power and prestige.

One feature of our interviews and the courses to which they related, one which we have not underlined in our previous discussion, is the always controversial area of assessment and standards. Within the area of the vocational educator there is a strong commitment to practice, to interdisciplinary assignments, to 'real-world problem-solving', to design-and-make, to establishing relevance together with practitioners in the field. The suspicions aroused from curriculum areas more wedded to the 'contemplative' liberal tradition may therefore be considerable. Here again, however, the traditions of the public-sector institutions, and the modes of assessment and review encouraged and supported by the National Council for Technological Awards and its successor, the CNAA, have been of major importance to the subject areas concerned in this sector. Questions of standards, however, have not related exclusively to the measurement of student performance and outcomes. They have also involved considerations of the purposes and resources of institutions, the extent of external influence, the academic and professional profiles of academic staff, the research base and prowess, the quality of student recruitment, and other less tangible factors to do with élite knowledge and hierarchies of other kinds. Again, responses to many of these charges from outside the public sector were clearly articulated in our interviews, but the strength of the continuing suspicion and its cultural foundations should not be underestimated. As in many other cases historically, changes in the structure of the system or of institutions may simply remove the conflict from one level or arena to another. The uneasy position of many professionally-related subject areas in the universities of the late nineteenth and early twentieth century has been translated into institutional terms in the late twentieth. Some of these disputed territories – teacher education is a good example – continue to have an uneasy position in terms of national prestige and acceptance in both sectors. Some, like business studies, community nursing, or sport and leisure studies have been largely located in the polytechnics and colleges. Community-work educators position themselves in relation to their field and to their public-sector institution, not to the mores of the university. While questions of standards are therefore shared across sectors, and forms of examination, the roles of external examiners, and the implications of course approval and review may have strong parallel features, in this as in other respects many vocational educators have important contextual differences depending upon their sector, or upon institutional identities within their sector. Teacher educators, for example, will find the nature of their operation, and therefore the means of evaluating its quality and effectiveness, easier to portray and to defend in an institution with predominant or strong roots in teacher education than in amalgamated institutions where their form of operation is a minority, ill-understood one. Some arguments in this connection point towards the retention, as in Scotland, of monotechnic teacher-education colleges, and other arguments, as in England and Wales, have pointed towards 'polytechnic' solutions. The argument here is not about the wisdom of one or the other, but about the ways in which vocational educators in general operate and defend their standards differently in different circumstances. A question such as that of determining and maintaining standards is therefore not merely a set of technical questions but a reflection of the relative identities and statuses of educators, and of the complex frameworks in which they operate and are differentially perceived.

If our discussion of vocationalism points towards implications for the educators, it also points to related policy implications. Throughout our discussions the emphasis has been strong on the withdrawing from positions at two ends of the spectrum – one of which might bear the label 'total utilitarian' and the other Patrick Nuttgens's label of 'specialised uselessness'. A liberal education which takes no account of the centrality of work, or expectations of work, or the crises of unemployment, evades the fact, as Ernest Boyer puts it for the United States, 'that our choice of work, our vocation, is overwhelmingly important in shaping our values and in determining the quality of our lives'. And yet, he continues:

> for some reason we have encouraged students to treat this fundamental choice as if it were a negligible concern. Many educators have suggested that collegiate traditions are demeaned if courses prepare students for finding jobs. Such a view not only distorts the present but also denies the past.
> (Boyer 1977: 150)

To meet this challenge policy-making has to come in from the extremes towards the centre if it is to take account of the diversity of tradition and the complexity of individual and social needs. What this implies also is the need for policy directions in higher education and in education generally which distance them from panic measures and the search for short-term economic and social solutions through education which fail to take account of explanations of the past and the complexities of the present. Meeting the challenge also means inviting higher education itself to reappraise, and to have the conditions in which to reappraise, its purposes.

Discussions of the relationships between higher education, or sectors of higher education, and outside constituencies – notably industry – have often been manpower-oriented on a short-term basis, and either confrontational or directed towards objectives of which the longer-term implications are neither clear nor considered. For the benefit of the long-term adaptability of higher education, its sectors, or its institutions, considerably more attention has to be addressed to the issues of importance to people like those whom we interviewed, and to the issues which have the international resonance that we have explored. Doing so would place policy-making more firmly in an explicit context of debate around the cultural meanings of technology or professional practice, the intentions and contributions of the vocational educator, the precise ways in which the landscape of higher education has been altered by the missions established by the new institutions of recent decades, and realistic appraisals of the power relations within institutions and between them and their multiple outside frames of reference. Policy, rather than the zigzags of national planning, requires attention to the underlying relationships between these contexts, and the kinds of conflicts and dichotomies we have discussed, and the curricula and institutional identities and roles of all levels of education. It is not some superficially comprehensive approach to the 'educational system' or to a packaged set of values to be transmitted through it for the benefit of a pluralist society that is indicated, but a firmer commitment than has been available in British policy-making to promoting analysis and debate at a more basic level. The gap is therefore not the absence of an ideal, but a serious consideration of salient, recent, and current realities.

What has been most apparent in public policy-making (policy debate has rarely occurred around such issues) has been the level of unexamined assumption that has been pervasive. Ministers have assumed they know what industry wants or needs. Universities have assumed they know what their central purposes are, and what those of polytechnics are. From the establishment of the polytechnics in the late 1960s parliamentarians, local government, and other interested parties have assumed they know what polytechnics and colleges do, or should do. Polytechnics and colleges have assumed they know their primary roles and purposes. The level of assumption has been accompanied by a level of proclamation, often necessary in situations of self-defence or crises of planning, resources, or confidence, not by the basic reappraisals needed but difficult to achieve in those situations.

The policy messages from this concern with the concepts that are central to understanding, in late twentieth-century terms, what precisely has happened and is happening to higher education are therefore directed towards policy and practice at the most global and the most local levels. The discussion is about the nature of all courses, not just of those in engineering or business studies. It is about the expectations, experience, and accomplishments of all students, not just of those in estate management or social work. It is about the relationships between all educational institutions and their labour markets, not just about polytechnics and their local industries. It is about putting educational traditions and ambiguities under sustained scrutiny. There is clearly, in the pursuit of such targets, the constant difficulty of balancing the desire for stability with the demands of change. None of those involved in designing and maintaining the courses we have examined, or in defining the missions of the institutions in which they take place, accepts either absolute values or total *ad hoc* responsiveness. The pressure of the argument is not for the abandonment of recognized values which underpin higher education – however strong some of the critiques of the universities are, or however firm a line is sometimes drawn between the intentions of the universities and those of the public-sector institutions. The pressure is for the re-examination of those values in changing circumstances, for the new meanings which emerge when old ways are juxtaposed with new needs and processes. Such a constant re-examination is often discussed in terms of the kinds of flexibilities, the range of graduate characteristics and skills, that carry forward essential change processes. The focus in some of our interviews on projects and problem-solving, and the explicit aims of courses to promote creativity and imagination and the capacity to take initiatives and decisions, point towards social and industrial needs as well as generous educational values. They argue that over-zealous pressure for responses to short-term needs are not only suspect educationally, they are also unproductive. The case, as is clear throughout, is for constant, understanding negotiation of positions – with the ultimate educational decisions being made within education. What policy-making can help to ensure in this connection is the process and the status of the negotiation. The partners in the exercise emerge very clearly in our interviews, as does their increasing willingness to participate. The essential message for that process is the centrality of the exploration of values in contexts of change. That is a long way from the politics of the rapid-swinging pendulum, and it suggests that the relationship between the profound changes visible over recent decades in society and the economy on the one hand, and public-sector and other higher education on the other hand, needs to be open to constant investigation.

A liberal vocationalism? 253

A final message from this study, one which has been inherent in the discussions throughout, is the need for wider opportunities for those involved in the kind of higher education we have considered to be heard. This is not a question of consultancy and committee roles, but of bringing into the centre of debate about pasts and futures those who are at the sensitive edges of the higher-education developments that we have investigated – those willing to accept the 'vocationalism' label with conditions. Discussions around higher-education policy have heard very little of their voices in recent decades. The dimensions of vocationalism have occasionally surfaced, but the scale and explicitness of the changes, represented particularly but not solely by public-sector higher education, have not received the kind of sustained attention in public to which they have been subjected in the contexts of course planning, academic boards and validation relationships with the CNAA. New institutional statuses and definitions being developed in the late 1980s, new forms of accreditation, new national funding arrangements, will affect the contexts we have discussed, and in uncertain ways the roles of those who plan, teach, and review courses of the kind we have considered. Those changes will not of themselves, however, solve the problems we have discussed, or produce the kinds of incentives and platforms for prolonged public access to debate about the basic purposes outlined in the kinds of course descriptions and tutors' explanations we have assembled. Other pressing concerns have occupied, and will no doubt continue to occupy, the scene, and other voices may continue to be the ones primarily heard. Those who have had a platform, through the written word and the interview, in this study have had little opportunity in the conditions of recent years to discuss *these* issues. The commitment that we have found to what we have termed a 'liberal vocationalism', and the questions it poses for other, firmly established or vague and tenuous, views of the purposes of higher education, need to be more systematically debated, both within the system and with employers and wider publics, collectively and individually, and in the hearing of those who attempt to influence, formulate, and implement policy.

Appendix

The interviews reported in chapters 7, 10, 12, and 13 were conducted by Harold Silver as follows (designations are as at the time of the interviews):

Humberside College of Higher Education

Mr L.M. Cutts	BA Business Studies course leader (3 June 1986)
Dr J. Earls	Director (25 March 1984 and 2 June 1986)
Mr C. Jones	BA Architecture course leader (2 June 1986)
Dr T. Tate	BEng Engineering course leader (3 June 1986)

Leicester Polytechnic

Professor P.J. Baron	Head, School of Economics and Accounting (5 June 1986)
Dr D. Bethel	Director (4 June 1986)
Mrs C. Gore	BA Business Studies deputy course leader (5 June 1986)
Mr H. Land	BSc Land Management course leader (5 June 1986)
Mr R. Rue	BEng Engineering Technology course leader (5 June 1986)
Mr L.E. Willmore	BSc Textile and Knitwear Technology course leader (4 June 1986).

Napier College, Edinburgh

Mr W.S. Bannister	BEng Energy Engineering course co-ordinator (on secondment to SCOTVEC) (28 February 1986)

Mr J.M. Glen	BEng Technology with Industrial Studies course co-ordinator (27 February 1986)
Mr P.W. McIntosh	Head, Department of Business Studies (27 February 1986)
Mr G. Rae	BEng Communication and Electronic Engineering (26 February 1986)
Dr W.A. Turmeau	Principal (22 November 1983 and 26 February 1986)
Mr D.C. Vettese	BA Business Studies (part-time) course co-ordinator (27 February 1986)

Napier College was also visited by Pamela Silver in December 1984 and help was given by:

Mrs K.J. Anderson, deputy principal
Mr J.S. Gilliatt, Technology and Industrial Studies
Mr J. Govan, Communication and Electronic Engineering
Mr J.P. Lowe, Science with Industrial Studies

Oxford Polytechnic

Mr G.T. Bennett	Acting head, Department of Architecture (21 November 1985)
Mr R.D.B. Booth	BSc Estate Management course leader (21 November 1985)
Dr G.R. Bremble	Head, Engineering Department (27 November 1985)
Mr J. Glasson	Head, Department of Town Planning (21 November 1985)
Dr P. Healey	Dean, Faculty of Architecture, Planning, and Estate Management (21 November 1985)
Mr R.W. Morris	BEng Civil Engineering course leader, Head, Department of Construction (28 January 1986)
Mr V.T. Owen	Acting director (27 November 1985)
Mr A.P.L. Pendlebury	BA Business Studies course tutor (3 February 1986)
Mr A. Smith	BEng Civil Engineering Integrative Studies tutor (28 January 1986)

Discussions were also held at Oxford Polytechnic with Dr W.J. Rea, Dean, Faculty of Technology, and Mr J.M. Dennis, Department of Civil Engineering.

In connection with the study of European Business courses the following institutions were visited by John Brennan between January and June 1984:

Buckinghamshire College of Higher Education
École Superieure de Commerce, Toulouse
Fachhochschule Osnabruck
Hochschule Bremen
Leeds Polytechnic
Trent Polytechnic

In connection with the study of engineering and business studies the following institutions were visited by Pamela Silver in April 1984:

Bloomsburg University of Pennsylvania
Carnegie-Mellon University, Pittsburgh
Lock Haven University of Pennsylvania
Massachusetts Institute of Technology
Pennsylvania State University
Slippery Rock University of Pennsylvania
University of Pittsburgh

Interviews at the Departments of Mechanical and Electrical Engineering at Pennsylvania State University were conducted by Harold Silver in January 1986.

Other institutions visited in connection with this study included:

Edinburgh College of Art
Middlesex Polytechnic

Bibliography

NB Prospectuses and course documentation are not included.

(US) Accreditation Board for Engineering and Technology (1980) *Criteria for Accrediting Programs in Engineering in the United States*, New York: ABET.

Adams, Mollie (1963) ' "Liberal studies" in technological education', *Universities Quarterly*, 17 (3).

Adelman, C. (1984) *Inside a College of Higher Education*, Uxbridge: Brunel University, Expectations of Higher Education Project.

Ahlström, Göran (1982) *Engineers and Industrial Growth*, London: Croom Helm.

Armstrong, P.J. et al. (1982) 'Undergraduate interdisciplinary projects', *European Journal of Engineering Education*, 7 (2).

Ashby, Eric (1958; edition of 1963) *Technology and the Academics*, London: Macmillan.

Au, Tung (1981) 'Some random thoughts on general education at CMU', *Focus* (Carnegie–Mellon University), 11 (3) (the first of five *Focus* articles by Au on 'The ideal of a liberal professional education').

Bailey, Roy (1983) 'Values in the curriculum', in Desmond Graves (ed.) *The Hidden Curriculum in Business Studies*, Chichester: Higher Education Foundation.

Bamford, T.W. (1967) *The Rise of the Public Schools*, London: Nelson.

Barnett, Ronald Anthony (1978) 'Knowledge and ideology in higher education', University of London Institute of Education MPhil thesis.

Battersby, G.A. (1983) 'New developments in engineering courses in UK polytechnics', *European Journal of Engineering Education*, 8 (1).

Ben-David, Joseph (1977) *Centers of Learning: Britain, France, Germany, United States*, New York: McGraw-Hill.

Berthoud, Richard and Smith, David J. (1980) *The Education, Training and Careers of Professional Engineers*, London: HMSO.

Beuret, Geoff and Webb, Anne (1983a) *Goals of Engineering Education: Final Report*, Leicester: Leicester Polytechnic.

Beuret, Geoff and Webb, Anne (1983b) *Goals of Engineering Education (GEEP). Engineers – Servants or Saviours?*, London: CNAA.

Birch, William (1981) *The Changing Relationship between Higher Education and Working Life*, Bristol: Bristol Polytechnic (mimeo).

Black, Joseph (1975) 'Allocation and assessment of project work in the final year of the engineering degree course at the University of Bath', *Assessment in Higher Education*, 1.

Bosworth, George (1971) 'The role of the polytechnics', *Further Education*, 3 (1).

Bosworth, G.S. (1964) 'Education and training of engineers' (three articles), *The Engineer*, 217: 5,653–5.

Bosworth, G.S. (1963) 'Towards creative activity in engineering', *Universities Quarterly*, 17 (3).

Boyer, Ernest L. (1977) 'The core of learning', in Dyckman W. Vermilye (ed.) *Relating Work and Education*, San Francisco: Jossey-Bass.

Boys, C.J. (1984) *Inside a Polytechnic*, Uxbridge: Brunel University, Expectations of Higher Education Project.

Boys, C.J. and Kogan, M. (1984) *Commentary on Three Studies of Higher Education Institutions ('The Providers')*, Uxbridge: Brunel University, Expectations of Higher Education Project.

Brennan, John and McGeevor, Philip (1987) *Graduates at Work: Degree Courses and the Labour Market. Final Report of a Survey of CNAA Graduates*, London: Jessica Kingsley.

Brennan, John and Pieniazek, Jolanta (1984) 'Students of psychology in Poland and Britain', in Gerhild Framhein and Josef Langer (eds) *Student Worlds in Europe*, Klagenfurt: Karntner Druck-Und Verlagsgesellschaft MBH.

Brillhart, Lia V. (1981) 'The engineer as educator', in Lawrence P. Grayson and Joseph M. Biedenbach (eds) *Frontiers in Education*, New York: Institute of Electrical and Electronics Engineers.

British Association for the Advancement of Science (1977a) *Education, Engineers and Manufacturing Industry: A Report to the British Association Co-ordinating Group*, Birmingham: University of Aston.

British Association for the Advancement of Science (1977b) *Education, Engineers and Manufacturing Industry: Support Papers*, Birmingham: University of Aston.

Brown, David (1983) 'Interdisciplinarity – a burnt-out case?', in Desmond Graves (ed.) *The Hidden Curriculum in Business Studies*, Chichester: Higher Education Foundation.

BTEC (Business and Technician Education Council) (1983) *Discussion Document on Education Policy*, London: BTEC.

Bud, R.F. and Roberts, G.K. (1984) *Science Versus Practice: Chemistry in Victorian Britain*, Manchester: Manchester University Press.

Bull, R.J. (1983) *A Practical Philosophy of Business Education*, Leeds: Leeds Polytechnic (mimeo).

Bull, R.J. (1985) *The Business Studies Degree – Towards a 'Core Curriculum'* (paper to the Undergraduate Courses Board of the CNAA Committee for Business and Management Studies), Leeds: Leeds Polytechnic (mimeo).

Burnhill, Peter and McPherson, Andrew (1983) 'The Scottish university and undergraduate expectations, 1971-1981', *Universities Quarterly*, 37 (3).

Calderbank, P.H. (1973) 'The balance between engineering science and practical experience', in R.E. Bell and A.J. Youngson (eds) *Present and Future in Higher Education*, London: Tavistock.

Carnegie Institute of Technology (1954) *Professional Education in Engineering and Science*, Pittsburgh: CIT.

Central Services Unit for Graduate Careers and Appointments Services (1984a) *CSU Statistical Quarterly*, 20.

Central Services Unit for Graduate Careers and Appointments Services (1984b) *Twelfth Annual Report of the Management Committee*.

Cerych, Ladislav and Sabatier, Paul (1986) *Great Expectations and Mixed Performance: The Implementation of Higher Education Reforms in Europe*, Stoke-on-Trent: Trentham.

Cheit, Earl (1975) *The Useful Arts and the Liberal Tradition*, New York: McGraw-Hill.

Chilver Committee (1975) *Education and Training of Civil Engineers*, London: Institution of Civil Engineers.

Christopherson, D.G. (1967) *The Engineer in the University*, London: English Universities Press.

Cohen, David K. and Garet, Michael S. (1975) 'Reforming educational policy with applied social research', *Harvard Educational Review*, 45 (1).

Commissioners for the University of Virginia (1818) *Rockfish Gap Report*, Charlottesville: University of Virginia (facsimile).

(US) Committee for Economic Development (1985) *Investing in Our Children: Business and the Public Schools*, New York: CED.

Committee of Inquiry into the Engineering Profession (Finniston) (1980) *Engineering Our Future*, London: HMSO.

Committee on Higher Education (Robbins) (1963) *Higher Education, Evidence*, pt 1, vol. B (Institution of Chemical Engineers, Federation of British Industries, Institution of Production Engineers); pt 1, vol. D (Joint Advisory Committee on Engineering Education), London: HMSO.

Conference of Engineering Societies of Western Europe and the United States of America (EUSEC) (1960) *Report on Education and Training of Professional Engineers*, vol. 2, EUSEC.

Conservative Sub-Committee on Education (1942), in *Staples' 'Reconstruction' Digest*, London: Staples.

Cornwell, A. and Newman, B. (1971) *Vocationalism in Higher Education*, London: North-East London Polytechnic (mimeo).

Cotgrove, Stephen (1962) 'Education and occupation', *British Journal of Sociology*, 13 (1).

Council for National Academic Awards (1965) Business Studies Board, *Minutes*, 19 March, London: CNAA (mimeo).

Council for National Academic Awards (1967-8) *Report*, London: CNAA.

Council for National Academic Awards (1969), *Minutes*, 29 January, London: CNAA (mimeo).

Council for National Academic Awards (1979) *The Council: Its Place in British Higher Education*, London: CNAA.

Council for National Academic Awards (1980) *Council's Response to the Report of the Committee of Inquiry into the Engineering Profession*, London: CNAA.

Council for National Academic Awards (1981) Committee for Business and Management, *Report of a Working Party on Undergraduate Business Education*, London: CNAA (mimeo).

Council for National Academic Awards (1982) *Policy Statement: Development and Validation of Engineering Degree Courses*, London: CNAA (mimeo).

Council for National Academic Awards (1983a) *Policy Statement: Engineering First Degree Courses*, London: CNAA.

Council for National Academic Awards (1983b) Working Party on Longer Term Developments, *Second Report to Council*, London: CNAA (mimeo).

Council for National Academic Awards (1984) *Response to the Scottish Tertiary Education Advisory Council's letter of 20 August 1984 headed 'Review of Higher Education in Scotland'*, London: CNAA (mimeo).

Council for National Academic Awards (1985) *Letter Commenting on the Interim Report of the Working Group on the Review of Vocational Qualifications*, London: CNAA (mimeo).

Council for National Academic Awards (1986a) *'The Development of Higher Education into the 1990s': CNAA's Response to the Government Green Paper*, London: CNAA.

Council for National Academic Awards (1986b) *Response from the CNAA to the Report by the Scottish Tertiary Education Advisory Council on its Review of Higher Education in Scotland*, London: CNAA (mimeo).

Council for National Academic Awards (1986–7) *Report*, London: CNAA.

Council of Engineering Institutions (1969) *Education and Training 1969: The General Principles of the Training of Professional Engineers*, London: CEI.

Council of Engineering Institutions (1975) *Education and Training 1975: The General Requirements for the Training and Experience of Engineers for Chartered Status*, London: CEI.

Cowan, John and McConnell, S.G. (1970) 'Project work for undergraduate civil engineers', *Universities Quarterly*, 24 (4).

Crosland, Anthony (1974) 'Pluralism in higher education', in *Socialism Now and Other Essays*, London, Cape.

Davies, Duncan *et al.* (1976) *The Humane Technologist*, Oxford: Oxford University Press.

Davies, John L. (1985) *Mission and Strategy of the Higher Education Institution: Main Issues for Management*, Chelmsford: Danbury Park Management Centre (mimeo).

Bibliography

Department of Education and Science (1966) *A Plan for Polytechnics and Other Colleges*, London: HMSO.

Department of Education and Science (1982) Circular 5/82: *Approval of Advanced Further Education Courses in England*.

Dewey, John (1914) 'Liberal education', in Paul Monroe (ed.) *A Cyclopedia of Education*, 4, New York: Macmillan.

Dewey, John (1917) 'The modern trend toward vocational education in its effect upon the professional and non-professional studies of the university', reprinted in Jo Ann Boydston (ed.) (1980) *John Dewey: The Middle Works*, 10, Carbondale: Southern Illinois University Press.

Diamond, J. (1970) 'University engineering education 1960–1980', *Advancement of Science*, 27.

Dore, Ronald (1976) *The Diploma Disease*, London: Allen & Unwin.

Edgerton, Russell (1986) 'Feeling in control: or, why would a humanist envy an engineer?', *Change*, 18 (2).

Edinburgh, Duke of (1962) 'The engineer in Commonwealth development', *School Science Review*, 63 (150).

Edington, G.A. (1969) 'The education and training of civil engineers: introduction', in *The Education and Training of Civil Engineers and Town Planners*, pt 2, London: Planning and Transport Research and Computation (mimeo).

Edwards, E.G. (1977) *The Relevant University*, Bradford: University of Bradford.

Engel, Arthur (1983) 'The English universities and professional education', in Konrad H. Jarausch (ed.) *The Transformation of Higher Learning 1860–1930*, Chicago: University of Chicago Press.

Engineering Council (1983) *Statement on Enhanced and Extended Undergraduate Engineering Degree Courses*, London: Engineering Council.

Engineering Employers' Federation (1977) *Graduates in Engineering*, London: EEF (mimeo).

Engineering Employers' Federation (1980) *Submission to the Secretary of State for Industry on the Finniston Report . . .* , London: EEF (mimeo).

Engineering Industry Training Board (1983) *The Training of Graduates in Engineering*, London: EITB.

Engineering Industry Training Board (1984) *EITB Scheme of Grants for Courses of Study in Advanced Technology*, London: EITB (mimeo).

Engineering Professors' Conference, *Evidence to the Finniston Committee*, London: EPC.

Fairhurst, David (1982) 'Where to draw the line in business studies', *Education and Training*, 24 (4).

Fiddes, Edward (1937) *Chapters in the History of Owens College and of Manchester University 1851–1914*, Manchester: Manchester University Press.

Finniston, Monty (1984) 'Overview of issues in engineering education', in Sinclair Goodlad (ed.) *Education for the Professions: Quis custodiet . . . ?*, Guildford: Society for Research into Higher Education.

Finniston, Monty (1985) 'Engineering the future', *International Journal of Applied Engineering Education*, 1 (1).

Fitzgerald, P. (1985), *An Alternative Model Business Studies Degree Scheme* (paper to the Undergraduate Course Board of the Committee for Business and Management Studies), London: CNAA (mimeo).

Fores, Michael (1972) 'University science and vocation', *Times Higher Education Supplement*, 7 July.

Friedman, Edward A. (1979) 'Technology as an academic discipline', in Lawrence P. Grayson and Joseph M. Biedenbach (eds) *Frontiers in Education*, New York: Institute of Electrical and Electronic Engineers.

Geiger, Roger L. (1980) 'The college curriculum and the market place: what place for disciplines in the trend towards vocationalism?', *Change*, 12 (8).

Gerstl, J.E. and Hutton, S.P. (1966) *Engineers: The Anatomy of a Profession. A Study of Mechanical Engineers in Britain*, London: Tavistock.

Glover, Ian (1980) 'Social science, engineering and society', *Higher Education Review*, 12 (3).

Goldberg, A.S. (ed.) (1973) *Proceedings of a National Conference on Engineering Education*, London: Education and Awareness.

Goldman, A. (1984) *CNAA Business Studies Degrees: Their Development and the Role and Value of the Work Placement* (paper to a conference, Regional and Community Colleges as Agents of Social Change, Israel), London: CNAA (mimeo).

Goodlad, Sinclair (1977) *Socio-Technical Projects in Engineering Education*, Stirling: University of Stirling, General Education in Engineering Project.

Gordon, A. (1983) 'Attitudes of employers to the recruitment of graduates', *Educational Studies*, 9.

Graves, Desmond (ed.) (1983) *The Hidden Curriculum in Business Studies*, Chichester: Higher Education Foundation.

Griffith, Dean E. (1981) 'Engineering', in Arthur W. Chickering *et al.*, *The Modern American College*, San Francisco: Jossey-Bass.

Haber, Samuel (1974) 'The professions and higher education in America: a historical view', in Margaret S. Gordon (ed.) *Higher Education and the Labor Market*, New York: McGraw-Hill.

Haines IV, George (1959) 'Technology and liberal education', in Philip Appleman *et al.* (eds) *1859: Entering an Age of Crisis*, Bloomington: Indiana University Press.

Hancher, Virgil M. (1954) 'Liberal education in professional curricula', *Journal of Engineering Education*, 44 (7).

Hanson, Norwood Russell (1957) 'Science as a liberal education', *Universities Quarterly*, 11 (2).

Harding, A.G. (1973) 'The objectives and structures of undergraduate projects, I', *British Journal of Educational Technology*, 4 (2).

Harland, John (1984) *The Diversified Colleges: The Graduate Perspective. Final Report*, York: Combined Colleges Research Group.

Harris, Robin (1955) 'General education in the British university', *Universities Review*, 27 (2).

Harrisberger, Lee (1984) 'Curricula and teaching methods in engineering

Bibliography

education', in Sinclair Goodlad (ed.) *Education for the Professions: Quis custodiet . . . ?*, Guildford: Society for Research into Higher Education.

Harvard Committee (1945) *General Education in a Free Society*, Cambridge, Mass.: Harvard University Press.

Hawkins, David (1973) 'Liberal education: a modest polemic', in Carl Kaysen (ed.) *Content and Context: Essays on College Education*, New York: McGraw-Hill.

Hazzard, George (1971) 'Engineering as a liberal education', *Liberal Education*, 59 (4).

Herbst, Jurgen (1980) 'The liberal arts: overcoming the legacy of the nineteenth century', *Liberal Education*, 66.

Heywood, J. et al. (1966) 'The education of professional mechanical engineers for design and manufacture', *Lancaster Studies in Higher Education*, 1.

Holloman, J. Herbert et al. (1975) *Future Directions for Engineering Education*, Washington, DC: American Society for Engineering Education.

Horner, David J. (1982) 'Expectations of the student', in Desmond Graves (ed.) *The Hidden Curriculum in Business Studies*, Chichester: Higher Education Foundation.

Huxley, Thomas H. (1899) 'Technical education', in *Science and Education: Essays*, London: Macmillan.

Institute of Civil Engineers (1980) *A Creative Career – Civil Engineering*, London: ICE.

Institution of Mechanical Engineers, Education and Training Group (1977) *The Education Debate and its Effect on the Future Supply of Mechanical Engineers*, London: IME (mimeo).

Isaac, P.C.G. (1982) 'The future of university education in civil engineering', in Institution of Civil Engineers, *Future Needs in Civil Engineering Education*, London: Telford.

Jahoda, Marie (1963) *The Education of Technologists*, London: Tavistock.

James of Rusholme, Lord (1971) 'York's attempt to balance vocational and general studies', *The Times*, 15 January.

Jarvis, Peter (1983) *Professional Education*, London: Croom Helm.

Jary, David W. (1969) 'General and vocational courses in polytechnics', *Universities Quarterly*, 24 (1).

Jenkins, D.E.P. (1983) 'Curriculum development', *European Journal of Engineering Education*, 8 (1).

Jobbins, David (1980) 'Employers want management status to follow job experience', *Times Higher Education Supplement*, 25 January.

Jones, Thomas B. (1985) 'Liberal learning and business study', *Liberal Education*, 71 (1).

Joseph, Sir Keith (1985) Speech to SRHE/THES conference, 9 July, in *Conference on the Green Paper on Development of HE into the 1990s*, Guildford: Society for Research into Higher Education.

Joseph, Sir Keith (1986) Reported in *Times Higher Education Supplement*, 14 March.

Kanigel, Robert (1986) 'Technology as a liberal art: scenes from a classroom', *Change*, 18 (2).

Kenny, Shirley Strumm (1984) 'Humanities and business: educational reform for corporate success', *Business and Society Review*, 48.

Kogan, M. and Boys, C.J. (1984) *Expectations of Higher Education: A Synopsis and Commentary on its Main Findings*, Uxbridge: Brunel University, Expectations of Higher Education Project.

Lane, Michael (1975) *Design for Degrees: New Degree Courses Under the CNAA – 1964–1974*, London: Macmillan.

Laycock, Mike (1978) 'The polytechnics and industry: the importance of social skills', *Journal of Further and Higher Education*, 2 (3).

Leverhulme Report (1983) *Excellence in Diversity: Towards a New Strategy for Higher Education*, Guildford: Society for Research into Higher Education.

Lewin, Douglas (1981) 'Engineering philosophy – the third culture?', *Royal Society of Arts Journal*, 129 (5,302).

London School of Economics (1984) *Response to UGC Circular Letter 16/83: Development of a Strategy for Higher Education*, London: LSE (mimeo).

Lucas, F.L. (1933) 'English literature', in Harold Wright (ed.) *University Studies Cambridge 1933*, London: Nicholson & Watson.

McCinnes, William C. (1982) 'The integration of liberal and professional education', *Thought*, 57 (225).

McCulloch, Gary et al. (1985) *Technological Revolution? The Politics of School Science and Technology in England and Wales since 1945*, London: Falmer Press.

McKenna, Eugene (1983) *Undergraduate Business Education: A Reappraisal*, London: London Chamber of Commerce and Industry.

McKenna, Eugene (1985) *Undergraduate Business Education* (paper to the Undergraduate Courses Board of the CNAA Committee for Business and Management Studies) London: CNAA.

Marris, Peter (1964) *The Experience of Higher Education*, London: Routledge & Kegan Paul.

(Massachusetts) *An Act to Incorporate the Trustees of the Massachusetts Agricultural College* (1863).

Meyerson, Martin (1969) 'Play for mortal stakes: vocation and the liberal learning', *Liberal Education*, 55 (1).

Meyerson, Martin (1974) 'Civilizing education: uniting liberal and professional learning', *Daedalus*, 103 (4).

Mill, John Stuart (1867) *Inaugural Address Delivered to the University of St Andrews 1 February 1867*, London: Longmans, Green, Reader & Dyer.

Miller, Kenneth (1985) Letter to *The Times*, 5 July.

Ministry of Education (1957) *Liberal Education in Technical Colleges* (Circular 323), London: HMSO.

Ministry of Technology and Council of Engineering Institutions (1977) *The Survey of Professional Engineers*, London: HMSO.

Moberly, Walter (1949) *The Crisis in the University*, London: SCM Press.

Monroe, Paul (ed.) (1914) *A Cyclopedia of Education*, vol. 4: *Vocational Education*, New York: Macmillan.
Montrose, J.L. (1952) 'A specialist approach to general education', *Universities Quarterly*, 7 (1).
Morison, Elting E. (1986) 'The new liberal arts: creating novel combinations out of diverse learning', *Change*, 18 (2).
Morrison, J.L.M. (1970-1) 'Educating engineers', in *Proceedings of the Institution of Mechanical Engineers*, 185 pt I.
Mosely, Philip E. (1971) 'The universities and public policy: challenges and limits', in Stephen D. Kertesz (ed.) *The Task of Universities in a Changing World*, Indiana: University of Notre Dame Press.
Mumford, Lewis (1946) 'Synthesis in American universities', in D.M.E. Dymes (ed.) *Synthesis in Education*, Malvern: Le Play House.
Murchland, Bernard (1982) 'Technology, liberal learning, and civic purpose', *Liberal Education*, 68 (4).
NAB (National Advisory Board for Local Authority Higher Education) (1983) *Towards a Strategy for Local Authority Higher Education in the Late 1980s and Beyond*, London, NAB.
NAB (National Advisory Board for Local Authority Higher Education) (1984a) *A Strategy for Higher Education in the Late 1980s and Beyond*, London: NAB.
NAB (National Advisory Board for Local Authority Higher Education) (1984b) 'The conclusion of the 1984/85 planning exercise', *NAB Bulletin*.
National Advisory Council on Education for Industry and Commerce (1964) *A Higher Award in Business Studies* (Crick Report), London: HMSO.
National Council for Technological Awards (1964) *Report of the Council's Industrial Training Panel on the Training of Engineering Students Following Courses Leading to the Diploma in Technology*, London: NCTA.
Newman, B. and Cornwell, A. (1971) *The Concept of Vocationalism*, London: North East London Polytechnic (mimeo).
Newman, Frank (1979) 'The traditional university in the United States' (editorial summary of remarks), in Daniel Heyduk (ed.) *Education and Work: A Symposium*, New York: Institute of International Education.
Newman, John Henry (1852) *On the Scope and Nature of University Education*, London: Everyman edn 1943.
Nuttgens, Patrick (1972) 'The new polytechnics: their principles and potential', in John Lawlor (ed.) *Higher Education: Patterns of Change in the 1970s*, London: Routledge & Kegan Paul.
Nuttgens, Patrick (1978) 'Learning to some purpose', *Higher Education Review*, 10 (3).
Nuttgens, Patrick (1986) Reported in European Association for Architectural Education, *News Sheet*, 16.
Oakley, D.J. (1973) 'Meeting conflicting demands', *Times Higher Education Supplement*, 5 October.
O'Flaherty, C.A. (1969) 'Education and training of engineers', in *The Education and Training of Civil Engineers and Town Planners*, pt 2,

London: Planning and Transport Research and Computation (mimeo).

Oxtoby, Robert (1972) 'Complementary studies and undergraduate degree courses in applied science and technology: an evaluation of developments in the polytechnics', *Journal of Curriculum Studies*, 4 (1).

Parkes, E.W. (1962) *The Education of an Engineer*, Leicester: Leicester University Press.

Pearson, Richard (1984) 'Graduates and employment', in CRAC, *GET '85: 2000 Employers*.

Pearson, Roland (1972) 'Education and industry', *Further Education*, 3 (5).

Percy, Lord Eustace (1950) Contribution to discussion of 'Industry's requirements of scientists and technologists and their education and training', in Association of Universities of the British Commonwealth, *Report of Proceedings*, 1950.

Petty, Evan R. (1983) 'Engineering curricula for encouraging creativity and innovation', *European Journal of Engineering Education*, 8 (1).

Porrer, Robert (1984a) 'Degrees of relevance', *Guardian*, 8 March.

Porrer, Robert (1984b) *Higher Education and Employment*, Leicester: Association of Graduate Careers Advisory Services (AGCAS) (mimeo).

Redwood, David (1951) 'The philosophy of university education in England from the reforms at Oxford and Cambridge (1877) to 1914', University of Manchester PhD thesis, 2 vols.

Reid, S.A. and Farrar, R.A. (1985) *What Makes a BEng Course? A Report of a Symposium Held at the University of Southampton*, London: CNAA.

Robertson, A.B. (1980) 'Sir Joshua Girling Fitch; 1824-1903: a study in the formation of English educational opinion', Newcastle University PhD thesis.

Robinson, Eric E. (1968) *The New Polytechnics*, London: Cornmarket Press.

Roizen, Judith and Jepson, Mark (1984) *An Employers' Perspective*, Uxbridge: Brunel University, Expectations of Higher Education Project.

Roizen, Judith and Jepson, Mark (1985) *Degrees for Jobs: Employer Expectations of Higher Education*, Guildford: Society for Research into Higher Education.

Rooke, Denis (1982) 'Business skills for student engineers', *Education and Training*, 24 (4).

Rothblatt, Sheldon (1968) *The Revolution of the Dons: Cambridge and Society in Victorian England*, Cambridge: Cambridge University Press.

Rothblatt, Sheldon (1976) *Tradition and Change in English Liberal Education*, London: Faber & Faber.

Rothblatt, Sheldon (1983) 'The diversification of higher education in England', in Konrad H. Jarausch (ed.) *The Transformation of Higher Learning 1860-1930*, Chicago: University of Chicago Press.

Royal Aeronautical Society (1964) *The Diploma in Technology in Aeronautical Engineering*, London: RAS (mimeo).

Rudolph, Frederick (1984) 'The power of professors: the impact of

specialization and professionalization on the curriculum', *Change*, 16 (4).
Runge, P.F. (1963) 'The menace of over-specialisation', *B.A.C.I.E. Journal*, 17 (3).
Sadler, Michael (1932a) *Liberal Education and Modern Business*, reprinted from *Journal of the Textile Institute*, 23 (5).
Sadler, Michael (1932b) *Liberal Education for Everybody*, London: Lindsey Press.
Saks, M. (1983) 'Removing the blinkers? A critique of recent contributions to the sociology of the professions', *Sociological Review*, 31.
Sanders, Jennings B. (1954a) *General and Liberal Educational Content of Professional Curricula: Engineering*, Washington, DC: US Department of Health, Education, and Welfare.
Sanders, Jennings B. (1954b) *General and Liberal Educational Content of Professional Curricula: Pharmacy*, Washington, DC: US Department of Health, Education, and Welfare.
Sanderson, Michael (1972) *The Universities and British Industry 1850–1970*, London: Routledge & Kegan Paul.
Saul, Anthony (1983) 'Survey of business studies degrees validated by CNAA', in Desmond Graves (ed.) *The Hidden Curriculum in Business Studies*, Chichester: Higher Education Foundation.
Scally, John (1976) 'Transvaluing: the humanities in a technical-vocational curriculum', *Journal of Higher Education*, 47 (2).
Schön, Donald A. (1983) *The Reflective Practitioner: How Professionals Think in Action*, London: Temple Smith.
Schreter, Debra J. (1976) *The Content of First Degree Courses in Engineering in Relation to the Knowledge Required of Professional Engineers in Industry*, London: EITB.
Scott, Peter (1984) *The Crisis of the University*, London: Croom Helm.
Scottish Tertiary Education Advisory Council (1985) *Report: Future Strategy for Higher Education in Scotland*, Edinburgh: HMSO.
Seamans Jr, Robert C. and Hansen, Kent F. (1981) 'Engineering education for the future', *Technology Review*, 83 (4).
Secretary of State for Education and Science (1972) *Education: A Framework for Expansion*, London: HMSO.
Secretary of State for Education and Science et al., (1985) *The Development of Higher Education into the 1990s* (Green Paper), London: HMSO.
Sills, Kenneth C.M. (1944) 'The useful and liberal arts and sciences', *The American Scholar*, 13 (4).
Silver, Harold (1983) *Education as History*, London: Methuen.
Silver, Harold and Silver, Pamela (1981) *Expectations of Higher Education: Some Historical Pointers*, Uxbridge: Brunel University, Expectations of Higher Education Project.
Simmons, Jack (1959) *New University*, Leicester: Leicester University Press.
Smith, Alex (1978) 'A sense of direction – some reflections on education and society', *Royal Society of Arts Journal*, 126 (5,262).

Smith, Elliott Dunlap (1954) *The Development of Humanistic–Social Education at Carnegie Institute of Technology*, Pittsburgh: CIT.
Smith, Elliott Dunlap et al. (1957) *The Role of Humanistic–Social Education in Making Professional Education Liberal at Carnegie Institute of Technology*, Pittsburgh: CIT.
Snow, C.P. (1959) *The Two Cultures and the Scientific Revolution*, Cambridge: Cambridge University Press.
Snow, Lord (1965–6) 'The place of the engineer in society', *Proceedings of the Institution of Mechanical Engineers*, 180 pt I.
Society of Education Officers (1983) *Key Issues for Industry and Education*, SEO Occasional Paper No. 3.
Stoddart, John (1975) 'Advance needed in business education', *Higher Education Review*, 7 (3).
Stoddart, J. (1981) 'Business education – trends and development', *Business Education*, spring.
Tarr, Joel A. (1980) *The Carnegie–Mellon University Program in Technology Humanities: A Five-Year Review*, Pittsburgh: CMU (mimeo).
Teare Jr, B. Richard (1948) *The Use of Problems and Instances to Make Education Professional*, Pittsburgh: Carnegie Institute of Technology.
Thatcher, Margaret (1970) 'The role of the polytechnics', *Guardian*, 17 February.
Thomas, Russell (1962) *The Search for a Common Learning: General Education, 1800–1960*, New York: McGraw-Hill.
Thring, M.W. (1967) 'The chartered engineer of the future', in Institution of Mechanical Engineers, *Trends in the Education and Training of Professional Mechanical Engineers: Proceedings*, 181 pt 3M.
Tolley, George (1982) 'Some reflections on education and training', in Science and Engineering Research Council, *Future Patterns in Education, Training and Work*, London: SERC.
Trow, Martin (1974) 'Reflections on the relation between the occupational structure and higher educational systems', in International Council for Educational Development, *Higher Education: Crisis and Support*, New York: ICED.
Truxal, John G. (1986) 'Learning to think like an engineer: why, what, and how?', *Change*, 18 (2).
Turmeau, W.A. (1982) 'Engineering degree curricula for the future', *Higher Education*, 11.
Turmeau, W.A. et al. (1982) 'The profession's lead for education', *Chartered Mechanical Engineer*, 29 (7).
Tustin, A. (1950) 'Broader education in a department of applied science', *Universities Quarterly*, 4 (3).
UGC (University Grants Committee) (1964) *University Development 1957–1962*, London: HMSO.
UGC (University Grants Committee) (1984) *A Strategy for Higher Education into the 1990s: The University Grants Committee's Advice*, London: HMSO.
UGC (University Grants Committee) (1985) *Response to Green Paper on Higher Education*, London: UGC (mimeo).

University of Maryland (College Park) (1984) *Liberal Arts in Business Program. A New Curriculum Offering Career Options for Undergraduates in the Division of Arts and Humanities*, College Park: University of Maryland (mimeo).

Van Doren, Mark (1943) *Liberal Education*, Boston: Beacon Press.

Venables, P.F.R. (1959) *Sandwich Courses for Training Technologists and Technicians*, London: Max Parrish.

Walker, Eric A. (1971) 'The major problems facing engineering education', *Proceedings of the IEEE*, 59 (6).

Warren, J.W.L. and Reid, S.A. (1981) 'The implications of revised goals of engineering education for curricula and teaching', in Polytechnics and Engineering Conference (Department of Education and Science Invitation Conference), *Proceedings*.

Watson, J. Steven (1973) 'Educating statesmen: a retrospect', in Eric Ashby et al., *The University on Trial*, Christchurch, New Zealand: University of Canterbury.

West Virginia Board of Regents (1979) *Profile of Progress: Higher Education in West Virginia*, Charleston: Board of Regents.

White Jr., Lynn (1967) ' "Civilizing" the engineer by "civilizing" the humanist', in William H. Davenport and Daniel Rosenthal (eds) *Engineering: Its Role and Function*, New York: Pergamon.

White Jr, Lynn (1968) *Machina ex Deo: Essays in the Dynamism of Western Culture*, Cambridge, Mass.: MIT Press.

White, W.H. (1906) 'The education and training of engineers – civil and naval', *Nineteenth Century*, 59.

Whitehead, A.N. (1932) *The Aims of Education and Other Essays*, London: Williams & Norgate; Benn edn 1962.

Wiener, Martin J. (1981) *English Culture and the Decline of the Industrial Spirit, 1850–1980*, Cambridge: Cambridge University Press.

Wilkinson, Rupert (1964) *The Prefects*, Oxford: Oxford University Press.

Williams, Gareth (1985) 'Graduate employment and vocationalism in higher education', *European Journal of Education*, 20 (2–3).

Young, Roger (1973) *Report on the Policies and Running of Stirling University 1966–1973*, Stirling: University of Stirling (mimeo).

Index

abstraction/application tension, 31
accountability, 7, 11, 32, 36, 52, 222
Accreditation Board for Engineering and Technology (ABET), 140, 141
Adams, M., 78
Ahlström, G., 21
Aims of Education, The (Whitehead), 14–15
American Assembly of Collegiate Schools of Business, 182
American Society for Engineering Education, 137, 140, 141
Anderson, Mrs K.J., 255
anti-industrialism, 18–33, 56, 248
application/abstraction tension, 31
apprenticeships, 6
architecture, 73; Humberside, 195–7, Oxford Polytechnic, 197–200
Aristotle, 3, 4
Armstrong, P.J., 89
arts, 56–8, 66–7, 80, 141–2, 239
Ashby, E., 11, 84, 242
Au, T., 139

Bailey, R., 151
Bamford, T.W., 19, 24
Bannister, W.S. (interview), 114–18, 254

Barnett, R.A., 237
Baron, P.J. (interview), 136–7, 254
Battersby, G.A., 84
Ben-David, J., 17
Bennett, G.T. (interview), 198–200, 255
Bethel, D. (interview), 219–23, 254
Beuret, G., 82, 86, 91
binary system, 16, 23, 55–6
Birmingham Polytechnic, 60
Birmingham University, 91
Black, J., 90
Bloomsburg University, 182
Booth, R.D.B. (interview), 204–6, 255
Bowdoin College, 10
Boyer, E.L., 29, 250
breadth (curricular), 16–17, 25, 28, 30, 85–7
Bremble, G.R. (interview), 124–7, 255
Brennan, J., 13, 145
Brighton Polytechnic, 60–1, 79
Brillhart, L.V., 141
Bristol Polytechnic, 61
British Association for the Advancement of Science, 87
Brown, D., 151–2
Brunel College, 78
Bud, R.F., 13, 21
built environment, 195–214
Bull, R.J., 153, 154, 155

Index

Burnhill, P., 34–5
business studies, 23, 52, 58, 88; courses; 157–83; curriculum, 73, 149–53, 154, 155, 156, 180–1; Europe (comparisons), 184–94; interviews, 158–78; project background, 6, 72–3, 144–56
Business Studies Board, 25
Business and Technician Education Council, 58, 148, 152, 154, 181

Calderbank, P.H., 87
Callaghan, James, 244
Carnegie-Mellon University, 137–9
Carnegie Institute of Technology, 138–9
case studies, 105, 132, 189, 196
Central Services Unit, 88
Cerych, L., 12, 184
Cheit, E., 27
Chilver Committee, 87
Christian-Hellenic tradition, 20, 29
Christopherson, D.G., 84–5
civil engineering, 127–31
CNAA, 15, 218, 223, 237, 240, 248; business studies, 25–6, 144–7, 149, 151–3, 156–7, 162, 169, 179, 183; engineering, 94, 97, 99, 101, 105, 109, 114, 118, 121, 123, 126–7, 131–2, 135; environments, 196–7, 200, 203, 206, 210, 211; policies, 60, 63–8, 238, 245–6, 253; project support, 71, 72, 73, 75; validation role, 6, 60, 63–5, 71, 75, 215, 222, 238–9
co-operative education, 32
Cohen, D.K. 76
colleges of higher education, 16, 23
Committee of Directors of Polytechnics, 60–1
Committee for Economic Development, 33
common core curriculum, 29–30
communication and electronic engineering, 109–14
communication skills, 83, 90, 100, 103, 107, 116, 128–9, 172, 179
competence, 31
Conference of Engineering Societies of Western Europe and the USA, 78
Conservative government, 14, 244
Council of Engineering Institutions, 81, 82, 91
Council for National Academic Awards, *see* CNAA
course-employment relationship, 41–52
course staff (business studies): Baron (Leicester), 163–6; Cutts (Humberside), 158–62; Gore (Leicester), 166–3; McIntosh (Napier), 170–4; Vettese (Napier), 170–4
course staff (engineering): Bannister (Napier), 114–18; Glenn (Napier). 118–21; Rae (Napier), 110–14; Rue (Leicester), 101–5; Tate (Humberside), 94–7; Willmore (Leicester), 106–9
course staff (environmental studies): Bennett (Oxford), 198–200; Booth (Oxford), 204–6; Glasson (Oxford), 207–9; Healey (Oxford), 209–11; Jones (Humberside), 195–7; Land (Leicester), 201–3; Pendlebury (Oxford), 175–8
courses (project), 71–6; *see also* business studies; engineering education
Coventry Lanchester Polytechnic, 78–9
Cowan, J., 90

Crick Report, 149, 152, 158, 160, 163, 170, 174, 177, 179, 180
Crosland, A., 23
culture, 7, 9, 11–12, 14–15; stigmas and, 21, 24, 26
curriculum, 5, 6, 9, 12–13, 15–16, 25; academicization, 44–51 *passim*, 214; breadth, 16–17, 25, 28, 30, 85–7; business studies, 73, 149–56, 180–1; common core, 29–30; engineering, 11, 13, 77–9, 81–2, 83, 85–92, 239
Cutts, L.M. (interview), 158–62, 254
Cyclopaedia of Education, A (Monroe), 3–4, 7

Davies, D., 89, 91
Davies, J.L., 215
decision-making, 162–3, 166, 169–70, 172, 175, 176–7
degrees: screening function, 37–52; *see also individual subjects*
democratic tradition, 4, 29
Dennis, J.M., 256
DES, 57–8, 59, 67, 215, 238
DESCAF, 185, 192–3
detachment/involvement tension, 31
Development of Higher Education into the 1990s, The, 56–7, 58, 66–8
Dewey, J., 4, 5, 10, 13–14, 15, 17
Diamond, J., 83
Diplom-Betriebswirt, 185, 191, 192–3
Diplom-Kaufmann, 185, 191, 192–3
directors (interviews), 216–29
Dore, R., 36

Earls, J. (interview), 97–9, 216–19, 254
École Superieure de Commerce, 190, 192

Edgerton, R., 243
Edinburgh, Duke of, 3, 85, 90
Edinburgh University, 225
Edington, G.A., 85
Education: A Framework for Expansion (White Paper), 54, 55
Edwards, E.G., 20
élites, 26–7, 35–6
employment, 241; business students, 145–6, 154–5, 179–80, 181, 191–2; engineers, 77, 80–3, 86, 88, 90, 94, 98, 123, 132–3, 134–6; open market, 38, 40, 48–51, 52; vocational preparation, 35–52
energy engineering, 114–18
Engel, A., 21
Engineering Council, 94, 222
Engineering Education, 140
engineering education, 6, 52, 57–8; curriculum, 11, 13, 77–9, 81–3, 85–92, 239; interviews, 94–131; project background, 72, 73–4, 77–92; stigma, 18, 91, 22–3; United States, 137–43; *see also* Finniston Report
engineering education (courses): emphasis (and explanations), 131–6; Humberside, 92–9; Leicester, 100–9; Napier, 109–23; Oxford, 123–31
Engineering Employers' Federation, 24, 82
Engineering Industry Training Board, 82, 91
Engineering Professors' Conference, 87
engineering technology course, 100–5
engineers (image), 86, 90–1, 131–2
environmental courses (comparisons), 195–214
estate management, 73, 203–6
Europe (business studies), 184–94

Index

Fachhochschulen, 12, 29, 184–94 passim
Fairhurst, D., 87
Farrar, R.A., 23
Federation of British Industry, 85
Fiddes, E., 246
Finniston, M., 23, 59, 84
Finniston Report, 21, 24, 59, 66, 81–4, 87–8, 93, 98, 122, 124, 131
Fitch, J., 21
Fitzgerald, P., 153–4
Fores, M., 20
France, 8, 12, 29, 74; business studies, 184–94
Friedman, E.A., 243

Garet, M.S., 76
GEEP project, 86, 90, 93, 98, 101
Geiger, R.L., 35
general education, 27–8, 29
generality/particularity, 31
Germany, 8, 12, 29, 74; business studies, 184–94
Gilliatt, J.S., 255
Glasson, J. (interview), 207–9, 255
Glen, J.M. (interview), 118–21, 255
Glover, I., 90
Goldberg, A.S., 80
Goldman, A., 156
Goodlad, S., 89
Goodman, P., 243
Gordon, A., 49, 145
Gore, C. (interview), 166–8, 254
Govan, J., 255
grandes écoles, 29, 184–94 passim
Grant, 82, 86, 90
Graves, D., 145, 154
Great Books approach, 139
Green Paper (1985), 56–7, 58, 66–8
Griffith, D.E., 137

Haber, S., 140
Haines IV, G., 20
Hancher, V.M., 242

Hansen, K.F., 140
Hanson, N.R., 20
Harding, A.G., 89
Harris, R., 84
Harrisberger, L., 140
Harvard Committee, 27
Harvey Mudd College, 137
Hatfield Polytechnic, 150
Hawkins, D., 27, 32
Hazzard, G., 243
Healey, P. (interview), 209–11, 255
Herbst, J., 27
Heriot-Watt University, 225
higher education: conflicts, 1–17; functions, 35–6; institutions (identities), 215–29; stigmas, 18–33
Higher Education: Meeting the Challenge (White Paper), 6
Holloman, J.H., 138
Horner, D.J., 146
Huddersfield Polytechnic, 61
Humane Technologist, The (Davies), 89, 91
humanities, 13, 57–8, 67, 78, 138, 139, 141
Humberside College of Higher Education, 73, 216–19; architecture, 195–7; business studies, 157–62; engineering, 93–9
Hutchins, R., 139
Huxley, T.H., 7
'hybrid phase', 233, 234, 245

Illston, J.M., 23
industrial studies, 118–23
industrialism (stigma), 18–33, 56, 248
Institution of Chemical Engineers, 86
Institute of Civil Engineers, 90–1
Institution of Mechanical Engineers, 81, 88, 91, 97

institutions (identities), 215–29
Instituts universitaires de technologie (IUT), 12, 29, 184
integrative studies, 129–31
intellectual de-industrialization, 19
interviews, 73–5; business studies, 158–78; directors/principals, 216–29; engineering, 94–131
involvement/detachment tension, 31
Isaac, P.C.G., 81

Jahoda, M., 78
James of Rusholme, Lord, 20
Jarvis, P., 77
Jenkins, D.E.P., 90
Jepson, M., 88, 145
Jobbins, D., 88
Jones, C. (interview), 195–7, 254
Joseph, Sir Keith, 57–8

Kanigel, R., 21
Kenny, S.S., 182
Kingston Polytechnic, 60
knowledge, 30–1, 56; conflict and, 4–5, 8–9, 13, 16; engineering, 77, 81, 86, 90; vocational preparation, 34, 35, 38–9, 50

Labour government, 244
labour market, *see* employment
Lanchester Polytechnic, 78–9
Land, H. (interview), 201–3, 254
land management, 73, 200–3
Lane, M., 81
Laycock, M., 90
leadership, 56, 82–3, 182
learning, 30–1
Leicester Polytechnic, 73, 219–23; business studies, 162–8; engineering, 100–9; land management, 200–3
Leverhulme Report, 218, 246

liberal arts, 9, 11, 23, 29, 62, 182, 226
liberal education, 3–5, 7, 9–11, 13–15, 17, 18–21, 25–7
liberal studies, 53, 77–80, 81, 89
liberal vocationalism, 233–53
Liverpool Polytechnic, 61, 150
London School of Economics, 22, 32–3
Lowe, J.P., 255
Lucas, F.L., 19

McCinnes, W.C., 78
McConnell, S.G., 90
McCulloch, G., 90
McGeevor, P., 145
Machina ex Deo (White), 89
McIntosh, P.W. (interview), 170–4, 255
McKenna, E., 153
McPherson, A., 34–5
management (in engineering), 88
Manchester Polytechnic, 150
Mann Report (1918), 137
Manpower Services Commission, 58, 67, 244
Marris, P., 88
'mastery', 77, 83
Meyerson, M., 11
Middlesex Polytechnic, 62, 151
Mill, J.S., 7–8, 13, 14, 16, 18
Miller, K., 24
Ministry of Education, 53
Ministry of Technology, 81
mission statements, 6, 73, 215, 252; Humberside, 216–19; Leicester, 219–23; Napier, 223–6; Oxford, 226–9
Moberley, W., 20, 29
Monroe, P., 3–4, 5, 7
Morison, E.E., 243
Morrill Act (1862), 10
Morris, R.W. (interview), 128–30, 255
Morrison, J.L.M., 82

Index

Mosely, P.E., 10
multidisciplinary courses, 101, 109, 210, 214
Mumford, L., 85
Murchland, B., 243

Nabarro, Sir Gerald, 80, 90
Napier College, 73, 80, 223–6; business studies, 169–74; engineering, 109–23
National Advisory Body for Local Authority (Public Sector) Higher Education, 55–6, 59, 61, 86, 238
National Advisory Council on Education for Industry and Commerce, 149
National Council for Technological Awards, 6, 25, 77, 248
Newcastle Polytechnic, 60
Newman, J.H., 8–9, 10, 14, 16, 18
Nuttgens, P., 21, 237, 250

Oakley, D.J., 88
O'Flaherty, C.A., 86
open market (employment), 38, 40, 48–52
over-supply (graduate), 41, 43–8 *passim*
Owen, V.T. (interview), 226–9, 255
Oxford Polytechnic, 62, 73, 226–9; architecture, 197–200; business studies, 175–8; engineering, 123–31; estate management, 203–6; planning studies, 206–11
Oxtoby, R., 66

Parkes, E.W., 79–80
part-time courses, 5, 64, 170, 238
partial regulation (employment), 45–8
particularity/generality tension, 31
Pearson, Richard, 88
Pearson, Roland, 86

Pendlebury, A.P.L. (interview), 175–8, 255
Pennsylvania State University, 141–2
Percy, Lord Eustace, 22–3
Pieniazek, J., 13
Plan for Polytechnics and Colleges, 215
planning studies, 73, 201–11
Poland, 12–13, 28–9, 74
policy, 15–16, 24, 33, 75–6, 244, 250–2; language of, 53–68
polytechnics, 3, 8, 12, 15–16, 22–3, 59–64; international comparisons, 184–94
Porrer, R., 86, 88
Portsmouth Polytechnic, 62
postgraduate business studies, 147–8
principals (interviews), 216–29
problem-solving: business studies, 162–3, 166–7, 169–70, 172, 175–7, 180, 182; engineering, 89, 94–5, 97, 100, 112, 123–4, 127, 129, 132, 138–9, 142; environmental studies, 201, 203, 207
professional studies, 7–11, 14; stigma, 21, 22, 27–8
professionalization, 37, 43, 47, 51
prospectuses, 62, 215; *see also* mission statements
public schools, 19, 24
public sector, 6, 16, 30, 31, 236–8, 240, 245

qualifications spiral, 36–7

Rae, G. (interview), 110–14, 255
Rankine, 82, 86, 90
Rea, W.R., 256
recruitment policies, 37–52
Redwood, D., 21
Regulations for Secondary Schools, 244

Reid, S.A., 23, 84
research degrees, 45
Review of Vocational
 Qualifications, 67
Robbins Report, 15–16, 84, 85, 86
Robert Gordon's Institute of
 Technology, 62
Roberts, G.K., 13, 21
Robertson, A.B., 22
Robinson, E., 77, 85
Rockfish Gap Report, 242
Roizen, J., 88, 145
Rooke, Sir Denis, 88
Rothblatt, S., 22
Royal Aeronautical Society, 86
Royal Institute of British
 Architects, 197, 212
Royal Institution of Chartered
 Surveyors, 200–3, 206
Royal Town Planning Institute,
 206, 209
Rudolph, F., 243
Rue, R. (interview), 101–5, 254
Runge, P.F., 85

Sabatier, P., 12, 184
Sadler, M., 19, 246
Saks, M., 37
Sanders, J.B., 11, 242
Sanderson, M., 16
sandwich courses, 30–2, 55, 64,
 65; business studies, 144–56,
 158–9, 165; engineering, 79,
 94, 105, 116–17, 122, 128,
 132–3
Saul, A., 152
Scally, J., 78
Schön, D.A., 243
Science Versus Practice (Bud and
 Roberts), 21
science, 7, 11–13, 54, 57–8; stigma,
 19, 20–1, 22–3
scientific humanism, 30
SCOTBEC, 223
Scott, P., 16

Scottish Tertiary Education
 Advisory Council, 24, 58, 68,
 109, 225, 226
Scottish Vocational Education
 Council, 114, 148, 223
screening process (degrees as),
 37–52
Seamans Jr, R.C., 140
self-learning, 126, 142
Sheffield Polytechnic, 62, 78
Sills, K.C.M., 10
Silver, H., 29, 88, 244
Silver, P., 88
Simons, J., 20
skills: engineering, 77–8, 83–4, 86,
 90–1; communication, 83, 90,
 100, 103, 107, 116, 128–9, 172,
 179; vocational preparation,
 38–9, 48–9, 50, 55–6
Slippery Rock University, 182
Sloan Foundation, 243
Smith, A., 66
Smith, A. (interview), 130–1, 255
Smith, E.D., 139
Snow, C.P. (Lord), 11, 18
social sciences, 63, 80, 138
social studies, 13, 67, 239
Society of Education Officers, 244
sole regulation (employment),
 43–5, 52
specialization, 5, 11, 16–17, 27–8;
 engineering, 79, 83, 84–6
stigmas (and dichotomies), 18–23,
 56; blame and failures, 24–5;
 liberal studies approach, 25–30;
 tensions, 30–2
Stirling University, 237

Tarr, J.A., 139
Tate, T. (interview), 94–7, 254
teacher educators, 249–50
teaching/learning tension, 30–1
teaching staff, 190–1, 247–8; *see
 also* interviews, course staff
Teare, J., 139

Index

technical education, 12, 14–15, 53, 58
Technical and Vocational Education Initiative, 58, 244
technological tradition, 29
technology, 7, 11–12; stigma, 20–1, 30
Technology and the Academics (Ashby), 11
Technology with Industrial studies (course), 118–23
Teesside Polytechnic, 150
textile and knitwear technology, 105–9
Thames Polytechnic, 60
Thatcher, M., 3, 15, 54, 244
Thomas, R., 27
Thring, M.W., 82
Tolley, G., 30–2, 145
town planning, 206–11
training, 38–40; completed, 41, 43, 45–6; educational base, 44–5, 47–8; part, 43–4, 46–7, 52
'transvaluing', 78
Trent Polytechnic, 150–1
Trow, M., 20, 35–6
Truxal, J.G., 21
Turmeau, W.A., 80, 82, 86, 90, 255; interview, 121–3, 223–6
Tustin, A., 91
Two Cultures and the Scientific Revolution (Snow), 11
undergraduates, *see* universities
United States, 9–11, 74; business studies, 181–2; engineering, 137–43
universities, 11, 12, 14–15, 16; stigmas, 18–23 *passim*; undergraduates, 5,6, 7–10
University of Bath, 89
University Grants Committee, 32, 54, 55, 57, 67, 86

University of London, 8
University of Maryland, 182
University of Virginia, 242

validation procedures. *see* CNAA
Van Doren, M., 11, 15
Vettese, D.C. (interview), 170–4, 255
vocational: ambiguity, 13–14; education (conflict), 3–17; educators, 247–8, 249–50; /liberal tension, 25–7, 28, 30; preparation, 34–52: relevance, 54, 57–8, 71–2, 87–8
vocationalism: higher education, 6–7, 11, 15, 17; liberal, 233–53; policies, *see* policy project, 71–6; stigma, *see* stigmas (and dichotomies)

Walker, E.A., 137
Warren, J.W.L., 84
Watson, J.S., 20
Webb, A., 82, 86, 91
West Virginia Institute of Technology, 242
White, L., 12, 89, 137–8, 142, 242
White, W.H., 82
White Papers: *Education: A Framework for Expansion* 54, 55; *Higher Education: Meeting the Challenge*, 6
Whitehead, A.N., 14–15
Wiener, M., 18–19, 24, 248
Wilkinson, R., 19
Willmore, L.E. (interview), 106–9, 254
Wolverhampton Polytechnic, 60
Worcester Polytechnic, 137

Young, R., 237